Sail. a Rousso $2

THE ENDLESS FOREST

The

ENDLESS FOREST

———

A NOVEL

Sara Donati

DELACORTE PRESS

NEW YORK

Copyright © 2010 by Sara Donati

Published in the United States by Delacorte Press, an imprint of The Random House Publishing Group, a division of Random House, Inc., New York.

DELACORTE PRESS is a registered trademark of Random House, Inc., and the colophon is a trademark of Random House, Inc.

LIBRARY OF CONGRESS CATALOGING-IN-PUBLICATION DATA
Donati, Sara.
The endless forest : a novel / Sara Donati.
p.   cm.
ISBN 978-0-553-80526-0
eBook ISBN 978-0-440-33902-1
1. New York (State)—History—1775–1865—Fiction.   2. Families—Fiction.
3. Frontier and pioneer life—Fiction.   4. Domestic fiction.
5. Psychological fiction.   I. Title.
PS3554.O46923E53 2010
813'.54—dc22   20009035381

Printed in the United States of America on acid-free paper

www.bantamdell.com

FIRST EDITION

2 4 6 8 9 7 5 3 1

Map by Laura Hartman Maestro
Book design by Dana Leigh Blanchette

This is dedicated to the ones I love: Bill and Elisabeth.
And to you too. I've enjoyed your company on
this long journey from 1792 to 1824.
I hope to see you again soon.

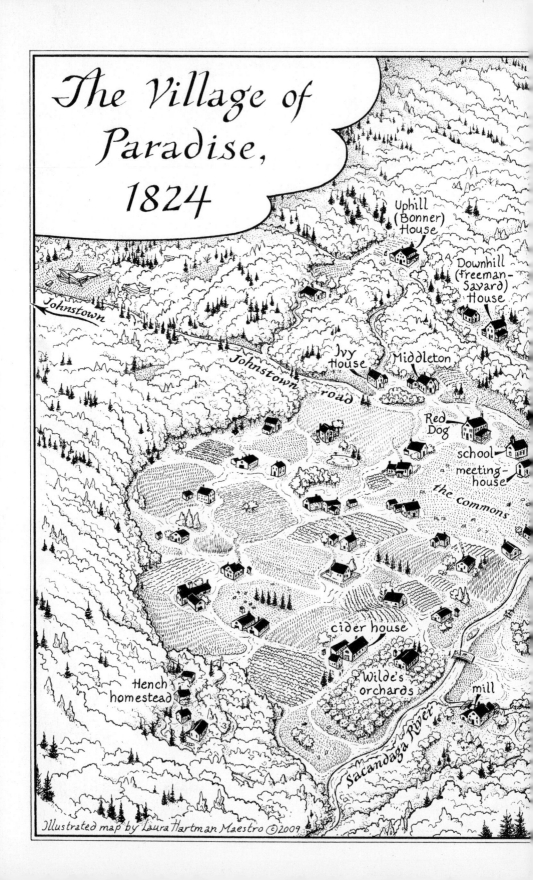

old
beaver
dam

Hidden Wolf Mountain

Lake in
the
Clouds

Half-Moon Lake

blacksmithy
livery

trading
post

strawberry fields

Little Muddy

Characters

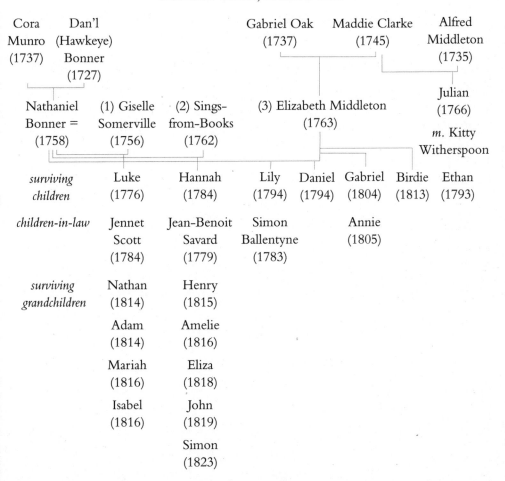

						Gabriel Oak	Maddie Clarke	Alfred

Cora Munro (1737) Dan'l (Hawkeye) Bonner (1727) Gabriel Oak (1737) Maddie Clarke (1745) Alfred Middleton (1735)

Julian (1766) *m.* Kitty Witherspoon

Nathaniel Bonner = (1758) (1) Giselle Somerville (1756) (2) Sings-from-Books (1762) (3) Elizabeth Middleton (1763)

surviving children	Luke (1776)	Hannah (1784)	Lily (1794)	Daniel (1794)	Gabriel (1804)	Birdie (1813)	Ethan (1793)
children-in-law	Jennet Scott (1784)	Jean-Benoit Savard (1779)	Simon Ballentyne (1783)		Annie (1805)		
surviving grandchildren	Nathan (1814)	Henry (1815)					
	Adam (1814)	Amelie (1816)					
	Mariah (1816)	Eliza (1818)					
	Isabel (1816)	John (1819)					
		Simon (1823)					

ADDITIONAL CHARACTERS

Martha Kuick Kirby, the daughter of Jemima Southern Kuick and Liam Kirby (deceased); Nathaniel's ward

Calista (Callie) Wilde, farmer, daughter of Nicholas and Dolly Wilde, both deceased; Nathaniel's ward, owner of the apple orchards

Levi Fiddler, manumitted slave, manager of the orchard

Curiosity Freeman, landholder, manumitted slave resident in Paradise; her surviving grown children also resident in Paradise

Daisy Hench, Curiosity's daughter, and her husband Joshua Hench, blacksmith; their adult children and grandchildren

Jemima Southern Kuick Wilde Focht, once of Paradise; Hamish Focht, her husband; Jemima's son, Nicholas Wilde Jr.

Lorena Webb and Harper Washington, two of the Fochts' servants

Charlie and Becca LeBlanc, innkeepers

Tobias Mayfair, Quaker, shopkeeper and owner of the trading post; his son John Mayfair, farmer and part-time attorney

THE ENDLESS FOREST

PROLOGUE

A Word with Curiosity

*W*ell now, look who's finally come round to call. Just yesterday I was wondering to Hannah if maybe you lost your way. But here you are, jumped right out my mind to stand in front of me.

It's been a long time. Early summer in the year '15, when Hannah and Jennet and everybody come back from New Orleans, you was here then as I recall. And wan't that a fine day? The Lord our God be praised. We have had a run of good luck that started right there, yes we have.

Did you go away again before Hawkeye come home? Ahuh, I thought me so. Now that's a shame. Was he a sight, walking up the road on a fine October afternoon? Like he was just coming in from checking his trap lines. Oh, and the stories. The things he saw in the West, my. Oh, yes, he was the same Hawkeye as ever was. Clear-eyed, like a boy of twenty in his mind at least. He died just after the new year, went to sleep and never woke up. Hawkeye never did like a fuss.

Scoot a little closer, I can hear your teeth chattering. The spring has got a chill of its own, don't it? But we got us a good fire. Ain't nothing like apple wood with a couple seasons on it. Sweet-smelling, but it got a backbone.

I bet you surprised to see me. You was thinking I'd be down to the graveyard next to my Galileo, the good Lord rest his soul. Most are, at my age. You know how old I am? Now's a purely dumb question. Of course you do. I will confess, I am proud of myself for getting this far. Come November I will be ninety full years on this earth, and I got ever tooth God gave me, haven't lost a one. I am up at first light, and I mostly tend my own garden. I can still catch a baby when needs must. Caught my fifth great-grandchild last summer, a sturdy little boy called Almanzo after his granddaddy. How many women can say as much? When I am feeling poorly, don't I got a doctor right here in the house?

These years have been good to our Hannah, my Lord yes. And high time too. Her and Ben just as sweet on each other as they ever was. Hmmm? Well a course they got children. Two healthy young people keeping house together, man and wife, children will come along.

You don't think I'ma tell you everything right off, do you? Some things you got to go find out your own self. Ain't that why you come?

Elizabeth and Nathaniel right there where you saw them last, just up this road a ways, the place that folks used to call the Judge's. Now mostly you hear it called Uphill House, and this place folks call Downhill House. Because folks just can't keep straight who belongs where.

You'll see, Paradise has changed a lot and mostly for the good, the Lord in heaven be praised. This place is filled to busting with new faces, Quaker almost ever one. Good folks, hardworking and fair-minded for the most part, though they like to keep to themselves. They know the land too. We got barley and wheat and corn and flax, so much that come harvest time, they got to tote it all out to Johnstown and sell it there.

I expect you'll get a shock when you see all the new houses and such Ethan decided we couldn't do without. When Leo and me got here in '61 there was maybe six cabins all together down by Half-Moon Lake, most just one room. Now we got an inn and a tavern and real houses like you see in Albany and Johnstown, all neat and proper. Some even got those little white fences around the garden couldn't keep a rabbit out.

These last few years have been prosperous for just about ever-body. Good weather and bountiful harvests, the good Lord be praised.

You got a question sitting on your tongue like a stray hair. Let me guess, you are trying to think how to ask about Daniel. I should have told you right off—it's a long time you been waiting and wondering is he alive or dead. My, if you could see your face.

Daniel ain't dead, far from it. But I cain't say he healed, neither. Those first few years was hard but little by little he come back to himself. I myself think it was teaching school got him through. These days seem like the pain mostly leave him be, but it is hard to know. He don't like to talk about it. Yes, he is still a bachelor, and maybe you are thinking he'll stay that way. What young woman wants a one-armed schoolteacher lives way out on the frontier? But I'll tell you true, the day he finds hisself a bride—and that day is coming—there will be weeping and a-wailing you can hear all the way to Johnstown and beyond. He could have his pick right here in Paradise, but he's waiting for something. Or somebody.

Now I said enough. You will just have to go find out for yourself about everybody else, Jennet and Luke and Lily and her Simon, the folks up at Lake in the Clouds, all those people you wanting to know about. There's enough going on to keep you busy for a good long time.

Don't you worry, you can come back here and set with me whenever you got questions. I ain't going nowhere for a while yet. Galileo fuss at me now and then in my dreams, wanting to know why am I taking so long to cross over?

I say, you Galileo, be patient! Don't be fussing at me when I still got work to do. I got some stories to tell. Stories I kept to myself, maybe too long. I was always thinking, not yet, not now, and while I was hesitating time run off on me.

Mayhap I was waiting for you to tell what I know. We'll find out, soon enough.

I

Letters

ELIZABETH BONNER TO HER
DAUGHTER LILY BALLENTYNE

4th day of August 1823

Dear Daughter,
This letter is overdue, I know. I hope you forgive me when you
learn that I have held it back in order to share good news.
Yesterday your sister Hannah was delivered of a healthy son.
Both mother and child are in good health and spirits.

Your nephews Henry and John are beside themselves with
joy, but the girls were disappointed. When Ben brought them in
to see Hannah and meet their new brother, Amelie patted her
mother on the shoulder in a consoling manner. Eliza told her to
never mind, the next one was sure to be a girl.

It was all Curiosity and I could do not to laugh aloud.

It is my impression that Hannah is finished with childbearing.

She said to me not so long ago that five healthy children are more than enough, though she believes Ben would cheerfully continue until they were overrun like the old woman who lived in a shoe.

You are wondering what name they have given to this newest Savard, but I have promised Birdie that she could be the one to tell.

There is quite a bit of news that will interest you. Now that Blue-Jay is remarried and settled at Lake in the Clouds we were all hoping for a peaceful autumn, but Gabriel has declared his intention to marry Annie straight away.

I must admit that I am concerned. Annie was to go to Albany to study at Mrs. Burrough's School next month. It is my sincere belief that she deserves that opportunity, but it must be her decision. My concern right now is making it clear to Gabriel that he must be guided by her in this. And they are so very young.

Daniel is in good health and seems to have less difficulty with his arm of late, but then it is hard to know exactly. You know your twin, and will not be surprised to hear that he cloaks his feelings much of the time, and we see less of him than we would like. If it were not for his responsibilities as a teacher I suspect he would follow Robbie MacLachlan's example and be content to live alone, far from any settlement. But he is the teacher, and a good one. Birdie finds him very strict in the classroom, but she does not claim that he is unfair.

In the village we Bonners continue as the main topic of conversation. Blue-Jay's marriage and now the promise of Gabriel's is of unending interest. Missy Parker—pardon me, I mean Missy O'Brien as of this winter past. I said the other day that I can never remember that she married Baldy O'Brien, and Curiosity laughed, and said that Missy must want to forget that herself.

So Missy came into the trading post while I was looking at fabric, and she told Mrs. Mayfair that the Bonners were reaping their reward for keeping such close quarters with Indians. Gabriel would be giving Mrs. Elizabeth Middleton Bonner red-skinned grandchildren and just how would she like that?

Then she turned around and saw me standing there and she hopped in place, like a very plump rabbit.

I plan to have a discussion with Mrs. O'Brien. It is unacceptable for her to speak so, when any one of Hannah's children—my grandchildren—might be close enough to hear.

Other friends are mostly well. Martha is still in Manhattan and it seems unlikely that she will ever come back here to stay. Apparently there is now a young man who calls on her. Young Callie has had more than her share of trouble. This past season she lost almost her whole crop, for the second year in a row. The season was wet, and apples are prone to rot. With Levi's help she presses just enough applejack to survive from one harvest to the next.

Now I will pass this letter over to Birdie. Your father and I, your sisters and brothers, we all send you and Simon our love and affection.

Your mother
Elizabeth Middleton Bonner

Dear sister and good brother:
Hannah and Ben have named their new son Simon. Is that not good news? Now that we have a young Simon, you must come home so old Simon can see his namesake. It would be the polite thing to do, and you know how much Ma likes it when we do the polite thing.

Some things that Ma should have writ: When I complained that if Gabriel got married and moved out of the house I'd be alone, our fine brother said that is what comes of being an After-Thought and Da said, I would call Birdie our Best Idea. So you see, if you and Simon were to come home that would be a great comfort to me.

I have finished my nine-patch quilt. I am sure I had to pick out every seam at least three times. If I never hold a needle again it will be far too soon, but Curiosity was talking about buttonholes just yesterday and giving me a look I did not like at all. I have come to think of it as her Woe-unto-thee-Birdie look. Last week Daniel showed me how to balance a knife on the palm and how to grip it properly, the first steps toward accurate throwing.

I have very little room, but Curiosity wants me to tell you that she tried her hand at that paste receipt you sent, but she fears she got it wrong. It took a prodigious amount of butter to get it down her gullet.

Your loving little sister
Curiosity-called-Birdie

30 September 1823

Dear Ma and Da, dear Everyone,
I write under separate cover to congratulate my sister Hannah and her Ben on the birth of a healthy son. Simon was very honored to learn that he now has a namesake.

We are just back from a long walk in gardens at the Villa Borghese, and now I sit down to share with you the decision we have reached after many days of discussion. Simon paces the room while I write and so I will take pity on him and put down our news in plain words, as my father and mother will approve.

It is time for us to come home. It is six years this month since we left on our travels. I have done what I set out to do and more, and we are both homesick. Your coordinated siege by post has brought me to surrender, although I will miss Birdie's letters especially.

To be very clear, I cannot promise that we will settle in Paradise permanently. Some part of this decision will depend on Luke's interests in Canada and what role Simon may play there. I can say that we have every intention of spending at least a full year with you, and we hope much longer.

We have had a letter from Ethan with the news that there is a new house in the village near his own, one that he would like us to have for as long as we require. This means we will not have to turn Mr. and Mrs. Lefroy out from our place, something we are loath to do. And so all the pieces have come together. We plan to sail as soon as we can sell this house and settle other business matters. If all goes well we will be home before the spring thaw.

Then we can sit together by the kitchen fire and tell our stories to each other. Now that the decision is made I wish I could grow wings and fly to you.

When we have booked passage I will write again with the particulars. With all our love and affection we remain your good-son & devoted daughter

Simon and Lily Ballentyne

2
———

$\mathcal{D}$aniel Bonner wakes in the deepest hour of the night with the sure knowledge that something is not right.

First he takes stock of his oldest and best-known adversary. In his mind he follows the pain as it moves from its cave deep in his shoulder to slide inch by inch down his left arm. At times Daniel thinks he can hear the nerves snapping and hissing, but just now it only flexes and turns, a big cat sleeping in the shade. If he stays very quiet and relaxed, the pain might settle and sleep come back for him. Three or four hours, if he is lucky. He thinks about sleep as another man thinks about a lover, with a pure yearning.

But there is something wrong, and so he sits up and swings his legs over the side of the bed to listen. The bed ropes squeak and the banked fire hisses to itself. From the main room, the faint tick of the clock on the mantel. There is a sound he doesn't hear, one that worries him. His nights echo with the sound of Bounder's wheezing hitch, the sound of an old dog struggling toward another day. Bounder is utterly quiet, and somehow Daniel knows without going to look that the dog is dead.

Now he realizes what it is that woke him: a dripping sound, from outside. From the eaves.

It is the first week in April. Three feet of snow would be no surprise, but the sound of running water is unexpected. Daniel goes to the window and opens the shutter. The thaw has a smell all its own, and it is thick in the air.

There is a figure standing outside, a dark shape against the coming dawn. A large man, strongly built. He has a blanket wrapped around his shoulders. What light there is picks up a glint of his scalp, shaved clean but for a topknot that still gleams yellow, though Throws-Far is a full sixty-six years old. Born to Yankees in the village of Paradise, Throws-Far is nevertheless Mohawk in blood and marrow. Since he came back to Paradise he often roams the mountain at night; Daniel has the idea he is trying to find his boy-self, the person he was before he took his rightful place among the Turtle clan.

"Throws-Far," Daniel calls out to him in Kahnyen'kehàka. "Why do you stand in the not-yet-light?"

The dark shape shifts and bends, arms extended to the sky. The voice that answers is deep and sure. "The Snow Eater is come. He brings the hundred-year water with him."

A rain had begun to fall, as soft and sweet as new milk.

"The Snow Eater is come," Throws-Far says again. "And I go."

The old man has been talking about leaving Paradise for a long time. About his wish to see his own children, who live far to the northwest on the other side of the great lakes. That he would pick up so suddenly, that things might change with a simple shift in the wind, this is not at all surprising. He doesn't think like a white man.

In Kahnyen'kehàka Daniel calls to him. "Be well."

Throws-Far raises a hand, and then he walks away into the rain.

In the light of the fire Daniel dresses, not to teach school, though this should be a normal day, but in lined leggings, a heavy flannel hunting shirt, and winter moccasins. Sudden thaw and rain together promise trouble.

The ground is still frozen and it will take more time than he has to see Bounder properly buried. He picks the dog up, the slack body already unfamiliar, and lays him in the root cellar. Birdie will want to help bury Bounder.

His knives are laid out on a linen cloth where he left them, along with whetstones and files, oils and soaps. They gleam dully in the fire-light, like a mouth full of crooked teeth. He puts small knives into loops inside the cuffs of each moccasin, another, larger and double-sided, in a sheath on his left hip. Two short-handled hatchets, one he inherited from his grandfather and the other made to his specifications, he tucks under the wide belt to lie along his spine.

Today or tomorrow or the day after, his sister will come home. His twin, who has been gone very long, who he has missed every day. She is coming with her husband, but not quite soon enough. The hundred-year rain has beat them home.

3

---

*W*hen the clock in the hall struck seven, Birdie roused herself out of bed, dressed in the dark very quietly so as not to wake her nieces, and went downstairs to Curiosity Freeman's kitchen. She might have slept another half hour but for excitement: by Birdie's calculations, her parents and sister Lily and good-brother Simon should have been back from the city three days ago. They would surely be home today.

She paused in the doorway and waited for her eyes to adjust to the brightness of firelight reflecting off polished copper and pewter. "Little girl. Come on over here." Curiosity was sitting at the long table, a tray of breakfast biscuits just out of the oven in front of her. When she smiled there was nothing halfway about it. At almost ninety she was proud to still have every one of her teeth, strong and white. Between the bleached linen of her head wrap and her smile, Curiosity's skin was as wrinkled and dark as an apple left to dry out to a sweet smelling husk.

"Bring me that plate of ham while you at it, would you?"

She was tying up a napkin of biscuits, which meant somebody couldn't wait for breakfast but would have to eat when time permitted, someplace out in the weather. Most likely it would be Birdie's oldest sister.

"Hannah?"

Curiosity nodded. "Missus Rountree in travail."

"Who brought word?"

"Why, your brother Daniel. The teacher his very own self."

This idea was so odd that for a moment Birdie couldn't make sense of it. Right now Daniel should be on his way from his little house on Hidden Wolf to the school, where he always arrived by quarter past seven at the very latest. But Daniel was running errands and bringing messages.

Curiosity was saying, "Missus Rountree got a good set of hips on her, I doubt she'll have much trouble though it is her first."

Birdie found herself staring out the window at the rain, and feeling suddenly sleepy again. The kitchen smelled of brewing tea and ham and fresh bread and it was warm, as familiar and comfortable as Birdie's mother's own kitchen. As she buttered biscuits and stacked them, she let herself be lulled by the familiar noises: Anje humming under her breath, the crackle of the fire, the soft creak that the cradle made as Curiosity rocked it with her foot. Birdie glanced down at the round face of her youngest nephew and saw that he was watching her too, content for the moment with the sound of their voices. Simon's eyes were the startling green-blue of spring lichen, a gift Ben Savard had settled on all three boys but neither of his daughters, whose eyes were hazel.

Nature ain't got no interest in playing fair. Another of Curiosity's many sayings that were true but shouldn't be.

Outsiders saw the household as odd, and in fact it had a reputation that reached to Albany and down the Hudson in one direction and to Quebec in the other. Once in a while a stranger came through and knocked on the door out of pure nosiness and bad manners, wanting to see the old black woman who had started her life as a slave and ended up with land and property of her own. And was it true she had a half-Mohawk woman who claimed to be a trained doctor living with her in the house, and a dozen children with skin the color of deep red clay? The rumor said that the only white faces in the household belonged to the maidservants. And if that wasn't a backwards picture, Birdie had heard a tinker say to his horse, then what was?

It *was* an unusual household in some ways, but to Birdie it was a second home. Noisier than her own maybe, when her nieces and nephews—known in the family as the little people—were all in the same room.

Rain was rattling against the shutters so loudly that at first Birdie didn't realize Hannah had come into the kitchen. She sat down at the table, tucked a stray dark hair into the scarf she had wrapped around her head, and then scooped up her youngest child and sat him, a solid six-month-old brick of boy, on her lap. He immediately began to bounce softly and sing to himself, thumping her breast with one little fist, as if demanding admission.

"You had your fill not an hour ago," Hannah said to him. "You just want to noodle."

"The sweetest child yet," Curiosity said in approval.

A soft rumble of thunder made the baby blink in surprise. Hannah nuzzled him, but she spoke to Birdie. She said, "Little sister, can you look after the children for me while I'm gone?" Birdie straightened in her surprise.

"But there's school."

"No school today," Curiosity said. "That's the other thing your brother come to tell us."

No school. A day here—a rainy day here—with the Savard nephews and nieces, the oldest not three years younger than Birdie herself, but twice as much trouble.

Birdie drew in a deep breath. "I don't understand. What's wrong? Where's Daniel now?"

"Out the barn with Ben and Runs-from-Bears and my Joshua and all the rest of the menfolk," said Curiosity. "Talking about the weather."

Birdie's eyes moved to Joan, who was opening the window in order to pull the shutters closed. The rain was falling in sheets, and Joan's face and arms got wet. She looked purely disgusted, but that was nothing new. Joan was always sour and her sister Anje was always sunny. Today Joan was especially sour because she didn't like coming to help out at Downhill House; and she was even more eager than Birdie to get back uphill.

To Hannah Curiosity said: "Thaw woke me up in the middle of the night. But then I suppose I was half listening for it anyway. The signs all there."

It occurred to Birdie finally that there was a connection between the weather and how long Ma and Da were in coming. They had traveled by sleigh as far as Johnstown and then booked passage down the river to the city. They would come back up the Hudson by steamboat—another adventure she was missing—and in Johnstown they'd get the horses and sleighs from the livery. The trip between Johnstown and Paradise flew by in a sleigh.

But the snow was going fast, and in its place there would be mud, and there wasn't a sleigh known to man that ran over mud. It would be a much longer and more difficult journey. All because of the early thaw, and the rain.

Birdie felt Hannah's eyes on her, the warm weight of her regard. "I wish Throws-Far had stayed up in Canada," Birdie said. "If he had to come back here, why couldn't he keep his old weather predictions to himself? It's not fair." She stopped herself because from the corner of her eye she saw Anje taking in every word and storing it away. Birdie glanced down at her feet and said, "I shouldn't talk like that. Da says Throws-Far is a good man."

Hannah was smiling at her. "A good man can also be a frustrating man."

"Amen to that," said Curiosity. "But Throws-Far, he always been one to shout out to the world the things he want to believe hisself. Even as a little boy. If he hadn't been raised among the Mohawk, I have no doubt he would have turned into a preacher of the fire-and-brimstone variety."

"But do you think he's right?" Birdie asked. "Is there such a thing as a hundred-year water?"

"I suppose we'll find out." Hannah's expression was clear and honest but not very comforting. When she was like this she most reminded Birdie of their father, who could tell you an unhappy truth and still make you feel safe.

Hannah leaned forward to smooth a curl away from Birdie's temple with one cool fingertip. "You can leave it to the men to do what can be done, you know. Not every burden is yours to carry."

Curiosity smiled grimly.

Hannah was saying, "You are a great help, little sister. You make me proud."

What Birdie thought to say, but kept to herself, was this: She had little choice. If Hannah needed her to help with the little people, then she would help. But what she wanted was for the rain to go away, so the grown-ups could stop talking about floods, and she could go to school and be distracted from her worries. There would be spelling to learn by heart, twenty words full of letters that popped up without sense or warning, from *exercises* to *receiving*.

If she could go to school and sit at her desk she could pretend that there was nothing to worry about and then when Daniel rang the bell that marked the end of school she could rush home and find them all there: her mother and father, her brother Gabriel, who had been allowed to come to Manhattan just to keep him out of trouble, Lily and Simon, Luke and Jennet and their brood. There would be a lot of talking and laughing and Ma would make tea and get out the cake tin and everybody would eat some and pretend to like it.

Curiosity said, "Child, where is your mind this morning?"

"Someplace between Johnstown and Paradise," Hannah answered for her.

With a deep sigh Birdie gave in. "Do you think—" She paused, wondering if it was a good idea to put her worst worries into words. Once spoken, thoughts were free. They could fly around the room and come swooping at a person's head when she could least protect herself.

"Go on." Curiosity wiped her hands on the piece of toweling she kept tucked into the waistband of her apron.

"I was wondering how much the thaw will slow them down."

Curiosity reached across the table and took Birdie's hand between both her own, and she smiled. "They be here just as soon as they can, you know that. Your Da will find a way."

Hannah said, "You needn't worry, sister. Before you know it we'll be overrun with Bonners. By the end of the summer you'll be glad to wave them off home."

"No, I won't," Birdie said, irritated now. "I would be happy if they stayed here forever, even if it would mean having the little people following me around everywhere. But at least Lily and Simon will stay even if Jennet and Luke won't."

"Hush," Curiosity said. "Don't you go borrowing trouble. It come to find us soon enough without you shouting out an invitation."

The clock in the hall whirred and struck seven, and Hannah got up. She put the baby in Curiosity's lap and set her doctor's bag on the table. It was old and very worn, the leather patched in more than one spot. But

Hannah opened it with care, and she studied what she saw there. Her doctor face was so different from her sister face that she looked like a stranger for a moment.

"You take Shorty," Curiosity said to her. "He the only horse sure-footed enough to get you where you need to go in this muck."

Hannah looked back at them over her shoulder. "Ben has already saddled him for me."

"Well, good," Curiosity said, huffing a little. "That's as it should be. You pay attention, you girls," she called to Joan and Anje. "Our Hannah had to go all the way to the other end of the country to find him, but she got herself a good man, one who looks to his own and takes a care. If you find yourself a man like Ben Savard you hold on tight."

Birdie wondered if Curiosity didn't see the expression that flickered across Joan's face, or if she just chose to ignore such things. Joan LeBlanc didn't appreciate the suggestion that she should find herself a husband who was red, black, and white all rolled together. She might like Ben Savard—it was hard not to like him—but there were boundaries, she had told Birdie once. Everybody knows about those boundaries but your family, she had added, and then looked afraid that she had said too much.

Birdie hadn't told anybody about that conversation, but she did try to work it out for herself, why Joan would say such a thing that was sure to cause offense.

From above came the sound of doors opening and closing and then a rushing down the stairs.

"Here they come," Birdie said.

"Hungry, too." Curiosity stood, her hands smoothing out her apron. "Best get some porridge on the table." She paused, her head tilted slightly to one side.

"My," she said. "Will you listen to that rain coming down?"

4
_____

In a boardinghouse on the outskirts of Johnstown, Mrs. Louise Kummer sat at her kitchen table scowling at her accounts book while the kitchen girl got breakfast started. A full house, down to the maid's own cubby. You could say this much for German girls, they knew better than to complain about spending a night on a pallet by the kitchen hearth.

Mrs. Kummer squinted at the point on her quill, decided it would have to do, and wrote down one last figure.

"There. Now watch nobody tries to sneak off before I settle with them. Keep an especial sharp eye on the folks up under the eaves, those Bonners. I don't know why I ever let them talk me into renting to them. I hardly slept a wink, worrying."

Herlinde might have said how clever Mrs. Kummer was; how many people could snore so loudly while wide awake? Instead she vowed to watch and report immediately if someone tried to cheat her mistress of her rent.

Mrs. Kummer thumped her coffee cup on the table, and Herlinde came over to fill it.

"Those Bonners are odd, every one. Now in some cases you can see clear enough where it comes from. He was brought up wild, like an Indian, but her?" She dropped her voice to a whisper. "Mrs. Bonner is an English lady brought up grand with maids to serve her, but what does she do? She comes over here to teach school in a godforsaken place like Paradise, and then she runs off with a backwoodsman and ends up with a whole houseful of brats."

Herlinde made a sound in her throat to show that she was listening. Mrs. Kummer did not like to be ignored.

"Nathaniel Bonner of all people," her mistress said. "And him with a half-Mohawk daughter."

Herlinde decided to chance a question. "Would that be the woman doctor?"

Mrs. Kummer drew in a noisy breath. "You've heard of her, I see. She does indeed call herself a doctor. I wouldn't believe it myself but for I saw Samson Vanderstaay with my own eyes. Went up to Paradise to see if she could do something about his belly gripe and came home right as rain. And he's not the only one." She waved both hands in the air as if to encompass all of Johnstown.

"For my part I wouldn't let a half-breed woman come close enough to touch me. But that's Paradise for you. Quakers and Indians and Africans living side by side. In the meetinghouse and classroom too. But then the schoolteacher is another Bonner."

Herlinde had come from Germany only six months ago, and sometimes her English couldn't keep up with Mrs. Kummer. "Mrs. Bonner does not teach school?"

"Oh, she did," Mrs. Kummer said, her whole face twitching in disapproval. "For years. But her oldest boy took it over, so she can write editorials. For newspapers. And what does a woman know of politics, I ask you, and who cares what she has to say? It's not what the good Lord gave us to do."

Herlinde tried to look disapproving, but in fact she was more curious. She had come to America with high hopes and now here she was, still working in Mrs. Kummer's kitchen. She liked stories of women who managed to do what they set out to do.

"And on top of all that," Mrs. Kummer said, "she calls herself a rationalist. Fancy word for heathens, you ask me." Her bright eyes cut suddenly toward the milk pail Herlinde had lifted to the table.

"You take the cream off and water that milk down proper before you start the porridge." She paused to pick the last of the bacon from the platter on the table. She tucked into her cheek like a squirrel. "Tonight half my rooms will stand empty. I'm not made of money, you know."

It was something she told Herlinde many times every day: I'm not made of money. Often Herlinde had had an urge, almost irresistible, to ask this woman who owned a house and a farm and ate meat every day exactly what she was made of. Mrs. Kummer's reaction would be swift. Pack your things and get out.

Herlinde had seen Mrs. Kummer put four girls out on the street in the last six months, and so she held her tongue. Work was hard to come by these days, and it wasn't as though she could ask Mrs. Elizabeth Bonner if she needed another house servant. As poor as her post was here in Johnstown, no one ever asked Herlinde Metzler to do for Africans, and certainly not for Indians. The very idea must give any Christian girl nightmares.

5

———

Just twelve days after their ship docked in New-York harbor and still many miles from home, Lily Bonner Ballentyne woke from a light sleep and tried to make sense of her surroundings.

A small room on the very top floor of a boardinghouse on the outskirts of Johnstown. A narrow bed that she was sharing, not with her husband, but with her good-sister Jennet. On a trundle jammed into the space between bed and wall, Jennet's daughters were still asleep. Sweet little girls, but busy and unsettled sleepers.

It was a small blessing to be the first to wake, one Lily was glad of. As much as she had missed her family, she now missed the solitude she had come to love. She thought of the small house in Rome, with its thick walls and deep shadows, the lemon and olive trees and the grape arbor in the garden where she spent so much of her time. The sound of bees, and the smells. Often she would go for hours without seeing or talking to anyone, drawing and reading and sleeping in the sun.

One of the twins twitched in her sleep. Lily was almost sure it was Isabel, but the girls were very much alike, and especially so like this, their faces relaxed in rest. Everything about them was round: chins and soft cheeks and the curls that tumbled around their faces. They had been born while Lily was away, but they were so much like their mother they seemed immediately familiar.

As much as her nieces amused and entertained her, Lily held her breath until the little girl settled again. In another half hour the tumult would begin, a party of adults and four lively young children on the last stage of a journey that had been fraught with delays and complications every step of the way. They should have been in Paradise days ago, and instead they were stuck here in Johnstown.

All the way across the ocean she had imagined coming home by sleigh, gliding over a winter's worth of hard-packed snow, tucked into a cocoon of furs. The way she and Simon had once come home to Paradise from Montreal, in the deep of winter, traveling fast and quiet because of the war and the troops that patrolled the border. Now she had to laugh at herself for such girlish fantasies, for her steadfast refusal to consider the unpredictability of spring weather. The snow was going, and the rain was rapidly turning the roads to mud.

Yesterday the men had gone about the business of arranging for oxen and wagons suitable for the transport of women and children, and for the storage of the sleighs over the summer. More delay.

Lily thought of setting out for home on foot, how good it would be to simply walk. Simon would laugh at such an idea, but he wasn't here to tease her into a better mood. He was rolled into a blanket, asleep in the barn along with the rest of the men and Jennet's two boys. Where they would all be sleeping at this moment, if Ma hadn't managed to talk the landlady into letting them have these tiny rooms under the eaves.

They had been lucky to get them, as Johnstown was overrun with people who had come to see a hanging. A thief, well known and widely admired for his style if not his morals, was going to the gallows today— just over the meadow behind Mrs. Kummer's garden, if they cared to join the crowd.

Not an auspicious beginning to this last leg of the journey home. Lily closed her eyes and brought up other images: the brother and sisters waiting in Paradise. Old friends, and Curiosity.

Then Lily realized that she was being studied.

"What are you thinking about?"

She turned on her side to talk to her niece.

"Curiosity."

The wide mouth split into a smile minus two bottom teeth. "I was thinking about her too. Did you miss her while you were gone?"

"Every day," Lily said.

"More than your ma and da? More than Birdie and Gabriel and Daniel and Hannah and—"

"Not more," Lily interrupted. "Just as much."

"Then why did you stay away so long?"

Jennet's daughters were as direct and unflinching as their mother. The only way to deal with any of them was to offer the truth.

"There were things I needed to do. Things I thought were important."

"And were they? Important?"

"Yes," Lily said. "They were."

The girl considered for a moment. "More important than having babies?"

Every day since she stepped off the ship Lily had expected this question. The first time she was alone with her mother, when the women sat down to tea together in her aunt Spencer's parlor, when she saw Jennet at the door and recognized the curve of her belly for what it was. But none of them had raised the subject. Curiosity would ask, of that she was very sure. And by that time she might be ready to answer.

"Not more important, no. But babies are born in Italy, you know. Every day."

"You didn't have one," Isabel said.

"No," Lily agreed. "I didn't. Tell me what you like best about going to Paradise."

Isabel wiggled with happiness as she talked about her Savard cousins. They were wild as ponies, full of life and noise and mischief, and fearless, too, in a way that made the uncles laugh and the aunts go very still.

As young as Amelie and Eliza were, Lily had no doubt that they had already discovered some of the secret places on the mountain and in the village. From Curiosity's letters and her mother's, it was clear that Hannah's daughters had no interest in dolls or quiet games played in the parlor, but they could run and climb as well as their brothers. And while the boys might be older and bigger, the girls had a powerful ally in their aunt Birdie.

"Birdie is ten," Isabel announced. "She is the boss of us all because she's the aunt. Even Nathan pays her mind, though he's only five months and sixteen days younger and he's already a head taller."

She ran the numbers all together, as if she announced the exact age difference with great regularity. Fivemonthsandsixteendays.

"Well of course he does," said Mariah, awake now. "She's Da's sister, ten years old or a hundred. If you bother her too much she makes you call her Dearest Auntie Caroline Curiosity instead of Birdie." She brightened. "Do you know *why* she's called Birdie?"

"I'm not sure I do," Lily said, trying not to smile. She had still been at home in Paradise when Birdie got her nickname, but she didn't want to discourage the twins from talking to her. "You go ahead and tell me the story."

"Well," Mariah said, spreading her hands over the covers. "When she wasn't even a whole year old, she looked out the window and saw a wren—"

"It wasn't a wren, it was a robin," her sister said.

"She saw a bird," Mariah said pointedly. "On the windowsill. And she stood up—she couldn't really walk yet, but she stood up because she was so excited, and she yelled *Burtie!*"

"Just like that," said Isabel.

"And the bird flew away," Mariah said.

"Oh, she was awful mad at the bird," said Isabel. "Kept yelling at it to come back. *Burtie! Burtie! Burtie!*"

"And that's when everybody started calling her Birdie."

"Except when she says not to," Isabel amended.

Lily pushed a curl out of Mariah's eyes. "So you don't mind this long journey every year?"

"Oh, no. Summer in Paradise is like—heaven." Mariah looked surprised at her own turn of phrase.

"I remember that," Lily said, mostly to herself. "I remember that feeling."

Jennet sat up and slowly stretched her arms overhead. "As do I. Though I never had so many fine playmates. A whole crackle of cousins."

"Do you think we'll get there today?" Isabel asked, climbing into her mother's lap like a much younger child.

"Not if we loll about in bed we won't."

Someone was knocking at the door.

"Maybe it's Uncle Simon, come to wish you a good morning," Mariah said, grinning at Lily.

But when Lily opened the door, she found her father standing there with an expression that did not promise good news.

"Tell me," Jennet said behind her. "What have my lads been up to now?"

In the earliest morning, in the fragile moment between sleep and not-sleep, Elizabeth Bonner heard the sound of children laughing and immediately time rolled away and gave up everything to her: the children she had raised, and those she had lost too young. All of them in the next room, laughing together.

For that brief moment it made perfect sense that they should all be together, and then her waking mind took over, and she recognized her granddaughters' voices.

She lay for a moment listening. Next to her Martha Kirby was still curled into a ball, determined even in sleep. The shadows under her eyes made her seem older than her years, but in a happy mood—as she had been just ten days ago—she was the liveliest of young women, one who drew attention to herself without trying to, and seemed to be unaware of the effect she had. It was her smile that drew people to her, more than her regular features or high color. Martha had her father's hair: straight and heavy, but where Liam had been coppery redhead, Martha's color deepened over time to a deep rich hue that worked brown in some lights and red in others. In the sun it burned a hundred shades, from copper to gold.

Elizabeth studied Martha's face, looking for some trace of her mother, some feature that she could recognize as Jemima. Others did see the connection, in the height of her brow and the line of her nose, but Elizabeth could not.

"They are mother and daughter, I'm not denying that," Elizabeth had said to her husband. "But they are no more alike than chalk and cheese."

"Boots, you see it that way because you like the girl," Nathaniel said. "You don't want to see Jemima Southern in her, so you don't."

That much was true. Elizabeth could not find any charity in her heart for the woman who had cheated a good man out of his property and abandoned her only daughter at the tender age of eleven.

Still asleep, Martha drew in a hiccupping breath, much as a very young child would when coming to the end of a long cry. She moved a little deeper into the covers and Elizabeth saw that she had been sleeping with a ring clutched in her right hand.

A beautiful ring held so tightly that there would be a bruise there, a faint stigmata. She had tried to give the ring back to her young man when he broke off their engagement, but he had refused. A silly, ignorant boy who was too easily persuaded by an overbearing mother. He was not worthy of Martha, though the girl could not see that, not now. Perhaps not for a long time.

There was a light tapping at the door. Elizabeth draped a shawl around herself and slipped out into the hall, where her husband leaned with one shoulder against the wall.

"Boots." He reached out and pulled her in to him, lowered his head to kiss her just under the ear. He had slept in the stable and the sweet warm smells clung to him.

Better not to think about Nathaniel in a barn; things could still get out of hand when they found themselves alone in one. She rubbed her forehead against his shoulder and sighed a little, suddenly sleepy. She should have slept beside him, and left Jennet and Lily to cope with Martha.

"How is she?" Her husband read her mind, a habit she had never been able to break him of.

"Melancholy," Elizabeth said. "But she is trying."

Nathaniel cleared his throat. "We've got a problem, Boots."

She closed her eyes. "Please do not tell me we don't have wagons and oxen enough. I don't know if I can cope with one more delay."

"Oh, we're fine as far as wagons and such go. We could get on the road right after breakfast—" He shook his head, unwilling to put whatever it was into words.

"Nathaniel."

"The boys," he said, rubbing his nose with a knuckle.

"Oh, Nathaniel," Elizabeth said. "They didn't—"

A door opened and Jennet was there, settling her cloak around her shoulders. "They did," she said. "The wee buggers ran off. And sorry they'll be when we've got them back again, I can promise ye that."

"But where?" Elizabeth asked.

Nathaniel said, "I'd wager they want to see the hanging and they'll stay hid until they do."

"If it's hanging they want I'm mair than happy tae oblige," Jennet said grimly. "Just as soon as I get ma hands on them."

Breakfast was a sorry affair with all the men gone off and no Jennet to keep them amused. Even the twins were subdued as they dutifully spooned up the watery and tasteless porridge.

Lily had no idea how to lift the mood at the table, as her own mood was quite low. The girls kept turning to look out of the dining room window, and for once they seemed to have no questions for Lily or Rachel or even their grandmother.

It was no surprise to Lily that her mother was a favorite with the twins. Children had always come to her classroom without a fuss. Her mother had been a strict teacher but scrupulously fair. Most of all, she was willing to listen to stories and to tell her own in turn. She handled her grandchildren in much the same way.

But right now she seemed distracted, her gaze unfocused and her brow furrowed. It was the expression she wore when she was trying to work through some challenge. In this state she could let milk boil over and simply not hear a knock at the door or even her name, spoken clearly. As Martha was trying to speak to her now.

"Mrs. Bonner?"

Lily's mother jerked out of her thoughts and turned to Martha. She said, "I know it is hard to break a habit, but I hope you will try to re-member to call me Elizabeth."

Martha looked surprised. "I don't know—"

"You called me Miss Elizabeth in school, after all. Will you try?"

Just that suddenly it came back to Lily, how frustrated she had some-times been with her mother, who would insist on her understanding of democracy even to the discomfort of others.

Martha was saying, "I will try."

Lily decided to rescue the girl. She said, "Martha, do you plan to have a house built in Paradise?"

The younger woman looked startled at this question. Her spoon hung frozen in the air.

"You could afford to build a grand house," Isabel said. "I heard Da say so."

"You weren't supposed to be listening," Mariah reminded her.

Isabel wrinkled her nose in annoyance and ignored her sister in favor of instructing Martha. "We stay with Grandpa and Grandma Bonner."

"And so will Martha," Elizabeth said. "Until she decides for herself what she'd like to do. I mean to say, if that will suit you, Martha. Unless you had other plans?"

A small muscle jumped in the girl's jaw. "That's very kind of you. I shouldn't like to put anybody out."

The girl was angry, all right. Lily could feel it radiating off her like a fever. She was angry but she had lived too long with the Spencers, and she would not sacrifice good manners to give vent to her emotions. Lily knew this because she had felt this way herself many times.

"You aren't putting us out," Elizabeth said. "But if you'd rather stay elsewhere you certainly may. What were you thinking?"

Martha's color rose a notch. "I don't know. Maybe I could stay with Callie at the orchard. If she has room."

"I'm sure she'd love to have you," Elizabeth said. "I know she has missed you very much. Have you written to her to say you were coming home to Paradise?"

"I should have, but . . . I am looking forward to seeing her. Mrs. Bonner—Elizabeth—" she started, and broke off. "Thank you," she said. "I appreciate all your help very much."

"I think you have a great deal to look forward to, though it might not feel that way right at this moment."

Lily watched Martha struggle with a landslide of emotions: sadness, anger, regret, hope. Finally she managed a small smile.

She said, "You are very good. I have no idea what I would have done without you."

"*I* know," Isabel offered with great seriousness. "You could become an actress. I think an actress is a very good thing to be. Far better than a wife." And she turned up her nose with such conviction that even Martha laughed.

Martha had started this day as she did the last seven: with a lecture to herself. It would get easier. She would stop thinking all day long about Teddy. She would be attentive to those good people who had taken her away from an untenable position and thus rescued what was left of her reputation.

When her mood dipped low, she would think of Teddy's face when he told her that they couldn't marry. How he had studied his shoes, and how that cowardly act shocked her as much as what he had to say. Making a list of his flaws could occupy her for a little while at least.

After breakfast they gathered their things and waited on the porch until the carts and oxen were in place and they could set off for home. Martha liked sitting out in the chill air. It made all the colors brighter, and the sun on her face was welcome.

Jennet's girls fussed with dolls and talked without pause. Lily had taken out a sketchbook, and Elizabeth was reading a newspaper. Martha wished she had something to do; even knitting, something she had always disliked.

How strange the world is, she might have said to Elizabeth. Right at this moment I should be on a ship, a new bride on my way to spend six months touring Europe with Teddy. But in a moment everything changed.

She had the urge to simply walk away, walk all the way back to Manhattan and the house on Whitehall Street. To the room that had been hers for so long, with its pretty draperies and wallpaper and the thick carpet on the floor. If she had to hide in her misery and shame, why not there? At first she had simply refused when this move was suggested to her, and then Mrs. Broos had cut her on Fifth Avenue. It wasn't until that point she realized how bad things really were.

She wondered what Amanda had done with her wedding gown. Most likely it was still hanging in the dressing room, a cloud of pale green silk wrapped in tissue. Now Martha understood why the matrons clucked over the new fashion of having a dress made for the wedding day alone. What a terrible waste.

A horse and carriage crawled past. The mud sucked at hooves and wheels and made the driver mutter to himself. And then Simon Ballentyne was there. Martha knew he had come before she turned around, because she had seen Lily's face and the way her expression softened.

Simon stood at the foot of the porch stairs, spattered with mud from head to toe. He was a tall, sturdy sort with a shock of thick dark hair as coarse as a bear's pelt, and a heavy beard shadow.

Lily stood, her sketchbook forgotten.

"No joy?"

"Not yet," Simon said. "The others are searching on the far side of the commons." He leaned on the rail with one hand while he worked a mud-caked boot off with the other. When he had it free he turned it over and a stone fell out.

"Stop fussing with your boot," Lily said, "and tell us."

He grinned at her. Martha didn't find Simon particularly attractive, but out in the open with his hair tousled by the wind there was something about him, something vital and alive. And his dimples flashed when he smiled, so that it was almost impossible not to smile back.

"There's naught to tell. Between the crowd and the mud and all there's small chance of finding two lads who don't care to be found. It may be best to wait until the business is done." He jerked his head in the direction of the fields behind the house. "They'll come back on their own when the crowd begins to shift."

Lily looked up toward the heavens and groaned. "I knew it; I knew there would be another delay."

"This is very bad," Elizabeth said. "Young boys should not be exposed to such things. But if it is as crowded as you say, perhaps they won't see anything at all."

Mariah looked up from her dolls, surprised.

"What is it, Mariah? Did you want to say something?"

The little girls exchanged a glance, and then Isabel spoke up. "Grandma, they won't be standing anywhere. They'll climb a tree and watch from there."

Elizabeth's mouth fell open and then snapped shut. "Of course. We should have thought of that. Why didn't you say anything, girls?"

Mariah and Isabel shrugged in harmony. "You didn't ask."

Simon started to put the muddy boot back on, but Elizabeth held up a hand to stop him.

"I'll go," she said. "There's no time to spare."

She thanked foresight for her own sturdy boots as she followed the crowds, people on an outing as though they were going to a fair, and expected to be well amused.

Where she could, Elizabeth ducked around larger groups—mothers and fathers and children, some still in arms. Then the field opened before them and she could see the gallows. The executioner stood, waiting patiently. So the prisoner hadn't yet arrived; she had time to find her grandsons and get them away.

There was little hope of meeting the rest of her party in such a throng, and so Elizabeth headed directly for the closest stand of trees. It was less crowded here, as this spot would give no view of the proceedings at all—unless you were sitting up high on a branch strong enough to hold two boys.

Elizabeth put her head back to look into the tangle of evergreen branches, squinting to sharpen her gaze—her eyesight was getting worse; she really should have made the time in Manhattan to see about spectacles—when many hundreds of people began to shout and cheer with such enthusiasm that she couldn't help but turn around.

The crowd made way for a cart drawn by a mule. On the flat bed was a rough coffin of raw wood, and on the coffin stood a man, his hands tied before him. He wore only breeches and a linen shirt open at the throat, a carefully laundered shirt that set off tanned skin and dark hair that fell down around his shoulders and lifted in the breeze. If he was cold there was no sign of it.

She could make out shouts from the crowd: *Murray! Murray! Murray! We'll miss you, Jim Boy. Jimmy Murray!*

The prisoner bowed gracefully from the shoulders, right and then left. He raised his bound hands in an awkward salute and the crowd responded with good cheer.

Elizabeth shook herself out of her preoccupation and turned back to the trees. She put her hands around her mouth and shouted up into the branches.

"Nathan Bonner! Adam Bonner!"

But it was no use, she couldn't be heard above the crowd. She couldn't even be sure that the boys were anywhere near. She hurried on, calling as she went.

On the gallows the mayor of Johnstown was reading from a piece of paper, his head thrown back and his arms extended to accommodate his shortsightedness.

"James Murray of Schenectady. You were charged with the roadside robbery and murder of Mr. Horace Johnson, tax collector—"

The crowd had a lot to say about Horace Johnson, and for a while their voices were louder than the mayor's. It seemed that many were thankful to Jimmy Murray for relieving them of Mr. Johnson's company.

Elizabeth worked her way from tree to tree, shouting the boys' names up into the dark and fragrant tangle of evergreen branches.

"And so!" bellowed the mayor. "You have been indicted, tried, and found guilty. The court has sentenced you to death by hanging. Do you have anything to say?"

Murray did indeed have something to say. Elizabeth hoped he would entertain the crowd for a good long while, as she hurried from tree to tree.

"He was a right bastard," Murray shouted, and the crowd agreed with him at length.

Elizabeth slipped between trees too young to support the weight of two boys and almost ran into someone she never expected to see here.

"Annie," she said. "What—"

But she could see what, and why, and understood that they had all been sent on a fool's errand. Nathan and Adam wouldn't be found anywhere nearby; most likely they were still someplace in Mrs. Kummer's barn. It had all been Gabriel's doing, and Annie's.

Her youngest son came out into the open without being called, his expression carefully neutral. Twenty years old, the tallest of all the Bonner men, taller even than his father by a few inches. The most stubborn of all the children, which was saying quite a lot. Nothing of embarrassment or regret nor even a trace of remorse.

"What exactly is it that you were planning?" She heard the tremor in her voice but could do nothing to stop it.

"We were married not an hour ago," Gabriel said. "By the dominie at the Dutch Reformed church."

Elizabeth drew in a sharp breath. "Oh, Gabriel."

"*You* eloped," Gabriel said.

"The circumstances were very different," Elizabeth said. A conversation they had had many times, and were about to have again while behind them a hanging ran its course.

"You and Da wanted to get married and your father disapproved," Gabriel said. "Seems pretty much the same to me."

"But I didn't object to you getting married," Elizabeth said, her voice rising and cracking. "All I was asking—"

"You ask too much, Ma," Gabriel said.

Elizabeth tried to gather her thoughts. She turned to look at the girl. The youngest daughter of Many-Doves and Runs-from-Bears, a child she had helped deliver. On her deathbed Many-Doves had asked

Elizabeth to look out for this daughter's welfare, and Elizabeth had sworn to do her best. What she had never imagined was that her own son would get in the way.

"Annie. This is what you wanted?"

The girl raised her head. She was so much like Many-Doves that the sight of her always gave Elizabeth a jolt, joy and sorrow intertwined.

"Hen'en." Yes. "I left the school."

"Of your own free will?"

Gabriel began to protest and Elizabeth shot him her sternest glance. He scowled, but stepped back.

"Annie. *Kenenstatsi."* Elizabeth switched to Kahnyen'kehàka, because it was the language the two used when they talked together. It was a language she spoke imperfectly, but she needed every advantage at her disposal.

"You must say what it is you want. It is your choice. Not Gabriel's, not mine. It is not too late."

A flash of anger lit up Annie's face. She said, "Aunt, I know who I am. I am Kenenstatsi of the Kahnyen'kehàka Wolf clan. I am the daughter of Many-Doves and the granddaughter of Falling-Day. I am the great-granddaughter of Made-of-Bones who was clan mother of the Wolf for five hundred moons. I am the great-great-granddaughter of Hawk-Woman, who killed an O'seronni chief with her own hands and fed his heart to her sons in the Hunger Moon, in the time when we were still many, and strong."

Her voice never faltered, but she paused, as if to gather her thoughts. Gabriel stood behind Annie, his posture stiff and his jaw set hard.

"Gabriel wrote to me and asked me to meet him here. I listened for my mother's voice, and in my dreams I ask my grandmothers to guide me. I am a daughter of the Wolf Longhouse, and it is my right to choose a husband."

All the tension left Gabriel's shoulders. The expression on his face was so full of emotion that Elizabeth felt it was an invasion of his privacy even to look at him.

To Annie she said, "My son is very fortunate to have won your favor."

Annie closed her eyes very briefly and then she smiled. For the first time in this very difficult discussion, she smiled. There was nothing of nervousness or agitation in her smile, but a kind of quiet calm that soothed some of Elizabeth's doubts.

In the field beyond them the noise of the crowd rose and then fell off suddenly. In the still they could hear the creak of the swinging rope.

Gabriel would follow in his father's and his grandfather's footsteps, and make his living hunting and trapping in the Kahnyen'kehàka tradition. He would never dream about leaving Hidden Wolf, as long as he had Annie with him. In his single-mindedness he was so much like his father at this age.

"I am sorry about the school, and the money you paid to send me there," Annie said. "But it wasn't the right place for me."

"I wanted you to be sure," Elizabeth said. "I thought you might like teaching."

"She's not you, Ma." Gabriel's temper, so easily aroused, flared up.

"And that is my misfortune." Annie shot back at him. "Do you show your mother disrespect on the very day you take a wife?"

The girl walked away and Gabriel watched her go, a stunned expression on his face. Then he ran to catch up to her. Elizabeth watched them both, and wondered how much she was to blame for this turn of events, and if at forty or fifty her youngest son would look back on this day and still find fault with her.

6
—————

On the mountain called Hidden Wolf the streams boil up, ready to breach their banks.

The ground is still frozen solid; a shovel wouldn't get far, and neither does the rain. The earth cannot soak up anything at all, and so the water begins to move, dragged down and down by its own weight, pulling debris from the forest floor along for the ride: branches, rocks, a whole hawthorn bush trailing its roots like a hundred knotty legs. The rain fills the burrows where small things tend their young. The water flushes out the deepest fox holes, and rouses a young bear from hibernation. From deep in the forest a moose bellows its irritation, but the sound disappears into the swelling water.

The water moves, and everything must move with it.

7

_____

They had a plan, and so the men who had gathered in Curiosity Freeman's barn set out into the rain. The river had been high many times, and it had even breached its banks once when Daniel was a boy. It was hard to imagine anything worse, and yet they must.

Ben Savard lent Daniel the use of a horse—his own horse, in fact, a big sorrel he called Florida. Daniel turned her toward the village and set off at a trot. He had to get the word out about school being closed, and it also fell to him to ask for volunteers to help with the sandbags. Too little and too late, but it was action. It was something.

And if his shoulder screamed to the heavens, he would get this done.

He headed straight for the trading post, the most logical place to find men who could be compelled into action. Daniel was wondering if there might be sacks somewhere in his mother's cellar and if Hannah would be able to put her hands on them when he first heard it.

A far-off sound, but big. Some large animal crashing through the underbrush. The hair on the back of his head stood up. Daniel turned in the saddle but found nothing that could account for such a noise, as big as the sky and swelling.

An odd memory came to him. One of the stories his grandfather Hawkeye had told about his years in the West. He had lived among the Crow for a few seasons, and hunted buffalo with them. The best stories were of the stampedes. A thousand buffalo pounding across the prairie so that dust rose like storm clouds. A hundred men in pursuit, because without the buffalo they would not survive the winter.

A hundred men. The hundred-year water.

The sound was louder now, and more distinct. The roar of an angry bear.

Daniel kicked Florida hard and galloped down through the village to pull up in front of the meetinghouse, where he leapt off and ran up a short flight of stairs. The alarm bell was housed under a small roof, open to everybody in case of emergency.

Now Daniel yanked the bell rope with all the power of his good right arm, and he kept yanking. The noise was tremendous, even through the rainfall, and the effect was immediate. Men came running into the lane from the trading post in their shirtsleeves. Joshua Hench appeared in the door of the smithy, a load of empty burlap bags over his arm. And from inside the meetinghouse came a half dozen men. The Quaker elders, who had been sitting in silence, as was their habit, while they prayed.

All across the village people were looking up at the sound of the bell. The first indication that they were in real danger, but from their windows they would see only more rain.

Daniel stopped the bell with his hand and then bellowed from the bottom of his lungs.

"Get to high ground! Get everybody to high ground! Flood!"

$\mathscr{T}$he storm bullied its way in and settled down on Paradise, merciless and unrelenting. Cold, but not cold enough to give way to snow. A miserable weather, in which nobody would want to be out. Nobody but Callie Wilde, who was exactly where she needed and wanted to be, in her apple orchard on the sloping hillside that ran down to the Sacandaga.

Callie worked steadily despite the weather and the low light, pausing now and then to wipe the streaming rain from her face and clear her eyes. She could not make room for the storm, not today. Not in the cusp between winter and spring after two years of crops lost to black rot.

Everything depended on the harvesting of this year's scion wood and the grafting of the Bleeding Heart, her best hope. Her only chance to turn things around.

She had found the tree by accident; a gift of fate. It began as an aimless walk on a Sunday afternoon in September with no thought but solitude and, if she was lucky, a few hours not thinking about the loss of her crop. The Spitzenburg to fire blight; the Seek-No-Furthers and

Reinettes and Newtons to black rot. The end result was a few bushels of sorry fruit, hardly enough to make pressing worthwhile.

As she wound her way along the banks of the Sacandaga, moving in and out of the forest and bush, she had asked herself for the first time what she would do if the next crop failed. It was a question she had always refused to consider, but now it stood before her and would not be ignored.

As this thought came to her, she looked up and there it was: a wild apple tree in a sunny patch of bristlegrass gone to seed. Just six feet tall and just as wide, its branches garlanded with fruit: small lopsided apples of a size that fit exactly into her cupped palm. Streaked red yellow at the crown deepening to a deep, rich true red. Wasps buzzed as they fed on the fallen fruit.

She picked up an apple and studied it. No sign of blight or mildew or rot, but that meant very little. It could be mealy, woody, bitter, without any taste at all, or simply inedible, as wild apples almost always were. It was silly to hope, and so she hesitated, picking up an apron full of fruit and studying each of them.

In time hunger and curiosity got the upper hand and Callie bit into the nameless apple from a solitary tree.

A crisp bite through tough skin into fine-grained flesh that gave up a mouthful of juice, sweet and tangy, with a hint of . . . she took another bite, and held the fruit in her mouth. Pear. Hints of pear. Nothing like any of the apples she grew or had grown.

Callie walked home at a steady pace. Levi was in the barn shoveling hay, his thoughts so distant that she had to call his name twice before he heard her. Levi was a hired hand, a freed slave who had been on this farm since Callie could remember, and who was as dear to her as a brother. Without his help she would have had to give up the orchard long ago. He had been trained by her father but he also had a feel for the work. Sometimes Callie caught Levi standing motionless in the orchard, his head cocked to one side and his eyes closed. She had the idea, silly but still somehow right, that he could hear the trees talking to him.

Callie handed him an apple from the wild tree. Something came over Levi's face when he bit into it. Maybe hope. Callie was pretty sure that's what he was seeing on her own face.

Here was the eternal problem: Even if she planted every seed from every apple on that miraculous wild tree, Callie would not get one like it. An apple tree could not be reproduced from seed, because apples never bred true.

Callie was barely six when her father began to teach her how to fool nature into making a tree that could not be grown from seed. How to identify scion wood, how to cut it, score the root end, and keep it damp until it could be grafted onto rootstock.

In the years since, she had grafted hundreds of trees and cared for them until their first bearing. The maybe trees, as she thought of them. They might produce a new fruit, perfect in every way, but more likely they would give her apples too sour or woody to eat, without any flavor at all, too acid to press, prone to aphids or maggots or fire blight. In all the years there had been two grafts that grew into trees worth keeping, and neither of them had been hardy enough to withstand insects or mold or rot.

Every year Levi pulled down the failed maybe trees, cut and stacked the apple wood for seasoning, and every year two dozen new grafts were set in those newly empty places.

The plan was to harvest scion wood from the wild tree, but that had to wait until winter was just about to give way to spring. In the meantime, there were other questions to ask.

Levi picked every apple on the tree and then Callie sat down with paper and ink and a new quill, and she wrote twenty-five letters.

Dear Sir. With this letter I send to you the first fruit of a tree
I have named Wilde's Bleeding Heart. If you would be so kind,
I would be exceedingly thankful for any thoughts or comments
you might have on the quality of this apple. Please share these
by letter, or directly with Levi Fiddler, a trusted employee, who
brings you this message. If you are interested in tasting the cider,
I will gladly arrange for it to be delivered at the end of the
winter.
Most sincerely yours, C. D. Wilde, New-York State.

Levi went off with the apples to call on growers from Schenectady to Albany, from Albany to Boston. When he came back three weeks later his portmanteau was bristling with letters. Every apple grower wanted to taste the cider of this new apple, as soon as it was available.

They had all questioned Levi closely, but he had not given them any satisfaction or even the vaguest hint of where C. D. Wilde was to be found in the great expanse of New-York State. Better to stay out of the public eye; they did not want a stranger showing up at the door until they had a few dozen healthy, bearing trees, mature enough to give up scion wood of their own. Without any discussion at all they knew that they could speak to no one about the Bleeding Heart.

Settlers might move ever westward and drag their laws with them, but Paradise sat on the very edge of the endless forests, a frontier that would never be tamed. There had been stories over the years of blood feuds over things as simple as a single tree.

That winter they pressed the small amount of fruit they had as soon as the temperatures dropped below the point of freezing. Ice covered the lake and made the lanes treacherous, but Callie and Levi welcomed the cold. Every morning Levi checked the three barrels of pressings from the Bleeding Hearts and removed the ice from the surface. This went on for a week. When the cider had a kick strong enough to get a man's unwavering attention, Levi pulled a ladleful and handed it to Callie.

She had been drinking applejack for as long as she could remember. From a single mouthful she could tell what kind of apples had gone into the press, how many nights of freezing temperatures it had been set out for, and if there would be a market for it.

This jack was very strong and fragrant. It burned a path down her throat into her belly, where its heat spread out a warmth that burrowed deep.

Levi said, "Well? What's it taste like?"

Callie took a deep breath and then a smile broke out across her face. "Money," she said. "It tastes like lots of money."

They fit as many quart jugs of applejack as they could in the bed of the wagon secured under a tarp covered over with straw. Levi set out again and was gone the entire month of March; in that time Callie harvested the first of the scion wood from the mother tree and grafted it onto her best rootstock. The Bleeding Heart grafts had gone into the ground in the rich soil at the bottom of the hillside, where they had some protection from the wind and even shallow roots could profit from the fast-running Sacandaga.

Now those saplings were in second leaf. The right thing to do, the way she had been trained, was to wait another two or three years until they were sure of the fruit before they began to graft the Bleeding Heart in earnest. This time they harvested the scion wood at the first opportunity. With the cuttings from the wild tree and this year's grafting, they should have more than fifty trees this year, and a half-dozen of them would bear first fruit.

The rain was coming down so hard that Callie finally took note. She pulled her hood more tightly around her face and shoulders, and cleaned her knife on her apron.

The ringing of the meetinghouse bell came to her on a gusting wind, as frantic as the beating wings of a caged bird. On a clear day the meetinghouse bell seemed loud enough to wake the dead, though it was almost a mile away. She turned to listen, and as she did, the ringing stopped. Most likely one of the Ratz boys getting up to mischief, but then the ringing started again and a knot pulled tight in her belly.

A fire or somebody underneath a fallen tree. Somebody in trouble. She folded her knife, put it in her pocket, and set out for the path along the river, the quickest route into the village proper. And then stopped at the sight of the Sacandaga, already breeching its banks.

Callie looked back to her saplings, but somebody was screaming. One of her neighbors, screaming loud enough to be heard over the rushing river and the rain.

She ran.

With Florida turning and dancing beneath him, frantic to be away, Daniel pulled hard on the reins and brought the horse to a shuddering stand so he could get a proper look.

On the far west slope a gash had opened up in the tree line, a long rip down the mountainside. As he watched, trees fell like children's blocks; the earth itself seemed to be moving, as a plank floor would give under the boots of a big man.

Even in the mildest winters it took weeks for the ice to break up, but today it shivered and shifted and then the ice began to crack. It sounded like a barrage of rifle shots.

The whole surface of the lake was pulsing and twisting, breaking apart into hundreds of pieces, some three feet thick and twice as long.

The force of water coming off the mountain was pushing the ice forward, and at that moment Daniel fully understood what this flood would do.

He turned Florida and galloped up the lane. All over the village people were running uphill. Some carried belongings—a candlestick, a small chest, a milk can—while others led cattle and goats. Many were without any kind of wrap or mantle and most were barefoot. Children were squalling in unison, confused and frightened. Michael Yarnell—the most fidgety student in Daniel's classroom—was running with a hen under each arm.

The sound of the water crashing along the valley floor was deafening.

Daniel pulled up hard and reached down to lift Jed MacGarrity up behind him on the saddle. The old man weighed next to nothing, but his whole thin body was alive with excitement.

"You just saved my sorry hide," he shouted into Daniel's ear.

"Don't make me regret it!" Daniel shouted back and Jed let out a squawking, terrified laugh.

A crowd had gathered in front of the Red Dog, it seemed because everyone believed the water would not come so far uphill. Daniel hoped they were right. He pulled up there to pass Jed over to the care of his daughter Jane, who broke into noisy tears at the sight of him. No one else took any notice. Every one of them was staring down toward the lake, expressions curiously slack but for the eyes that scanned the scene, back and forth. Daniel turned to watch.

The wall of water came on with an almost regal slowness, roaring like a charging bear. Whole trees and boulders and huge clumps of ice tumbled before it. The bridge broke in two and disappeared into the churning waters.

Whole buildings were lost in a heartbeat. Ice flew through the air in chunks, like dried corn left too close to the fire. A piece as big as a door flew hundreds of feet through the air and hit a bawling cow. Later Daniel would tell himself that he had only imagined the sound of the cow's spine cracking. Then the animal was gone too, sucked into the melee.

Around him many voices were raised in prayer. Others shouted to each other the things they were seeing but didn't want to believe. Couldn't believe, until they saw the truth of it all in the faces of neighbors.

"Hast thou seen Friend Amos? What about the Crispins?"

"I fear Grandmother May didn't get to safety in time."

The crowd had doubled and continued to grow as people staggered in, many of them soaked and muddy, some bloody. Daniel wondered where Hannah was. For a moment panic overtook him and then he remembered she had gone to a birthing at the Rountrees, farther up the hillside. Surely the flood waters couldn't reach that far. Surely not.

That thought was still in his head when Lincoln Coleman came galloping up shouting for Becca. When she turned, he tossed a screaming, thrashing infant into her arms, wheeled about and was off again.

Daniel came out of his daze. He turned Florida and kicked her to a gallop. Ethan passed him going the other way, two white-faced children crowded together before him.

The first group Luke came across was Maria Oxley with her children. Her left arm hung at an unnatural angle, but she had one child on her back and another one on her right arm. She looked close to collapsing. Daniel pulled up beside her, took the reins in his teeth and leaned down with his good right arm to grab hands and pull the bigger children up, one behind and one before him. Maria passed the babies up for the older children to hold and then sat down just where she was. The children were screaming, and his bad arm was screaming, and the earth itself seemed to be screaming.

Callie Wilde came around a corner, mud-covered and barefooted. She had a bulging sack over one shoulder and her expression was murderous. Furious with God himself, and ready to do battle. Her orchards were right on the river. Daniel had a brief image of her apple trees popping out of the ground one by one.

She shouted, "Go ahead. I'll bring Maria along."

A man might hesitate at such a moment, knowing full well that if things took a bad turn, these two women would be dead within the quarter hour. But Daniel had been well trained, and he would not allow himself such weakness. He kicked Florida hard, pulled her head around and galloped away, hung about with wailing children who stank of piss and vomit and fear.

9

Martha Kirby had a hard time working out for herself exactly when she had last visited Paradise. She believed it must have been two years ago, just after New Year.

In the middle of winter Paradise was a peaceful place. Even the most constant sounds of water rushing downhill, of the river and the lake were hushed by the cold, slowed down and then stopped. That last visit the ferocious cold had surprised her, how absolute it was. At the time they had teased her, asking if she had forgot everything about home while she was away, and whether she needed somebody to show her around.

She had stayed with the Bonners for that visit too, because Nathaniel Bonner was one of her guardians. Nathaniel and his sons had been out on a week-long hunt, and so they were a household of women: Elizabeth and Birdie and the two LeBlanc girls who came every day to cook and clean. Curiosity and Hannah came by almost every day, always with Hannah's children in tow. There were visitors enough, and still there had been little to do but help with the household chores, read and write letters, and pay visits.

The only person she cared to call on was Callie Wilde. Callie was not a blood relation but she was a stepsister, and the only family Martha would claim. The hardest part about going to Manhattan had been leaving Callie behind. She had asked about taking her stepsister with them to Manhattan, but Callie herself had no interest in that proposition.

Even at that young age her friend's only interest was the orchard her father had started, and the pursuit of the perfect apple.

The storm picked up its rhythm when they were less than a half mile out of Paradise, and Martha realized that some would take it as a sign: a turn for the worse in the fortunes of the village. Most likely some would hold even this against her, and truth be told, she couldn't be sure they were wrong.

Lily hunkered down under the oiled tarp and told herself yet again that it would not do to scream at the heavens. So close to home after so long, and the oxen had slowed to a painful crawl, their heavy hooves sending up sprays of mud and water with every jolt forward.

The irony of it was not lost on her. She had left Italy with doubts; then one day she had come up on deck at first light and there was the shoreline, Long Island stretching as far as she could see. Everything in her had clutched in joy and fear; she was sure, at that moment, that they had been right to come home.

And it was at that very point that things began to go wrong with the journey. Broken axels, lamed horses, lost trunks, misplaced letters of credit. They had finally boarded the steamboat that would take them up the Hudson in a fraction of the time it had once taken to sail the same route, but even that had not gone to plan. She had given up counting the delays after the third time they were required to disembark because of trouble with the boilers.

People were burned to bits every year when steamboats caught fire, she reminded herself each time she made her way onto the shore. Better to arrive home like this than not at all.

Once they finally reached Albany the men had been keen to have a look at how the great canal was coming along. Even Simon, who understood how much she wanted to get home, even Simon couldn't hide his fascination with the idea of double-stair-step locks. Only the promise of more bad weather put an end to the discussion.

"Better to wait until it's done," Simon had said—to console himself alone. Lily would go to see it with him, but for his sake rather than her own. She would draw the locks and the boats and the mules who trod the towpath, but it was Simon who looked forward to the outing. And they had not even reached Paradise yet.

"Next year you'll be able to travel from Manhattan to Albany to Lake Erie without a single portage," Luke added. "It's a great advance for commerce."

No doubt it was, but at that moment Lily wouldn't care if the whole thing collapsed upon itself and sunk into the middle of the earth. She wanted to be home. She was desperate to be home.

Now the wind rose in eddies, picking at wet bonnets and capes. It set the trees to twisting and bowing low to the ground like agitated old ladies, all flutter and creak. The sharp crack of a branch giving way made them all jump.

So close to home, and the storm dug in its heels, sending down a cold driving rain that cut right through the stoutest boiled wool mantle. Were the little girls weeping? Lily thought she might join them.

"Almost there!" Luke rode up alongside the wagon. His voice had the hearty tone that was meant to comfort his frightened children, but the boys only scowled at him and the girls wouldn't meet his eye at all. Lily saw him exchange glances with Jennet, a whole conversation in a flash. Worry for their children bound them like a sturdy rope, intricately knotted.

As they came around the last curve and onto the road that led down through the village and to the west branch of the Sacandaga, the rain began to slacken again.

"One last bluster," Jennet announced. "The storm is played out now. I can feel it."

The children immediately perked up and began to look about themselves, but the oxen took no note of the weather one way or the other and plodded along at their usual pace; it was enough to drive a person mad.

Adam said, "The road is a river. Look, the oxen are pulling us down a river." Nathan giggled. Neither of the boys were concerned; they were enjoying the novelty of being out in the weather. They had already forgotten the morning's scolding, but then it had been Gabriel who had been taken aside, he and Annie with him, for a discussion that had taken the defiance from his expression and replaced it with something else, far more thoughtful.

The nieces and nephews loved the idea of Gabriel and Annie getting married. And despite the surprise of it all, Lily found she liked it too. It seemed right, once she saw them together. It was one more bit of evidence of what she had known in theory: Everyone had gone about their business while she and Simon were away. Gabriel was a man, as good a shot as their grandfather had been. "Better than I was at his age," Lily's father had told her. "Better than I was at my peak. As good as Daniel was."

Nobody said, before he lost the use of his arm. But they thought it, every one of them.

The little girls were asking questions, anxiety raising its head once again. Jennet clucked and comforted and began a story about a rain so hard it made the trees go hide.

"There," said Nathan, interrupting his mother in his excitement. "There's Uncle Ethan's new house; he wrote to us about it, do you remember?"

It was a neat, well-built house with a satisfying symmetry. Lily could imagine her cousin Ethan there with no difficulty. What she couldn't understand was why every house window as far as she could see down the main street was dark.

"Where is he? Where is everybody?" The only light was in the window of a building that was new to Lily, but must be the Red Dog.

She had had many letters from home about the changes in the village, but still the sight of an inn on the Johnstown road was a surprise. Another one of Ethan's projects: an inn that catered to locals and travelers alike, with a tavern on the ground floor and rooms to let above. There would be an apartment for the innkeeper and his family. Then he had hired Charlie LeBlanc to manage it—a daring experiment, as her mother had written, but one that might eventually take a happy ending, not so much because Charlie showed a talent for innkeeping, but because his wife would. What Charlie lacked in ambition, Becca made up for.

The Red Dog was a popular place, one Lily had heard about a great deal in the letters that came from home. A lively place, her mother had written. Except not this day. The shutters were closed and everything seemed very still.

There was something very wrong.

Lily started when her father nosed his horse up right next to her, rain still coming off the brim of his hat when he turned his head. It was so good to have him near, she regretted being cranky about something as inconsequential as rain.

"We've got to get to high ground." He raised his voice so it would carry, and then his gaze fixed on Lily's mother, sitting with her arms around the twins.

"Boots, take the blackberry path, the one that starts from behind Ethan's place. Move smartly. Carry the girls if you must."

"Very well." She caught Lily's eye and gave her a firm, determined smile. "Who wants an adventure?"

The men went down to the village on horseback to see what help they could be, and the women and children abandoned the wagons and oxen where they stood. Simon left too, raising a hand to Lily before he turned his horse's head and trotted off. He was glad to be here, among family, among the men, with serious work to do.

The women and children waded through ankle-deep snow water and mud that tried to suck the boots off their feet. The land behind Ethan's house inclined sharply and then disappeared into the forest, where the trees gave the group some protection from the rain and wind. The path was littered with broken branches and last year's sodden leaves. Wet snow fell from the trees in huge, unwieldy clumps.

It was a path Lily had walked hundreds of times in her life, and was full of memories: games, rivalries, feats of bravery, and utter foolishness. It was immediately familiar but strange too. At the top of the rise the woods would open up onto a clearing, and in the middle of that clearing she would see what some people still called the doctor's place, though Richard Todd was dead many years and the whole homestead belonged to Curiosity Freeman.

And maybe that house would be dark too, and empty.

Lily shook herself to dislodge the image. They would stop first at Curiosity's kitchen, where the fire in the hearth would warm them, and the teakettle would be whistling, and where Hannah and her family would be waiting, and little sister Birdie and Curiosity herself. Lily's heart was racing in her chest, and it had little to do with the steep uphill climb.

She was concentrating on her footing and so lost in her thoughts that

she bumped into Martha Kirby. They were stopped because at the front
of the line Lily's mother had stopped.

At first Lily wondered if her mother was trying to catch her breath,
but then things shifted and she got a better view. Lily knew every one of
her mother's expressions; six years or sixty years apart from her made no
difference. What Lily saw in her mother's face was surprise and deep
concern. Elizabeth Middleton Bonner, normally unflappable, was watching something happening in the village through a gap in the trees, and it
frightened her.

The boys scrambled up to see for themselves.

"What is it?" the girls cried out. "What's wrong?"

"It's a flood!" Nathan shouted back, putting all his strength into the
last word so that it seemed to echo. "The whole village—"

Jennet stepped in front of him and then they were moving again,
faster now. Lily told herself she wouldn't look when she came to that
open spot in the trees, but it was no use. The village of Paradise had been
her whole world for most of her life, and she could no more turn away
from it than she could from Ma or Da.

There was enough light to make out the trading post, the school-
house, the smokehouse, a half dozen cabins—houses, Lily told herself.
These were proper two-story houses with glass windows and curtains.
But there was something odd, something that made no sense.

Then she had it: Some of the buildings seemed to have moved
around, like pieces on a chessboard. The trading post had been on this
side of the Sacandaga when she was last home, but now it stood on the
far shore.

Annie seemed to read her thoughts because she offered up the explanation.

"The whole village is afloat," she said. "The hundred-year water
Throws-Far told us about."

"But it's—" and Lily stopped, because now it was all too obvious. The
river had become a lake. All the buildings at the heart of the village stood
in at least five feet of water, maybe more.

There was some movement. A canoe, paddling toward the schoolhouse.

"Did they get everyone out?" Lily asked the question though her
companions knew as little about what was happening in the village as
she did.

Annie said, "The river will drop. It will seek its own level fast, unless there's more rain."

Martha gave a hiccupping laugh that was so odd, Lily had to turn to look at her.

"What are you laughing about?"

Martha lifted a shoulder. "Quite a lot. Just the other day Mrs. Peyton—who was to be my mother-in-law? Mrs. Peyton said to me—" Martha stopped.

"What?" Lily said. "What did she tell you?"

"Oh, a great many things," Martha said. "She told me I was unworthy of her son, that I had been found out for the deceitful wretch I was. This was just after Jemima paid her a call, you understand. And she said—"

That odd and disturbing smile, once more.

"She said that sooner or later, water must seek its own level."

Martha turned back to the path and picked up her pace.

10

When the sky outside the kitchen door began to shift color, Birdie re-signed herself to the fact that she would not see the rest of her family today. Usually such an admission would have put her in a very sour mood, but she really had to be thankful that her people were far away from the flood.

She was helping Hannah put a splint on Maria Oxley's arm, and she had to concentrate very hard with all the noise and confusion in the kitchen.

Maria's oldest was telling their story again, in a hoarse and whispery voice. There was no stopping him. Nor should they even try, Hannah said.

"It started up the very same minute we heard the fire bell," he was saying. "There was a noise like a tree falling. Like a hundred trees ripping themselves out of the ground, and Mama stood up so sudden the bowl in her lap fell and broke. Then she was shouting and pushing us to the door, saying that we had to run, we had to run right now and we ran, I carried Joseph but it was hard, the ground was muddy and it was raining so. And when we stopped to catch our breath I turned and saw it, a— a—fist of water. A giant's fist punching, pushing trees out of the way. It flipped the Low Bridge like a pancake, and snatched up Miz Yarnell's milk cow; I saw it, it's true. That fist lifted our roof like I would pick up a wood chip from the ground. It was like standing on the brim of a bucket filling up fast." He blinked. "It was like the hand of God."

Birdie wanted him to stop. She wanted to go away and hide. But she could do neither; she must hold the basin of water for Hannah.

She glanced up and caught sight of Curiosity holding a cup of strong tea to Jimmy Crispin's mouth. Jimmy was fourteen but he was so good at numbers that his folks didn't make him quit school like most boys would at his age, to help on the farm. Sometimes Daniel took Jimmy and Birdie and Jamie McCandless aside for a math lesson, just the three of them. Jimmy was Quaker but he was friendly, with a wicked sense of humor and a quick smile.

Curiosity had swaddled Jimmy like a baby and settled him close to the hearth, and he still shivered. Almost everyone was shivering, even the people who hadn't got caught in the flood waters directly. The continual coming and going robbed the room of its heat, though Curiosity's grandsons laid on wood almost as fast as they could carry it in. Birdie was wrapped in shawls but she shivered too, so that it took all her effort to concentrate on what Hannah needed her to do.

On the far side of the kitchen a woman began weeping as though her heart would break. Mrs. Oxley kept trying to lift her head to see who it was.

Hannah spoke to her in a low voice. She said, "Still now, while I'm working."

Mrs. Oxley seemed not to hear her. "Is that Friend Molly? Where is her daughter? Where are her grandchildren?"

Hannah turned to Maria's oldest boy. "Joshua, please go over and speak kindly to Mrs. Noble. Find out if there's anything we can do for her."

For the first time a faint smile showed itself on Mrs. Oxley's face. "Yes," she whispered. "Joshua, thou must go and see to Friend Molly. And please see if there's any tea to be had."

The boy looked at his brothers and sisters. They were wrapped in a variety of blankets and sheets and every one of them looked dazed. Mrs. Oxley saw her son's hesitation and understood it.

"The little ones are safe. Go to Friend Molly."

Joshua looked as though he might be sick right where he stood, but he did as he was bid. He wound his way through the crowded kitchen to crouch down beside the elderly Molly Noble and speak to her. Joshua was just Birdie's age—they sat near each other at school—but she rarely saw him outside the classroom.

"Such a good child," Mrs. Oxley said. "Sweet-tempered and biddable. He's been in charge of the sheep for three years now, and he's done very well with them." She paused. "I fear we lost the whole herd."

"Maria," Hannah said. "You must brace yourself now. I'm going to set the bone. It will hurt, but it will be over quickly."

"May all our conflicts and trials be sanctified," Mrs. Oxley said, her eyes on her children. "May the merciful God in heaven keep and protect us all."

The travelers came in Curiosity's front door and found themselves in the middle of what looked like a hospital ward. The hall was filled with refugees from the flood, many of them in an exhausted sleep and others who barely took note of yet more people arriving. Lily didn't see a single familiar face and for a moment she couldn't remember where she was, exactly.

"Friend Elizabeth," said an older woman, holding out a hand. "Is there any news? Is the river still rising? If I might ask of thee, is there word of my sister and her family?"

Lily's mother crouched down and spoke a few words. Her tone was so soft and gentle that while it was impossible to make out what she was saying, there was still comfort to be had.

Raised voices could be heard in the kitchen, and one of them was Curiosity's. Lily went ahead, her muddy traveling cloak trailing behind her, her boots squelching with every step.

"You'll want to get out of them clothes right quick," said a man with a bandaged head and a mouthful of bloody teeth. "Or you'll take a chill." Then she recognized him: Jim Bookman, who had been a militia officer in the last war, and now was sheriff and possibly even a magistrate— something she might have been able to remember if not for the crusted blood on his face.

"Yes," she said. "Of course. Thank you. Has my sister seen to your wounds?"

He had eyes the color of periwinkle, as blue as her own, but the expression there was sharper, as if he saw more and better than anyone should.

"There's others hurt worse than me," he said. "I can wait."

The kitchen door swung open and she stepped through.

"I won't have it," Curiosity was saying. "Not in my kitchen."

The young girl in front of her was weeping, though her expression was mutinous. The cause of Curiosity's displeasure was the basket in the girl's arms, and what looked to be a half dozen raccoon kits.

"But their mama left them," the girl wailed. "They'll drown."

"Better them than you," Curiosity said, but she huffed a little. "Take that basket out to Miz Hannah's laboratory and give it over to Emmanuel if you must. He's got a fire going and they'll perk up quick enough. But if they leave their droppings all over that clean floor it'll be your hide Miz Hannah will be looking to tan."

The girl was gone before the last word was spoken.

"You are as soft-hearted as ever you were," Lily said.

Heads came up all over the kitchen: those who had nearly drowned, others who had broken bones or torn flesh in their struggle to reach dry land, children separated from their parents. And a girl who looked so much like the face Lily saw in her looking glass that it could only be Birdie.

Curiosity broke into a broad smile. "Look who the cat drug in, and soaking wet too. Birdie, child. Don't stand there. Your big sister standing right there in front of you. Go and give her a hug."

It was eight o'clock and full dark when the Bonner men came back from the village, Nathaniel bringing up the rear with his long, loose-jointed stride. Every one of them was worn down to a nub; the smiles they gave her were sincere but strained.

Elizabeth shifted the baby sleeping on her shoulder and quickly stepped out of the way lest her grandchildren bowl her over in their eagerness to reach their fathers.

"Are you whole?" Elizabeth asked her husband.

"We are," he said. He cupped her head in one hand and kissed her on the temple. "And hungry, and wet." He pulled back a little to examine the sleeping baby's face, and then he brushed a lock of dark hair off a brow the color of faded roses. Young Simon had helped himself to the best features each parent had to offer. He could be taken for Kahnyen'kehàka or Seminole or North African. Nathaniel saw nothing of himself in the boy's looks, but it didn't concern him. His grandsons would never have any doubt where they came from.

"Ballentyne," he called. "Come, man. Let me introduce you to your namesake."

Simon studied Hannah and Ben's youngest for a long moment. "Aye," he said. "The resemblance is uncanny."

They were still laughing when Lily came out on the porch and stood there with a hand pressed to her mouth, as if she feared the things she might say.

"Sister," Daniel called to her. "You've traveled so far, stay there and I'll come this last little distance to you."

Elizabeth found herself blinking away tears. Beside her Nathaniel cleared his throat and then he put an arm around her.

"That's a fine sight," he said.

It was a fine sight indeed to see the twins reunited. Elizabeth would have said so, if it had been within her power.

In Curiosity's kitchen the men were poked and prodded until the women convinced themselves that no one was making light of a serious injury. The worst they had among them was Ben's broken toe. And there was good news: The river had stopped rising.

That simple sentence ran through the house, rousing the injured and the exhausted alike to cheers and renewed conversation on how long it would take to clean up and rebuild, whether they might still be able to get the crops in the ground on time, what steps could be taken to replace the lost livestock, how much cash all these steps would require.

It was just at that point that Curiosity had said they needed to get home, and showed them the door. The only reason Ma and the rest agreed to go was by that time Curiosity's daughter Daisy and her two grown daughters had come to help, and the kitchen really was too crowded to get anything done.

The talk about the work that would need to start in the village followed them as they walked the short distance from Downhill House to their own. The mud made tough going of it, but Birdie could have skipped, she was so delighted. Lily and Simon were home, and everyone was safe, and soon they'd be sitting together around the table.

She knew it was wrong to be so cheerful when so many people had lost so much, but it was hard. For days she had been so worried, but they were all home now—including Gabriel, who was married. That idea made her stop just where she was.

She hung back a little to take stock. Ma and Da were at the front of the line, then Jennet and Luke with their children, Hannah and Ben with theirs, Gabriel and Annie, who stopped more than once to whisper to each other, Daniel, Ethan, and best of all, Lily and Simon. It was a wonderful sight, but something was missing.

Martha.

"Ma!" she called. "We forgot Martha!"

"Go fetch her, then," her mother called. "And don't take no for an answer."

That was easier said than done. Martha didn't want to interrupt or interfere, and said she would sleep on the settle in Curiosity's kitchen rather than get in the way.

"Ma said I was to fetch you," Birdie told her again. "Do you want me to get in trouble? And anyway, my da's your guardian, and how can he guard you if you're all the way over here?"

She held out Martha's boots, and after a moment's hesitation, the older girl took them.

By the time they got to the house the fire in the hearth had been fed and the kettle was boiling, but there were no women in sight.

"Gone to put the little people to bed," Ethan told them. "They'll be back soon."

Birdie tried not to show her disappointment. "Did Lily have to go too? And Annie?"

"Your nieces seemed to think so," said Birdie's father. "You could go up and join them, if you wanted. Both of you."

What Martha thought of that idea they never found out, because the door swung open and everybody came back. Or everybody except Hannah and Jennet, who would still be busy answering questions and tucking in.

Birdie's ma said, "Daniel, I've waited all day to hear your account of the flood. Are you too tired to tell it all again?"

They were all tired, but not one of them was willing to wait and so they talked in turns. Daniel and Ben had been right in the middle of things from the beginning, Daniel on one end of the village and Ben on the other. In the middle of their stories Jennet and Hannah came back to the kitchen and Hannah joined in.

"Birdie was a great help to me," she said. "She was calm and she did exactly as I asked her. She has the makings of an excellent assistant. It's true, Birdie. Why are you making such a face?"

It came bursting out of her then. "We can talk about the flood to-morrow," she said. "We'll be talking about it all summer. But I want to hear from Lily and Simon. I want to hear about their trip, and what took you so long to get back home, and what they brought in their trunks. Where are the trunks, anyway?"

Lily sat up straighter. "That's a very good question. The last I saw of them was when we abandoned the wagons to walk up here." Then she slumped back against the settle. "Not that I'd have the energy to go after them."

"No need," Ben told her. "We got them sorted through. They're sitting in the kitchen in the house Ethan offered you, drying out in front of the hearth."

And that was the first Birdie heard about Lily and Simon going to live in the house next to Ethan's, the one folks called Ivy House. It struck her as a very bad idea, and she was about to say so when Lily smiled at her.

"I hope you will come and visit with me every day," she said.

"After school," Daniel prompted.

"And chores," said her da.

"Yes, after school and chores," Lily agreed. "But then you and I will have a lot to talk about, just the two of us."

Birdie paused and rethought her arguments. It might not be so very bad to have Lily and Simon in a house of their own. There was a great deal to be said for privacy, and there would be precious little of it here over the next months.

"She likes the idea," Jennet said. "Clever lass."

Daniel was sitting beside Lily, leaning into her with the warm famil-iarity of a twin. He turned to her. "Now you," he said. "Birdie there is about ready to bust, wondering what held you up so long. What's this I hear about a hanging?"

Tea was poured and the biscuit tin appeared on the table, followed by cheese and bread and pickles, and more tea, and more talk. Elizabeth, as tired as she was, found it impossible to stay seated. She roamed back and forth, passing dishes, pausing to touch a shoulder or lay her hand on a head. This was not the way she had imagined Lily's homecoming, but the most important thing was to have them all here, whole and healthy. This one summer they would have together, all of them. In the fall Luke and Jennet would go back to the city and maybe Lily and Simon would move on too. She must not let herself hope for anything more.

It was silly to borrow trouble; she knew that. She stood to fill the teapot, and Nathaniel caught her by the wrist and made her sit again.

"You're as nervous as a cat," Nathaniel said to her. His eyes moved over her face. He understood; he always did, when it came to the children. She wondered if today he had thought of the others, the sons they had lost as infants. Sometimes they talked of those boys, how old they would be now, and who they might favor. It was a comfort, that freedom to talk of children thirty years in their graves. To know that they were not completely forgotten.

"Ethan, you must have some more soup," she said, starting to rise. "You are too thin."

"No you don't," Nathaniel said, pulling her back down again.

"Ma," Birdie said in mock irritation. "You'd scold me if I kept jumping up from the table."

"Leave her be." Luke winked at his stepmother. "It's her best broody hen imitation."

Ethan said, "I couldn't eat any more, Aunt Elizabeth. But maybe there is something I can do for you? Shall I trounce these louts for their impertinence?"

"They may tease me all they like," Elizabeth said over the laughter. "Today I can't be ruffled."

That silenced them for a moment, thinking of the village and the families who had lost so much.

"How bad is it?" Hannah asked.

"Not good," Gabriel said into his bowl.

"Six missing," Daniel said. "All three of the Sampsons, Noah True-blood, Grandma May, and the Crispins' youngest, Alexander."

"One of your students?" Lily asked her brother, and he nodded.

"Ten years old, good with numbers. Quiet boy, polite."

"He's got family on the other side of the river," Ben said. "He might be there. Could be that the Sampson brothers and all the rest of them are sitting in the kitchen at the mill house drinking cider."

Nathaniel said, "Let's hope so. What we do know for sure is, a lot of stock went down the river. Oxley's sheep and some goats too. A dozen or more milch cows."

"And a good lot of Callie's trees are gone," Daniel added. "Maybe three quarters."

When Daniel spoke of Callie Wilde it was always with a certain amount of warmth. Elizabeth had once had the idea that something more might grow out of their friendship, but that had never come to pass.

For the first time Martha Kirby spoke up to ask a question. She said, "And Callie herself? Is she safe?"

"She's a little banged up," Nathaniel said. "But last I saw her she was walking and talking. Becca gave her a bed at the Red Dog."

Daniel's eyes had settled on Martha and stayed right there while the conversation moved off in a new direction. It struck Elizabeth then that he didn't recognize her, or maybe he was in too much pain to take note. The lines that bracketed his mouth said very clearly that he had strained his shoulder today and must now pay the price. Anything that might distract him would be welcome.

Elizabeth said, "Daniel, you must remember Martha Kirby."

He started at the name and came up as if out of a dream, already rising from his seat. He leaned over the table and extended his good right hand to Martha.

"I haven't seen you in five years at least. I guess I was away when you visited the last few times."

Martha shook the offered hand and agreed that it was a very long time since they had seen each other. She looked as tired as any of them, but she bore it well: a dignified, friendly young woman, sure of herself without any hint of arrogance, though she was rich by most men's standards and had spent half her life in the city. To look at her you wouldn't know that just a week ago the life she had built for herself had fallen to pieces.

Elizabeth had taught Martha as a child, and looking at her now she saw that she had not changed very much after all. There was a quiet strength about her, a dignity that was easily read from the way she held herself. And sometime since they had arrived back in Paradise she had lost the stiff posture of the last weeks. As if she recognized that this place was truly safe, and she belonged here.

She wasn't the only one to take note. All the men watched Martha when she crossed the kitchen. There was nothing untoward in it; they watched her as they would watch any well-favored young woman, with appreciation. The simple pleasure of looking at a girl in her first full blush. Martha had her father's heavy, thick hair, though hers was many shades darker. Her complexion was clear and high in color, and her features strong. She might be shy of men for some months or even years, but if she showed any interest at all she would have proposals enough to choose from, before the summer came to an end.

"She'll have to rebuild," Martha was saying about Callie.

"I'd have her up here," Elizabeth said. "But every bed is occupied, some more than once."

When the laughing stopped, Elizabeth was content to sit quietly at the table and listen as the men talked about the work that would have to start the next day. How many houses would have to be torn down, how many might be repaired, if it might be possible to salvage materials from the great piles of rubble that marked the passing of the water.

Then the apple grunt went around and Elizabeth felt Nathaniel looking at her.

"You and your apple grunt," she said, but she smiled.

"I'm fond of apples," he said, winking at her. "Always have been."

Martha got up to gather plates and take them away, and Daniel watched her go.

He said, "No apple grunt for you, Martha?"

Under the table Nathaniel bumped Elizabeth's knee with his own and then he leaned forward to whisper in her ear, his warm breath stirring a few wayward curls.

"Stop it."

She began to protest and his hand pressed into her leg, fingers sliding provocatively.

"If he gets a whiff of what you're thinking you know he'll run in the other direction. That ain't what you want, is it?"

Elizabeth leaned into him. Nathaniel smelled of river water and mud and sweat, but he was healthy and whole. She said, "It is very shallow and selfish of me, but I do resent the fact that Lily's homecoming has been ruined."

He narrowed one eye at her, suspicious of this change in the subject.

"I wanted it to be—"

Nathaniel looked around the table, and then looked at her again, pointedly. "What could you want more than this?"

She could not challenge him on that point. He was perfectly right.

"A search party will be going out at first light," Simon was saying. He didn't add what they all knew, that the searchers were unlikely to find much to rescue.

"Aye then," Nathaniel said. "Time we got to bed. Daniel, you planning to walk up the mountain after the long day you've had?"

Daniel barely looked up from his cup. He didn't seem to notice that the table had gone quiet in anticipation. Elizabeth couldn't remember the last time he had agreed to stay in the village, or when she had dared ask him to stay.

"I want to walk down to the village with Simon and Lily," he said finally. "And then I'll see."

Gabriel and Annie declared it time to set out for Hidden Wolf, and would not hear of bedding down in the parlor or anywhere but their own cabin beside the waterfalls. At the door Elizabeth took Annie's face between her hands and kissed her soundly on the forehead. She was so much like her mother, and her mother was so missed. How young they were. Children, setting off on their own. Tomorrow, when she had slept, Elizabeth would sit down and think it all through.

By ones and twos they began to drift away to their beds, until she and Nathaniel were alone in the kitchen with the only light coming from the banked hearth where coals pulsed hot beneath the cinders.

"We've got the whole summer and into the fall," Nathaniel said. "Right now it's time we slept."

Up the stairs, stepping quietly with Nathaniel behind her, Elizabeth stopped at the top and stood to listen. From behind Luke's door they could hear the soft rise and fall of voices. The small chamber Martha had for her own was quiet, and the children's rooms were just as silent.

"You'll wake them," Nathaniel said. He was right, of course. But still she hesitated at the door, listening for some sign. She imagined the girls asleep, all four of them wound together in a bed meant for two adults. The twins on their backs with chins pointed to the rafters, and Hannah's two girls back-to-back. The boys would be on the floor in the next chamber, all of them claiming to be more comfortable on hard board than soft mattress. Sometime in the night one or all of them would climb into the bed, half asleep, and have no memory of doing so the next morning. Or none that they would admit to. They were good boys, but in such a hurry to grow up and prove themselves. As her own boys had been, to her constant worry. When the next war came—and it would, she could not deny the inevitability of it—she hoped these children would be wise enough to know better.

And if they did not, she would remind them. Wherever they were, she would remind them. It was increasingly clear to her that Paradise would one day be too small for Hannah's children. Their alternatives would be few and limited. She had become fully aware of this when she took Henry with her to Johnstown when he was just three. People stopped to stare at him without hesitation or apology, because he was beautiful. Because he was long-limbed and graceful. And because his eyes were turquoise and his features symmetrical and his complexion the color of copper seen through old honey.

Like a painting, strangers stop to say. Like an angel. And: Such a shame.

Most people could not imagine a place in the real world—in their own world—for a mixed-race child. In Henry's face were the best features of every race that populated the continent, white and red and black, and there was more. The bright and intelligent eyes, the naked curiosity in the way he observed the world. He had never known a hateful word, but the day would come. For all of them, that day would come. Others would pronounce them worthless and unclean.

Elizabeth would spend the rest of her life making sure that these grandchildren—every one of them—learned their own true value. They were healthy and whole, full of light and promise. Not of her blood, but hers just the same.

There would be others. It seemed now that Gabriel might be the first to bring her a grandchild, something she would have never imagined even ten years ago. She had believed for a very long time it would be Lily. In those first few years while they were away, Elizabeth opened every letter in a state of excitement and then folded it away more thoughtfully.

Why this should be, Lily had never written, and Elizabeth had never asked. Some things were too fragile to put on paper, but tomorrow she would sit with her daughter, her most loved firstborn, and Lily would tell her those things she had been holding back.

Because Elizabeth could not wonder in silence another day.

$\mathcal{B}$ecca LeBlanc said, "Charlie, you'll have to go out and look for her. She should have come back by now. I wish I had never let her go."

It was full dark, and all through the Red Dog people were trying to let go of the terrible day they had survived in order to sleep. Every bit of floor space was taken up, and every bed with the exception of one.

"Callie Wilde is too smart and too tough to get herself in trouble," Charlie said, folding his hands over his middle. "If she gets it in her head to go check on her trees, then there's no stopping her. You know that yourself."

"But it's so late," Becca said, not for the first time. "What can she be doing?"

Charlie yawned noisily. "My guess is she's over there with a lantern taking the toll."

Becca woke sometime later to the sound of murmured voices. Charlie had already gone to their chamber door and opened it a crack. He listened for a moment and then he closed it and came back to bed, stubbing his toe in the process.

"I told you," he said. "Now will you stop fussing about Callie Wilde? You need all your strength for tomorrow's worries. We all will."

The finest room at the Red Dog was the one that looked down over the lane. It had a big bed hung with faded curtains and an adjoining room no bigger than a closet with a single bed, a servant's lot.

The entire Cunningham family had crowded into the bigger room and now slept uneasily, older children wrapped in blankets on the floor and what looked like two or three grown-ups in the bed with Jane's youngest between them. Callie stepped carefully by the light of a tallow candle and then closed herself into the servant's cabinet.

It was narrow and stuffy, but she had it to herself for the simple reason that there was not room enough for anyone to stretch out on the floor. She sat down heavily and started to peel herself out of clothes that were drenched with water and dirt. Her face and arms were tight with dried mud, but the very idea of looking for a washbasin and water was so absurd that it brought out a small smile.

When she was naked she wrapped herself in the rough wool blanket, put out the candle, and lay down.

The dark was a comfort. Absolute and unyielding, she made a place for herself inside it. A safe place, where she could let her iron grip loosen for a little while. She wept until her eyes were swollen shut, silent tears that burned like lye. For the first time in her life, she understood what it meant to want to go to sleep and not wake up again. She understood why her father had simply . . . walked away.

Callie wished for the thousandth time that she hadn't sent Levi to Johnstown for supplies. But she had, and so had spent the day alone, walking her property lines back and forth for hours, venturing as far as she could go before water and mud stopped her.

With some effort she turned her mind to other things. The cider house still stood, minus a few shingles but otherwise intact on the hillside above the orchard. Inside, the cider press, rows of jugs, and stacks of baskets and barrels, all as she had last seen them. She continued on, a quarter mile into the woods to the spot where Levi's small cabin stood in a circle of birch trees, undisturbed. It was one thing to be thankful for.

And they still had three dozen trees that had survived and might still bear fruit this year. Even poor fruit could be made into applejack, and applejack would carry them through yet another disastrous year.

In the close, damp dark she found she could not keep control of her thoughts, or of the images she had gathered by the light of a pierced tin lantern.

Every single Bleeding Heart was gone, and in the rushing and confusion of the escape from the flood, she had lost her scion wood bag too.

As soon as Levi got home she would ask him to go searching downriver to see what he might find. There must be something, and if there was not, then she needed to know about the wild apple tree.

If God was at all merciful, the wild Bleeding Heart would be there. Callie tried to pray, and had time to realize she didn't know where to start before sleep overcame her.

Levi came back from Johnstown with the supplies, spent ten minutes listening to Callie's halting story of the disaster that had come upon them, and then set out immediately downriver. He took two axes with him, a bucket, and a long rifle on his back, and told Callie he might be gone until dark or after.

She swept out the cider house, fetched water, built a fire to heat it, and scrubbed the press and the buckets clean of dust and mold. Her hands were red and swollen with work, and she was so light-headed that sometimes she had to sit for five minutes until her vision cleared.

In the village they would have started the digging out, but Callie had no intention of leaving this place until she knew the whole story. She would wait for Levi if it meant sleeping on the bare ground.

It was midafternoon when she looked up and saw him coming toward her, and the only thing she felt in that moment was fear. The strongest urge, almost too strong to resist, was to turn her back and run. The things he had to tell her, the things he must tell her, were the things that would break her in half or set her on the road back to herself.

He put down the bucket so she could see that it was filled with scion wood. Callie glanced up at him and he shook his head.

This wood was not from the Bleeding Heart, then. A shudder ran through her, but Levi took no note. He was reaching behind himself to undo something strapped along his spine.

A three-year-old Bleeding Heart sapling, its root ball wrapped in wet and muddy cloth. Two branches had been broken off, but there were three others.

"I found it sitting right on top of a mountain of deadwood and rock twelve feet high. Still got your tag on it."

They had been hoping for fifty Bleeding Hearts, and had now only this one.

She said, "Tell me about the wild tree."

He didn't answer until she raised her face to look at him.

"Gone," he said. "Ripped right up out of the ground and pounded to pulp, is what I guess. No sign of her anywhere. But we got this one, Miss Callie. We got a healthy tree, and that's all we had two years ago. We just got to start again."

12

_____

Just past dawn, and Elizabeth watched Nathaniel dressing to go down into the village. Into what had been the village. There would be search parties and salvage parties. Everyone strong enough to lift a shovel would be set to work digging what was left of Paradise out of the mud.

Elizabeth had dreamed of the women from the village wading through the mud, pulling out fine silver spoons and porcelain chargers rimmed in gold, beeswax candles by the dozens, delicate little mantel clocks, shoes with sapphire buckles, portraits of laughing children in ornate frames. Everything beautiful, sparkling clean.

She had come to give credence to dreams over the years. More often than not there was the spark of truth in them, but presented from such an odd angle that her waking mind could dismiss them. Many-Doves would have had much to say about this dream. It had been her gift, the ability to reach inside the images Elizabeth recalled in bright snatches, and pull out a single truth hidden among the silver and jewels.

In the village women would be digging in the mud for fragments of far simpler lives. Tin plate ware and barn clogs much mended. An old

Farmer's Almanac handed down from grandfather and father. A family Bible, a spinning wheel. Even the smallest thing precious.

She sat up suddenly.

"Boots?" Nathaniel half turned toward her. His hair was still unbound and it flowed over the bulk of his shoulders, black and silver in the firelight.

"I can't stay abed, not with—not with the trouble in the village. I'm going with you."

For a moment he considered arguing with her; she could see it working in his face. And then he gave it up as a lost cause.

When Nathaniel had a choice, he walked. Raised up by a father who looked like a white man but thought and acted like a Mahican, he had learned to value the silence of the forests, and the things that could be learned from them when a man was on foot. A horse was a fine creature, but of little use to a man who was out looking for game.

In fact, Elizabeth couldn't remember the last time she had seen him mount a horse for so short a distance. But today he insisted on riding. And it made sense; the mud would be a foot deep and more.

Nathaniel rode Romeo, named by Birdie for his beauty, and for Elizabeth he saddled Pepper, a mule as dependable as the sunrise, and devoted to Elizabeth.

"Because you feed him apples." Birdie wanted it recorded for posterity that her mother was willing to bribe mules for their good behavior, a tactic she never employed with children.

It was good to be out in the weather in the early morning, even such gray weather as this. And the birds were coming back. There was birdsong all around; veeries, thrush, phoebes, robins, all announcing their presence and claiming territory. She was very glad to be home.

The trip to Manhattan had been unusually difficult. First waiting for the ship to dock—three days, listening for the messenger who would bring word—and then so overwhelmed with the fact of her daughter that her mind could not be still, even when she slept. If things had gone differently—

Beside her Nathaniel said, "The best-laid plans."

Elizabeth made a face at her husband. "It's very rude, the way you read my thoughts."

He grinned at her. "How does the rest of it go?"

"I can't recall. How odd." She frowned. "Once I would have remembered the whole poem, word for word."

"You've got a lot less space in that head of yours than you used to. Close to thirty years of raising up a family and teaching don't leave much room for poetry."

He always knew how to distract her. Elizabeth straightened in the saddle to relieve the ache in her back, and said as much to him. "I don't like to think of it that way, in years. Thirty years! That can't be correct."

It was a conversation they had often, but she had never been able to adopt Nathaniel's matter-of-fact way of looking at things. Time moved on, and so must they.

They passed the Downhill House, and the smell of wood smoke and baking bread drifting from the chimney. Curiosity came to the kitchen window and waved a floury hand to them as they passed.

"I'd like to stop by to see Lily," Elizabeth said suddenly.

Nathaniel made the thoughtful face, the one that meant he had reservations but would keep them to himself. That one expression was more effective than any argument; as much as Elizabeth liked to depend on reason in her deliberations, Nathaniel was far better at holding that line when it came to dealing with the children.

Then they came around a corner and saw the village, and for the moment all thought of Lily left her.

Elizabeth had imagined a flood as a lot of water pouring into a basin that eventually drained away through a plug at the bottom; the receding water would leave dirt and scum and unpleasantness. But what was before her was nothing as simple as that. What she saw before her was disaster.

The river had retreated far enough to release the schoolhouse, the smithy, and a few other buildings, but the meetinghouse and the trading post were closer to the Sacandaga and still stood in four good feet of water.

Between the new waterline and the place the horses had come to a stop, the ground was littered with debris. Whole trees, branches broken like toothpicks, great tangles of roots. Stones too big for a man to lift; slabs of ice, mud-covered and leaning together. Heaps of gravel that had yesterday been buried in the riverbed. Beaver traps, shingles, a pitchfork already rusting, a window frame with most of the glass knocked out, a half door. A whole henhouse, intact, filled with muddy carcasses. A piece of railing from the bridge that had been washed away. On top of a table half submerged in mud sat a battered tin cup. A length of linen, twisted like a ribbon. A child's shoe.

In the distance, just above the receding waterline, a group of people were trying to pull what looked like a pig out of the mud.

"From the smokehouse," Nathaniel said.

She hadn't thought of the smokehouse. The men had got together some years ago and built it for the use of the whole community. A dozen families had the entire winter's worth of meat stored there. All gone.

There were scavengers everywhere, mud-covered and grim as they searched for anything that might be used to rebuild. Katie Blackhouse went by with a chamber pot under one arm and a cooking pot under the other.

Joshua Hench and his sons were at work shoveling mud out of the smithy. At the trading post there was a makeshift raft tied to the hitching post, and they watched as the Mayfair sons threw bundles and sacks and parcels out of the window and onto it.

"That's enough," their father called to them, ready to take up his pole. But even as he spoke a small barrel came flying out the window and thumped onto the raft, which immediately listed and began to sink.

"Nails?!" he shouted. "Hast thou lost thy head, Samuel?" He was trying to lift the keg of nails to hand it back through the window, but instead he lost his balance and fell backward into the muddy waters. There was a great cry from inside the trading post and from the smithy as well. Three Mayfair sons catapulted themselves out the window to their father's rescue and, in the process, sank the raft and everything on it. Tobias Mayfair came up coughing, the keg of nails clasped in his arms.

The schoolhouse stood on dry land now, and it looked to be intact. Two windowpanes had broken and some boards were missing from the steps, but the roof was whole and in general the building had survived. What it must be like inside, Elizabeth could hardly imagine. She very purposefully turned her mind away from the question of schoolbooks.

"There's Daniel," Nathaniel said. He pointed with his chin to a group of men who were examining what was left of the smokehouse. Gabriel was there too, prying something out of the mud with a crowbar. Luke and Simon would be nearby.

"This is so much worse than I imagined." Elizabeth turned to Nathaniel and saw that his attention was elsewhere, somewhere behind her, and that there was something wrong.

The first scream was so loud and piercing that everyone turned together, like ladies and gentlemen performing a country dance. The screams doubled and then tripled before Elizabeth could locate the source.

A group of women stood pointing, all of them, toward the far shore of the bloated river. Men were running from every direction, jumping over debris, swerving around fallen trees. Jumping from safe spot to safe spot rather than risk sinking neck-deep in the muck. And all the time the keening spiraled up and up.

Elizabeth did not want to look, but she felt helpless to resist.

For twenty years on the mountain she had never feared the wolves it was named for. Not once had she seen a wolf attack a man, or even threaten. They never lacked for prey, even in hard winters. But now a large wolf—an animal she recognized by the blaze on his forehead and one damaged ear—was pulling at a human form, half submerged in the river. He had grasped it by the wrist in a pose that looked almost dainty.

"Who is it?" someone shouted. "Who is that?"

It was impossible to tell, battered and muddy as the body was. The wolf tugged harder and the corpse turned.

"His eyes are open!" Jane Cunningham moaned.

"It's one of the Sampsons," shouted a man's voice.

Old Father. The wolf's name came to her suddenly. They called him Old Father, for his calm dignity, and for his intelligence. Now he had judged himself safe from the humans across the water, or his hunger had overridden such calculations.

Old Father tore into the soft, bloated belly of the dead man on the ground.

Nathaniel took her horse by the bridle and was turning her away, but she couldn't leave, not yet, because Daniel was moving.

He ran forward, his good arm hooked behind his back to grab a tomahawk. That same arm came up and around in an arc and then the tomahawk was flying, flashing as it turned over and over, like a child's whirligig.

The heavy thunk of the blade burying itself in bone was loud enough to hear over the rushing river water.

"By God," said someone nearby. "I doubt there's another man living who could have made that kill. An angel of death with a bloody tomahawk instead of a scythe."

"You see," Nathaniel was saying. "Daniel's took care of it. Come, Boots, come away now."

13

$\mathcal{A}$long with Ivy House, that had been made available for Lily and Simon for as long as they cared to stay in Paradise, came a Mrs. Thicke. The housekeeper was a widow and good-sister to Ethan's own house-keeper, another Widow Thicke; both had come with him from Manhattan when he moved back to Paradise.

"Ethan would tear every building down just to build it up again, if we let him." Lily's father had told her about this soon after they arrived in port, in one of many long conversations about the changes she would see at home. Ethan had hand-picked families to take up vacant farm-steads in Paradise, and made sure that they would bring the skilled labor he wanted. There were carpenters, joiners, cabinetmakers, and masons. Farming was a risky business in the Sacandaga valley, but Ethan kept finding things to build or rebuild, and he paid the skilled workers well.

Lying in bed that first morning Lily took in the details that had been lost on her yesterday. Carved lintels where rabbits played among foliage; a washstand with a marble top; the hearth lined with beautiful tiles of a type she had never seen before, with a raised pattern in deep cobalt blue.

When she finally managed to get out of bed, Lily found that Mrs. Thicke had put out a full breakfast, from fresh biscuits to shirred eggs and bacon.

Simon grinned at the housekeeper from over his teacup. He had washed and shaved and found clean clothes in the confusion of their trunks, which meant he had risen long before. Simon was abominably cheery in the early morning, a habit Lily had not been able to break him of, nor could she bring herself to approve it.

She said, "What's happened to Daniel?"

Mrs. Thicke's eyelids fluttered. "He was leaving as I came in, just after sunrise. Wouldn't stop for coffee nor tea nor anything else, either. Now they say you and he are twins, is that right?"

"We are twins," Lily said. "But I'm the elder, by a good half hour."

Simon leaned across the table to kiss her when Mrs. Thicke's back was turned. "I'm off to see if I can be some help in the village, hen."

"Well, of course you can be a help," Lily said, a little grumpily. "You'll have a dozen people asking you to build for them before the day is out."

"And do ye object to the idea?"

Simon was looking at her with a patient expression that she disliked intensely. It meant that he was prepared to wait out her bad mood and could not be goaded into arguing.

Lily drew in a deep breath and concentrated. Did she wish to start out this new chapter of her life like a fishwife?

"Of course not." She gentled her tone. "I'll come down in a bit and see what I can do. Right now I've got trunks to sort through."

There was a knock at the front door.

"And company to visit with, forbye." Simon got up before Mrs. Thicke could even turn toward the door.

"Please permit me."

The housekeeper giggled like a schoolgirl, something that often happened with women when Simon flashed his dimples at them. A long time ago he had promised Lily never to let his beard grow again, but lately she'd begun to reconsider. As satisfying as it was to know that other women found her husband handsome, it could be tiresome.

"Now that's a fine man you've got there, Mrs. Ballentyne," Mrs. Thicke said in a conspiratorial whisper. "Good-tempered, sweet, but a man all the same." She sighed her way through a memory. "My first husband was a Frenchman, you know. Jock come over here from Paris,

France—as a young man. For to make his fortune. And a sweet talker, oh my, with that accent. Like a dove cooing. I do like a man with a foreign accent so long as he's got a good deep voice, like your—"

She broke off because Curiosity stood at the door.

Lily jumped up from the table, her surprise and pleasure banishing the last of her mood. "You are out very early."

"Child, half the morning is gone," she said. "Couldn't wait no longer to see your sweet face again. With all the trouble yesterday I hardly got a chance to look at you."

"Is Ma coming too?"

"She be by soon enough," Curiosity said. "Went down to the village with your daddy, see what help they could be. Let me set, my joints aching this morning something fierce. Here now, that will be Hannah and Birdie at the door."

Lily went to let her sisters in, and was enveloped immediately in Birdie's strong hug. It seemed as though the youngest of them would take after Da in terms of her height, because she was almost as tall as Lily at just ten years old.

Hannah had her Simon tied to her chest in a large square of linen folded into a sling. The baby peeked out like a very comfortable and satisfied owl as Hannah leaned forward to kiss Lily on the cheek.

Birdie was breathless with excitement. "I wanted to come an hour ago but Hannah said to wait, you needed to catch up on your sleep. The nieces and nephews wanted to come too, but they can't, not yet." Said with considerable satisfaction.

Birdie continued, "The boys had a plan to sneak out of the house to go down to the village, but Ben saw right through that, and he took them all off with him to check his lines. If he's got any left."

Hannah didn't reply to this, which was sound practice; it seemed to Lily that her little sister was looking for something to worry about.

"Will you take your nephew?" Hannah asked, and then passed him over to Lily without waiting for an answer. The large, warm, squiggling lump of boy regarded her for a long moment and then broke into a very wide smile.

"He's got a tooth." Lily leaned forward to examine the crest of white peaking out of the gum line.

"Believe me, I'm aware of that." Hannah made a face at her son and he burbled back at her.

Curiosity said, "You won't break the child, Lily. He so fat that if you did drop him he'd bounce."

And so they sat together as if it were the most normal thing, as if they did this every morning and always would. The baby played with Lily's buttons and Birdie called out commentary from one room and then another. Curiosity picked up a sketchbook and began to look through it while Mrs. Thicke went about her business, contributing now and then to a conversation which ranged from the treacherous weather and flood damage to the quality of the most recent batch of flour from the mill, to Friend Lincoln Matthews's propensity for doing arithmetic in his head, and had they heard about young Billy Crispin, carrying a goat almost as big as himself away from the flood?

Finally Curiosity stood up. "Mrs. Thicke, I am going to ask Lily to show Hannah and me around this pretty little house."

Mrs. Thicke's small, round face wrinkled in thought, as though Curiosity had spoken to her in a language she didn't know, but needed to understand. Then her expression cleared as the underlying request revealed itself to her.

"Oh, sure. I'm just finished here. I'll go across and see if my sister needs any help; she's baking this morning. If that's agreeable?"

Lily nodded, because there was a knot in her throat. For such a long time she had wished for these women to talk to, and time to talk, and privacy. But first she would show them the house, which she assumed they knew better than she did. She had been so tired the night before that she had gone to bed without taking in anything at all.

It was a very pleasing house, carefully planned and built with a great deal of attention to small details. Cupboards and shelves and drawers everywhere she looked, carved lintels and a beautiful tiled oven that was fed, very cleverly, from a grate in the kitchen next to the wood box.

The three of them walked at Curiosity's pace, from hall to parlor to bedchamber, to the small dining room and finally to the study.

To give you another reason to come home, Ethan had written. *There's a study with good light; it would serve as a studio.*

The room would be sunny indeed—if the sun ever came out again. And there were cubbyholes and shelves enough for her supplies.

Hannah said, "Ethan likes to build with somebody particular in mind."

"Ma didn't put him up to this—" Lily gestured around herself.

"No, she did not," Curiosity said. "But I'm glad Ethan did all this without being asked. That boy has got a feeling for family. I have rarely seen the like."

They settled in the parlor, where Ethan had hung some framed drawings—Lily's own work, some of it fifteen years old and more. When she was still feeling her way along and learning the shape of the world. It was like seeing through her own girlhood eyes.

"Snug," Curiosity said. She lowered her head as if she were looking at Lily over the top of spectacles. "So you planning to stay put for a while?"

"Oh, yes," Lily said.

Hannah smiled at her with such kindness and understanding that Lily felt herself relaxing.

"Well then." Curiosity looked around the parlor with satisfaction. Finally her gaze came back to Lily and settled there. "So tell us, is it that you cain't catch, or you cain't keep?"

In her surprise Lily expelled a soft puff of air and then a small laugh, which triggered a bigger one. In response, her nephew let out a husky chuckle from deep in his lungs. It was such a pure and natural sound that it set them all off, and then Birdie came in to see what she had missed and what they were all laughing at, and really, did they need to treat her like a child? She understood quite a lot; they should realize that much.

Hannah sent her off with the baby and orders to see that he went down for his nap on Lily's bed. Birdie took him with a resigned sigh. At the door she said, "Lily, your trunks aren't unpacked yet."

"Go ahead," Lily said. "You can sort through whatever interests you."

"But keep an eye on that child," Curiosity added. "Or he will roll right off that bed and put a dent in the floorboards."

And then the three of them were alone again. Lily felt at ease, the one thing she had not expected to feel when this subject was finally raised. There was the vaguest sense of embarrassment and even anger way down deep—that these women who had borne their children so easily would sit in judgment of her, who could not. Or would not; she could tell them what she liked and they would take her word. She might claim that she and Simon had decided that they didn't want children. That thought stayed with her for no more than a second; she was superstitious enough not to tempt the fates.

They were watching her. An old black woman who had been as

much as a grandmother for all Lily's life, and her half sister Hannah, who had been Birdie's age when Lily and Daniel were born.

"I think it's both," Lily said finally. "I have—" she hesitated over the word, and decided that the alternatives were not very appealing. "I have caught three times since I've been—married." Since before I was married, she corrected herself, but silently. "Three times that I'm sure of. And I lost each of them very early on."

"And this time?" Hannah said. "How far along are you this time?"

Lily blinked. "How do you—how did you—"

Curiosity said, "Between Hannah and me we got close to a hundred years experience taking care of womenfolk. I don't think there's much we ain't run across. I myself have seen a fair number of women who couldn't bear for one reason or another. Sometimes just because they just didn't know how the business was supposed to go."

Hannah and Lily looked at each other, and then at Curiosity.

"You mean they didn't know—" Lily bit her lip.

"That's right," Curiosity said. "They didn't know nothing. I won't tell you who this was, and I don't think you could guess. It was a long time ago, a young married girl comes to me. A little bit of a thing, no more than nineteen. She came to ask for could I give her some tea or pills to make a baby come along? So I set down with her and ask her a few things. Oh, yes, she says to me. She love her husband something fierce. He so kind and considerate. So I come right out and ask her, how often do you two have relations?

"That girl look at me like I was speaking Latin. No idea what I'm trying to say except that it some business it ain't polite to talk about. But in the end she want that baby more than she want to keep her pride. So I ask her, how often does your husband cover you at night? Once or twice a week, or more? Did she look scandalized? She say, why, I have a coverlet every night. He wouldn't let me be cold. He a good man.

"Can you imagine?

"She been lying next to that man of hers for close to six months and he hadn't ever done no more than touch her hand. She thought that's all they was to it—a woman and a man and a bed. So I told her what she didn't know already.

"Now, I don't know what she said to her husband or how she explained what they were supposed to be doing, but nine months later she brought a little girl into the world. Just as pretty as the morning. She went on to have another five."

They were laughing quietly, for fear that Birdie would come to demand to hear the story.

Lily said, "Well, I can tell you that whatever has gone wrong with me, it hasn't been for lack of trying. I decided to come home in the fall because I know if you can help me, you will. Then sometime on the journey—"

"You caught," Hannah said.

"I thought I was seasick," Lily said. "But it's been ten weeks since I last bled. . . ." Her voice trailed off.

Hannah said, "You are frightened to the bone. You don't know if you could stand another loss."

Lily felt the blood draining from her face.

"Why are you surprised? We women too," Curiosity said. "Hannah and me, we know what it is to lose a child. Your mama know, and just about every woman old enough to bear know well enough. I don't doubt it the same way the world over. Ain't you have nobody to talk to in Italy?"

Lily's gaze dropped to her lap. "There was an English doctor. I saw him once."

"An English doctor," Hannah echoed.

Curiosity's mouth twitched. "Tell us what the great man had to say."

"It will make you mad."

"No doubt," Curiosity said.

"Do tell," said Hannah.

"He said that as long as I persisted in pursuing male activities and denying my true nature, I wouldn't be able to bring a child into the world."

"Lord have mercy. Save us women from educated men. I'd like to have a word with that English doctor, I surely would." Curiosity shook her head.

Lily was so relieved that tears sprang to her eyes.

"You didn't start to believe that nonsense, did you?" Hannah looked at her as if she might have a fever.

"I tried not to," Lily said. "But there was no one else to ask—"

"That's when you decided to come home?" Hannah asked.

She nodded.

Curiosity said, "And high time too."

"Do you think you can—" She paused, afraid to say the words. Her gaze shifted from Hannah to Curiosity and back again. "Is there a chance?"

"There is a chance," Hannah said. "But you are going to have to follow orders very closely."

"That wan't never your strong suit," said Curiosity. "You always had to do things your own way."

Lily managed a smile. She said, "I look forward to surprising you."

14

A full week after the flood pretty much everybody was still out of sorts: short-tempered, prone to crying fits, distracted. Plain old sad. Birdie understood why. It could hardly be otherwise, with so many families still without a roof. The repairs went on from first light to last, and still many houses and cabins were uninhabitable. It was a new word for Birdie, one she liked.

Since the flood she had learned a lot of new words, because when Ma was worried, she started to talk like a book. Other people might babble when they were scared, but Birdie's ma would talk more slowly, and her sentences got longer, and her words got bigger. Birdie's list was longer every day: *chaotic, debris, indestructible* (because the schoolhouse had mostly survived), *turbulence,* and the best of all: *Mesopotamian* and *aqueduct.* Those she got from a conversation at the table—the very crowded table—when Ma had told them all about how people farmed long ago, and what benefits were to be had from floods. Then Adam had asked if Mesopotamia was in Ohio territory, and Ma had got out the atlas to show them the world, with Da and Ben making comments now and then that had them all laughing.

There was a lot of talk at home, and even more in the village. People asked altogether too many questions and Birdie got more than her share. When a Bonner came into the village people wanted to know was it true that Gabriel had married the Mohawk girl Annie from Lake in the Clouds? And wasn't that a surprise? And where were the happy couple living, and did they have one of the cabins at Lake in the Clouds for themselves or were they living with Blue-Jay and Susanna?

Blue-Jay and Susanna were another subject people never got tired asking about. Not the Quakers, of course, but everybody else. The Quakers had turned her out because she fell in love with a savage, or at least that's the way people talked about it, though Birdie knew better. Her ma had explained how it all worked, but she never corrected people when they said stupid things. They wouldn't have listened to her anyway.

The hardest thing was when they used words like *savage*. Which was being used even more now that Gabriel had gone and married Annie. One of the good things about that was clear right away. The talk about Susanna was put away for a while at least.

One day Mrs. Reed asked Birdie about Annie's wedding clothes and Birdie stopped in her tracks and frowned as if she were trying to remember. "You had best ask my brother Gabriel," she said finally. "He's right behind you."

Later Mrs. Reed complained to Ma that Birdie was rude, but that was only because she had jumped right out of her skin and then flushed the color of plums when it turned out Gabriel was miles away hauling timber. Ma only furrowed her brow at Birdie. There wasn't even a talk about common respect and dignity in the face of provocation. Ma was tired of questions herself.

That first night they were home, the day of the flood, Ma had wanted Gabriel and Annie to stay in the village until the weather settled, but they had gone off, walking ten miles out of their way to get on the other side of the waters and then climbing the mountain from the north side. The next day Gabriel had come back again to help in the village. Not happily, exactly, but as if he had something to prove. He was a man full grown and didn't need to be reminded of his responsibilities to friends and neighbors.

That very evening Runs-from-Bears came by to talk with Ma and Da, but even that came out lopsided, in Birdie's view. Uncle Bears wasn't worried about Annie eloping, but he was concerned about the fact that Gabriel's half sister and father were both of the Wolf clan, as was Annie. In the Kahnyen'kehàka way of things this was like marrying a sister.

And so that evening after a long day of work that involved wading in cold mud, Da and Daniel went up to Hidden Wolf. For once Birdie didn't ask to come along, because she knew what was going to happen. The men would sit in a circle around the fire and each of them would talk and tell long complicated stories, and then they would pass the pipe or throw tobacco on the fire and talk some more, and then someone would say, we have no clan mother here, and this is the province of the women.

And everybody would look at Blue-Jay, whose first wife might have been a help if she hadn't run off and got herself drowned, and whose new wife was plainspoken and wise, but still feeling her way into this new life, and unwilling to be put on the spot. It could go on like that for hours and if not for the flood, maybe days. Gabriel and Blue-Jay and Daniel would sit opposite Runs-from-Bears and Throws-Far and Da, and none of them would ever yawn or look bored.

Birdie wondered if Runs-from-Bears might send to Good Pasture for a clan mother, but Hannah said that it was more likely that Gabriel and Annie would be sent to Good Pasture to make their case before all the elder women. But the trapping season had been cut short by the flood and Gabriel wasn't going anywhere until he had secured or repaired his lines. He was the head of a family now and it mattered, how many furs he had to sell.

The next morning Da and Daniel came down at sunrise. They let Ma fuss over them and feed them, but then they went to the new graveyard on the far side of the village above the orchards, where the four people who had not gotten out of the way in time were being buried. Birdie went because it was the right thing to do and because she was curious, which embarrassed her, but she owned it anyway.

A few hours later, Gabriel and Runs-from-Bears came too, and they got in their canoes and started looking for things that could be dredged out of the lake. It was the perfect task for Gabriel. He was helping, but at the same time he was too far away to be asked questions about his new bride or his wedding.

All in all Birdie didn't mind the fact that Gabriel was married. She wouldn't really be alone until the fall, when Luke and Jennet took the children home for the winter. Even then, Birdie reminded herself, she would have Lily, who needed her help.

And exactly that was the plan. Birdie would make herself indispensable— a word she looked up in Ma's dictionary—and that would convince the grown-ups that it would be best if she didn't come back to school this year. Instead, she would move in with Lily and Simon in order to be there whenever Lily needed anything at all.

It was perfectly logical and reasonable. She just had to convince the grown-ups.

When Hannah went out on a call, Birdie went with her and spent that time sweeping mud or washing down walls, scrubbing clothes, toting firewood, pumping endless buckets of water, and most usually, entertaining the children. She ran errands for Curiosity and Ma and anyone else who needed things fetched. She liked it best when somebody sent her down to the village, so she could see for herself how much progress was being made.

The old trading post had already been pulled down and they were just starting to lay the foundation for a new one, which would be larger, with room for things like plows and bathtubs.

Missy O'Brien found this not to her liking at all. "They talk about plain," she said. "They are mighty good to themselves."

Birdie heard her say this to Becca LeBlanc outside the Red Dog.

"Well then," Becca said in her driest tone. "I guess you'll be going all the way to Johnstown for your buttons and salt."

Becca could draw blood with the dull side of her tongue. Most people didn't even notice when they'd been tweaked until five minutes later. She had a high spot on Birdie's list of grown-ups who could be counted on to teach her something.

Every day, as soon as her errands and chores were done, Birdie ran down to Ivy House to see what she could do for Lily. Sometimes there were other people there—Ma or Da, Hannah or Jennet or Ben or Luke. Neighbors and old friends. Even the nieces and nephews were allowed to come, but only under close supervision. To Birdie's relief, they were never allowed to visit for very long. Nathan and Henry and Adam thought this was unfair and took every opportunity to argue about it with her.

Today Birdie stopped at the door and listened. No voices, which meant Lily was alone or asleep. She went in as quietly as she could and stood beside the window in a puddle of light.

Lily slept with a book opened over her belly. She didn't have a bump yet, but some women took a long time to grow one, or so Curiosity said.

Birdie crept around quietly, bringing some order to the parlor. Or at least, trying to. The little house had been stood on its head. Simon hung the chairs on wall pegs to make room for what Ma called a chaise longue, but really was just a chair with a long bit attached so you could stretch out your legs. The whole thing was covered over with a feather bed and sheets and blankets. Lily could recline on a chaise longue, which made it better than a bed with a lot of pillows.

After the first day Birdie had to admit it had been a good idea, because Lily looked like a princess in her pretty dressing gown, with her feet in velvet slippers the color of roses, with daisies embroidered in white silk. And she was allowed to sit up halfway, which meant she could drink the tea Mrs. Thicke brought her every hour, and she could read and draw. The only time Lily was allowed out of bed was to use the chamber pot behind a screen Simon had put up just for that purpose.

There were plenty of rumors in the village about why Lily had taken to her bed only one day after coming home, some of which were funny and others that were not. The first thing Birdie did when she arrived every day was to give Lily all the gossip. She was ready with it when Lily woke up with a little start.

"Little sister." She yawned. "How long have you been here?"

"A quarter hour, maybe a bit more. Look, Mrs. Thicke just made fresh tea. I'll pour you some."

Lily said, "What news in the village today? Anything interesting?"

Birdie considered what to offer first. "Friend Katie Blackhouse thinks you must be consumptive," Birdie announced.

"Does she? That would be very dramatic, wouldn't it? Any other good bits?"

Birdie recited it all in a rush. The Brodie house had a roof again; Simon and some of the other men had shored up the Meeting House so maybe it wouldn't have to be pulled down altogether; and the Truebloods had gone back home, and high time because Cyrus was driving Leyton Yarnell to distraction.

Birdie paused in her recital to make sure Lily was comfortable and didn't need anything.

"You fuss like Ma," Lily said. "Go on."

The last bit of news was that Magistrate Bookman had gone to Johnstown on official business but ended up coming back with the kind of supplies the Friends didn't want or need—alcohol and ammunition—as well as three dozen hens and a single rooster.

"Missy said how the poor old bird would work himself to an early grave, but he'd die happy."

It was rude to tell such stories, but it did make Lily laugh aloud, and that was the idea.

Lily said, "You bring so much light into the room, like a hundred candles at once."

Birdie tried to look modest, but she was so pleased that it was hard. She went to get a fresh pillow slip and brought back the brushes to work through Lily's hair.

"You spoil me," Lily said. "If I were a more suspicious person I would think you were plotting something."

Birdie managed to smile, and hoped that her sister wouldn't see the crack in it.

On her way home again Birdie was feeling satisfied with her afternoon's work. Maybe she really did have a chance of convincing Ma and Da that school was not the right place for her, at the moment at least. But then Jane Cunningham waved her down outside the post to ask had she heard the news? Maria Oxley had died sudden in the night, just when she seemed to be getting back on her feet. And all those children left behind. Wasn't it true that Birdie was there, helping, when Hannah set Friend Maria's broke wrist?

Sometimes there was no help for it but to be rude. Birdie turned on her heel and started straight up the hillside, forgoing the road or anything that might have served as a path.

15

Martha heard the news about Maria Oxley from Hannah, who came by one midafternoon to share it.

"Where is Birdie?" Hannah wanted to know. "I need to be the one to tell her, because she'll take the news hard."

"Were they very close?" Martha asked.

"Not especially," Hannah said. "But she helped me set the arm, and she will want to know."

Maria Oxley was now the seventh casualty of the flood. On the first day one of the Sampson brothers had been pulled from the far side of the river; his two brothers hadn't been found and probably would never be.

Noah Trueblood, Grandma May, and Alexander Crispin were put to rest in graves that took a long time to dig because the earth was still frozen in the new graveyard, and now Mrs. Oxley would join them. People kept telling each other that it could have been much worse; that it was God's own mercy to have saved so many of them. Martha thought that Daniel Bonner deserved a good part of the credit, as he had been the one to sound the alarm.

That afternoon she took the mending outside to work in the fresh air. She found a spot in the sun on the side of the springhouse that faced the kitchen. Nearby Anje was tending the week's washing, a task that required all her attention and thus spared Martha a conversation that would be awkward at best. Anje was the best of the LeBlanc sisters, but even she was given to asking questions that Martha had no intention of answering.

She slipped the darning egg into a sock and chose a bolt of thread from the workbasket. As she threaded the needle she wondered who would come by to talk to her today. The children would find her eventually, but Martha hoped that Curiosity would come too, and spend a few minutes. She liked talking to Curiosity, who seemed to see things nobody else saw, or at least to credit the things nobody else considered important.

The wind came up from the village and with it the sound of hammering and sawing, faint but persistent. Every man who could be spared had been put to work, and as a result most of the families who had lost their homes in the flood would have roofs over their heads within another week. Sooner, if it weren't for the spring mud.

Sometimes Ethan came by and gave her news from the village or read the newspaper to her while she mended or sewed. From him she learned which houses needed roofs and which families were in most need of food or an encouraging word. Not that she provided these things; she stayed on the hill and did what she could to help the Bonners. But Ethan clearly needed to talk of these things, and it was an old habit between them, something left over from Manhattan when he had been her tutor.

The Spencers had first enrolled Martha at Miss Martin's School for Young Ladies, but she had felt out of place there and terribly unhappy. Letters went back and forth between Manhattan and Paradise, and one day Amanda presented a proposition. The Bonners believed Martha was too intelligent to be satisfied with a curriculum that went no further than needlework, deportment, and rudimentary French. She should learn Latin and the classics, algebra and philosophy, and anything else that interested her. Italian? History? Tutors could be had for any subject, really, and in the comfort of the Spencer's house.

In the end Ethan had taken most of the responsibility for her schooling. Miss Anne Schubert was hired as a singing tutor—Martha had no interest in pianoforte, but she did have a clear and very sweet alto voice worthy of training, or at least the adults claimed that to be the case. There was a drawing teacher as well, and from Amanda she learned the fine points of crewelwork embroidery.

The only problem, as Martha saw it, was that Ethan's concern for her education was something he took far more seriously than she did herself, at least at first.

He gave her books to read and long lists of verbs to conjugate and memorize. At a weekly supper he would draw her into conversation about her studies. This was not so terrible, because Will and Amanda were always there and the discussions were often too interesting to be thought of as examinations.

Then Ethan had moved back to Paradise, leaving her with the injunction to keep working on the list of books he had left behind.

It had been a relief at the time, not to have to bother with conversations about taxes and trade, Cromwell and Richard III. No more French subjunctive clauses, or dusty old Latin historians. When Ethan left Manhattan Teddy had just begun to court her, and with Teddy on her mind there was no room for anything else. Martha rarely thought of Ethan at all—she was embarrassed to admit this to herself, but it was true—until the day Teddy broke off the engagement. The Spencers did their best for her, but she would have liked to have Ethan nearby as well.

She was not the only one who felt his absence. Ethan Middleton was one of the most eligible young men in Manhattan. He had a great deal of money and property both; the men all thought well of his skills in business and his financial dealings; he was personable and good-looking and he could dance so well that when he did make an appearance at a ball, many heads turned eagerly in his direction.

In New-York he had presence and a sterling reputation, but here in Paradise they saw him differently. It most likely had to do with his Bonner cousins. In a crowd of Bonners, Ethan seemed to fade away. Martha had talked to Amanda Spencer about this more than once, because it struck her as unfair.

"His whole posture changes," Martha had said. "As if he doesn't want to be seen."

Amanda couldn't disagree with Martha's observations, but she knew more of Ethan's history and saw the matter differently.

"He is very much like his father," she said. "But only in his appearance.

The high brow, the shape of his head and hands and fingers, all except his coloring—he is the image of Julian. But in all other ways he is nothing like Julian at all. Not in temperament nor in spirit. Julian had no ambitions at all, and Ethan—why, you see for yourself. There's hardly a charitable cause that he doesn't support. He is always hard at work on one project or another." She drew in a short breath and held it for a heartbeat. "Cousin Julian was a difficult and unhappy young man."

Which was all Amanda could be coaxed to say about Julian Middleton, who had died of burns from a fire he had set himself, only a few hours before Ethan was born. There was a great deal more to the story, but those details had proved impossible to extract. Plenty of people knew about Ethan, but nobody was talking.

With that thought a possible explanation came to mind and so she asked Amanda directly. "Can you tell me just one thing? Does Ethan know the things you won't talk about?"

Amanda nodded. "Oh, yes," she said. "There were people in Paradise who made sure of that."

Which meant, Martha understood, that it was her own mother who had had some part in telling Ethan things that would hurt him most. His mother had been vain and silly and died too young, and his stepfather had little use for him until he was old enough to take over the more unpleasant tasks that came a doctor's way.

To Martha's eye, at least, Ethan seemed to have survived all that and prospered. He had inherited almost seventy percent of the land in and around Paradise, not to mention properties from Johnstown to Albany and beyond; he need never raise a finger if he didn't care to. But he worked without pause, as if the village's welfare rested entirely with him. He was never so talkative as he was when the subject was Paradise and improvements that might be made.

Now he was talking about the flood damage, which houses had roofs and which needed shutters, how difficult it was to get hinges and every other kind of hardware that was needed. Joshua Hench was an outstanding blacksmith and he was more than hardworking; since the flood it seemed that the sound of hammering came from the smithy twenty hours a day. But even Curiosity's son-in-law could not conjure raw material out of thin air.

Martha liked it when Ethan talked to her like this, as a woman grown, someone capable of discussing the situation and contributing her thoughts. It was very different from the hours she had spent going over the readings he had assigned her in philosophy and current events.

She looked up from her mending and saw that Curiosity was walking toward her, moving more quickly than a woman her age could or should. Her cane kicked up sharp-edged divots of earth.

"Came by to see Elizabeth," she announced. "Asked about you and now here you are, working."

"It's not very much," Martha said. "Just a little darning. Jennet's boys are hard on their socks, and I might as well make myself useful."

Curiosity called over to Anje. "Been at it since sunup, have you?"

Anje nodded and wiped a strand of hair from her face with the back of one wrist. "Joan should be coming to take over any minute now," she called back.

Curiosity lowered herself onto the second stool and pushed out a deep breath. She said, "Don't you have a nice hand with a needle. But then I always did like darning; it put me in a peaceful state of mind. Some women darn too heavy, but see there, you got a smooth edge all around."

Martha made a humming sound and bent down to the thread basket, taking her time to find what she needed.

"You modest as you ever was as a girl and just as hard a worker," Curiosity said. "Why do you blush and look away when you hear the truth spoke plain?"

"You give me too much credit," Martha said. "I'll take on any work that gives me an excuse to stay out of the village another day."

A smile flickered across Curiosity's face. "You planning on staying up here on the hill for good?"

"It's a tempting idea," Martha said. "I certainly wouldn't ever be bored as long as the Bonner grandchildren are nearby. They want to go down to the village as much as I want to stay here, and somehow I've become the person they bring all their arguments to. I don't make those decisions, but they seem to like to practice on me."

Curiosity crossed her arms over her middle and rocked back and forth, laughing softly. "They are a rascally bunch. I can tell you, all this pestering about going down to the village will stop just as soon as Daniel opens the school back up. Then you'll see how much work they got to do right here. Now you, you'll go down when you ready. I expect you'll want to see Callie sooner rather than later."

"I think about her every day," Martha said. "But then I always find a reason not to go."

Curiosity thought about that for a while. "Ain't much of a welcome home you had, but I don't expect you wanted one."

"No," Martha said. "Not especially."

"I had my doubts when they took you away to Manhattan," Curiosity said. "But you turned out a fine young woman, and I'm glad to see you back here again."

Tears filled Martha's eyes. "Thank you," she said, her voice hoarse.

"Now I'ma say something to you, and I want you to listen close. That young man—what was his name?"

"Edward Peyton," Martha said. How strange it sounded, spoken out loud. "Teddy."

"You can count yourself lucky to be shut of such a weak-willed boy. Maybe you don't see it yet, but so it is."

"Oh, I see it," Martha said. "I had a letter from him yesterday that made everything clear to me. Do you want to hear it?"

"If you want to read it to me, I'll listen."

"I put it in the fire, but I can recite it word for word. It went like this: 'My dear Miss Kirby, I should like to have the ring I gave you returned to me at your earliest convenience, as it was my grandmother's and is meant to stay in the family. Sincerely, Edward Peyton the Third.'"

In the small silence that followed, Martha gathered her thoughts. "I did try to give it back to him on the day he broke the engagement off, but he could not get out of the house quickly enough." The rest of what she was thinking came out almost against her will. "No doubt he is about to enter into another engagement. I'm sure I'll hear about it soon, in next week's post or the one after that."

She wondered at herself that she could be so calm as she told these things, but it all seemed so small and far away. The very idea of Teddy left her hollow, nothing of anger or resentment. A kind of echo, and no more. Now there was a lightness, a feeling of having taken the right path, though it had not been her choice at the time.

"Not the right young man for you, no indeed," Curiosity said. "You need somebody you can count on when things get rough. Because they going to get rough this summer, and I know you feel it coming."

Martha came up out of her thoughts at this change of tone.

"You mean Jemima."

"I do. That exactly who I mean. The only good thing that woman ever done was to bring you into the world and then leave you with us when she run off. But she back now, and the only reason for her to come looking for you is, she want something. She won't stop coming at you until she got it."

"What?" Martha said. "What could she want from me? Money? I'd give her everything if it meant being shut of her."

"Don't matter," Curiosity said. " 'Cause even if you give her every penny, she ain't gonna be satisfied. It ain't in her nature. So now, we know something's coming, but there's nothing to be gained by sitting around and worrying about it. I want you to go on about your life and settle down here in Paradise. Try to put Jemima out of your head and re-member, we look after our own."

Just as Curiosity got to her feet with the intention of going on to talk to Elizabeth, Anje called over. Could Martha watch the fire while Anje went to see what was keeping her sister? She still hadn't had her midday meal and there was the matter of the Necessary.

Martha had not tended to such chores for many years, but she could not turn down such a reasonable and polite request for help. She tucked away her mending and took Anje's place, waving to Curiosity as she set off for the house.

It was immediately familiar, the heat and steam and the many strong smells.

"Just keep stirring," Anje said. "One of us will be back before the fire needs tending."

Within a few minutes Martha's clothes were soaked with steam and sweat, and the stirring stick felt as heavy as a tree. She was concentrating so hard that she didn't notice Birdie until she had walked right up to stand on the far side of the fire pit.

"You need to tie your skirts up higher and tighter. You could catch fire. That's how Anna from the trading post died; she didn't pay attention and her skirts caught and—she died."

Without comment or argument Martha stepped back from the pot and pulled a handful of her skirt up through her belt. Anybody who came by would have a clear view of her stockinged legs from knee to shoe, but she never saw anyone here but the Bonner grandchildren and Curiosity or Hannah.

"That's better," Birdie said, still indignant. And: "Did you know that a person can die from a broken arm, even when it's been set?"

Martha took her time answering. "I think I had heard that. Sometimes the marrow gets infected, or the blood."

"I helped my sister set Friend Maria's arm," Birdie said. "My brother Daniel brought her to us, and Hannah told me how to help, and we set her arm. And I told her children that she would be well again soon."

Martha had no idea what Birdie needed to hear, so she asked an obvious question.

"I've never seen it done. How do you set a broken bone?"

Birdie told her. It was a long and involved story because she stopped constantly to tell Martha where she had learned one fact or another and who had taught her. She had an astonishing memory for details, but Martha kept this observation to herself and said very little, unless it was to ask a question that would send Birdie off again.

"Friend Maria wasn't even thirty years old," Birdie said. "And her youngest just a year. What will they do?"

Now Martha understood why Birdie had come to her rather than her mother or one of her sisters, or even Curiosity.

Birdie was saying, "Missy O'Brien says they'll have to go to an orphanage in Johnstown because a man can't take care of so many little children unless he remarries right quick. And she said that she had faith that God would look after them. He never gives us more to bear than we can carry, that's what she said."

Her color was rising. "Do you believe that?"

"No," Martha said. "It would be a happier world, if it were true. But people buckle and break every day under the weight they carry." She thought of Callie's father, who had simply walked away from home after Jemima cheated him out of everything he held dear.

Birdie turned suddenly, as if something had tapped her on the shoulder.

"I'm going to write an essay," she said. "About burdens and happiness. Ma will help me, and Da and Lily and Hannah and—will you?"

"Of course," Martha said, though she was not quite sure what she was agreeing to.

Birdie's narrow back straightened as she walked toward the kitchen door. Which stood propped open, because Daniel Bonner was leaning against it, watching them. He caught Martha's gaze and then he smiled, which was ever so rude. The polite thing to do would be to turn away and pretend he hadn't seen her with her skirts hiked up and her legs visible. But he stood there still, grinning at her. Curiosity's voice came from the kitchen, asking if he intended on holding the house up like that forever, and if not, he had best make a decision about in or out, and right now.

Martha closed her eyes and counted to ten, and then the smell of burning roused her. The fire.

She grabbed for the stirring stick but Daniel was there to take it out of her hand. She should object, but she was too flustered and in spite of Anje's reassurances, the fire did need feeding. She ignored Daniel while she got an armful of wood from the stack up against the springhouse door. When she allowed herself to look again, he was stirring. His one arm moved the paddle effortlessly, where Martha had struggled with both.

Daniel said, "You've burned yourself."

Martha didn't know what he was talking about. She looked down and saw that there was a blister rising on her hand.

"It's nothing," she said. "But thank you for your concern. I can take over the stirring again."

"I'm sure you could," Daniel said. "But I'm not ready to stop."

She held her breath for two beats, and then said, "You have better things to do; you must."

He looked toward the house. "I'm supposed to meet Ben, but he's late. So no, at this moment I have nothing better to do. It's not too often I lend a hand at this kind of thing, you know. Be a shame to waste the opportunity."

He stirred for a full moment while Martha tried to find something to say, but then he had had enough of waiting.

"You mad about something?"

"Not in the least."

"Now see, I would say you're plenty mad by the look on your face."

"I am not mad," Martha said with all the polite nonchalance she could muster. "Thank you kindly for your help."

"Mad," Daniel said. "As a wet hen."

It took a great deal of effort to calm down, but Martha managed. She drew in a deep breath. "If I was being short with you, I apologize."

Daniel nodded. "Well, that's to be expected. You come back here after all those years in the big city, your manners ain't what they used to be."

"My manners?" Martha heard herself squeak. "*My* manners! What about your manners?"

He raised an eyebrow in what was clearly mock surprise. "And here I thought I was lending a hand."

"You did. You are. But—"

"—one road or another I managed to make you mad."

Her color was rising; she could feel it. "You you you—watched me. And my skirts—I'm not—You watch me."

"What's wrong with me watching you?"

"It's unseemly."

"It don't seem to me anything out of the ordinary to look at a pretty girl all flushed from the heat. That's not what you're mad about. Not really."

"You are being—" Martha stopped. "I see. You are winding me up."

He laughed outright. "Why would I do that?"

"I don't know," she said, giving him her most severe look. "Why would you?"

The very hardest part, once she turned away, was banishing anything that might be taken for a smile from her own face.

---

16

*A*t supper Jennet kept them all amused with her day's adventures. She had spent part of it with Lily, part of it with the children, and the third and more difficult part in the village, sweeping mud.

"I've never been so dirty," she declared. "Not even that spring we spent on Nut Island. Do you remember, Hannah? We even had mud in—" she paused and looked around the table. "Places where mud isnae welcome."

Martha had been wondering how to raise this very subject, and now she took the opportunity. "Would that be the time when—" Everyone was looking at her, but not in an unkind way. It was Hannah who first understood.

"Yes," she said. "It was then that your father came into the garrison gaol. He died a few days later, of his wounds."

Elizabeth was surprised. "Hasn't anyone ever told you about this?" She looked around the table. "Three of you were there. Jennet, Hannah, and Daniel."

"And Blue-Jay," Daniel said.

"Yes, of course."

"You can't remember very much of those days," she said to her son, as if her command might keep away things best forgot.

"I remember," he said.

Martha felt his gaze on her. His tone was unremarkable, easy.

"We talked, Liam and me, more than once. He asked me about you, Martha."

This afternoon she had sworn to herself that she would avoid Daniel Bonner at all costs, and now she was eager to ask him a dozen questions.

"We all have stories about Liam," Nathaniel said. "Maybe it was thoughtless of us to think you knew them too."

"Yes, it was thoughtless," said his wife. "But it's a mistake that can be rectified. He really was the sweetest, friendliest boy, but he had a talent for getting himself in trouble. Wouldn't you agree, Nathaniel?"

"I can still see him peeking in the schoolhouse window," he said.

"Oooh," said Birdie. "Is this the story about the ink bottle and a winkle?"

Daniel watched Martha's face as she took in the stories, one after the other. He had a story of his own about Liam and Jemima both, but he would not share it at this table, and maybe not ever. Lily was the only one who knew the whole of it, and she wasn't here. He wondered if his sister thought of that summer's day, and if her memories were as clear as his own.

It had been some years later that it had occurred to him that what they had stumbled upon that day at Eagle Rock was the act that resulted in Martha's presence in the world. When he brought this up to Lily, she had looked surprised.

"All you have to do is count the months," she said. "Or easier still, look at Martha. From the day she was born she looked like Liam."

They had been children themselves, hardly nine years old. Not ignorant of the ways of men and women—they had grown up on the frontier, with every kind of animal around and unconcerned about a child's curiosity. What a strange, disturbing day that had been, but if it had not happened at all, Martha would not be sitting at this table; she would not exist in this world.

His father was saying, "I don't know that we should talk about Billy, at least not now."

But Martha insisted that she wanted to know everything about her father and her uncle both, good and bad.

And then of course she was shocked. As the story was told, her expression went still and the color drained from her face. She clenched her hands together and held them on her lap as if she were afraid of what she might do with them.

"I don't understand," she said at one point. "You sound as if you liked Liam—"

"Oh, we did," said Nathaniel.

"But he caused you such harm." She looked as if she might cry, she was blinking so furiously. "I thought that at the least—"

She couldn't say it, but they knew, everyone knew what she was thinking: My mother was so very bad, so cruel and destructive, I was sure my father must have been a good man. And if he was not, what will I turn into?

"No one here subscribes to a theory of inherited evil." Hannah's tone was almost sharp, and certainly uncompromising. "You stand on your own feet and make your way as best you can."

Daniel said, "What Hannah is trying to say is, the sins of the fathers got nothing to do with the children. You don't have to apologize for the mistakes Liam made. He wouldn't want you to, that much I know. Because Liam was a good man, down deep, and he did a lot more good in this world than he did bad."

Martha's expression relaxed, but not by much. When she finally drew in a deep breath and let it out with a sigh, Daniel wondered if she was giving in, or just hiding what she couldn't bear.

She closed her eyes for the merest moment, and then got up to help clear the table.

Daniel felt a hand on his arm and he turned. "Lilac has got a sore foot," his father said. "Would you come out to the barn with me and have a look?"

17

*S*o what is it you wanted to talk to me about, Da?"

Nathaniel looked around himself, surprised. "Didn't I say? Lilac has got a sore foot."

Daniel wasn't convinced but he kept his thoughts to himself. If his father had something to say, he would say it in his own good time.

With the lantern held high, they went into the stable. It was like calling out a greeting; all the animals—the cow and her calf, the mule, all the horses, and the oxen—stuck their heads out of their stalls. Lilac gave a loud and insistent nicker.

"She was waiting," Daniel said.

"Must be worse off than I thought."

Daniel gave his father a sharp look. "You're up to something, I can smell it."

"First things first. Let's have a look at that hoof."

A few minutes later Daniel said, "I think you need to have Joshua Hench look at this, or Hannah."

"I fear you're right."

"You knew that full well yourself," Daniel said. "Why did you really want me out here?"

"Hold on a minute. Let me herd my thoughts together."

Daniel leaned back against the wall and closed his eyes. The familiar smells would cling to his clothes for a day. Cow and hay and ointment, leather and dung. Comfortable smells.

"Your ma and me, we're glad to see you spending more time down here in the village."

Daniel opened his eyes and saw a rat the size of a small dog digging at something in the corner.

"Now my position—"

The movement came to him so easily that his father didn't even register what was happening until the knife struck its target. Nathaniel glanced over his shoulder and then back again, unwilling to be distracted.

"What I was saying was, I'm guessing you want to spend time with Lily, and that's what keeps you from going back up to your own place."

"I've been back," Daniel said, going to retrieve his knife. He wiped the blade on a bit of burlap sack. "I went up yesterday."

"And you came right back down with clothes and books. Now I hate to admit this, but you just about proved your ma's right about what you got on your mind."

A flutter of alarm deep in the gut, but Daniel knew better than to let his anxiety show. "And that would be?"

"You're glad to have Lily home, but it's mostly Martha you're hanging around for."

The surprise struck him dumb for a minute. "Ma thinks I'm interested in Martha Kirby?"

"You spend a lot of time looking at her."

"I look at a lot of people."

"So you're saying your ma's got it wrong?"

Daniel walked away in his irritation. Everything he might say could be taken and turned around.

He said, "If she is right—I'm not saying she is or isn't—why would she be worried?"

His father rubbed the bridge of his nose with a knuckle. "I never said she was worried, did I? Not about you, at least."

"She think I'm out to ruin Martha once and for all?"

His father shot him a look that let him know he had gone too far. "The girl's tender and still hurting, that's the point."

The best option in this situation was to say nothing at all. The habit of silence was one he had courted for years, and could draw on as easily as any Quaker.

Finally Daniel said, "I'm off to the Red Dog with Ethan."

His father nodded his acknowledgment, and Daniel walked out of the stable, uneasy with the way he was leaving things.

"Daniel?"

He turned around.

"You ain't asked, but I'll tell you anyway. She's grown into a fine young woman, never mind who her ma is. That's all I'll say for now."

There were questions he might have asked, but Daniel realized that he wasn't ready for the answers.

$\mathcal{B}$irdie, stuck in the house with her younger nieces and nephews, fretted. She wanted to go down to Lily, but her mother had decided that given the cold rain, it would be best to stay indoors this day.

"Martha went down to the village." Birdie was careful to keep her tone even and respectful, as if she were opening a discussion. If you could hold on to your temper and sound like you were talking about this year's crop of onions, you could say almost anything to Ma. "Is there some other reason I shouldn't go sit with Lily?"

Her mother was looking at her with that thoughtful expression that did not bode well. She put down the book she had been reading.

"You have spent a great deal of time with Lily, and I'm glad of it. You are a good companion and a great help to her. She has told me these things, plainly spoken. The decision to keep you here for the day has to do with the weather and the fact that the little people need distraction, and they love no one so much as you when it comes to games. Curiosity and Jennet are with Lily this morning, so you needn't worry that she's alone or in need of help."

The hot rush of tears to her eyes was something Birdie could not hide, but Ma was too clever and kind to say anything. It was up to Birdie to counter the arguments Ma had made. But there was nothing to counter; it was all logical and true.

"Ma," she said, "Don't you think that maybe, just sometimes it's right to let feelings get the upper hand and leave reason fend for itself?"

A great smile broke over her mother's face and she held her arms open so Birdie could come and put her nose to the soft spot between shoulder and breast where her mother's scent was strongest.

"That is the most concise description of falling in love I have ever heard," she said against Birdie's hair.

Birdie sniffed a little, and Ma rocked her. And that was good, almost as good as being allowed to go down to Lily.

"The worst kind of weather," Curiosity said, her brow furrowed. "The very worst. Every kind of wet there is, and cold? And a mean wind coming down off the mountain." She looked up from her knitting to Jennet and Lily, who were winding yarn, Lily from her chaise longue and Jennet beside her in a chair.

If Lily closed her eyes she could imagine herself at eighteen or sixteen or ten, just like this. Talking to Curiosity about the weather, yawning in the warmth of the hearth and tending to knitting or sewing. How uncomplicated her life had been, and she had never noticed. And perhaps that was the very definition of childhood.

"Put some more wood on the fire, would you, Jennet?"

Lily almost jumped in her surprise. "Isn't it warm enough in here? I could do without some of these." Lily pushed a quilt away.

Curiosity reached over and put it right back. "Those covers staying right where they are."

"But I am sweating like a . . . like a—"

"Pig?" Jennet suggested amiably. "Did you forget the art of plain speaking while you were away?"

"I can speak plain," Lily said, her temper rising.

Curiosity was unmoved. "Sweating is good for you, get all the dark humors out. Good for the little one too."

That was the one argument that Lily could not counter. She was some four months with child, and as of this day, she had seen no sign of bleeding. Hope was a luxury she wanted to deny herself, but oh, it was hard. Her body wanted her to hope; it gave her every reason, not least the swelling of her belly. Just a gentle curve for now, but she focused all her energy on it, willing the child to speak to her with that first quickening.

In the evenings Simon sat with her in the parlor and then when they both were yawning, he carried her to bed. To their chaste bed. When she raised the topic, he had shushed her.

"I can do without," he said. "I won't have you worrying about that."

She loved that hour before they fell asleep, when they talked about everything and nothing at all. Simon made her laugh with his stories, and she brought him up to date with the gossip brought to her by Birdie and Mrs. Thicke.

They rarely talked about the thing they thought about most, but sometimes Lily found the words rising up, wanting to be spoken. She said, "Curiosity thinks the summer will be very hot this year. I'll melt into a puddle."

"Nonsense." He turned on his side to look at her, and put his hand low on her belly. "By fall you'll be as round and plump as a blueberry."

She had laughed as he meant her to, but the image stuck in her mind like a burr and wouldn't be shook off until she took up paper and began to draw. She drew blueberry bushes and a foraging bear, blueberries spilling over a bucket into the grass, single berries in excruciating detail. All in pencil, because she had got the idea that the sharp smells of her paints might be unhealthy for the child she had already started thinking of as Blueberry.

Maybe it was superstition to think that smells might make the difference, but it made Lily feel better, and wasn't that the whole idea behind such beliefs? She would take whatever help she could find. Because once she had taken childbearing for granted, foolish girl she had been.

She glanced at Jennet's rounded belly and caught her eye, as well.

Jennet said, "I've been waiting for ye to ask, Lily. Midsummer, by Curiosity's reckoning. So you'll have some practice with newborns before your own comes along."

"Unless the cold rain get the better of all of us," Curiosity sniffed.

Lily caught Jennet's half smile. Curiosity often got into a temper about the weather. She held long lectures that seemed to be directed to a minor god directly responsible for the trouble that came along with a cold wind.

Jennet said, "Martha picked an unpleasant day tae go intae the village for the first time."

Lily drew her knees up and turned toward Curiosity. "The first time? But it's been weeks—"

Curiosity thumped the table piled high with baskets of thread and yarn so that they leaped. "Leave Martha be. She got enough on her shoulders; she don't need you talking mean behind her back."

That brought them up short. Jennet was the first one to find her voice. "But Curiosity, we like the girl. If we talk about her it's no different from talking among ourselves about Mariah's cough or Eliza's nightmares—"

"Now see," Curiosity interrupted her. "That's the problem, right there. You think about Martha like she was a child. Maybe you ain't noticed," she said directly to Lily. "But some see her for what she is, a woman grown. Some have taken note, yes, Lord."

Jennet looked intrigued, but the idea that was churning in Lily's gut was not pleasant.

"Who are you talking about?" And, after a pause: "Ethan? Is Ethan seeing Martha in a—a new light?"

Curiosity shook her head and turned back to her knitting. "I'ma hold my tongue. Said too much already."

"Too much about what?"

Jennet caught her eye and gave a small shake of the head, but Lily knew she had misspoken before she saw the expression on Curiosity's face.

"I got nothing more to say."

For the rest of the visit Lily's thoughts circled back again and again to Martha Kirby. If it was true that Ethan was really interested in Jemima Kuick's daughter, then that was Lily's business. He was her cousin, after all. And so good-hearted that he would be willing to put aside all the things he knew of Jemima. And maybe that was right and good, because she knew nothing but good of Martha.

She knew more about Martha than anyone in the whole village except her twin. She could close her eyes and remember a hot summer afternoon when she had learned firsthand what Jemima could do.

She would have liked to talk about this, but Curiosity had declared the subject closed, and she would not change her mind. It wasn't until much later that it occurred to Lily that Ethan might not be the one they were talking about. There were others who could have taken an interest in Martha Kirby.

And oh, how terribly complicated that would be. She hoped her brother had more sense.

19

*E*than came up for supper and brought a note from Callie, just a sentence scrawled over a bit of newspaper: *What is keeping you?*

Martha read it aloud and Ethan smiled. "Not one to waste words, is she?"

"Is she angry with me, do you think?"

"Oh, no." Ethan ran his hands through his hair. He was muddy from helping in the village and in spite of a severe scrubbing, his hands were stained. This was not the Ethan she had known in Manhattan, but the younger version of himself she had known growing up here in the village with Daniel and Blue-Jay as his companions. The boys had seemed to possess some kind of magic, something that protected them from harm. Or so it had seemed to Martha.

He said, "If Callie were mad at you, she'd come right to the door and tell you so. The simple fact is that she's been too busy trying to put things back together to come up here. Now she's asking you to come down."

"Then I'll go tomorrow morning," Martha said. A difficult lesson, one she had learned imperfectly, was how to take criticisms—well deserved criticisms—with good grace.

At table the Bonners talked about affairs in the village, progress made or delayed, the difficulty of getting enough hardware, and the fact that in the next days the trappers would start coming out of the bush with the winter's work. Luke would spend all his time in the Red Dog meeting with them and negotiating prices, and then the drinking would start. The worst of them would lose every penny made in trade at cards or dice.

Martha listened but she didn't take part, and still she had the strong sense that someone was watching her. If she kept her eyes on her plate, the sensible thing to do, she never need know who.

In the morning Martha stopped in the parlor where Elizabeth was talking to Anje and Joan about the week's dinners and what was left in the root cellar.

Elizabeth smiled at Martha as if the interruption were of no importance, but behind her back Joan scowled.

"I wondered if I could do any errands for you while I'm in the village. Is there anything you need?"

Anje said, "We are low on sugar, if there's any to be had."

"White or brown?"

The LeBlanc girls looked at each other and laughed, for which they got a very sharp look from Elizabeth. She explained, "It's rare that we see white sugar here. When I go to Johnstown I bring some back, but mostly we use brown."

"What do people eat in Manhattan, then?" Joan wanted to know. "Honey on your biscuits and white sugar in your tea?"

Martha felt her face flush warm.

"Joan," Elizabeth began, but Martha put out a hand to stop her.

"I'll hear worse, I'm sure, before the day is done. You can't protect me from everything, though you are so good enough to try."

Anje's whole face twitched. Trying to hold back a laugh, Martha thought. Or a snicker.

"I will bring what sugar I can find."

Voices followed her through the door and down the hall. The girls and Elizabeth, back and forth. She must see about lodgings of her own. She had been a burden on the Bonners for long enough.

Martha remembered very well what the weather could be on the edge of the endless forests, and so she had dressed carefully: wool stockings and two underskirts and her thickest boots, along with a cape lined with fox fur with matching mittens, a muff, and a scarf that itched terribly but kept out the cold like nothing else. She had to leave her good bonnet on the shelf, and took instead the one of boiled wool lined with fur.

All that, and she was still cold. She hurried along as quickly as was safe, keeping an eye on anything that might cause her to lose her footing. Before she had reached the crossroads her skirts were heavy with mud to the knee, and she was breathing loudly. It was really very odd, that she should have been cold a half hour ago and now be dripping with perspiration. But none of that was important.

She should be thinking about Callie, who waited for her at the Red Dog.

"Why the Red Dog?" she had asked Ethan before they went in to the table.

"Because I wouldn't let her sleep in the cider house, which is the only proper building left standing on her property."

Martha saw something in his expression that she had never seen before, distress or unhappiness of some kind. Now she wondered if there was a connection. It had never occurred to her before, but why should Ethan not take an interest in Callie?

"Why hasn't she started rebuilding?" Martha asked.

"Because she doesn't have the money, and she won't mortgage the orchards, and she won't accept gifts. At least, she won't accept them from me or Luke or Daniel or Nathaniel either, though we've all offered more than once."

Martha said, "She might accept an offer from me. I could afford to build a house for her, isn't that so?"

His smile was a rare sight. "You could afford to build a dozen houses and it would not make a dent in your account books."

Every year she sat down with Will Spencer and Ethan to hear the report on what they liked to call her holdings or her investments, and every year she deliberately tried not to listen. She could not conceive of such amounts of money. It only made her think of her mother, and what Jemima would do if she knew about it.

"I don't know that Callie will accept your offer any more than she took mine," Ethan said.

"Nor will we, unless I ask," Martha said.

This conversation played itself over in Martha's head as she walked carefully downhill, her skirts gathered tightly in one fist so she could watch her feet. The other way to the village—the one that went right by the Downhill House—would have been faster, but Martha was unused to muddy lanes and preferred the longer, not quite so difficult alternative.

She turned onto the Johnstown road, and then turned again in the direction of the village.

At the crossroads she let out a sigh of relief, when the worst was behind her. The main lane was heavily traveled and deeply rutted, but there was also a footpath that ran along it, hard-packed and secure. And just up ahead she could see the front door of the Red Dog and light shining from the windows.

This wasn't so very bad, she told herself, and with that thought the earth beneath her left foot disappeared and her leg plunged up to the thigh in cold mud.

Even as it was happening the thought came to her: How had she forgotten about Big Muck, well known to every person with two good feet within fifty miles?

She scrambled backward and tugged, but Big Muck wasn't having any. Her leg slipped down another notch, and her skirts began to follow. Martha yanked again, and this time Big Muck let go with a sound like a drawn-out and very wet kiss.

She found herself on her back, looking into the stormy sky. Lying prone on the lane while rain plopped into the mud and onto her face, Martha hiccupped a laugh. She raised a hand to her nose and recalled too late the sorry condition of her gloves.

This time the laughter came in fits and starts between bouts of spitting out mud and struggling to sit up. When she finally managed that small task she sat leaning back on her hands as though she was on a picnic in a meadow. Her skirts and mantle were caked with muck and dripping water. The muff was lost, probably never to be found. And down at the end of her left leg, five muddy toes.

Big Muck had sucked the boot off her foot and taken the stocking for good measure. She wiggled her muddy toes and lay down again on the lane, and now the laugh came up from deep in her belly and she was helpless to do anything more than hold her sides.

"Got you but good," a voice said over her.

Daniel Bonner. She closed her eyes, but there was no ignoring the fact that of all people, Daniel Bonner had come across her like this.

"Can't remember last time somebody walked right into Big Muck. Maybe you're the first," his disembodied voice went on amiably.

"A dubious honor," Martha muttered. There was still mud on her mouth, caked in the corners. And on top of all that, the rain was picking up its tempo.

"I came over to lend you a hand, but you look happy just where you are."

That brought Martha up. "You were watching me?"

His broad-rimmed hat kept rain off his neck, but it also left his face in shadow and hid his expression. Martha suspected that he was smiling.

He said, "We had this very conversation just yesterday as I recall."

The sound of a window being thrown open made them both look in the direction of the Red Dog. Callie Wilde was leaning out, and she did not look happy.

"Daniel Bonner, you help her up right this minute and don't take no for an answer." And then: "Martha! Come on in here, girl; you'll catch your death."

Daniel held out his hand. It was a big hand that was stained with ink and dirt too, callused and hard. Martha grabbed with one muddy glove, and he pulled her up and onto her feet. She wobbled for a moment and then her balance came back.

"Your bonnet?"

She looked around herself and shrugged. "Lost, I fear."

"Well, one good thing came out of this little adventure, then."

She was about to protest the idea that her bonnet was not worth saving when Uz Brodie came around the corner on his old mule, and Martha let out a resigned sigh. By noon everybody in Paradise would hear all about Martha Kirby standing in the crossroads, mud-covered, bare-headed, and half barefoot. Holding on to Daniel Bonner's hand.

"Maybe he didn't recognize me," she muttered, taking her hand back with a jerk.

"If that makes you feel better," Daniel said.

Martha stomped along beside him, as lopsided as she was mortified.

"I'm sorry we have got to do this in the kitchen," Becca LeBlanc told Martha. They were standing between a screen and the cooking hearth, she and Becca and Callie, all of them peeling off layer after layer of mud-caked linen and cotton and wool.

Martha hadn't imagined her visit with Callie this way; the whole situation was so absurd, she had trouble not laughing aloud.

Becca said, "Lift up your foot so I can get this skirt off you."

"I really could manage on my own," Martha protested, and Becca put her hands on her hips and pursed her mouth.

Martha lifted her foot. Becca was so lean and wiry that she seemed to have no bosom or hips at all. Mostly she was a cheerful sort, as anyone married to Charlie LeBlanc would have to be.

"I know this is embarrassing," Becca said. "If I had a room free you'd have some privacy, but with the flood and all, every room I got to let is spoken for."

"My goodness," Martha said. "Please don't apologize. This is very kind of you, and I appreciate your help."

Alice LeBlanc poured another bucket of hot water into the hip bath and wiped her forehead with the back of her wrist. She said, "Talk is cheap."

Callie jumped on her before Martha had even drawn a breath.

"Well now, Alice, maybe you can tell me. Has Martha here ever run up a debt she couldn't settle? I'm asking because you talk like you know her to be somebody who doesn't pull her own weight. One thing I know for certain, and that is that Martha could outwork you hobbled and half starved. But I guess you must have had some bad experience with her, some reason to talk to her like that, so rude and disrespectful."

In her confusion, Martha turned to Becca, ready to offer payment for the use of the tub and the towels, but Becca wasn't even looking at her.

"Alice," Becca said. "Your mouth is hanging open. Close it. The next thing I want to hear is you apologizing to Martha here. You'll apologize; otherwise, you and me, we'll have a private conversation in the washhouse. I don't care how old you are, I won't tolerate such rude behavior. As for you, Martha—" She paused to take a breath.

"I am glad to see you back here in Paradise, and I hope you'll stay, though I'd understand if you didn't, what with the welcome you're getting." She glared at her daughter. "I know you got some bad memories, but I'm a great believer in starting over fresh, and I think you could be happy here, I really do. Now Alice," she turned back to her daughter. "You got something you want to say?"

The girl stood there with her arms crossed and her face turned to the wall. Her whole body trembled with anger.

"Alice!"

"I apologize if I was rude." She spoke to the wall.

Becca flapped her apron. "Do you want me to take my hand to your backside?"

Alice turned to face them and Martha was shocked to see that she was trembling with anger. She couldn't imagine why Alice LeBlanc would hate her so sincerely.

"I am sorry that I was rude to Martha. I shouldn't have said what I said. But I can think it, and I do think it, and you can switch me to Albany and back again, Ma, but that's the truth. Why did she have to come back here when—"

"Ah." Callie's smile could be frightening, and it was focused on Alice. "It's that way, is it?"

The high color in Alice's cheeks drained away just that easily. She turned and walked so quickly from the kitchen that she was almost running.

Becca was looking at Callie. "What do you mean, it's that way? What way? Alice may be testy at times but she's always been a good girl."

"Good girls fall in love just like bad ones," Callie said.

"Who is she supposed to be in love with?" Becca demanded. "Has she been making eyes at that Yarnell boy?"

Martha said, "And what does that have to do with me? Why is she so mad at me?"

Callie's small, narrow face turned to her. There was a sadness there, and a good amount of resignation.

"It's about Daniel. He's a rare prize, and more than a few girls have set their caps for him. Nobody's happy about you coming back and grabbing him for yourself."

"Grabbing? I've been *grabbing* after Daniel?" Martha was horrified. "But that's—that's—"

She wanted to say it wasn't true, but something held her back.

"It don't matter if it's true or not," Callie interrupted her. "Alice thinks it is, and if she thinks it is, then everybody else does too. Now you had best get into that water before it's cold again."

Martha was relieved to be able to disappear, even if it was only behind an old carved screen. She needed to make sense of what Callie had said. She felt herself blushing. Completely irritated with herself, she stripped off her chemise—even that was muddy at the hem—and stepped into the hip bath. The water was blessedly hot, and she sank into it thankfully.

On the other side of the screen, Becca had come back into the kitchen and was proclaiming her thoughts on the whole matter.

"Foolishness," she said. "I won't have it. Those girls of mine will get an earful this evening, I promise you that. Chasing after a man who ain't interested, like a, like a trollop! Did I raise my girls that way? No, I did not. I will see to it your brothers hear about this, you mark my word," Becca called loudly. "They care about this family's good name even if you don't. Pete will set you straight, that he will. I'll see to it."

There was a sound of a stool scraping along the floor and then Callie's voice from the other side of the screen.

"I have to say, Martha, you took your time coming down to the village, but then you did it with style."

Martha closed her eyes and shifted so that the water came up to her shoulders. "I might as well have hired a drummer to walk in front of me."

But she had to smile, a little at least. Sometimes the only thing you could do was laugh at yourself, and this seemed to be one of those times.

Callie was saying, "Flood dirt is stubborn. Here."

A cake of soap came flying around the corner of the screen and plopped into the water.

"Don't use it on your hair," Callie said. "That coarse stuff would do awful things to it and that would be a shame."

Martha slid down further into the water. "Callie?"

"Hmmm?"

"Have I ruined what good name I had?"

Callie barked a short laugh. "You worried about your reputation?"

Yes, Martha should have said. *Yes, I am.*

"It's none of my business anyway," Callie said.

Becca called from the other side of the room. "Ain't nobody asked me but I think Daniel could do a lot worse than Martha. And he ain't getting any younger. But Martha, if you want to look around a bit, don't you forget about my Roy. He's the best worker at the mill, so says Marcus Reed; you can ask him yourself."

Martha clamped her mouth shut hard on the urge to giggle, but Callie wasn't amused.

"Why would you go putting ideas in her head?" Callie snapped. "Why is everybody so interested in pairing people up? Is there an ark somewhere I overlooked? Daniel is happy the way he is."

"Is that so?" Becca said, mildly.

"It is so," Callie shot back.

Martha raised her voice. "Could we please stop talking about Daniel Bonner? I am here to see you, Callie. Tell me how things stand."

There was a short silence and then Callie made a sound deep in her throat. "Why would you want to talk about that sorry subject?"

"Because I want to know," Martha said. "Because I'd like to help if I can."

"You can come shovel mud anytime you got the urge," Callie said, her dry humor coming to the surface again.

"Do you have to joke about everything? I'm serious."

There was a moment's silence, and then Callie reeled off a list of things lost in the flood, from her home to her chickens.

"What about your stock?"

"I lost some trees. But the cider house came through fine, and no damage to the press," she finished. "I could fix up a little place for myself right there in the cider house—there's room for a bed—but Ethan Middleton has got it in his head that it wouldn't be seemly—"

Martha laughed.

"Now what in the name of perdition is so funny about that?" Callie demanded, all sputter and spark.

"You. You are funny, always finding a way to deny yourself the things everybody is entitled to. A home, for one. And don't try to tell me the cider house could be your home, because that argument would be beneath you."

Martha reached for the linen towel and stood up. The water was a deep gray-brown and she was nowhere near clean, but she couldn't loll all morning in Becca's hip bath and to ask for more water would cement her reputation as spoiled and wasteful.

Callie found her voice again. "I don't want to talk houses anymore; it's all I hear about. Now I have got to get back to work. I'm sorry we didn't have much of a visit, but you're welcome anytime. I come in about sunset. Becca, stop making faces. I do come in about sunset."

"About a couple hours after," Becca said. She seemed to be one of the rare people who was not in the least put off by Callie's temper.

While they were arguing the point Martha was dressing as quickly as she could manage. Becca had loaned her an old-fashioned skirt and bodice and a white linen blouse soft with many washings. No stockings, but she would have to send for her second pair of boots and another pair of stockings anyway.

She stepped out from behind the screen feeling a little shy.

"Aren't you a sight?" Callie said. She pressed one hand to her mouth, but she couldn't hide her smile. "With that linen wrapped around your head you look like an old widow woman."

Becca turned suddenly toward raised voices at the kitchen door. She said, "You two had best scat. That sounds like Charlie and he'll pin you down talking all day if he finds you in the kitchen. Go on."

There were five tables in the tavern where travelers could take food and drink, and Martha was relieved to find them all empty. In the normal way of things there would be a full room of people wanting to hear just what happened, and how, and why, and by the way, what was she doing back in Paradise, had she learned something about the wider world, and her place in it?

So she was thankful for the empty tables, but her good luck had its limitations: Daniel sat on a stool in front of the raised hearth, examining a book from the stack on the floor next to him. He looked up briefly and nodded. His expression was distracted and severe, and Martha had the idea that it might be a face his students saw quite often.

"Set by the warm," Callie said behind her. "You can't go back up the hill until you are good and dry, or Curiosity will give me the sharp side of her tongue, and she'd be right too. And I expect it will be a while before Becca finds somebody to go fetch your dry boots. Daniel!" she called. "Scoot over, make some room. Maybe Martha can give you a hand with those books. And now I am gone, I have got to go look at Mayfair's mule before somebody else buys her out from under my nose."

Daniel had a great many things spread out over the apron of the hearth: buckets of water, piles of rags, knives, a scissors, and a whole range of brushes. Some of them looked like Lily's paintbrushes, but she must be mistaken about that. Lily treated her tools with great care and would hardly give them up without an argument. She and Daniel had been very good at arguing, as she recalled.

As she watched, Daniel stood to hang a dripping book from a dowel rack over the hearth. Then he took each of the others hanging there one by one, gently shook the pages, and put it back to dry some more. He worked so quickly and efficiently that a stranger might not have noticed straight off that he worked without the use of his left hand.

"I won't bite," he said without turning around. "And I could use some help."

His tone was matter-of-fact, and so Martha took an empty stool and accepted the primer that he offered her. It was damp and already smelled vaguely of mold, but the covers still opened and individual pages could be turned with a little coaxing. It might have been the very primer she used when she had gone to the Paradise school, when it was still halfway up Hidden Wolf in an old cabin.

Becca swept into the room with a tray. "Before he puts you to work you'll drink down this tea. It's Hannah's recipe for a cold in the lungs."

Martha accepted the cup thrust at her because there was no other option. "I don't have a cold in the lungs."

"Not yet, anyhow. You drink that; I don't want to hear any excuses. Daniel, you need anything?"

"No, ma'am, but thank you anyway." His attention had already turned back to the book in front of him.

The thing about Daniel Bonner—about all the Bonner men—was that they responded to a woman's directions as if there were no differences between the sexes. In Manhattan things didn't work that way, but the Bonners and some of the other people in Paradise had never learned the rules that people in the city lived by, and more, they seemed to do fine without them. There was even talk that when the Quakers held their prayer meetings, a woman could stand up and preach like a man. Martha remembered talking to Teddy about that.

"That little village you come from is the perfect place for Quakers," Teddy said. "They like forward women and Negroes and most likely Indians too. I can't think of another group of whites who would be willing to live in such an unnatural setting."

With time, Martha was remembering more about Teddy, things that she had somehow overlooked or failed to credit. Unpleasant things, most of them. Though he had been right about one thing: She couldn't see herself preaching under any circumstances. Martha tried to decide what woman of her acquaintance would be comfortable in a pulpit and a few did come to mind: Curiosity, first and foremost; Elizabeth Bonner, if she were permitted to talk philosophy and rationalism. Jennet would tell stories that would keep the congregation laughing in spite of themselves. And the Mohawk women—if you gave any of them the chance, they would be fine speakers.

"You don't need to help if you don't care to."

Martha started. She was still holding the primer in her hands. She picked up a dry rag from the pile and began to press the pages dry, one by one.

Sometime later, when they were working in a companionable silence, Daniel said, "You were far away in your thoughts."

"Was I?" She kept her eyes on her work. "I was thinking about how the Quaker women are allowed to preach."

"Ah," Daniel glanced at her. "Writing a sermon to deliver to friends and neighbors, are you?"

"Me? Oh, no." She laughed aloud at the idea. "But there are others in Paradise who could do it in a heartbeat. The Mohawk women, first of all."

"You thinking of our Hannah?"

"Well, actually, it was Blue-Jay's wife who came to mind. I once heard Terese get into an argument with Anna MacGarrity. Even with her English the way it is, she had people agreeing with her and nodding."

Daniel was looking at her with a puzzled expression.

"What?"

"Terese died some two years ago. She got tangled up in an old fishing net and drowned. You didn't know?"

"No, I didn't. I'm sorry to hear it. I haven't seen Blue-Jay since I've been back, so the subject was never raised."

"And you likely won't see him," Daniel said. "He remarried a year ago and he mostly stays out of the village. Hasn't even been down to see Lily yet, and you can believe she's hopping mad about that."

"Did he marry somebody from Good Pasture?" Martha asked.

She felt Daniel's gaze and wondered for a minute if he would just refuse to discuss the matter, and why the subject was so clearly difficult for him.

"You ever meet the Mayfairs when you visited?"

"Well, sure," Martha said. "Susanna and Sally, and—John, is that the oldest one? You don't mean to say that Blue-Jay married into the Mayfairs?"

His mouth worked, but out of irritation or insult she couldn't tell. "He married Susanna."

"Oh, I see. And her family disapproves."

"It's more complicated." Daniel smiled. "But most things are, when you come down to it."

While he told her about Susanna and Blue-Jay, Martha was reminded that he came from a family of good storytellers. It went along with being a good teacher, in Martha's experience.

Blue-Jay and Susanna were living at Lake in the Clouds in the house nearest the falls, the one Daniel's father built. Gabriel and Annie were in the cabin nearest the cornfields. Runs-from-Bears moved back and forth between the houses as he pleased.

"There are others who come and go," he finished. "But mostly the Lake in the Clouds folks stay among themselves and they're happy that way."

"She must miss her family."

"She sees John and Sally now and then. But sure, I guess she does miss them."

"In Manhattan they talk about Indians a lot," she told Daniel. "But none of them have ever really known an Indian. They asked me rude questions, at first. And then in time they just seemed to forget where I came from and that I might know more than any of them did about the Hodenosaunee. They are full of opinions. What should be done about them, mostly."

"They think they can decide that?" Daniel's tone was half amused and half affronted.

"They think they can decide most things. I'm ashamed now to think back at some of the things I heard said. Some of them talked about Indians as they would talk about a rat infestation, but I didn't say a word. I just left the room."

He was looking at her; she could feel the weight of his regard. It made Martha wonder why she had said so much, and if he would think badly of her now.

"I am a coward," she said. "Is that what you're thinking?"

"No," he said, turning back to his work. "That's not even close to what I was thinking."

The door from the hall opened with a bang and Sam LeBlanc came in. He was a couple years older than Martha, but they had been in Elizabeth's classroom at the same time. Now he grinned at her and presented a basket with a deep and cheeky bow.

Sam had been a terrible tease, she remembered now. As if she didn't have enough to cope with at the moment.

"Thank you," she told him. "Very good of you."

"I'm a helpful sort," Sam agreed. He sat down beside her. "What else can I do for you, ducky? Your wish is my command. But first tell me this: Are you home for good? Say yes and you'll make me a happy man. Why are you laughing?"

"I'm not," Martha said. "I'm just wondering why Becca didn't mention you. She's already tried to get me interested in Roy."

"Roy!" Sam looked sour at the very idea. "I see I'll have to talk to Ma straight away."

While Sam flirted with Martha, Daniel reminded himself that the best thing to do was to keep his focus on the book in front of him. It made no sense to be put out with Sam LeBlanc, who was his usual cheerful self. Odd, though, that Daniel had never noticed before how grating Sam's voice could be. He could find some humor in Sam's clumsy and harmless flirting, and something to admire in Martha's response—not unfriendly, not exactly cool, but standoffish. He wondered if that came to her naturally, or if there had been lessons in poise and bearing. How to speak to young men who were forward, how to discourage them or reprimand as the situation required.

When Sam finally went into the kitchen to find his ma, Martha took up the basket he had brought her. She put the heel of one bare foot on the edge of the stool and began to pull on a stocking, rolling it along her foot and up. She rested her chin on her knee and a great swath of hair—as straight as Daniel's was curly—fell down over the long arch of her back and over an arm to brush against the hem of her borrowed skirt.

It was an everyday sight. Women put on stockings and took them off with regularity, and often before the hearth in the kitchen, when the weather was cold. Nothing unusual, but he found it difficult to look away.

Martha's foot was slender with a high arch, the skin as white as paper. Each of the long toes ended in a perfect nail without flaw or scar, and was cushioned with a round pad of pale pink. Martha Kirby had the most delicate and narrow ankles, with a sprinkling of freckles.

She raised her head suddenly, and their eyes met.

As a boy learning to hunt in the endless forests with his father and uncle, Daniel had come to understand the importance of holding himself contained, absolutely still and calm. It hadn't been hard. He was swift and quiet, and he could trail a doe all morning and then drop her before she ever got a hint of danger.

And why had that thought come to him?

Two seconds passed, and then three and four, and neither of them looked away.

Finally Martha raised a brow. "Do I offend you?"

Daniel could make no sense of the question. "What?"

"Do my bare feet offend your sensibilities?" Her tone was cool and impertinent, and the urge to laugh out loud came to him as unexpectedly as a hiccup.

"I've seen bare feet before. I've seen your bare feet before, Martha Kirby. As girls you and Callie were always running in and out, uphill and downhill both."

He did have clear memories of those days when Callie and Martha had been inseparable. Sisters in spirit, at least, though no one would mistake them for blood kin. Martha was a head taller, with shoulders a little broader than might be expected. As a girl—he was surprised how quickly this memory came to him—she had been the fastest runner, long-legged and lithe. Callie was strongly built, in the way of a muscular small pony; she could work all day without ever sitting down or even thinking about it. She had her father's dark complexion, an intelligent expression, and a generous spirit. If those things didn't get her the husband she deserved, he had heard his mother say, then the farm and orchard would.

Daniel tried to clear his head of memories. He said, "You were always barefoot back then."

"But not by choice," she said. "The winter I was eight I outgrew my old pattens and Ma said I'd have to stay home. She said there was nothing being taught in the schoolroom that she couldn't teach me herself. But the real reason was, she didn't care to spend what little cash she had on shoes I'd outgrow in a few months. I do believe she would have bought them if she could have, because she didn't like having me in the house and school kept me away for a good part of the day."

Her tone was matter-of-fact, telling this story into the fire.

"But you did go to school that winter, if I remember right."

Martha nodded. "One morning there was a basket on the doorstep when I went to fetch wood. With boots and wool stockings and a hat and gloves. Jemima was angry, but we didn't know who had left them. In the end she gave up and let me go to school. I always thought it was Callie who did it, but then I asked her and she said it wasn't, and I should have known better. They didn't have the money for that kind of thing either."

In that moment Daniel wished she would look at him. There was little he could do for her but listen, but he could do that without reservation or judgment. If she would look at him again, he would smile at her. Because she struck him as someone in need of a smile, someone who was coming up from a long sleep fraught with terrible dreams.

All the money and land she had inherited from the father she had never met—that didn't matter. Those things couldn't make her childhood memories sweet. Nothing could undo the damage her mother had done. Jemima Southern had torn apart more than one family, but first she had cut her teeth on her own.

He was surprised to hear himself asking a question that could only be called impolite. "So what happened with this Teddy you were set to marry?"

"My mother," she said. "Jemima happened. But when people ask I'll only say that we both had a change of heart."

She had told him the truth without hesitation, and for some reason he couldn't put a finger on, that pleased him. Daniel wanted to say so, but before he could put the words together the door opened. Martha turned her back and finished pulling on her stockings and boots while Baldy O'Brien waddled into the room.

"What's this?" he bellowed in a voice that was meant to shake the glass in the windows. "What's this? Young aristocrats wasting away the hours in front of a fire while the rest of us work to put roofs over our heads."

O'Brien meant to look menacing but he always put Daniel in mind of a dumpy little teapot. He was as bothersome as a wasp; his voice was loud and his tone harsh, and he could make a nuisance of himself faster than anyone else between Paradise and Philadelphia. Worst of all, if you had a conversation with him, Baldy insisted on pushing his face as close as he could, and his breath stank. In fact Hannah's professional opinion was that he didn't have a sound tooth in his head and that if they all came out his temperament would improve. No one mentioned this to O'Brien, as he would have scoffed at the idea of taking advice from a half-breed Indian, and a woman at that. The only person he seemed to dislike more than Hannah was Curiosity.

"Baldy O'Brien." Daniel kept his voice as neutral as possible. "Good morning to you."

Martha was so tense he could feel her humming with it.

Baldy came closer. His whole face was in motion, squinting and twitching, his jaw working as he chewed his usual plug of tobacco, the evidence dripping down his chin. "Who is that with you hiding her face? She got a guilty conscience?"

"Mind your own business," Daniel said, still in the same neutral tone.

"Oh, it's little Martha Kuick. I was wondering if you'd have the gall to show yourself. Come running home from the city to sit on your money like a broody hen on her nest."

Daniel stood. "O'Brien, you've got money hid away in every nook and cranny, most of it skimmed off the tax coffers. Or did your treasure chest get swept away in the flood?"

O'Brien ignored him. He had Martha in his sights and wouldn't give up so easy.

"You come home on the very day of the flood, ain't that right? Trouble follows you around, girl. No wonder they chased you out of the city."

Martha's back straightened slowly. There was a look on her face that Daniel hadn't seen from her before: a quiet but forceful anger.

Baldy was saying, "I'll tell you, I thought you'd have the sense to stay away, after what your ma did. If they find you one morning with your throat slit, it won't be a surprise."

Daniel's hand moved to the knife sheath of its own accord, and O'Brien took a step backward. "I didn't say Jemima murdered anybody, did I? But she had her ways, yes she did."

Martha put a hand on Daniel's arm. "Don't," she said. "He may be a blowhard without an honest bone in his body, but he is right about Jemima."

O'Brien's mouth fell open to show his teeth, discolored and broken.

"And of course, you knew my mother better than most, didn't you? You knew Jemima very well."

There was a moment in which the only sound was the fire in the hearth and the hitch of O'Brien's breathing. Daniel felt almost as surprised as O'Brien must.

Martha stood there, straight of back, head held high. There was a dignity to her that O'Brien could never touch, and even he seemed to know it. The old man backed away, clutching his hat and muttering under his breath. Then the door closed behind him and the air seemed to go out of Martha. She closed her eyes.

And so Daniel had leave to look at her. Really look at her. The hair that fell around her in a river of color, the sharp line of her jaw and cheek. Strongly marked eyebrows, like wings. Faint lines on her forehead at—how old was she? Nineteen? Twenty? She was pale, but there were shadows around her eyes, like smudges of faint blue ash. She was long of limb, and lithe, and the idea struck him just that easily that he could fall in love with Martha Kirby. That he was well on his way already, and didn't know how to stop, or even if he wanted to.

20

_____

$\mathscr{T}$he spring and summer in Paradise were anything but peaceful, most especially not at the Uphill House, nor the Downhill. Both of them were bursting at the seams with children and thus every day brought a selection of catastrophes small and large. Elizabeth was never happier. She had looked forward all winter to having Luke and Jennet come to stay.

Once or twice Luke had raised the possibility of building a house in Paradise—usually after a rainy day with all nine of the grandchildren together under one roof. It would be a sensible thing to do, he contended, as they spent a good half of their year here—but Elizabeth always found a way to dissuade him. Nathaniel liked having the little people nearby as much as Elizabeth did, and took her side. Jennet kept quiet during these conversations, but she was ready to jump in if things seemed to be swinging Luke's way. She had no intention of taking on the running of another household.

And now Lily was come home, and Daniel had begun to spend less time alone.

The twins were her own, her firstborn. When Elizabeth first saw Lily standing on the dock with Simon beside her, everything in her had clenched very tight and then, finally, let go. Later she told Nathaniel it felt as if she had been roused from a deep sleep.

She loved every one of the children, but Lily had always been, would always be, the child of her heart. Through the winter Elizabeth had wondered what was bringing them home just at this time; if one of them was ill, or if there were problems between them. Or maybe, she told Nathaniel, it could be that they were homesick. All through the fall and winter she had asked questions that had no answers. Nathaniel listened in his own patient way, maybe because she was putting words to things he felt himself, but couldn't express.

All those long days and nights of waiting, and then the week in Manhattan and the difficult journey home, in all that time Lily had not spoken of her condition to anyone. She had saved that news for Curiosity and Hannah. In some ways this was perfectly logical; Elizabeth herself had never talked about a baby on the way until the news announced itself to the world.

Elizabeth told herself that Lily simply hadn't wanted to get her mother's hopes up. But it did sting that she was not the first to be told. She must admit that at least to herself. She was more like her twin than she would ever admit: Lily would suffer in silence, even should it dearly cost those who loved her best.

The hours Elizabeth spent with Lily were the most important of the day. They talked, it seemed to Elizabeth, without pause, about everything but the child Lily carried, and the ones she had lost. They discussed each of Curiosity's family members, and the possibility of sending her grandson Markus to a music conservatory in Paris or London. They never seemed to tire of talking about Birdie. They talked about Ethan and Blue-Jay and his new wife, and most of all about Daniel. When they were silent Elizabeth could almost see the words hanging in the air between them, but Lily did not speak them, and she must wait.

Finally Elizabeth took her frustration to Curiosity.

"I was wondering when it would wear you down," Curiosity said by way of greeting. "Don't look so surprised, Elizabeth. You never could hide anything you was feeling."

But for the longest time they sat silently. The questions that she had come to ask were stuck in her throat, though they roamed around her mind freely enough.

She cleared her throat. "All right," she said. "Tell me."

Curiosity glanced up at her and then back down at the fleece she was combing.

"I told you already what there is to know about her condition. You think I'd try to hold anything back on you?"

Elizabeth kept her gaze on Curiosity and said nothing.

Curiosity said, "You cain't take Lily's trouble on yourself. It ain't your fault. Something else I been wanting to say to you since she got home—this ain't the time for you to get all fluttery on the girl."

Elizabeth jerked up. "Fluttery? Fluttery? When have I ever been fluttery?"

"Now see," Curiosity said, widening her eyes as if she were surprised. "I knew you was in there some place. Betimes I have got to poke you real hard to make you wake up."

"I assure you, I am awake."

"I ain't so sure," Curiosity said. "You going to lose your nerve when Lily need you most?"

"I haven't lost my nerve. I just want to—"

"Fix things. I know you do. And you know you cain't. What you can do you already doing. You go down there every day and sit with that little girl of yours, and you talk to her and read to her like you do for any of us when we feeling low. You make sure she has got good fortifying food, red meat to feed her blood. When she get restless you distract her."

"But I'm running out of things to distract her with," Elizabeth said.

"Far from it. Ask the girl to teach you how to draw."

Elizabeth barked a short laugh. "Draw? Me?"

"Why not?" Curiosity shrugged. "It's something she can do that you cain't. It might help her to remember that her mama ain't perfect."

Curiosity had surprised her many times over the years, but for a moment Elizabeth was truly speechless.

"Perfect?" she said finally. "Lily couldn't think—" She broke off, lost in her thoughts.

After a moment Curiosity said, "You brought six healthy children into this world. The ones you lost were carried off by illness ain't nobody but the good Lord hisself could fix. Why, you had Birdie when you was almost fifty. There was a time Nathaniel only had to look at you cross-ways and you fell pregnant."

To her consternation Elizabeth felt herself blushing.

"How old were you when your mama died?"

"You know the answer to that. I was ten."

"You still think about her?"

"Every day."

"You remember how it felt when you done something that disappointed her?"

Elizabeth closed her eyes. She remembered her mother's voice and her hands and the set of her shoulders. Her features had faded and could only be called back by means of the miniature Elizabeth kept on the table near her bed. But she remembered snatches of conversations, and games played and books read aloud in the nursery at Oakmere. She remembered her mother's accent and way of speaking, how it had set her apart from everyone—from Elizabeth herself—and how she had tried to sound more like her. And she remembered how easily her mother could deal with Julian when he was frightened or moody.

"I remember a day in July just before she fell ill. It was very hot," she told Curiosity. "I was wearing a new bodice and it was terribly scratchy, so I was out of sorts. And I—I was cruel to Julian. He came crying about something, and I shook him off, like a fly. And when I turned around I saw my mother standing there, watching. I remember her expression, very sad and disappointed. My stomach lurched into my throat, because I knew I couldn't take back what I had done. Then she turned away from me and called Julian to her and took him on her lap to comfort him. I was in agony until she came to talk to me, and then I wept as much as Julian had."

She paused. "Are you saying I need to let Lily weep?"

"Mayhap," Curiosity said.

Elizabeth walked to the window and stood there for a moment.

"I'd much rather have Lily whole and healthy than have a grandchild. Curiosity." Elizabeth inhaled very deeply. "Tell me, what are her chances?" The question that kept her awake long into the night.

Curiosity took her time, thinking it through. Elizabeth pressed her forehead to the cold windowpane.

"Lily had a hard time these last years," Curiosity said. "From what she told, I have got to doubt whether she can bring a living child into this world. But we will do everything in our power to save Lily. You know that we will."

"I can't lose her," Elizabeth said. "I couldn't bear it."

Curiosity left her chair and came to stand next to Elizabeth at the window. On the sill Curiosity's hand looked frail, the skin as thin as silk tissue with age, the joints swollen. Elizabeth's own hand was chapped from cold and wet, and the first faint old-age freckles were rising up out of her skin to remind her that she was sixty years old. When that thought came to her, she always had the urge to laugh at the absurdity of it.

"Listen to me now." Curiosity's voice was low, and the tone familiar. It was the voice she used when she was talking to a woman who had been so long in travail that she was close to giving up.

"Listen close. If that day come, if Lily has got to move on, you will do what you got to do. You be right there beside her to help her go, the same way you brought her into this world. The last thing she see should be the faces of the people who love her best. You know that you will be there to do for her. And she know it too, that's why she came home."

A shudder ran through Elizabeth, so that her whole body shook. "You think she expects to die?"

"No," Curiosity said. "The girl come home because she want to live."

21

Since Martha's first eventful outing to the village, Curiosity seemed to find a reason to send her every day, sometimes twice.

Today she was supposed to take a pound of salt, a jar of tea, and a loaf of new bread to Joshua at the smithy. Joshua was Curiosity's son-in-law and she was always sending little things over to him or to her daughter Daisy. The Hench family lived on the other side of the village up high on the hillside, with three married children in their own small houses in a half circle, like chicks to a hen. Curiosity had bought the land with her own money and then gifted it to her Daisy and Joshua, who had in turned divided it up among those three children who had married on in Paradise.

It had turned cold again, and Martha wore her warmest things. It was good to be out in the open, and she made it down to the village without falling even once. She might run into someone who wished her ill—Alice LeBlanc or Baldy O'Brien were the first names that came to her—but she would do everything in her power to maintain her dignity.

A flock of geese was coming toward her on the lane, waddling with a purpose, propelled by a young girl with a stick and a very serious expression. She dropped her head in shyness or uncertainty before Martha could greet her, much less ask her name. One of the Blackhouse girls, Martha thought, though she couldn't be sure.

It was a beautifully clear day, and the air was clean and sharp. All around the evergreens were alive with the wind. The faintest smell of spring was in the air, a sweetness that meant the first flush of color was about to show itself, a green so tender that it verged on the color of April butter.

She would be here if it should happen tomorrow or weeks from now. For once that thought didn't upset her. Martha still woke in the morning expecting to see her room in the house on Whitehall Street, but the disappointment that followed didn't last through the day, as it once had.

The turn in her state of mind had come the very day she sent the packet with Teddy's pearl ring and watched until the post rider disappeared.

And if the weather were to turn wintery again? Would her spirits survive that?

Blizzards in late April were not all that rare. As a girl she had feared such storms, because they kept her indoors with Jemima. As she had been the day that Callie's mother walked past the kitchen windows, heading up the mountain and into a blizzard dressed as though she were going to see a neighbor on a Sunday afternoon in May.

A court of law could not find Jemima guilty of murder, but her neighbors had their own way of seeing things and an older, much bloodier understanding of the law. Jemima had not reached out to stop Dolly Wilde from walking into the storm, nor had she allowed Martha to go after her. A bullet would have been kinder, people had said.

Today there was no snow, but it might come. All around the forests seemed untouched, untouchable. Waiting for winter's last breath.

As she came into the village proper the sound of voices and saws and hammers came up from the river. The building of the new bridge was something that interested everybody and there would be onlookers. No place for Martha, at least not yet.

As she passed the schoolhouse something caught her attention. Martha stopped to study it for a moment and realized that someone had painted a neat black line on the wall of the schoolhouse, about a foot in length and considerably higher than Martha's line of sight. Six feet, four inches high, declared the writing below it. There was verse too. Her curiosity got the better of her and she went closer, up on tiptoe, to read it.

> To this high point the flood water reached
> when the hundred-year water breached
> the banks of the mighty Sacandaga.
> ~Anno MDCCCXXIV~

Standing as she was, she sensed rather than saw someone coming to the window just above her and to the right.

Daniel, of course.

Martha held very still, studying the verse on the wall and waiting for him to turn away.

They had seen each other many times since the unhappy episode with Baldy O'Brien at the Red Dog. She always smiled and nodded; Daniel smiled and inclined his head. Quite often he ate his dinner or his supper at his mother's table and sometimes stayed into the evening to sit in the parlor and talk. The evening visits were great fun. Every one of the Bonners was an excellent storyteller, and sometimes they would sing or Elizabeth would read aloud from books that her cousins sent her from England and Manhattan. Twice Simon had carried Lily all the way from the village so that she could sit with all her family at once. On those evenings every one of the Bonners did their best to make her laugh, Daniel most especially.

Martha found it was hard not to let her eyes follow him around the room.

At night these short meetings kept her awake and sermonizing to herself. Really, did she mean to make a fool of herself mooning over Daniel Bonner? What kind of weak-willed person was she? She had been engaged to marry Teddy just weeks ago and now her head was full of someone else. It would simply not do.

But still, if she heard Daniel's name raised in a conversation she could not help but stop and listen. Sooner or later someone would notice, and her reputation would be compromised once and for all.

And now Daniel Bonner was standing there watching her. Martha recited to herself a list of facts: He was ten years her senior; he was a veteran of the last war, and a schoolteacher. He was without the use of his left arm, but he managed well enough. He could have any unmarried woman he wanted. He was friendly but not overbearing, and she could not predict what he might say or do, from one moment to the next.

Most of all: He was a Bonner, and she was Jemima's daughter, the granddaughter of Moses Southern, whose sins against the Bonners were too many and too awful to contemplate.

Now he stood there in the window, motionless. She determined to turn away, but instead stood there, looking at him from the corner of her eye. His shirt was plain homespun, soft with washing. The right sleeve was folded up neatly to just below the elbow. His weak arm was kept close to his side by a sling made of doeskin. His hair was shorn very short, and he was clean shaven.

From Amanda Spencer, Martha had learned that calm could be won by nothing more than deep breathing. Deeply and slowly, no matter how dire the situation. Now she took three very deep breaths and turned toward the livery to complete her errands.

"Martha!"

Another very deep breath, and she pivoted. Daniel had opened the window with its new glass panes and leaned out toward her.

She called out, rather than come any closer. She said, "I was just admiring your verse."

"Not mine." He looked like he was going to laugh at the idea. "That's Birdie's composition. Simon painted it for her."

"With Birdie's close supervision, no doubt."

"Exactly. Where are you off to?"

Where was she off to? For a moment she couldn't remember.

"Ah, the livery," she said finally. "Curiosity sent me down to bring some things to Joshua. And then I was going to see Callie."

"You never sit still."

She looked away. "I like to be busy." And: "I should be on my way."

"Scaring you off, am I?"

"No!" She sputtered. "Of course not. There's nothing to be scared about."

"Then come in," Daniel said. "I'll give you a tour."

"Of the schoolhouse?"

"Have you seen it before?"

She had to admit she had not; she had left for Manhattan before it had been put into use.

"Then come in, have a look."

———

Daniel's sisters chided him for his lack of playfulness and spontaneity, and how surprised they would be to see him invite Martha Kirby into his school on a moment's whim. Out of curiosity, he told himself. Simple goodwill toward someone who had come home after a long absence.

The truth was, he hadn't expected her to agree. She'd fluster and make excuses or she'd hold herself very straight and decline with dignity. Or—and this thought came to him too late—she might laugh outright.

But she had accepted, after the smallest hesitation.

Daniel closed the window, listening to her run her boots over the scraper. He went out into the foyer to greet her.

"Martha. Maybe I spoke too quick—" He stopped, disconcerted by the way the color rose up from her throat and fell again. From deep red to white. As if she had been slapped.

"I only meant to say that tour is too big a word for this little school-house."

"Oh," she said, visibly relieved. She made a small ceremony of putting down her basket and retrieving her handkerchief from her cuff, and then hid her face in it.

He had flustered her so badly that she had lost her command of language. For some reason, that pleased him. But he was not heartless, and so he turned away to give her time to gather her thoughts.

"My mother designed it all," he said to the wall. "The two classrooms, with the cloakroom between—"

"She was always coming up with new ways to keep mud and wet out of the classroom," Martha said. She had regained her composure. "It seems like she found the solution. And there?" She inclined her head to a door at the other end of the hall.

"The teacher's apartment. We'll have to put it to rights before Mr. Moss comes in the fall or he'll turn around and leave again."

Daniel sounded more and more like his sisters, talking so fast that he himself was having trouble making sense of it.

"It's all very nice," Martha said, quite formally. She looked uncomfortable again, but then Daniel felt uncomfortable himself for no good reason. He said the next thing that occurred to him.

"Did you know you've got a bucket on your head?"

She blinked, and a ghost of a smile ran across her face. "You don't like my bonnet? I bought it from the very best milliner in Manhattan."

Daniel put his good hand on the wall and leaned into it. "You familiar with every milliner in the city?"

"Of course not," she said. "Very well, I should have said he's the most fashionable milliner in the city."

"And this Mr.—"

"Henricks."

"Everyone wants one of his buckets."

"That's right," Martha said, her smile widening.

"Because his shop is fashionable."

"Oh," she said. "I see what you're about. You mean to point out a logical fallacy on my part. An *argumentum ad populum*. But I won't walk into that trap."

"*Argumentum ad populum?*" Daniel found himself smiling too. "You took your philosophy and rhetoric studies seriously, I see."

"Your cousin Ethan is an exacting taskmaster."

"And you liked your studies."

"Don't tell anyone," she said. "It was very unladylike of me. I should have detested philosophy and longed for a pony to go riding in the park."

"You didn't like to ride?"

"I did," she said. "But I liked my lessons as well."

She crossed her arms at the waist and lowered her chin until it touched the buttons at her throat. As if she were trying to remember something, or maybe she was sorry to have said so much.

"So what does a young lady do with an education in Manhattan?"

She raised a shoulder. "Why, nothing. In fact it's wise of her to keep her education to herself, if she intends to—" She studied her own feet for a moment and raised her head. "Of course, if she must support herself that's a different matter. If she is very quick, she might find a school who will hire a female teacher, in a small village or town. Otherwise, there are more female clerks in the shops these days, so she might end up—selling hats."

"Like the bucket you're wearing."

"Bucket?" Martha lifted the bonnet off her head. She held it up on the flat of her hands to examine in a patch of sunlight.

"You may be very well educated," she said. "But clearly you know nothing about fashion or the workmanship that goes into something like this. Do you see the way the silk seems to glow, and how the colors complement each other? That is all by design. And see how smoothly the shape tapers from front to back. This kind of ruching is very difficult, especially with such delicate material. The workmanship is impeccable."

"Maybe so," Daniel said. He took the bonnet from her and held it at arm's length. "But being well put together and being pleasing don't necessarily go hand in hand. This bonnet of yours is plain ugly, girl. Admit it, even a goat would have to be mighty hungry to bother with it."

Her mouth fell open. "I'll admit no such—" She drew up. "Now you are teasing me." And her expression was so affronted that Daniel had to laugh.

"And? Don't young ladies get teased in Manhattan?"

"Daniel Bonner," Martha said. "You are trying to distract me, because I have argued you into a corner. I find this bonnet charming and beautifully made, and that's the end of it. Aesthetics have nothing to do with logic. *De gustibus non disputandum*. Now may I have my bonnet back?"

"Of course." But he turned it around, examining it. It was a desperate move on his part, a play for a few moments in which to figure out what he was up to, flirting with Martha Kirby in the deserted schoolhouse.

With a sigh he leaned forward and placed the monstrosity of a bonnet on her head. Her hand came up to hold it in place, and without thinking about it at all, he caught her fingers in his and held them there.

He saw the muscles of her throat working when she swallowed.

"Thank you," she said. "I believe I can manage."

And when he failed to step away, she raised her face and looked at him with a combination of doubt and irritation.

"Do you realize that the little bit of reputation I have left will dwindle to nothing if someone finds us—"

"Kissing?"

She stepped backward, and he forward.

"I said nothing about kissing."

"Not with words. But your mouth is all set to do just that."

"Daniel Bonner," she said, her breath coming fast. "Let my hand go."

The door opened, and Daniel released her.

Martha turned from the waist to look over her shoulder, and a ray of sunlight fell across her face and hair and slanted over her throat. For that moment she might have been an apparition, color and form and movement conjured up like a magical being.

Callie Wilde said, "Oh ha. Am I interrupting?"

"You are most certainly not interrupting," Martha said, too loudly. "Come in."

"Come in," Daniel echoed. His voice creaked a little.

"I'm filthy," Callie said. "I just wanted to leave this basket. Will you take it up to your ma, Daniel? I promised to get it back to her. I'll say good-bye, then. Sorry to have interrupted."

The door closed before either of them could deny the obvious.

$\mathcal{M}$artha ran so that when she caught up to Callie, she was flushed and out of breath.

"Let me walk with you," she said. "I've been meaning to come by and see how things stand."

Callie gave her a lopsided smile that Martha took to be an invitation. She fell in beside her friend and for a minute they walked in silence. Martha considered things she might say, but every one of them only made the situation worse. Better to be still.

All over the village people were still busy putting things to rights, repairing the flood damage, digging and sweeping, sawing and hammering. Some of them called out to Callie, and she answered without slowing. I might as well be invisible, Martha thought, and didn't know why she minded.

They passed the Cunninghams' place, one of the few old-time cabins left in Paradise. A new door hung from leather hinges and there was a pile of shingles sitting on the ground. Through the window Martha caught a glimpse of women at work. Everyone was busy, but there was nothing frantic about it. The sun had come out and the air smelled of growing things, of wood drying out and of lye soap and sawdust.

"Would you have thought things would be back to normal so quick?"

Callie rubbed her nose with a bent wrist. "I wouldn't exactly call this normal," she said. They stopped on the rise where the orchards came into sight. In the fullness of spring this would be the prettiest spot in Paradise, when the first apple trees were in blossom. If there was to be a crop this year.

Of course things were not back to normal and might never be again for either of them.

The Wilde farm was on a long sloping stretch of land that ran along the river on one end, three quarters of it orchard. The buildings that made up the homestead—the house and barn and outbuildings—they were all gone. The only evidence that they had ever existed was a scattering of stone where the chimney had stood.

"It was your home too," Callie said. "Do you ever think about that time?"

To be truthful, Martha did her best not to think about that year when she and Callie had truly been stepsisters.

"I try not to," Martha said. "I try to give my—to give Jemima as little thought as I can manage. I don't know how I'd live with what she did, otherwise."

"You mean marrying my da?" Callie asked. "Or forcing him out?"

At that moment Martha was glad that the orchard house was gone. So many bad things had happened there, she had never wanted to cross the threshold again, and now she wouldn't have to. Now Callie could start over again.

Just across from where they stood was the cider house, still intact, and all around it evidence of Callie's hard work. A few dozen split oak baskets had been scrubbed and set out in the sun to dry; a goat and a mule both grazed within a hastily fenced pasture, and chickens hunted through the sparse late-winter grass. From behind the cider house came the sound of an axe on wood.

"Levi?"

Callie nodded. "Most of the trees we salvaged couldn't be saved. At least we'll get firewood out of them."

Martha had the sense that Callie was holding something back. Something too awful to talk about for fear of what those words might trigger. The only thing Callie cared about so much was the orchard and the trees.

She cleared her throat. "How many did you lose?"

Callie held herself very still. "Too many. Do you remember what Cookie used to call you and me? Working fools."

Martha smiled. "I dream about Cookie sometimes."

Callie drew in a deep breath. "Me and Levi, we talk about her a lot and I dream about her almost every night," she said. "Mostly about the way she talked to my ma, like there wasn't a thing in the world wrong with her. Other folks were afraid of Ma, but not Cookie."

"She knew how to talk so your ma heard her. She took care of all of you."

Cookie had died in the same blizzard that killed Callie's mother. In Martha's view of things, Cookie was the greater loss. Not that she could say such a thing out loud, but it was true. Cookie had been an irritable and prickly old woman, an emancipated slave with no good opinion of white people, with the exception of the Wildes. She ran the household and kept an eye on Dolly, who would wander off if not watched. It was Cookie who had raised Callie.

"She deserved better than she got." Callie's voice had taken on an edge.

"They both did," Martha said.

Martha wondered if they would start up the old conversation again, the one they had had so many times. How Cookie had died, if she had fallen from the icy bridge by accident, or if she had been pushed. Whether she had gone out to find Callie's ma before she got lost in the storm, and how Dolly had slipped away in the first place.

They had been young girls and ready to buckle under the weight of what they dare not tell the adults. And if they had come across solid proof that Jemima had pushed Cookie to her death, they still would have been silent. They had only each other at that point, and in their minds and hearts they believed that if Jemima were to go to the gallows, Martha would be sent to a workhouse, or worse.

I couldn't bear it, Callie had said. *I can't lose you too.*

How frightened they had been, and how foolish.

In the end the court had dismissed the charges against Jemima for lack of evidence, and the two girls had cried themselves to sleep out of anger and relief.

"We should have told," Martha said. "If we had told—"

"She wouldn't have come back again," Callie finished for her.

Martha said, "If I could empty out the half of my blood that comes from Jemima, I would do it right here, on this spot."

"Cut it out, bad from good."

"Just so," Martha said.

"There's things I'd cut away too, if I could. Did you know my ma's grandma was just as mad as Ma? It comes down through the bloodline. Sometimes I feel it in my brain, like a seed waiting for rain so it can come up out of the ground and bear fruit."

Martha drew in a shocked breath. "Do you really believe that, that you could turn out like your ma?"

"Yes," Callie said. "I do believe it."

For a long moment Martha listened to the sound of the axe meeting wood, the steady *thunk thunk thunk* and then the pause before it started again. The wind was rising cool on her hot cheeks. At this moment, standing next to Callie, she was overcome with regret and sorrow. She had left Callie behind, in the end.

"I wish I had never gone to Manhattan," Martha said.

To which Callie said nothing, and rightly so. It did no good to worry about things long gone. Things she couldn't change. Martha cleared her throat.

"Where are you going to build?"

Callie had taken a few steps forward, and she looked back at Martha over her shoulder. "I'm not sure yet. Why do you ask?"

"Because," Martha said. "I can't stay with the Bonners forever. I shouldn't even be there now. If I left, there would be room for Lily and Simon. Nobody has said as much to me, but I know Elizabeth thinks about it."

Callie's arms were crossed against her waist, her head lowered as though she saw something crucially important in the mud in which she stood. "I can't build yet," she said. "It will be a good while before I can get enough money saved up. What little savings I had went with everything else."

"That's what I wanted to talk to you about," Martha said.

As children they had often read each other's thoughts, and Callie still had the knack. She said, "I couldn't take money from you."

"You wouldn't have to," Martha said. "You supply the land, and I build a house big enough for the both of us."

Callie went still, her whole body stiff and wary. Martha wanted to apologize for giving offense, but Callie cut her off with a movement of her hand.

"Tell me this," she said. "When you want to get married and start a family of your own, what then?"

"I could ask the same of you," Martha countered.

Callie looked up sharply. "I'm never going to get married."

She was so vehement that Martha was taken aback.

"Don't look at me like that. If you think it through you'll know that it's the only reasonable thing for me to do. Ma didn't lose her mind until I was born. I don't want children, not if it means turning into—that."

Martha hesitated. "You won't be lonely?"

Callie grimaced. "No," she said sharply. "I'm far too busy to be lonely."

When Martha had disappeared from sight, Callie walked slowly down to the farm where she had been born and worked for all of her life, past the cider house to the new nursery. A small plot of land with a new-woven fence of beech saplings eight feet high all around it, as close as was possible to deer-proof.

On the other side of the fence was the single Bleeding Heart Levi had found and brought back, along with five new grafts from that same tree. Whatever other chores he turned his hand to, Levi was always within sight of the nursery. Every day he wove new wood into the fence that surrounded it; he had closed the gate with a complicated twisting of wires that were not easily undone. Levi's vigilance was the difference between success and failure. They bore the burden together, and told no one about the Bleeding Heart.

23

Martha was on her way back to the Bonners for supper, lost in her thoughts, when a hand tugged at her mantle from behind and she let out a small cry in surprise.

"Birdie," she said. "You startled me."

The girl had been running, and she took a moment to catch her breath. She said, "I've been wanting to talk to you."

Birdie had the same dark and unruly hair as her brothers and sisters, and some of it had escaped the plaits to dance around her face. She was flushed with running and her eyes—an odd mixture of green and brown—seemed almost to glow. Birdie wouldn't be called pretty, but there was an energy about her that drew a person in. As tired as Martha was and as preoccupied by her conversation with Callie, she stopped to listen to what Birdie had to say.

"My da says it's best to be straightforward when you've got a favor to ask. So I'm asking." She hesitated anyway, as if waiting for permission.

"Go on," Martha said. She couldn't think what Birdie might want, unless it had to do with the trunk of books she had brought with her from Manhattan. The girl loved to read, and was always looking for new stories.

"I think you would make a very good teacher," Birdie said. "And I'd like you to think about teaching at the Paradise school."

This request was so unexpected that Martha stopped where she was. Birdie reached out and tugged Martha's cuff.

"You don't have to answer now," she said. "Just think about it."

Martha would have preferred to put such a nonsensical suggestion out of her mind completely, but it stayed with her until the adults were all gathered around the supper table. And of course Lily and Simon weren't here, but Hannah and Ben had come over so all in all there were the three married couples, each sitting side by side. Daniel and Ethan sat at one end of the long table, and Martha and Birdie at the other.

It was Birdie's first time at the adult supper table. She had been campaigning for a place for months, Elizabeth told Martha.

"She's not even six months older than her eldest nephew," Elizabeth said. "But she claims precedence because she's of his father's generation."

"And how did that go over with Nathan?" Martha asked. The Bonner grandchildren were the source of many dramas every day, many of them oddly compelling.

Nathan was a sensible boy, she was told, and he knew better than to take on Birdie on such a matter as this. He had gone off to bed with the rest of the grandchildren without a fuss and now Birdie sat next to Martha, looking around herself as if she had landed in Aladdin's cave.

Surely, Martha consoled herself, surely Birdie would not raise the topic of teaching at this supper table.

The LeBlanc girls came in with platters and bowls until the sideboard was filled, and then the long process of passing plates began. There was a lot of small talk around the table, Jennet and Hannah had their heads together about something, while Luke was telling Ben something complicated in a combination of French and English. A living French, nothing like the parlor language she had learned. She could discuss painting and music and the health of relatives, but the language she had been taught had been stripped down and, in the process, crippled. She found herself listening. Birdie was just as interested, her head swiveling back and forth between the two men, as if she needed to see the mouths making the words to understand their meaning.

Then came the small silence that always preceded the very first topic of discussion. The question that had no answer, and Martha herself was the cause. She could taste it on the air.

"You look tired, Ma," Daniel said from the other end of the table. "Not sleeping well?"

Elizabeth smiled at Daniel in the hope that he would let the subject go, but Nathaniel answered for her.

"Hardly sleeping at all."

"Lily really is doing well," Hannah said. "If it's her health that's keeping you awake at night."

"I am satisfied that Lily is well," Elizabeth said.

"Curiosity?" Jennet asked.

"She may outlive us all." Hannah said this in a perfectly serious tone. Elizabeth's stepdaughter could laugh and joke when the mood was on her, but never when she talked about her work.

She could trust Hannah; Elizabeth knew that. Lily was being well looked after, and she seemed in high good spirits when Elizabeth sat with her. And still she lay awake at night, wondering what more could be done. The truth was, she felt Lily's absence like a burn, but it was something she had to keep to herself. Short of building an extension onto the house, something she could not in good conscience ask Nathaniel to do, she saw no immediate solution. Not while so many families were still living rough after the flood.

"Today Lily drew Mrs. Thicke's likeness," Birdie was saying. "But she left the big mole with three hairs out. She meant it as a kindness, I think. But Mrs. Thicke asked about it straight away."

"And what did Lily say to that?" Nathaniel encouraged Birdie, which was probably not the best strategy, to Elizabeth's way of thinking.

"She said, 'Give it back and I'll add it in,' but Mrs. Thicke clutched it to her bosom and scuttled away to the kitchen like a beetle."

"Birdie," Elizabeth said. One word of warning that the girl understood immediately.

"I like Mrs. Thicke," she said, as if she must explain herself. "She's very friendly and she makes jellies every day because she thinks they're good for Lily. But mostly Simon eats them."

"With your help," Hannah prompted.

"Yes," Birdie said. "I like jellies too." Not a hint of embarrassment.

"An admirable lack of artifice," Ethan said.

"Don't encourage her," Daniel said, but he winked at his little sister.

Elizabeth had been so concerned about Lily that she hadn't been paying Birdie the attention she needed and deserved. For weeks now she had been running wild. Elizabeth was thinking back over that period of time, trying to remember where Birdie had been and what she had done, so deep in her thoughts that it took her some time to realize that Martha was answering questions about Callie Wilde and her plans for rebuilding.

"That won't happen anytime soon," Nathaniel said. "She's short on cash."

"You know Ethan will lend her what she needs," Hannah said.

"Or I will," Martha said.

All heads turned toward her and her color rose.

"Why should I not?"

Nathaniel cleared his throat. "You just took us by surprise. It's a fine thing if you can help Callie out. That's a hardworking young woman."

Daniel was watching Martha thoughtfully. He said, "Did she ask, or did you offer?"

Martha seemed confused by the question at first. "I'm not sure. Does it matter?"

"Of course not," Elizabeth said, irritated with Daniel.

"A day out in the open air agrees with you," Luke told Martha.

"It does," said Ben. "Your skin glows."

Martha put the back of her hand to her cheek in surprise and unease.

"Stop," Jennet said, but she was grinning. "You're embarrassing the puir thing. Never mind them, Martha."

Into the silence that followed came Birdie's voice again, this time directed to Daniel at the other end of the table.

"Is it true school will start again next week?"

"Barring unforeseen circumstances," he said. Elizabeth caught his gaze and he raised a brow. Birdie's voice took on a certain tone when she was about to announce a plan of some kind, and it was there now.

"It's aye high time," Jennet said, and then when everyone looked at her, she ducked her head in embarrassment. "I love the bairns one and all, but it's enough to wring a woman dry, having all of them about at once."

Luke put a hand on her shoulder and rubbed it. "I can take the boys with me, you know. You only have to say."

"Och, I think not." Jennet laughed and brushed his hand away. "The last time I let them go with you to buy furs they cursed like sailors for a month."

"I look forward to having your monsters at school," Daniel said. "But I will be glad to have the new teacher here in the fall so we can split the class in two."

Luke looked up from his soup. "When do you expect him?"

A whole chorus of voices answered him: "September."

"Not that we're anxious," Ben said dryly. "Except of course Birdie. Little sister is more than anxious."

Birdie sat up very straight, her mouth pressed into a hard line. Arguing with herself, wondering if she dare say what she was thinking or if she would be banished to the children's table if she did such a thing. In the next years she would learn to hide what she was thinking, but for now Elizabeth could still read her youngest child's face like words on a page.

Ethan's attention was on Birdie. He said, "I think you like school more than you want to admit. Martha was just like that, always pretending not to be interested."

Martha looked surprised at this observation, but Birdie gave her no chance to respond.

"I don't like school," Birdie said, each word pronounced clearly, like a finger tapping on the table.

"But it's only because the classroom is overcrowded," Elizabeth said. "When there are two classrooms and Daniel can give all his attention to the more advanced students, Birdie will stop chafing."

"I should hope so," Nathaniel said. "You're made of sterner stuff than that, Birdie. You can survive the rest of this school year. And—" he looked at her intently, "you can do it without complaint."

"But Da, that's not the only problem," Birdie said, her tone rising. "Everything moves so slowly—I know, the others need a chance to learn too, but it's so frustrating. Sometimes I feel like I have to scream."

"Surely not," Elizabeth said firmly.

"But I've got a solution," Birdie said. She looked around the table. "Will you listen?"

Everyone stilled at the idea of one of Birdie's plans, but Martha flushed so deeply that the color touched her hairline.

She said, "Birdie, please don't."

"I must," she said, and her next words came rapidly, as if she expected to be physically stopped, but was determined to get as much said as possible.

"I think Martha could take the other classroom for the two months left in this school session. Wait! Let me finish. Ethan saw to it that she got an excellent education and she's good with children; you've seen how the little people follow her around and pay attention when she talks."

She stopped to draw in a breath, and Martha stepped in.

"I want to say clearly that this was not my idea, and that when Birdie raised the subject to me, I told her no."

"You said you'd think about it!"

"I did not," Martha's color was still high, but her tone was calm. "You asked me if I ever thought of teaching and I said I didn't have the training. Ethan, please tell them I don't have the education I would need."

Ethan raised an eyebrow. "Truth be told, I don't think I can say such a thing. You went through the entire trivium. It's true you rebelled now and again, but you were an excellent student."

Martha's expression lifted. "Why then, Ethan, why don't you take the second classroom until the session ends? You do have teaching experience."

"Now, that's an idea," Nathaniel said, turning in Ethan's direction.

"One I already thought of," Daniel said. "Maybe you'll have more luck talking him into it than I did."

"Daniel asked and I did think about it," Ethan said. "But there's so much rebuilding to get done, I just don't see how I could manage."

Martha turned to Elizabeth, a pleading look on her face. "I have no experience, you know that. Would you please put an end to this discussion?"

Elizabeth knew that she should do just that, but instead something entirely different came out of her mouth. "You have more formal education now than I did when I began teaching, and just as much experience."

With the floodgates opened, everyone began to talk at once, questions and declarations bumping into each other so that nothing sensible came out anywhere. In the middle of all that, Daniel was quiet, his expression thoughtful. Not happy or unhappy, but alert and watchful.

Nathaniel raised a hand, and just that simply the talking stopped.

"One at a time," he said. "Boots, did you have anything else to say?"

"Well," Elizabeth began slowly. "I see some advantages to the idea, if all parties were agreed. That is, both Martha and Daniel have to come to the conclusion that the arrangement would be a beneficial one. For everyone."

"Daniel?"

He cleared his throat, and then cleared it again. His good hand moved to touch his left shoulder, a gesture Elizabeth recognized and which she was very surprised to see at that moment.

"But you must see," Martha said, her tone almost insistent. "This has put Daniel in an awkward position. So please let me say, Daniel, if you will speak sense on this matter I would be thankful. Let's let this subject go, can we please? It is very hard to refuse you, you've all been so good to me in these last weeks—" She paused to catch her breath

Elizabeth watched Daniel, the son she knew best and understood least. He had withdrawn from them all to nurse his wounds in isolation, and she had watched him go and despaired. For years she counted herself fortunate if she saw him at their table even once a week. But since they were come home from Manhattan that had changed. Now he came to the house every day, and usually stayed for supper. There was something in his expression she had not seen for a very long time.

Openness, for want of a better word. Open to the world around him. It had something to do with Lily coming home, but it also had to do with Martha Kirby. And she was beginning to believe that Martha was the primary source of the change in his behavior.

Now he was smiling, but it was a quiet smile and there was nothing of teasing in it.

He said, "It's premature of you to reject a proposal I haven't even made yet, don't you think, Martha?"

Elizabeth heard herself gasp in surprise, and she was not the only one. Martha looked ready to bolt, in embarrassment and anger. She stood suddenly, but Daniel kept talking.

He was saying, "I think there would be some advantages to having Martha's help, but it was rude of Birdie to raise this subject at the supper table. It was selfish of you to raise the subject at all, Birdie. I know you are frustrated with school, but that is no excuse for embarrassing Martha in front of her friends."

All the color left Birdie's face. She turned stiffly toward her father. "God-kissing carrion, Da. If she's embarrassed it's because Daniel's flirting with her in front of everybody."

"Enough," Nathaniel said in the tone all the children recognized. "And please, Birdie, if your ma can resist quoting Shakespeare at table, you could do as much."

Birdie dropped her head and studied her plate, but her expression was mutinous. She was mumbling to herself, her whole person twitching with frustration. They all listened to this for a moment. Even Martha stayed where she was, turned toward the door.

"Go on then," Nathaniel said. "Say whatever it is you've got stuck in your throat. And then go up to bed. We'll not see you at this supper table again, not until you've seen the error of your ways and made amends."

Birdie stood up, wounded and angry that her plan had come to nothing. She said, "I am not being selfish. I am not. It's for Lily; the whole idea is for Lily."

"How would my teaching help Lily?" Martha asked, her tone calmer.

Jennet said, "Ach, that's the plan." And to the table: "Birdie is thinking that Martha could move in to the apartment in the schoolhouse and then Lily and Simon could move up here and take her chamber."

"It's small, but I don't think they'll complain about cramped quarters," Birdie said, trying to sound dignified.

Luke said, "But that would mean that Martha would have to live alone in the apartment. There would be a lot of talk."

Daniel said, "Exactly. Which is why it's out of the question. Not the teaching—that's something I'd want to talk about—but Martha living alone in the schoolhouse, no."

Birdie opened her mouth as if she had something more to say, and then slumped back down into her chair when she saw her father raise a single eyebrow in her direction.

"Are ye saying that the people in the village would keep their children awa in protest?" Simon asked.

"It's likely," Daniel said. "An unmarried woman living in the schoolhouse just wouldn't sit with most anybody."

"He's right," Elizabeth said, and all eyes turned toward her. "Even if Martha wanted the apartment, it wouldn't be a good idea. She came home hoping to start fresh and avoid the gossip that made her life so difficult in Manhattan. But we've been talking about this as if Martha had no voice and could not speak for herself. Martha, what do you think?"

The girl's complexion was splotched with color and her eyes flashed in the candlelight; she was holding back tears.

"It would cause talk," she said quietly. "That's true."

Birdie was bouncing in place in her earnest need to be heard.

"Birdie, go on."

"Ma," she said, resolutely refusing to look at Daniel. "You are always telling us that we have to make decisions based on our own understanding of right and wrong. It's the way we're supposed to live our lives. It's our way."

"Birdie," Martha said. She drew in a deep breath and let it go. "Birdie, you forget, I am not one of you and I won't be judged as if I were. I also understand now that I am the one who has been selfish. Your plan was meant to bring Lily back home, and that's as it should be. She should be here. Tomorrow I'll go see about taking a room at the Red Dog. I should have done that on the first day."

Birdie reached out to take her wrist before she could walk away.

"I never meant to drive you away! That wasn't the idea at all!"

"Now ain't this a mess," Ben said. He pitched his voice just so, and they all turned to him. "Everybody's so wound up you can't see what's sitting right in front of you. Martha, stay a minute and hear me out, and if you'll listen, I'll see if I can untangle things. Elizabeth? Nathaniel?"

Nathaniel made a sweeping gesture with his hand, an invitation to go ahead.

Ben Savard didn't often speak up, but when he did people paid attention. His eyes were a strange and compelling blue-green that even the most conservative of matrons, the ones who disliked Africans and Indians on principle and were horrified by the very idea that nature would allow a human being of mixed race to survive birth—even they could not look away when Ben Savard smiled. Elizabeth had seen it happen more than once in the village, and it happened again around the table as postures relaxed.

"Fifty years ago they would have called him a witch," Hannah had once said about her husband. "He only has to look at you hard and say a word to get his way."

Ben said, "Now bear with me while I work through this and make sure I've got it all right. We know Lily needs watching over, and everybody would be happier if Elizabeth could do that right here, at home. That's not to say Birdie ain't done a good job, because she has."

"Yes," Elizabeth said. "She has done an excellent job."

"But Birdie belongs in school," Ben said. "She wants to be in school too, but not until she can be in the upper class and away from the little ones. What she's looking for is a way to make that happen before she has to go back to school, and so she was hoping her ma and da would keep her out of the classroom to help look after Lily. Ain't that so, little sister?"

Birdie crossed her arms and gave a curt nod.

"That's answer enough for me," Ben said and to his credit he didn't even smile.

"So then there's the fact that the new teacher won't be here till the fall. There's two months left in the school year and things are about to get more crowded still.

"Now have a look at Miss Martha Kirby standing there. She's got an education—Ethan ain't one to praise without cause—and nothing to do all day long except darn socks and settle arguments between little people. Seems to me that if Martha were to take over the school for the rest of the session, Luke could take the older ones into the second classroom and they can move along at their own pace. Birdie would get that much of what she wants, anyway.

"Now here's the last piece, something nobody has brought up. Think it through. Once Lily and Simon move up here, ain't their house empty? Ethan built it and it still belongs to him. I doubt he'd have any objection to Martha living there until she can build a place of her own. You can work out the question of rent between you. Mrs. Thicke would stay on to keep house and quiet the gossip. So there you are. If there's some problem I'm overlooking, I think that would solve most of what's got everybody tied in knots."

"But Martha said she won't—" Birdie began, and Elizabeth cut her off.

"We'll not get into that discussion again. Ben has given us a great deal to think about, and we need to do that before we talk about this any further. The truth is that we could spend the whole night arguing about the teaching situation, but it's not our decision. Those are questions for Martha and Daniel to decide."

Nathaniel rubbed his jawline with the flat of his hand. "Daniel? You got nothing to say to Ben's idea?"

Daniel cleared his throat. "In all of this I think the most important thing is that Lily move back home so Ma can look after her and get some sleep at night. If Martha is agreeable to taking over Ethan's house." His tone was gentle and friendly and still it was insincere; he understood, as they all did, that if nothing else came out of this conversation, Martha would be leaving the household. She would not stay, and the thought made Elizabeth sick at heart. It was not the way she had wanted to resolve the problem.

"You don't have to teach," Daniel said, looking directly at Martha. "Unless you want to. I'd be glad of the help."

In her surprise, Elizabeth did not know where to look. She wanted to see how Martha was reacting, but more important was her son.

Daniel had his father's ability to hide what he was feeling, the deepest emotions—anger, fear, hate, love—behind a personal dignity. He was doing that now, but for once she could see what it cost him, the tension in his back and jaw. And if Martha should reject his—what was it exactly he had offered her?

Nathaniel said, "Well, there you are then, Martha. Daniel's made you a proposal, and you'll have to make some decisions about what you want to do. Now will you sit down and finish your supper? You could use some meat on your bones, girl."

There was a tone Nathaniel used when he wanted to put an end to a discussion, and it was in his voice now. All around the table his children picked up spoons and applied themselves to soup that had gone cold.

Slowly, awkwardly, interrupted conversations came back to life. Jennet and Hannah were talking about the children, and the fact that Adam was in need of new clothes as he had already outgrown those handed down to him by his brother a few months before. Ben was talking to Luke about the quality of the winter's furs and the market in Manhattan, whether the call for beaver pelts had let up any and if so, what other fur would bring the best price. Ethan asked Nathaniel about the hardware for the bridge, and whether they should send to Johnstown.

But there were islands of silence around the table. Birdie focused on her food, sniffing once in a while until Elizabeth handed her a fresh handkerchief. Martha ate, lost in her thoughts, and at the other end of the table, Daniel did the same.

Ethan said, "Aunt Bonner, you are very quiet."

"I was just thinking," Elizabeth said. "I hope you and Martha will come down to the village with me when we are done here. I'd like to present Ben's plan to Lily and Simon."

Birdie looked up, all eagerness restored to her face. "But how will Lily get here?" she asked. "Simon will break his back carrying her up again."

"Hardly," Hannah said. "But we'll find a way."

Nathaniel leaned into Elizabeth so their shoulders touched, and put one hand on her knee. A companionable gesture, a reminder that he was beside her, as he always was and would always be.

He said, "I guess there are enough of us to carry her on our shoulders, like a queen on a throne."

An image flashed through Elizabeth's mind's eye: six men carrying a box on their shoulders. She shuddered so that Nathaniel looked at her, concerned.

"Oooh." Birdie was saying. "Like one of the Roman ladies who never put a foot on the ground."

"Yes," Elizabeth said, her voice hoarse. "Exactly like that."

24

$\mathcal{I}$n a day's time, when it had all been accomplished and Lily was safe at home, Elizabeth found herself alone in the kitchen with Jennet. Jennet looked around herself to make sure she wouldn't be overheard, and asked a question Elizabeth had been waiting for.

"I havenae seen Daniel, not since all this moving about was decided at the supper table. Have you?"

Elizabeth had not. Daniel made himself scarce through all the tumult of moving Lily up and Martha down to the village. She told herself that he stayed away because if he could not be of help—and he could not carry anything over a certain size—he would rather not watch others do that work. But there was something else, something wrong.

"Do ye think his shoulder is paining him?"

Elizabeth touched her skirt and heard the comforting crackle of paper. The letter was addressed to Hannah, but it fell to Elizabeth to share what it said with Daniel.

"I don't know," she said. "Though I doubt it. If the pain were bad enough to send him to ground, he wouldn't be around at all, and Daniel has been spending most of the day at the schoolhouse."

Jennet pushed out her lower lip as she thought. "I thought he would come to see Lily as soon as she put foot over the threshold—oh aye, but ye ken what I mean. It's been a full day and no sign of him. Are they at odds again?"

The little bit that Elizabeth knew she would not volunteer, nor did she want to talk about her suspicions. Because she did have them, and they had to do with Martha Kirby.

"Do ye ken if he's been by to see Martha?"

That their minds had moved along the same series of questions did not surprise Elizabeth, but neither did it move her to talk about what she could not know for sure.

More to herself than to Jennet she said, "The only sensible thing to do is to ask Lily directly. If—when her mood settles."

"Aye," Jennet said. "I can do it, if ye like."

There would be some advantages to having Jennet take on this conversation with Lily in her current fragile mood. Especially if Lily was fretting over the idea of Martha Kirby and her cousin Ethan.

There was nothing between Ethan and Martha, but there might be something—given time and opportunity—between Martha and Daniel.

Of all the Bonners, Lily was the one who was most vehement about Jemima. There were reasons for Lily's animosity, certainly. But Daniel had the same history with Jemima, and he was far more detached when the subject came up. Certainly he did not look at Martha and see Jemima, while it seemed that Lily could not or would not distinguish between daughter and mother.

In the end, none of it was Lily's business, just as Daniel had had no business meddling when she had first shown an interest in Simon Ballentyne. Such personal matters should remain personal, and Elizabeth must trust her adult children to make reasonable choices. She would not follow her father's example. Judge Middleton had wanted Elizabeth to marry Richard Todd; her refusal and his interference had set a series of events in motion that ended badly. Nathaniel had lost his grandfather Chingachgook and Jemima her father.

To Elizabeth it seemed that any hope for Jemima had gone to the grave with Moses Southern. Since that day she had blamed the Bonners, and her hate for them had grown to encompass everything that stood between her and the things she believed were owed her.

But once there had been hope for her. As a young girl in Elizabeth's classroom she had been surly and uncooperative in that first year, but toward the spring she had begun to take pleasure in her small victories. She was very good with numbers and she had a beautiful singing voice. Unfortunately she also had a sly way that made her unpopular with her classmates.

Just lately Elizabeth had been thinking a great deal about that first winter and spring in Paradise, how very different it had been from her imaginings. Elizabeth found that she was protective of her younger self, that woman on the verge of thirty who came to teach in a wilderness school with such earnest and naïve goodwill. At sixty she could see many things that had been unclear still at forty or even fifty.

Often these days she had the sense of herself nearby, watching. In those moments she had the strong urge to speak to her younger counterpart in encouraging words. She would use the same tone she did when Lily and Hannah needed comforting.

The future is mysterious and frightening to you now, but in the end all will be well. There will be great happiness and great sorrow, you will have a family, you will find yourself capable of things you cannot now imagine. But you will persevere, and one day you will look around yourself and know that your life is good and that you are, in spite of all your early doubts, happy.

"Elizabeth?"

Jennet touched her wrist, and Elizabeth startled up out of her thoughts.

"Pardon me," she said with a small laugh. "Woolgathering."

"We were talking about Lily. Whether I should approach her and try to find out what's got her upset."

Elizabeth nodded. "I think she would respond more openly to you. You are sensible and you understand her condition. I remember the affinity I felt for other bearing women when I was increasing."

"Women going off to battle together," Jennet said with a grim smile. "Ye neednae fash yersel, I'm not easily put off and should she throw paint pots at my head, as was once her habit."

Elizabeth was content to leave it at that, but she reminded herself that Lily was not sick. She was with child, a condition that was always

dangerous but natural nonetheless. She herself had had a difficult deliv-
ery with Birdie, and with less experienced midwives she might well have
died. Now Many-Doves was gone, but Curiosity would be there, and
Hannah, and Friend Molly Noble, whose skill and experience Curiosity
and Hannah respected. And Simon. She would have Simon, who had
loved her from the beginning though she fought her own emotions and
strove to deny the attraction. Sometimes with words, and sometimes
with paint pots.

Jennet said, "I was wondering—"

"What is it?"

"I was wondering about Martha Kirby. She's a different lass already
from the one who left Manhattan with us, is she no?"

"Yes," Elizabeth said. "She is come back to herself."

"Do ye think she'll start teaching come Monday?"

"I don't know," Elizabeth said. The question confused and even irritated her. She must not interfere in her children's lives, but neither could
she look away, no matter how much trouble they made for themselves.

"Ye think it's a good idea?"

Elizabeth gave her a tired smile. "It's too early to know," she said. "But
I think it might work out quite well."

"Aye, weel," Jennet said. "I admit I'm more than a wee bit curious.
Were Daniel to walk in this minute I'd come out and ask him."

Elizabeth said, "Maybe I will be able to put the question to him today.
I have to speak to him on a different matter, and the subject could come
up."

"He's aye fond of her," Jennet said.

"Yes," Elizabeth said. "He is fond. And more than fond."

Jennet was frowning as she wrung her cloth in the water basin.

Elizabeth said, "Come out and say it. Are you thinking of Martha's
connections?"

"I am," Jennet said. "And so must you. Does the idea of sharing
grandchildren with Jemima—what is her name now? Wilde, is that
right?"

"As far as we know, yes. I can't remember at this moment how she
signed her letter to Martha."

"Would she no be within her rights to demand to see her grandchildren?"

Elizabeth thought about that for a minute. Then she said, "I have nine grandchildren, soon to be ten—" she inclined her head to Jennet's middle. "And not one of them is related to me by blood. But they are my grandchildren. I could feel no different about them if I had given birth to Luke and Hannah. Do you feel differently about Adam than you do about your other three?"

Jennet and Luke had taken Adam in as a newborn just before they started home from New Orleans. Nathan had been no more than six or seven months old and so the boys had no understanding of themselves as anything but brothers. One towheaded and the other dark, they had slept forehead to forehead for years. Lily had done many studies of them as infants, in just that pose.

For some reason Elizabeth had never been able to work out for herself, even those people who refused to recognize blacks as human beings would smile and coo at an infant, no matter what color. And so it had been with Adam, who had been a beautiful child. But that was changing. He had shot up in the last year; he was tall for his age, well built, strong. In his birth state of Louisiana he would be someone's possession, already working in the fields. He'd know nothing of books, and most likely even less of kindness. It hurt even to imagine it.

"Aye, when you put it that way—" Jennet turned her head as if she were trying to hear a voice far away. "Were Adam's faither to rise from his grave tae claim him, I wad put a knife in his heart rather than let him touch the boy."

Elizabeth said, "Jennet, someday he will fall in love and want to marry. What if the girl's family forbade it because they knew Adam's father for the scoundrel he was?"

"But they couldn't know," Jennet said, flushing with irritation. "So far as the world kens, Adam is Luke's son."

Elizabeth held her gaze, and Jennet closed her eyes briefly. Then she said, "Aye, aye. I take your meaning. It's the color of his skin that will cause him heartache. Martha's situation has naught to do with color, but to be turned away for her mother's sake—aye. But Elizabeth, Adam's father is deid and can do the boy no direct harm. Jemima is alive, and stirring in whatever hidey-hole she found for herself."

It was an image that stayed with Elizabeth for the rest of the day.

———

She was determined to find Daniel and have a discussion with him before the morning passed, and so Elizabeth hurried through the long list of decisions and directions she dealt with every day. She talked to John Henry, the husband of Curiosity's granddaughter Solange, who was come to start double-digging the vegetable garden. She wrote a little in her current letter to her cousins in Manhattan to ask for some French bean seeds she had been wanting to try, and a new pair of shoes for Birdie. She spoke to the LeBlanc girls about the meals for the next days; how salty the ham had been and if the remainder should be put to soak, how long the store of potatoes and carrots might last, or if more would have to be purchased, if there were enough eggs to make custard for everyone, or if they would make do with stewed dried apples and leave the rich eggs and cream to Lily and Jennet.

Having Lily and Simon at home meant more to do in the household, which put the maids in a justifiably sour mood. Elizabeth solved the problem by asking if one of the other LeBlanc sisters might like to come to work.

That brought her the first faint glimmer of a smile. Matilda would start tomorrow, at the same wages as her sisters.

The Bonners were one of the few families in Paradise who paid with coin rather than bushels of cabbage or ells of cloth, and cash was always welcome. They had four LeBlancs working for them—Joan and Anje in the house, and Sam and Carl in the stable and garden. It was why the girls stayed on, Elizabeth knew very well. They had the best places in the village and would keep them, no matter how offended their sensibilities might be.

When Elizabeth could put it off no longer, she got dressed to go down into the village. Adam and Nathan had been waiting for this, as it was their turn to go with her. She started off with the boys to either side of her, hindered by the mud and distracted by their antics. There was a long story about a honeycomb, the Savard cousins, Curiosity's kitchen cat, and a wager. The story bounced back and forth between them, and Elizabeth grabbed what she could as it sped by.

"I believe you've just confessed to larceny and gambling. And beyond that, you've given away your very advanced and frightening grasp of the principles of hucksterism."

The boys frowned at each other. Elizabeth could almost hear their thoughts: Grandmother Bonner had started to talk like a book, and so early in their outing too.

Adam said, "If you mean we cheated the girls, I guess we did." Adam had a talent for the truth. Sometimes when she was talking to him, she remembered the stories she had heard about the father who had abandoned him before he was born, how strange the ways of nature when a seed from such a poor tree thrived and grew into something straight and strong.

"It wasn't much of a wager," Nathan said. Even at the end of a long winter his hair was almost white-blond. In their physical selves the two boys could hardly be less alike, but in mind and deed they were cut from the same cloth exactly.

Adam did his best to change the direction of the conversation by pointing out a towhee perched on a pine branch, raccoon tracks, the remains of a squirrel that had run into a dog and never run away again. He talked until Nathan worked up his courage to ask a question.

"Our folks won't let us do anything or go anywhere since the flood. We haven't even been to Lake in the Clouds yet. Why is that? The flood was so long ago."

"To your way of thinking it was a long time ago," Elizabeth said. "But you must think of those who still do not have a roof over their head. It won't be much longer before school starts again."

Nathan's smooth face scrunched into thoughtfulness, and it made him look very much his mother's child.

"What worries you so?" she asked him. And then, after a silence: "You needn't tell me if it's a secret. As long as no one is in danger, you needn't tell me."

"Is it a danger to make Aunt Birdie mad at you?" Adam asked, and Nathan flashed him a warning look.

"If it is, something is very wrong," Elizabeth said.

The boys exchanged another glance, and then Adam spoke up. "Why doesn't Birdie want to be in the same classroom with us? She's only five months sixteen days older than Nathan, so why shouldn't she be in the same classroom?"

For the rest of the walk into the village they discussed the family generations, where Birdie stood in relationship to her own brothers and sisters, and what it was like to be stuck between them and her nieces and nephews. By the time they had come to the Red Dog, the boys seemed much less agitated and more thoughtful. Elizabeth sent them off to say hello in the smithy and then to go watch the men building the new bridge, with firm directions on where they may go and where they may not.

The boys were off before the last word was spoken and Elizabeth turned toward the schoolhouse, trying to organize her thoughts and not getting very far. Both subjects she wanted to discuss with her son were difficult, and both were important. As she walked up the steps to the schoolhouse door, she was surprised and a little ashamed to realize she was holding her breath.

But Daniel wasn't in the school. She walked from classroom to class-room to the apartment in the back that he had so vehemently denied Martha—the rooms swept and scrubbed now, and free of all traces of mud.

On the lane she asked Friend Emma Michaels, but Emma hadn't seen Daniel and neither had any of the others Elizabeth stopped. In the shell of the new trading post the noise of hammering was so loud that she had trouble getting anyone's attention. That gave her a moment to study the improvements.

There had been a large hearth and a Franklin oven, but those things were gone now. The men who had gathered here to exchange news and opinions about everything from crops to presidents had already begun to migrate to the Red Dog, but now they would have no choice. So many memories tied up with the old trading post, most of them good, some of them so funny that she smiled even now when they came to mind. It oc-curred to her for the first time that the only gaol Paradise had—Anna's pantry, as they still called it—had been lost with the rest of the trading post. She wondered if they'd build another one, and where. It was a ques-tion she wouldn't put to Tobias Mayfair, who was very difficult to draw into conversation even on topics as uncontroversial as the weather.

It was odd that the Mayfairs should be living here in Paradise for so long but still did not understand—or care to understand—the most basic of facts about their neighbors. They would build a larger and better lit and cleaner trading post, but their business would decline because they made no place for men to sit and talk. But maybe that was what Mayfair wanted; he might be hoping to bring in women, with pretty fabrics and ready-made clothes. The younger women showed little interest in spin-ning and weaving, after all, but just as much interest in fashion as their mothers and grandmothers before them.

The new sign, freshly painted, was propped against the wall to dry. In strong black letters it declared the place to be Mayfair's Mercantile. Anna could have told him, if she were still alive, how fruitless it was to try to rename things in Paradise. She herself had tried to call the trading post an emporium, but had to give it up as a bad job when Magistrate Bookman asked her what she meant, if she was declaring all Paradise an empire or just her piece of it.

When Elizabeth finally had the attention of one of the Mayfair sons—which one she could not say, there were so many of them—and he had gone around to ask, she learned that Daniel had been seen in the early morning, but not since.

Elizabeth stood in the soft spring sunlight and considered. Daniel might be helping Callie or working with Ethan; he might have gone to call on one of his student's families, or he could have gone home to the small house he had had built for himself in the strawberry fields, an hour's walk up Hidden Wolf. A walk she would not have hesitated to undertake even a few years ago. A walk she would have enjoyed, because it was her favorite time of year in the endless forests, when small things woke up and reached out. If you stood very silent for long enough, you could hear it happening, like the whispering a butterfly made working its way out of a cocoon.

She read herself a short sermon: The smells of spring were in the air, and the light had a buttery color that was particular to this time of year. The walk would do her good, even if Daniel was not at home. Why, she could continue on to Lake in the Clouds and visit with Susanna, who was always glad of company, most especially company of women who had been married longer than she herself. It had been a long time since her last visit, when the snow was still deep and the cold unyielding.

Or she could go home again, and see how Lily was faring. If she had found a way to be comfortable in mind and body both.

The letter she carried crackled as if encouraging her to hurry along. *Don't be a coward.*

She said this to herself aloud, and then she turned toward the lake, where most of the men—including some of her own—were trying to get the new bridge finished. People had had enough of waiting to be ferried across the river. Even fifteen minutes in the company of Willy LeBlanc was daunting, for the boy was as garrulous and distracted in conversation as his father. To Becca's credit, he was a much harder worker. As were all the LeBlanc children.

"Boots, if you were any deeper in your thoughts you'd drown."

Nathaniel grabbed her shoulders before she walked directly into him, and then he kissed her and let her go.

"You look less than happy to see me," she said. "I suppose because I was lost in my thoughts."

For years he had been trying to impress upon her the importance of paying attention to her surroundings, especially in spots such as this one, where trees cut off the view of both the lake and the village center. When she was first in Paradise she had heard many stories of panthers— or painters, as the woodsmen called them—attacking the unwary. Then she had seen it for herself, and thus should be all the more cautious, but still over the years the fear had faded.

She could try to make this argument to her husband, but it would get her nowhere. Primarily because he was right.

"I'm turning into a forgetful old lady," she said. "But I will try harder. Where are you going?" She cast a pointed look at the empty bucket he carried.

"Nails," he said. "If Joshua has got the new batch done. And what about you, Boots? Why are you wandering in the woods? Never mind, let me guess. You're looking for Daniel."

He was grinning at her. A long strand of steel gray hair was caught up in the simple silver hoop he wore in his ear, and she reached up to smooth it. Nathaniel took the opportunity to grasp her hand and raise her wrist to his mouth.

"Ow!" Elizabeth pulled away, laughing. "You nip like a bull calf. And don't you dare start, I won't have one of your conversations here in the open."

That made him laugh. "You are looking for Daniel, ain't that so?" With the heel of his hand he pressed the spot between her breasts and was rewarded with the crackle of paper before she could slap his hand away.

"I knew you were up to something when Hannah brought that letter and the two of you shut yourself up with Curiosity."

"And how do you know it has to do with Daniel? It could be Lily or anyone else."

"Because I know that look," Nathaniel said. He let a long breath go and pulled her to him with one arm. "And because there's a lot of talk about a box that came all the way from India, addressed to our Hannah."

It would do no good to deny any of it, and so Elizabeth looked around herself and then lowered her voice. "I promised Hannah I would talk to Daniel before I told you or anyone else."

His brow folded down, and then he inclined his head. "Fine then, Boots. But don't make me wait too long."

"The sooner I find the boy, the sooner you'll hear for yourself."

Nathaniel turned to look over his shoulder into the woods. "You don't hear him?"

"I hear hammering and geese but I don't hear—" She stopped and concentrated. And there it was: the sharp, abrupt sound of a knife penetrating wood.

Nathaniel nodded. "He's been at it an hour at least. Give him a reason to stop, he won't fight too hard."

25

When he was agitated and ill at ease, Daniel worked with his knives.

At just nineteen he had taken his rifle to war to make a name for himself, as his father and grandfather had done before him. He came home with an arm that could not support the weight of a book, much less a long gun. It took a year for him to accept that he wouldn't ever be able to handle a rifle again, and another year before he turned all his effort and attention to throwing.

He started with the tomahawk that belonged to his great-grandfather Chingachgook, practicing every day until his good arm shook and he couldn't make a fist anymore.

One day he came upon a doe and without giving it much thought he threw and killed her with one clean blow to the neck. He had to hold the doe's head down with one boot to wrench the blade from the spine where it had lodged.

Once he had mastered the tomahawk Daniel began working with smaller blades. Now he had a half dozen different weapons of all sizes and types, some of them of his own design, forged in the smithy. He carried five or six blades with him at all times, as he would have carried his rifle.

Daniel was proud of the fact that he hunted for his own table, cleaned and cooked what he brought down. Rabbit and squirrel, grouse and turkey, ducks, and once a wild swine. He left the larger game for the most part, because he couldn't get it home on his own and disliked the waste of field dressing. The skins he brought to Annie for curing, and paid her for her help.

Now a knife came as easily to hand as a fork or spoon. Daniel tested the weight of the heavier hatchet before he let it go. It made the *whoop-whoop-whoop* sound of an eagle flying overhead, and then it severed a witch hazel branch as thick as his good wrist.

He was sweat-soaked but not so weary that he didn't hear the sound of his mother coming through the woods, a full five minutes before she stepped into the clearing.

The sight of Ma out here in the open always surprised him, though he knew it should not. Thirty years ago she had gone into the bush a new bride and come out again changed. Able to care for herself in the endless forests, if need be. The wife of a backwoodsman.

"You could cut a few more branches," she said to him. "And put them in your classroom. They smell so sweet."

Daniel had to laugh at this suggestion. All her years in Paradise among trappers, and she had never resigned herself to the stink of sour clothes stiff with grime. She never gave up on trying to improve what she called the miasma of the classroom, and retiring from teaching hadn't damp-ened her ongoing dedication to a problem that Daniel could live with.

He said, "Ma, I'll cut some for you if you like. To put by your window for when you're working."

"That would be lovely."

A woodpecker rattled overhead. Daniel went about caring for his weapons; his mother would raise whatever topic sent her looking for him soon enough. But she surprised him, reaching out to take his grand-father's tomahawk from him to run her fingers over the carving.

"Hawkeye told so many stories," she said. "And most of them had to do with war. This is the hatchet that saved your grandmother Cora's life on more than one occasion. But that was three wars ago."

She seemed to be talking more to herself than to him as she traced the carving.

"You are very pensive today," he said. In his mother's company his vo-cabulary began to stretch and grow and words he never used anytime else—except in spelling lessons—would come out of hiding.

"Am I?"

"You've got all of us together in one place; what is there to worry about now?"

"Lily. Lily worries me. Her health and her state of mind both."

Daniel wished now he could take back the question. His mother did enough worrying without his encouragement.

"Ma," he said. "Did you come to talk about Lily?"

She cast a frowning glance and then turned away to look into the trees, her arms folded over the ends of her shawl and her head canted forward, her gaze focused on the ground beneath her feet. She was patient, and demanded the same of her children. The words would come when they presented themselves in the proper order, and not be-fore.

"There is a letter," she said. "It came with the post yesterday, for Han-nah. She asked me to talk to you about it."

Elizabeth was braced for what must come next, and so she watched the animation leave his face and his jaw settle hard. Inscrutable. The very image of his father when he sensed a battle ahead.

He said the one word.

"No."

"Daniel," Elizabeth said quietly. "I want you to listen until I'm fin-ished, without interrupting me. Will you please do that for me?"

Oh, how he wanted to deny her. She could see it in the way his gaze jerked away into the woods. But he was a good man and he had been trained well by his father. It took a concentrated effort but he calmed himself.

"Go on."

She sat down on a fallen log and took the letter out of her bodice. Fine paper, closely written. Not a watermark or crease beyond the folds. It had come in a chest with medical supplies and books, and a manu-script written in the same clean, tight hand.

"Do you remember Hakim Ibrahim?"

"Only from stories," Daniel said. He would not volunteer anything, and in some ways that made her task easier.

"Hakim Ibrahim and Hannah have been corresponding for many

years, before she went west with Strikes-the-Sky, and again since she came back from New Orleans after the war."

Hannah corresponded with so many doctors and healers of every stripe. Sometimes she recited bits of their letters when they had a meal together, but for the most part the tone and subject were of interest to Birdie and Curiosity and no one else.

"Apparently she asked his advice about your nerve damage," she went on. "Some years ago."

The muscles in Daniel's jaw jumped, but he stood his ground.

"Hakim Ibrahim is recently returned to his home in India after five years in China."

She paused then, searching for the right words, and with that he let out a sigh.

"What is it? Another herb? Another tea? I've had enough, Ma. A few green things steeped in water can't fix what's wrong with me. I'll never have the full use of the arm again. If I can live with that, why can't you?"

It was an old argument, and one they both hated.

"Let me ask," she said, her voice firm. "Have we brought anything to you recently? In the last two years, even. And let me remind you, we have not. If Hannah and I are willing to risk your anger and another week's long disappearance, does it not seem reasonable to you that this time what we have to propose must be something very out of the ordinary?"

She was breathing rapidly and made an effort to calm herself. When she looked up again, some of the tension had left his face. His expression was still aggrieved, but there was a good amount of reluctant acquiescence there as well.

"So," he said. "Go on and tell me about this miracle cure that comes all the way from China by way of India. I'll listen, but that's all."

"Very well. Hakim Ibrahim spent his time in China studying a medical procedure that involves targeting specific nerves. The evidence indicates that this treatment will have a positive effect in the majority of patients."

"But not all," Daniel said.

"Not all," Elizabeth echoed. "But there is some reason to believe it might help your symptoms. There is no tea or herb or ointment, no medication in the traditional sense."

His mouth contorted. He was interested in spite of himself.

"A scalpel, then," he said.

"No," Elizabeth said quickly. "No surgery."

His patience was at an end. "What then, Ma? Will you spit it out?"

"Needles," Elizabeth said. "Long, very thin needles. Hakim Ibrahim has sent Hannah a full set of these needles in a beautiful ebony wood box, along with a hundred-page treatise on their application and use. Dozens of illustrations. Hannah was up until very late studying them, and today she has a headache. She should know better than to read by candlelight—"

She stopped herself, because the corner of Daniel's mouth was twitching.

He said, "And Hannah would like to try this procedure. She'd like to turn me into a pincushion to see if she can put things right."

"Hannah would like to sit down with you and Curiosity, if you agree, to talk it through. And then, if everyone is agreed—"

"What?"

"She will turn you into a pincushion."

He turned his head away sharply. "I need to think about this."

"Of course," Elizabeth said. She got up and brushed her skirts. "Would you like to read the letter? Hannah thought it might answer some of your questions."

"I'll read it," Daniel said. "But that's as far as I'm willing to go."

It was hard to suppress her own relief, but Elizabeth closed her mouth hard on the things she might have said, promises that would be worse than any knife cut and take longer to heal. She held out the letter, and after a moment, Daniel took it.

Elizabeth knew that there would be no more discussion until Daniel had had time to think through this new information. Which meant that the other subjects she had wanted to raise would have to wait. But he surprised her.

"Did you want to ask about Martha?"

"Actually I was thinking more of Lily," she said and for that she earned a narrowed look, one that said he didn't believe her, not for a moment.

"She was expecting a visit from you yesterday," Elizabeth said.

"Martha—" he stopped himself. "Lily was expecting me?"

Elizabeth couldn't hide her surprise. Daniel himself was surprised; he looked away, rubbing his beard stubble with the flat of his good hand.

"Lily would like to see you, but I think Martha would also be glad of a visit. Have you made a decision, then, the two of you? About the second classroom?"

"Haven't had the chance to talk to her about it."

When he was a young boy she could usually read his state of mind from his posture. Over the years he had learned to mask his thoughts more thoroughly, but just now she saw him as a fourteen-year-old, unhappy with the direction a conversation was taking.

Should she withdraw the question, or push, ever so carefully? She still hadn't reached a decision when Gabriel came into the clearing. Daniel wasn't surprised to see him, which was more evidence that Elizabeth's woodcraft had declined past the point of return; she hadn't heard him approaching. She pushed that thought away and focused on her sons, the two surviving sons of her body. They were tall and strong and handsome. Pleasure and pride rose in her so that for that moment all the other things to worry about fell away.

"You make more noise than an army in the bush," Daniel said, but he was smiling. "Has marriage got you so turned around?"

Gabriel's color was high, his eyes bright. He looked happy, and Elizabeth was sorry that she had ever stood in the way of his marriage. He understood his own needs, even when she did not. A recurring theme for the day, she pointed out to herself.

Daniel was saying, "I had the idea you never came off the mountain unless it was to hunt."

"Ma," Gabriel said. "Would you tell my big brother he's being rude? He could at least pretend to be glad to see me." And he winked at her.

"Oh, no," Elizabeth said. "None of your games. If there's a message we'll hear it now, and not be made to jump through hoops first."

Gabriel put a fist to his chest with mock surprise. "You cut me to the quick, Ma. And here I am to say tonight's the ice-out party."

Elizabeth's first thought was for Lily, who would miss this annual party to celebrate the spring. There was no viable way to transport her all the way up Hidden Wolf. Unless she were to ride, which Hannah and Curiosity had strictly forbidden, and a wagon on the bumpy path was out of the question.

"Short notice," Daniel said. "But I'll be there."

"You better be, or we'll track you down and force-march you all the way up."

As a boy Gabriel had found ways to distract Daniel when everyone else had given it up as a bad job, and it seemed he didn't intend to let that advantage go.

He was saying, "Blue-Jay wants you to know you had best bring along a woman of your own. He plans to be the only one Susanna pays any attention to."

The corner of Daniel's mouth jerked. He said, "Blue-Jay mistakes me entirely. It's your wife I intend to monopolize tonight."

"You can try," Gabriel said. "But I think you'd have better luck with Martha Kirby."

---

26

*L*ily roused from a light sleep to find Simon sitting on the edge of the bed, grinning down at her. She turned her head to scowl into the pillow, and turned back again when he leaned down and kissed her shoulder.

"I brought you a tray."

She yawned. "How am I ever supposed to work up an appetite, spending three quarters of the day asleep? Curiosity won't be satisfied until I'm as fat as a Christmas goose."

But Simon knew her too well to be drawn into a discussion like this, when she was half asleep and cranky.

"What a horrid crabbit old witch I am these days. I apologize."

"There's naught to apologize for. Come, take some tea."

To Lily's disgust, there were great fat tears running down her cheeks. She buried her face back in the pillow and wailed.

When it was over she was glad of Simon's warm presence and his calm.

He said, "Scootch."

"You mean to come back to bed? But you're dressed."

"And you are not. Scootch."

"Your shoes."

"I promise not to kick, no matter how you provoke me. And if you'll recall, it's no the first time we've been in this very bed with clothes on. Some clothes, at least."

Against her will Lily laughed, and then she gave in and moved. The bed was narrow and Simon was very big. It had always been a comfort, the long length of him like a wall between the world and her small spot in it.

"I remember that," she said to the ceiling.

"I should hope so," Simon said. He put his laced hands behind his head and stretched. "We had some memorable times in this room, if I do say it myself."

Lily put her face to his shoulder. She was mortified, embarrassed, angry, and there was nowhere to go with any of that, except to pour it out on the people who loved her best.

They settled into a silence that was less than companionable. Simon would wait her out; Lily knew that. He had that talent, as did most of the men in the family. She might just drift off to sleep waiting for him to say the first word, and when she woke, ten minutes or ten hours later, he would still be there, waiting.

"I want to be here."

"Aye."

"But I can't keep myself from snapping at people, like a—like a—"

"Like a lioness in a cage." Simon turned on his side to look at her. "I thought you might take Hannah's head off yesterday. It's a good thing she's so quick on her feet."

She pressed a fist to her mouth.

"Lily." His tone had deepened, and she braced herself.

"Lily. Spring is in the air. Ye want tae be oot in the sun."

She said, "You must really be worried. You're speaking Scots."

"Aye, I am."

"Because I was cranky with Ma and Hannah?"

"Because something is wrong. Something has ye worried, but ye canna speak of it and so ye pick at everything else. Martha Kirby, for example."

Lily tried not to scowl. "My worries about Martha Kirby are well founded. And don't grunt. It's true."

"We'll leave the subject of Martha Kirby's love life for the moment, shall we? Noo, are ye claiming there's naught else pressing on ye but the idea that your brither is fond of yon Martha?"

Lily had known this moment would come, that Simon would corner her and draw her fears out like thorns. In a way she was relieved. She was certainly thankful that Simon was the kind of husband to take note.

She hated to put the words into the world, but he was right; they were poisoning her.

Simon said, "Are ye bleeding, is that it?"

"No," Lily said sharply. "I wouldn't keep that to myself."

"What, then?"

Lily drew a deep breath and put her hands on the rise of her belly. "I haven't felt the baby quicken."

He didn't jerk or startle; his voice came in its normal warm tone. "And it's owerlate for the quickening?"

Lily nodded, because her throat was full of tears.

Simon was watching her face. He said, "Have you spoke to any of the women about this?"

She shook her head. He leaned forward to touch his brow to hers. "Afraid?"

"Terrified." And then: "But I know, I know I have to talk to Hannah about it. I wanted to yesterday, then the little girls came in to tell a story, and—I lost my nerve."

"And ye canna gae someplace quiet to think," Simon said.

A very large yawn escaped Lily, which seemed to cheer Simon. He smiled. "It's no surprise ye need to rest after putting that burden doon."

He rolled off the bed and ran his hands through his hair. "Sleep, Lily. And when ye wake ye'll talk to the women. Whatever it is they have to say, we'll go on together, as we always have."

"The two of us," Lily said softly.

Simon said, "And if it should stay that way, I will still count myself the luckiest man in the world."

But she could not. She would not. She turned her face away to hide from him what he already knew.

———

It wasn't Hannah but Jennet who came to see her next, bringing her lunch. Jennet, who had given birth twice and would do so again, in a matter of weeks. Lily tried not to look at her cousin and good-sister too closely, as she avoided all women with child. It was pure superstition, but it felt like a necessity. She wondered if Jennet noticed, and if she took offense, and then she laughed at her own vanity. Jennet had a busy life and would not spend her time wondering what anyone thought of her.

Now she dropped into the bedside chair and blew out a long sigh.

"So," Jennet said. "I've brought ye lamb stew, and I am under strict orders to see that ye eat all of it. While you're applying yourself to that, I have a story to tell. But first I have a confession to make."

Lily sat up a little straighter.

"When I was carrying the twins, the midwife feared I would deliver too soon, and so she ordered me to stay abed. She banished me from my own household, and complain as I might, Luke wouldnae budge. He swore he'd tie me tae the bed if I couldnae follow orders, and so there I stayed for close to two months.

"The lads were at that age when ye cannae turn awa for even a moment for fear they'll be dancing on the roof or digging up roses, just tae see how deep the roots could go. Oh, they were awful." She said this with quiet delight.

"When did they grow out of that?" Lily asked, happy to play her part in this family story.

"Grow out of it? What man ever grows so old? You and I, we could tell each other tales for days and never come to the end of it. Why, not a month ago Luke took Nathan and Adam down to the docks and had them racing each other up the masts. And then the lasses wouldnae let up until he took them too. Thank providence they're too small still to reach the handholds."

Jennet's outrage was only halfhearted, which gave Lily permission to laugh out loud.

"So there I was, abed. We had Mrs. Landry—you met her, our housekeeper—and help enough, but I couldnae rest easy wondering what devilment the boys wad think up next. It put me in a terrible mood, and I turned sour and crankit as a June apple. It was the worry, Luke said time and again, as if to excuse me. But it was more than that.

"Now I'll tell ye something I have never said tae anybody, not even Luke.

"I wasna ower pleased when I fell pregnant with the lasses. The very idea of another babe in arms made me weary to the bone. But I had naught to complain about, with a guid man who looked after us and saw to it we had everything we could need or want. And that made it all the worse. I was resentful, and guilty for feeling that way, and angry that I couldnae be reasonable and happy.

"Every day I spent in bed listening to the house go on without me made it worse, but I couldnae say anything to Luke or even the midwife for fear that they'd tell me what a miserable excuse for a woman I was.

"And then your mither came to call.

"It was in the afternoon. I heard her and your da in the hall and then I heard her step on the stair, and then there she was standing in the door, all smiles, and before she could say a word, I began to weep and wail. And can ye guess what she did?

"She closed the door and sat wi me while I wept. She held my hand and waited, and when I had no tears left she called for tea and sent everyone who came to the door awa and sat down again to wait.

"And when finally she did speak, she surprised me. She said, 'Every woman fears childbed and will say so, but few are honest enough to talk about what comes after. What it's like to be held hostage, how it chafes.'

"Aye, she said just those words. And she talked about how each time she came close to her time she was torn. She couldnae wait for the baby to come, and dreaded it all the same. 'You see,' she told me in her calm way. 'Everyone will praise the new baby, even the women with children of their own who know the truth.'"

Jennet paused.

"Go on," Lily said, a little breathlessly.

"It's just this. A newborn child is a tyrant. A merciless despot, far worse than Napoleon or King George or any other mannie ye could name. But there's no cure but time itself. With the second pregnancy most women spend the whole nine months gathering up courage not so much for childbed, but for doing battle with a wee dictator.

"'Now, Jennet,' said your mam. 'Of course you're angry. You thought you had another month of freedom, but no. That wily child you would gladly die for has wrestled you to the ground already, and there's naught to do but submit.'"

Jennet's expression was so serious, but Lily could not help herself. She hiccupped a laugh.

"My ma said this."

"Och, aye."

"Why hasn't she told me the same thing?"

Jennet raised an eyebrow, and so Lily answered her own question. "I wasn't ready to hear it. At least not from her. So the advice you're giving me is—"

"Surrender gracefully. In time you'll find it was worth the sacrifice. But it will require time and patience and perhaps most important, a sense of humor."

Later, when Jennet had gone, Lily felt as if she had been relieved of some great weight.

She wondered if she could do what was required of her. If she could simply give up, and surrender to her fate. The idea didn't shock or frighten her, which she realized must mean she had already taken the first step.

With that idea drifting around her, she slipped away to the very edge of sleep, and then was suddenly awake again.

A gentle tapping. A fluttering that came and went and came again. The child quickened just now, as though she had passed a test, and earned a reward.

On the way into the village Daniel put the idea of Hakim Ibrahim's letter out of his head. There were more immediate concerns, and more pleasant ones.

The ice-out party was something he looked forward to every year. There would be music and dancing and food enough to feed the crowd three times over. Friends he hadn't seen in a good while would be there, and if he handled things right, Martha Kirby might be there too.

But first he'd have to call on her and ask, and the fact was, he had never invited a girl—a woman—to anything before in his life. And another fact: He hadn't seen her since she moved in to Ivy House, and she might be offended at that, or hurt.

When he thought about it, he realized he would much rather make her mad than unhappy. When Martha was mad her color rose and her eyes flashed and her whole body trembled. He had made her mad a couple times just to see it happen, and he had the idea he'd be doing that again soon.

The truth was, the idea of calling on Martha made him jittery. He didn't know who he'd come across there, and what conversations he'd get caught up in. There were already rumors running around the village about Martha coming to teach, and that was a subject he wanted to talk to her about alone. There were a lot of things he needed to talk to her about alone.

Why he couldn't just walk over to see Martha, what exactly was holding him back, that wasn't so clear. Either she'd be glad to see him and want to see more of him, or she wouldn't. There wasn't any way to know until he showed up, and so he only wasted his time worrying over it. It was the reasonable way to think about the issue, and it gave him no peace at all.

Daniel turned onto a deer path that would take him around the village and right to his mother's door. If he was going to call on Martha, he'd go see Lily first. Sparring with his twin always sharpened his wits. And he owed her a visit too. He hadn't been to the house since Lily came home and Martha went to stay in the village, as his mother had pointed out so clearly.

Once the decision to move Lily was decided, he had slipped away and stayed away. There was little he could do to help—a one-armed schoolteacher wasn't much use when it came to carrying trunks and baskets and pregnant sisters up and down hillsides—and he hadn't yet mastered the art of standing by while other men worked. It raised all kinds of feelings, none of which made him suitable for company.

He came into the clearing just a hundred feet from Curiosity's front porch, where his nephews had been put to work cleaning shoes and boots. They were deep in an argument that had to do with a bear and they didn't see him at first, but then they were all flying off the porch yelling his name as if he were deaf.

Dirty faces surrounded him, raised up to his with an expression that made his heart ache.

"Tell us the story about Bump and the bear, will you? Will you?"

There were places for him to be, conversations he must have before the day was much older. But he was an uncle, and uncles had responsibilities, the most important of which was telling of the family stories. Beyond that, it would give him a few more minutes before he saw Lily.

"All right, then," he said, and sat down on the porch to tell the tale.

Johnny promptly climbed into his lap. He was a sturdy boy of four, no longer Hannah's youngest but still in need of noodling now and then.

"The porcupine that killed a bear, you want to hear that one again?"

They did indeed.

"From the beginning," Johnny said, "and this time don't leave anything out."

Martha found that she was delighted with the little house, and contrary to those worries she had kept to herself, she wasn't in the least bit lonely. Being back in the village meant that people came by to visit, which kept her busy answering questions and passing teacups.

The one subject nobody dared to raise was Jemima. She was thankful for that, and for the many kindnesses people showed her. Most folks brought little gifts to welcome her. A few eggs, a cutting from a favorite geranium, a small basket woven from reeds; Becca came with a quart of her best gooseberry preserves.

"A peace offering," Becca said.

"But why a peace offering? You have been the soul of generosity."

Becca grunted. "I'm right put out with my girls. Alice most especially. She had no call to talk to you the way she did, and if I know her she ain't finished yet."

"No one has done me any harm," Martha said. "Alice will come around eventually, and if she doesn't we will keep out of each other's way."

Becca seemed to relax. She drank a cup of tea, provided what news there was from the rest of the village, and finally went back to the Red Dog looking determined.

All in all, the move had been a good idea, though Elizabeth seemed to be ill at ease about it. She had come to say good night to Martha the night before the move and apologized for what she called her rude behavior. She wanted to keep Martha at Uphill House, and she needed to have Lily at home, and she could not at first think of a way those two things could exist side by side.

"But it occurs to me," she said. "That it would take less than a week to add on a room. Nathaniel and Simon believe it can be done, and then you can come back and stay with us as long as you like."

Martha tried to say something, but Elizabeth held up a hand to ask for another moment.

"I am making a muddle of this, but really what I want to say is that we would like to keep you here with us, despite all the talk about getting Lily home. We'd like to have you here, and we will do whatever is required."

"Lily is your daughter," Martha told her. "There's no need to apologize. Of course you need and want to have her here, and really, with all the building that needs to be done in the village, it would be very selfish of me to let Nathaniel and the others drop everything to see to building me a chamber. Ethan's little house will suit me very well."

"I still am very unhappy about the idea of you on your own," Elizabeth said.

"There's Mrs. Thicke," Martha reminded her, but it didn't seem to help. The crux of the problem was that she had no people of her own. No matter how loved and cared for she had been in the Spencer household, in the end she was not related to any of them by blood, but only goodwill. And now even that was at an end; she was able to see to her own affairs; she was an adult, and responsible for her own welfare.

Here she was, situated in a small, very pleasing little house with no one to call master. The idea was shocking. Revolutionary. Exciting. She could spend her days as she wished, sleep late mornings or walk around from room to room in her chemise.

Where that odd thought came from she wasn't sure. Martha turned her attention to her trunks. Clothes and shoes and hats, boots and shawls and cloaks. She put her brushes and combs out on the dresser and then spent some time considering where she wanted her books.

It was true that she had a great many books, including a collection of novels that she often reread. It was a bit scandalous of her—she had never got up the courage to tell Teddy or his mother that she read such things—but now there was no need to hide her preference. In Paradise no one looked down on novels; at least, no one who had ever had Elizabeth Bonner for a teacher. When the class had been particularly productive or well behaved, Miss Elizabeth had rewarded them with a half hour or even an hour of reading aloud.

Martha put her books on the mantelpiece in the parlor and was pleased by the way the light picked up the gilded letters on the spines.

All through the day visitors dropped by, mostly out of curiosity. The women old enough to be her mother did not hesitate to ask her pointed questions. Who was to do her washing, then, and had she brought plates and bowls and such all the way from New-York City? Surely she must have had such things, if she was about to get married.

A significant pause always followed this observation. It was Martha's habit to ignore such comments and questions, and in the end most people gave up and went back to household matters. They wanted to know about her pewter and where she would get her firewood, if she would buy soap and candles from the trading post or send to Albany or Johnstown for such things. If she was afraid, a single young woman alone with only Mrs. Thicke nearby. If she feared for her good name or her virtue. That last from Missy O'Brien, whose red, wet nose twitched as she went from room to room, determined to sniff out whatever secrets hid behind doors and in cupboards.

After a simple dinner Martha took the crumbs from the table outside for the birds and stayed a minute to feel the sun on her face. She thought of sitting here with a book, but then she was an object of enough gossip, and there would be more talk if she was seen reading in the full light of day. As if there were no work in the world worth putting her hand to, when in fact she had stockings to mend, and shoes to polish, and letters to write. She turned to go back in and saw Callie coming up the lane.

She wore an old gown, singed at the hem and much mended. On her head was a straw hat with a hole in the brim.

Somehow Callie had learned a trick that Martha knew she could not master. Callie followed her heart and her conscience and her good sense, and damn what the neighbors thought. She didn't care for fancy clothes and didn't seem to mind the loss of all her things in the flood; she wore what people loaned her without complaint. It was an admirable thing, but an odd one.

If Martha were to say as much to her, Callie would just laugh and agree that she surely was odd, and hadn't Martha known that all along? She was the daughter of a woman who wandered through the village at night, ate dirt, forgot her own name. And no one had ever let her forget it.

To Martha's way of looking at things, Callie had done more than well for herself. She had—or had had, before the flood—a well-run farm and orchard, and the respect of her neighbors, and the satisfaction she got from every day's hard work. Martha had been spoiled by opportunity and money, and she knew it.

"Hello," Martha called to her. "Will you come in and have some dinner?"

Callie squinted up at Martha, her expression close and guarded. She was angry about something. Whatever it was, Martha would hear about it before she left again. Callie couldn't keep such things to herself. She was quick to take offense but she didn't hold a grudge, at least not in Martha's experience of her.

Mrs. Thicke had gone off to see her sister, and so Martha fixed Callie a plate and sat down with her.

"Don't worry," she said. "It's not my cooking."

"I don't remember you having any trouble in the kitchen."

Martha drew in a long breath. "You're right. I don't even know why I said that."

What she really didn't know was, why she was so nervous around Callie. Why she should feel uncertain and anxious. Maybe it wasn't obvious to Callie, because she applied herself to the roast pork and put-up butter beans, pausing every once in a while to look around herself.

"Like a doll's house," she said. "I don't know why it should seem so small. It's twice the size of the cabin I grew up in."

A little warmth had crept into her tone, and her color was coming up.

"When's the last time you sat down to eat a proper meal?" Martha asked.

Callie glanced up sharply. "Do I look to you like I need mothering?"

Martha jerked. "Are you sitting on a tack? Because otherwise I'm at a loss to explain your tone."

"Hmmmpf." Callie stabbed the last piece of meat on the plate and took her time chewing it.

Finally she said, "I should have known you wasn't serious when we talked about building a house on my land. But you could have told me so yourself instead of me finding out from Alice LeBlanc, with a smirk on her face too."

Martha said, "Why would you credit anything Alice has to say?"

"I see what I see," Callie said.

Martha let out a bark of a laugh. "You are jumping to conclusions. What makes you think I'm settling in here for good?"

Callie shrugged. "Never said that."

"If you haven't guessed already," Martha said, "I'm here because Lily needed the room at Uphill House and this was the only logical place for me to go."

"There's the Red Dog." Callie chased a bean around her plate as if it were a matter of life and death.

"You aren't thinking this through," Martha said. "If I turned down the house offered me for a room in the Red Dog, how churlish and small-minded would that make me look? Elizabeth was falling all over herself as it was, trying to think of a way not to send me off. I think if I had said I was going to the Red Dog, she would have slept in the hay barn and insisted I take her bed."

Callie grumbled into her cup.

"What was that?"

"I said, the Red Dog is good enough for me."

"Lord give me strength. Did you come by here set on an argument? You remember that mule of Mr. Glove's, the one so stubborn and ill-tempered that he just up and shot it between the eyes?"

The corner of Callie's mouth jerked.

Martha said, "If you had given me the chance, I was going to ask you if you had any interest in this place. There's another chamber with a good bed in it, and Mrs. Thicke doesn't much like cooking for just me. Now you can talk, if you've got something to say. You might want to start by excusing yourself."

Callie cleared her throat. "Is it true you're going to take over the second classroom at the schoolhouse?"

In her surprise Martha stammered. "It's not true. Or at least, the subject was raised and it hasn't been settled yet."

Callie looked at her coolly. "But if he asked, you'd do it."

"He did ask me," Martha said. "But the conversation never took an end. I haven't seen Daniel in—two days, at least. What is that look, Callie? Are you accusing me of lying?"

"Oh, I think you may be lying," Callie said, more easily. "But mostly to yourself."

She pushed her plate away and stood. "Thank you kindly for the meal, it was good. And I'm sorry for being so sharp, but it was a disappointment to hear about the change in plans."

"What change in plans?" Martha said, looking up at her. "I don't see why we have to put aside the plan to build that house."

"You don't?" Callie shook her head. "Well, I do. And his name is Daniel Bonner. I expect you'll marry him before the summer's out."

And finally, there it was, in the open. That moment in the sunlit schoolhouse with Daniel Bonner, when Callie had walked in and startled them.

She could make excuses, but Callie would see through them and would like her even less for it. The truth was very plain and undeniable: There was something happening between her and Daniel. When she remembered that moment in the schoolhouse before Callie came in—as she did, quite often—Martha felt the same pressure and tingling just under the heart, that fear and joy and anticipation all wound together. Once she had had that feeling when she was with Teddy, and here it was again, unexpectedly. Even against her will. What it meant, where it was likely to go, she had no idea. At this moment she wasn't sure what she wanted herself, though Callie seemed to know exactly.

Martha folded her hands together to keep them from trembling. "Where do you get such an idea?"

"I've got eyes in my head."

"But there was nothing to see," Martha said. "He never touched me—like that."

Callie turned her face away. "Seems to me that a girl would take some care, so soon after she got her heart broke. Or maybe you're tougher than I thought. You got over Teddy quick enough."

Martha froze, unsure of what she had heard until she saw the challenge in Callie's face. A flicker of embarrassment and then another, sharper, of anger.

"That was both unfair and unkind," Martha said. She said this very quietly, very evenly, but Callie held up her head and set her jaw.

"Thank you again for my dinner," she said. Nothing remarkable in her voice, as if they were hardly acquainted. Martha followed her to the door, trying to gather her thoughts together and find something to say.

"By the way," Callie said, pausing in the open door. "The ice-out party is tonight at Lake in the Clouds."

Martha found it difficult to take this information in. "A party at Lake in the Clouds? Tonight?"

"Short notice, but you don't have to get dressed up fine. You'd only ruin a good gown. There's a big fire and dancing and food."

"Who will be there?" Martha asked. Her voice came a little hoarse.

"The Hidden Wolf folks, and most all the younger Bonners from Luke down to Gabriel. The children they leave at home with the grand-parents. A few friends and cousins from Good Pasture."

"Oh," Martha said. The question that came to mind was not one she wanted to ask Callie, but she didn't need to put it into words any-way.

"I expect he'll be by this afternoon to invite you," Callie said.

"What I was wondering," Martha said, "is if you'll be there."

Callie met her eye. "Maybe," she said. "Maybe I will."

Lily woke to find Daniel sitting beside her.

"There you are," he said. "Ma said she'd have my liver if I woke you. Did you know you snore, little sister?"

Lily tried not to smile and found that a very difficult trick. She said, "I'm still older than you and always will be. And you'd snore too, if you were tied down day and night."

"Maybe so." And then: "Ice-out tonight, did you hear?"

"It would be hard to miss. The whole house is in an uproar."

He met her gaze. "I was wondering if maybe we should have ice-out down here this year."

"That's kind of you, but it wouldn't feel right to ask for everybody to change their plans. And if you did all come down here, what would I do? Watch you from the window?" She shook her head. "Ice-out belongs to Lake in the Clouds. You go, and don't worry about me. Ma has got something planned, her and Curiosity and Birdie."

There was a small silence.

She said, "Would you stop rumpling your face like that? I don't mind staying behind, I really don't. There's a reward coming down the line for all this good behavior."

His gaze wandered to her middle and something moved across his face. Worry? Discomfort?

Finally he said, "That makes sense. But once you've got that baby safe on the outside of you, we'll have a party. You still like a party, don't you? I can't imagine Italy would have changed you that much."

"Oh, I like a party," she said. "So you came by here to try to cheer me up?"

"I suppose."

"Ah," she said. "There's something else, I can see it on your face."

Daniel was pleased to be able to nudge his twin toward a better mood, and for a moment he thought they might have a whole conversation without an argument. But he wasn't a coward, and so he said it.

"I'm going to invite Martha to the ice-out."

Her expression shifted, so subtly that a stranger wouldn't think much of it.

"You think that's a good idea?"

"I do," he said evenly. He held her gaze.

When they were young Lily could scold her brother and cousins into a corner and keep them there until there was no choice but to concede the folly and repent whatever scheme they had in mind. Daniel had the distinct feeling that such a scolding was coming his way, and he didn't like the idea.

He said, "You can't talk me out of it, Lily. We're not ten years old anymore."

She said nothing for a long time, putting together her argument. Daniel waited patiently because there was nothing else to do. They would have this conversation sooner or later, and it might as well be now.

She was saying, "You have waited so long, Daniel. Why must you settle all at once on Martha Kirby?"

Daniel made her wait, as he had waited. "Why do you dislike her so much?"

"Oh, Daniel." Lily sighed. "I don't. I don't dislike her."

"So it's about Jemima. You can't see the difference between Martha and her mother."

A muscle in Lily's jaw fluttered. "Of course I can see the difference. If Jemima was gone for good—" She paused as if thinking through what she was about to say, and he interrupted her.

"If we got word tomorrow that Jemima was dead, you'd welcome Martha into the family with open arms. Is that what you're saying?"

She shook her head. "I'm not thinking that far ahead, and I hope you aren't either. What I do know is that Jemima could show up here any time and if she does—when she does—she will look for any opportunity to cause us harm."

Daniel found it hard to imagine what kind of harm Jemima might cause the Bonners, but he could see how much Lily believed what she was saying, and how distressed she was.

"The only person who really has cause to be afraid is Martha herself," he said. "And Jemima's already stripped her of the life she had in Manhattan."

Lily put her hands flat on the coverlet and smoothed it. "We were there, Daniel. We were there on the day Martha was conceived at Eagle Rock. I know you reckoned it out for yourself. You can't deny it. You saw Jemima, what was in her face when she caught sight of us. I doubt many people have ever seen her true nature as we did that day. Do you think that's gone away? Do you think she's sitting in Manhattan or Boston or Albany wondering how to put things right? The simple fact of the trouble she set out to ruin Martha's engagement makes it clear that she's as bad as she ever was. Can you disagree with that?"

His voice came hoarse. "No."

"Of course not. She's been biding her time these years to come back here and get even with all of us. She'll tear Martha apart if that's what it takes to get what she wants."

"If that's true, you think I can stand back and watch it happen?"

"It's not your concern," Lily said. "It's Da's. He's her guardian, and he's more than equal to Jemima. Let him handle it."

"I could," Daniel said. "But I don't want to."

That, finally, reached her. Lily closed her eyes briefly and produced a strained smile.

"Is it that far gone?"

Daniel wouldn't allow himself to look away. "Yes," he said, and he realized that he had made a decision. "I keep thinking of the day you told Ma and Da about Simon and Angus Moncrieff, that connection. Da said Simon had proved himself and that was good enough, and Ma agreed. Doesn't Martha deserve the same consideration?"

"No," Lily said shortly. Her color, already high, deepened.

"And why not?"

"Because," she said. "Because Angus Moncrieff is dead, and Jemima is very much alive."

"Once you trusted me," Daniel said. "When did that change?"

"I trust you," Lily said, tears in her eyes. "You aren't the one who worries me."

Daniel leaned over and kissed her on the cheek.

"You take care of you and yours," he said. "And I'll do the same."

On his way back to the village, Daniel crossed paths with Ethan.

"You look somber for a man on his way to a party," his cousin said.

Daniel shook his head. "I just had one of those talks with Lily." He didn't need to explain any further; Ethan knew Lily's ways as well as Daniel did.

"You're not going to let that spoil things, are you?"

"No," Daniel said. "I'm not. But I do need some time to think. Ethan, would you do me a favor? Please take Martha my best wishes and ask her if she'll join us for the ice-out party. I'll meet you all up there."

With Daniel gone off to invite Martha Kirby to ice-out, Lily found herself at a loss. The thing that would have settled her—a long, hard walk—was out of reach. Simon would have been able to distract her, but he was off, working on the Blackhouses' barn.

She put a hand on her belly.

"Your uncle Daniel," she said. "What should we do about him?"

She heard the little people come into the hall and she called out.

"Eliza, would you call Ma for me please? Ask her to come if she can spare the time."

Eliza's head appeared in the doorway. "Are you all right, Auntie?"

She spoke in Mohawk, which took Lily by surprise and delighted her all at once. In the same language she said, "Nothing wrong with me. I just need Ma."

———

For the rest of the afternoon Lily kept herself occupied with her mother's first drawing lessons and exercises in line and perspective. While the preparations for the party went on around them, Lily concentrated on paper and the pencil and explained as she drew.

Her mother sat back and put her fingers to her mouth, clearly trying not to laugh.

"What?" Lily said.

"Geometry," her mother said. "How you resisted learning it, the arguments and rationalizations—they were really very creative. And here you are teaching the practical application of geometrical principles to me."

Lily's own mouth twitched at the corner, because really, it was rather funny. She did remember those discussions, carefully worked out with dramatic gestures for emphasis. Much as Birdie had made her case about school at the supper table.

"I suppose the really odd thing is, all the while I was avoiding learning geometry from you, I was practicing it on my own."

"You had something to prove to yourself," Elizabeth said. "And now will you please show me again how to find the vanishing point?"

Within an hour she was drawing boxes in three dimensions, her mouth pursed in concentration. Working like this in the soft afternoon sunlight, Lily could see more clearly than ever that her mother had aged. The gray in her hair, the softened line of jaw and throat, the network of lines, most distinct at the corners of mouth and eyes.

"You study me very closely," she said. "Am I to sit for a portrait?"

And so Lily took out paper and charcoal and worked at catching her mother's likeness as her mother worked on the very simplest exercises.

She was as serious a student as she had always been a teacher. When she wanted to understand something, Elizabeth Middleton Bonner had no pride; never would it occur to her to pretend that she knew more than she did. She asked questions, listened closely to the answers, probed for weak spots, and asked more questions. Out in the world—anywhere, really, that wasn't Paradise—ladies did not show such an interest in politics or philosophy, architecture or history. And that, Lily recognized once again, was why her mother had found her place here, so far from all polite society.

Now she had set herself the task of learning how to draw, and she would not leave off until she had satisfied her curiosity and come to the limits of her own abilities, or to the end of what Lily had to offer. There was no doubt that her enthusiasm was completely sincere, which really did do something to lift Lily's spirits while the others went about getting ready for the ice-out party.

The little people ran back and forth in wild high spirits—their parents were going off for the whole night, and they could all stay together here with their grandparents and Lily and Simon. Even Birdie was in high good spirits. Since she had got her way about school she was much less irritable and kinder to her nieces and nephews.

From the kitchen came the sound of Curiosity's voice raised in mock outrage, followed by high giggling that only ended when the door shut abruptly.

"Sometimes," said Lily's mother, "I think of this house as it was when I first came to Paradise. When my father was alive, and your uncle Julian. I wonder what my father would make of things as they are today. His grandchildren and great-grandchildren."

"Would he be shocked?"

"Oh, certainly. This is not the life he imagined for me."

Lily thought for a moment. "Do any of us have lives as you imagined?"

Her mother looked up, her expression thoughtful. "There are things I wanted for you, and ways I imagined that those things might come to be. You are the closest, I think, to what I hoped."

"Because I went off traveling."

"Because you went off to find your calling, and you were persistent, and look what has come of it." She put a hand on a pile of drawings. "And because you and Simon are so well matched and clearly happy together."

"And Gabriel?"

This time her mother put down her pencil. "Gabriel is not so much my child as your father's, if that makes sense to you. He belongs here, and would be happy nowhere else. Birdie, on the other hand—Birdie, I think, will not be satisfied to stay in Paradise. She will end up in Manhattan or Boston."

"In the short term," Lily said. "But eventually she will settle much closer to home than that. She is as attached to you and Da as Gabriel is to the mountain."

"I would like to believe that you are right," her mother said. "But my reasons are very selfish. I like having all of you nearby. Not necessarily here in Paradise, but within a day's travel. You are working your way around to Daniel, Lily. What do you want to know?"

She should have known that her mother would hear the things that she did not say directly.

"I'm worried about him. I know we've all been worried about him since he went off to join the militia, worried about his health and state of mind. But this is different."

"You are concerned about Martha Kirby's connections."

Lily pushed down the first flush of irritation. "I am worried about his health and state of mind, now as before. I don't understand how he could have fallen in love so quickly."

Her mother studied her own folded hands. "There was a time," she said, "when I thought he might take his own life."

Lily jerked in surprise.

"I believe you were in France then," her mother said. "The pain was much worse, and he came close to despair. Your father was with him quite a lot, and they talked. I think it was those talks that got Daniel through the worst of it."

"You never wrote to me about this. Why did you not tell me how badly off he was?"

"Because I didn't want you to come home for that reason. Daniel would have been very distressed if you had. He didn't want every decision we made to be about him. I believe at one point he convinced himself that it wouldn't be right to marry, and that's when he asked your father and Ethan to help him build himself a homestead in the strawberry fields. He needed a lair, a place where he could retreat and tend to his own needs.

"Little by little, he did find a way to live again. He put all his intelligence and energy into the school, and he worked at learning how to hunt with knife and tomahawk. In time he started visiting friends, and going to Good Pasture once or twice a year. But there were things that never mended in him. His sense of humor. His teasing ways. He was such an open boy, with such a joyous nature, and there was nothing left of that. Until Martha came back to Paradise."

"I came back too," Lily said and she was immediately ashamed of her childish tone.

"And he is as delighted as the rest of us are to have you here," said her mother. "But that day of the flood when he came into the kitchen and saw Martha—I happened to be looking at him in that moment. Something came back into his expression I had almost forgotten about."

"Do you mean he was attracted to her?"

Her mother's brow lowered, the look she reserved for times when her students were being studiously oblivious.

"I mean hope," she said. "I mean that something he had closed off in himself and given up on opened up without any conscious effort."

Lily said, "Surely you must understand, Ma. Her connections scare me. They must scare you too."

"Does Martha scare you herself?"

Lily looked up in surprise. "No, of course not. I like her."

"That's all that's required of you," her mother said. "That, and show ing some faith in your brother's ability to make his own decisions. Now, I want to fetch the drawings you made in Paris and Geneva and those northern Italian villages. I think they will provide some more insight into this issue of multiple vanishing points."

The folder she got out of the desk was full of sketches that Lily barely remembered doing. Many of them from the first few years in Europe when they stayed no more than a month in any one place. Bruges, Paris, Lyon, villages along the Rhine, and then the mountains in Switzerland. The long journey from Lake Constance to the sea coast and into Italy, where villages had been carved, so it seemed, out of the rock face and clung there stubbornly. Vineyards in the fall. The mountains that ran down Italy like a spine, the valleys that echoed with the bells of grazing sheep. Florence and Umbria, circling around Rome to visit ruins at Pompeii, and into the villages perched high enough to look out over the Middle Sea, the whole world a gauzy, hazy blue. The village called Por- cile where they had stayed for weeks in a house built of stone, rented from the mayor, who was also the owner of all the orchards, a man who desperately wanted to discuss politics though he had little English, and their Italian wasn't equal to the task. How cool it was in the dim rooms at the height of the day, and how in the evening the air was ripe with the smell of olives crushed underfoot and sun hot on tile roofs. And then finally Rome. The shock of it. The thrill of standing before the Coli- seum. The little house with its gardens and grape arbor and the bed where she had conceived and lost and lost again.

"Do you miss Rome?"

They were studying a drawing of one of the hundreds of Roman side streets. A flight of stairs that curved up a hillside, flanked by clay flower-pots on every step. The houses on either side had their shutters closed against the sun. The hottest part of the day, when everyone retreated until the late afternoon. In those first years she hadn't even felt the heat, and she liked having the city to herself.

"No," she said. "Or maybe I should say, there are things I miss about it, but I'm glad to be home." She did not say, safe at home.

For that moment Lily was keenly aware of the curve of her belly. She willed the baby to move again, but Jennet was right; she was at its mercy and had no control at all.

The little people appeared in the open doorway to report on progress in the kitchen and tell tales on one another. Adam wondered aloud if Auntie Lily might be willing to teach anyone else how to draw, and the girls informed him that he wouldn't need to borrow charcoal or a pencil, he had so much dirt under his fingernails. This sent them running to the kitchen again, where they would all insist on scrubbing their hands. What one must do, so must they all. Her own child would join in these games, and the one Jennet would birth this summer.

"Now that it's getting warmer you should be spending at least part of the day in the air," her mother said, bringing Lily up out of her thoughts.

Lily didn't answer, because she wasn't required to. There was always talk in her presence about where she should spend her time, the right combination of sleep and sunlight and interaction, tea and milk, red meat, new greens. They were worried for her and she loved them for it, but sometimes it did grate. Except today. Today she could bear any amount of coddling. Her baby was alive.

"They're going!" one of the boys called from the front porch.

"Not yet," Hannah said, coming into the doorway. She was dressed for the walk up Hidden Wolf, but she carried a tray that she set down where Lily could reach it. Covered plates and bowls, and lovely smells.

"My share of the party?"

"There's more in the kitchen." Hannah's gaze moved over her face and torso. Her doctor look, brow lowered to a sharp V. Lily didn't like to think too much about what went through her sister's head. The calculations she went through, every day, on Lily's progress toward bringing this child into the world.

Hannah said, "We're off in a minute."

Elizabeth said, "Will you tell Gabriel and Annie that I expect them for supper next Sunday? And whoever else wants to come from Lake in the Clouds. Where is Daniel?"

"He's gone ahead."

"With Marrrrthaaaaaa," called Isabel from the doorway in a long singsong that ended in a giggle.

"Silly geese," Hannah said. "Martha is going to walk up with us."

She kissed Lily on the cheek and smiled at her, but Lily found it hard to return the smile.

27

They set out for Hidden Wolf when the first hint of dusk was in the air. They were on foot and everyone carried a basket or box. Ethan had a keg of cider strapped to his back, which was odd indeed. If Martha were to ask Lily to draw him like this and she sent the drawing to Manhattan, no one would recognize him. He had shaken off that other person, the city version of himself, and he seemed healthier if not happier for it.

The procession on foot was part of the ice-out tradition, Jennet told Martha. And in truth Martha didn't mind the long walk. It would give her time to gather her thoughts and try to sort out exactly what was going on.

Callie had been gone not a quarter hour when there was a knock at the door, and Martha went to answer it with her heart in her throat. But it wasn't Daniel, as Callie had predicted. Instead Ethan had invited her to Lake in the Clouds for the ice-out party. Ethan had accompanied her dozens of times before—to recitals and museums and receptions—and this invitation felt no different. Friendly, detached. She asked for a half hour to get ready, and spent the whole time wondering where Daniel was.

She shifted the basket she carried over her arm. Again she wondered if she should have brought gloves, warmer boots, a scarf, and again she reminded herself that there was no cause to be so nervous. This was a party, after all, and she would be among friends. Certainly there would be pelts enough at Hidden Wolf to keep everyone warm, even if the weather should turn.

Up ahead of her on the path there was talk and laughter, but Martha moved more slowly. It had been such a long time since she had come this way, and with every new view she found herself stopping to look out over the river valley that ran away to the east. As the gloaming came over the mountains every tree seemed to be outlined with light, while behind her the shadows stretched through the woods like the gentle touch of a mother's quieting. Thrushes and finches were settling down for the night while the nightjar and owl roused themselves. Grouse scratching in the underbrush, and the cooing doves, the bark of a fox. It was so beautiful, and somehow she had simply forgotten what it was like. What it was.

Hannah called her name and Martha hurried to catch up, casting a glance back over her shoulder. Still no sign of Callie. The full impact of the afternoon's conversation had not hit her until an hour later. Then she sat, trembling hands folded tight in her lap, and tried to reason her way through what had happened and what she was feeling.

It was no use; there was no way to put a better face on what had passed between herself and the person she still thought of as a sister. The memory wouldn't be denied or even put aside for very long. Martha pushed it down once again, Callie's anger and hurt—there was nothing else but to admit that somehow, without thinking, she had caused Callie great hurt—and once again it rose to leave a sour taste in her mouth.

And something else. Something she had always feared but never felt before, with Callie. For the first time Callie seemed to be envious. The orchard was everything to her, but she envied Martha, and why, exactly? Did it come down to something as simple as money?

Liam Kirby had left her his considerable fortune. Before Jemima ran off, when she had thought of herself as Martha Quick, she had day-dreamed about her real father coming to claim her. He would take her away from Jemima and she would keep house for him, and if he had no fortune she never would have missed it. Instead he had died in the war and now she had his money instead, and with it came the Spencers, her guardians, and a new home in Manhattan. She had never asked for any of it.

She thought Callie understood that much. Callie *did* understand that much, or at least, she had once understood it. This was not the friend Martha had grown up with. Something was far wrong, and it had only partly to do with changed plans for a new orchard house. Martha determined that the only way to get to the heart of it was to sit Callie down and demand the whole truth, come what may. She would do that as soon as she got back to the village. In the meantime, she would not let the party be ruined because Callie Wilde had got her head full of foolish ideas.

She set herself that goal, and one more: She would see that the orchard house was built, whether or not she ever set a foot in it. Callie could protest; she might insist on paying back every penny, but she would have the house.

Once Martha put Callie out of her mind, she found herself just as wound up with thoughts of Daniel, who hadn't joined the group for the walk up to Lake in the Clouds either. Whether this meant he wasn't coming, or had gone ahead, that Martha couldn't know without asking. Something she would not and could not do.

Out of sight Luke was telling a story about a trapper named Malone who had come into the Red Dog and tried to pick a fight, and how Charlie LeBlanc had made an effort to talk him out of it with liberal helpings of schnapps, and failed. Malone had just about got it into his head to take a swing at Ethan when Jim Bookman showed his face and things settled down.

Once the trappers had gone all the way to Johnstown or Albany to trade their furs, but now they came only as far as Paradise, where they got fair prices from Luke Bonner. But that also meant fistfights and sometimes worse, fueled by hard drink and short tempers.

Today Martha seemed to be overflowing with memories, things that hadn't come to mind for years. Most likely, she told herself, it had to do with the fact that this was the path she had walked to school and home again, when home had been the big mill house that overlooked the river and the village. Martha had made herself look at it as they passed. Recently painted a light gray with white shutters, every windowpane polished, crisp white curtains. The brass door knocker winked in the late afternoon sun. A young woman with a baby in her arms stood at one of the uppermost windows, a room that had been closed off when Martha was a girl. As most of the rooms had been. They had lived in the kitchen and two tiny chambers. In the deepest, coldest part of the winter they had sometimes slept on pallets by the kitchen hearth where some small amount of heat came from the banked fire. And still Martha remembered waking with her breath frozen on the blanket over her face.

It seemed all her memories of the house where she grew up were of cold. Drafty rooms with great damp splotches of peeling wallpaper, the smell of mice in dim corners. The casements that weren't shuttered were boarded over because where was the money to come from, Jemima would ask out loud, to replace a dozen windowpanes? When Martha had nightmares, which was not so often in the last years, she always found herself in that house with its smells of cooking beans and cabbage, dust and lye soap. Chilblains kept her awake at night, listening to the sound of Jemima's pacing.

Martha straightened her shoulders and tried to pay attention to the world around her. Not much farther to the cabin that had been Elizabeth Bonner's school. Where she had taught her own children and almost everyone else as well. If you lived in Paradise, were under forty and knew your letters, you most probably had learned them from her. As Martha had, and both her parents. As Callie had too.

Martha paused and shifted the basket Curiosity had given her to carry. The smell of fresh cornbread and new butter made her stomach growl.

"Martha!" called Ben Savard. "Make tracks!"

It wasn't safe to walk the mountain at dusk without a weapon. When darkness fell the big cats came out to hunt, and the first bears were about with empty bellies. Martha knew all that but somehow the danger didn't feel real until she heard the tone of Ben's voice. She picked up her pace and caught up to the others at the old schoolhouse.

For a moment it seemed that time had rolled backward yet again, because there were children sitting on the cabin porch or playing nearby. Then she recognized the Oxleys, who had so recently lost their home and mother both.

The children were telling stories to the unexpected visitors. Martha heard one of the older children politely offer tea and Ethan's carefully worded refusal, always laced with easy good humor. He was very good with children. Good with everyone, really, able to put people at ease, though he himself never seemed to be.

Mr. Oxley came to the door, or Friend James, as they called him. A tall and painfully thin man, his cheeks so sunken he could not have many teeth. But when he smiled his whole face erupted into a landscape of wrinkles, and it turned out he did have teeth, though not so many of them as most.

They spent some minutes talking about the progress he was making rebuilding his own place near the river, how much help he had gotten and how thankful he was, and what a shame that Lily couldn't join the party on such a fine spring evening. Hannah wanted to know how the children were getting on, who was doing the cooking, whether there was someone to take care of the littlest Oxleys and look to the endless list of chores a mother with five young children and a household must face every day.

"My second cousin Belinda is coming," Oxley told them. "A widow with two children of her own, older boys."

So the women gossiping in the village had been right. A man like this one must remarry quickly or lose his children. James Oxley had acted quickly, and Martha liked him for it. Callie's father had not dealt so well with loss and disappointment, while Martha had never once seen her own father in the flesh.

Finally they walked in silence for a while. Martha wondered if the men were still thinking of the Oxleys or if their minds had gone on to other things, the evening ahead or the work that waited tomorrow, whether it would be necessary to go to Johnstown for supplies before long, the things that needed mending, chairs and traps, a hoe, shingles.

The women's minds were still with the Oxleys, there was no doubt of that. Jennet had a look Martha had come to recognize, determined to accomplish something others told her she could not. The Oxleys wouldn't want for clothes or food as long as Jennet had a say. Hannah kept her thoughts better hidden, but Ben must have known what was going on behind those dark eyes, because he leaned over and whispered something in her ear and she laughed and batted at him. With that the melancholy spell was broken and they began to talk again.

The woods thinned and then they were in the strawberry fields, a long narrow meadow that would be fragrant with fruit in the height of summer. As girls she and Callie had often played in the ruins of an old cabin right off the deer path that angled from one corner to the other, but even that had changed. A newer house stood where the old cabin had been. This one was larger, and in the shape of an L with a porch across the front. Daniel Bonner's place, then. She had known about it but never come so far up the mountain to see it on any of her visits. It hadn't interested her enough then, but she was interested now. Her pace slowed as they passed so she could take in more details.

There was one old oak in the meadow, close enough to the house to provide shade in summer. Daniel had planted a few more trees to make a half circle that would protect the spot from the worst of the winter winds, once they had grown in. There was no garden unless it was on the other side of the small barn.

The house itself she recognized as similar to the ones Ethan had built on the Johnstown road. Not fancy or fussy, but pleasing to the eye. She had been expecting a cabin similar to the one she had grown up in: two rooms at the most, and just as many small windows to break up the squared log walls chinked with clay.

Martha was looking so hard that she walked right into Ethan, who had come to a stop on the path without her notice. He grabbed her shoulders before she could fall over.

Jennet said, "He's gone ahead to Lake in the Clouds, or we might invite ourselves in."

Her tone was unremarkable, but Martha was aware of the way the others were holding themselves, as if they were intruding on something private. Martha might have corrected them. She could have said there was nothing to be secretive about; she had no claim on Daniel nor he on her. If she felt some inexplicable urge to tell everything, all she could confess to was a few conversations. The only time he had touched her was to help her up out of the mud, and of course there was the episode with the hat—

"We're losing the light," said Luke and so they went on. Martha resisted the urge for one look back at the cabin and concentrated on keeping up with the others, now that they were in the woods again and the way was growing steeper.

A nightjar called and its mate answered, and Martha's skin rose in goose bumps all along her spine.

Daniel stood out of sight in the woods for no other reason than to watch Martha Kirby.

The party passed single file on the narrow path, Luke up ahead, Ben at the rear, Ethan in the middle, all of them carrying their rifles cradled and ready. Ben looked up to the spot where Daniel stood out of sight, and for a moment Daniel was sure he had been sensed if not seen. But if Ben knew he was not willing to show himself, he also knew why and was not in a hurry to draw attention to Daniel's odd behavior.

Because it was odd. He had come right out and made his interest in Martha clear at the dinner table, after all. He had startled himself, speaking up so early when it was clear that Martha was interested but not ready, not yet, to consider him. His own interest, the depth of it, unsettled him. Now Daniel watched Martha, who walked the path through the woods with the easy stride of someone who had grown up on this mountain. Contained within herself, but aware of everything. As she moved away Daniel told himself she could be anyone. Any woman running an errand, a basket on one arm and another on her back, the very last of the sunlight tracing her shape, gilding the curve of her shoulder. The light caught her hair and set the red in it to sparkling.

He had yet to kiss her. There was nothing more between them than some teasing and a few conversations that he remembered word for word. And the fact that some nineteen years ago he had come upon her mother and father coupling in the light of day, in the hour she was conceived, as Lily had reminded him.

When they were gone far enough ahead that he could no longer hear them, Daniel got up and followed.

28

———————

$\mathscr{B}$irdie knew she was being unreasonable, but she was out of sorts, though she had tried hard to hide it all day. The little people had all been put to bed—though by the thumping that came from overhead, she was sure they were far from asleep—and she was allowed to stay up, which was a very good thing. On the other hand, it seemed she would never be old enough to go to ice-out at Lake in the Clouds. Today she had asked Da when she might be asked along and he had put his hand on her head and rocked it back and forth.

"Why such a hurry to grow up?"

She tried Lily instead.

"How old do you think I'll have to be?" she asked. Too late she realized that her sister was likely feeling very low herself. She had missed a lot of ice-out parties and now she was going to miss another one.

"Oh, someday," she said easily. "When you're old and gray and you have grandchildren of your own."

In spite of herself, Birdie had to smile at such an odd idea. She decided she had been shirking the job of keeping Lily occupied and distracted, except she did seem to be in a better mood. It was right that she was at home, but Birdie did miss the long afternoons together.

"I think you and I are a great deal alike," Lily said.

"And what am I like?"

Lily looked out the window and studied what she saw there for a moment. "Not easy. Certainly not complaisant. At odds with the world, and always fighting your way forward. Birdie, I am not scolding you. Those are good qualities in a woman who has dreams for herself. I wish the same for my daughter, though at times I'm sure I'll wonder what I was thinking."

Birdie sniffed, mollified. "How do you know it's a girl?"

The question seemed to catch Lily by surprise. "I'm not sure. It just feels to me as if it must be."

"Is it worth not going to the ice-out party?"

"I think so," Lily said. "The ice-out party and much more. And you know, I like the idea of some time with just you and Ma and Curiosity."

"That's good," Curiosity said as she came into the parlor. " 'Cause that's just what I had in mind."

Curiosity said, "I been thinking about this all day, just the four of us. Here's your mama with the tea."

"Gingerbread," Birdie breathed happily. "Oh, gingerbread."

"We got to have a little party of our own, don't we?" Curiosity leaned over and tugged on Birdie's plait.

It took a moment to pass the teacups and plates, and then there was silence while proper attention was paid to the food. Birdie looked through her mother's drawing exercises while she ate, and held each one up to make a comment or ask a question.

"You see," Elizabeth said to her. "I am struggling, but I think I grasp the concept. Lily is a good teacher."

Lily swallowed and said, "Ma, you're the teacher. You and Daniel. I don't have the patience."

"You're patient when you're drawing," Birdie said. "You concentrate so hard I think you wouldn't notice if the roof fell in."

"That's different," Curiosity said. "That's Lily's gift. Handed down from your daddy, Elizabeth."

The silence that followed was so sharply defined, Elizabeth imagined she could hear the beat of her own heart. Everyone was looking at her. Birdie with some confusion, Lily with dawning surprise. Curiosity sat, her hands folded in front of her, nothing of fear or hope in her expression. Elizabeth had been waiting many years for Curiosity to raise this subject, but now that it was here she felt a trickle of fear at the back of her throat.

"What?" Birdie said, looking between them. "What?"

Elizabeth took a sip of tea to steady herself, and then she put the cup down on the table.

"Is it time?" She wanted to look away, but she forced herself to hold Curiosity's gaze.

"I think so," Curiosity said. "High time."

"What are you talking about?" Birdie said, her voice rising. "Lily, what are they talking about? Time for what?"

Lily smiled at her. "Curiosity is going to tell us about Gabriel Oak. Isn't that right, Curiosity?"

"Gabriel Oak?" Birdie's forehead creased and for a moment she looked so much like her infant self, determined to make sense of the world, that Elizabeth's heart ached. The story Curiosity wanted to tell them—needed to tell them—was one Birdie might not understand fully, but it was right that she was here. The four of them, together.

Elizabeth wondered if Curiosity's choice of time and place had mostly to do with Lily, whose discontent over Daniel's growing attachment to Martha Kirby she didn't even attempt to hide. Her concern for her twin was such that she might do more harm than good, though she could not see that, just now. Why Gabriel Oak should be relevant was not at all clear, but Elizabeth had a strong feeling about this. Curiosity's stories were carefully timed.

She cleared her throat. "Birdie, you must let Curiosity talk without interruption. She is going to tell us the story of why my mother left Paradise and went to England."

"What does that have to do with Gabriel Oak?" Birdie said.

"Everything," Curiosity said.

"Do you know this story already, Ma?" Birdie was looking at her sharply, her tone both surprised and offended at the idea that she had not been told something of such clear value.

"I think I do," Elizabeth said. "Over the years, I think I have worked it out for myself. But I don't know any of the details. We must let Curiosity tell us."

*C*uriosity began:

Back then things was a lot different.

Only a few families, and the wood come right down to the marsh in most places. In those days the Mohawk was still strong and the other tribes too, hadn't none of them give up the fight. The only reason the settlement survived at all was Hawkeye. He was on good terms with the Mohawk and just about everybody else, except the Huron and they didn't come this far south. Hawkeye had him a reputation. Those that didn't like him were sore fearful of making him angry, and so the tribes made a circle around this little village, for a few years at least.

You know the first thing I saw, when we came into Paradise? It was your man, Elizabeth. Three years old, and so full of life, you had to smile just to see that boy. We come out of the woods—the forest came all the way down to where the trading post stands today, back then, oh, yes. We come out of the woods and there was Half Moon shining in the sun, bright enough to make your eyes water. Somebody was chopping wood, and there was birdsong all around, and the air smelled so good you would want to eat it. To all that came the sound of a little child laughing. You know that laugh the little ones got, so full and deep you got no choice but to laugh along with 'em? And there was Nathaniel roughhousing with Maddie. With your mama, Elizabeth. They were playing some game with pinecones and did she have that boy wound up?

She was the prettiest thing I ever saw, was Maddie. Wasn't much to her, you understand. Built small, but oh she was tough. She could work all day in the field and never once slack off. I never heard her complain. That morning she had just washed her hair and left it free to dry, and it floated around her like a cloud, as if those curls had someplace else to be. I can see her still when I close my eyes, how she smiled at us so open and free, and she come and took my hands in both of hers. She looked me in the eye, the way she did when she had an idea somebody needed help. Real direct. Not nosy, you understand. Not forward. She had the clearest eyes and ways of looking, I have never seen the like since. And she said how happy she was to see us but most especially me, because there wan't any other woman her age to talk to.

You cain't know what a shock that was. A white woman talking to me like that, like I was just the same as her. I am ashamed to say that I thought at first maybe it was a joke. Me and Leo talked it through for a long time, trying to understand how things could be so different here than they was back in Pennsylvania.

The judge came along just then. I say the judge because I cain't think of him no other way, but back then he was just Mr. Middleton. Alfred. He cut a nice figure as a younger man, not big but right nimble, and with a fine head of fair hair and a good smile. He was proud to show us the house he built for his bride, for your ma, Elizabeth. I could show you just where it stood if we was to walk down to the lake together. There was the main cabin, three rooms—which let me tell you, was a palace back then—and windows with glass in them just about wherever you looked. There was a smaller cabin out back; the judge give that to me and Leo. All the years after, whenever I got so mad at the man I was ready to walk off, I remembered what it was like, that day.

I don't know can you imagine it. Just a week before we was slaves, and that day we had a place to call our own. Where nobody could come in without knocking, and we could sit quiet in the evening, talking or studying. I set myself to learning to read just as soon as we got settled in, and Maddie helped me. Then when I had the trick of it, I taught Leo.

I know, I am wandering all around this story like a lost calf. Ever since you come to Paradise I know you been wondering why I ain't ever told you about that first year. I kept it back too long, and now I ain't sure how to go about the telling of it.

I will say something you know already about your mama. Maddie was the sweetest, most loving soul the good Lord ever put on this earth, and hardworking? She hardly slept, from what I could tell. She could be sharp when it was called for, but never spiteful. Many times I heard her tell the judge that he was acting in a way that wasn't proper, but she said it so soft and sure not even Alfred Middleton could take offense. She say, Alfred, it ain't right to take advantage of the trappers who don't speak English. And he say, Maddie, of course you are right. They may figure it out one day and take their furs elsewhere. And she would sigh and shake her head, like you do sometimes yourself, Elizabeth, when you frustrated or disappointed.

The judge just could not see Maddie for the woman she was. He loved her to distraction, but he never did understand her. If she asked something solid of him, soap from Johnstown or a paper of pins, he jumped right up and made sure she had it. But there were other things she needed and she couldn't ask for, and truth be tolt, those things she wanted, he didn't have to give. He wan't the man she wanted him to be.

Things went along like that, oh, close to a year, and every day she seemed a little smaller in herself, as if she was losing sight of something important that she never did mean to let go. Something was draining out of her, I could see it plain, but the judge never took note. So long as she was there to listen and put his supper on the table and keep his shirts mended, he was happy.

I suppose things might have gone on that same way for twenty years or more, but just about a year after we first got here, Gabriel Oak came to Paradise.

All that summer and into the fall we worked side by side in the garden and house, worked hard. We planted cabbage and beans and squash and a half acre of corn too. Cora showed us how to do it the Mohawk way. She spent a year at Good Pasture—I'll bet you didn't know that—just after she and Hawkeye got married—and she was always ready to help. Oh, and was she fond of Maddie? You could see it in the way she smiled.

Cora lost her own sister in the wars and I guess Maddie helped fill that
hole in her heart at least a little bit.

The three of us, we sat together many evenings with sewing or
mending, and we talked. It took a long time for me to understand that it
was real, that they wanted me there for more than fetching things.

She was hungry for stories, was Maddie, always wanting more. Little
by little she got me to talk about my mama, and how I got sold away
from her when I wan't no older than you are now, Birdie. How I first saw
Galileo on the auction block and how calm he was, how that gave me
strength. Master Paxton, he bought six slaves that day and me and Leo
were the youngest. She wanted to hear all about what it was like when
we was young, but her favorite story was the day her daddy come and
bought us away from Master Paxton. She went all quiet when I talked
about her daddy. Not mad quiet, you understand, but thoughtful. I had
the idea she missed him more than anybody else, but it was a good long
time before she told me about how she left her family and friends to
marry.

We got through the winter, spinning and weaving and grinding corn,
baking and cleaning. Sewing and mending. The men spent most of the
time out of doors, hunting or hauling wood, doing what men do. In the
evening folks would stop by sometimes. I would have gone off to the little cabin me and Galileo had for ourselves, but Maddie wouldn't allow
it. Not everybody was willing to take tea with a freed slave, but not even
Mrs. Todd was brave enough to say so to Maddie. She had a way of looking at you when you disappointed her, went straight to the heart like a
thorn. She was stubborn and righteous both, which suited me just fine
but didn't sit so well with other folks.

Alfred Middleton wan't a bad man, really. He could get on my nerves
quicker than any man born of woman, but with her he was always kind
and gentle and he never touched hard drink, which is more than some
women can say. I think it surprised him new every day to remember
how well he had married. But newly wed only last so long, and by
March of that winter he had backslid into some of his old ways. You see,
the problem was, he couldn't ever stick to one thing. Ever' day he had
some new scheme, grand plans he didn't ever see through. He would
spend weeks explaining to anybody who'd listen how things just went
wrong and it wan't his fault, no sir, it never was.

Maddie never said a word to me about all that. She went pale when he started talking that way but she never gainsaid him, not in my hearing. But as spring come along, she got quieter and more thoughtful and sometime it seem she wan't sleeping hardly at all, she had such dark circles under her eyes. If I asked her was she feeling poorly, she'd brighten right up and turn the talk to something else. But I saw it.

Later on after things took such a turn, I looked back and saw it clear, how she was disappointed not so much in him—though she had a right, if you ask me—but in herself. I been thinking it over many years now and I come to believe that Maddie married Alfred Middleton knowing full well that he was a leaky vessel, but thinking she could fix him which, let me say this clear, Birdie, and you hear me: Don' ever take a man on because you got the idea you can change him into something you might could love some day. Tears will follow, that I promise you.

But Maddie was young and her mama never taught her what a girl need to understand about men. All she saw when Alfred come along was a man who had traveled far and wide and had stories to tell. And he was a good storyteller, that much is true.

So now here Maddie was, just about two years later, in a cabin on the marsh way at the back of beyond, with a husband she couldn't depend on except not to be there when she needed him. It was a hard lesson, but she didn't shirk it. That wan't in her nature. She didn't blame nobody but her own self. Marry in haste, repent in leisure, so the Bible say.

And then that spring when me and Leo been here a year, Alfred got the idea in his head that he had to go off to Albany to talk to some banker. I cain't hardly remember any more what the scheme was he cooked up but the idea was always the same: He promised her he'd come home a rich man and buy her a thousand acres and build a big house right in the middle of it. And she said—she always said—that she didn't need no thousand acres and that the house she had suited her just fine. But did he take heed? Of course not.

That was the judge in a nutshell, always sure he had more coming to him, and overlooking what was right there for the taking. So off he went, leaving Galileo behind to look after us and see to it we had meat on the table.

For the first week or so Maddie was quiet. Now, it wan't an unusual thing for her to keep her thoughts to herself. She had that Quaker habit. Quiet contemplation, she call it. I got to like it myself, listening to the world without making any noise to add to it. Sometimes I wonder if maybe she was thinking she might go back home again to her people, stand up in front of the meeting to say she had made a mistake. I admit I was afraid she'd do just that, and then what was to happen to me and Galileo? We'd have to find work someplace, and that had to mean going out to Johnstown or Albany or even farther, with no cash money. The judge didn't have nothing to pay us, you see. So there we'd be, two freed slaves with nobody to say a good word for us. Scared me half blind, that idea.

Whatever it was Maddie had in mind, it all changed on a morning in late May, when Gabriel Oak and Cornelius Bump come to Paradise.

The sun has warmed the earth enough to sow the seeds she put away so carefully, each in a folded paper labeled in her careful hand: love-in-a-mist, black-eyed Susan, columbine, sweet william.

It's not so much a garden as a smallhold where they will plant corn and squash and beans. She and Curiosity will spend the summer tending the crops that will sustain them through the winter: cabbage and corn and lima beans, potatoes and carrots and turnips, onions and leeks.

But one corner she has put aside for the flowers she loves. This morning she has dug the plot once and then again until the earth, dark and damp, is loose and the sweet smell of it soaks everything. She will have morning glories trained up the fence and in August the sunflowers will raise their round faces up to the sun. The flowers are what make the long hours hoeing corn pleasant. A simple pleasure, one even her mother could not fault.

She is so focused on her work that she doesn't notice that a shadow has fallen. The shape of a man, stretched out so that it reaches across the entire expanse of the garden. A prickling on the back of her neck makes her pause, but the things she fears are nonsensical. If the Mohawk raid, they will not come like this, so quiet. She raises her head and considers the man standing on the other side of her fence. The men, she sees now. There are two of them. One very tall and straight, and the other only half his height because his back is twisted into an oxbow. His head is canted sideways, and lies against one lumpen shoulder.

"Good day, Friend Maddie. I was told I would find thee here, but I hardly believed it."

She stands, wiping her hands on her apron and searching her memory. A Friend by his speech and dress, and someone she once knew, by his tone.

"Good morning," she says, turning a little so the sun is out of her eyes and she can see her visitors more clearly. "Do I know ye?"

The taller man extends his hand and she takes it. Large and firm and cool to the touch. His fingernails are cleaner than her own. From under the brim of his hat he looks down at her with eyes the color of periwinkle. His brows are very dark, and when he smiles at her the left one lifts into a peak, as if he doubts her word. And now she recognizes him.

"Friend Gabriel," she says. "How—what—"

"First may I introduce my good friend to thee? Maddie, this is Cornelius."

"Cornelius Bump," the other man tells her as he shakes her hand. Bump is a man of twenty-five or so, with milky white skin and hair the vivid color of blanched carrots. Even his whiskers are copper bright. In the polite conversation of strangers he tells her he is come to Paradise to visit his sister and good-brother, the Todds.

She hears Curiosity at the gate. "Come," she says. "Come and meet our visitors. This is Cornelius Bump, Martha Todd's brother."

"Half brother," Cornelius Bump murmurs, and Maddie nods her acknowledgment.

"And Gabriel Oak, of Baltimore."

"Family?" Curiosity extends her hand gracefully, first to one and then to the other man, and neither of them hesitate to take it.

"Gabriel is an old friend of my family," Maddie says. "Our fathers are—" she pauses to work it through, and Gabriel answers for her.

"Second cousins, once removed."

"And you've come all the way from Baltimore." Curiosity's eyes are bright, her expression easy and friendly. She has that talent, she can speak to strangers in a way that makes them comfortable.

She says, "Should I put on water for tea, Caroline?"

"Caroline?" Gabriel Oak looks between them, that brow peaking again.

"So I am known here. It is my husband's wish."

"Ah." He doesn't look away, and she takes this to mean that he has had news from home, that he knows about her marriage. "I will try to remember. Where is thy—?"

The wind plucks the paper of larkspur seeds out of her hand and sends it flying. Gabriel Oak follows it, and she takes the opportunity to ask Cornelius Bump a question.

"Will ye take tea? There is new-made bread this morning, and butter."

"I must go on ahead to my sister," he says. Then he raises his voice so that it will reach his friend, who is striding back toward them, the folded square of paper in his hand. As they watch Gabriel takes off his hat—he still wears the broad-brimmed, low-crowned hat favored by the Friends he grew up with.

"Gabriel, you must stay for tea," Bump calls. "There is time enough for you to meet my sister and her family."

Time enough.

What that might mean is something that Maddie thinks about without pause for the next hour. While tea is poured and bread cut and the pot of butter brought up from the cellar, she wonders how long Gabriel Oak intends to be in Paradise.

Instead they talk about news from home. The little that Maddie knows she tells him, and he returns this favor. He is better informed than she is; the mother of an old friend has died, children have come into the world, Friend Michel Learner has lost all he owns to speculation.

"Have you been to Baltimore recently?" Curiosity asks, and he shakes his head. He has a kind smile that comes slowly but then stays. "I have letters now and then from my sister Susan."

Galileo comes in to fetch some line for fishing and stops to be introduced. Gabriel studies Galileo closely, almost as a doctor studies a patient, to see how he is put together.

He says, "May I take thy likeness, friend?"

And there it is, the subject Maddie has been hesitant to raise. The reason Gabriel Oak left Meeting and his family and went off to wander through the world. He draws.

Now he takes some paper and a tin box from his pack and puts them on the table, spreading the sheets to show. The world, as he has seen it.

Vanity and excess and worldly indulgence, and unacceptable to the community of Friends. To his father, who was such a quiet, serious man. Strict in every sense of the word.

Galileo and Curiosity can hardly believe what they see spread out before them. The streets of Manhattan, a place they have only heard about in stories. The harbor at Baltimore. Boston, and a half dozen villages north of there in the Massachusetts wilderness. People of all ages and races, at work or rest, children playing under a stand of oak trees, chickens in a barnyard, an old woman scouring a pot.

"It's like a—" Galileo hesitates, reaching for the right word. "It's like looking through a glass window."

"You have been just about everywhere, seems like," Curiosity says.

"Yes," Gabriel tells her, his gaze on Maddie. "I have traveled far."

These are the things she remembers about him: how on a first day in June he gave testimony at meeting, and never once said the name of the Lord God or of his Son Jesus Christ. That the girls watched him with pleasure, and he returned all their glances but never showed favor to any one of them in particular. How he helped her carry a heavy basket home when they met in the street one day, and spoke to her of the evening light in a way that opened her eyes to color. How terribly concerned his parents had been. How tenderly he helped his sister into the carriage, when she was heavy with child. The troubled looks when his name was mentioned. How exciting it was, and how frightening to know that someone sixteen years old might leave everything and walk out into the world. How she envied him. How she wondered about him for years, and listened for news whenever she crossed paths with any of his people.

She remembers too the first day she met Alfred, and how his dark hair and the color of his eyes reminded her of Gabriel Oak.

Much later when they are alone again, Curiosity looks up from the loom when Maddie comes in and she says, "You never mentioned to me that you don't like to be called Caroline."

She looks up in surprise. "I don't dislike it," she tells Curiosity. "It is my name, after all. Maddie was my girlhood name. I suppose I think of it that way."

She doesn't say how much she liked being called Maddie again.

"But you like it," Curiosity said. "And it suit you better than Caroline. I'ma call you Maddie from now on."

Maddie says, "Certainly, if thou feels called upon to do so."

For a long minute Curiosity says nothing, but then the questions Maddie had hoped to avoid begin.

"Tell me about him, about your friend Gabriel. Is he disowned too?"

"Oh, yes," Maddie tells her. "I was there when the elders read their statement at quarterly meeting."

She was not there for her own disownment, but she has a copy of the declaration; she keeps it with her wedding lines.

"Because he wanted to draw?" Curiosity can't quite understand. Maddie doubts that anyone but another Friend could.

"He could not live his life according to the principles," she says. "And so he left."

"And his family won't own him."

"No!" Maddie's tone is too sharp, and so she takes a deep breath and attempts to explain.

"A Quaker who cannot or will not live by the principles is warned and prayed over and given every chance, and when it is clear that he has no intention of changing his ways, he is disowned by the meeting. It only means that the meeting no longer owns him. He might still attend if he likes. He is welcome everywhere in the hope that he will find the light again and return to the Quaker way of life."

"But his family put him out," Curiosity says. "Because he has a gift for drawing."

"Not exactly," Maddie says. "People are sometimes disowned by the meeting but rarely by their families. In his case, his father would not allow him back into the house unless he gave up his worldly ways."

"Like your mama did to you," Curiosity says. Her tone is not unkind; she is a sensible person and not given to displays of emotion.

"Yes," Maddie says. "That is true. Though thou has seen, my father still is concerned with my well-being. He sent ye to us here, and I am thankful for thy help and company every day."

"He don't want you to be lonely," Curiosity says.

To that Maddie has nothing to say; she is overwhelmed, as she often is these days, by the depths of her loss. How much she gave up, for something that never existed.

He comes again when she is working in the garden, and his hair is damp and she thinks he must have gone swimming in the lake. He has an exuberance of hair, thick and healthy and anything but plain. Her own curly mass she keeps tightly braided and hidden away under a white linen cap. She is no longer a Friend, but some habits she cannot leave behind.

"Let me help thee," he says and without waiting for her answer he takes up the spade and starts turning the earth with sure, quick movements.

For a long while they work in silence. Without asking he takes the bushel of seed potatoes and begins to plant them, his fingers moving in the earth. Maddie realizes that she is staring and she goes back to her carrot bed. She has many questions, none of which she can think of a way to ask.

He says, "Tell me about thy husband. How ye met, and why ye married."

From anyone else this question would be too rude to answer, but he is a Friend, someone from home. He is asking for her testimony, in this oddest of ways and settings. Maddie finds, to her own surprise, that she doesn't mind. In fact, she feels some relief that he has asked so directly.

"Alfred came to see my father on business," she tells Gabriel. "And my mother invited him to table. He told us stories of his travels. He is English, you understand. He came to the colonies when he was just five-and-twenty and decided to stay."

He works on as if he doesn't hear her, but she knows that he does.

"It was very exciting," Maddie says. Her trowel makes sharp punching sounds as she digs. "Such tales as he told. He spoke of the Russian winter, and the villages ruled by robber barons. He told of Paris and Barcelona and the African coast. He spoke of Sweden and the Lowlands. He traveled through the mountains in Switzerland and Austria on his way to Italy. Oh, how he talked about Rome and Florence. He is a good storyteller, and he made it so real, I could smell the very air. And he had plans to travel farther. He wanted to go to China, and start a business importing silk."

What she doesn't say, not yet, not now, is simpler: Most of what Alfred told was no more than fantasy. He is a storyteller first and foremost; he does not credit any difference between truth and imagination. Something she realized far too late, after she had married him and left her family for this wilderness.

The simple truth is, he has no more been to Russia than she has. All his plans and grand schemes will never be more than that, ideas that never come to life. If not for Galileo and Dan'l Bonner, who bring meat and fish for the table, they might well have starved in the past winter. She and Curiosity spend every spare minute spinning and weaving to trade cloth for things they cannot afford to buy and Galileo can't make.

It has been three months since she had a sheet of paper, anything at all that she might write on. Her father will wonder, and worry. That is the hardest thing, not having her father's ear, even in this disjointed fashion.

She doesn't say any of these things, but it seems that he may be reading them from her face. It would be a gift to have another Friend—a former Friend—to talk to about these things, but maybe it would not be wise.

"It is a quiet life here," she says finally. "And a good one."

"So I see." And then: "But not the life thee expected."

"I am young," Maddie tells him. Too young, her mother had said, but that thought she puts aside. If she thinks of her mother she will weep.

"I am young," she says again. "There are many years to travel."

To that he says nothing at all, and she knows now that he is wise where she cannot be.

It is the next day or the day after when he asks her. He says, "What wilt thou do if he doesn't return?"

That question that beats like a drum in her head. Alfred has been gone almost three months, the longest time he has been away without any word at all. He may be dead, or he may sit in a gaol somewhere, or maybe he has just lost track of time, wandering as he loves to do. As Maddie had once thought she would do with him.

"Go home," she says. "I will go home to my family."

"Thou might do that anyway, if this life does not suit."

"I was married before God," she said. "I made a promise."

"And so did he, but is he here to keep it?"

There is something still in his expression, something watchful. As if this is an assignment he sets her, this question.

"I thank thee for thy concern," she says. "But I will wait for my husband a while longer."

"Then may God send thee children to brighten thy days," says Gabriel Oak, and when she looks up in surprise she sees that he knows more than she could ever say.

"Ma," said Lily. "This is not talk for Birdie to hear."

Her mother's gaze was distant. She came back to this room, this day, with reluctance, blinking like a child roused from a nap.

"Ma," said Lily.

Birdie scowled at her sister. "Curiosity wanted me here and Ma wanted me here and you can't send me away. Can she, Ma?"

"No," Elizabeth said. "We won't send you away. I think Curiosity is almost done with her story. Is that not so?"

"Almost," Curiosity agreed.

"I want to hear the rest of it," said Birdie, still glaring at her sister.

"So do we all," said Curiosity.

———

It is clear that Galileo and Curiosity are concerned. Curiosity says, "You watch yourself, Maddie. You watch out for yourself."

Another time Maddie hears them talking in the garden.

"First time I seen her smile like she mean it," Galileo was saying.

"Headed for heartbreak," answers his wife.

When Sixth month passes into Seventh and the visitors have not yet moved on, Martha Todd and Mary Witherspoon come to pay a call. Mrs. Todd's firstborn, a sturdy little boy with hair the color of ripe corn, runs ahead of her and jumps into Maddie's lap where she sits in the shade of a birch tree, mending a shirt.

Mrs. Todd is heavy with child, her belly so extended that it almost comes to a point, like the prow of a great ship. Her face is red with the sun and perspiration runs off her brow like rain.

Maddie offers them water, and they accept with thanks. When Mrs. Todd puts the jug down her gaze fixes on Maddie, and her mouth presses itself into a line.

"Mrs. Middleton. Caroline. We are here," she says in her clipped Boston way, "to tell you that your immortal soul is in danger. Send the man away."

She has been expecting this for some time, and she is ready. "Friend Gabriel comes and goes as he pleases," she says. "He is not mine to command."

Mrs. Witherspoon's thin mouth curves downward, but she leaves the talking to her friend.

"Is he not?" Mrs. Todd's tone is flat. "Well then, suit yourself. What will you tell your husband when he comes home?"

"I am sure you will tell him whatever needs to be told," Maddie says. "Which is nothing at all."

When they are at the door Mrs. Witherspoon speaks for the first time.

"Whose shirt is that you're mending, Mrs. Middleton?"

When Maddie doesn't look up and keeps her silence, her neighbors go out into the heat of summer.

Gabriel says, "Come away with me."

Maddie thinks of the cabin, of the garden and the ripening corn, of Curiosity and Galileo. She thinks of Cora, who has been so kind, and the other friends she has here. Anneliese Metzler, who is often ill and needs help. Axel, who makes her smile with his tall tales.

"We'll go to Russia," he says, laughing down at her. This is a joke now, one they tell each other quite often.

"Russia in the winter?"

He is so close, the smell of him rubbed into her skin so that she is loath to bathe.

"And in the spring. And summer. And fall. Maddie, come away with me."

High summer, in the cool of the woods.

"Wilt thou think about it?"

She says, "I do little else."

"Tomorrow," she tells him on a day when rain has driven them indoors. "Tomorrow is the anniversary of my marriage."

"What marriage?" Gabriel says. "I see thee alone here on the very edge of the frontier."

"Tomorrow," Maddie says. "Tomorrow Alfred will be gone for six months. If he does not come tomorrow, I will go with thee."

The day comes and goes. Thunderheads build in the west and then descend to pelt the small settlement on the lake with fistfuls of hail. The wind tears down the fence and the corn within the fence and the twining morning glories from the fence. When the lightning finishes they go out, Maddie and Gabriel, Curiosity and Galileo, to save what they can. They are soaked to the skin within seconds.

Curiosity and Galileo go off to their small cabin and Maddie stands across from Gabriel, dripping onto her scrubbed plank floor. The first time she saw this room there was only the beaten earth. But she wanted a floor, and Alfred saw to it she got one. The men who did the work have still not been paid.

The sun has come out, only to set. Gabriel stands in the open doorway watching the last of the sunlight reflected in every water drop. A cave of wonders, jewel-bright.

Maddie says, "Come now. Come, it is time."

Later they talk of where they will go. Or Gabriel talks and Maddie listens, stopping him now and then to ask a question. Tomorrow, she thinks, she will remember little of this, but no matter. He will tell her these things again. As often as she asks, he will tell her because he will be right there, beside her. His body, the long bones of him, the muscles that flex and tighten under her palms. His mouth. His lovely mouth.

She sleeps, one hand cupped over her own belly. Over the child she has con-
ceived with this man who is not her husband.

And the next day her husband comes home.

Elizabeth was pale, her gaze fixed on her folded hands. "Tell the rest of
it," she said without looking up.

"I think you know," Curiosity said. "But I got to tell it anyhow.
Gabriel Oak asked her to go away but she couldn't, not with her husband come home. So he left without her. Said he'd be back in the spring
to ask her again, and every year after that until she said yes. In November Alfred was gone again, off to Montreal for one thing or another. Man
could not sit still. Neither of her men could."

"But why did she go to England?" Birdie asked. "Why didn't she go
home to her ma and da?"

"I expect she didn't want to lie to them," Elizabeth said. "And she
wanted to be far enough away that her husband couldn't come after her
easily."

"She did write to her family," Curiosity said. "Borrowed paper from
Cora to write a letter and borrowed money to send it. And waited until
an answer came back. A draft on a bank in Manhattan and a note from
her daddy, saying her ma wouldn't have her back but she should write
for money when she needed it. And that same day there was a letter from
England, from her good-sister, your aunt Merriweather, Elizabeth. Saying she wished Alfred and his wife would come home to England. She
worried about him with all the Indian trouble."

"But what about Gabriel Oak?" Birdie asked and her voice had a
tremble to it. "How could he not come back?"

Curiosity was looking at Lily. "You know, Lily, don't you? You
guessed it."

Lily looked from Curiosity to her mother and back again. "Yes, I suppose I did. I told Simon a long time ago that Gabriel Oak was most
likely my real grandfather."

For a moment Elizabeth thought Lily would want to tell them how
she had come to such a conclusion, as Elizabeth herself had in that last
summer Gabriel Oak spent in Paradise. Like Lily, Elizabeth had talked to
Nathaniel about it, but otherwise kept the idea—one that had grown

from suspicion to a certainty over the years—to herself. But then it seemed Lily was as impatient as Elizabeth was to hear the rest of what Curiosity had to say. To confess.

Lily said, "He did come back, didn't he. He came back and you told him she was gone. Did he give you a letter?"

"Yes, he did," Curiosity said. "He come back here at Christmastime, couldn't wait any longer is what he say to me. We sat at the table and I told him not the way it was, but the way I wanted it to be. And then I watched him write a letter for Maddie. He gave that letter to me to make sure she got it, and he went off and didn't come back for a long time, some twenty years."

"Did you have a letter for him?" Elizabeth asked. "Did she give you a letter for him when she left for England?"

Curiosity closed her eyes briefly and then nodded. "I didn't give that over neither. If I had done what they ask me to do, most likely she would have come back. It was me kept them apart, may God forgive me my pride. And you know why I did that? Lily?"

"Because you thought you knew better," Lily said. There were tears on her cheeks now. "You thought you knew what was right, and you were so sure you made that decision for her."

"Yes, ma'am," Curiosity said. "In my pride and vanity I thought I knew better than your grandmama. I tole myself that Gabriel Oak couldn't be trusted to take care of her and a child too. Him with that itch to always be off moving. I was bitter about her going off, though I didn't see that right then. And so I tampered where I had no business, no matter how much I loved Maddie. I had no business. I have prayed every day that the Good Lord might take mercy on me for my wickedness. When the letter come from England saying you was safely come into this world, Elizabeth, there was a note for me too."

She reached into her apron pocket and brought it out. A single piece of paper, yellow with age. Elizabeth took it when Curiosity held it out to her, and after a moment she opened it. She read aloud:

If thou shouldst ever see Gabriel again, please tell him that I bear him no ill will. He gave me a beautiful daughter and I am content.

"Right then I knew what a terrible thing I had done. I had to tell Maddie, but I kept putting it off. I thought if I could find Gabriel first and confess to him, he'd go to England and claim Maddie and his child.

I wrote to him, I did. Whenever I could get together enough money I sent off another letter, to all the places he talked about. Wrote on it, *for Friend Gabriel Oak, Artist Originally of Baltimore, Should He Pass Through.* I did that right until the judge went off to England hisself to bring Maddie home. Then I waited all those months until he came back, every day telling myself that when she was back, when I could look her in the eye, I would confess it all.

"But she didn't come back and I never had word from Gabriel either, not until he come through Paradise some twenty years later, when Maddie was long in her grave, may the Good Lord rest her soul.

"I can see the question you afraid to ask on your face, Elizabeth. So let me just finish this sorry story and say yes, I did tell him then. I tolt him what I had done and I tolt him he had a daughter, born and raised in England in the belief that the judge was her daddy.

"I tole him all that and he just sat quiet, the way he had. Thoughtful. I wished he would shout at me but no, he just sat and thought for a long while. And then he ask, real calm, what was it did I want from him? As if he owed me something. As if I thought I deserved his forgiveness. I was going to say that, but then something else come into my mind. Something I could ask for, not for me, but for you, Elizabeth. I ask him for a picture of his own face, a portrait. So that I could send it to you one day and say, this is your daddy. Your mama loved him very much.

"And he say, yes, he would see to it that you got to see his likeness one day."

"Oh," Lily said. Tears trailed over her face but she made no attempt to wipe them away. "That day he asked me to draw him. You were there, Curiosity."

"Yes, I was. I held him to that promise."

Birdie sat up straight. "Is that the picture hanging in your room, Ma? Of the man with the—" she used her hands to describe the broad-rimmed hat Gabriel Oak had worn.

"Yes," Elizabeth said. "Lily gave me that drawing as a gift. I look at it every day."

"That's the story I been holding back all these years. I expect I'll have to tell it again when I stand before God, and I won't have no excuses because it was wrong, what I did. I will tell him what I'm telling you now, Elizabeth. I am heartily sorry."

"I can see that," Elizabeth said. "I can see that you are. But Curiosity, the penance you have inflicted on yourself has been too extreme. All these years of self-recrimination and guilt—"

"I was guilty," Curiosity said.

"Yes," Elizabeth said. "If you need to hear me say it, then yes. It was a mistake, and you should not have done it."

Birdie came over and leaned against Elizabeth with all her slight weight, as she had done as a very little girl when she was uncertain and in fear of losing her balance. In a voice that was swollen with the tears she was trying to hold back, she said, "I don't want you to be mad at Curiosity."

Elizabeth put her arm around her youngest daughter's waist. "I know," she said. "But you must understand that the anger and sadness will pass with time. What will not pass are the feelings of love and affection and gratitude I feel for Curiosity. She has been the truest friend, as much a mother to me as my own."

Curiosity had closed her eyes. The muscle fluttering in her cheek was the only proof that she had heard what Elizabeth was trying to tell her. Then she seemed to force herself into action. From her apron pocket Curiosity drew out two letters. Her hand was shaking when she held them out to Elizabeth. They were brittle with age, and neither of them had ever been opened.

"Many times I imagined this, of what it would be like to give these to you. All these years I been thinking on it. I never read them; you can see the seals ain't never been broke. So now I am going to go back to my own place and set a while, leave you three to talk among yourselves. When you are ready to talk to me, Elizabeth, I will abide by whatever it is you want me to do."

"But I know that already," Elizabeth said. "I want you to stay here. Right here with us, where you belong."

There was a small silence. Then Curiosity took a deep breath and let it go slowly. "So," she said. "That teapot has gone and emptied itself again. I'll be right back."

She left the room without a backward glance, and Birdie would have started after her had Elizabeth not held her where she was.

"Leave her for now," Elizabeth said. "Leave her a few minutes. She'll come back to us. Wait and see."

30

At Lake in the Clouds the party had already started when the walkers came into the clearing. The others greeted their arrival with shouts and laughter, everyone so happy to see one another and determined to have a good time that Martha was immediately drawn in, all her doubts gone just that easily.

Hannah took her by the hand and introduced her to the people she didn't know—Susanna, Blue-Jay's wife of a year; Susanna's brother John, who had come up from Paradise earlier in the day; a young Mohawk brother and sister called Jumping-Bird and Little-Tree who were visiting from Good Pasture in Canada, and a few others whose names escaped her as soon as she had heard them.

Though the new dark limited what she could see, Martha had the sense that very little had changed at Lake in the Clouds. The house and the cabin stood no more than a minute's walk apart, each with a clutch of outbuildings and a scattering of trees. The long mountain glen led to the waterfall and the lake that gave this place its name. Cornfields at the other extreme, and beyond them cliffs and a steep drop.

In the clearing between the house where Daniel had been raised up and the lake, a great bonfire was burning, putting out heat that Martha felt standing at the edge of its light. Another, smaller fire had been set farther away, where a boy of ten or twelve was turning a calf on a spit. He was in deep conversation with Annie, who was pouring something over the meat, liquid that spattered into the fire and sent up clouds of fragrant smoke. The smell came on the breeze and again Martha's stomach cramped in protest.

Annie caught sight of her and smiled. Martha raised a hand in greeting. She had last seen Annie on the day of the flood and she was surprised and a little ashamed to realize she had not thought much about her at all, though they were of an age and had been friendly as girls. And here she was, the new bride opening her doors to a crowd of people and showing a confidence and ease Martha had to both wonder at and admire. She might have been doing exactly the same thing in a very different setting, but that seemed more like an odd dream now, something apart from her real self.

On the last leg of the walk Ethan had explained to her how things were ordered at Lake in the Clouds, to spare her the need to ask embarrassing questions. Annie and Gabriel lived in the cabin nearest the cornfields, the one where Runs-from-Bears and Many-Doves had raised their family. They shared their home with friends and cousins who came to visit from Good Pasture in Canada or even farther. Blue-Jay and Susanna were in the house nearer the falls, where Daniel's parents had lived until they moved into the village. Runs-from-Bears stayed with them there. Martha was curious about Susanna and would have liked to talk to her, but that would have to wait. There was food to get ready—a great deal of food—all to be put out on two long plank tables set upwind of the bonfire.

The women unpacked baskets and called out to one another, telling stories as they put out platters and bowls, shooed the hounds away, and laughed for the simple pleasure of it.

There were three different kinds of bread, apple butter and honey and dried berries stewed to a jam, a side of smoked bacon cut into thick slabs, bowls of beans, pickled tomatoes and cabbage, the sharp smell of cider vinegar and dill bringing Martha's appetite up to a roar. Jennet put a plate of gingerbread on the table and then rapped her husband's knuckles when he reached for a piece.

"As bad as the bairns," she told him, and he laughed.

Martha took part in a half dozen conversations, answered questions, and asked some of her own, though she had to raise her voice to be heard. It was very noisy with the sound of the waterfall and the fires and so many people with so much to say to one another in English and French and Mohawk.

When Gabriel brought the first great platter of roast meat to the table, steaming and fragrant, people filled their plates and settled down to the business of eating.

There had been no sign of Daniel, but Martha thought he would show himself now. He must, she told herself, and planned how she would greet him, how friendly her tone should be without giving away—what? What really was there to hide, anymore? People seemed to have decided for her, and she could fight against that or ignore it. Try to ignore it.

"Friend Martha?"

She looked up from her food, suddenly aware that Susanna's brother was talking to her. John, she recalled. He had read law and these days he ran the mercantile for his father. A sturdily built man of some twenty-five years, as fair as his sister with his hair tied back into a neat queue and as thoughtful and quietly observant as an owl. Martha was surprised to hear his voice at all. "I'm sorry, I didn't hear you."

"I asked thee, could I please have the water?"

As she picked up the pitcher Martha realized it was empty. It was a chance to get away and calm herself before she did something truly awful, and so she got up from the bench and announced she was going to fill it.

As soon as she walked out of the light of the bonfire Martha realized how cold the evening had grown, and she wished for her shawl. To go back for it now seemed silly, and so she drew the cold air as deep into her lungs as she could and held it there for a moment. A trick she had learned as a girl, and it still seemed to work.

At the edge of the lake a variety of water buckets stood on a low stand. There was a rope tethered to a stake in the ground and a bucket at the end of it, so she could lower it into the water, and a winch to haul it back up again.

A misting from the waterfall fell light as silk on her face as she went down on one knee, folding her skirts carefully. Then she leaned over the mossy flat rocks and plunged the jug directly into the water.

Balanced on the heel of one hand, she looked back over her shoulder to the tables where the others were busy eating and talking. Martha caught the sound of a male voice raised in protest and then an explosion of laughter that echoed off the cliff face and back again.

A feeling came over her, something familiar but hard to place in that first moment. Not happiness, not exactly, but a kind of contentment she hadn't known in many weeks. She was among friends, safe among friends, and down in the village she had a small house to call her own, and work, if she wanted it. She could be useful. And if teaching did not suit, if she failed at it, why, it was only a matter of weeks. She could manage for that long. In the fall the new teacher would arrive and she would have to figure out what she wanted to do with her time. For now she didn't need to answer that question. At this moment she simply needed to leverage the filled and very heavy jug out of the lake without falling in.

Martha was digging in with the heel of her free hand and her knees when she caught a movement out of the corner of her eye. A pale flickering in the dark water, like the flexing of a great fish.

She moved back instinctively, but too late. A hand punched up out of the depths and grabbed her wrist so that she let out a small scream and dropped the jug. She tugged, but her balance was a frail thing. Another scream, louder, but not loud enough to be heard over the waterfall.

She was going to fall in; she was going to be pulled in, pulled down and down into the cold and dark. Martha began to struggle in earnest but in that split second a head and shoulders broke the water.

"Daniel Bonner!" she roared his name in her surprise and outrage. "What—"

Another pull and she was tilted forward as though she were about to dive. In the flickering light of the bonfire the water in his curly dark hair glimmered, and she saw that he was laughing. Laughing.

"You—" The things she wanted to call him were unladylike. That was the last coherent thought Martha could summon, and then he was kissing her. He let go of her wrist and settled his wet palm against her throat, fingers spread, to hold her where he wanted her, and he kissed her full on the mouth. His skin was cold and his mouth shockingly hot. Martha felt it like a blow to the chest, a blow that traveled to the deepest part of her where something only vaguely imagined sparked into sudden life.

A kiss that lasted three seconds, no more, and then he was smiling at her. She opened her mouth to say something but he pressed his fingers there, gently, and shook his head.

"I'm sorry I scared you," he said, still smiling. "Go on back, I'll be there shortly."

She hesitated for the merest second, her thoughts were tumbling so; a mistake.

"Or if you want to wait—" He made to climb out and she stood abruptly. Daniel looked up at her like one of the selkies in Jennet's stories, sleek and dark. In one movement she pivoted away and then remembered the jug, stopped her movement but too suddenly. One boot lost its purchase on the wet rocks and then she was falling, aware of the tangle of her skirts as she kicked, aware of the wave of cold air off the waterfalls and of Daniel, a quick view of his surprised expression and then she was in the water, the cold shutting out everything else.

A strong hand grabbed at her and missed, grabbed again. Martha would have reached up but her arms were suddenly so heavy she couldn't lift them.

An arm closed around her waist and with a great upward thrust her face broke water.

"Easy," Daniel said. "Easy."

He wasn't smiling anymore, at least there was that much. As Martha caught her breath she could see that he had been as scared as she was. And still her fist came up of its own accord with every intention of cuffing him over the ear. Daniel caught it easily, but he had to let go of her to do it and with that Martha realized a few startling things. First, he was standing on an outcropping of stone that served as a step beneath the waterline, so that he had footing, while she had none. Second, he had not a stitch of clothing on. Daniel Bonner was stark naked.

She stood pressed against a naked man in a mountain lake on a spring night and the only thought in her head was that he was going to kiss her again, and she wanted him to.

"We weren't planning on swimming," boomed a voice above them. "But you always were one for the unexpected, Daniel."

Martha closed her eyes and drew in a deep breath. When she looked she saw that they were all there. With the light to their backs she could not make out the faces, but she could name them every one, anyway. Hannah, Ben, Jennet, Luke, Annie and Gabriel, Ethan. Ethan, who had

been her teacher and should be outraged, but she was sure he was smiling. The others, the ones she had just met were definitely smiling,
though they were trying not to.

All that took no more than a heartbeat and then Susanna was coming forward.

"Blue-Jay," she said in a no-nonsense tone. "Help Martha out of
there. Daniel is in no position."

"Oh, I see his position all right," Blue-Jay said. He leaned over and
extended a hand, and Martha took it. He pulled her up onto dry land
with a flick of his wrist, as if she weighed no more than a trout.

There were a dozen conversations going on, but Susanna had her by
the shoulders and was propelling her toward the house. "Dry clothes, hot
tea," she said. "Quickly."

Martha tried not to hear the teasing Daniel was taking. At least he was
responding with an easy humor, something she herself could not have
done. She wondered if he was going to climb out of the lake as he was,
in front of everybody. If nobody would mind him walking across the
glen naked.

Suddenly she stopped and turned.

"He did not pull me in!" she shouted. "He didn't! I fell!"

There was a split second of silence, and then Jennet called back.

"Och, aye. I fell right here mysel, lass. Most Bonner women do."

For the second time since her return to Paradise, Martha found herself
being put to rights in front of a blazing fire, stripped of her own clothes.
At least this time there was no mud and no LeBlanc daughters to come
in and glare at her.

Susanna and Hannah wrapped her in blankets and put her in the
good rocking chair, which was positioned as close to the hearth as they
dared. Then Hannah took up toweling to rub her hair and head dry, and
if she were honest, Martha would have to admit what a wonderful thing
it was to be tended to this way. She had nothing to do but sip her tea and
study her surroundings.

The house was well made, the walls thick enough to reduce the noise
of the waterfalls to a hush, but oddest of all, it smelled pleasant. After a
winter of scraping and curing pelts it should have been ripe, but there
was only the faintest odor of bear grease and gun oil. It was true that

Susanna had hung bundles of dried flowers and herbs from the rafters along with the last of the stores of corn and squash and onions, but in Martha's experience those things could hardly be enough.

"She airs every room out, twice a day," Hannah said, "no matter the weather, and she leaves many of them open all night. It was one of her conditions."

"For marrying Blue-Jay?"

Hannah laughed. "For living up here. I don't think there's any force in nature that could have changed her mind about Blue-Jay."

From the chamber that opened off the main room Susanna called out to them.

"The skirts will be a little short, but the stockings are good wool."

Martha's voice creaked. "I'm glad of whatever you can lend me. Truly."

Her own things were hanging in front of the hearth, dripping into the hissing fire.

Behind her Hannah said, "You could stay here and rest, if you like."

It was a reasonable thing to offer and Hannah's tone was unremarkable, but Martha tensed. Another decision to make, and she could hardly organize her thoughts enough to drink a cup of tea. Daniel Bonner had kissed her, and she had kissed him back, and somehow or another she had to make sense of that before she walked out of this house and had to look him—and everybody else—in the eye.

"Daniel swam in that lake every day, winter and summer, from the time he was old enough to walk until he built his own place," Hannah went on in a conversational tone. "He still comes up to swim two or three times a week at first light. He's hardened to the cold in a way you can't be. I'm worried that you may come down sick."

"Oh," Martha said. "You think it would be wise for me to stay here by the fire, is that what you mean?"

"No," Hannah said. "I hope you'll come back to the party with us, but I don't want you to feel as though you must." And then she hesitated. It was odd to see such an expression on Hannah's face. To Martha she seemed the most self-possessed and confident woman she had ever known. It was something of a relief to realize that others found the situation as awkward as Martha did herself.

Hannah said, "Daniel didn't mean for it to go so far, I'm sure of that. He would never put you in danger."

Martha tried to look interested but not overly so.

"You couldn't know this," Hannah said, "but it's been a very long time since we've seen Daniel so playful. We have you to thank for that."

"It wasn't anything I did," Martha said. "I just happened to—" her voice trailed away, because if she didn't believe the things she was about to say, Hannah certainly would not.

Hannah was smiling now, a soft smile with a great deal of understanding in it. She said, "You haven't asked me for advice, but I'm going to give you some anyway. As embarrassed as you are now, one day you'll look back on this night—on this whole summer, is my guess—and the memory will warm you."

"I forget sometimes that you're old enough to be my—to have a daughter my age," Martha said.

"Oh please." Hannah laughed. "I'd rather you thought of me as a sister."

Before Martha could think of a response to such a surprising statement, Susanna appeared with an armful of neatly folded clothing. Underskirts and skirts, sleeves and a fitted bodice and the stockings, as promised.

Susanna had a bright smile and the kindest of eyes. A friendly girl, people said of her, always attentive and sincere. And how her parents had grieved when she turned her back on the Friends and went her own way.

"Are you happy here?" Martha heard herself ask the question and wished she could take it back, but Susanna seemed to take no offense.

"Dost thou mean, do I miss my family and my home? Thou sees that John comes to call whenever he can, and that helps a great deal. But I am happy here, so happy that sometimes I fear that I might wake up and find it was all a dream."

She glanced at Hannah, who smiled at her. "This is where I am meant to be," Susanna said. "I want no other life."

"Listen," Hannah said, straightening.

"Who is that with the rattle?" Susanna said after a moment.

Martha thought it was a question for its own sake and expected no answer, but Hannah had one.

"Standing-Elk is come. Listen, the Round Dance is starting."

Hannah looked so excited and pleased that Martha felt her own pulse leap.

"Then you should go ahead, both of you," she said. "As soon as I'm warm through I'll dress and come out, I promise."

———

The bonfire had been built up so that the flames shot into the night sky and pulsed with the beat of the drum. It had a life force of its own, and as it danced it threw shadows around it like a many-layered skirt.

Daniel retrieved his pack from where he had left it on the other side of the lake, and standing there in the shadows, he dressed. First he exchanged the wet sling for a dry one, and then he pulled on breeches and a loose shirt, moving gingerly and praying that his shoulder would leave him in peace this evening. At the moment the pain was small and far away; cold water could do that, and the excitement. And most likely, he told himself, the kissing.

He cast one more glance at the cabin and saw his sister and Susanna closing the door behind themselves, without Martha. But she would come. He felt the truth of that deep in his gut. In those few seconds when he held her and her whole body softened, he understood that she wanted to be here, with him. She was frightened, but more than that she was curious and open, and that was enough, for now at least.

As he walked back to the fire he watched Gabriel strip down to loincloth and leggings and then join the circle of men moving into the dance. Runs-from-Bears and Standing-Elk sat with Sky-Wound-Round on benches, the big water drum between them. Standing-Elk had horn rattles in both hands, and all three of them were already caught up in the singing. At Good Pasture there were sometimes a dozen men gathered around two or three water drums and another three or four with horn rattles, but here at Lake in the Clouds they had their own ways, and they were good.

Daniel came into the heat and light and moved into the shuffle-kick-step of the dance behind Blue-Jay, just as the women came up to form another circle inside their own. Martha would join them, and the dancing would go on and on until they were all breathless with laughter. As this thought came to him, Daniel saw that Martha had come out on the porch and John Mayfair was walking toward her with purpose.

As soon as Martha stepped off the porch John Mayfair appeared—seemingly out of the shadows—and startled her so that she jumped. She would have fallen—for the second time in one evening—if he had not caught her by the elbow and steadied her.

She had never seen a man so determined to apologize. He should not have let her go fill the water jug on her own, and he hoped she would forgive him for his thoughtlessness. Martha had forgot about the jug and about John Mayfair too, but she hoped her expression didn't give that much away.

It was hard to talk over the crackle of the flames, the drums and the singing and the dancing, but she wanted to put his mind at ease.

"You are not to blame, and there was no real harm done. Won't you join the—" She stopped herself, but not quite in time. "Pardon me, I forgot. Of course you're not dancing."

He shook off her apology. "While I have the opportunity, may I ask thee a question?"

Martha pulled up short. She gathered the borrowed shawl more closely around herself and gave a brief nod.

John looked away into the trees and when he looked back he was smiling. A small and apologetic smile. "Will Callie be joining the party, does thou know?"

For a moment Martha was so surprised that she couldn't organize her thoughts. He rushed ahead before she could respond.

"Callie and I are—I like to think of myself as her friend. I—" He paused. "I am interested in her work. We sometimes talk about apples. About grafting. Thou must know. . . ."

He looked a little panicked, so that Martha's initial surprise gave way to the impulse to reassure him.

"Oh," she said. "Yes, I know. We spent so much time following her father around the orchard. I believe I can name all the different trees. Snow and Seek-No-Further and the Spitzenburg. There was a very good one called Duchess."

He nodded avidly. "It's one of Callie's favorites. She had a graft of the Duchess on the Red Moon that produced its first fruit last year. I do believe the new apple was as close as it is possible to get to perfection. It was medium-sized, with a skin of red and yellow both and a crisp bite with the most flavorful juice. The new apple—she called it Bleeding Heart—would have made her fortune. If not for the flood."

Understanding and regret brought sudden tears to Martha's eyes. She was ashamed of the small worries that had kept her from seeing the depths of Callie's loss.

"Few people know about this," John Mayfair said. "So I suppose it is wrong of me to tell thee. But I am worried about her, and thou art her friend. Is that not so?"

"I am," Martha said firmly. "And now it is my turn to ask, what are you to Callie?"

He seemed to be anticipating the question. "I am her friend. I can be nothing else." His gaze moved across the scene before them and dwelled on his sister. The speed of the dance had picked up and Susanna was flushed with excitement. The two circles were moving in opposite directions and as they watched, Susanna and Blue-Jay passed each other. Susanna's face, tilted up toward Blue-Jay's, was as bright as the firelight.

Even among such well-favored men, Blue-Jay stood out. When Martha was a girl it had been everyone's pastime, watching Blue-Jay and admiring him, though few would admit such a thing. In the old days the Bonners and their Mohawk relations had been respected and feared by all, but most kept their distance; certainly no white girl would admit that she liked an Indian boy. It would have been like standing up in church and announcing that you preferred the devil to the angels.

It surprised nobody when Gabriel Bonner married Annie, but Susanna Mayfair binding herself to a full-blooded Mohawk, that was too much for her people to bear. Thus Birdie had explained the situation to Martha, and it seemed that her perceptions were very much in line with the truth.

Susanna had been brave and strong enough to come to Blue-Jay. It took great courage to step beyond the line drawn by faith and duty and habit.

"She's happy," Martha said. "Whatever it cost her to leave you all, she is happy."

"Yes," said Susanna's brother. "She is. And as much as she is missed, I am happy for her."

Someone called out *yo'-ha'* and both the inner and the outer circles jumped in place to change direction. Most of the men had shed their shirts, and sweat shone on skin of every shade, from Ben Savard's rich deep red-brown to Ethan's pale winter white. Every one of them was built in the way of men who worked hard, with heavy muscles that flexed across shoulders and down thighs, the flow and flex almost too beautiful to watch.

Martha looked away for a moment. She could not ask John Mayfair what it was he wanted, not only because it was too forward a question and none of her business, but because she had an idea of what he might say, and she had no answers for him. Just a few months ago Martha might have spoken of love and fate and the need to follow one's heart. She had been smitten with the very idea of love, and wanted nothing more than to have everyone else join her in that state. Now she knew better.

She said, "I am glad that Callie has a friend such as you, John Mayfair. I will try to be a better one."

When she looked up again, Daniel was standing there. He was breathing hard, sweat rolling down his face even this far from the bonfire. He held out his hand palm up, and his fingers curled in invitation.

"You're wanted at the dance," John Mayfair said. "Please, don't let me stop you."

The bonfire made an undulating island of light in the darkened glen, and Martha let the women pull her into it. More than that, she was glad of it.

She had seen the Mohawk dance once or twice as a girl, when the whole school had been invited up to the Midwinter Ceremony at Lake in the Clouds. She remembered the excitement of those visits well, but few of the details; she didn't know the names of the dances or what was required of her. None of that seemed to matter.

The women danced together, in a line or circle, interwoven with the men or separately, and the steps were easy enough to follow. Sometimes someone would call out *yo'* and the other men would respond *ha'* but the driving force, the animating force, was the water drum. She felt the pulse of it move up from the ground and through her feet, along the length of leg and backbone and into the very bones of her skull.

When the women finally retired to the trestles the men kept dancing. The Robin Dance, Annie told her, handing her a beaker of water. It was very cold but Martha was too thirsty to worry about her stomach or good manners; she gulped, and then Jennet filled it again for her. Jennet was so flushed with color and so clearly happy, in the light of the fire she might have been no more than twenty if not for the child she carried so unself-consciously.

The drum's rhythm was speeding up steadily. There was little talk now and less laughter, they were all so focused on the dancing. Because it was beautiful, there was no other word for the sight of men in their prime moving for the sake of movement. As a student Martha had been taught to observe line and proportion, but this—men in the flesh—no sculptor could equal it.

Martha watched Gabriel spin in place with his long hair flying around him, his feet moving so fast that a dust cloud reached his knees. She thought of her friends in Manhattan, of Marianne and Catherine and Luisa, whether any of them could watch this and see it for what it was, or if training and habit would blind them.

When she could resist not one moment longer, Martha turned to watch Daniel.

He wore his hair cropped short, but now a few damp curls fell forward over his brow. His whole face was streaked with sweat. His expression was not joyful; Martha didn't know what she saw there, beyond deep concentration. At this moment it seemed his whole world was drum and rattle, and so for once she could watch him and he wouldn't catch her at it.

All the Bonner men were big, so tall that finding one of them in a crowd was no difficulty. As tall as Daniel was, his younger brother was an inch or two bigger still, as was Blue-Jay. Both Gabriel and Blue-Jay were woodsmen, heavily muscled in chest and shoulder, back and leg. Daniel spent most of his day in the classroom, but it was hard to see any evidence of that. He was long and lithe and powerful in the way of the big cats who hunted in the forests.

His left arm was back in its sling. Martha forced herself to look at it directly. There was a lack of symmetry, certainly. The muscles of his good arm were more developed, but the left side was not withered, as she had expected. Martha realized how little she really knew about the nature of the injury.

Hannah had come to sit down beside her. She said, "You know he was in the militia in the last war?"

Martha nodded but didn't look at Hannah. "Of course. Under Magistrate Bookman."

For a while it seemed as if Hannah would say nothing more, but then what came next was as fluid as it was detailed.

"There is a spot in the shoulder where many nerves come together. That bundle of nerves is protected by muscle and by the collarbone. It's very hard to reach on a healthy person, though I have known men who could do it. Dig in hard with two fingers to compress the nerves at the juncture, I mean. It's a pain that can't really be described. I think probably only a severe burn is worse."

"And that's what Daniel lives with?"

"It isn't as bad as it once was, but I can't tell you why. Whether the nerves are healing with time, or if he has just learned to shut it out of his mind, at least some of the time. Such things are possible."

"How do you know the pain is less than it was?" Martha asked. "Does he talk of that?"

"No," Hannah said. "He doesn't need to. For the first year he wasn't able to do much of anything, the pain was so crippling. But you see him now, able to go about his life and do most things. Most of the time," she added.

"The pain comes and goes?"

She lifted her own shoulder in a shrug. "When he disappears for a day or two without warning, it means the pain has got the upper hand. It doesn't happen often. He has learned to protect the arm and shoulder and not to overextend himself."

Runs-from-Bears had begun to chant, and the men were answering.

"Might it continue to get better?" Martha asked, and this time Hannah turned toward her sharply.

"He is what he is," she said. "If by some magic the damage was healed instantly, it would be very hard, maybe impossible, to bring the left arm up to strength. He knows that, and because he knows he flatly refuses to see surgeons who might be able to help at least ease the pain. There has only been one exception, something an old teacher of mine sent to try. A treatment that comes from China."

"But it didn't work," Martha concluded for her.

Hannah looked at her, surprised. "That is yet to be seen. We haven't tried it yet." She stood. "The last dance," she said. "You'll need your shawl."

"Watch me," Annie told Martha. "It's not hard."

There was something new here, something about this last dance that was different, but no one seemed to think it necessary to explain it to her. But to retreat now would be silly, and more than that, Martha didn't want to.

The water drum started up. They danced in two lines, men and women facing each other, half on one side of the water drum and half on the other. The pace was easy at first as they moved forward and then back, but soon enough the tempo began to increase with each pass. Someone let out a high yipping cry—Gabriel, Martha saw from the corner of her eye—as the women swept in a circle around the man opposite, shawls held in outstretched hands to give them wings.

Her shawl brushed against Daniel and then she was gone again, turning in time with the others. Breathless, she danced in place as the men came forward. Daniel's gaze was on her face, but there was nothing frightening there. He was enjoying himself; he liked the dance. And this was nothing more than that, an evening's entertainment in this circle of light and sound. To step outside that circle into the cold seemed an impossible thing, though her face and neck and back were damp with sweat. All of her body was damp, so that the sweep of the shawl as she turned brought a welcome relief.

In some part of her mind she tried to recall the last time she had danced, and while the details came to her easily enough—her gloved hand on Teddy's arm, the brush of silk skirts against delicate slippers— she could not see her own face, or remember what she had been feeling.

But this, this she would never forget. She knew that as they swept forward for the last time, shawls held high and wide and pausing for a moment, for no more than a moment, while she looked into Daniel's eyes and saw the question there before she revolved and lowered her arms to let her shawl fall onto his shoulders.

In the sudden echoing quiet all Martha could hear was the rush of her own harsh breath and the thump of her heart at the base of her throat. She could not have moved; she might have forgotten how to walk, but Daniel's hand touched her elbow and steered her toward the house. There was a lot of quiet talk but little laughter. Somehow the mood had shifted. She wanted to know what was coming, but she didn't want to know, not really.

The men carried the benches into the house and after some moving and shifting, the whole party was sitting in a half circle before the hearth. The great room was very warm now and Martha was glad of it. She was glad too that Daniel was sitting beside her, but his quiet disconcerted

her. He might be in pain, if she had understood Hannah correctly. That
he wouldn't want to be asked, she knew even without being told.

He sat straight of back, his good hand rested on a knee. Martha could
feel the heat coming off his skin. He smelled of healthy sweat and wood
smoke. Suddenly his face turned to her and smiled as if he had just remembered who she was and why she was sitting here at all.

"Storytelling," he said. And just at that moment Runs-from-Bears
stood, a big man unfolding to his full height.

Daniel inclined his head toward her and translated.

"It's a prayer. 'Great Spirit who gave us the darkness in which to rest.
In that darkness we send our words to you.'"

Runs-from-Bears turned and cast tobacco into the fire and the smell
filled the air. Then he started to talk again.

"It's an old story," Daniel said. "How a raiding party came to Hidden
Wolf. When He-Who-Remembers claimed both the Todd boys to replace the sons he had lost in battle."

Martha had heard bits of this story over the years, many fancifully
embroidered. Now she learned about how children were adopted into a
longhouse, of training as a warrior and going into battles.

One story led to another.

They all took turns. Ben told of the journey from New Orleans to
Paradise, where he had made his home with Hannah. Luke spoke of his
grandmother Iona, and Gabriel of the first bear he killed on Hidden
Wolf. Blue-Jay told a story Martha knew, about a time two great hogs
had got stuck under the schoolhouse floor. The stories, long or short,
were well told and the small audience was receptive. Martha wondered
if Daniel would take a turn, but after a longer pause Jennet got up and
told the story of how she left her home in Scotland to come and claim
Luke as her husband.

"Fine and good," said her good-sister Hannah. "But what of the fairy
tree?"

"I've had my turn," Jennet said. "What of Susanna?"

All heads turned to the young woman who sat beside Blue-Jay with
her hands folded in her lap. She had a pretty smile, but she seemed reluctant. Martha could understand that very well. It had just occurred to her
that she might be called on too.

"I've got another idea," said Susanna. "I will sing for thee."

Later Martha would remember the singing as her favorite part of the evening. It started slowly, but then one song led to another and everyone joined in. Sometimes Hannah or Susanna sang harmony, and sometimes all voices fell away to leave someone singing alone for a moment.

Beside her Daniel was as enthusiastic as all the rest of them. He had a steady, strong baritone that could be heard clearly among the other voices. It pleased Martha greatly, and it came to her that she had missed this kind of music. In the city there had been recitals and concerts and dozens of young ladies eager to show off their skills at the pianoforte, but rarely had anyone sung like this. Just for the joy of it.

She had no intention of singing herself, though she had a good voice. An excellent voice, her music teacher had told her more than once, and how sad that she chose not to use it. While other young ladies got up to sing after dinner, Martha only listened politely and tried not to notice the dropped notes and sour turns.

Jemima had a good voice, and so Martha preferred to pretend that she did not.

And then suddenly it was over. Susanna was directing people to beds and pallets, and Gabriel and Annie were at the door, saying good night. Runs-from-Bears and the visitors from Good Pasture had already gone.

"You'll be comfortable here," Daniel was saying.

Martha couldn't hide her surprise. "You're leaving?"

"It's the hayloft or the road for me," he said, smiling. "I prefer my own bed, and it's not so far."

For a moment she wasn't sure what to say. The thought foremost in her mind—that she didn't want him to go—that could not be spoken aloud. Or the next thought, that she would rather go back to her own little house than stay here without him—

"I'm away home," said John Mayfair. "I can see Martha back to the village, if she'd rather go."

There was a silence that lasted two heartbeats. In that time Martha saw something come over Daniel's face, irritation followed by—jealousy? That seemed unlikely, but whatever was there, at least John understood. He stepped back. "But then I have to go now, and that may not suit thee—"

Many pairs of eyes were on Martha as John Mayfair took his leave.

Then Hannah said, "You could just mark your territory the way the wolves do, brother."

There was a burp of laughter that swelled into something much bigger.

Daniel laughed too, embarrassed now, which suited him far better than surly jealousy.

"I can take you into the village," Daniel said. "We have to talk about school on Monday; we could get that out of the way."

"It'll be dawn before you get back to the strawberry fields," Ben said.

"I'm a good walker," Martha said, and with that the matter was settled.

He knew the mountain. He knew every trail on the mountain, and a dozen ways to get from Lake in the Clouds to his own homestead. Even going the fastest way it would take close to an hour to get Martha to her own front door, and by that time it would be light enough that somebody would see them. The sensible thing would be to take the most direct route, along the ridge and down.

Daniel turned the opposite direction, and within a couple minutes they were deep in the forest.

Martha went along willingly enough, yawning now and then until they had worked up a good pace. Twenty minutes of hard walking without hesitating; more proof that she was at home here. That she belonged.

He stopped to check on her. It was very dark, but Daniel could still see the shape of Martha's face quite clearly, and it was tilted up toward him.

"You worried about getting lost?"

"Of course not," she said. Not in a talkative mood, probably regretting passing up the warm spot in front of Susanna's hearth.

"Did you like the party?"

She glanced up, surprised or maybe just plain suspicious that he would be making small talk right here and now. Daniel didn't understand it himself.

"Yes," she said. "I did. Thank you." And: "Where exactly are we? For all I know I could be walking over a cliff face." Her tone was pricklish.

He said, "I've got that feeling myself."

Another hour, at least, and Martha's energy began to flag. It would be light soon and that would mean a whole twenty-four hours without real sleep. She had no regrets, she told herself. Not even this long hike through the forest in the dead of night.

When the trail got steep and muddy Daniel reached back to take her hand. They might have been sister and brother, Martha thought as he led her along the trail. His hand was hard and warm and his grip no-nonsense, and wasn't she a foolish twit for wanting something else? What exactly was she hoping for? He had already kissed her—kissed her twice—and that was supposed to be enough for any girl of good family. More than enough. The thing was, and she could admit this to herself at least, that she had once thought she didn't like kissing. Teddy's kisses hadn't suited her at all, dry and rough and hard, but Daniel went about it in a whole different way.

He was saying "Watch your step," but too late, she had already lost her footing. He caught her up before she could hit the ground and set her back on her feet.

"We seem to do this a lot," he said. He was smiling; she could hear it.

"I am normally quite graceful." And, "What I mean is, I usually am able to stay on my feet."

"I knock you off balance."

She stiffened, but managed to count to three. "If you prefer to think of it that way."

That made him laugh out loud.

She scowled to herself. "Where are we now?"

He put a hand on her shoulder and turned her to face away from himself. "North." Another gentle push. "West." And another, so that she was directly facing him. "South."

Martha realized it was light enough now to see his shape. "Five minutes at this pace and we're at the strawberry fields. Or that way"—he turned—"and we'll be in the village in twenty. But it's steep."

"It's almost a sheer drop," Martha said. "I grew up on this mountain too, remember. I thought you wanted to see the sunrise. Which way is that?"

"East," he said, and her hand came up of its own volition and pushed him.

"All right." He laughed. "All right. That way."

"You said that was the trail to the strawberry fields. Or is it Eagle Rock you're thinking of?"

———

Daniel saw the idea come to her, too late.

Of course she would jump to the conclusion that he was taking her to Eagle Rock. He cursed himself for his lack of foresight because he was very sure of one thing: He would not take Martha Kirby there. Not now, not ever, if he could help it. Eagle Rock would always make him think of Jemima on a hot summer's day when he and Lily had been Birdie's age. Jemima with her clothes pulled open and splotches of color on her exposed breasts, and the smell of sex on her, as pungent as tar. Liam Kirby had slipped away, but Daniel had seen him too, the copper flash of his hair in the sun. His daughter's hair was a deeper color, but it flashed too when the sun touched it.

She took a step back as if she feared him suddenly.

"Did I say something wrong?"

"No," Daniel said. "Nothing at all. But there's not time enough to get to Eagle Rock."

He leaned forward and kissed her, a fleeting kiss meant to reassure, but the curve of her lower lip fit exactly between his, and what was there to do but kiss her properly? Pull her up against him and kiss her like he meant it. Because he did. God help him, he was completely besotted.

For the smallest part of a second she was stiff, and then she relaxed against him and a little sound came up out of her throat, surprise and pleasure. Whatever she had been doing with that idiot of a fiancé, this was new to her, and she liked being kissed as much as Daniel liked kissing her.

When he let her go they were both gasping. She pressed the fingers of one hand to her mouth, her eyes wide with surprise, but nothing of unhappiness there. The beginning of a smile, more like.

"The sunrise from my front porch," he said. "We can still get there in time if we hurry."

Now she was smiling, but still trying to hide it. She managed a nod. Daniel took her hand and set off for home.

In the first faint wash of light they passed through stands of beech and ash, witch hobble and ferns just beginning to curl up out of the earth, and came then to the stream that separated the woods from the meadow.

Daniel crossed it in three steps almost without looking, and Martha followed his path from rock to rock, her skirts firmly in hand. She was determined to stay on her feet. Such focused attention had another benefit: She had no time to ask questions of herself, or answer them either.

The meadow was just coming to life, clumps of new-growth grass rising up to remind her of a badly shaved chin. Somewhere nearby a frog was singing to itself. Among the tumble of rocks thick with moss, she caught sight of the first trillium and Solomon's seal shoots, violets and jack-in-the-pulpit. In a matter of days the woods and fields would be full of spring flowers, and there would be livestock grazing in the strawberry fields, the Bonners' horses and Curiosity's goats and cows. One of Curiosity's grandsons would have the job of driving them back and forth from pasture to town and watching the flock during the day. You couldn't leave animals on the mountain unattended unless you meant to provide for every wildcat, bear, and wolf. Martha realized that she was babbling to herself, and that she was so nervous—so excited—that her hands were trembling.

"Here," Daniel said. Martha looked up and realized they had come to his place. A small homestead like an island in the meadow. Not made of split logs but framed and shingled, a house that would not look out of place in Johnstown. There was a covered porch along the side that faced the valley. "No dogs?" The Bonners always had dogs, smart and well trained.

"Bounder died," Daniel said. "The day of the flood I buried him under that beech sapling. I'll be looking for a pup soon." He opened the door and stood aside to let her pass, but Martha pretended she didn't see. She sat down quite deliberately in one of the two chairs on the porch. He laughed softly and went in without her.

"We can't see the sunrise from inside," she called.

He was back in a moment with an armful of blankets.

"It's cold sitting still. Take a couple of these."

And so they sat, side by side, wrapped in blankets and watched the sun's light first seep and then pour over the horizon, bringing color back into the world. Shades of gray gave way to every kind of green. The moon, still visible, rested on the long spine of the mountain called Walking Wolf.

"It's so—pretty is too small a word," Martha said. "I don't think there are words to describe this."

He smiled at her. There were lines at the corners of his eyes, the green of the forest in high summer. His hair was still a shambles, determined to curl though it lacked any length. He had his mother's hair and much of her expression, but otherwise he was Nathaniel Bonner's son through and through. Not just his face and build, but the very way he held himself when he was at rest. He was the picture of good health, but for the left arm in its sling, tight against his chest.

She said, "Are you in pain?"

It wasn't a subject she had meant to raise, but the question was there between them and couldn't be ignored. He looked away for a moment and then back. The muscles along the line of his jaw clenched and then relaxed.

"I'm sorry," she said. "It was a rude question."

"Not rude," he said. "Took me by surprise, though. My mind was someplace else entirely." He leaned forward until their noses were almost touching. "Just about right here."

He was smiling. A slow smile, but cheeky.

"You are very sure of yourself. Or me."

"Is that so?" His breath touched her face. He had been chewing on something, some herb that made his breath sweet. "You saying I'm mistaken about what's happening between us two?"

Martha considered herself braver than most girls her age, but now her hands were trembling so that she had to fold them together. This was the last thing she expected when she came home to Paradise. It had happened so fast, but there was no denying it.

And he smelled so good. He smelled of evergreen and wood smoke and herbs, and of something else; maybe it was only himself, his own smell.

"That what you're saying?"

"No—"

He leaned forward just that last inch, inclined his head, and caught her mouth before she could finish her thought. It was a tentative kiss, one that came with a question. She let herself be drawn in and he broke away for the smallest moment to look at her, his composure intact, but his breath coming faster.

Martha reached out and touched his hand with her own and in response he brought it up to cradle her head and pull her back to him. Then everything was gone but the kiss, deep and true. His tongue touched hers and a shudder ran down her spine. Martha heard herself make a sound and she saw that it had pleased him. He smiled against her mouth and then drew her back down into the kiss.

At some point—when she couldn't say—that same hand had come around to cup her throat and then it moved to her shoulder. Fingers trailed down, tracing the curve of her breast. She caught it and held herself away.

He raised a brow.

"What *is* happening between us?" It came out in a coarse whisper.

The question distracted him enough to make him sit back. It was full light now and as far as she could see, trees were lit up like candles at the first touch of the sun. Her heart was pounding, for fear of what he was going to say.

He leaned forward and touched his forehead to hers.

"Why don't we just get married?"

It sounded like a question, but his expression made it more of a challenge.

Panic flowed through her, and worse still, she could see that he knew what she was feeling. He saw it, but what did he make of it? Disappointment? Anger? Amusement?

She sat back and folded her hands together in her lap, as tight as she could.

"Um, I thought you wanted to talk to me about teaching."

Daniel grinned, clearly pleased to have flustered her so completely. "Will you help out at the school until the end of term?"

She nodded, because she didn't trust her voice. There was a tic at the corner of her mouth, a smile that wanted to show itself. Which was utterly ridiculous; this wasn't a game they were playing.

"That's settled then. Now what about getting married?"

She expelled a sharp breath. "You're serious."

"I am serious. And if you're honest with yourself, you'll recognize it's right. You can feel it in your gut, I know you can."

She took his hand in her sincere wish to be heard. "Daniel Bonner, we hardly know each other."

He gripped the hand she had given him and his thumb moved across her wrist in a motion so light and so shocking that she jerked, as though he had stuck her with a hidden pin.

He said, "How well did you know your Teddy?"

Annoyed, Martha turned her head away. "Don't call him that. Don't call him my Teddy. And the obvious answer is, I didn't know him as well as I thought I did."

Daniel was not in the least put out by her irritation, and was that not impolite? Though some small voice pointed out how refreshing it was to be able to say what she thought without worrying about it being wrong somehow. She wondered what it would take to make Daniel Bonner angry, or to turn him away. A question she had never asked herself about Teddy, but she had found out the answer anyway.

He was saying, "Do you think I'm after your money?"

"No!"

Martha got up and walked to the end of the porch. She should be collapsing with weariness, but every nerve was tingling. A breeze had come up and with it, the smell of things greening. Birds darted in and out of shadow, small flags fluttering under the canopy of trees where the evergreen branches were tipped with new color. The light irritated her eyes. Martha squinted and wished for the handkerchief she must have left behind at Lake in the Clouds. She was not near tears, she told herself sternly. In no way or manner was she about to weep. No matter how confusing and shocking this sudden proposal, no matter how—thrilling.

Daniel Bonner wanted to marry her.

Something bright had blossomed in her as he said the words, an excitement and pleasure she couldn't remember ever feeling before, though surely she must have, when Teddy proposed. What had been in her mind then? How had she felt? Relieved, certainly. But otherwise she had no memory beyond the fact that he had a smudge on his cheek, one she wanted to tell him about but certainly could not, not in the middle of his very formal, almost—

"Still got Teddy on your mind?"

She jumped. He was directly behind her. Martha shook her head and then turned and gave him a reluctant nod. "It is hard not to think of him—" her voice trailed away.

"I reckon his proposal was a lot fancier," Daniel said flatly.

"Oh Daniel." She put her forehead on his chest and his arm came up around her. "It was very awkward, to tell the truth. He meant to sound sophisticated but he—" She stopped, searching for a word that wouldn't sound cruel.

"He's a boy," Daniel said. "I'm not."

She lifted her head and put her chin where her forehead had been. "I know that. I know."

He smiled at her then. A small, knowing smile that made the knot in her chest draw tighter. When he kissed her there was some hesitation, as if he expected to be rebuffed. If he only knew what he made her feel, that was the last thing he need worry about. The very thought made her flush, and at that moment his tongue touched hers, a tentative brushing that raised gooseflesh along her arms and back. She opened her mouth to him on a sigh, and he pulled her up tighter against him. A kiss that spun out of all imagining and experience. His cheeks were rough with beard but she hardly noticed, the recklessness of the kiss was too overwhelming. She felt it everywhere. Everywhere.

"Come inside," he whispered. "Come."

Oh, she wanted to. She wanted nothing more, but there were other considerations, things she could barely admit to herself.

"What?" His expression was puzzled.

"I don't want people to think of me as they did of my mother." There. It came out that simply. She heard herself going on, a little breathless. "She was—immoderate. She was—" Words failed her, as they must. How could she speak of something she barely understood?

But Daniel knew. He swung around to half sit on the rail and pulled her to him. This way they were face-to-face and so there was no way to hide what she was thinking.

"Jemima used whatever tools she had to hand to get what she wanted," Daniel said. "To get what she thought she needed. Is that why you're here with me?"

She shook her head.

"Nobody could confuse you with Jemima. Nobody with a brain. Nobody with an ounce of fairness in them."

Now tears did rise and threaten to fall. She blinked them back. "But there will be people like that. Thoughtless and cruel. I don't want to give them anything to hold against me. Against us." The last came in a whisper, but it made him smile.

"Is that an answer I'm hearing?"

Talk was terribly overrated in these situations, Martha told herself. She kissed him and he smiled against her mouth.

"I'll have an answer," he said.

She nodded. "Yes. Yes."

His smile grew broader. "A proper answer. A full sentence. 'Yes, Daniel Bonner, my love, my life, I will marry you and gladly.'"

She opened her mouth to protest and he kissed her. Thoroughly. His hand moved over the line of her hip and down, rested flat on the curve where leg met hip.

Martha felt herself beginning to unravel.

He broke the kiss. "You can say it here, or you can say it inside." He rocked her toward him with his hand spread over her bottom. Nerves jumped and kicked.

"Yes," she said. For the third time.

Inside he pressed her against the closed door and kissed her there in the dim empty room. With one hand holding her face he kissed her until something came awake in her, a need she hadn't known about. But he had underestimated her, or overestimated his powers of persuasion, because she pushed him away with a hand against his good shoulder.

"Wait," she said breathlessly. "Wait. I have to say something. I have to ask you a question."

It took a moment to master himself, but then Daniel nodded. He tried to focus on her eyes, though his gaze was drawn to the curve of her lip. Her lower lip, full and plump as a berry.

She said, "Jemima is going to show up here, you know that."

The hem of her skirt was already in his fist, and he let it go.

"Let her come," he said. "She don't worry me."

"She'll be your mother-in-law."

"You'll be my wife; that's the important thing."

She held him off, still. "Daniel, you need to think this through. What it means."

"She's nothing but a bully," Daniel said. He was leaning over her with his hand stemmed against the wall. He bent his elbow and came in closer. "I never could abide a bully."

Martha curled her hands in his shirtfront and pulled his face down to hers. "People will talk, you know."

"They do that anyway. Might as well make it worth their while."

He ducked his head but she held him away to examine his expression. "They'll say it's too fast. And maybe it is."

"I'm not an impetuous man," he said. His tone was patient. "I could have got married ten times over these last years, but I was waiting for you."

Her mouth dropped open in surprise. "You were not."

"I was," he said. "I just didn't know it 'til I walked into my mother's kitchen and saw you standing there." He gave her an intense look, just edged with playfulness. "Now, if you're trying to say you don't want me—"

Martha went up on tiptoe and kissed him, or tried to. Daniel turned, his head cocked at an angle at the sound of voices.

He said, "That's my sister and brother and the rest of them on the way home."

They stood there against the door for five minutes and then another five, listening as the others passed. The talk was far more subdued this morning than it had been last night, but that would have mostly to do with lack of sleep. Daniel waited for one of them—Hannah or Jennet, most likely—to call out a hello. Or Ben or Ethan might just come and open the door, see if he was back from the village. Ask if he had done any swimming this morning and did Martha get home all right? With a grin and a nod. Nothing mean about it, all good-natured.

The truth was, he didn't care to talk to anybody just now, no matter how well-meaning. They were just about to settle some things, he and Martha, and they didn't need any interruptions. With luck this was something a man only did once in his life, and he wanted to do it right. Now that he had made the decision.

Just exactly when that had happened, he couldn't say. The moment she settled the shawl around his shoulders at the end of the last dance, right then it was clear to him he had known for days what he wanted. He'd marry Martha Kirby as soon as she'd have him, and count himself lucky. She was one of the strong ones, though she didn't seem to realize it herself.

Women on the edge of the endless forests grew up tough or they didn't last long. A steady stream of girls left Paradise for Johnstown and Albany and beyond. They took jobs as servants and cooks, nurses and seamstresses, married and settled, and never came home again.

Some who shouldn't have stayed did, and turned mean. Martha's mother was a prime example, as people kept reminding him. As his sister Lily kept reminding him. She would take this hard, but Simon was there to talk sense to her. In the end Martha herself would need to win Lily over, but that would happen. He didn't doubt it for a minute.

There was something whole about Martha, something solid that he had never known in women outside his own family, and that was something even Lily couldn't ignore. It was a fine thing and a rare one and she couldn't begrudge him. It was true it had happened fast, but he argued with himself as he would with Lily: He was old enough to know his own mind. And then the voice that came to him wasn't Lily's or even his mother's, but Curiosity's. Telling him he might know his own mind, but did Martha know hers? Or was he sweet-talking her into something she wan't ready for? She was a rarity, all right, and she would suit him just fine. But why the hurry?

That was a question he would be asked by Curiosity and his mother and every other woman he knew. Why the hurry?

He closed his eyes and reached for an answer, but all he got was Martha, the smell of her. He had the urge to put his face to the line of her neck and pull in her scent until it filled his lungs, but she was already anxious, breathing shallow and quick. When he looked he saw that she had turned her head hard to the side, listening still for voices. He studied her profile in the half-light from the one open shutter and saw how high her color was. Her upper lip and her forehead were damp, and as he watched a single drop of sweat moved from her hairline to travel down her temple, though the room was cold.

Where the light touched her hair, the rich dark color sparked a deep copper. Her skin was milky, the faintest blush of color high on her cheekbones and at her earlobes. Like sugar candy that would taste of strawberries.

She gasped when his lips touched her neck and then again, a small sharp intake of breath when he reached her earlobe. Now she would push him away, walk away and stare at him from across the room, accusing him and rightly. Instead she turned her head sharply and their mouths met. Something gave way, some last bit of barrier between them. She was so close that he could feel the shape of her legs against his own, the curve of hip and breast. He was aroused beyond all experience, but he made himself stop. To remind himself what she was owed. What was right and reasonable. Of his mother's infernal categorical imperative.

Think for a moment. Think if everyone were to handle this kind of situation and act as you are acting now.

Martha was very still, but for the triple beat of the pulse at her temple. "What is it?"

"I've been standing here reading myself a sermon," he said finally. "Am I trying to take you someplace you don't want to go?"

Her eyes widened. "And where would that be, exactly?" The grin surprised him. A little uncertain but a grin nonetheless. Whatever she was feeling, it hadn't robbed her of her wits.

Daniel found that he was grinning back at her. "You want me to say it plain?" He ducked and nipped at her earlobe.

She wiggled and she was gone, on the other side of the room with her arms wrapped around herself, almost rocking on her heels. Ready to run a race.

"Don't smile like that," she said. "It's too early to congratulate yourself."

Daniel began to cross the room at a casual pace that fooled neither of them. But she held her ground until he was in front of her, looking up as if there was something written across his face in bold letters.

She said, "There's too much to think about. It's too complicated."

So the play was over for the moment. Daniel took her by the hand to the settle that stood at right angles to the hearth, and when they were seated he took a deep breath.

"It ain't complicated. People get married every day with no fuss at all. Unless you were wanting a big party and a new dress and all that. Is that it?"

Martha studied the hands folded in her lap. "No," she said. "I've been through all that and I didn't like it the first time. But there are things to be settled, Daniel. If you'll only stop and think. Where are we to live? Here? In the village? Some other place? And forgive me for raising this subject, but all my property will pass to you as my—my husband."

"I don't care about that," he said. He was hot now, a churning in his gut. It was something he hadn't wanted to think about, but she was right.

"People will care," she said. "People will say—"

He took her hand and squeezed it hard. "But I don't care," he repeated slowly. "We'll go to a lawyer and see about getting papers drawn up, so you can keep what's yours. Signed and witnessed. Let people talk then, we'll know the truth."

"Will that be enough to convince your sister?"

"She didn't ask my permission when she married," Daniel said, more calmly now. This, at least, he had thought through. "If she had, I wouldn't have given it. And I'd have been wrong. Simon is right for her. Can you leave my sister to me?"

Martha's gaze was steady. After a moment she nodded. "Yes, I think I can. I mean to. But there's still the question of Callie."

It was as if she had spoken a name completely unfamiliar to him, so confused was his expression.

"Callie? What about her?"

"She came to me—why, it was only yesterday," Martha said. "She was very agitated, and she said some things—I wouldn't care to repeat them. But she predicted this." She lifted their clasped hands and let them fall.

His brow rose. "She did?"

"She said we'd be married before the summer was out. And she was so angry, Daniel. She said it was about the house, about the idea that she and I would build a house and live together there, but I wonder now if she isn't in love with you after all."

If he was feigning surprise he was a very good actor.

"Callie Wilde is not in love with me."

"I don't want her to be hurt," Martha said.

"Nor do I," Daniel said. "But this is between you and me and nobody else."

There was something so focused and knowing in the way he looked at her that gooseflesh rose along Martha's spine in one long unfurling.

"We will make our lives in this village," Martha said. "We can't pretend it doesn't matter, what others think."

"If I was a suspicious man," he said, his voice low and sweet, "I'd wonder if you had your eye on somebody else. John Mayfair, maybe."

She straightened. "Don't be silly. I met him for the first time yesterday evening. It would take a great deal more than that to make me fall in love with him. Another evening, at least."

His fingers curled into her waist and she shrieked with laughter and tried to pull away, but he had her where he wanted her. And, Martha admitted to herself as his hand moved to her breast and his mouth covered her own, she wouldn't want to be anywhere else.

———

She had never swooned in her life, but a half hour later Martha thought she understood what it must be like. She was a stranger to herself, so given over to feeling that even simple language eluded her. Daniel wasn't having that problem. Between long, deep kisses he talked to her in a low whisper, his voice muffled against the skin. The words themselves searing into flesh.

In the village he was known to be quiet, even severe, but the things he said to her were extravagant, opulent, full of images of herself, as he saw her. The color of her skin, the taste of it at the hollow of her throat. The shape of her lip and earlobe, the smell of her hair just behind her ear.

Her breasts. Somehow they had come so far. Somehow it had seemed imperative, and she had helped. In a frenzy to know the feel of his touch exactly there. And then the reality of it, his open palm moving over puckered flesh in a soft circle until she gasped and twisted, unable to get close enough. Wanting more. Wanting everything. He whispered to her, smiled against her mouth, touched her tongue with his own. His hand cupping her face while his beard scratched her throat and then the shock of his mouth closing over her nipple. Her body jerking in response to that slow suckling, as if he had taken her already. As if he had climbed inside her.

Daniel was the one to pull away. The cool air on her wet breast made her shiver; his absence was so absolute that she could hardly fathom it. He slid to the far end of the settle, breathing as though he had never tasted air before.

"What?" her voice creaked and wobbled.

"We could be married tomorrow," he said.

"There's the school to open tomorrow." She shocked herself, and yet she couldn't deny what she was feeling, and that was simple: She wanted more.

"Then by the end of the week," he said. His eyes were wide open. Deep-set eyes the color of ivy, something in the expression: shock, or disgust? It struck her then, the truth.

"I've shocked you," she said. "I'm—immoderate."

His smile was completely unexpected, and then he laughed.

Martha turned away, sudden tears spilling over as she tried to put herself to rights.

"Martha."

"How dare you, how dare you laugh at me." The sob came up like a stone.

"I am not laughing at you." He took her arm. She tried to pull away but she was already up against his chest, her tears seeping into his open shirt. The crisp dark hair against her cheek and the beat of his heart, these things robbed her of the urge to pull away.

"I am not laughing." He said it again. "I'm happy. Martha. I'm happy. And let me make one thing clear to you, right now so there's no mistake. There's no such thing as immoderate, not between the two of us. You could never be too eager. I'll prove it to you, when the time is right."

After a moment she nodded, and then she pulled away gently and went back to trying to make some semblance of order out of her clothing. He was waiting for her to say something, but everything that came to mind was monstrously unladylike. She drew in a shuddering breath and stood.

"I need to tell you the rest of the story. About Teddy and his mother." She made herself meet his eye, because this must be done and be done properly, if they were really to continue as they had started.

He nodded, his expression neutral. "Go on, then."

"I haven't been able to talk to anybody about this," she said. "But I think you should know."

"You trying to scare me off?"

"Yes," she said.

"Go on, then," Daniel said with a calm smile.

She tried to put the story together in some rational order. Mrs. Peyton's parlor, the heavy velvet and damask draperies always drawn to protect the furniture. Mrs. Peyton herself, still in mourning though her husband was six years gone. Her mouth pressed and pursed until it was ringed with a rigid white line, her whole frame trembling with anger.

The words she had used. Wanton. Unworthy. A look of hatred so plain it must have been very close to the surface all the time Martha had known her. The many kind things she had said and done—it seemed none of that had been sincere.

I hope you are not breeding, my girl. If you are, my son will not own you or it. The wages of sin will be yours alone to bear.

She stood up for herself, because Teddy did not. Standing in a shadowy corner, bent forward as if to study the pattern in the carpet, he said nothing.

I have never allowed your son such liberties. She said it firmly, and promised herself that she would not cry or faint or show these people anything but calm. Mrs. Peyton had pushed her to the limit of her endurance.

Liar, she called her. And worse. Far worse.

But Martha held her ground. Swallowed down her own outrage and anger and terrible sadness and held her head high.

Martha told Daniel all of it, sitting just far enough away that he wouldn't touch her. All the noxious memories of that last interview came pouring out of her.

Like mother, like daughter. And: *No wonder you pretend that she doesn't exist. No wonder you lie with so little effort.*

"But I didn't," Martha told Daniel. "I've never been able to tell a lie. Not because I'm an especially good person. I simply have no talent for it."

While Mrs. Peyton talked Martha kept her gaze fixed on the hall table heaped with wedding presents, all topped by a silver bowl overflowing with calling cards and notes. The wedding of the season.

She finished. "She called me *degenerate.*"

That word had struck harder than anything that came before, because it was not new to her. It was the word she had chosen, after many years of careful thought, to assign to her mother. And Mrs. Peyton hung it around Martha's own neck, tied it with knots that might never be undone.

Daniel was shaking his head. "No," he said. His tone calm and sure. "That word does not apply to you."

"How can you know?" She wiped her wet cheeks with the back of her hand. "Wasn't this—". She gestured at the settle with its flattened cushions. "Doesn't this prove her point?"

He took her chin between his fingers and tipped her face up to him. "It's a gift you give to me," he said.

"One you don't want?"

"Of course I want it. I want you. But I've pushed this hard. Maybe I've just overwhelmed you. Maybe tomorrow you'd wake up and know you made a mistake. I wanted to give you time to think it through before we—before we took this last step."

"Is that what it is?" Martha drew in a deep breath. "Is that what you call it, a last step?"

His eyes scanned her face, and then he lowered his head and kissed her. "And the first too. You have to know, Martha. I'm not one to jump to conclusions. I know my mind, and I know that I want you more than I want anything else in this life." He drew in a sharp breath.

"Except for the use of your arm," she said. "You can say that. You must be thinking it. Anyone would."

"Except," he said slowly, "for the use of my arm. That's something else we need to talk about. But not right now."

Right now he used his good arm to bring her up against him, and Martha went gladly.

$\mathscr{B}$irdie was up first on Sunday morning, even before her father. She dressed as quietly as she could and made her way downstairs into the silent kitchen, where she got right to work.

She brought in water, stirred the fire in the hearth and got a good blaze going, cut what was left of yesterday's bread, and fetched butter and the last of last summer's plum preserves from the cellar. When her father came downstairs the table was set and Birdie was just setting out a platter of cold bacon and cheese.

He didn't look particularly surprised to see her. Late last night he would have heard Curiosity's story from Ma, and he was quicker than most men when it came to figuring out moods.

"I want to go down to the village so I'll be there when Hannah and the others come over the bridge," she said. "I've done all my chores. I would have started the porridge too, but I can't reach the big kettle. Can I go?"

Her da could look right through her, it seemed to Birdie. After a minute he said, "No farther than the bridge."

Which was all the permission she needed. Before Ma or the little people could appear and spoil her plan, Birdie flew out the door. She held her breath as she passed the Downhill House, for fear that she would be seen and hailed. Before she talked to anybody about last night, she needed to talk to Hannah.

Hannah was the one most likely to understand the dreams that had plagued her. Somehow Curiosity's story had got all tangled up with the flood and other things and Birdie just didn't know what to make of any of it. In some things Hannah was far more Kahnyen'kehàka than white, and reading dreams was one of them. She would take Birdie's worries seriously.

As would her mother, of course. But she wasn't ready to talk to Ma yet.

She was glad to be outside so early. The growing weather had settled in and the morning was very clear, so bright that it seemed as if she could see each pine needle and budding leaf. She did mean to ask Lily if there were names for all the different greens in the world. To Birdie it seemed impossible but somehow necessary. Without names it was very hard to recall the exact shade of the new leaves on the sugar maple, something she wanted to be able to do, though she couldn't say why.

Birdie found a spot on an outcropping of rock where she could warm herself in the sun and see into the village as far as the bridge. As soon as she caught sight of the others she'd run to meet them, take Hannah's hand, and pull her aside so they could talk the rest of the way home. Before she was overrun by little people who would be as happy to see her as Birdie was.

It was so good to be warm like this that she felt herself slipping away into sleep more than once, and then had to get up and run in place. A walk up the mountain would keep her awake, but Da had said she mustn't, and so Birdie turned her back on the bridge and focused on the pastures and fields. Friend Blackhouse was crossing the Rountree's pasture on the far side, carrying a rake over one shoulder and a pannier on his back. He was wearing a wide-rimmed straw hat against the sun, but it was Arthur Blackhouse; Birdie could tell just about anybody by the way they walked. Just the same way a person could name a bird, by the way it moved itself through the air. Shapes within shapes.

The planting would begin just as soon as there was no more chance of a frost at night. The best thing about this time of year was the smell of sunshine on newly turned earth.

The faint sound of horses coming toward town on the Johnstown road came to her. More than one horse, and the rumble of wheels. The only people who were away that Birdie knew about were Praise-Be Cunningham, who had gone to buy some lambs, and the Magistrate, who had taken off for Albany on a big gelding called Popeye. Whatever was coming, there were four horses or more, pulling something bigger than a flatbed wagon.

In the ten minutes it took for the travelers to come into view, Birdie debated with herself on whether she should withdraw to a more hidden spot. Then she saw them and forgot everything else.

The four horses were perfectly matched and very beautiful, and they pulled a carriage the likes of which Birdie had only ever seen in Johnstown or heard described. A closed carriage, very large, it was painted a shiny black with yellow trim around the doors and curtained windows. The wheel spokes were bright red where they weren't covered in mud. There was a lot of luggage tied to the top, and two coachmen who sat on the box. They were perfectly matched too, so alike in face and figure that they could only be twins. They were strongly built, with complexions a far deeper black than any of the Africans Birdie knew. The coachmen wore red coats with brass buttons, high-crowned beaver hats, and fawn-colored breeches spattered with mud. They must have set out from Johnstown long before dawn, which was in itself so odd that Birdie could hardly make sense of it. Who would do such a thing, and why?

She wouldn't have been surprised if a queen had stepped out of the carriage, but when the coachmen opened the door the woman who appeared seemed just another lady, maybe as old as Hannah and Jennet. She was very finely dressed, in a beautiful traveling cloak of deep red velvet with embroidery around the hem, and fur on the cuffs and collar. Her bonnet was made of the same heavy velvet, with a scoop brim so deep that Birdie couldn't make out anything about her face. She held out a gloved hand and one of the coachmen helped her down. She didn't seem to mind the poor condition of the lane. She just looked around herself, turning in a circle to scan everything from earth to sky. Birdie wondered what she was looking for.

The man who came out of the carriage behind her was older, with a full iron-gray beard. He was just as fashionably dressed with his long coat and high hat.

He turned to speak a word to somebody and then a boy came out.

An ordinary boy, no bigger or smaller than most, brown of hair, pale, but dressed like the grown-ups in clothes too fine for traveling.

The three of them stood there for just a moment while the man spoke at the boy, who was nodding as though he didn't like what he was hearing but knew better than to speak back. Then the lady turned her head and called out. "Helene!" in a strong, vaguely displeased voice.

Two more people stepped out of the carriage, both of them as dark-skinned as the coachmen, and both dressed plainly. Servants, their arms filled with leather satchels and boxes.

Who were these people, and what were they looking for in Paradise? Birdie was so absorbed in watching them that she didn't hear the others approaching from behind her until Hannah was standing there. Her sister put a hand out and Birdie took it, coming down from her perch in a hop. But Hannah wasn't looking at her at all; her attention was on the newcomers.

Jennet said, "Hannah? Do ye ken those folk?"

Ethan came forward to stand beside Hannah. Birdie saw then that Daniel was not among the party-goers. Nor was Martha. What this might mean would have to wait, because there was something wrong. Hannah and Ethan wore identical expressions, faces wiped clean of all emotion. Ben came to stand beside Hannah, his expression concerned and watchful.

Without turning her head Hannah said, "Little sister, has Martha come down the mountain yet?"

Birdie almost jumped, she was so surprised by this question.

"No," she said. "Isn't she with you?"

Ethan said, "Ben, could you please go back and find Daniel and Martha? Tell them Jemima is come, and they should sit tight where they are. As soon as we figure out what's going on, we'll bring word."

Jemima. Birdie's mouth fell open and she shut it with a clicking sound. That lady in the fine clothes was Jemima Southern, as close to a witch as Paradise had ever come.

Hannah looked down at Birdie and managed a grim smile. "Run," she said. "Run home and fetch your ma and da and Curiosity. Tell them Jemima is come back to Paradise and she's at the Red Dog. Go now, as fast as you can."

Birdie ran.

Nathaniel said, "Boots, will you let me do the talking?"

It was a quarter hour since Birdie had come bursting through the door with her news. Elizabeth's expression had gone very still, in a way Nathaniel rarely saw. In the grip of an anger like this, all the common sense and rational thought she valued so highly went missing. This angry she could do anything at all. March into the open when men were shooting at each other, for example. She had done that once, and taken a good year off his life.

He almost felt sorry for Jemima.

Nathaniel looked behind himself. He hoped it would take a while to get Curiosity's Ginny hitched to the trap. The longer it took Curiosity and Birdie to get back to the village the better. He didn't want to have to worry about Curiosity's heart giving out or Birdie getting in the way of trouble. Of all the children, Birdie was most like her mother.

"Boots?"

"I have no wish to speak to that woman," she said tersely.

"I know that," he said. "But your temper has the upper hand right now."

"You think I am not equal to dealing with the likes of Jemima Southern?"

"I know you are," Nathaniel said. "It's not you I'm worried about. It's Martha, and that boy. Whoever he is."

She pulled up short and looked at him, her brow lowered. "You know I won't do anything to compromise Martha's well-being."

Nathaniel wondered if it really was Martha, or mostly Daniel on her mind. Or if maybe there wasn't much difference now, in the way she looked at things. He leaned down and kissed her briefly. "I do know that, Boots. That's why I'm asking for you to step back and let me have a go at her first."

She didn't respond, and that was a good sign.

There were a lot of people in the lane outside the Red Dog. Few Quakers, but most of the folks who knew Jemima from way back. Old Jed MacGarrity and his daughter Jane, the Camerons, Pete Dubonnet, a half dozen others. Word had spread fast.

Jemima didn't have any friends in this crowd; folks were not likely to forget nor to forgive the things she had done.

Nathaniel and Elizabeth didn't stop to talk, though many called out to them. Nathaniel smiled and raised a hand in greeting as if there was nothing more pressing on his mind than ale and Becca's rabbit stew. He caught sight of Ethan and Luke and steered Elizabeth that way.

Luke said, "Now that you're here I'll go over to the schoolhouse. Hannah and Jennet went there to wait for you. The other one—" he clearly did not want to say the name aloud—"is in the Red Dog. With her party."

Ethan stayed behind. He didn't seem uncomfortable, but then he never did. There was a calm about Ethan that came from deep inside, and was his own. Nathaniel had the idea he was lonely, though he couldn't have said why.

"Go on to the school," Ethan said. "Hannah will be glad to see you."

There was no time to ask for impressions, and it wasn't something Nathaniel wanted to talk about in front of so many people, anyway.

"Just as soon as we say hello to 'Mima," Nathaniel said, and Ethan stepped away, glad to be out of the drama.

Elizabeth lowered her voice. "Martha?"

"Still on Hidden Wolf with Daniel," Ethan said. "Ben ran back to tell them to stay put for the time being."

"Good thinking," Nathaniel said, and he squeezed Ethan's shoulder. "So, Boots," he said. "Let's go on in and see what Jemima has on her mind."

Elizabeth had been imagining the young woman Jemima of ten years ago when she left Paradise, big with child. This woman was Jemima and she wasn't. The same face and frame, but she held herself differently, as if the fine clothes she wore pressed her into a new shape. She was watchful, but otherwise there was little to read from her expression. But then she had been preparing herself for this meeting, and there she had them at a disadvantage.

She held a boy by the hand. Her son, and Nicholas Wilde's, or at least, Elizabeth thought, that's what she meant them to believe.

That idea made her deeply uneasy. She thought of Callie and Martha, who would both be half sisters to the boy. How they would feel to learn of his existence; whether there would be resentment or animosity or simple disbelief. The truth was, nobody in Paradise would believe anything Jemima said. She had lied too often and too well.

Martha was safe on Hidden Wolf for the moment, but where was Callie on this Sunday morning? She should not be expected to deal with her stepmother or the boy, not yet. It occurred to Elizabeth then that Ethan was still outside because he meant to intercept Callie before she could walk into this situation.

Elizabeth had known Jemima for a very long time. When she first started teaching school Jemima had been in her class. Not a dull child, by any means, but dark of spirit and view of the world, distrustful, and above all other things, ruthless. Even as a very young girl she had not hesitated to take what she needed for herself and never cared about the repercussions. She had manipulated Isaiah Kuick into a sham marriage, and after he died and her plans were thwarted, she had stewed in her anger in the old mill house. How Martha had survived that household and remained sweet-natured, that Elizabeth would never really understand. It made no sense for a child to take after a parent it had never known, but Martha was most like Liam Kirby. It ran contrary to Elizabeth's own theories about personality and heredity. All of which she would have to reexamine anyway, given the revelations of the last day.

As much as Jemima had been disliked in the years after her first husband died, people had recognized how hard things were for her, a widow woman with a young child, no way to earn a living beyond taking in laundry and leasing out the millworks for a fraction of its value. Then she had married Nicholas Wilde under circumstances that people were still talking about and would continue to talk about for years to come. On occasion Elizabeth heard parts of these conversations in the trading post.

Poor out-of-her-head Dolly, wandering around in a fog since she gave birth but still, didn't nobody have the right to let the woman walk into a blizzard barefoot, and wan't that exactly what Jemima had done? No sir, there wan't any excuse for that, and if you was to look at it real close, why, you'd have to agree that it was most likely Jemima who had clunked Cookie over the head and tipped her over the rail of the old bridge into the lake. Because Cookie would never have let Dolly wander away in the first place, everybody knew that. And all that because Jemima set her sights on poor Nicholas. And then Nicholas running off and getting himself killed. Of course Callie was odd after all that bad fortune come down on her, wouldn't you be too?

Elizabeth never participated in these discussions. There was nothing to be gained. And now here was Jemima come back to the place where she started.

She was saying, "If you can refund the money we sent to hold the rooms, we will seek accommodations elsewhere."

As if they stood in the lobby of a hotel in Manhattan or London. Her voice and tone and modulation, all so changed that it was hard to credit. She had made herself over into—what, exactly? It was Jemima; of that there was no doubt. She had never been beautiful, but as a younger woman she had been comely, with glossy brown hair and regular features. She might have been pretty if she ever truly smiled, but she had been consumed by dissatisfaction and anger for all of her life, and those things showed as clear as tattoos on her face. But something had changed.

"I can't give you a room I don't have," Becca was saying. "Since the flood I'm full up, and those folks have got nowhere else to go until their homes are livable again."

Charlie said, "And we don't have the money neither. You could take your meals here and we'll give you a bill of credit for the rest."

Even Charlie LeBlanc knew how silly that offer sounded, because the color rose right up to his bald head and he started fiddling with the buttons on his shirt.

"You could just go back to where you came from." Jane Cunningham spoke up clear and loud from the back of the room. "Get in that fancy buggy of yours and go."

Missy O'Brien pushed past Elizabeth. "I'm surprised you have the nerve to show your face here, you murder—"

There was a quick movement as the man beside Jemima turned. The look on his face was so cold that Missy swallowed hard and took a step back.

He said, "Let me give you fair warning, Mrs.—" He waited until Missy croaked her name.

"Mrs. O'Brien, then. If you finish that sentence and accuse my wife of crimes she did not commit, I will sue you in a court of law for libel."

His tone was perfectly reasonable, and his tone utterly serious. Missy was nothing if not courageous, and she tilted up her chin at him in a way that put Elizabeth in mind of an affronted and overfed cat.

"And your name, sir?"

"Hamish Focht."

"Mr. Focht," Missy said, her voice wobbling ever so slightly. "I know a thing or two about the law myself, and I'm not the only one in Paradise who does."

There was a short silence, and then Jemima said, "We must find a solution to this problem, Charlie. We are here to conduct important business and we will not leave until we have done so."

A small hand touched Elizabeth's arm and she turned. Becca's two youngest girls, twins, were so alike that she couldn't be sure if this was Maggie or Kate. Whoever it was, she crooked her finger toward the hall. Elizabeth caught Nathaniel's eye and he nodded.

Out of the room the girl said, "I've got a message from Callie. She cleared out her room and she's gone off. She'll stay out of the way until Jemima's gone."

Elizabeth tried to make sense of it. "She saw them arrive?"

Maggie—now Elizabeth saw the small letter M embroidered on her bodice—nodded eagerly. Clearly she was enjoying her part in the drama. "It wasn't five minutes before she had her things tied up into an old pillow slip and off she went."

"She didn't say where?"

"She said Ethan would know where to find her, if you needed to talk to her."

"Ethan," Elizabeth echoed. And then: "Why don't you tell your ma that the big front room is available for the Fochts now?"

Maggie's eyes rounded in surprise. "You want them to stay?"

"What I want is beside the point," Elizabeth said. "What I know is somewhat simpler. Jemima won't leave Paradise voluntarily, and certainly not today."

In the common room the discussion was still revolving around Jemima's demands and Becca's steadfast refusal, with Charlie alternating between looking sheepish and chagrined. No doubt it would have gone on all day in the same way if Maggie hadn't announced the new vacancy.

Becca cleared her throat. "Well, then. I'll see that it's cleaned and aired straight away. If you'll take a seat, it will be a half hour or so."

She didn't wait to get an answer from the Fochts before she turned and walked into the kitchen. Charlie followed her, glancing behind himself as if he still couldn't believe it was Jemima Southern standing in the middle of the common room.

Elizabeth raised her voice just to that point that people would have to be quiet to hear it; an old schoolteacher's trick.

"Now that this problem has been settled, may I ask everyone to leave so that Nathaniel and I can speak to Mr. and Mrs. Focht?"

From the corner of her eye she saw Jemima bite down on the impulse to say something cutting. In fact, everyone fell into an uneasy moment of silence, but then people began to move. They had been her students once, many of them, and they were still inclined to follow her instructions. And as much as they wanted to see Jemima dressed down and hear all the news there was to hear, they remembered her too well to relish what was to come. In a word, she frightened them.

As she does me, Elizabeth admitted to herself. Nathaniel squeezed her elbow and she was glad of him. More than that, she was happy to let him take the lead in this conversation.

When the room had emptied Jemima said, "Where are my daughters?"

"Hello to you too, 'Mima," Nathaniel said. The use of her girlhood name struck almost visibly; two bright red spots appeared high on Jemima's cheekbones.

"Ain't you going to introduce us to your husband?"

One side of the stranger's mouth curled up. "I am Hamish Focht," he said. "Attorney-at-law."

"And the boy? Your son, Mr. Focht?"

Jemima jerked as if stung. "This is my son, Nicholas Wilde. Named after his father."

The boy raised his head and looked at them. Elizabeth was struck by his expression, which was not exactly empty, but perhaps best described as confused. Nothing of suspicion or caution or worry; a child sure of his place and people. The boy smiled, and the whole face was transformed, as bright as the summer sky. That smile turned an ordinary face into something otherworldly.

Elizabeth studied him and couldn't decide if he favored the Wildes or not. Certainly his coloring was like Callie's, but there were thousands of children between New-York City and Boston exactly like this: about nine years old, brown-haired, brown-eyed. She admitted to herself that she had hardly any memory of Nicholas Wilde's face and could not judge who the boy favored. If anyone.

He said, "Hello." Jemima's hand came to rest on his shoulder, not to quiet him but simply in a protective gesture any mother must recognize. There was something about the boy, something Elizabeth couldn't put her finger on. She would most likely never have the chance to talk to him alone, but she would have liked to do that. Very much.

"I know who you are," Focht was saying to Nathaniel. "You claim guardianship rights over my stepdaughters Martha and Callie."

"Where are my daughters?" Jemima said again. "I'd like to see them now. I'd like them to meet their brother."

Elizabeth caught the twitch at the corner of Nathaniel's mouth. He was as surprised as she was to hear Jemima claim Callie as her daughter. According to the law she had that right, of course, but why she should want it, that was the question. A demonstration of motherly concern was so out of character for Jemima as to be unimaginable. But then there was the boy. Could one child have had such an effect on her?

"I don't know where they are, exactly," Nathaniel said. "Elizabeth?"

She started out of her thoughts. "Nor do I. If they want to see you, Jemima, I'm sure they will come by."

Jemima said, "It would be best for everyone concerned if you could convince them that they should do just that." Her tone was chilly now. More of the old Jemima.

"We won't be put off," said her husband. "The law is on our side."

Nathaniel shook his head in the way that meant he was sorry to see somebody make a fool of themselves.

"You're a stranger here, Focht, but I guess your wife could tell you, I don't scare so easy."

"You mistake me, Mr. Bonner. I have absolutely no interest in you. I couldn't be bothered to exert myself so far for such little reason."

Oh, how he reminded Elizabeth of her uncle Merriweather. That twitch of a sneer, and the cool efficiency with which he could take apart an enemy's arguments. Except of course Uncle Merriweather had never dealt with Nathaniel, who could remain—had remained—steady in the face of much worse.

"Well, then," Nathaniel said, not in the least ruffled. "Maybe it's Callie and Martha you want to scare, could that be it? Because let me tell you plain, I have been guardian to those girls since your good wife there deserted them. All done legal, with attorneys before a judge."

Jemima blinked but otherwise she seemed unsurprised.

Focht said, "We will go to law if we must."

There was a small silence. Elizabeth fought for something to say, but Nathaniel was ahead of her, as he usually was in such situations that aroused emotion.

"Now you see, we do have business," Nathaniel said. "We'll just call on our attorney before we take this any further."

Curiosity turned the trap onto the lane just in time to see Birdie's ma and da come out of the Red Dog. Before Birdie could even wave to catch their attention they were surrounded by a crowd—thirty people or more, and most of them looked angry or worried. No sign of Hannah or Jennet, who were probably inside. There was no time to ask one of the bystanders for information, because Curiosity was calling out to a group of boys who stood by, watching.

Her grandson Leo heard her voice and came trotting straight over. Curiosity's grown grandchildren loved her only slightly more than they held her in awe. Which Birdie understood, because she felt the same way. Or had felt the same way, for all of her life until last night. Now she didn't know exactly what she should feel. Odder still, she had no sense of her ma's feelings about the whole business. It had happened so long ago, but then again it was her own ma who had suffered.

While Leo helped Curiosity—mostly by lifting her like a small child and setting her on the ground—she told him what she wanted him to do with the horse and trap, and with Birdie too.

"Take the girl on down to the smithy with you," she said. "This ain't no place for a child, not right now."

Birdie's surprised squawk didn't even give Curiosity a moment's pause, and before she could think of how to protest, Ginny lurched into a walk.

"Don't fuss," Leo said to her. "It won't do no good."

It was irritating to be told things you already knew, but Birdie held her tongue. For all his quiet nature, Leo was as stubborn as his grandmother, and the only thing to do was to wait until her chance came. Which didn't take long; as soon as the wheels came to a standstill outside the smithy Birdie's feet hit the ground and she sprinted off, back the way they had come. She would get a closer look at Jemima Southern. The only way Leo could stop her was to tie her hand and foot. If he could catch her first, which would be hard as she wasn't so foolish as to go right up the road.

Birdie slipped along behind the schoolhouse, mud sucking at her bare feet. Just as she came to the spot where she'd have to walk into the open she heard familiar voices. She pressed herself to the wall and held her breath.

Curiosity was coming along between Birdie's ma and da, gripping their arms so that her feet barely skimmed the ground. They went into the schoolhouse and the door closed firmly, the latch catching with a sharp click.

A great stroke of good luck. Now Birdie could go see what was going on at the Red Dog and get a look at Jemima and the boy while her people huddled together on the other side of the very wall where Birdie stood and talked about what was to happen.

Jemima could wait a few minutes. From what Curiosity said of her, she wasn't the kind to tuck tail and run at the first sign of trouble.

Birdie slipped around to the rear door. She knew which steps creaked, and how to slip the latch so quietly that no one—not even her father with his hearing like a bat—would know.

Once in the hall she had little choice. The only place she could be sure of hearing them talk was the cloakroom, which opened onto both classrooms. She hesitated for less than a heartbeat before she made up her mind.

Jennet said, "Well, is this no a fine mess? What a good thing Daniel kept Martha behind. Jemima willna dare step foot on Hidden Wolf."

"Please Jesus," Curiosity said. "Now I'm wondering where has Callie got to. Do you know, Ethan?"

"I have a good idea."

"We have to have some kind of plan," Elizabeth said. "Some unified approach."

"I wish Ben would get back," Hannah said. "I'd like to know what Martha wants."

"To be free of her mama," said Curiosity. "Same thing Callie want."

"I wonder if he's really a lawyer," Luke said.

"Or if the boy is who she say he is," said Curiosity. "I don't know what to make of any of it. You saw the child, Elizabeth. What do you think?"

Elizabeth drew in a noisy breath and let it go. "I have no idea, and I doubt there's any way to prove or disprove her claim about the boy's parentage." She thought about saying more and realized that her impressions of the boy were so vague and unsettling that she could not express them to her own satisfaction.

"We really do need a lawyer," she said.

"Well, now," said Curiosity. "Here come John Mayfair. Ethan, you sent for him?"

"I knew we'd need an attorney, and John is very good. I believe we can trust him."

Birdie had to be very still to hear, but she had had a lot of practice and she knew how to be patient. When she paid calls with Hannah to see how a wound was healing, or went with her father to check his trap lines, everything required patience. A hunter had to disappear into the woods, and Birdie could disappear into dim corners.

They were talking to John Mayfair, who sounded weary but very sure of his facts.

For a moment Birdie wished she had just gone on her way. Much better to be at the Red Dog, waiting for a fight to break out between Becca LeBlanc and Jemima. Maybe Missy Parker would come by too, or even Baldy. There were many stories about Jemima and Baldy O'Brien, and at least a few of them had to be true.

But she had come here to sit on the cold floor—still damp too—with her ear pressed to the crack in the door. Ten minutes just like this and she was no the wiser. What she wanted to do was ask a question. Or many questions, because she wasn't even sure what John Mayfair was talking about, or what it had to do with Jemima. There were words like *ecclesiastical* and *tenancy* and *tort*. The others did ask him questions, but most of those didn't mean much to Birdie either.

Hannah was saying, "There really is no other option?"

"Not if it is important to thee that Martha and Callie keep their independence," John Mayfair said. "If ye are agreed, I will write the document for your signature, Nathaniel. Two must sign as witnesses."

There was a lot of talking and moving around but in the end Jennet, Hannah, and Luke went back home to see to the children, and they took Curiosity with them. Finally there was only the familiar sound of pens scratching. Now and then John Mayfair asked a question and got his answer, and then the scratching started again.

"This is very hard," said Birdie's mother. "To send them off like this. It's not what I imagined at all."

Birdie sat up straighter. If only someone would come out and say the word *elope,* so she could be sure of what she was hearing. It was an exciting idea but it frightened her too, hearing the tone in her ma's voice.

"We don't know that they will go off, Boots. It's their decision. Or better said, it's Martha's decision. Daniel knows what he wants."

"But it's all so rushed. You and I, we had the whole winter before we—" her voice trailed away.

"When it's right it's never too late, when it's wrong it's always too soon," Ethan said.

John Mayfair let out a small laugh. "True words."

Ethan said, "Come, let's get this done. I'll go fetch the things they'll need and saddle horses. Then I'll take the letters up to them, unless you want to do it, Uncle."

Birdie couldn't help herself anymore. She opened the cloakroom door and peeked out.

"Finally," said her da. "I thought you fell asleep in there."

He was smiling, but there was sadness in the way he looked too.

"I'm sorry," Birdie said. "I shouldn't have done it. But Ma, I'm as worried about Daniel and Martha as you are."

"And we've shut you out, haven't we." Her mother held out a hand, and Birdie went to stand beside her. The urge to put her head against her mother's breast was very strong, but she was too old for such things.

"I want to be there when they get married." Her voice came a little hoarse.

"If they do get married," said her da.

"Of course they'll get married," said Birdie. She leaned into her mother and was glad of it. "Martha tries to hide it but she's crazy about Daniel. And he doesn't even try to hide it."

"You think they are a match, then." Her mother's hand smoothed her hair, and Birdie could have fallen asleep right there, though it wasn't even noon. "I said so from the beginning. Didn't I say so right from the start?"

32

Martha had no sense at all of the time; whether it was twenty minutes or two hours later that they closed Daniel's cabin door behind themselves and set out for the village. She was so tired that she was light-headed, and how could she be anything else after the events of the last twenty-four hours? She had come up the mountain an unmarried girl essentially alone in the world but for her stepsister, Callie, and now here she was, on the brink of getting married. Again. So soon. Maybe too soon.

It was what people would say, and there was no use pretending otherwise.

But she would be one of the Bonners. It was a thought so odd that she might have laughed aloud. She had never imagined herself as a Bonner, though they invited her into their home and treated her with such kindness.

"When I was little," she told Daniel, "I used to hope that your ma would want me as a servant one day. So I could be near all of you."

He only smiled down at her when she told him that, which was enough. To have the right to say the things she was thinking—no, it was more than that. He liked it when she talked to him, as odd as that seemed. She wondered if she would ever really understand what he felt, and what he wanted from her.

Martha cast a small look out of the corner of her eye, suddenly shy but needing to study him nonetheless. Unshaven, his clothes the worse for two days' or more wear, weapons hung all about him and his left arm in a sling, he might have stepped out of one of Jennet's pirate stories. There was white in his shorn hair and deep lines bracketed his mouth and eyes, but he still had that way about him, the look of all the Bonner men. When he smiled some of those years fell away. It made him almost beautiful; Martha could find no other suitable word. He was tall and lean, hickory hard. When he turned his head his neck reminded her of an elk's, which was such an odd idea that she was too embarrassed to pursue it.

His mother would ask hard questions that would require answers.

Why? Why him, why now? What was it she hoped from marriage to Daniel?

The first word that came to mind was not one she was proud of.

Safety. As Daniel Bonner's wife she would be safe. She would belong. Jemima couldn't hurt her anymore if she was married to Daniel Bonner.

But there was a great deal more to it than that. If asked, she would make herself say the rest of it, why she was drawn to him. Why she wanted him.

The way he looked at a problem from all sides and then came up with an answer that should have been obvious from the start. How impatient he got with a certain kind of talk, and the way he struggled to hide it so as not to offend. Out of courtesy and respect, or maybe simply because he knew how to pick his battles. His loyalty to his family, and the easy dry humor, the way he talked to his nephews and nieces.

How he dealt with Birdie, as prickly as she was, and as demanding.

"Your little sister," Martha said aloud.

He grinned. "She'll be insufferable."

"I don't see why she shouldn't have some of the credit," Martha said, and Daniel laughed aloud. Then he turned sharply toward the village, his head inclined.

"What?" Martha asked, pulling up short.

"Ben," said Daniel. "And he's moving fast."

It seemed that Ben Savard could move very fast indeed when the need was on him; Martha barely had time to wonder what was wrong before he was in shouting distance. He ran loose-limbed and hardly seemed to be breathing hard.

He raised a hand in greeting and Daniel and Martha both returned the gesture, and then he was there. His shirt and face were damp with sweat.

"You barely had time to get to the village," Daniel said. "You must have turned right around to come back."

"What is it?" Martha tried to sound as calm as Daniel, but she heard the tremor in her voice. Ben looked at her and smiled, his odd blue-green eyes flashing against the dark of his skin.

"No need to panic," he said. "But it would be a good idea if you turned right around and went back to your place, Daniel."

And just like that they did turn around and start back. In those ten minutes of walking neither Daniel nor Ben said anything, and Martha thought she would scream with needing to know.

As soon as the door closed behind them, Ben took a deep breath and wiped his brow with his sleeve.

"I don't like to bear bad tidings, but Martha, your mama came into Paradise not an hour ago." It didn't take long for him to tell the rest of it.

"She remarried?" Martha wondered why this possibility had never occurred to her. "And there's a boy?"

"That's the claim. We all thought you should stay here until they've got a sense of what she wants, and how to handle the situation. A couple of hours, maybe."

Martha's throat was so dry that she had to clear it twice before she could make her voice obey her. She said, "I can't go down there at all. I don't want to see her. Them."

"I know that, darlin'," Ben said. "It's got to come as a shock. But just hold tight, can you do that? Any message you want me to carry down, Daniel?"

Martha saw none of her own surprise or unease on Daniel's face. Instead he looked grim, even angry.

"No," he said. "Just bring us word as soon as you know anything."

And just that simply Ben was out the door and sprinted away, this time leaving the path to cut through the forest and down the mountain-side.

"And now what?" Martha said.

"That's easy," Daniel said. "First we're going to eat something, and then we're going to sleep. Or you could sleep first. You look like you're ready to collapse."

There was a small silence that seemed to grow between them while Daniel took cornbread, ripe cheese, and some dried meat from the food safe. He put these things on the small table with its two chairs and then went into the workroom that ran along the back of the cabin.

Martha took a pinch of cornbread between her fingers and then let the crumbs sit on her tongue. She walked the short distance to the small chamber that opened off the far end of the room, and stood for a minute in the doorway.

A bed, unmade. Clothes hanging from hooks. A cold hearth. A Betty lamp on the mantelpiece, and a candle stub. A few books, well read.

From the window she could see Daniel at the pump. He looked around himself now and then in his usual watchful way. A knife sheath lay against his thigh, easy to hand. She wondered if that knife could stop a bear or a panther, and if he'd ever brought a man low that way.

You fought with the weapons you had to hand. Something her mother had told her so many times, without talking about her own weapons or how she had used them.

And now she was back. It was as if Jemima could somehow predict the worst possible moment to interfere in her daughter's life. Another truth presented itself: Whatever plans Jemima had, they were already under way and nothing short of death could stop her.

The boy might be Martha's brother. Her half brother, and Callie's. She didn't know how to think about that, or even how to stop thinking about it. If it was true, the boy was the only blood relation she had in the world beyond Jemima.

A shiver ran up her back and following close on its heels, the first tickle of nausea at the back of her throat.

She moved to the bed and took a moment to straighten the covers and tuck them. Then she stretched out on her side, her head bedded on the crook of her arm. Weariness rolled over her in waves so that she passed from waking to sleeping in an instant, unaware that she had crossed the threshold.

When Martha started awake, the window had been opened and a soft breeze touched her face. She was alone, and for the first moment confused. She sat up just as the chamber door opened.

"I thought I heard you," Daniel said. "There's tea, if you want some."

And he walked off without waiting to hear if she had an answer. Martha followed him. The cold hearth had been stoked and fed, and a pot sat on the grate next to a battered kettle.

"You needed sleep more than food," Daniel said.

Her stomach growled in agreement. She took the teacup he offered her and sat at the table taking small sips and trying to make sense of things.

"How long did I sleep?"

He cocked his head. "Maybe two hours. I was asleep myself for most of the time. On the settle." A small curve at the corner of his mouth, as if she had accused him of something silly.

"And no word?"

"Not yet," he said. "But I doubt it will be much longer."

She said, "You can take it back. It's not too late."

Because, she couldn't quite bring herself to say, they hadn't gone very far beyond kissing, and wasn't that fortunate? He owed her nothing.

Daniel took the cup from her hand and set it aside. "What are you talking about, I can take it back. What can I take back? You think I'm so scared of Jemima that I'd tuck tail and run?"

"No," Martha said, and she felt herself smiling. "I don't think that, but I wanted to give you the chance to prove me wrong."

He studied her face for a long moment and then he cleared his throat. "We could just take off," he said. "Elope, right now."

"That would be very ungrateful after all your mother's kindnesses," she said, and that earned her a real smile from him.

She studied the wood grain in the tabletop, and when she had gathered her courage she said, "Maybe we should just go down to the village."

"I can think of a few reasons why not," he said slowly. "But the most important one is, my folks are down there right now with their heads together, and they'll come up with a plan. They always do. We can give them a little more time, can't we?"

Martha nodded, but he saw her hesitation.

"What?"

"I feel like a fish in a barrel," she said.

He seemed to understand that. "We could go back up to Lake in the Clouds," he said. "Or under the falls, even. That's a tradition in the family, hiding out under the falls."

There were many rumors in the village about a secret hideaway on Hidden Wolf, and Martha had heard them all. And still, she found it hard to credit the notion.

"Behind the falls?"

He nodded. "Two caves. We store food there, and pelts. Only the family knows how to find the opening. And that includes you now too."

She felt herself coloring with surprise and pleasure. Martha hardly knew what to do with the extremes that day had brought, and might continue to bring. Fear and embarrassment and utter happiness and anger that gripped her like a fist. She could not think of her mother without bile rising into her throat, but then there was Daniel. His calm certainty and absolute conviction about her, who she was and what she could be. And what if he was simply wrong?

"It's a lot to deal with in one day," he said to her. "And I understand if you need to keep to yourself until you sort it through. One thing though is, I'm not going to get mad at you for speaking your mind. I can see you've got things to say, so go on and say them."

That made her laugh aloud. "You never get mad, Daniel Bonner? What kind of saint are you?"

He looked surprised. "I didn't say I wouldn't get mad. I don't doubt we'll have our share of disagreements, and I can lose my temper now and then. What I meant was, I wouldn't ever strike out at you in anger. I may walk away to get myself under control, but I'll always come back."

Just that simply he stole her breath away, but he wasn't finished.

"I expect the same from you," he said. "It's the way my folks have always handled things and I think it will most likely work for us too. We can get through anything that way."

"Your ma and da can get through anything that way," Martha heard herself say. "What makes you think I'm equal to your ma?"

His smile faded and he slipped his hand behind her neck to pull her face up close to his. "Are you trying to scare me off? Because let me make something clear, Martha Kirby. I see who you are, even if you cain't see yourself."

She lowered her face so her forehead touched his. "I never thought I'd say this, but my mother did me a good turn."

Daniel turned his head and his breath moved the hair at her temple. "And how's that?"

"If it weren't for her, I'd be married to Teddy right now and on a ship headed for England. And I think that would have been a mistake."

His mouth trailed from her temple, across her cheekbone and down to her mouth. The kiss was short, a brief soft touch that set every nerve on edge and made her collapse forward, into the sheltering curve of his arm.

Martha felt him tense. He turned away from her, his brows folding together in concentration. He said, "Horses."

They moved toward the door together. Martha's stomach lurched and for that moment she would have lost the little she had eaten but then she saw that it was Ethan who had come. He was riding his own roan and leading two others, Ben's Florida and Hannah's Jiminy.

He pulled up hard and was on the ground before his Scout came to a full stop.

"How bad is it?" Martha called out to him, and Daniel's hand came up to the small of her back.

"Let's not give Jemima so much credit," he said. "Ethan, what news have you got for us?"

Ethan said, "Best we go inside to talk, don't you think?"

He accepted a cup of cold tea and emptied it in two swallows, and then he drew in a deep breath.

"First off, she calls herself Jemima Focht now. Brought her husband with her, a lawyer. John Mayfair has stepped in to represent your side of things, Martha. Our side."

"And the boy? Ben said there's a boy."

"There is. She says she named him Nicholas Wilde, after his father."

Martha wondered what Callie would make of that.

"What do they want?" Daniel's tone was steady. "Do you know?"

Ethan said, "I'll tell you what it looks like so far. Martha, Jemima is going to try to challenge the portion of your father's will that assigns guardianship to Will Spencer and my uncle Nathaniel. They'll claim that Liam Kirby had no right to make such provisions for you, as you are legally the daughter of Isaiah Kuick, which makes—"

"Jemima my legal guardian," Martha finished for him. "And if the boy is who she says he is, he has a right to half Callie's property. So that's it; they're after the money and property."

She folded her hands tight to keep them from trembling.

"Can I just—give her everything? Let her have it, as long as she leaves me in peace."

"If the courts rule in her favor, she'll get everything anyway, and still have control over you. And there is a good chance that they will in fact rule in her favor. There was always the chance she'd come back to make such a claim."

"You never said as much to me. Nobody did."

"We saw no need to worry you about something that might never come to pass. Martha, there are strong factors in your favor. She abandoned you. Kuick admitted in writing that he wasn't your father, and Liam Kirby claimed paternity. And there was that questionable episode with the deed to the orchard."

A knot fixed itself in the back of Martha's throat, and her gorge rose to meet it. She pressed her lips together and made an effort to gain control over her stomach and her mind both. Now was not the time to wilt. It had come, as she knew it must, but she would not have to meet it alone.

Ethan was saying, "John wrote this for Nathaniel's signature, and there's a letter too." He pulled two sheets of paper, already much rumpled, from the same old battered leather bag he had been carrying for years.

The first, smaller sheet of paper was folded in half, with Daniel's name written in a hasty hand across it.

"My father," Daniel said.

He opened it and held it to the side so that Martha could read it too. The pen strokes were dark and hard enough to have torn the paper in places.

Son—ask the girl to marry you, and then go straight to
Johnstown. Make sure Jemima don't have men there watching
for you and if there's no trouble, go see Mr. Cady. He's familiar
with the history and he'll be able to arrange a wedding straight
away. That's the quickest and safest way to put an end to Jemima's
scheming. If Martha won't have you, then take her to Johnstown
anyway and ask the Cadys to take her in and hide her until we
can figure out a way to solve this. In any case don't bring her
back to Paradise unless she's legally married and has got a
husband to speak for her. I hope that's you.

At the bottom his mother had added a few lines:

Dear Martha
The future is mysterious and frightening to you now, but in
the end all will be well. There will be great happiness and great
sorrow, you will have a family, you will find yourself capable of
things you cannot now imagine. But you will persevere, and one
day you will look around yourself and know that your life is
good and that you are, in spite of all your early fears, happy.
    We hope to see you next as our daughter. That would be true
no matter the circumstances.

    Martha folded the sheet carefully and tucked it into her bodice. It was
a note she wanted to read again, in privacy and solitude.
    The other paper was more formally written, this time in a stranger's
hand.

    I, Nathaniel Bonner, legal guardian of the minor Martha Kuick
also known as Martha Kirby, born in the village of Paradise on
the west branch of the Sacandaga in New-York State on the
4th day of April in the Year 1805, do find her to be of sound
and moral mind and of healthy body and competent to enter
into the state of marriage, and therefore I grant my permission—

    Martha had stopped breathing. Everything had stopped, it seemed,
because the only sound she could hear was the rushing of her own blood
in her ears. Daniel and Ethan were looking at her.

"I already asked you three times in the last couple hours," Daniel said. "You never did give me a straight answer. I said I didn't want to push you, and I meant it. I can get you settled safe somewhere in Johnstown, Martha."

Her mother was in the village right now, putting one of her plans into motion. The thing was, Jemima's schemes usually did work out in her favor.

Martha said, "Do we have to go right now, in the clothes we're wearing?"

"Jennet packed a saddlebag for you," Ethan said. "There's money and a bill of credit and even some food. Birdie was very concerned that you two didn't starve on your way to getting married. She begged to come along, but your ma wouldn't have it."

And then the first tears did come. Martha dashed them away. She said, "Will you tell Birdie thank you? Tell them all?"

"Of course," Ethan said.

"And tell her that the best part of marrying her brother is getting her as a sister."

There, she had said it.

"Hey," Daniel said, but he was smiling. "That's a mighty odd way of accepting a proposal."

"It was an odd proposal," Martha said.

Ethan cleared his throat. "I had best get back."

"Wait," Martha said. "About Callie—"

He said, "Don't worry about Callie, I promise I'll take care of her."

Martha had her doubts, but there was another matter that concerned her more. "If she needs a place to stay, she should take Ivy House. Will you tell her that?"

"That's where she is now," Ethan said. "I'm headed that way."

"It's unfair that I should have everything and she be left alone," Martha said. "Whatever she needs, she should have. No matter how put out with me she may be, I want to be sure she is safe and comfortable."

Ethan leaned over and kissed Martha on the cheek. Something he had never done before, but it felt right.

"Hey," Daniel said again, but he stepped forward and hugged his cousin with his good arm. "Ethan," he said. "Will you talk to Lily, try to put her at ease with this?"

"I don't think you need worry about Lily anymore," Ethan said. "It was her idea that you two go straight off and don't come back until you're good and married."

Of all the strange and disturbing news Ethan had brought them, this was certainly the one that would occupy Martha for the longest time. She saw the confusion move across Daniel's face too, and then it was gone, and in its place, grim determination.

"I wish there was time to write a note," Martha told Ethan.

"And I wish I could paint like Lily," Ethan said. "I'd paint the two of you standing on the porch against the sky with the mountains all around, and you'd see how you look when you're happy. As it is I'll just have to remind you when you forget. Now will you two get a move on?"

They waited for a moment until Ethan reached the curve in the path and then they raised their hands in farewell.

"Well, then," Daniel said. She felt him looking at her. "If you're sure."

Nothing seemed sure to Martha right at this moment. The world had tilted out of its orbit.

Jiminy pawed the ground impatiently, and Florida followed suit.

"Everything is going so fast," Martha said.

"Too fast, maybe." He was standing away from her, too far to touch. And right now she wanted that, she needed that assurance. Maybe he saw it in her face because he reached out a hand, palm up. Martha took it and he bent his arm so that she came up against him. They stood there in the shade of the porch for a minute and then another, and little by little the tension drained away. Martha rested her head against his shoulder and shut out everything but the feel of his shirt against her cheek, the solid shape of him, and the smell of the sunshine hot on skin and leather and muslin, and the slow steady blossoming of something that could be, that just might be happiness.

It was the last thing she could have imagined about this moment. Martha's mother was come to claim her, as she had always feared might happen. Her mother was here, but so was Daniel. First and foremost, Daniel was with her.

---

33

*T*hey were on their way home when Elizabeth realized where Callie must have gone. To Nathaniel she said, "I want to go sit with her. She'll be very agitated and she shouldn't be alone."

And so they changed direction and found their way to Ivy House. There was a pot of violets on the front rail, velvety deep purple with touches of yellow that seemed to glow. There was beauty to be found even in the most difficult and sober of times, but Elizabeth doubted Callie would see it that way.

Joseph Crispin went by leading a donkey cart laden with empty chicken crates. They paused to speak a few words with him, and in that time Elizabeth had the sense of somebody watching them from the window. She put her hand on Nathaniel's arm.

"I think it best if I go in alone," she said.

He thought about that for a moment and then nodded. "But I don't want you walking home alone past dark, do you hear me?"

Elizabeth's first impulse was to shake off his caution, but then she thought again of Jemima and she nodded. "I don't imagine I'll be here that long, but come at dusk if I'm not home yet."

He leaned over and kissed her. "We can take the girl home with us if you don't like the idea of her alone here. I'll sleep in the hayloft if that's what it takes."

Elizabeth caught his earlobe and brought him back down so that she could kiss him back, properly. They had come this far together and survived much worse than a spiteful and greedy Jemima Southern. And they had slept in the hayloft more than once. She would do it again, and gladly.

"Not without me," she said, and then she went in to Callie.

The girl was sitting at the kitchen table with her hands folded before her. The little house was still and obviously empty.

"Mrs. Thicke's gone to help Curiosity," Callie said. "I told her to stay there until somebody sends for her."

Elizabeth's worry for the girl shifted and turned into unease.

She said, "I'll make tea and see what there is to eat."

If she moved slowly and with caution, Elizabeth thought that Callie might relax enough to start the conversation herself. She warmed the teapot, sought out the milk jug, set the table properly. It wasn't until she put the tea and the plate of buttered bread down and sat herself that it happened.

"Martha?"

"She's safe," Elizabeth said.

"On Hidden Wolf."

"Yes. For the moment."

Callie looked so stricken that Elizabeth reached out to touch her, but the girl jerked away. A scratching at the door, and her face was suddenly alive with hope.

When Ethan came in, it all seeped away, like a candle flame stuttering out. Slowly, though, something new came into the girl's face. Contented relief, perhaps. Resignation. Ethan was a friend she trusted who had come to help, and she was glad of it.

Without explanation or introduction Ethan said, "Here's what's happened so far."

Elizabeth listened without interrupting as Ethan told Callie in great detail about what Jemima and her new husband had said and claimed, and how they had been received. He described the boy who was meant to be her half brother, and he described him carefully, noting the things that Elizabeth had seen: a sweet child, unafraid.

"Does he look like my father?"

"I think that's for you to decide," Ethan said.

He told her about the meeting in the schoolhouse, and the plan they had put together on such short notice.

And then, looking at Elizabeth as much as Callie, he told them about his ride up Hidden Wolf, and how he found Daniel and Martha, and the conversation they had had about the documents and the choices before them.

In all of that Callie never said a word. Instead her breath came more slowly and the little bit of color in her face seeped away until Elizabeth feared that she might faint.

Her voice rasped. "You are telling me that Martha is gone off with Daniel. Eloped with Daniel."

"That was the suggestion put to them," Ethan said. "I believe that is what they are going to do, but we can't know for sure."

Elizabeth said, "It is Martha's choice, Callie. No one would try to force her."

"They'll be married," Callie said dully. "Because of Jemima."

Elizabeth caught Ethan's gaze. He gave a small shake of the head.

"What we're worried about right now is you," Ethan said.

"I want to go to Johnstown," Callie said.

Elizabeth started, but Ethan seemed not at all surprised.

"I want to go to Johnstown now," Callie said. "Will you take me, Ethan? Or lend me a horse and I'll ride by myself."

And just that simply, Ethan agreed. "Yes," he said. "I'll take you."

It seemed that Ethan saw nothing odd in this plan, but Elizabeth was not so fortunate.

"Callie, what do you hope to accomplish?" Elizabeth asked, in as gentle a tone as she could manage.

Callie looked puzzled, and so Elizabeth tried again. "Why is it you want to go after them?"

"To be with her," Callie said simply. "To be there. She's all I have left."

Her tone was unremarkable. Elizabeth glanced at Ethan again and he shook his head at her, one sharp movement that asked her to leave this line of inquiry alone.

"We have to go straight away," Callie said. She stood and looked at Ethan. "There's no time to lose."

Elizabeth said, "Callie, first we should talk about Jemima. I fear you are just as much at peril as Martha. Jemima will take what she can."

Suddenly the animation came back into Callie's face, as quick as a strike of lightning.

"Oh, no," she said with a disconcerting calm. "No she won't. I'll kill her first. I'd go to the gallows happily for that pleasure."

"But right now we're going to Johnstown," Ethan said. "We can talk about Jemima later."

He was speaking to Callie but looking at Elizabeth, asking her for some understanding and latitude in a matter she could not fathom.

The whole episode took less than twenty minutes and now they were gone, on their way to Johnstown. Like thieves in the night.

And why did that phrase come to mind?

Elizabeth felt vaguely nauseated, and so unsettled that her hands shook when she held them out in front of herself.

When her children or grandchildren were undone by emotion, unable to act or react, she had tried to teach them to articulate their fears for themselves. Even as very young children they had found it useful. Now she must try to follow her own advice.

What scared her about Callie?

The girl was not herself. In fact, she had not been herself since the flood. Since the day they all came back from Manhattan, Lily and Simon and Martha. Something about the confluence of those two events: the flood that took everything, and the stepsister who came back unexpectedly. Then today Jemima came, and Martha, the only family Callie cared to claim, had gone.

Long ago Elizabeth had convinced herself that Callie had no feelings for Daniel, but now she wondered if she had perhaps been wrong.

It was Lily Elizabeth came across first, and Lily wanted to know everything. She lay on her daybed, propped up on pillows with one hand resting lightly on the curve of her belly. Her expression was difficult to read;

just another indication that they had been too long separated and knew each other too little.

Elizabeth made an effort to relate the details as thoroughly and objectively as possible. The differences ten years had wrought, the style and cut and expense of Jemima's clothing. The changes to the way she spoke and held herself. The boy, what he had looked like and his demeanor. The things Jemima had claimed, or her husband had claimed for her. The implicit threat to Martha and Callie both.

She said nothing about Ethan and Callie's plans for fear of saying too much.

Lily levered herself into a more comfortable position with the help of a bolster, but the whole time she watched her mother.

"You observe me sometimes like a bug in a jar," Elizabeth said when she was finished.

That made Lily smile. "Do I? Really I was just thinking about the hundred questions I've got."

"I doubt I have so many answers, but I can try. What have I left out?"

Lily pulled back in surprise. "Between you and Da, I think I've heard pretty much everything. And anyway, it's not Jemima I want to hear about. In fact, the less said of her, the better. But you could tell me about Daniel. Da wasn't very forthcoming."

"Whatever your father told you," Elizabeth said, "I hope he remembered to thank you for supporting your brother's wishes."

Lily's expression turned thoughtful. Elizabeth held her breath, alarmed and unsure. For one uneasy moment she wondered if she had misunderstood Lily's position on her brother's choice of a bride.

Just as suddenly as she had disappeared into her own thoughts, Lily turned back, her expression so open and full of light that Elizabeth knew what had happened even before she spoke.

"Mama," she said. "The baby is moving." She caught Elizabeth's hand and placed it on her belly.

"Do you feel it? A fluttering."

Elizabeth nodded. "Yes," she said. "I do."

She had always been prone to tears in happy situations, but now they came in a rush. She stood up, and then leaning over, pressed her lips to her daughter's head. For that moment Lily rested against her mother's breast and Elizabeth was too overcome to speak even a single word.

It had been so long since she had held Lily like this.

When she sat down again she accepted the handkerchief Lily offered and wiped her cheeks; a fruitless exercise, as the tears continued.

"It started some days ago," Lily said. "But I wanted to be sure before I said anything. I swore Simon to secrecy."

Elizabeth was smiling through her tears, and now Lily was weeping too.

"What an awful harridan I've been," Lily said. "I apologize, I really do. It was just that I couldn't stop worrying—"

"I understand," Elizabeth said. "Of course I understand."

"And what's all this, then?" Nathaniel was at the door, his expression wary.

"Come in, Da," Lily said. "There's nothing wrong. Daniel's run off to marry Martha and I couldn't be happier."

Nathaniel came into the room and crouched beside Elizabeth's chair. One side of his mouth curled. "I see Lily's not alone in her unbridled happiness." He used a thumb to wipe her cheek. "If we're going to celebrate we should call the whole family in."

"Ethan," Elizabeth said, catching Nathaniel's hand. "You don't know yet that Ethan and Callie have gone to Johnstown."

Nathaniel's brows knit themselves together, and Lily went still.

"Callie insisted. She wanted to follow Daniel and Martha," Elizabeth said. "And Ethan agreed."

Lily said, "To attend Martha at the ceremony?"

"Or to stop it," said Nathaniel.

"But why?" said Lily. And then: "Do you think she's in love with Daniel?"

They looked at each other for a long moment.

"That's one possibility," Nathaniel said. "But we'll have to leave it to them to sort out. Could we get back to the weeping for happiness?"

"I'd like to hear more about the little boy," Lily said. "Does he favor Nicholas Wilde?"

"I couldn't say." Nathaniel put a hand on his daughter's head. "I hardly remember what the man looked like to start with. Dark hair is all I recall. Did you think the boy favored Nicholas, Boots?"

"I wish I knew," she said. "It's really a question that Callie has to answer."

Lily said, "It's strange, but I am most worried about Ethan just at this moment. I can't imagine what he hopes to accomplish, taking Callie to Johnstown." She sought out her father's gaze. "Da, do you have any idea?"

Clever Lily, who could see below the surface. Now that Elizabeth looked, it was clear to her too. Nathaniel was not entirely uninvolved in whatever was going on, but neither was he willing to talk about it.

She hoped he would change his mind before things got out of hand.

34

_____

They arrived at Cady's offices at three, spent an hour in conversation and the drawing up of papers, and at five they assembled in the parlor to be married by the hastily summoned justice of the peace and county clerk. Cady was a personable man but first and foremost he was a good lawyer, and knew how to tie a knot.

Mrs. Cady had offered Martha a chamber where she could wash and change, a kind and thoughtful gesture that Daniel, at least, could have done without. He didn't like having Martha out of his sight. For his own part, he needed no more than ten minutes to strip himself out of the rumpled clothes he had been wearing for three days and put on the things he had packed in such haste.

At home he was most comfortable in a hunting shirt and leggings, though in the classroom he substituted breeches, a linen shirt, and a workday coat. Now neither of those options would do and so he had brought the clothes he wore on those rare occasions he had to go farther than Johnstown. He slipped on his best linen shirt, made for him by Curiosity's daughter Daisy, a vest embroidered with leaves and twining vines Ethan had brought him from Manhattan, and his good dark blue broadcloth coat. Both the shirt and coat sleeves were cut unfashionably wide, which was the only way he could get them on. Daisy had also made his trousers, cut narrow from ankle to waist, with silver buttons to close the front fall. He hoped he wouldn't be an embarrassment to Martha.

Finally washed and dressed, he folded and tied a fresh square of linen into a sling, eased his arm into it, and went outside to deal with the pain in the relative seclusion of Mrs. Cady's garden.

The wind had picked up, and the sky was darkening fast. Daniel forced himself to breathe in and out at a normal pace and then he turned all his attention to his arm. The pain had come up full force on the ride from Paradise, and now it radiated down his arm and into his hand in jolts as resonant as a hammer striking an anvil. He had been pushing himself hard for days; the only real question was why it hadn't happened sooner.

With his eyes closed and his face raised to the wind Daniel went through the exercises he had learned from Many-Doves and the healers at Good Pasture, turning inward to address the pain itself. Speaking to it like the living thing it was, and asking for peace. On this of all days. He pushed it gently and watched it retreating, along the nerves that ran through wrist and forearm to pool, for one excruciating minute, in the angles of his elbow. Sweat rolled down his face even in the cooling wind.

Another few minutes and it fell back into his bicep and finally it burrowed like a rat into the nest of nerves deep in his shoulder.

Cady came to the door and called his name. He wiped his face with his handkerchief and went inside to his bride.

She had washed and changed and put her hair up in a neat roll on the back of her head. A few damp strands lay against her nape and touched the lace collar of her gown. It was what his mother would call a morning dress, of some light fabric the color of rich cream, with lace along the layered hems of the skirt and sleeves. There was embroidery across the bodice, gleaming white on white, a pattern of small birds and flowers. Against the dress her coloring seemed almost flagrant, from the rich bronze of her hair, the deep pink of her mouth, to creamy skin that darkened to rose along her cheekbones and on her earlobes.

Her smile was small and anxious, but there was courage there too. He took her hand and kissed her lightly, just a brushing of mouths but he felt the jolt of it move through her as it traveled the length of his own spine.

Throughout the ceremony her hand trembled in his, though her voice was calm and strong when she spoke. His own caught a little and she glanced up at him. And then she squeezed his hand, and that made him smile. So they were both grinning like idiots when the final words were spoken.

While the lawyers and the notary were busy with the documents Daniel leaned over and whispered into her ear.

"Sorry you let me talk you into this?"

"No," she said. And then, with a grin that was meant to be cheeky: "Not yet."

It cheered him beyond all reason to see that she could tease. There was nothing of panic or unhappiness in her expression. What was there he wasn't sure. Shock, perhaps, at how suddenly her life had changed. For his own part he felt relief and thankfulness and the distinct stirrings of his body in response to hers.

The next challenge was to feed her properly and find a place to stay the night. He said this to her as soon as they had taken their leave. Martha had changed again, this time into clothes suitable for riding. Because as much as they both disliked the idea, the wisest thing would be to stay the night somewhere other than Johnstown.

"If we push we can get there before the storm comes in."

"Get where? Where are we going?"

"To Michael Allen, an old friend of mine. It's a big house and I know he'd be happy to put us up."

It was a big enough house to spare two rooms, but that was something he couldn't say just at the moment. The truth was, some things didn't have to be rushed. There were notarized copies of their wedding lines in Cady's safe, in the courthouse, and in Daniel's saddlebag, and so now they could take the time to stop and think. Or rather, Daniel admitted to himself as they set out at a trot, he would give Martha the time she needed to come to him of her own accord. He hoped it wouldn't be too long. He hoped he would be equal to the business when that moment came.

Overhead the sky lowered and flexed, and all around trees bent with the force of the buffeting winds. The horses nickered uneasily, and broke into a cantor at the vaguest, lightest touch. The first fat drops of rain fell just as they crested a hill and Allen's farm came into view.

An old woman with a twisted back answered Daniel's knock. Behind her the house was in shadow, and silent.

"Mrs. Allen," Daniel said. "It's very good to see you, ma'am. May I introduce you to my wife?"

Beside him Martha jerked to hear those words spoken. He hoped not in displeasure.

"Daniel Bonner," said the old woman. "Come in out of the rain, young man, and bring your bride with you."

35

Two miles out of Johnstown Callie's mare threw a shoe and shortly after that, the storm came in, so they arrived at Mr. Cady's home later than planned, and soaked to the skin. It was Mrs. Cady who told them that Daniel and Martha had left some two hours earlier. No, Mrs. Cady didn't know where exactly the newlyweds had been headed, but could she help them in any other way?

One look at Callie's face made it clear that she wanted nothing to do with Mrs. Cady, whose curiosity was open and avid. Ethan thanked her and they walked on into the center of town, where he took two rooms at the White Horse Inn. Then Callie stayed behind, dripping onto the hearth, while he went out to take care of matters that could not wait. She barely looked at him when he told her where he was going, so lost was she in her own thoughts.

In the next hour, while he roused the blacksmith from his Sunday rest and made arrangements for the horses to be stabled overnight, Ethan tried to plan what he was going to say to Callie and failed completely.

He had only a vague idea of what was wrong, but one thing he knew for certain: She wouldn't welcome empty promises.

She was waiting for him by the front door of the inn when he got back. Her clothes were still wet, and her hair lay in clumps and snarls on her shoulders.

"You know all the same people as Daniel," she said. There were hectic spots of color high on her cheeks. "You know his friends. Where might they have gone?"

The one question Ethan had hoped she wouldn't put to him, because in fact he did have some ideas. Daniel had a few very close friends, one of them a carpenter here in Johnstown, and another who lived due west on a large family farm. Both men had served with Daniel and Blue-Jay in the militia, and Ethan had met them now and then over the years. But he had no intention of telling Callie about those friends, because she seemed now to have regained some of the frantic energy that had driven them here in the first place. The idea of intruding on Daniel and Martha at this most sensitive time was not acceptable to him, but Callie would insist.

Hope faded from her face, and she went back to her room without another word.

Ethan ordered a meal and tea, and arranged for the innkeeper's wife to find some dry clothes for both of them and then he went up to Callie to see what could be done. On the way he thought of Curiosity, and tried to imagine what advice she might give, if she were only nearby to talk to.

He said, "If we could find them this evening, what would you hope to accomplish?"

At first it seemed as if Callie hadn't heard him. She stared at the untouched food on her plate and then slowly raised her gaze to him. "I don't know. Nothing, I suppose."

And then, to his horror, a tear ran down Callie's cheek. Callie Wilde was the most pragmatic, sensible, least emotional person he had ever known, and now she was weeping for reasons she couldn't or wouldn't name. But she would not appreciate soft words, and so he cut to the heart of the matter.

"If you love Daniel, you could have told him so at any time in the last years."

Her eyes flickered toward him, unsure, and then away again. Rather than embarrassment what he saw on her face was something like annoyance. "What gives you the idea that I love Daniel Bonner?"

"Don't you?"

"No," she said. "I think of him as a friend, and nothing more. As I think of you." She looked at him directly, as if she thought this might cause him pain and she was glad of it.

"I feel the same way," Ethan said.

"About me, or Daniel?"

Her tone was stark and even strident, but Ethan found that he couldn't take offense. "I think of Daniel as a brother. He would want to help you if he were here, but he is not, and I am."

"I don't want your help," Callie said. "I don't want Daniel's help either."

"But you would have let Martha help you."

She regarded him coolly. "Martha is to me what Daniel is to you."

Ethan was determined to meet her cruelty with calm, just as he was determined to continue the conversation until he had the answers he needed. Callie was angry; she had been angry for years, but she had never let it out, as though she were afraid what might happen if she let go. Others had seen only her sharp wit and sharper tongue, until recently. Until the flood, and Martha's homecoming.

With Callie the best approach was usually the most direct. He said, "Why are you so angry at Martha?"

She jerked as if slapped. Her face, when she turned to look at him, had drained of all color.

"You think I'm angry. At Martha."

"I do think so, yes." Calm in the face of the pain.

"And why would I be angry at her?" Callie asked, her voice low.

"She left you once, came back, and now suddenly she's left again."

She struck out like a viper, the flat of her hand meeting his cheek with enough force to bring water to his eyes. Ethan caught her wrist before she could strike again.

The last time Ethan had seen Callie weeping was the spring they buried her mother. Even then she had cried reluctantly, her whole being stiff with resistance while the tears rolled down her face. Only Martha had seemed able to reach her.

She broke away, turned her back to him and shuddered with the effort to control herself. Ethan waited, five minutes, ten minutes, a full half hour before she was willing to look at him again.

She said, "I do not begrudge Martha her good fortune. I do not."

"But?"

She drew in a hitching breath. "She is always being rescued. First her inheritance and Manhattan, and when that went wrong everyone came to her aid and brought her home as though she were as fragile as an egg. And now—now—"

For a moment he thought she could not go on, but she found her voice again.

"I have things to lose too, but nobody seems to remember me. Everything turns around Martha. What about me? What about the orchard?"

"Jemima hasn't said anything about your property," Ethan said. "Do you think she wants it?"

"She'll take anything she can get. It's her nature."

"Yes," he said. "I suppose that's as true a thing as has ever been said of Jemima."

"Can she do it?" Callie's voice sank to a whisper. "Could she take the orchard?"

"Yes," Ethan said. "I think she could. We could fight her in the courts—we will do that—but she has some grounds."

The tears had started to flow again. Callie pressed her weathered, work-scarred hands to her eyes and made a sound deep in her throat.

"Callie," he said. "There are ways to put you out of her reach. Ways to turn the law so that it stands between the two of you, to your advantage."

"As Martha is doing," she said. "By marrying Daniel."

He said nothing, and watched the ideas work. She was putting herself in Martha's place and wondering if she could be comfortable there.

Finally she said, "You'd be willing to do that. To marry me to keep me safe from Jemima."

"Yes," Ethan said quietly. "I am willing."

She walked to the window and back again. Ethan was surprised to note how calm he was, almost to the point of numbness. What happened in the next few minutes could solve multiple problems, or it could be disastrous.

Callie said, "I don't love you as a woman loves a man. I couldn't—I couldn't—" She broke off.

"That's just as well," Ethan said. "Because I couldn't either."

He might have laughed, if the situation were not so dire. Her expression was so comically torn between confusion and hope. She sat down across from him.

"I don't understand."

"I think you do," Ethan said. "But for the sake of clarity, here is what I'm proposing. A partnership. A legal marriage, but one that is platonic."

"You don't want to share a bed?"

He shook his head. "No."

She scowled at him openly. "You will change your mind, and what then? I do not want children, and I don't want the business that goes into making children either."

"I promise you," Ethan said calmly. "I will not change my mind. And I am content to remain childless."

Her brow furrowed. "Are you—incapable?"

It was only a word, one that would give her the assurance she needed. "Yes," he said finally. "I am incapable of being a husband to you in that one way. But I will be your friend and supporter. You'll have my protection and my resources and my family to claim as your own. Jemima will not be able to touch you."

"But she might still challenge me in court," Callie said. "She might still claim that she has a legal right to my father's property."

"She will try," Ethan said. "But it is me she'll be challenging as your legal husband. I know many excellent lawyers, Callie. If they can't stop her outright, they will tie the matter up in the courts for the rest of her life. Or if you prefer to have this settled more quickly, I'll pay her to drop her case and leave us in peace."

"That would be expensive."

"My stepfather left me a great deal of money, and I've invested it well."

She was studying her folded hands. Without raising her head she said, "Why would you do this for me?"

"Because I love you as a friend and I like you very much," Ethan said. "And because I'm lonely."

That seemed to reach her as nothing else had. Her expression soft-ened, and Ethan knew it was more than time to leave her to sort things out for herself.

He stood. "You need time to think. We can talk again in the morn-ing."

"And you might change your mind," Callie said, looking at him di-rectly. A challenge.

"I'm not going to change my mind," Ethan said. "If you decide you want to accept this offer, we can be married tomorrow before we set out for Paradise."

He was closing the door behind himself when she stood suddenly. Ethan raised an eyebrow.

She said, "Where would we live?"

"Wherever you like," he said. "We could build a house in the orchards or stay where I am now. We could live in Manhattan for part of the year, if you like. Or Boston, or London. The look on your face, Callie. I can't tell if you're horrified or delighted."

"I never thought I'd ever see any of those places," she said. "I never let myself wonder."

Ethan bowed from the shoulders. "I will be yours to command."

And there it was, finally. Callie laughing. In surprise, and disbelief, and the first glimmerings of hope.

36

*W*hen a servant had taken the horses away to the stable, Daniel and Martha followed Mrs. Allen into the kitchen, the warmest room in the house. It smelled of new bread and a stew rich with gravy and vegetables. Martha's stomach growled so loudly that Mrs. Allen laughed.

"Food first, by the sound of it. If you'd get down two more bowls—"

Martha was glad to have something to do. She set the table and poured water into the teapot while Daniel hauled water and wood and saw to the fire. The hardest part, as far as Martha was concerned, was trying to look disappointed when Mrs. Allen told them that her son Michael and his whole family had gone to a wedding in Little Falls and wouldn't be back until late the next day.

"It's too far for me to travel," she told them without even a hint of regret. "But truth be told, I'm glad of the quiet. Children are a blessing, but a noisy one. So I've sent the help away home, all but Henry who took your horses and will see to the livestock. It's just me and Molly and the quiet."

Daniel's head jerked up. "Molly stayed behind?"

"Aye," said Mrs. Allen, pointing with her cane. "She's right here if you want to have a word with her. Molly!"

There was a rustling in a box on the other side of the hearth and then a dog appeared. Not especially big, black with white markings, and a grin that looked distinctly human. She came straight to Daniel, who made a great deal of rubbing her head and talking to her.

"Molly's grandsire followed Michael to the war," he told Martha. "Hunter stayed with us all through the campaign on the St. Lawrence."

"And Molly is cut from the same cloth," said Mrs. Allen. "Didn't Michael promise you a pup from her next litter?"

Daniel admitted that he had.

"Well, then, your timing is just right," said Mrs. Allen. "Have a look."

A puppy was climbing over the edge of the box, followed in short order by five more, each of them in pursuit of their mother. When Martha thought the parade had come to an end a seventh came rolling out of the box in an ungainly ball. This last puppy was twice the size of the others with a round belly and a satisfied air.

"That's Hopper," said Mrs. Allen. "Born three days ahead of the rest of them."

Martha looked up in surprise.

"Oh, aye, it's true," said the old lady. "Out he popped, alone. We didn't know what to make of it. Molly seemed glad enough to see him and he went right to the teat, but anybody with eyes could see her belly was still full of pups, all of them as jumpy as crickets. Three days later she got down to work again and along come the other six. And did Hopper make hay while that sun was shining? I have never seen a pup so fat."

"He looks exactly like his mother," Martha said. "The same markings."

"Aye," said Mrs. Allen. "And he's just as smart. Isn't your lad clever, Molly. Three full days with all those teats to hisself."

Daniel leaned over to scoop up the puppy, who squirmed not to get away, but to get as close as he could. In no time at all he had found a button and was tugging at it with great seriousness.

"Looks like you've got your dog," said Mrs. Allen. "And now I have to get these old bones to bed."

"We are intruding on your peace," Daniel said. Martha held her breath because it was certainly true, but what could be done about it, unless they were to ride away into the night? In which case she would surely collapse of plain exhaustion.

"Not unless you decide to play bowls in the parlor at ten of the evening. Which my grandsons did, not a week ago."

At the door she paused and turned laboriously. Then she used her cane to point at the ceiling over her head. "Two chambers, fresh made up," she said. "Take one or both, whatever suits. Extra coverlets in the chest if it should happen you need 'em. We're in for some more weather."

When they heard the sound of Mrs. Allen's chamber door closing, Daniel smiled at her.

"Didn't expect to be bringing a new dog home from this trip." He dumped the pup onto Martha's lap and laughed to see him start from scratch, nosing into Martha's bodice and under her arms, pulling on buttons and tugging at ties until he reached her throat and began the process of licking her into submission. She laughed, but that only seemed to encourage him.

When she turned to Daniel he was watching her with an expression that she had seen before. Early this morning, sitting on the porch while the sun rose on this very long, most extraordinary day. Without taking his eyes from hers he reclaimed Hopper and put him with the rest of the litter, where he immediately wiggled his way to a free teat.

"So," he said. "Let's eat."

Later, Daniel banked the fire while Martha wiped the bowls and put them away.

"I'll take our bags upstairs."

She said, "I'll come behind with the candle. Unless the stories are true and you can see in the dark."

He laughed. "Now that's one I haven't heard before."

"I think there must be many stories you haven't heard about yourself. You have always been a staple of conversation among the schoolchildren." She said, "I knew you couldn't make deer and wolves and otters obey you. You couldn't even make Lily obey you, try though you might."

"So you saw through me even then."

She might have said, *I loved you even then,* but her bravado only reached so far.

The two chambers above the kitchen were simply furnished, each with a dresser, a small table under the windows, a few chairs, and a bed. In the second room the bed was very old-fashioned, high enough to require steps, with curtains that could be pulled closed to keep out the sun, and a canopy of faded fabric heavily embroidered. It was a bed for a princess, and the very sight of it made Martha step backward over the door swell.

Daniel seemed less overwhelmed. He went straight to the windows that looked out over pasture and woodland. When he turned around again he seemed to have come to some kind of decision.

"You need sleep," he said. "I'll take the other room."

Before she could think of how to respond to this surprising declaration, he was most of the way out of the room, turning his body so he could slip past her. Martha caught his hand and he stopped. The two of them stood together in the narrow doorway, his gaze so intent, as if he meant to see into her head and see what she was thinking.

She said, "Wait."

"It's all right," he said. "We've got years ahead of us."

She forbade herself to drop her gaze. "I am very tired," she said. "But can't we sleep in the same bed? Just sleep?"

Now there was a question.

Daniel doubted that such a thing was possible, but he also was determined to give her what she wanted. It was the least he could do after such an abrupt wedding, without so much as a proper wedding supper. And worse still, without a wedding ring.

In the hurry to get away it was the one thing that hadn't occurred to him. They were almost to Johnstown when he realized what was missing, and he told her immediately. He was ready to see unhappiness or disappointment on her face, but she only looked puzzled.

"There's no goldsmith in Johnstown," Daniel told her, "but there is an Irishman who fixes clocks and he sometimes has things to sell. We could stop there—"

She stopped him with a soft shake of the head.

"Is a marriage legal without a ring?"

It was the first question they asked of the lawyer, who assured them that the law did not insist on a ring. But it still felt wrong, no matter how unconcerned Martha seemed to be. He would have to put it right as soon as possible.

Now Martha was sorting through her bag and making neat piles of things. He saw something edged in lace, a set of hairbrushes, a tin of tooth powder, a pair of rolled stockings.

She said, "I won't be long," and without waiting for a response she ducked behind the dressing screen. When she came out she was wearing a night rail that brushed against her bare feet, with their high arches and long toes. She had plaited her hair and it swung as she walked, bumping the base of her spine.

She climbed the three steps to the bed and sat on the edge, her hands folded in her lap.

"I think this will be a very comfortable bed to sleep in. Come, Daniel, I'm not going to bite. Come and sleep."

Sleep was going to be hard to come by; now he had not only her bare feet to put out of his mind, but curiosity about how exactly she might bite him, should things ever get that far.

The last person Martha had shared a bed with was Callie, when they were girls. After Callie's father disappeared and Jemima ran off, Curiosity took them both in and gave them a chamber together. It had seemed too large a gift at the time, a quiet, safe place where they could talk without worry that they would be overheard.

What a treat it had been to sleep in a bed made up with cool linen and pillow slips that smelled of lavender. How comforting it was to have Callie sleeping beside her, better than a warming brick on the coldest nights. Every time she went to bed with a full stomach she had wondered how long she could count on what she had.

Now that old feeling of safety and comfort came back to her, and she slipped away, contented, half asleep before Daniel ever came to lay down beside her.

She woke to the sound of rain drumming on the roof and the smell of apple wood on the hearth. Had she ever been so comfortable before in her life? If so she couldn't remember. It would have been the most natural thing in the world to slip back into sleep.

If it wasn't for the fact that there was a man in the bed with her. Daniel Bonner, who was, oddly enough, her husband. Martha turned onto her back slowly so as not to wake him and saw she was too late.

He smiled at her. A sleepy smile that asked nothing of her but acknowledgment. She said, "Good morning. What time is it, do you know?"

"The hall clock struck six not long ago."

"You've been watching me sleep."

"Do you mind?"

She shook her head. It was interesting to her that he watched her openly and without excuse. For her own part, she found both things very difficult. Daniel had worn his shirt to bed, open at the top so that his throat was plain to see. Why it should move her so strongly she couldn't say. Looking at classical sculpture she was most often drawn to the strength of leg and arm and back, but now the sight of Daniel's muscular throat started a warm pulsing that moved up her spine and spread out.

Of course she could do as she liked. She could run her fingers along Daniel's jaw to feel the bristle of his beard or kiss the hollow at the bottom of his throat and test his pulse with her lips. Any of those things were her right, but for the moment she was content to study him as he studied her.

Martha had heard quite a lot about the etiquette of the wedding night from her friends who had married first, marching into foreign territory armed with the advice of mothers and older sisters and grandmothers. The trouble was, there was no consistency in any of the reports. Some of it was shocking and some of it was frightening, and some of it was even funny, but there was precious little practical in the guidelines handed down to a bride or even in the firsthand accounts.

Her own engagement had ended before Amanda could bring herself to speak of such things. She wondered now what Amanda might have said. It seemed unlikely that sweet, quiet Amanda would give advice as Sylvie Steenburgen's mother had. Mrs. Steenburgen had told her only daughter not to worry, the business was messy but it didn't last long; she herself used the time to compose menus.

Margaret Bickman's mother had told her to submit once a week and no more, and that complaining would do her no good; in fact, it might only serve to drag it out. And, most important: She was never to lift her night rail higher than her waist.

Dorothea Ennis had heard from her grandmother that it was a great deal of fuss about nothing at all and that once she had three children she should come again and ask how to keep from having more.

And Annie Chamberlain's mother, Martha's favorite of all her friends' mothers, had said that if it turned out Annie didn't like it, why that meant her husband was as new at the business as she, or if not, he was a selfish bugger who needed an education. If they worked at it, Jane Chamberlain explained, they'd soon find it was a fine way to spend an evening alone, and the best way there was of really getting to know each other.

Technically Martha understood what was supposed to happen. Certainly animals had provided a lot of information over the years: dogs in the garden, pigeons on her windowsill, cows at pasture. None of whom kissed, which brought her back to the original problem. If he didn't kiss her, what then? Was she to wait until he was ready? And did it mean she was not attractive to him?

He said, "You look as though you're trying to do long division in your head."

That made her laugh, a little at least.

Then he sat up and, without another word, got out of bed. Martha was so surprised she didn't know what to say. Maybe he wanted to go right back to Paradise, but it was raining so hard, that seemed unlikely. He disappeared behind the dressing screen and began the noisy business of emptying his bladder into the commode. Martha wondered if all men took such a long time. She knew so little about the way they were put together. There was splashing at the washbasin, and when Daniel appeared again he was damp and half dressed.

He said, "I'll be right back," and to her astonishment, he went out and closed the door behind him.

Martha sat up in her surprise and tried to make sense of what had just happened. Apparently there was to be no kissing—he hadn't even kissed her after the ceremony in the lawyer's office—and nothing else either. Why this should be the case was unclear. Certainly no explanation was coming her way. She didn't know if she should be insulted or thankful. Or simply sad.

There was nothing for it, and so she lay down again and watched the rain pearling on the windowpanes.

There was no sign of Mrs. Allen in the kitchen, but she had left a note. It was written in a spidery, uphill hand and announced that her daughter had fetched her to help deliver her eldest granddaughter's first child, and she would likely be away until tomorrow. If they cared to stay they were welcome. She had made up a breakfast tray, and they were to help themselves to whatever else they found to eat. There was a bath in the workroom and if anybody wanted to bathe she suggested the best place to do that was before the kitchen hearth. In any case she hoped they would stay. Michael would be pleased if they did.

Daniel thought of the horses, and remembered that one of the farmhands was there to see to them.

By blind good luck they had come to a place where they could be alone. They had the house to themselves, and firewood enough, and food. It would be foolish to set out for Paradise in a downpour when there was no pressing need.

Molly's litter was playing in front of the hearth. He whistled and they all looked his way, but Hopper was the only one who came running in his tumbling puppy way. Daniel took a minute to rub the potbelly and let his fingers be nibbled.

"So," he said to the pup. "I have to go back upstairs. I'm as nervous as a girl, but that stays between the two of us, if you please."

The tray was heavy with dishes: warm biscuits under a folded tea cloth, a lump of new butter sweating water, a plate of bacon, a jar of gooseberry preserves, and a jug of water.

He found Martha seated on the edge of the bed with her hands folded in her lap. She was watching the storm, and she gave him no more than a glance as he put down the tray.

He had done something wrong, clearly. Rather than ask about it he sat down beside her—he didn't need the stairs as Martha did—and took her hand and folded his fingers through hers.

Martha shifted a little, as though she might want to get up and walk away.

He said, "The biscuits are still warm. Aren't you hungry?"

She looked at him then, and he saw that he had insulted her somehow but that she was trying to control her feelings. They would eat breakfast, her look seemed to say, if that was what he really wanted.

What he really wanted was something very different, but again he reminded himself that she should be the one to set the pace.

The truth was that Martha really was hungry and so they went about filling plates and then they sat there on their perch on the side of the bed and ate. Daniel told her about Mrs. Allen's note, but his tone didn't indicate how he felt about any of it. And why, she asked herself, was she so ready to be insulted?

The food helped. The biscuits were tender and the preserves sweet and tart at once. She would have liked tea, but the water was very cold and good. None of that changed the fact that Daniel had run off without even kissing her, but on the other hand it was nice to sit beside him like this in the quiet house with the rain coming down. Outside the world was wrapped in mist, but this chamber over the kitchen was warm. She felt her irritation seeping away, and try as she might to call it back, it was soon gone for good.

She heard herself sigh.

"That bad?" He was smiling, but there was a wariness about it.

What an odd thing marriage was. Two people who could—by laws of man and God both—do what they pleased together, who liked and even believed that they loved each other, though those words hadn't been spoken out loud. Who had spent a good part of the previous day wrapped together on a settle, trying to stop doing what they now could not start.

She said the first thing that came to mind. "This butter is very good."

"It is," he agreed. And then: "But you're meant to eat it, you know. It won't do much as a face cream."

And before she could raise a hand to her face, he leaned toward her and licked the corner of her mouth clean. Just that simply every muscle in her body flexed toward him, and her mouth opened on a silent sigh.

For a long time they kissed in that awkward position. Plates on their laps, side by side, his body turned toward hers and his head canted. Daniel smiled against her mouth and broke away to take the plates and put them aside. Then in one fluid movement he turned back to her and took her down onto the bed.

And this was what she had hoped for. Kissing Daniel was something wondrous and strange; serious business, certainly, but not a humorless one. Even now his smile drew her in, and she caught herself laughing.

At one point he left her for what could have been no more than three seconds, long enough for her to take stock of the way her body was reacting to him; the heavy thud of her pulse in her wrists and throat; her mouth, already swollen, and most disconcerting, how damp she was in places that had never perspired before. Then he was back, two fingers thick with butter.

"What—" she said, but he had already smeared it over her lower lip and down her neck to the base of her throat. When he kissed her this time his tongue touched hers and the bright taste of new butter blossomed between them.

He worked his way down and down, nipping and licking and drawing her flesh into his mouth. His amazing mouth, so warm and tender and fierce. It robbed her of her ability to draw a breath. She moved to push him away—just for a moment, just for the chance to let her mind catch up to her body—and then froze when her right hand encountered the jut of a shoulder beneath the sling he wore to protect his ruined arm.

She looked into his eyes and for that moment the playfulness was gone. He said, "As long as I don't put weight on it or lift anything heavy I should be equal to—this."

"I should hope so," Martha said, and then blushed and blushed again when he laughed. He rubbed his face against her breast, and why did it seem so natural? If anyone had described such a thing to her she would have been—

Intrigued.

"Don't," he said. "Don't look away. You never need apologize to me. I like that you're curious. Do you want to touch my arm? You can, you know. You can touch me anywhere."

It was something he wanted her to do, and so Martha ran her fingers lightly from elbow to wrist, tracing the shape inside the sling. "That doesn't hurt?"

"Oh, no," he said. "You couldn't hurt me, not like that."

Impulsively she bowed her head to kiss the injured hand. Then Daniel pulled her back up so they were face-to-face.

The next kiss was so deep that Martha thought she might melt into a puddle. The soft, often washed cotton of her night rail felt like sackcloth against her skin, so that it seemed the most natural and important thing in the world to rid herself of it. Daniel helped her, nudged her this way and that until he could lift the gown up over her head and raised arms.

"You have beautiful breasts." He used the tips of his fingers to trace around a nipple in a hypnotic circle that made her arch toward him.

"I have freckles," she said, breathlessly.

"And I intend to make myself familiar with every one of them. For example, right here."

Oh, the things he did with his mouth. The licking and tugging and soft suckling went on and on until she gasped and would have turned away, except he had spread his hand on her back to hold her there, where he wanted her. She was the sole object of Daniel's attention, and she burned with it.

Martha found herself lifting her hips, something that surely must mark her for a wanton. Except he liked her like this; he had said so. She needn't pretend.

The feel of him, the rough beard and the calluses on his fingertips and the muscles that clenched and rolled under his skin, the expanse of his back, these things wound her up in a fog that she might get lost in. And still she wanted more. She wanted everything.

"Come," he whispered against her mouth. "Will you come to me now?"

She nodded, though the truth was she was sad to have the kissing part over so quickly. Men didn't much like kissing, her newly married friend Sally Roth had told her. Oh, they would kiss if that's what it took to put a wife in a receptive mood, Sally said. But once that goal was achieved there would be no more kisses until he wanted to start over again.

"Like a highway toll," said Sally. "One he will shirk if he can."

Daniel pulled away suddenly and looked her in the face.

"Where is your mind?" he asked. "You went away there suddenly."

So she told him about Sally and Sally's pronouncements on the proclivities of men.

Daniel laughed out loud.

"It's not true, then?" Martha said. She was embarrassed to sound so eager for an answer.

"It's not true," he said. "Or maybe it's true for some men, but not for me. I like kissing. Or better said, I like kissing you. A lot."

"Oh," Martha said. "Good."

His mouth twitched as though the effort not to laugh cost him dearly. "While we're talking," he said, "are there other mysteries you'd like cleared up?"

"Dozens of them," Martha said. "But I'm happy to wait and see if I find the answers on my own. I'll let you know if I run into any difficulties."

She shrieked when he grabbed her and pulled her up against his chest, both of them kneeling now in the middle of the bed. She was entirely naked but he still had his breeches on, though they had slid down his hips. That was her last observation for a good while, because he seemed intent on demonstrating to her how very seriously he took this kissing business.

Poor Sally, who had married her father's law clerk for his reliable ways and calm good sense.

"You're thinking again," he said. And: "I can fix that."

He moved her on the bed, nudging gently as he tasted and rubbed and suckled, her flesh pebbling and flushing hot with his attention. Then oddly enough she was lying crosswise on the bed with her legs dangling over the side, pillows under her head and shoulders. Daniel stood before her and, bending at the waist, he covered her. Hip to breast she felt him hovering there, with his weight on his feet. It left his good arm free for things other than holding himself over her.

And he made excellent use of that good right arm and hand and every finger on it. Except he hadn't yet touched her where the ache was worst. She was wondering if she dare ask him for such a thing when his hand moved up her thigh into the soft folds of her sex. At the same moment he drew her nipple into his mouth and suckled so hard that something deep in her belly flexed and began to flow. The sound she made shocked her but she could no more be silent than she could stop breathing.

There was no place to put her legs; she drew her knees up and then dropped them, ran her heels down his thighs rock hard with tensed muscle and she realized first, that he had lost his breeches somewhere along the way and second, that she had wrapped her legs around him and his sex was pressed up against hers.

At that moment he let her nipple go with a soft plop and she saw down the length of her body to his. Her new husband, naked and fully aroused. Clearly what they were about to do must be possible, but now the mechanics struck her as absurd.

"Dear Lord." She put her head back and closed her eyes. Then Daniel was beside her, flat on his back.

"I meant to distract you," he said.

She burped a small laugh. "I have this image in mind, of somebody trying to put a cucumber through a buttonhole."

She pressed a hand to her mouth, and giggled anyway.

Daniel lifted himself up over her on his good arm, his expression blank. Then his mouth twitched and they were laughing, both of them, like loons.

She said, "Is it hopeless, do you think?"

Daniel cupped her face. His smile was so open and sincere she had to love him just for that. He said, "I'll do my best to get you ready."

She wanted to ask what he meant, how it was possible to make her ready and what that had to do with the pain she knew was coming. But then they had talked enough, and Daniel's expression was so focused and intent that she was drawn in and curious and eager, less worried about pain than she was fearful of disappointing him.

At first the lightest of touches, nothing more than the brushing of his mouth against her neck and cheek and brow. Then his teeth nipped at her earlobe, worried her lower lip. Before she realized what she was about, she reached up, grabbed one earlobe, and brought his mouth to hers so she could kiss him properly, a tender kiss that made her whole body soften and open to him.

Because she did want him; that was the simplest truth.

He moved, his mouth sliding down her chest, back to her breasts where he lingered until she was gasping, and down farther and farther until he was kneeling on the floor, his head buried between her legs.

Her breath hitched and caught as he spread her flesh with two curious fingers and then kissed her, hot and openmouthed, where she had been expecting an invasion of another kind.

Martha moved under his touch, twisted and opened, wrapped herself around him.

She was trying to catch her breath when he got to his feet to stand between her legs and press himself against her. Arched over her, he

whispered into her ear, his voice deep and sweet, every word as powerful as his touch. He told her things she never realized she wanted to hear,
about her own body and the feel of her skin and the taste of her. Salty
sweet, like the sea.

She said, "I'm ready now. I think I'm ready." That she could blush in
this situation was a mystery, but she felt her color climbing.

He said, "I'll be the judge of that." And he went back to his work,
though she was already dissolving like sugar in hot water.

And when it was time, when the urge to lift her hips to welcome him
was irresistible, then he came to her. Sealed their marriage by penetrating her body with his own, stretched her to the bursting point and filled
her to overflowing.

The pain was sharp, upward-spiraling, all-consuming, and then it fell
away to a throbbing ache. He inhaled her cry and spoke to her, his voice
reedy with the strain, and breathless. *Hold* and *wait* and *feel me. Feel me inside you.*

With his forehead pressed to hers she could not hide what she was
feeling, or ignore the things she saw in his face. Concern, worry, and a
flickering of pleasure that caught and flared. His whole body trembled
but he held himself still while she shifted and adjusted herself around
him. He throbbed within her like a heart grown suddenly too large.

When the pain began to fade Martha let a long hitching breath go.
She realized then that his hand was on her breast, cupping it as gently as
an egg. One finger traced the lower curve and then he opened his hand
and touched her nipple with his palm. A strange sound came from her
own throat and he dropped his head and drew that nipple into his
mouth. Her muscles began to twitch and spasm around him and her hips
rose of their own volition as if to ask for more.

He pressed deeper and deeper still and Martha cried out not in pain
so much as welcome.

He moved inside her, and the dance began.

When the clock struck eleven Martha startled awake. Daniel, sitting
cross-legged beside her on the bed, watched it happen.

His own sleep had lasted maybe a quarter hour, and then the pain had
roused him as effectively as a sharp stick to the ribs. It was the way of

things, and any vague idea that this time might be different had to be put away.

While he waited for Martha to wake he tried to sort through the logistics of getting back to Paradise and the problem of the weather, what the best way would be to come face-to-face with Jemima, where they would live, if Martha would want to be so far from the village. These things occupied his mind but it was the sight of Martha asleep that eased him as the pain ebbed.

Her plait had come undone and her hair was spread around her and over one breast. The rise and fall of her breathing was enough to make his flesh stir, impervious, apparently, to both pain and common sense. At least when it came to Martha.

He had had many years' practice subduing his natural urges and he drew on that now. It would be brutish to expect more of her, as tender as she must be. Hours in the saddle would only make that worse. It might be days before he could touch her again. Long after they were back in Paradise and had taken up housekeeping.

When he woke in the morning she would be there, and when he came through the door at the end of the day, she would be there. For as long as they lived they would sleep in the same bed and eat together at the same table.

On the long ride to Johnstown Daniel had asked himself if he was sure about what he was doing. If maybe he had a picture of Martha in his mind that had nothing to do with the truth, out of loneliness and the need to have a woman in his bed. But then, he knew where to find companionship when the need was unmanageable. Twice a year, at most, he had sought that kind of release. At Good Pasture there was a woman who welcomed him warmly, a woman he liked, but one he rarely thought about in the long months between visits. The time they spent together had never been anything like the last few hours with Martha, who was unschooled and anxious but who came to him without hesitation. She had been through a lot in the past weeks, but she always held tight to her courage and her wit.

A cucumber through a buttonhole.

He pressed his mouth hard, determined not to wake her by laughing.

———

Martha woke and was immediately aware of her surroundings. Daniel was sitting beside her, naked, which brought to mind what had been going on in this bed. Tentatively she flexed muscles to see which of them could be relied upon.

Everything was sore, but the worst was the deep burning itch that reminded her of the obvious: She was well and truly married.

She sat up. "You've been watching me again," she said. "Second thoughts?"

He leaned forward and kissed her. "Not me. You?"

"Of course not. But then I got the better deal. I got you and all the rest of the Bonners, and you got—well, you know who you got."

She was babbling, but he dealt with that by kissing her again. The weight of his arm around her shoulders was so comforting, she could almost hear the unspoken words.

I'm here. I'm here, and I'm not going anywhere.

He said, "I'm not worried about the baggage that comes along for the ride."

"Oh, Jemima would like that, being called baggage." She tried to hold on to her smile but it faltered.

Daniel touched his forehead to hers. He said, "She can't hurt you anymore."

Martha wanted to believe it was so, but she would need time before she could trust her good fortune.

They were having a conversation about what came next when there was a pounding at the downstairs door. It was at that moment Martha realized that the storm wasn't going away. In fact, the sky flickered with lightning.

Daniel raised one brow and inclined his head to say she should stay where she was. Then he pulled on his breeks and went down the stairs three at a time to answer the door. Martha, wrapped in her night rail, came out onto the landing.

The boy who stood there was perhaps Birdie's age. He wore an old wool tricorn that was too big for him, water rolling off it in a steady stream. He was saying, "A message from the old Mrs. Allen, sir. She said it was important."

"Go on, then, I'm listening."

The boy straightened.

"Mrs. Allen says, don't you think about setting off for home in the middle of a storm. She says that Michael will stay put in Little Falls until it's safe to travel, and so should you. Stay here, not Little Falls. At least I think that's what she meant. Why would she tell you to stay put and go to Little Falls as well?"

"I understand what she meant," Daniel said. "Go on."

"There's food and firewood enough, and you aren't to worry about the animals because Henry will take care of all that. She wants you to stay another night so you can meet up with Michael tomorrow. And I'm to take back word what you want to do but hurry if you would, Mr. Bonner, I saw a cow struck dead in a thunderstorm last spring and I don't care to find out what it felt like."

Daniel glanced up at Martha. The idea of staying another night appealed, certainly more than going out into the weather. She nodded, and Daniel sent the boy on his way with his answer.

Before he could close the door, the boy was back again.

"I forgot something. Mrs. Allen says I should say about the hip bath in the workroom. Please help yourself to towels and whatever else serves."

Martha said, "Bath?"

37

---

*E*than and Callie ate breakfast together at nine in the hotel dining room. She studied the food on her plate as though it were a painting, and picked up her fork with reluctance. She had done her best with soap and water, but her scrubbed hands and face only made the traveling dress she had worn yesterday look worse.

He had hoped that she would be rested enough to talk about what was before them, but now Ethan doubted it could be done. He was wondering how best to proceed when she looked up at him.

"About the boy she named for my father," she said. "He could be anyone, an orphan she picked up off the street."

"True."

"I don't believe he's my brother. I think it's one of her tricks."

"You may be right," Ethan said.

"That's her plan," Callie said firmly. "If she can't get everything, she'll get at least half, through the boy."

"And the good news about that," Ethan said, "is the nature of the law.

They can file a claim on the estate, but that's the kind of thing that can take years to make its way through the court system."

Callie snorted softly. "And in the meantime she'll be sitting there like a spider, just waiting. I don't know why I agreed to this plan; she will have her way in the end and there's nothing you can do to stop her."

Her tone was so bitter and fraught that at first Ethan couldn't think how to reply. She was prickly and always had been, but her temper was always countered by a sense of humor and love of the absurd. Now she seemed to be on the verge of something much darker.

Maybe, Ethan reminded himself, because she had no illusions about Jemima. Jemima knew no bounds and accepted no limits. And of course the boy might be who she said he was. Callie's half brother. Her only blood kin in the world.

He said, "If he is your brother, he's your last tie to your father."

Her expression softened. He had said aloud the thing she wouldn't allow herself to hope for.

"If he is," she said. "If he is my half brother, I don't want her to have the raising of him."

Ethan studied the pattern of bluebells on his plate and tried to think of a way to tell her the truth. No court of law would take a son away from a mother to be raised by an underage sister.

She said, "If I were married, it would be easier to make the case, wouldn't it?"

"It would make many things easier," Ethan said. "But not everything."

She went away into her thoughts, her gaze fixed on a point somewhere behind him. Finally she raised her gaze to his.

"When would we go to see Mr. Cady?"

"In the afternoon," Ethan said. "If that suits you."

In the long silence that followed he was almost sure she had decided against the whole plan.

"And what do we do in the meantime?"

"Shopping," Ethan said. "We go shopping."

She started to object, and then stopped herself. Callie had lost everything in the flood, and so for the past weeks she had been relying on borrowed clothes, ill fitting and much the worse for wear. He knew that as much as she disliked the idea of a trip to the shops, she was too practical to deny the need.

"All right, then," she said. "Let's go."

———

They borrowed an umbrella from the innkeeper and made their way across the cobblestones to the dry goods store, trying to avoid puddles and mud and only partially succeeding.

Just before they reached it, Callie said, "I wonder where they could have gone."

Ethan was spared the necessity of a reply by Mr. Turner, who came to the door to welcome them, with his wife standing just beyond. The Turners were always very happy to see Ethan and they greeted Callie too, as though she were dressed like a lady of means rather than a farmwife in difficulties.

With a minimum of fuss Mr. and Mrs. Turner took Ethan's list—he saw Callie glance at it suspiciously as he handed it over—and began to gather things together. Mrs. Turner paused now and then to cast an experienced eye over Callie to gauge her size, and in a very short time the counter was piled high with chemises, stays, vests, petticoats, two pairs of fashionable drawers that made Callie's eyebrows peak; six pairs of cotton stockings, six of wool and one of silk, garters, a substantial shawl, a hooded mantle, a pair of light slippers for indoors, a pair of fancy leather boots such as a lady wore on the street, another pair of solid work boots, neckerchiefs, and gloves.

The gowns were the most difficult, as Ethan knew would be the case.

She said, "I have no use for finery like this when I'm in the orchard or cider house."

From the corner of his eye he saw the vaguest hint of surprise pass over Mrs. Turner's face.

"Mrs. Turner, we'll need three very simple workday gowns, of solid construction. What do you have that will fit Miss Wilde?"

There wasn't much of a choice in ready-made gowns, but they seemed to suit Callie's sense of what was appropriate. Sturdy osnaburg in muted colors, without ornamentation, cut unfashionably full in arm and shoulder. Made for a woman who ran a household and kept her own garden.

"And that one." Ethan stepped forward to touch one of the gowns that had been set aside. A simple printed summer-weight cotton, pale yellow with a scattering of small flowers and trailing greenery. There was a simple ruffled collar and a green plaid ribbon to go with it, and a matching straw hat with a scoop brim lined in pale yellow.

"I don't need it," Callie said. "Three gowns are enough."

"Nevertheless," Ethan said calmly.

Callie's expression darkened, and then she seemed to tire of the conversation. She walked away to examine buckets on the other end of the crowded store.

"If you would please have these things delivered to Miss Wilde's room at the White Horse right away," Ethan said. "We have another list."

They bought split-oak baskets, barrels and spigots, buckets, shovels, rakes of three different sizes, pitchforks, a sturdy shovel, two tin washtubs, a gross of gallon jugs, rope and wire, nails, saws, axes, a turnscrew, mallets and hammers, a ladder, and a great variety of other tools and supplies that had been lost in the flood. Halfway through this process Callie seemed to come awake, and some color came into her cheeks.

Ethan said, "I think a Franklin stove would be a good addition to the cider house."

She turned to look at him, and there was not a hint of anger or cynicism in her face. "Ethan. You will bankrupt yourself."

"Hardly. Mr. Turner, will you make sure that the stove comes on the wagon with the rest of the supplies?"

Her mouth pursed, as if she had to resist the urge to argue with him.

Ethan said, "You could go back to the inn, if you like. I have a few more matters to settle, but I will join you for lunch."

It was still raining, but Callie took her new umbrella and after studying the mechanism for a moment, opened it and went out into the street to make her way back to the White Horse. With a certain girlish pleasure she stepped hard in every puddle she passed.

Herlinde Metzler, employed in the kitchen of Mrs. Louise Kummer's boardinghouse until that substantial lady was felled by apoplexy, was busy in the scullery at the White Horse when she was called to the front desk. She had joined the staff just two weeks earlier, but the innkeeper and his wife seemed to be satisfied with her work, and thus far she got along well enough with the other servants. A better place than the one she had had with Mrs. Kummer. More than she had dared hope for.

Now the mistress directed her to take hot water and fresh towels to the young lady who had checked in yesterday afternoon. "And whatever else she requires," said Mrs. Mulroney. "Spare no effort."

Which was what an innkeeper said when a guest was known to make free with his purse.

A half hour later she knocked lightly at Miss Wilde's door and was surprised almost beyond speech by the appearance of the young woman who answered. Slightly built and no more than plain, Miss Wilde was wearing a bodice and skirt that should have long ago been cut up for rags. The hem had been dragged through the mud, and brushing had not taken away the stains; there was a hole in her stocking the size of an egg, and the seam where bodice met skirt was gaping. More telling still, her hands were red and rough with work, and her skin sun-darkened.

Herlinde saw all this in a few seconds, and then bowed her head not to give away her thoughts, which were very simple: What was a country-woman of no means doing in this room in the finest inn in Johnstown?

Instead she said, "Your bathwater, Miss Wilde."

The young woman stepped aside.

Herlinde went about her work. She stoked the fire and poured hot water into the basin, folded towels and set them out. All the time her gaze kept drifting back to the slight figure standing at the window.

She was about to withdraw when someone scratched at the door. A glance at Miss Wilde made it clear that she had no intention of answering, and so Herlinde went.

Young Matthew Turner held out a package, rain spattered, and danced from foot to foot until she took it from him. Then he dashed away.

"From the dry goods store. Shall I unpack it?"

Strictly speaking this was not something she should offer to do; she was not a lady's maid or secretary. She was a maid of all work, and nothing more. But it had been such a long time since she had had the pleasure of opening up a parcel, and she was curious about this odd young woman who dressed so poorly and seemed so out of place.

Miss Wilde nodded without turning around. "Please."

It wasn't until that point that Herlinde noticed the bed, and the piles of new clothes, some folded, some laid out, that covered its entire surface.

In spite of herself, Herlinde was interested. Most of the things she could see were plain, but all were of very high quality. There was no lace, nor any embroidery or fancy pleats but still, a small fortune spent in carefully made, good quality gowns and the other things a lady needed to consider herself properly attired.

This young woman of no means or style, in this room with all these riches. An odd and intriguing combination of facts.

Herlinde sat down on a stool to open the parcel, carefully setting aside string and paper. Inside she found fine milled soap and talc that smelled of lilacs, and a dozen fine lawn handkerchiefs with lace trim, tied together with a silky blue ribbon.

And finally, a dresser set with carved ivory handles on mirror, hair-brushes, and combs. A very expensive dresser set, as Herlinde knew well because she had been visiting it regularly at the mercantile. She had even reckoned out how long it would take for her to save enough money to buy it, on her meager salary. At least two years, if she put aside every penny she could spare and did without other things she liked.

But here was the beautiful and very valuable dresser set, and Miss Wilde wouldn't even turn to see it. It was silly to moon over fancy things she did not need and would never have; Herlinde was determined to be sensible and make the best of her situation, which was considerably better today than it had been a month ago.

"Miss Wilde," she said. "If there's nothing else, I'll go."

She turned, and the misty half-light lit her face so for a moment she looked not so much pretty, but striking.

Her voice came a little hoarse. She said, "I'm getting married this afternoon."

In her surprise Herlinde paused. "Oh," she said. It was not enough, but nothing else came to mind. In English you were never to congratulate a lady about such a thing, that much she knew. The phrase came to her.

I wish you joy. No, that was too forward.

"May I wish you joy?"

Over the next few hours while she went about her work, Herlinde thought of Miss Calista Wilde, who had clearly come into a reversal of fortunes as many people dream of but few achieve. And yet, to Herlinde she looked like a person in mourning.

———

They were married in the same parlor where Daniel and Martha had married, almost exactly a day later. Callie wore the yellow gown Ethan had bought over her protests, along with the straw bonnet with its ivory silk roses and pale yellow buttercups clustered on the brim. It suited Callie, he was glad to see. At the right moment he produced a simple gold band and put it on Callie's finger.

She looked very young, with a glow to her face that came from prodigious scrubbing, Ethan was sure, rather than any kind of bridelike emotions.

When the paperwork was out of the way Mrs. Cady stepped up to offer them supper.

"Your cousin and his bride wouldn't stop yesterday, but I hope you will, Mr. and Mrs. Middleton. I'd like to hear the news from Paradise. We've all been so worried since word came of the flood."

Ethan glanced at Callie. "Shall we stay for supper?"

"We aren't starting for home?" She looked toward the door.

Mrs. Cady's eyes went very round at such a rude reply, but her husband picked up the thread of the conversation.

"I certainly hope not," said Mr. Cady. "Not in this weather."

Another storm was coming on, pushing shards of light before it.

"Oh," Callie said in a voice nothing like her own. "Well then, yes. Thank you, we will stay for supper. You are very kind."

Mrs. Cady served them a roast of spring lamb, chicken and onion pie, and a veal ragout. There was a big bowl of sauerkraut and the last of the potatoes from the cellar as well. She would have rather given them the first of the new peas and beans and a salad, but the garden was late coming on this year and so they must make do, and Mrs. Middleton, won't you try the sweet pickle relish?

Ethan was glad to see that Callie had lost some of her distracted air if only to apply herself to her food. He himself had had to produce an appetite out of thin air. He did justice to the cook's skills out of obligation, at first, and then with some real admiration for her talent.

The whole time he talked with Mr. Cady about the damage done by the flood, what rebuilding had been done and what still waited, how much time and money would be invested before they were finished.

About the casualties, which had been fewer than one might have expected but still enough to rock the village hard.

"Your own home?" Mrs. Cady asked. "I hope you didn't lose that as well."

"Callie lost her place," Ethan said. He glanced at Callie and smiled. "But we're going to rebuild. I've already started working on the plans."

The look she gave him, wonder but also irritation, that he would assume so much.

The kitchen maid cleared the table and brought out a gingerbread cake, fragrant and glistening with sugar. At a word from Mrs. Cady she retired back to the kitchen, but on the way she sent one wistful look back to the untouched cake.

Mrs. Cady had drawn Callie into a conversation about the quality of the last batch of meal and where the very best molasses was to be found and did she think tomatoes were truly safe to serve? Because she, Millicent Cady, had never touched a tomato even when the mayor's wife served them to her on the finest china. Then she asked about apples, and Callie's expression turned from wary to thankful. Ethan couldn't tell if Mrs. Cady's interest was sincere, or if she was being charitable.

When they were ready to leave the lady took both Callie's hands in her own and kissed her on the cheek.

She said, "I wish you joy, Mrs. Middleton. And when you next come to Johnstown, I hope you will visit with us again."

Outside the rain had given way, finally, to the golden light of a summer evening. Overhead the sky was clear and blameless. Ethan offered Callie his arm just as the door behind them opened again and Mr. Cady called to them.

"Mrs. Cady says if you'll wait just a moment she'll send some provisions with you for your journey tomorrow. I believe she intends to give you a large slice of her gingerbread."

He turned as if listening to someone in another part of the house, and left them there outside, half standing in the open door.

Voices drifted to them down the hallway, Mr. Cady speaking to a man, and then the kitchen maid who had served them, speaking to another servant as dishes clattered.

She was saying, "Looked a fright, didn't she, when they showed up yesterday. Like a drowned cat. But today I hardly recognized her in that new gown. Everything new from stem to stern, looked like to me, and don't it make you wonder?

"I'm not saying any such thing, Henrietta, and I'll thank you not to put words in my mouth. Of course he can spend as much money as he likes on his wife, I wouldn't dispute that. But all that expensive finery for somebody who'd rather be out working in the fields and don't care a bit about those pretty things. It's a waste, say I.

"Will you look, Henrietta, you've missed a spot right in the middle of the table and you know how she likes the whole thing to shine. Now what was I saying? Oh, yes, that nice Mr. Middleton, a good-looking man and educated and good-hearted and generous to a fault, and money to burn. And her. It don't make any sense at all, not unless—"

Ethan reached for the door to shut it, but Callie caught his arm and forced it away.

"I'm just saying I wouldn't be surprised if she's got something growing under her apron. Why else would a man like that marry such a awkward ugly little thing with nothing to her name but some tore-up old apple trees?"

The walk back to the hotel took no more than ten minutes, and every one of them was utterly silent. Ethan considered things he might say and then rejected each one. When he ventured a glance there was nothing to read from her expression. No trace of anger or hurt. Just the same expression Callie wore every day of her life. Focused on some goal just out of sight.

When they were within sight of the inn, she stopped. Without looking at him she said, "What is in this for you?"

Swallows reeled overhead against a darkening sky. On his face the breeze was warm and damp, and he realized how very tired he was.

Callie was waiting for his answer. He wondered if there was any way for him to say the right things, and decided there was not. He would have to settle for the truth.

Ethan said, "I'm tired of being alone."

She snorted a short laugh. "You've got the whole Bonner clan, all those cousins."

"I do," he agreed. "I am welcome at my aunt's table whenever I care to show my face, and the same is true of all my cousins. They are glad to see me, and they like my company as much as I like theirs."

"But?"

"I'm a cousin, but I go home eventually to an empty house and I don't like it. You're alone in the world too, and we have always got on just fine. I thought we could help each other. Are you regretting this already?"

"You're the one who should be having doubts. You heard what that serving girl said. That's what everyone will be thinking, that I trapped you, and forced you into marriage. Nobody will understand why you'd take me otherwise."

He said, "Nobody whose opinion I value will think that."

"I think it." She turned to face him.

"I find that sad."

She flushed. "You made some promises."

"And I will keep them."

"Separate beds."

"Yes. No marital relations, no children."

"How is that possible?"

Ethan looked at her directly. They had come to the sticking point. He said, "I am incapable of that act that produces children."

"Physically incapable. You have tried?"

"And failed. I am reconciled to my situation."

"Ah." She drew back a little. He wondered if she would ask more pressing questions. Not now, he thought, but someday. Someday her curiosity would get the better of her. And maybe by then it wouldn't matter.

He said, "So you see, we are well suited. It will be just the two of us, but we have friendship and mutual understanding and common interests. Those things can be enough. I believe that."

She let out a small laugh, one that sounded almost pleased. She said, "That's more than most people get."

"Exactly," Ethan said. "That is exactly what I was trying to say."

"People mustn't know," she said. "No one needs to know, do they?"

"It's no one's business but ours."

"And if Jemima—if anybody should ask—"

"Ah, well. That's a question. If you're willing to go along with it, I will tell anyone who needs to know that this is a proper marriage."

"That it's been consummated."

"Yes. If you're agreed."

She looked as though he had handed her a treasure beyond counting. A gift more valuable than any of the things he had paid for with coin, something she had never thought to have. Callie took his arm and they walked on. "Yes," she said. "We are agreed."

38

"*If* I didn't know better, I would swear you arranged all this," Martha said.

They were at the kitchen table with the remains of their midday meal spread out before them. Daniel sat across from her with his head resting on his right hand.

She said, "Why do you stare at me?"

That only made him grin, which made her want to pinch him.

The storm was directly overhead now, and a strike of lightning made the window glass shake. Another long, stuttering bluish flash came almost immediately, and then the double boom.

He said, "Why shouldn't I look at you? You are very nice to look at. And oh, yes, you also happen to be my wife."

Odd how two words could cause her color to rise.

Daniel got up and leaned over the table to whisper in her ear. "Do you know what we're going to do now, all alone in the kitchen?"

Her throat was too dry to produce even a squeak.

He said, "We're going to drag the tub out here and heat water so you can have a bath."

Her fist came up of its own accord and he caught it neatly before it could connect with his ear. Then laughing, he pulled her up against him and kissed her soundly.

"Bath first," he said. "And then you can do with me as you like."

He was her husband, but Martha had no intention of stripping down for him in the Allens' kitchen. Once the bath was filled with steaming water she banished him, and then she eased down into it inch by inch, drawing in a hissing breath as the heat reached those places that were raw and sore and still, oddly enough, pleasantly aching. Her hair smelled of Daniel. There were other, more practical reasons not to wash it just now, and she listed those for herself. Better to wait until they got home.

Home, to Paradise. Martha rested her head against the edge of the tub, closed her eyes, and for the first time let herself think about what was to come.

Would they go directly to Uphill House? It seemed likely. Almost certainly his family would be waiting for them to do just that. His very large, very opinionated family who had done her so many good turns. Hannah, Ben, Luke, Jennet, Lily, Simon, Gabriel, Annie, and Birdie. Ethan, who had been her teacher. His brothers and sisters, his cousin, father, and mother—who had taught her how to read and write and work long division. His people, and now hers too.

And at some point, when she was ready, Jemima.

From the doorway Daniel called to her. "Do you need any help?"

She drew in a deep sigh. The temptation was great, but bigger still was the fear that Mrs. Allen would come home after all to find them—

"No," she said. "I'm on my way upstairs now."

It was the most self-indulgent, decadent thing imaginable, but Martha did it. Wrapped in towels she went back to bed in the middle of the day, climbed up the steps to burrow under sheets and coverlets, soft and fragrant.

Daniel sat beside her on the edge of the bed. He looked very serious, but that wasn't what she was hoping for from him, not just now.

"Won't you come—rest?" Her voice cracked, and that made him grin.

When they were lying side by side with the storm still howling all around them, Daniel took her hand and folded their fingers together. It was a comforting thing, and Martha found herself on the brink of tears, for no good reason at all.

Daniel said, "This is nice."

It was. It was wonderful, in fact.

"Nobody knows where we are," Martha said. "We might as well be on Mr. Defoe's island, cast away."

"You like the idea?"

She lifted a shoulder. "I like the idea of a few days of quiet and rest."

"Just the two of us."

"Yes."

"A wedding trip. A honeymoon, is that what it's called?"

"Oh, no," Martha said. "A honeymoon is hard work, for the bride most especially."

He barked a surprised laugh.

Martha pressed her mouth hard and said, "That's not what I meant, and you know it."

"Fine," Daniel said. "Tell me what you did mean."

He would wait for her answer and so Martha began, a little grumpily. "In Manhattan when young people go off on a wedding trip, their time is hardly their own. They have to call on any and every relation within twenty miles all along the way, and sit in parlors and try not to look bored when all they want is—"

The corner of his mouth jerked.

"All they want is some quiet time together."

"And how do you know this?"

She turned onto her side to look at him. "Girls talk to each other."

"Of course you do. About kissing."

Martha felt herself coloring but she was determined to hold on to her dignity. "Among other things."

Now she had his interest.

"Such as?"

Her irritation was about to get the upper hand. She said, "You're asking me to betray confidences."

"I'm asking you to confide in me."

She pushed herself up on one elbow. "Since we seem to have run aground on this topic, I should be able to ask you the same things."

One brow arched. "What do you want to know?"

"Well," Martha said slowly. She lay back down and concentrated on the canopy overhead. "Where did you learn all—that. The things you know. I can't imagine you sitting around with Gabriel and Blue-Jay, talking about such things."

"Oh, men talk," Daniel said.

For some reason Martha was irritated by this. "You are saying that you know what you know—you learned what you know—from listening to other men talk about what they do with their wives?"

"Hell no," Daniel said. "I don't want to hear what Gabriel gets up to behind closed doors."

"Well then, where—" she broke off. "Never mind. I don't think I want to know."

There was a long silence. A full minute, by Martha's reckoning.

Daniel said, "You do want to know. Admit it."

"Not every curiosity has to be satisfied."

"Oh, but some do. Some curiosities beg to be satisfied."

She put her face into the pillow and screamed.

When she came up for air he said, "I'll tell you, you know. I don't mind."

Very calmly, with all the dignity she could muster, Martha said, "Your history is your business alone."

"In great detail, if you care to hear."

She glared at him and he raised one brow in response. It made him look disreputable, with his beard stubble and tousled hair. It made her want to slap him, or run away and hide, or laugh. She said, "There is something very unsettling about this side to your personality."

"I understand," he said. "But if you'll let me explain—"

"Daniel!"

He was trying not to laugh. "Don't ever play at cards, Martha. You'll go bankrupt in a half hour."

She said, "Let me be clear. I really don't want to know about other women you've been with." She thought: in Paradise? here in Johnstown? girls I know? And she bit down hard on her lip.

He was saying, "Why do you assume I've been with a lot of women?"

It was a reasonable question. She took a moment to think about it. "It would be better than hearing about one special person."

He ran a finger down the length of her arm and she jerked. "There isn't anybody like that. I'm not bound to anybody by affection or habit. I would have told you so."

Martha let out a breath. "All right then."

"But that still leaves your curiosity unanswered."

She threw up her hands. "Go ahead and tell me. I want names and dates and details."

"That I can't give you," Daniel said with mock seriousness. "But I could show you."

She heard herself draw in a shocked breath. "I have no interest in meeting—whoever it is you're talking about."

Daniel rubbed a knuckle along his upper lip.

"I don't know why you jump to the worst conclusions. There's nobody to introduce you to. What I know I learned from a book." And: "Martha, if you could see the look on your face."

"I don't believe you," she stuttered. "I don't believe such a book exists. Who would write such a thing? Who would read it? Why did *you* read it? Never mind. I don't want to know. Do booksellers have such things available for anyone who asks?"

"Not every bookseller, no. I ordered it from a bookshop in London. It's a novel, but of a particular sort."

"A novel. Like Miss Austen's *Pride and Prejudice,* or Mr. Scott's *Ivanhoe,* or that novel that your mother dislikes so much, what was it called—"

"*The Pioneers.* A work of fiction, a novel. Yes. That's what I mean. Though I am fairly sure my mother has never read *Adventures of a French Lady of Leisure.*"

He was neither embarrassed nor flustered, and moreover, it was clear he was not going to drop the subject. Nor could she really criticize him for that because she was having a difficult time convincing herself—much less him—that she had no interest in this book of his. If it existed.

He was saying, "It's about a young Frenchwoman named Marie-Rose de la Force. She is very curious about the world."

Martha bit her cheek but the question came out anyway. "A Frenchwoman?"

"*Oui,*" Daniel said, and she heard herself giggle. It was time to take things in hand.

She said, "Don't tell me any more."

"As you wish," Daniel said. "It would be easier to show you, anyway."

She went still. "You have the book with you?"

"Your enthusiasm makes me cheerful. It bodes well for our marital happiness."

She pinched him.

"Ow!" He laughed and pulled away. "Of course I don't have it here. It's at home. We could read it aloud in the evenings if you like."

She knew she was sputtering, and she knew too that her outrage was not completely sincere; what she was feeling was more a tingling curiosity. A book. He had read about those things they had done in this very bed in a book. About a French lady.

Better to put it out of her mind.

He had moved closer, and now he whispered in her ear. "It's a long book," he said. "It will take us ages to work through it."

A flush ran up Martha's body from deep in her belly. Her breasts felt heavy and her nipples had hardened enough to make her chemise peak.

"If you are trying to seduce me," Martha said, "you're investing a great deal of effort for a foregone conclusion. And if I may say, I hope I'm at least as interesting as a book."

"Darlin'," he said. "You've got my undivided attention."

This time there was something new between them. A playfulness, as rough as puppies but far more serious.

Daniel lifted his head to say, "Do you know what this is called?"

And she batted at him so that he laughed harder and pinned her wrist down, levered himself over her and kissed her breathless.

Oh, she was curious. She had to admit that to herself at least. There were so many questions she might have asked, but Daniel's touch made them all go away. Once again standing over her, he lifted her up to him with his good hand, and she watched him, every nerve firing, as he fit himself to her and then settled exactly where she needed him to be.

"Oh," she said. *"Ooh là là."*

39

In Paradise the rain came down in winding sheets and mist rose up from the ground and hovered over the town, like a lid on a boiling pot, rattling angrily and threatening to fly off. Not even noon, and two storms had already passed through. And more was coming, by the smell of the air.

Birdie tried to block out the conversation behind her, but without luck.

Adam was saying, "They might still be back today. And then school will start tomorrow."

The little people could hardly wait for school to start. Even John, who was two years shy of being able to go himself. The only one of them who was unhappy about all this was Eliza. Her sister Amelie and her cousins Mariah and Isabel would be going to school, and she would have to stay behind with the babies. Her eyes swam with tears that she tried to blink away. Birdie felt protective of Eliza, who was just a little too young to fit in.

"Not tomorrow," she said. "New-married people go off together to be alone."

"Ooooh," said Adam. "Can we go with them?"

"Then they wouldn't be alone, would they?" Birdie wished she could take back her tone, but it was too late.

"You are grumpy," said Mariah. "I thought you liked the idea of having Martha as a good-sister."

"Of course she does," said Henry, and she threw him a thankful glance.

"Then there's no call to be so short," Nathan said. "Especially now that you got your way about splitting the class in two."

Unless Martha didn't want to teach, now that she was married. Birdie kept that distressing idea to herself.

"Children!" called Curiosity from the kitchen. "Come on in here now. Food's on the table."

Things got a little better then. The little people liked to eat and they liked nothing better than to eat all together at one table. As long as someone was there to fill bowls and cups, they would all settle in and forget their arguments while they worked their way through soup and cornbread and dandelion greens stewed with bacon.

It was a relief, or at least Birdie expected to be relieved by the quiet, but to her own surprise she found she couldn't keep her thoughts to herself.

To Curiosity she said, "Do you think they'll be back today?" and all faces turned to her. Even Hannah looked up from spooning gruel into Simon's open mouth.

"You know I ain't never been good at telling weather," Curiosity said. "Now Jennet, she the one can read the sky like a book. You think the rain going to stop anytime soon, Jennet?"

"Och, aye," Jennet said, handing Isabel a piece of cornbread. "It won't last the afternoon. But the roads will be a misery and I doubt we'll see any of them before midday tomorrow."

"And then school will start," Adam said firmly.

"We'll see," Hannah said. "There are things they'll need to attend to."

By which she meant Jemima.

———

Birdie had spent much of Sunday trying to find a way to get a good look at Jemima Southern. She gave up finally and went home, and not an hour later Jemima had come to Uphill House, her husband beside her but no sign of the little boy, who interested Birdie just as much as his mother did.

If she was his mother. There was some debate about that possibility going on in corners in the village. If her ma and da were thinking the same thing, they weren't talking about it where they might be over-heard. She herself was trying to come up with a way to raise the subject to her ma when Jemima arrived.

Birdie thought right away it must be Jemima, because nobody else from Paradise would knock. A visitor opened the door and hallooed, and somebody hallooed back. You could tell who it was by the halloo itself. Birdie considered herself a pretty good mimic of other people's halloos; she had once got in trouble for making Curiosity think Becca LeBlanc was at her front door.

That hour of Jemima's visit was hard. First Ma wanted her to take the little people over to Curiosity, something Birdie most sincerely did not want to do but would have to; she had never directly disobeyed her ma, and knew that it would be a bad time to start. Ma was worried about too many things to count, and angry too, and so Birdie had walked with the little people over to Curiosity's, listening the whole time to Nathan and Henry and Adam talking about the Fochts' horses. Boys would get caught up in the least important thing, and then they called girls flighty.

Once she had delivered the little people—waving to Curiosity from the distance so as not to get caught up in having to tell everything—she flew back home as fast as she could, coming around the long way through the woods and in by way of the kitchen door so as not to dis-turb the grown-ups where they stood talking on the front porch.

And that was an odd thing. It meant that Ma hadn't invited them into the parlor, a breach of what Ma called etiquette that was hard to credit. She gave even the smelliest trapper a better welcome, offered him food and drink and a bath, if he wanted one. Anyone who took the bath was welcome to come eat in the house and otherwise she sent out a plate.

The trappers mostly didn't take her up on the bath, because they sewed their clothes on for the season and wouldn't be bothered. But the point, Birdie told herself, was that Ma would let a trapper eat at her table if he was willing to take a bath, and there stood Jemima in fine clothes and Ma wouldn't let her over the door swell.

Jemima had come to Paradise with her coach and her servants and her trunks of clothes (four of them, Anje LeBlanc had reported, with shiny brass fittings) and she had turned everything upside down and inside out. Not all of that was bad. Daniel and Martha eloping was a very good thing; everybody seemed to be agreed on that much. To Birdie it was exciting and irritating at the same time; she hoped nobody had the idea that since they got married in Johnstown they could just do without a wedding party.

Birdie thought this through while she tiptoed through the hall and up the stairs to her own room, where she could stand at the window and hear every word spoken on the front porch.

It seemed like Jemima was doing all the talking, but if she was mad, she was holding her temper in check. Her voice was even and reasonable-sounding, but when she paused she never got more than a couple of words in reply, and all of them from Da, who was good at getting his point across with nothing but a sharp look.

Now Mr. Focht was talking, a man like a swollen keg ready to burst at the seams. His hair standing out straight and stiff from his ears and nose and eyebrows and even from his knuckles, like porcupine quills. Asking about legal documents and court hearings and other things that Birdie didn't understand, and could not even remember long enough to write down in her notebook.

Jemima asked better questions. She wanted to know about Callie, where she was living since the flood and how was it that the Bonners took it upon themselves to hide her own stepdaughter from her; could he explain that? Because it didn't seem right. And there was a rumor in the village that Daniel and Martha had gone off together. Did they have anything to do with that?

"Our Daniel is a man grown," Da said finally. "We don't keep him on a leash."

"I have a right to know where my daughters are," Jemima said again, her voice a little strained now.

"Of course you do," Da said. "You've always had that right. When you walked off and left them with nothing and no way to fend for themselves, for example. Surely you must remember the day you abandoned those girls you're wanting to see so bad. Or have I got that wrong?"

"Don't answer that," Mr. Focht said.

Birdie would have liked to see her ma's face. She wanted some idea of how she was taking all this.

"We'll go, then," Jemima said stiffly. There was a long pause and she said, "The rumor is that Daniel and Martha have gone to Johnstown to be married. If that's so—"

"Spare us your threats," Ma said.

"On the contrary," Jemima said. "I would be delighted."

40

"Tell it to me again," Curiosity said.

They were sitting at Curiosity's kitchen table over teacups. Elizabeth was weary to the bone but this conversation couldn't wait, and so here she was.

"She is willing to go to court to force her hand," Elizabeth said.

Curiosity let out a noisy breath. "I think she should go right ahead. She can stand there in front of God and man and explain herself. I for one would like to hear it."

Elizabeth finished the last of her milky tea, and then spent a moment studying the dregs on the bottom of her cup. She said, "Curiosity, we haven't talked about your story."

She felt the older woman tensing ever so slightly.

"It must have been very difficult for you, I realize that. And I am thankful. Otherwise I would never have known the truth about myself."

Curiosity's head snapped toward her. "That story wan't about *you*. That story was about me, and what a foolish, vainglorious thing I did. I caused your mama harm and your daddy too, and I am truly sorry for it."

Elizabeth said, "You shouldn't have withheld the letters, that's true. But I think the outcome would have been the same."

"Well," Curiosity said. "You free to believe what you like. She was your mama, after all."

She was irritated and ill at ease, and so Elizabeth put two opened letters on the table between them. Yellowed paper, darker along the edges where the pages had been folded for so many years. All the years of Elizabeth's life.

"No," Curiosity said. "Sixty years I been looking at those letters and I don't care to look no more."

"Nevertheless," Elizabeth said. "I am leaving them here with you. If you can bring yourself to read them, you may find a way to come to peace with the past."

The old woman looked up at her and her eyes were wet.

"You think so." Not so much a question as a challenge.

"I do," Elizabeth said. "Read them, and decide for yourself."

"If you want me to know what's in those letters, then you have got to read them to me. Read them aloud so's I can hear her voice."

Elizabeth drew in a deep breath, and then she picked up the first of the letters.

Dear Gabriel,

I write to thee to thank thee for so many things, it is hard to know where to begin. The gifts of fellowship and love thou gave me were then and will always be precious to me. When I was cast down, when I was in danger of never finding my way out of the shadows, it was thee who came to my aid. And I have found my way. Here in England I have a place in my good-sister's fine home, and work to keep me busy, and Augusta's friendship.

But the primary source of my joy is our daughter, Elizabeth. If I had thy talent I should draw her likeness, so that thou couldst see what a beautiful, healthy child she is. Already at eight weeks she is so curious about the world, and so dear to me. The Lord has blessed me with a daughter to raise, and I am thankful.

We two are welcome at Oakmere, and this is where we will make our permanent home. It is my intention to never return to the New-York frontier.

It is best this way, Gabriel. In thy heart thou must know that in the end, we should both chafe at the other's needs and grow resentful, and that I could not bear. I regret nothing. I am only sorry that I will never be able to tell thy daughter about thee and that she will never know the pleasure of thy fellowship.

And so I wish thee well and happy in thy travels, my love. May our Lord's light shine upon thee.

Maddie

Dear Maddie,

It is a year since I returned to Paradise to hear from good friend Curiosity that thou wert gone away to England, there to stay. At first I could not credit this report and I promised that I would come back every season to see if thou might have left word for me.

Now it seems I must accept that thou art gone away from this place, from thy husband and from me. I know thee, Maddie. I know thee in thy bones, and I know thou would not do such a thing lightly.

Thou hast removed thyself from temptation's way, and still I wonder, if one day thou should see me at thy door, so many miles from here, how wouldst thou greet me? As a friend, or something less? I confess I cannot bear the thought that thou might turn away from me.

But above all things I care for thy happiness and well-being, and so I must also respect thy wishes. There is an expedition leaving in a few days' time for Spanish Florida and beyond, and I have been invited to join the company. It will be a difficult two or perhaps three years before I return to this part of the world. Every day I will think of thee and pray that thou might find fulfillment and joy in thy life. To honor thee, I can do no less.

With all my heart, my love

Gabriel

After a long time, when she was calm, Elizabeth reached across the table and covered Curiosity's hand with her own.

41

Late that night Elizabeth lay sleepless beside Nathaniel, her thoughts dashing one way and then the other. Daniel, Martha, Curiosity, Ethan, Callie, Curiosity. Jemima. Curiosity. Curiosity.

Nathaniel rolled onto his side and said, "I can hear you thinking, Boots. Talk to me."

"We've been talking all day," she said, her voice wavering. "Do you think another conversation would help?"

He smiled sleepily. "I do. This is me you're talking to, and nobody else listening in. No need to hold back."

"I haven't been holding anything back."

"No?"

Elizabeth tried to gather her thoughts. "Do you mean about Curiosity?"

"I'd say the fact that you brought her name up so quick means something. That story she told, that's not something you can hide away and forget you ever heard."

Elizabeth recognized the wisdom in this, even if she wasn't particularly eager to pursue the discussion.

"I think the thing that surprised me most was the way she looked at me when she had finished. She truly believed I would turn her away and never speak to her again."

"Sixty years holding that story back, I don't doubt she was worried. And maybe rightly so. Talking about what happened so long ago has raised ghosts, is all."

"She's thinking about my mother."

"And Gabriel. Boots, do you think your mother was unhappy?"

Elizabeth closed her eyes and sent her mind back to her ten-year-old self, just Birdie's age. That last good summer before the sudden illness that took her mother's life. She had so many clear memories of those few months. Over the years her mother's face had faded, but still Elizabeth had a sense of her expression. Always calm, often cheerful. A poor relation, Quaker, an odd American with strange ideas but still valued and respected in Aunt Merriweather's household. She had been the voice of reason and logic tempered with kindness, and all the children had come to her in times of hurt and uncertainty. Never once had Elizabeth heard her mother complain, but she had often heard her laugh.

"I don't think she was unhappy, but what do children really understand of adults?" Elizabeth said. "Perhaps she wept every night."

"She had the chance to come back here, but she stayed where she was. I think that means something."

"I've wondered about that too," Elizabeth said. "What a shock it must have been when her husband showed up, wanting to claim his wife and daughter both and take us back to Paradise. I wonder if she felt anger or only sadness. I think the fact that she conceived Julian during that visit is evidence enough that she struggled with guilt and remorse."

"If she had brought you back here right then, we would have grown up together."

"That's an odd idea," Elizabeth said. "I wonder what would have become of us."

They were quiet for a long minute and then Elizabeth realized that Nathaniel had drifted off to sleep. As if to say, where else could we possibly be, but together in this bed, with children and grandchildren sleeping soundly nearby. Because neither of them could imagine a life without the other in it.

---

42

*W*hen they had been husband and wife for two days the rains stopped and the sun came out with a fierce purpose, and so Daniel and Martha started for home at dawn. The puppy slept in a basket tied to Martha's saddle, apparently unruffled by the bumpy road. The plan was to reach Paradise by early afternoon and to go directly to his family at Uphill House.

"There will be some sort of party," Daniel said, as if she might not like the idea. In fact, Martha did find it a little disconcerting.

"I suppose there's no avoiding it."

"Not if you want to stay in Birdie's good graces. She dearly loves a party."

"Just family?"

She felt him looking at her. "Today, yes. I can't promise what will happen tomorrow at school."

"Oh, that I don't mind," Martha said. "You don't think it will be awkward, me taking over the younger students?"

"Hell, no," Daniel said. "It'll be a lot easier all the way around. A new bride puts most people in a cheerful mood."

"I hope you're right."

He squinted at her.

"Is there somebody specific you're worried about?"

"Let's just say that I don't have many admirers among girls my age."

"Aha," Daniel said. "Alice LeBlanc?"

"Among others."

"They'll get over it," he said.

Which was certainly true, but how long it would take and how awkward the process might be, those questions seemed not to interest Daniel. She had finally found one thing in which he and Teddy were alike.

Maybe, she reasoned to herself, this disinterest had to do with the fact that male friendships were never quite so intense or close as those females forged. Or, a less charitable interpretation was simply that now that they were married—she still stumbled over that idea—she didn't need anyone else in her life. She had him, and his family, and what else was necessary?

Daniel was saying, "We could go to Lake in the Clouds and stay there until the business with Jemima is settled. You never have to see her if you don't want to."

"Tempting," Martha said. "But hiding from my mother has never worked, and I wouldn't want to give her the satisfaction. I have to stand up to her if I'm ever to have any peace."

Daniel's slow smile said that she had surprised him, or pleased him, or both. For her own part, she could only hope she could live up to the goal she had set for herself.

"And anyway, I don't like the idea of leaving Callie to deal with it all. It wouldn't be fair."

"If you put it that way," Daniel said. "It makes sense. But I should point out to you that the Bonner men will keep an eye on Callie and make sure she's left alone."

"I'm not so sure she wants to be alone," Martha said.

She wondered if it was possible to explain how she felt about this, and decided that she must try.

"Everyone has abandoned her, all her life," she said. "Her mother, Cookie, her father. Jemima. And then I went to Manhattan, and that must have been the hardest blow. She's distrustful and with good reason. I want to try to make her understand that she can depend on me. Though I have to admit I didn't get off to such a good start.

"I should never have spoken so quick," Martha finished. "She was in a fragile state of mind and I should have known better. She is very angry at me. I only hope I can mend things between us."

There was just too much to worry about, and so Martha turned her attention to the day, bright and clear with a warm breeze that lifted the hem on her skirt and made the grass dance. Deadwood and debris from the flood was everywhere, but things were already surrendering to the force of nature, disappearing under layers of moss and serving as home to countless numbers of small creatures. Now and then they caught a glimpse of the river running on its way to the sea. Just weeks ago it had roused itself to strike, an image which explained why the Mohawk called the west branch of the Sacandaga *twisting snake.*

Martha shifted in the saddle in an effort to find a more comfortable spot. Or a less painful one. When she saw Daniel padding the saddle before they set out, she had found herself as capable of blushing as she ever was. Somehow it hadn't occurred to her that Daniel would be aware of how sore she was, but then it was his doing, after all.

In that moment she was glad the trail had narrowed and he was ahead of her, because she was red all the way to her hairline and worse still: He would know what she was thinking about if he caught sight of her face.

He sat easy and straight in the saddle. Beneath the loose linen shirt and the knives and tomahawks—such a great number of them—she could see the shape of him and the way the muscles moved. All the museums in the world and all the sculpture could not have prepared her for the reality of Daniel Bonner. She kept discovering things that took her by surprise, things that she would have asked him about if she had had the words. And the nerve.

"What are you thinking about?" He was looking back at her over his shoulder.

Your buttocks, she might have said. *As round and firm and smooth as fruit. The texture of your skin. The smell of you.*

His mind was somewhere else entirely. He was saying, "We'll find a way to put Callie at ease."

"Yes," she answered in the most serious tone she could summon. "I know we will."

But there was a gulf now between Callie and herself, and in truth she didn't know if it could be breached. Callie had no interest in a family of her own and Martha was a wife; she would have a household, a garden to look after, and a husband to talk to about her day. And children. If they went on the way they had started, children would not be long in coming.

Martha wondered if it was quite normal for a new bride to be so preoccupied with sex. The subject was never far from her mind. What she had seen, and how it had felt. Especially how it felt, the things Daniel did with such focus and determination. He watched her so intently that she sometimes wondered if she was doing something wrong. Maybe the next time she would ask him straight out.

Whenever the next time might be. How long would it be before he turned to her with that expression she had already learned to recognize? And if he wasn't turning to her, why wasn't he, and what did it mean that she was hoping he would. Did a wife ask for her husband's attention? She could hardly imagine it.

There were other things—important things—to worry about; she might even have been able to focus on those things for a few hours at least. If not for the fact that she was sore, and on horseback.

Just two miles out of Paradise where the road ran along the Sacandaga, Daniel came to a sudden stop for a reason that Martha couldn't see right away. Then she followed his gaze down to the river, where two riders were watering their horses.

Seen through the trees Martha could make out very little about them, but Daniel didn't have the same problem.

"Ethan," he said.

"Ethan?"

"And Callie."

"Ethan and Callie?" Like an echo, and just as empty of sensible thought. "But—"

"Here they come," Daniel said. "We can ask them."

At first Martha believed Daniel must be mistaken, because the young woman was unfamiliar to her. She held herself very well, which suited the plain but excellent cut of her clothes, from traveling cloak to boots.

Then she met Callie's gaze beneath the scoop brim of her new bonnet and understood that something monumental had happened.

Callie was transformed from the anxious, bitter young woman who had come to call on Saturday, who had said her mind with such disapproval. That was the last time they had seen each other, because Callie hadn't come to the ice-out party. And this, this was a different Callie altogether.

Then the sun caught the ring on Callie's finger, and it all came clear.

Martha tried to pin down a single thought that she might put into words. *I see you are married,* or *May I wish you joy,* or *This is a surprise,* or *Did you not swear to me just a few days ago that you would never marry, and scold me for my foolishness in considering such a thing?* But she could say none of those things for fear of being misunderstood. Or, she admitted to herself, of being understood too well.

Daniel was saying, "We sat out the weather at the Allen place. You were in town?"

Martha would have poked him, had she been close enough. He was being dense.

"We got married, just about exactly a day after you."

"In Mr. Cady's parlor," Callie added. The first words she had said.

Daniel blinked. "I'd be lying if I didn't say I was surprised. But I'm happy for both of you. Congratulations. If we had known what you had in mind, we could have traveled together."

At that Martha had to press her mouth shut, because the idea struck her as outlandish.

Ethan spoke to her directly, "I'd congratulate Daniel but he's too proud of himself already. So I will wish you joy, Martha."

How very awkward and silly it all sounded; this was the way people talked to each other in Manhattan salons, not on country lanes.

"You have gone very still," Callie said to Martha. "I suppose we have shocked you with our news. We did try to find you in Johnstown."

"Not at all," Martha said, and she made an effort to put all the warmth and sincerity she could muster into her voice. "I am very happy for you, Callie."

"The idea wasn't to make you happy," Callie said shortly. "It was to make your mother unhappy."

There was an awkward pause. In the end Martha simply turned her horse's head and walked away.

"There's a lot to talk about," she heard Daniel say behind her. "But this isn't the place for it. Will you come home with us to see my folks?"

"That would be very nice," Callie said. "I would like that."

For the rest of the short trip Martha wondered what she might have said or done different, but there was no help for it. The four of them would arrive at Uphill House together. Her anxiety, already high, soared to the breaking point.

The idea wasn't to make you happy. It was to make your mother unhappy.

Within five minutes they had left the Johnstown road and were following a deer trail uphill, single file. No chance to talk to Daniel or Ethan or even Callie. If she could voice her opinion, what then? She'd come across as mean-spirited, and maybe that was the right word.

Martha asked herself the hardest question: If it made sense for her to marry Daniel, why shouldn't Callie marry Ethan? She needed protection and support; she had no money of her own and if Jemima should try to take the orchard from her, it would be much more difficult now. Ethan had put himself between Callie and Jemima, as Daniel had done for her.

Then what was wrong?

The answer came floating up without prodding at all. *She doesn't love him.* Then again, it was none of her business who Callie loved or didn't love. Ethan was no fool, and he had married Callie of his own free will.

When they came out of the woods at the back of the clearing behind the Bonners' place Martha's heart leaped into her throat.

Daniel leaned over and squeezed her hand. "Chin up," he said. "You have nothing to prove, you know. They already love you."

From the corner of her eye she caught Callie's expression. Reserved, watchful, and determined. She looked nothing like a bride, which made Martha think of what she herself might look like to the world after two days of Daniel's attentions. Just then it came to her, as simple and clear as water: Callie's marriage was truly one of convenience only. They had not shared a bed, and maybe they never would.

A face appeared at the kitchen window followed by a flurry of activity.

"Here they come," Daniel said.

The kitchen door opened and disgorged the little people, as frisky as calves and bellowing almost as loud. Curiosity stood behind them leaning on her cane.

"Hold it right there!" she shouted. "You run out into that dooryard you'll be knee-deep in mud, and then you be stuck right there with the rest of the creatures what don't know no better while we in here visiting with the newlyweds and eating cake."

The children went back the way they had come, looking disgruntled, so it was Curiosity who greeted them first, with Elizabeth and Nathaniel close behind.

"Now look at you," Curiosity said, her eyes moving from Martha to Callie and back again. "Here we was expecting one wedding party but it looks to me like we got two brides here. Ethan! Did you go and marry Callie Wilde?"

Ethan had dismounted and he came over to bend down and kiss Curiosity's cheek. "I did."

"Two brides, then. Martha, did that man of yours forget you needed a ring?"

Martha was momentarily sorry to have taken off her gloves.

"Never mind!" Curiosity said, waving a hand in the air. "I got the idea Elizabeth already got that sorted. Daniel, where's my sugar? Martha, Callie, you two come on now, everybody waiting to see you. Ain't ever day we get two brides at once. In fact I can't remember that ever happening. Don't worry about those men of yours, they know the way."

Martha caught Daniel's eye and he smiled at her, a quiet smile that said she had nothing—they had nothing—to worry about. She belonged here now, and so did Callie. It was a comforting thought, that they were facing this change together, as they had faced so many other, far less pleasant things.

But when she reached out to take Callie's arm, all she got in return was a sharp look as unforgiving as broken glass.

43

Sometimes, Elizabeth told herself, it made no sense to even try to sleep. Certainly after a day like this one she found it hard to imagine she might find any rest. It had been so full of emotion, so overwhelming, that it was stuck in her head like a melody.

The house had never seemed so small, though there was no one in attendance but family. It had to do with the little people, of course, who had not yet learned to temper happiness and excitement with common sense. Even Birdie had given in to it, the usual carefully maintained seniority over nephews and nieces left aside.

"It was a good party," Nathaniel said. He was sitting on the edge of the bed, unlacing his moccasins. When she had no reply he glanced at her and his hair fell over his shoulder, black shot with silver.

She said, "I was thinking of Birdie. It won't be very long before she leaves us too."

He leaned over and kissed her. "I don't know, Boots, but eight, ten years strikes me as a good while before we have to worry about that."

"It will go by very quickly," Elizabeth said.

"Only if you let it."

"And I'm worried about Daniel."

He stripped off his shirt and slid under the covers. With his head propped up on one hand, he studied her face.

"I cain't recall the last time I saw him so happy."

"Oh, I know he's happy with Martha and she with him. It was a joy to see them together. But he was in pain this afternoon, you must have noticed."

Nathaniel was quiet for a long moment. This was a conversation they had had many times over the years. She told him about the things that concerned her, and Nathaniel took it all in without providing false comfort.

"I wish he would talk to Hannah about the treatment Hakim Ibrahim has suggested."

"He's got other things on his mind just now," Nathaniel said. He ran a thumb from her throat down between her breasts. She caught his hand and held it to her.

"You'll forgive me if I don't care to think much about that."

He grinned. "I forgive you. With all that worry in your head, you got any room for Ethan?"

Elizabeth closed her eyes in the hope that would keep her husband from reading her thoughts.

"Boots."

"Hmmm?"

"You're not worried about Ethan and Callie?"

"How could I be anything else?"

She stayed just as she was while he blew out the candle and then settled down for sleep. For a moment she thought she had evaded the worst, but then he slid an arm around her and pulled her close so he could tuck her head under his chin.

"I'll tell you what worries me," he said. "I don't know if it will help or hurt with Jemima."

She sighed. "It makes my head spin to think about it. Nathaniel, did they seem happy to you, Ethan and Callie?"

He rubbed his chin against the crown of her head. "Depends on what you mean by happy, I suppose. They just may suit each other in ways that don't make sense to you and me."

"That's a nice thought," Elizabeth said. And it was enough of a com-

fort that she could let her worries go, just now. In the sweet dark, tethered to her place in the world by Nathaniel's voice and the sound of his
heartbeat.

Simon said, "You need your sleep, Lily, and so do I."

He reached beyond her for the candle, and she caught his hand to
stop him.

"It's your own fault," she said. "You started the conversation. You
asked me what I thought."

He fell back against his pillow and blew a long sigh toward the ceiling.

"God above help me, so I did. All right, then. Now what toll is there
to pay before we can sleep?"

Lily still had his hand in hers, and she smoothed it for a moment
while she thought.

"You can explain Ethan to me."

He let out a rough laugh. "Darlin', I can't even explain you."

This surprised her. "There's nothing complicated about me," Lily
said. "I have everything I want and need, and all my family are settled and
happy. Do not make that face, Simon Ballentyne. I am happy for Daniel.
I see now that Martha is the right choice."

"Come out with it, lass, and say it."

"All right. I was wrong about Martha. And I'm glad that I was wrong.
But I am still confused about Ethan and Callie."

He was silent for a long moment. "Tell me this," he said finally. "Is
there aught we can do but wish them well?"

Lily could think of nothing to say, and so Simon put out the light. She
had begun to slide toward sleep when it happened.

"What?" Simon said. "Is there aught amiss?"

"Feel," she said, and she put his palm on her belly. "As soon as I settle
down to sleep, it starts. A tumbling, like a leaf in the wind."

"Aye, well," Simon said, rubbing gently. "It's only when you're asleep
that wee blueberry can get a word in sidewise."

Hannah came to bed in the last hour of dark, stumbling a little in her exhaustion.

"And?" murmured Ben.

"Mother and child both safe. A girl. Small but I think strong enough to survive."

He reached for her. "You know, I think I could manage another girl," and she rolled away, or tried to.

"Behave yourself." She laughed and wiggled away.

"But why would I do that?"

"We're not the newlyweds," she said.

"Oh, but I feel like one. And so do you."

He had her on her back and soon enough she was kissing him, long, deep slow kisses. In the dark she could make out only the shape of him, but her hands told her the rest.

"Come," he whispered at her ear. "Come to me now and you'll sleep all the better for it after."

It was what he always said, even when she needed no coaxing. And he was right, she couldn't deny it. She couldn't deny him, or her own need. It blossomed with the touch of his mouth on her neck and the gentle bite at the curve where shoulder and throat came together.

She made a sound and he closed the space between them.

"Now let's see," he said. "Let's see if I can remind you what you felt like as a bride."

Under a setting moon two shapes swam in the lake under the falls high on Hidden Wolf. Slender and lithe in their youth and strength, they played together like otters and then disappeared behind the curtain of falling water.

In a fine bed made with linens that smelled of lavender, Callie Wilde started awake, her heart thudding.

An oil lamp cast a soft circle of light over the bed. Why had she gone to bed by lantern light? And what was this room? A carved mantelpiece with a mirror above it, a garderobe, a table covered with a white cloth on which sat a brace of good beeswax candles, a chaise longue.

And a man asleep on it. Ethan Middleton.

He was breathing deeply, shoulders rising and falling, and his face turned to the wall.

A solid, dependable man, who kept his promises. Who had married her for no reason she could see but his kindness and generosity and friendship. Because he was lonely, and had seen the same in her.

He had presented her to his family, as was right and proper, and they had welcomed her as if it were the most natural thing in the world. Her new husband had no brothers or sisters, but he had cousins. Cousins who loved him and would love her for his sake. They treated her as if she had always belonged, and could never belong anywhere else.

From across the room he had smiled at her, and she smiled back while the children fussed over her, bringing her dolls and toys to admire, the littlest ones climbing into her lap. Telling her stories about their games and adventures. They asked about her apple trees, and she told those few stories she had.

She had not told Ethan about the Bleeding Heart. Out of superstition. Out of fear.

The adults brought her tea and refilled her plate and asked her questions about things that interested her. Everyone took pains to make her feel wanted and welcome. Everyone except Martha, who had once been her only family and was now just one of many.

Martha sat on the other side of the room and was surrounded, just as Callie was surrounded, by children and adults. The only difference, as far as Callie could tell, was that Martha had a puppy on her lap. In fact, the children seemed more interested in the puppy than anything else.

When it came time to say good night, she and Ethan had left the horses in the stable and walked the path through the woods, down the hillside, to his house. To her new home. Just as Martha had gone with Daniel to his house in the strawberry fields.

Callie slept in a fine bed by herself. Her husband had gone to his own narrow bed cheerfully, without complaint, and fell straight away to sleep.

What had she been dreaming about, to wake in such panic? Her whole body was damp with sweat and her heart still raced, and how silly that was. She was safe and well fed and comfortable and tomorrow she would be the same, and the days after that, for the rest of her life.

She wondered if Martha disliked sharing a bed, and how well she slept in it.

---

44

*F*orce of habit woke Daniel at first light. Sunlight filtered through the joints of the closed shutters along with the vaguest hint of a breeze; a perfect May morning.

What came next he didn't need to think about; every school morning looked like the last. Get up and dressed, eat whatever there was to eat in the larder, wash and scrape the bristle from his face, rinse his mouth with salt water, and head out for the schoolhouse at a trot, using that time to work through the day's lesson plans.

In the normal course of things he would have been impatient to get back into the classroom after the long break forced on him by the flood and its aftermath. But normal had shifted on its axis, and Daniel wondered how he could best shift himself to suit.

Beside him Martha slept deeply, curled on her side away from him so that he could count the knobs of her spine. Next to her his own skin seemed so dark, and the contrast still took him by surprise. So many things about her surprised him.

There was a small whimpering and then the puppy wiggled out from under the sheet to look at him sheepishly.

"How did you get up here?"

The tiny tail thumped twice in response.

"Lie down with dogs, wake up with fleas," Daniel reminded him. "You've got a basket to sleep in. Best get used to it."

The puppy yawned and tucked himself up against Martha, unconcerned with Daniel's tone, and clearly very pleased with himself.

He could let Martha sleep on. Write a note and go off to teach. Tomorrow would be soon enough for her to start with the younger students, he'd tell her. But it would mean leaving her alone and that went against every instinct he had, given the situation with Jemima. Short of locking her in the cellar, sooner or later Martha would come face-to-face with her mother, and the best he could do was to make sure that when it did, he was right there.

And it was high time he got back to the classroom. He had to go, and so she had to come along with him. It was the plan they had made and they would hold to it, no matter how peaceful she looked sleeping. Or how distracted the process of waking her up turned out to be.

That was the most pressing reason for wanting to wake her, but plain common sense and good manners held him back. He was not a boy of seventeen anymore; he could control his base instincts and leave her be. But that didn't mean he wanted to get out of bed, not quite yet.

He leaned over and put his chin on the shelf of her shoulder and resisted the urge to slip his arms around her.

"Time to get up, teacher."

She couldn't have roused more quickly had he poked her with a pin. Her expression was almost comical, but then again her anxiety was real and so Daniel bit back a smile.

He said, "Unless you've changed your mind."

She sat up and the vaguest hint of a wince crossed her face. Daniel cursed himself for an immoderate fool and vowed to leave her in peace for at least a full day.

"Of course not," she said. "You realize I know nothing of teaching, and I will most probably make a muddle of it."

"Most likely," he agreed.

She pinched him and he yelped.

"Are you sure you want to start a wrestling match right now? Because I could go without breakfast, but you are going to need your strength."

"I don't know about that," Martha said. "I intend to race you down to the village, and to win. You had best eat hearty."

She made him laugh. That was the biggest surprise, how easily she made him laugh, and how often.

The children were waiting by the time they got to the schoolhouse. Daniel could read their mood from a long distance, and this morning there was a lot of excitement barely being held in check. Last night they had promised the nieces and nephews that Hopper would be attending school with them, and Martha realized now that the puppy was a wonderful way to divert at least some of the excitement from herself.

"Eager," Martha remarked.

"Curious," he answered.

"Fair enough," she said. "I'm curious myself." But she kept casting glances up the lane toward the Red Dog that said quite clearly how nervous she was, and for more than one reason. They had talked about this at length, and her position was clear: She would not seek out Jemima, but neither could she hide. When the time came, they would cope with it.

"I'll be within calling distance," he had reminded her. It seemed that idea didn't provide her with much comfort, because she only nodded nervously.

He said, "You think she might walk into the classroom to confront you."

"Yes," Martha had said. And then: "What are you thinking?"

"Not much. We can lock the doors once I sound the last bell."

She looked surprised, and then thoughtful. "You think it will be so easy?"

He shrugged. "If we let it be."

And that was the end of the conversation.

Now the children pushed every other thought and worry out of her head. All fourteen of the littler ones gathered around her and vied for her attention. Six of them were Martha's newly acquired nieces and nephews, which would require a bit of diplomacy. Luckily all of them seemed to be on their best behavior. No doubt they had been closely tutored about what was expected of relatives in the classroom. Birdie would take great pains with that, and Daniel had said a word to the older ones himself the evening before.

Birdie caught Daniel's eye. She stood near the door, her hands folded in front of her and looking so much like their mother trying to hold on to her patience that Daniel almost laughed.

To Martha he said, "Can you cope?"

She shooed him away like a buzzing fly.

When she had her students assembled in the classroom, Martha found that her mind had gone blank; all the plans she had discussed with Daniel were simply gone.

Then Henry raised his hand and asked with perfect manners if she would like help calling the roll, a hint that she accepted thankfully. She found the sheet of paper in the top drawer of the desk and saw immediately that there were twenty-two names.

"Is Alois Cunningham here?"

Lottie Mayfair popped up from her seat. "Friend Martha," she began, "Alois hasn't been here since January and he's not about to come back. Wouldst thou care to hear the particulars?"

Martha would, and so the longer story was told with contributions from all the children; it involved a complicated incident with a plow, a pig, and Alois's grandfather Jed. Martha let them tell her whatever they seemed to think was important about all the names on the roll without children to claim them, an exercise that grew into a longer discussion of the flood and the aftermath of the flood. The conversation was informative, amusing, and best of all, it ate up some of the time she had to fill until recess.

From the next room came the murmuring of voices, Daniel's chief among them.

"Children," Martha said, her voice catching. "If you'll take out your readers—"

The door, warped by water and ill-fitting, creaked when it opened, a sound that sounded to Martha like a rifle shot and just as welcome. Daniel had forgot to lock the door as he had planned, and when she turned, her mother would be standing there.

An African woman stood in the doorway, neatly dressed, her expression neutral. She held a boy by the hand. He was about nine, and he looked to be fit and strong as any child his age. He was supposed to be her half brother, but as far as she could see he had none of his mother's features, or of his father's. Which might mean nothing, or everything.

The African woman said, "My mistress say, this is where Master Nicholas must be, in school. I leave him with you now. He will make his own way back come dinnertime."

Before Martha could think to ask her name, the woman was gone. The boy was looking at her with a guileless and open expression, perfectly calm and even eager to please, as if he had never known anything but kindness and could not perceive of any other treatment. Behind her Martha felt the children stirring, uneasy with her silence and with the boy.

He said, "That was Elfie. Elfie didn't want to bring me. Lorena wanted to bring me but Ma said Lorena coddles me and she'd let me run off and play, but I don't mind coming to school. I wouldn't have run off."

Martha said, "Nicholas, we are glad you've come to join us. There are a number of empty desks. Please pick one and sit down."

Younger children, her new mother-in-law had told her, needed movement and distraction and if she could provide those, she would have more success turning their minds to arithmetic and reading and geography. Elizabeth had only given this advice when Martha took her aside to ask her about the best way to approach the class she was supposed to take on the very next morning.

It was the little people revolving around Martha like a carousel during the wedding supper that reminded her what was ahead, and how unprepared she was to walk into a classroom.

Elizabeth's advice made sense to Martha and no doubt it would have been the key to success, but for the unanticipated distraction of a new student who had come to the village and brought so much excitement with him. If Martha's attention was drawn to the boy again and again, despite her earnest intention to treat him just as she did the others, then who could expect any more of the children?

The son of a farmer or a cobbler would have been a matter of great interest—any new child in the village was a momentous event for these children—and still they would have waited until recess to satisfy their curiosity. But Nicholas Wilde was Jemima's son, and even the littlest of

Paradise's young had heard stories of Jemima. Sooner or later Nicholas would find himself at the center of a crowd of children bent on interrogation. He would be overwhelmed by questions he had no way to answer, and rumors that would make no sense to him.

Some children stood up to such treatment and maintained their dignity by stalwart silence; a few tried to fight their way to the respect of their classmates. In any case, Martha could not raise the subject without intensifying the effect. She would keep an eye on him during recess, but children could be both sly and cruel, and it would be impossible to defend him against all comers. Martha had grown up in Paradise as Jemima's daughter, and those memories were very close to the surface as she went about her business. While she bent over water-buckled primers, passed out slates and chalk, she watched Nicholas from the corner of her eye and wondered how he would cope. Each time this thought crossed her mind, she reminded herself that because some of her own classmates had been cruel and mean-spirited, that didn't mean that Nicholas would necessarily receive the same treatment.

When she had set all the other schoolchildren work and it could no longer be avoided, Martha called Nicholas to her desk.

He stood before her, a likely young boy with a head of wavy brown hair and mild eyes the color of caramel. His smile was shy and trusting both.

She said, "Nicholas, how far along are you in your primer?"

He seemed confused by the question, and so she tried again. "Did you learn from a primer like this one with your last teacher?"

"Oh," he said. "No, ma'am."

"You may call me Miss Martha. Then what books did you learn from?"

He seemed pleased to have an answer to this question at least. "The newspaper."

"You learned your letters from the newspaper?"

"Yes, ma'am. Every morning Mr. Focht reads the newspaper and then he passes it along to me."

"And who taught you to read?"

A set of lines appeared on his brow, as though she had spoken to him in Japanese. "Nobody," he said finally. "Ma showed me but mostly I learned on my own."

With a dread sense, Martha thumbed through the primer until she found a list of vocabulary words.

absent	*abhor*	*apron*	*author*
Babel	*became*	*beguile*	*boldly*
capon	*cellar*	*constant*	*cupboard*
daily	*depend*	*divers*	*duty*

"Do you recognize any of these?"

His gaze ran dutifully across each line, and then he shook his head. "Guess I haven't got to those ones yet."

She tried again. "And these?"

> *Age*
> *Beef*
> *Cake*
> *Dead*
> *Eat*
> *Neat*
> *Gate*

Again the solemn consideration, and then a bright smile. He pointed. "There," he said. "My name starts with N, and there it is, N."

"And so it is," Martha said. "Can you read the word that starts with N?"

"Well, I don't know," he said, his brow furled. "I'm not sure I can."

Over the course of the next few minutes Martha discovered that young Nicholas Wilde was a biddable, pleasant child, apparently devoid of all artifice. She learned too that he had only the most rudimentary arithmetic skills, and that he could, when coaxed very patiently, recite the alphabet up to and including the letter K.

At recess Martha sent the children off and then watched from the window as they ran, full of mischief, leaping and skipping, into the warm midmorning sun. Nicholas ran with them, as frolicsome as a colt, full of movement and joy.

From behind her Daniel said, "How did it go?"

He came up and put a hand on her shoulder and she leaned into him. "It went well," she said. "But I have a new student."

She could almost hear him frown. His gaze shifted to the children at play and his posture straightened.

"Is that—"

"Yes," Martha said. "That is my half brother Nicholas."

Daniel drew in a sharp breath. "She is sly," he said finally. "Using the boy to get places she herself can't go."

Martha couldn't see his face, but she could feel a fine thrumming tension running through him.

"What do you think she means to accomplish?" Martha said finally.

"Hard to say."

"There's something else. He's slow-witted."

Daniel started and she looked over her shoulder at him.

"How do you mean?"

She said, "Do you remember Dora Cunningham's youngest daughter? She looked perfectly healthy and normal, but there was something wrong. She always seemed far younger than she was. I remember asking Hannah about it."

"And she said?"

"That sometimes if a birth is very difficult and prolonged, the full extent of the damage won't be known for a year or more. The strain of the birth can injure the brain so that it doesn't fully develop. She used more medical terms, but that's what it was, in essence."

"Does that seem to be the case here?"

Martha lifted a shoulder. "I really don't know. It's unlikely Jemima will allow Hannah to examine the boy, and possibly nothing would come of it anyway."

They watched the younger boys who stood in a circle, heads bent together to study something one of them held in his hands. Nicholas was one of the group.

"I thought he'd have a far harder time fitting in," Martha said. "But they've accepted him without a moment's hesitation."

"He is no challenge to them," Daniel said. "And now what are you going to do?"

"I suppose I'll see if I can teach him anything. He's very eager to please."

"That's not what I meant."

She let out a deep sigh. "I know what you meant. What can I do? It would be wrong to simply turn the boy away."

"Jemima is using him like a Trojan horse."

"She means to," Martha agreed.

"What of Callie?"

Martha said, "I sent Henry with a note. It seemed the right thing to do."

"You realize that they may be watching for her, in the hope of getting you together in one place."

"I don't know," Martha said slowly. "My sense is that they won't try to approach Callie or me directly. They're hoping the boy will do that work for them. But I suppose we'll find out."

Daniel stepped to the side, out of view of the window, and pulled her with him. There in the shadows he turned her around and held her against him. She put her cheek on his shoulder.

"This is playing with fire."

She smelled of lavender water and chalk dust and soap, and who would have thought that such things would render a man incapable of speech? When she lifted her face to look at him, he kissed her. A slow, deep kiss that was meant to prove her point. Then he let her go.

"A good slow burn," he said. "That's what I was aiming for. It has its rewards down the road."

It wasn't until a few minutes before the end of the school day that Callie appeared at the classroom door.

The transformation that had so taken Martha by surprise on the Johnstown road was still in evidence. Callie was wearing a simple gown of dove gray linen, and instead of the usual head scarf, a small bonnet. Ethan stood just behind her, and Martha was especially glad to see him.

She went into the hall to greet them. "I didn't know if you'd come," she said. "I don't even know if it's a good idea."

"Does he look like my father?" Callie craned her head to see into the classroom.

"I'm not sure," Martha said. "You must decide for yourself."

She gestured for them to go ahead, and then she followed them.

The children went very still. They darted looks at one another and then dropped their gazes only to raise them again. It occurred to Martha that most of them might not even know that Callie and Ethan had married, but there was no time to worry about that, or how to remedy it.

As it turned out Ethan was ready to handle what might have been a very awkward situation. His whole demeanor changed when he stepped in front of the class; with the suddenness of a finger snap he was the teacher she had known.

Ethan was good with young children. He spoke in an easy tone that engaged their interest, asking questions of each of them and answering questions in turn.

Finally he said to Martha, "I see you have a new student."

"Yes," she said. "Nicholas Wilde joined our class this morning."

The boy looked back and forth between them, a little uncertain.

"Nicholas," Ethan said. "You are visiting Paradise with your parents?"

The boy stood up. "No, sir."

"No?"

The boy said, "A visitor comes and goes away again. I don't think we are going away."

Martha turned because she couldn't govern her expression. She could only hope that the boy was mistaken; the idea of Jemima settling permanently in Paradise was more than she could face, just now. She reminded herself that to do so, Jemima would have to purchase land, which required more than money.

Unless, of course, she was assuming she had the right to make a home for herself at the orchards.

All Callie's attention and concentration were on the boy. For one moment Martha imagined Callie striking out; she would use her fist like a hammer. The image was so strong that she shifted, but only Ethan turned to look at her.

Callie's eyes were fever bright. She was saying, "Do you know who I am? Does the name Callie mean anything to you?"

That angelic smile spread across his face. "My sister?"

"That's right," Callie said. Her voice wavered and caught. "That is exactly right."

45

*B*irdie stood in the open doorway of the classroom and hoped no one would send her away. This was far too important and interesting a meeting and the details needed to be recorded. Grown-ups always got things wrong when it fell to them to tell such stories, and so it was up to her.

Strangely enough, it seemed as though Callie took one look at Jemima's son and knew right off who he was. All the worry and doubt of the last few days, people wondering out loud what kind of trick Jemima was trying to play, and then this simple end because Callie looked at Nicholas and saw her father.

Birdie had asked both her ma and da if there was a resemblance, and neither of them had been sure enough to say. Curiosity had been a little clearer. She raised a shoulder and let it fall.

"Could be," she said. "Might not be."

And so Birdie had gone to Lily, who had the best memory for faces of all of them.

Lily said, "I have more than one drawing of Nicholas Wilde in a box somewhere."

"Could you draw him again, without the old pictures?"

She looked surprised. "You want me to draw him now?"

"I thought you'd have his face by heart."

That made Lily smile. She caught up her little sister's hand and pulled her down so she could kiss her cheek. "There is only room for so many faces on a person's heart."

"But Hannah says you were sweet on Nicholas when you were my age. You wanted to marry him. Why are you laughing?"

Lily bit her lip and then tried to govern her expression. "I'm sorry, Birdie. I'm not laughing at you, I'm laughing to hear that Hannah still recalls that conversation. She was so irritated with me for going on about Nicholas Wilde."

"But didn't you love him?"

"In a small way, I suppose I did. But it was a love without foundation and so it couldn't grow."

"And then he married Jemima."

"Yes," Lily said. "I was very insulted at the time, but not for any good reason. Tell me again why you are so interested in my drawings of Nicholas. Does it have to do with Jemima's son?"

Birdie plopped down on the stool beside the divan and let out a deep breath. "I thought maybe we could see if the boy looks like Nicholas. If he does, maybe the gossip and talking will stop."

"You feel bad for the boy?"

"Yes," Birdie said. "Hardly anybody has even spoke a word to him and they're taking him apart already like a Christmas turkey."

"You do realize," Lily said slowly, "that even if there is a strong resemblance, people might not admit to seeing it."

"But we'll never know one way or the other without the drawing."

"And I suppose the drawings I gave to Callie were lost in the flood."

"With everything else."

Lily said, "I tell you what, let me talk to some other people and see what they think. If everyone agrees the drawings would be some help, I'll give you leave to sort through all my boxes to find them. What will you do if it turns out the boy looks nothing like Nicholas Wilde?"

Birdie said, "I don't know."

"Exactly," said her sister. "Exactly that is the problem."

Birdie had thought about that for a long time. She tried to imagine what Callie would see when she looked at the boy who was supposed to be her half brother. If she was capable of seeing him at all. Martha was less of a worry to her. Martha would take her time making up her mind, because that was her way.

And then at recess she had come out to play with her head full of algebra, and there he was, playing with the other boys as if he had grown up right here in Paradise. They had worked Hopper into such a frenzy that the pup had finally collapsed, and now he slept tucked into Nicholas Wilde's shirt.

Birdie said, "You've got a way with animals, Nicholas."

He stopped just where he was and smiled at her. "Do I? I like them. Would you like to play?" And without waiting for an answer he threw her the ball. This was a good sign; the boys tended to be possessive about such things and reluctant to include girls.

She caught it with one hand—she was a Bonner, after all—and for the last five minutes of recess they talked while they threw the ball back and forth. By the time the bell rang Birdie hadn't discovered anything that might help understand what Jemima wanted or why she had sent the boy to school, but she did know something important about the boy himself. He was what Curiosity called a gentle soul, someone who lived in the world but was not really part of it. Someone without the ability to see danger coming, and even lacking the most basic instincts to protect himself.

"Like an egg come out with no shell," Curiosity had said. "A body got no way to give that egg what God saw fit to hold back. His ways are mysterious to behold."

"Ma says weak shells come from not feeding the chickens right."

Curiosity had put her head back and laughed. "That too."

So now there was Callie, crouched down next to Nicholas, and he was smiling at her. For her part, Birdie didn't like it when strangers came so close. You could smell what they had been eating on their skin, and sometimes worse. Clearly Nicholas wasn't as fussy as she was, because his smile just got bigger.

From the corner of her eye Birdie saw the little people waiting on the porch, trying to gather the courage to come in and stand beside her so they could hear what was going on. It had to do with them too, now that Ethan and Callie were married.

Mariah slipped her hand into Birdie's and leaned against her.

"Why does that boy have Daniel's new puppy? Is it because he's our cousin?" she whispered.

"No," Birdie said. "He just likes dogs, and they like him."

"Everybody likes him. Callie too, because he's her brother."

"It looks that way," Birdie agreed.

"So she got a husband and a brother all at once. But does it mean that she'll have to let Jemima be her ma again?"

A flush of gooseflesh ran up Birdie's spine. "I don't want to talk about Jemima," she said. "And it's time we went home."

They trooped home up the hill together, and there was nothing Birdie could think to do to distract the boys from the one topic that interested them.

"You knew Callie's father," Adam said to her. "Does Nicholas take after him?"

"Nicholas Wilde went away before I was born. And anyway, not all children resemble their parents."

"I sure don't," Adam said. Adam with his skin the color of burnt sugar and his dark eyes.

"You look like one of us," Henry said. "You look like a Savard."

"Well, why not?" Nathan said. "We're cousins."

The truth was, Adam had been raised to be as much a Bonner as any of them. She doubted he ever thought about the family he had been born into. It occurred to Birdie now that Adam knew exactly who he was and where he belonged, but someday he might be curious about what might have been. If he asked, no doubt Jennet would tell him, and how would he feel about that?

"Bonner is as Bonner does." That was the way Curiosity always answered questions about Adam.

Birdie broke into a slow trot, and the others followed her lead.

Curiosity said, "Slow down and start from the beginning. What is it troubling you?"

Nathan cleared his throat. "I think I know what Birdie means. If Nicholas does stay here in Paradise, sooner or later he's going to hear some stories about his ma he won't much like."

Curiosity looked at Birdie closely. "Is that it?"

That was it, or at least part of it. She didn't know how to say the rest, and so she simply nodded.

"You little people, listen to me now. All of you, go on out in the sunshine, you going to turn pale as slugs if you stay in this kitchen much longer." It was the tone Curiosity used when she wasn't in the mood to argue and every child recognized it. When the door closed behind a scowling Amelie, Curiosity said, "Come on out with it, little girl. You got something else on your mind."

Finally she said, "It's about Callie. It's about the way Callie looked at Nicholas. It wasn't—it didn't feel right."

"She mad?"

"No."

"Unhappy?"

"No, not unhappy at all. Eager, maybe. But not in a good way eager."

Curiosity's hands stilled. "Go on."

"Like she had a fever on the mind," Birdie said. "But that's not right either."

"But as close as anybody likely to come," Curiosity said. She stared at nothing for a long moment, and then she sighed.

"Callie has had some hard times. Harder times than most twice her age. She strong, no doubt about that, but everybody got a breaking point. I think for right now we got to trust Ethan to help her come through."

"Because he's her husband now."

"Because he her friend, mostly," Curiosity said. "The two of them, they understand each other best. But we'll keep an eye on her anyhow. Do that put your mind to rest?"

"I'm not sure," Birdie said. She might have simply lied, but Curiosity would have seen it in her face.

"Lord have mercy," Curiosity said. "Me neither."

Martha said, "Callie, we have to let him go back to the Red Dog. Otherwise someone will come looking for him."

They were standing in the hall, talking in low voices while Nicholas played with Hopper in the classroom. He was dragging a bit of string along the floor while the puppy stumbled all over himself trying to catch it. Young children often mishandled puppies out of pure excitement, but Nicholas seemed to have no such problems. Maybe he was slow when it came to some kinds of learning, but he was quick to understand other things.

Nicholas looked up and caught Daniel's eye. When he laughed, he had a kind of beauty.

"Really, that would be the worst way to open up a conversation," Martha was saying. "If you want to keep the boy here."

"What do you mean, 'if'?" Callie frowned. "Of course we need to keep him here. He's your half brother as well as mine. Surely you can see that."

Martha started to say something, but Daniel put a light hand on her shoulder.

Ethan said, "If we try to hold him back now and fail—and I think we would have to fail—we might never see him again."

Callie had on her most stubborn expression. She said, "We can't leave him with her. God knows what kind of monster she'd make out of him."

Daniel felt Martha startle, but Callie didn't notice, or maybe, Daniel had to admit, maybe she meant to strike out.

"I think we could give him a good home," Ethan said. "But it will take some planning to make that happen. As strongly as you feel about this, it's plain reasoning we need right now."

Daniel resisted the urge to ask Callie if she was seriously considering kidnapping the boy, because he could see the answer on her face, and it unsettled him. He was tempted to say as much to Martha as they made their way up Hidden Wolf, but then his own common sense got the upper hand.

Instead he said, "I don't think I've ever been so glad to set out for home."

That got him a smile. "It would be nice to just stay put for a while, but I don't suppose that will be possible. We'll have to fetch my things up from the village sooner or later."

"My da took care of that already," Daniel said. "He's got a couple more loads. Maybe you were too distracted to notice him going by."

"That is a relief," Martha said. "Did you ask him?"

The question surprised him, but he took a moment to look at it from her perspective. Then he said, "He didn't need to be asked, Martha. He saw what needed to be done and he did it. He would have done the same for any of his daughters."

He saw the emotion rise up in her face, and then settle again, slowly.

"I see I'll have to remind you where you married into once in a while," Daniel said.

She gave a strangled half laugh. "And Callie will remind me where I came from. Who I came from."

"Do you think she meant to be unkind?"

"Yes," Martha said without hesitation. "I do."

"I've got a suggestion. Let's not talk about any of that until tomorrow evening when we sit down at Ma's. Just let it go."

After a moment she said, "We'll have to leave the horses with Ben tomorrow."

"Do you mind?"

"Not really. I like the walk."

"You may well change your mind in January. I've been meaning to put up a stable, anyway."

They talked about stables and horses and hens, and if Martha wanted a cow or would rather buy milk; whether she would put in a garden and if she needed a washhouse, and if she might want a girl to come up from the village to help. It took a lot of work to keep a household going, and it was work she hadn't turned her hand to in quite some time.

"Which reminds me," she said. "I need to get pennyroyal ointment from Hannah."

"You can't be bit already," Daniel said. "The blackfly won't be out for a while yet."

"Well, you neglected to tell them," Martha said. "Because I've got bites on my ankles and they itch."

Daniel said, "I've got some bear grease that would do the trick."

She laughed at him. "I hope you can do better than that." And: "Daniel Bonner, you are hatching some kind of plan. I see it on your face."

She didn't protest very hard, and if she was entirely truthful with herself, she had half been hoping for something like this. For Daniel to lead her off the path into the woods, where they'd be out of reach and could really leave everything else behind for a short while at least.

The horses began to huff as the climb got steeper.

"Where are we going?"

"Wait and see."

Martha didn't know the mountain as Daniel did, and she doubted she could ever learn as much, even if she dedicated every waking hour to that pursuit for the next twenty years. He seemed to recognize every tree and rock, and found his way without even the vaguest trace of a trail. At times he held branches out of her way and then she could see how pleased he was to be showing her the places he loved. For her part she knew better than to ask a lot of questions. Woodsmen preferred silence in the bush, and she understood why. Though the horses made noise enough, the birdsong continued all around them and small things rustled, unimpressed by their presence.

Daniel pulled up and let her come next to him. Martha was about to ask him what he meant her to see, but from that spot it was too obvious. It looked as though someone had taken a dull knife and hacked a wedge out of Hidden Wolf. A rift had been gouged out of the forested mountainside, from a point near the top all the way down. Trees lay scattered like a child's building blocks tossed hastily aside. The stark white of the exposed trunks worked like a thousand bone-deep slashes.

She hadn't thought it could be so very bad, but now she realized that things could have been so much worse. If the main thrust of the flood had come a half mile farther west, the whole village would have disappeared. And, she supposed, that might still happen one day.

They sat there for five minutes, and in that time Daniel said nothing. He trusted her to understand for herself. It was a gift he gave to her.

In the cool of the woods, surrounded once again by growing things in every shade of green, she tried to imprint it on her mind so that she would be able to look back at this short time and remember the feel of it, no matter how old she might grow.

It wasn't until she heard the waterfalls that Martha realized Daniel had taken her by a roundabout way to Lake in the Clouds. She had thought they might spend the rest of the day alone, but to her own surprise she realized she was glad to be here. And it was right to have come; these people were Daniel's family too.

The falls kicked up a cool breeze as they came into the clearing; the sun played off the water and cast rainbows into the clouds of mist. The horses trotted forward and Hopper, who had slept for much of the ride, began to squirm in his basket. Daniel leaned over and lifted the pup out as he dismounted. Hopper wiggled out of Daniel's grasp and galloped off toward the lake, skidding right over the edge and landing with a splash.

"He's got the idea," Daniel said, helping Martha dismount. But then doors were opening and people were coming out to greet them. Runs-from-Bears, Susanna and Blue-Jay, Annie and Gabriel. To Martha it seemed as if they were expected, and when she looked at Daniel he nodded.

"Annie wanted it to be a surprise," he said. "They wanted to give us a wedding supper too."

Martha struggled for a moment with a flash of discomfort—she had never liked being the center of attention—and with regret that she would not be able to follow Hopper into the lake.

The pup climbed out of the water and shook himself.

Daniel said, "You'll get your turn, girl, and soon."

Watching her for the next half hour, Daniel saw that Martha was pleased and touched and terribly embarrassed. Somehow her shyness stirred him. She could stand up to cruelty and keep her composure—her upbringing had taught her that skill—but she found it hard to believe that these people would simply accept her as one of their own. She would learn to trust in time, and he was looking forward to proving it to her.

It wasn't individuals who put her off. She didn't hesitate when Runs-from-Bears took her hands and leaned over to talk to her. Bears frightened a lot of people; he was a big man, battle-scarred, his face and arms tattooed; Daniel had seen men go pale when Bears looked at them in a certain way. But with his own people—with Martha, now—there was nothing of that in him. His manner was almost courtly.

Blue-Jay was saying, "Good thing he was smart enough to get you in front of a judge before you had time to reconsider."

"What he did," Gabriel said, "was inspired, I have to admit it. Kept her walking after the ice-out party until she could hardly put one foot ahead of the other. At some point she was so desperate to sit down she just gave in and said yes." He elbowed Annie, but she elbowed him right back so that he jumped.

"Don't pay them any mind," Susanna said to Martha. "They must have their fun at Daniel's expense, but if they know what's good for them, they will leave thee out of it. Now Annie and I have work to do."

"I'll come help," Martha said, and Susanna caught Daniel's eye.

"What?" Martha said, looking between them. Gabriel was trying not to smile, and not succeeding very well.

"We've got something to do before we eat, you and me," Daniel said. "We'll be back in an hour."

She followed Daniel out of the clearing, back into the forest and uphill, but what she really wanted to do was very different. Martha wanted to sit down just where she was and go to sleep.

In Manhattan she had had a reputation for restlessness, and it was true that she disliked sitting in one place for very long. She was a great walker, and did as much of it as the weather and common sense allowed. Her friends saw this habit as odd, but not unexpected, given the fact that Martha had grown up on the edge of the endless forests where things were not exactly civilized.

But in the last few days her stamina had been tested, and she wondered how much longer she could hold up. So the question was very simple: If she were simply to sit down exactly where she stood, if she demanded a slower pace or refused the walk altogether, what then?

Daniel might laugh at her, or listen to her, or try to persuade her that yes, she really did want to be trudging up Hidden Wolf in the heat of the late afternoon, after three days of monumental upheaval. She had no doubt that he would find it very easy to talk her into any number of things she had never considered before. It had something to do with his voice and the way he used it.

They were passing through plantations of beech and maple, yew and wild cherry. There was still enough mud to give her pause now and then, but she was determined to manage on her own.

They came out onto a rocky plateau and the world opened itself like a gift. The sky was so bright that Martha had to squint until her eyes would focus.

She had grown up here, but still the view took her breath. The endless forests stretched out as far as the eye could see, a world of trees too large to comprehend. The mountains marched off toward the horizon, and while she knew that there was indeed something on the other side of them—Canada, to be exact—at this moment that seemed improbable.

The sound of the falls was quite distinct, and suddenly Martha knew where they were going. The caves under the falls, of course. Where, according to Jennet, sooner or later all Bonner women fell. It was an odd turn of phrase, one that could mean many different things. She tried to convince herself of that fact. The effort kept her occupied while they made their way along the ridge and came finally to a great outcropping of rock.

They were standing just feet away from the point where the water came out of the mountain to fall, first unrestricted and then layer by layer into the lake below. The pulse of the water in the rock beat like a heart.

It seemed that they would have to make their way down a loose and very steep path. Martha remembered now that Daniel had produced moccasins this morning and suggested they'd be more comfortable than her fancy city shoes.

"You just happen to have moccasins sitting around?"

"Borrowed them from Ma," he said. "Until Annie has time to make you a pair."

So he had been planning this yesterday when they sat in his parent's parlor. It seemed Daniel had the habit of making plans and keeping them to himself until the last minute. She didn't know whether to be pleased or put out about that in general, but at this moment she was overcome with affection and happiness; he had planned this, for her.

"I'll go first," Daniel said.

"Good," Martha said, a little breathlessly. "You can catch me."

He winked at her. "Always, darlin'."

A bolt had been driven into the bedrock, with a heavy rope coiled beside it. Daniel threw the rope down the incline and then started after it. He moved easily, never losing purchase or even hesitating about where best to put a foot.

Now was not the time to lose confidence. When he was just out of sight, she started down after him.

When the rope ended they were standing on a small plateau. Daniel pointed out a fissure in the rock face, and then he simply disappeared into it. Martha counted to ten and followed him. The cave opened directly onto the falling water, which acted like a curtain that admitted light to dance on the walls.

It was a simple cave, with nothing to mark it but the wolf skulls that had been wedged into a cleft in one wall. At the back, where the shadows were deeper, she could see that a boulder stood like an open door and that from there, a passageway led deeper into the mountain. Daniel put his ear to her mouth and raised his voice.

"Another cave, just about this size, but quieter. Do you want to see it?"

But of course there was little to see; they had no fire to light a torch, and here the light from the falls did not penetrate.

His voice echoed. "We used to store furs up here, and food. Back in the old days when the mountain still belonged to my grandfather Middleton."

She knew that story, and she knew too that her grandfather Southern had a role to play in it that was nothing to be proud of.

"You don't store things here now?"

"Sometimes we do. Not just now."

"It must be very cold here in the winter."

"There's a pile of furs here at that time of year, some basic provisions. We'll have to come in January and you can see for yourself."

Martha didn't doubt his word, but at this moment perspiration was running down between her breasts, and she was glad to get back to the cool breeze in the foremost cave. Daniel came up behind her and she said what was on her mind.

"Everybody knows we're here." And bit her lip, because it sounded so girlish, almost coy even to her own ear. She tried again.

"They think we're—we're—"

"Most probably," Daniel said. His tone was patient and easy and infuriating.

She leaned back against him and let out a sigh. "I suppose that's part and parcel of being married. But I don't like it."

Daniel's hand came around and opened in front of her. On the flat of his palm was a ring. The band was gold, its flat surface incised with a twining vine and tiny leaves and flowers.

"I hope you'll like this."

Martha drew in a sharp breath and nodded. It wasn't until Daniel had put the ring on her finger that she could take her eyes away long enough to look at him.

"It's beautiful. How— where—"

"Joshua does a little fine work when he has the time," Daniel said. "He made this a few months ago. If you want something different he can do that too, but not until the rebuilding is finished."

"I like this one," Martha said, twirling it on her finger to demonstrate that it was a little too big. "Maybe I'll grow into it." And she laughed at her own joke.

"Joshua will adjust it for you. You want me to take it for now, so it doesn't get lost?"

"That's not likely," she said.

"It is if we go swimming. You did say you wanted to swim, didn't you?"

"Yes, but don't we need to get back for supper?"

"We'll take the shortcut," he said.

Daniel walked right up to the edge, where the cave floor dropped away into the falling water, and held out his hand. She went to him, but cautiously. Her skin rose in goose bumps all along her back.

"We'd have plenty of time if we started from here." He was looking at her in a particularly calculating way, and in that moment she realized what he was suggesting.

"You don't mean it," she said. Shocked and excited too.

"Oh, I mean it."

"It must be dangerous."

"We all do it. I've been jumping into the lake from here since Da taught me to swim."

"What if *I* can't swim?"

He looked at her.

"All right, I can swim. But—but—" She laughed. "Whatever they imagine us doing, this is not it."

"Nothing predictable about this, you're right."

She shivered, and he squeezed her hand.

"We don't have to," Daniel said. And the truly wonderful thing was, he meant it. He would not be angry or disappointed if she told him she couldn't, for any reason at all.

"I want to," Martha said.

"Well, then," he said. "Strip down to your chemise."

That brought her up short, and he cocked his head at her.

"My chemise?"

"Long skirts won't do much for your backstroke. You reconsidering?"

Daniel's thumb was stroking the indentation at the juncture of palm and wrist, and somehow that made it all the harder to order her thoughts.

She said, "What are you going to wear?"

"You don't remember?"

She did, of course. Daniel naked in the water, and the way he had kissed her. The shock and pleasure of it.

"You don't mean it."

"Darlin'," he said, leaning closer so that his warm breath stirred the hair on her temple. "We're married now. We can do whatever we like."

She could be a coward, or she could do this thing. This crazy, exciting thing. "Very well," she said. Before she could change her mind, she turned to offer him her back. That in itself was something it would take a long time to get used to. There had always been a woman nearby to help with dressing and undressing, and now this task fell to Daniel.

It was almost off-putting, how easily he coped, one-handed. In no time her gown was around her ankles; her short corset and petticoat followed, and then her moccasins—she steadied herself with a hand on his shoulder when he lifted one leg and then the other—and finally her stockings. Then he reached for her drawers, and she stepped away.

"I don't think silk and a bit of lace will slow me down at all," she said.

His hand was still on her leg, moving upward with a gentle and devastating touch. "Maybe not you," he said. "But these things are sure in my way. Since when do women wear drawers, anyway?"

She scowled at the change in the direction of the conversation, but she answered. "I suppose it's a French fashion. I think they had just been introduced when I first moved to Manhattan. Now everyone wears them."

He raised a brow.

"Everyone of my acquaintance. All the ladies of my acquaintance. In Manhattan."

He was tugging at the lace edging of her drawers, very softly. "But how do you know who's wearing them? And more important, why do you wear them?"

In her irritation, Martha said what she otherwise would never have said. "Because the silk feels good."

His hand was moving again. "So it rubs you in the right way."

"Daniel."

"Hmmm?"

What was it she meant to say? She couldn't think like this. It felt as if she was dissolving, as if her flesh had turned to liquid and was flowing toward him. With tremendous effort she pulled away.

She said, "I want to swim. Right now."

"Hold on, girl. Let me get out of my breeches."

She didn't trust him, but neither did she want to go without him and so she stood there while he stripped, sling first and then shirt—it was shocking, how few clothes he wore, really—and finally his breeches and moccasins.

He was fully aroused, and completely at ease. Martha, coward that she was, closed her eyes and when she opened them again, he had slipped the sling back into place and was holding something out to her. A long strip of fabric.

"Will you help me bind my arm in place? It'll go quicker if you do."

It was the first time he had asked for her help, and it struck her that she had been waiting for this. Wondering when he would let her close enough to do what she could for him, if he could trust anybody with that. Her whole body flooded with relief and thankfulness and love. It was a word they hadn't yet used, but at this moment she might have.

Instead she did as he asked. When she had finished to his satisfaction and her own, they stood for a moment in the light of the falling water.

He said, "Do you trust me?"

She took his hand, and they jumped.

———

Her hair flowed around her, a long dark flag that sparked with color and then fell like a cloak over her shoulders as they broke the surface.

She blinked water out of her eyes, put back her head, and laughed.

"I'd like to do that again." With a wiggle she dove underwater and swam away.

The simple truth was, she made him happy. Daniel stayed just where he was to watch her moving through the water, sleek and fast, as flexible as a reed.

When he caught up with her she moved in so close that she must feel the fact of his arousal but now there was nothing of embarrassment or shyness in her expression. Treading water he could feel the warmth of her, the curves of breast and hip as she pressed against him, but he couldn't reach out for her.

It struck him then: She was teasing him. The idea surprised him, but he kept that out of his expression.

"Aren't you the brave one." He looked past her shoulder. "You're giving Gabriel quite a shock."

She jerked around then shrieked; no sign of Gabriel or anyone else.

"You rotter. You fiend!"

Daniel laughed. "Tease and thou shalt be teased."

She was off again, swimming toward the falls. Daniel passed her and kept going, pushing right through the curtains of water to the other side. To his satisfaction she followed him without hesitation or pause.

Martha pulled up short, treading water and turning one way and then the other.

"It's a little cove." Her voice echoed against the rock face. "How is it you're standing and I can't touch the bottom?"

"Boulders," he said. "Come and see for yourself."

For the moment she stayed where she was. "It's quieter here."

"That has to do with the angle of the water on the rock. You are as nervous as a cat. Come over here, girl."

She made a doubtful face but came closer anyway. "Where does that opening go? Another cave?"

"Not much of one," Daniel said. "Go look."

She found her footing and walked toward the cleft in the rock wall, her chemise floating around her in the water. In the shallow opening she stopped, and Daniel, coming up behind her, stopped too. A shiver ran through her that had nothing to do with cold, he was sure of it.

"This isn't a cave," she said, a little breathlessly.

"I said it wasn't." He moved closer still until all that was between them was a thin layer of wet linen.

She turned and then stopped suddenly, as if the sight of him surprised her. He touched her face and she turned her cheek into his cupped palm.

"What?" he said.

She shook her head, and Daniel had the strong impression that she wanted something from him—that she wanted him—but was unsure of how to say so.

"Tell me," he said.

She frowned. "I don't remember what I wanted to say."

"Ah," Daniel said. "Then let me remind you."

It was her own fault; Martha had to acknowledge that much. She had teased him and played games, and here was the price to pay. Or the reward to claim.

"It's not seemly," she said against his mouth, but then the kiss drew her down and down and she couldn't hold on to the argument she had wanted to offer. Something to do with privacy and public places. Something to do with adults capable of self-control. Which at this moment was simply not true.

Daniel said, "I told you these silk drawers of yours would be in the way."

She started to say that she did not want to part company with her undergarments, but his fingers were very clever and all that came out of her mouth was a sigh and a gasp.

The plain truth was that all her concerns about privacy could not stand up to the pleasure of kissing Daniel. He was slipping her chemise over her shoulders when she realized that her drawers were already gone, but for the moment at least she couldn't remember why she had resisted in the first place. Daniel turned her until the rock face was at her back and her legs were hooked around his waist beneath the water, his good hand cupping her buttock, lifting her leg to position her for his thrust.

He made a sound deep in his throat as he entered her and then he was still. For two, four, six heartbeats he stayed just as he was, embedded to the very core of her while the water flowed around them. He pressed his brow to hers.

"My God," he muttered.

Martha put her head back against the wall and made herself relax, drew in a deep breath and centered all her attention on the point where they were joined.

"Please," she whispered, and he let out a short, sharp laugh as he surged into her, harder and deeper than she would have thought possible.

"Please," she said. "Don't stop."

He worked over her, strained into her again and again, but it wasn't enough, somehow it wasn't enough; she shifted and spread herself and reached down to clutch at him, to bring him into her hard, harder, to touch that one spot that yearned toward him, tighter and tighter until every nerve in her body thrummed in the same rhythm.

When she thought she could bear the spiraling ache no longer, when she was sure she must die, it burst and she cried out. It came upon her in a rush that made her hips and legs jerk convulsively, a wave of feeling so intense that she was lost in it, defenseless. It washed over her once, twice, three times, and then left her, breathless and shaken.

Daniel thrust one last time hard into her and held her there, split open around him and filled, his whole body trembling.

He kissed her then. A soft kiss, slow and gentle, and she felt how his heart was racing, as her own raced.

Daniel shifted and drew away from her. It felt like a terrible loss, an inestimable loss, and there were tears on her face.

"Shhhh." He pulled her closer and moved through the water with her just as she was, wrapped around him, until he found the place he was looking for. Then he sat on the outcropping of rock and held her until the tears and the trembling had passed.

He said, "You didn't know about that, did you? What just happened to you."

She sat up to look him in the face. "I may be naïve, Daniel Bonner, but I am not simple. I know what we just did. Or at least, I know what it's called."

"No," he said, and he was trying not to smile. "Not the act, what happened to you toward the end. That rushing feeling."

"Oh," Martha said, pressing her forehead to his shoulder. "I didn't think you would notice."

Now he did laugh. "It was hard to miss. You reached a climax."

After a moment's silent contemplation Martha said, "I'm not sure I can talk about this."

"Ever?"

She bit him, gently.

"No need to go after my good arm," he said. "We can put off this discussion for a while. Or at least, until next time."

Her mouth fell open and she closed it with a click. "That could happen again?"

"If we're lucky and we work at it," Daniel said, "it should happen pretty much every time."

Someone had left them blankets for when they finally came out of the water, and someone else—Gabriel or Blue-Jay, most likely—had retrieved their clothes from the cave. But for once Martha was too preoccupied to worry about what others saw or imagined.

While they sat down to eat, all during the long conversation about Johnstown, about Ethan and Callie, Jemima and young Nicholas, about crops, her thoughts kept wandering away and jolting back when someone asked her a question.

She made an effort to answer thoughtfully and then as soon as the discussion moved on, her thoughts slipped away again.

Pretty much every time.

The things she wanted and needed to talk about could not be raised at this table, or at any table she could imagine. Even if her best friends from Manhattan should magically appear, Martha had no idea how she would put such things into words. She would have to talk to Daniel about this, or be content to live in ignorance.

Pretty much every time.

She felt him watching her. She had pleased him, there was no doubt of that, but he also seemed pleased with himself.

"You're hardly eating," Gabriel said to her and it was true.

"It's the heat," Susanna suggested.

Martha smiled at her in thanks, and Susanna put her hand over Martha's and squeezed it.

"It's a grand adventure," she said quietly. "But ofttimes a disconcerting one."

The puppy nosed around her ankle and Martha took him onto her lap.

Annie said, "So does he favor Nicholas Wilde? The boy?"

From one uncomfortable conversation to the next.

"To be truthful, I don't know," Martha said. "I have a hard time remembering what Mr. Wilde looked like at all. I was no more than Birdie's age."

"It's strange that Jemima waited so long to bring him here to meet his sisters," Gabriel said.

Susanna had never known Jemima or Nicholas Wilde at all. The others had: Runs-from-Bears, Blue-Jay, Daniel himself; they knew her own story as well as she did. The miraculous thing was, it didn't seem to matter. She was one of them; it was as if by marrying Daniel she had forsworn the family that went before, and cut her connection to the woman who had borne and raised her.

They had done the same for Susanna when she walked away from her family because they would not or could not come to peace with her decision. Of course, Susanna had left something worthwhile behind, something she must miss every day.

Martha wondered if Susanna was someone she could talk to. If she could be the kind of friend that once Callie had been, someone who understood without a great deal of explanation. There was a calm about her that Martha liked and trusted. She studied Susanna's profile, the freckled skin, strong nose, wide-set eyes. She had a kind smile and an uncommonly even temper, though she had seemed ready to skin Daniel alive for bringing Martha through the falls.

Every now and then glances passed between Susanna and Blue-Jay, as they passed between Annie and Gabriel. As they might have passed between Martha and Daniel, were she to look up at him.

Runs-from-Bears said, "You are very quiet, Martha."

"We've had an unusually eventful couple days," said Daniel.

"I'd say so," Annie said. "Martha got married and started teaching school and Jemima showed up, all at once."

There was a small silence, and Martha decided that it would be best to break it.

She said, "I have no complaints. Just the opposite. I am very glad to be here. You are all very kind, but you don't need to spare my feelings. I know what my mother is, and what she is capable of."

"That's not you," said Runs-from-Bears.

"So I've been telling her," Daniel said. "But it's taking a while to sink in."

"Well then, you'll have to come up here regular," Gabriel said. "And not just to swim."

Gabriel's smile flashed, and in that moment Martha had a memory of him from their days at school together. He was always up to something, organizing races or baggataway games in the lunch recess. Together with Annie he had taken every chance to go explore the far—and forbidden side—of Hidden Wolf. They were much closer to her in age than Daniel and Lily, but still they seemed older and settled.

She said, "I will visit, I promise."

"Good," Susanna said. "I should like that very much."

"In case you're not hearing us plain enough," said Runs-from-Bears, "you're at home here. The mountain is your place now, and Lake in the Clouds is where you come if you need help."

"Thank you," Martha said. Her voice wavered and broke, but no one was rude enough to take note.

"Don't get too excited," Annie said with a half smile. "Most of the time we'll put you straight to work."

As tired as she was, it still took Martha a good while to fall into a deep sleep. All the things that had happened in one day, so many it would take her a long time to sort them all through. Her wakefulness rose and fell on the night breeze. A tumble of faces and conversations swelled and receded, and followed her into sleep.

$\mathcal{E}$than had a mantel clock, a pretty thing of polished cherry wood with delicate hands to point out the time.

On her first night in this house Callie had hardly noticed the chiming. It certainly hadn't kept her from her sleep, but then, she reckoned to herself, she had been bone weary and overwhelmed, a word she did not like to use in relation to herself. She could never afford to let her guard down or give in to fear. And she didn't need much sleep; she never had.

She counted the soft chiming of the mantel clock at ten, at eleven, and now at midnight.

Ethan slept soundly; she could not see him in the darkened room, but she could hear the steady rise and fall of his breathing. Of course, Ethan had a clear conscience and nothing to really worry him. He had land and money and the respect of everyone in the village; he had an education, and freedom to do as he pleased. Ethan had lost his father and mother long ago, and his stepfather as well; he had no brothers or sisters to look after and worry about.

Yesterday Callie had believed the same of herself; she was alone in the world but for a stepsister who had once been her best friend but who had grown distant and unfamiliar. Today she had a brother. A half brother, it was true, but still, a human being of her blood. Her father's son. A handsome boy, with bright eyes and a good smile, strongly built and quick. Somehow or another, he had survived Jemima, where their father had not. She had broken Nicholas Wilde like a dry twig over her knee, but the boy—the boy was made of stronger stuff.

When the clock chimed half past midnight, Callie got out of bed. By touch she found her clothes and in a matter of minutes she was closing the house door behind herself.

It was the kind of night she liked best, full of wayward breezes and sudden smells. The sky overhead was crowded with stars that lit her way from the porch steps to the path, from the path through the kitchen garden to the lane. It felt good to be barefoot after a day in shoes; the earth was still vaguely warm, reluctant to give up the last of the previous day's sun.

Every window at the Red Dog was dark, including the one that had been her own just a few nights ago. Where Jemima slept next to her most recent husband.

Most likely the boy would be in the little parlor that opened off the bedchamber, on a trundle bed. Jemima would want him nearby, within reach. She guarded her possessions closely, no matter how she had got them.

Finally Callie turned away, speaking harsh words to herself, words like patience and fortitude. Words a preacher might use, standing in front of his congregation. She had no use for preachers or churches, but she knew the value of self-control.

She headed for the orchards almost without thought, her feet taking her where she needed to be. The only place she could really think; the one place she belonged. The idea that her home was now a small house on the Johnstown road was too ridiculous to credit. She would come back to the orchards. Ethan would rebuild the house and she would live there, with or without him.

She was sorry, suddenly, that she hadn't taken the time to talk to Levi before she went to Johnstown with Ethan. What had she been thinking, to go off without a word and leave him to care for the animals and everything else? She had been able to run away and escape Jemima because Levi was there to look after things.

She had let her time be taken up with far less important things, visits with neighbors who came to satisfy their curiosity and wish them well; an awkward conversation with the Thicke sisters about how she wanted the meals to be handled and the washing to be done. Things that had never interested her, and would never interest her: she had given them a free hand and the distinct impression that she didn't care to be asked about any of it.

Through all that, she had meant to come to the orchards, but time had slipped away and then came word from Martha: The boy was at the schoolhouse.

She forgot about everything else. This was what she had wanted, a chance to see the boy without Jemima nearby. She had been so wound up in the idea of a brother that she had never given a thought to Levi, who would have an opinion on this matter. Levi's history with Jemima was as bad as her own.

Levi slept as little as she did, and so Callie took a chance. She ran most of the way and stopped when she was near enough to see a thin ribbon of light around the one shuttered window of Levi's cabin. She called, and in a moment the door opened.

He came out on the porch and stood there quietly, looking at her.

"I'm sorry," Callie said. "I should have come yesterday. I'm sorry."

He said, "Let's go set."

When she was a girl he would have invited her to sit right there on his little porch while they talked about work to be done, but that had stopped when she turned sixteen. Wasn't seemly, he told her. People might get the wrong idea. It seemed silly to her still today; his mother Cookie had raised her, and Levi was much like an older brother. Then Cookie died, and Levi's brother went to Johnstown and married there, but Levi had stayed behind to work the orchards. How anyone could think badly of him was a mystery to her. He was a big man, that was true, and his skin was very black, but he was also acknowledged to be one of the hardest-working men in a hundred miles, generous, soft-spoken, and so good with animals that folks came to him with sick cows and goats and horses.

They sat on stumps just outside the cider house double doors, as was their habit. It took a lot of weather to chase them inside.

"It was a sudden thing," she told him. "We decided to do it so Jemima couldn't make a claim on this place."

Levi was quiet for a long time.

She said, "It doesn't change anything. As soon as I can rebuild the house, I'll be moving back here. There's money for that now; we won't have to wait. And oh, there's a whole wagonload full of supplies coming. Wait 'til you see."

When he turned his head to look at her, she could make out nothing untoward in his expression.

"Mister Ethan is a good man," he said finally.

Callie sighed with relief. "Yes, he is." She let her eyes wander over the saplings, though that very act made her heart race with fear.

"How is it?"

She didn't need to be specific; Levi knew exactly what was on her mind.

"Good," he said. "I'll tell you this for sure, there ain't an apple tree in all God's creation better looked after." And then, more softly: "Won't be many days now before she blossoms."

The apple blossom days had always been her favorite, second only to the harvest and far better than any holiday. This spring she had been hoping for fruit from three of the Bleeding Hearts; sometimes she could forget, for a little while at least, about the true depths of her loss.

"Did you tell your husband about the Bleeding Heart?"

She started to hear Ethan called her husband, but more disturbing still was the knowledge that she had not even considered telling him the secret. Could not imagine telling him.

"I didn't," she said. "And I won't."

"Why not?"

She looked Levi directly in the eye. "I suppose I'm being superstitious, but I want to keep it between the two of us. Does that seem odd to you?"

"No," Levi said. "That make perfect sense to me." His expression relaxed a little, and Callie had the urge to leave things just where they were. But she couldn't, in good conscience.

"You know about Jemima."

There was the slightest stirring from him. A tightening of muscles that came and went almost instantly. As seldom as this subject came up over the years, Levi's reaction was always the same. He went from quiet to silent, and nothing could make him talk about Callie's stepmother.

"I'm sorry to have to say any of this, but do you remember, was she pregnant when she went away from here?"

In the silence she knew that they were both reliving those few difficult months when Levi had lost his mother and Callie had lost everything.

She cleared her throat. "She brought the boy back here. He's here. I saw him, Levi. I talked to him. I think—I know that he's my half brother. When you see him, you'll know it right away too."

Levi stood very slowly, his arms hanging straight at his sides. He said, "I got no interest in seeing that woman's child, and neither should you."

Callie stood too, her heart beating so hard she could feel it in her hands. "Levi, he looks like my father. He *looks* just like my *father,* and—"

"Miss Callie," Levi interrupted her. "Let me tell you plain and you listen to me now. She playing games with you. She want you to let that boy close so she can get close her own self. Don't you be took in. Don't let her do it."

Levi turned without another word and walked away into the dark.

47

_M_artha had always considered herself a composed person, not easily overwhelmed by stressful or demanding situations.

It was a characteristic that she valued in herself and in others, but over the course of the next ten days, she came to believe that she had overestimated her skills. She was a new bride in a new household, teaching for the first time and dealing with the sudden and unwelcome reappearance of her mother and the boy who was supposed to be her brother. It was a great amount to deal with all at once, but long conversations with Daniel and the rest of the family had been helpful. It would not be pleasant when she finally had to face Jemima, but she could manage, when the time came.

Except it didn't. A week after Jemima had first come to Paradise, Martha had still not seen her, nor had she had any other kind of communication. Every day she went into the village to teach, fully expecting to come face-to-face with her mother. Every day her mother stayed away.

There were reports of her. Mr. and Mrs. Focht ate their meals in the common room at the Red Dog, and went walking every day after dinner and supper both. Young Nicholas was often with them. They spoke to no one. Becca conducted all business through the Fochts' servants, who were utterly polite and efficient.

All of this made Martha supremely uneasy, but there was more.

Oddly enough, she saw nothing of Callie either. There were a dozen excuses, but in the end it was impossible to deny the truth: Callie was avoiding her.

If not for Daniel's calm support, Martha thought she might have given in to anxiety and gone into hiding as Callie had. But she was newly married, and married into the large and complex Bonner clan, which turned out to mean that she had no opportunity to indulge in worry and self-pity.

She had a household to manage, something she had not thought about at all. Within a day she had to laugh at her own temerity. A house on a mountainside more than two miles from the nearest neighbor—and uphill miles, at that—had nothing to do with a town house on Broadway with a dozen servants and daily calls by the butcher and baker and dairyman. To her immense relief, Daniel seemed to realize what would be required before she did, and so he arranged for Betty Ratz to come up from the village every morning, bringing new bread and a bucket of milk with her. While they were teaching, Betty cleaned and washed and kept an eye on the puppy, who was too much of a distraction to take into the classroom every day.

Teaching turned out to be not quite so hard as she had feared, but those five hours from nine to twelve and one to three drained her of every ounce of energy. She was always ravenously hungry and ate until she was satisfied, and still the waistband on her skirts was looser. It was all the walking up and down the mountainside, she told Daniel.

"Is that what you want to call it now?" he asked, and ducked before she could swat him.

She really did need to get more sleep, she told herself every morning. But then when she climbed into bed at night her body responded to Daniel's without hesitation. That was another, newer kind of hunger that could hardly be stilled. She would catch sight of Daniel talking to a student, and her whole being flushed with need so that she had to turn away and use all her powers of concentration to remember what four times four made.

The children were very good at distracting her. They were full of stories that erupted with no warning. Martha knew she should be teaching them about self-discipline and the rules of polite discourse, but they were so earnest and their stories often so funny that she found it hard. She would only be in the classroom for a few weeks, after all, and the children did seem to be learning something.

Or at least, most of them were learning.

Young Nicholas Wilde fit into the class seamlessly, as biddable and sincere and cheerful a student as she could imagine, but clearly one who might never learn to read or handle calculations beyond the simplest sums. The blessing was that he didn't seem to see this as a lack in himself, and maybe it was for that reason that the others resisted teasing him for sitting every day with the most basic primer, each time approaching it as if he had never seen it before.

The only reaction Martha had witnessed happened during morning recess when Pete Ratz asked Nick why he couldn't read at his age. Adam had stepped in immediately to ask why Pete couldn't throw a ball, and that had led to a competition, one that ended with Nicholas and Henry tied for first place.

The Bonners didn't like to lose. When it did happen they were gracious in defeat; even the little people had learned that lesson early because their parents and grandparents would tolerate nothing less. But then, Martha suspected, it was easy to be gracious when they so seldom lost.

They had taken Nicholas in as their own, and that was as much protection as any child could hope for.

As tired as she often was, Martha could not even retreat to the empty apartment at the back of the school to sleep during lunch recess, because one of the Bonners was sure to drop by to bring her something or pass on an invitation or ask a question or simply talk. Lily, still confined to her bed, sent notes that Birdie delivered every morning and then waited to hear read aloud. Within days the whole lower class had joined in and the reading of Lily's letters had become a morning ritual. When Lily heard about this, she started illustrating her notes, so that Martha found herself holding up a sketch of the raccoon who had got his paw stuck in a bottle, or Amelie wrinkling her nose over a bowl of porridge.

The work in the village had finally been finished, which meant very little to her until the afternoon when she and Daniel came home to see that the Bonner men had started building a stable behind their house and would start on the extension to the house itself once she told them what she wanted.

If I only knew, she told her new father-in-law, who laughed and went back to sawing. The next day Ethan brought her a dozen drawings to consider. She might want an addition of one larger room or two smaller ones, a bigger workroom along the rear of the house, or set off at a right angle. Should they dig a bigger cellar? It would be difficult but not impossible. Or would she rather have a springhouse?

Martha took the plans out on the porch to look at them only to discover Gabriel, waist-deep in a hole that would eventually be a well and then, with luck, have a pump, so that she didn't have to go as far as the stream for water.

"Ethan has got some idea about putting a pump right in the kitchen," Gabriel told her. "Sounds crazy, I know. You'll have to be careful or he'll rebuild the whole house around you."

On Sunday morning Martha woke very late to the sound of Daniel's knives thudding as they found their targets. She felt a twinge of irritation, that he should need so little sleep when she felt as though she could spend the whole day where she was in the cool shadows with a breeze washing over her. She had wondered if she would be able to live in such an isolated place and found that she loved the quiet.

She would drift back into sleep if she wasn't careful, and they were expected at Uphill House for supper. Really she should get up and wash her hair. And she was hungry. All good reasons to get out of bed, but she was so comfortable and more relaxed than she could remember being for a very long time.

Maybe she did drift off again, because she woke to find Daniel standing beside the bed. His hair was tousled and his shirt wet with perspiration, but it was his expression that concerned her.

"What is it?"

"Jemima," he said. "And her husband. I told them to wait on the porch. Should I send them away?" His tone solidly neutral; he wanted this to be her decision.

Martha pressed her face into the pillow slip for a moment and then slowly, she sat up.

"I think it would be best to get this over with."

Daniel nodded grimly. "That's my take on it too."

"Give me ten minutes," Martha said.

Daniel said, "Take twenty. They can wait."

He waited on the porch with their unwelcome, not entirely unexpected visitors, his gaze fixed resolutely on a point in the middle distance. They made no attempt to talk to him and had nothing to say to each other, which alarmed him, oddly enough.

Daniel was patient; he could wait just as he was for hours, as he had done often enough when hunting. He wondered if Jemima had changed so much that she could do the same. She had always been short-tempered and impatient, unable to keep her tongue or her opinion in check. Now she simply sat with her gloved hands folded in her lap and her gaze fixed on her own shoes. There was a look of concentration on her face which struck him as preoccupied.

Time passed and the day grew warmer. Daniel closed his eyes and listened, breathing deeply to find that point where his feelings could be stored away. His job here was to provide support for Martha, which meant he couldn't lose his temper.

By the time she came out onto the porch, he thought he was almost there.

She was wearing a simple gown of sprigged cotton, and she had wound her hair around her head and covered it with a cap. He hadn't ever seen the cap before, and decided that it must have come from Manhattan. Maybe from the same milliner who had sold her those awful hats she liked so much.

Daniel stepped up beside her and took her hand. Her skin was clammy.

Jemima and her husband rose.

There was a long moment's silence while Jemima studied her daughter from head to foot, as if to reassure herself that this was indeed the girl she had borne and raised up. Now a corner of her mouth twitched, whether in satisfaction or distaste was impossible to say, though it made his hackles rise to think she might be finding fault.

Martha's tone was even. She said, "You wanted to talk to me?"

Jemima drew in a deep breath. "Yes. It is good to see you so healthy and happy."

She didn't rise to the bait, and Daniel was glad of it.

"What is your business here?" Martha asked. Her tone still steady and remarkably cool.

"I come to ask a favor of you," Jemima said.

It was the last thing Daniel had been expecting, but Martha didn't seem surprised. She said, "Why do you think I would be inclined to do you any favors? You abandoned me to the care of others without a word, and then you appear out of nowhere in Manha—"

She broke off. Daniel stepped closer so that she could feel him there, ready.

"Seems to me you should be thanking me for getting you out of that marriage. Didn't things turn out better for you in the end?"

Martha jerked as if she had been slapped. "It was none of your business," she said coldly.

"I had my reasons."

"I'm sure you did. Just as I'm sure they had nothing to do with my well-being, and everything to do with your own."

Jemima said, "You don't belong in Manhattan. You'd never fit in there. You belong right here, where you were born." And she gave Daniel a sharp look, one that made the hair on the back of his neck rise.

"Leave," he said. "Both of you, right now."

"First I need an answer," Jemima said.

Martha coughed a laugh. "Why would I ever want to do you a favor?"

"It's not so much for us," said Focht, "as it is for your brother."

With her head averted, Martha listened. Mention of the boy demanded that much.

Daniel still had hold of her hand, and he held it tight as Jemima told them that she and her husband needed to leave Paradise, and that they would be gone two or even three months. It had to do with business that couldn't wait, and they could not take young Nicholas with them.

Without looking at her mother, Martha said, "Do I understand correctly that you want me to take your son in?"

Focht said, "If you will not take your brother in, Nicholas will stay at the Red Dog with Lorena and Harper—"

"Which is more than you did for me or Callie when you ran off," Martha interrupted, speaking directly to her mother.

"He'd be happier with you or your sister," Focht finished. "And you needn't worry that he'll take up too much of your time. Harper can keep him busy exploring, when you don't have any other use for him."

Daniel felt Martha stiffen, something that Jemima caught as well. Her mouth twitched and a satisfied expression crept into her eyes. While she was making no progress convincing Martha, her husband had found a vulnerable spot. Daniel wanted to point out to her that any thinking person would be put off to hear children spoken of in such a way.

There was something not quite right about this whole subject. Daniel cast back in his memory for Harper. A boy who had a lot of leisure time, though he was one of Focht's servants. Unlike the rest of Focht's servants, from what Daniel had seen.

And the boy asked a lot of questions, something no servant would do. Daniel was uneasy now, and so he resolved to look more closely at Harper.

Martha was saying, "This is something I need to discuss with my family before I can give you an answer."

For the first time Jemima flushed. "You must mean your husband's family," she said. "I am your mother. We are your family."

"You are a stranger to me," Martha said. "I repudiate you."

"You'll keep a civil tongue in your head when you talk to me," Jemima said.

Daniel said, "Now see, there you are. The real Jemima. Didn't take much to make you shake off that mask you wear these days."

The small twitch at the corner of Jemima's mouth gave him some satisfaction.

Focht said, "There's no need to be—"

Daniel said, "You'd best stay out of this."

"And why is that?"

Daniel looked the man directly in the eye and held his gaze for three full heartbeats. The skin under Focht's eyes and along his jaw sagged, and his complexion had an odd cast to it, like a man who was recovering from a long illness that had kept him indoors. He might be clever, but he didn't have the wherewithal to stand up to Daniel. Focht dropped his gaze.

Jemima said, "If you must have your vengeance on me, at least leave your brother out of it. He is innocent. Surely you've seen that much over the last week."

Martha's smile was cold. "I wondered what you were angling for."

"Yes," Jemima said. "I sent your brother to school so you could get to know him and see that he is no threat to you or your sister. Will you take him in, or not?"

"You can leave now," Martha said. "And I'll send word to you tomorrow."

She went into the house and closed the door behind herself.

"We have to leave today," Focht said to Daniel. "Within the hour we'll be gone. I've paid Mrs. LeBlanc in advance for room and board for the boy and two servants. If you take him in, send Lorena back to Boston if you want, but leave Harper. Nicholas should have someone familiar nearby."

Daniel counted to three and then he turned to look at Jemima. He said, "You don't fool me, you know. As sure as you're standing there smug and superior, I know you have got some scheme going. I don't know what it is you want, but you can be sure I'll figure that out soon enough. There's one more thing I can promise you. Nobody will take revenge on that boy. That's not the way we think, but you wouldn't understand that. Now you are trespassing on Hidden Wolf. Get gone, and don't come back here uninvited."

Jemima's jaw tightened and her eyes narrowed. He might have been able to drive her further, all the way to that place where she could no longer conceal her real motivations, but Focht put a hand on her shoulder.

Finally she drew in a deep breath, and turned her back on Daniel. He stood and watched them go, and then waited until he had mastered his breathing and his temper both. Then he went in to see what he could do for Martha.

48

Sunday mornings toward the end of the school year, Birdie was preoccupied with what she considered a great responsibility: One way or another, they had to come up with a prank before class let out for the summer.

The students had been talking about it among themselves for a long time, because while it could be great fun, it was never easy. Daniel had rules: Nobody could get hurt. No property could be destroyed, and no student held up to mockery or ridicule.

The teacher was another matter entirely; even Daniel understood that much. He had come up with pranks in his own time, some of which were still talked about. It was hard being the youngest of Nathaniel Bonner's children.

On Sunday morning Birdie called a meeting in Curiosity's hay barn right after breakfast and chores. Of the boys, Nathan, Henry, and Adam were there, and of the girls, Isabel, Mariah, and Amelie. The youngest three had to be distracted somehow, but fate had provided: This morning Callie and Ethan had come to spend the day. Ethan had understood right away what was going on, and drawn the littlest of the little people into a game of hide-and-seek.

Now Birdie explained her plan, and then she explained it again.

"Wait," Isabel said. "Whose chickens are we going to use? Who has four chickens all the same color we can borrow?"

"We don't need four chickens," Adam explained. "Haven't you been listening? We need three. We number them one, three, and four, and we let them out in school."

The boys put back their heads and laughed, so delighted were they with this plan. Birdie thought it was a good prank, maybe her best yet, and their reaction put her in a fine mood.

The girls were excited too, but they had a more practical approach to these things.

Mariah said, "Maybe Aunt Lily can make us the signs to pin to their backs."

"I suppose we could ask her," Birdie said. "But I'd worry about her saying something to Daniel."

They all considered this for a moment and decided that it was true; they couldn't really tell any grown-up about this before the fact. They talked too much among themselves and anyway, Daniel would be on the lookout for hints. He knew something would happen, and he knew Birdie would be at the middle of it.

"How hard can it be to make some signs?" Nathan said. "All we need is paper and ink. I can do that part."

"But what if it rains," Amelie said, "and the ink runs?"

"Never mind the ink and the rain," Henry said. "We don't even have chickens yet."

"We could pay," Mariah said. "I've got five pennies. We could rent them."

Nathan held out his hands as if to offer a question. "Who ever heard of renting out chickens?"

"Biddy Ratz rents out George. I had to fetch him for Curiosity just a few days ago," Adam said.

Isabel said, "But a goose is another matter entirely."

"You know anybody who's got two geese look exactly the same? And why did Curiosity rent a goose in the first place?" Nathan was getting cranky.

"Slugs," said the others in unison.

"George is mighty fond of slugs and they've been a plague in the garden, that's what Curiosity says," said Henry. "And she don't much like geese so she just borrows Biddy's now and then."

Birdie already knew where she would get the hens, but the discussion had run away and she couldn't see a way to reel it back in. And besides, it made her laugh.

"What about Missy and Ma'am and Mimi?" Isabel said.

Finally, Birdie thought.

"Curiosity would skin us alive," said Henry.

"She likes those chickens better than she likes us." Mariah wrinkled her nose.

It was an exaggeration, but not much of one. Curiosity had a flock of eight hens and one rooster that she wouldn't let anybody else care for. In the evening she went herself to make sure they were snug in the henhouse before full dark, and if she heard them fussing in the night she'd go out with a stave in case she needed to beat back a sassy wolf or a wolverine looking for a way in.

Of all the hens, her favorites were the three oldest, glossy black, called Missy and Ma'am and Mimi. Curiosity talked to them as though they were her sisters, and they seemed to talk right back.

"We won't hurt them," Adam said. "We'll just take them . . . for a walk."

"We'll scare the eggs right out of them," Henry said, but in a resigned voice. Anybody could see that they had already settled on this plan.

Birdie was more than satisfied. When they let the hens out, there would be a lot of squawking and screeching while grown-ups and students chased them back and forth. If things went well, Birdie thought, they could take bets on how long people would go on searching for the number two chicken that didn't exist at all.

With the plan mostly in place, the girls went back to Curiosity's kitchen to help with dinner, but the boys stood in a semicircle giving one another sharp looks. Birdie knew those looks too well.

"What?" Birdie said. "Tell me."

"If we hurry," Adam whispered, "we could go to the beaver dams and be back in time for dinner."

It was one of those times when she knew exactly what she was supposed to do: Remind these three that they had been forbidden to go to the far end of the lake because of the flood damage. She was the aunt, and she was the oldest, and for the last few days she had thought about little else but doing just what the boys were suggesting.

She cast a glance at the house, and made herself a promise. She would count to ten, and if no grown-up showed themselves in the meantime, they would go.

"What's she doing?" Nathan whispered, and Henry hushed him with an upraised hand.

She counted to fifteen for good measure.

"Maybe we should tell somebody," Adam suggested.

"No," Birdie shook her head. "It will be easier to ask for forgiveness than permission. Let's go."

They only got as far as the Johnstown road, where a small crowd had stopped in front of the Red Dog. The Focht's big carriage stood right in front with all four horses hitched up and ready to go. The servants were busy strapping luggage to the roof.

"They're leaving?" Birdie said to no one in particular. "Just like that? Going away?"

"Just the mister and missus," Pete LeBlanc answered.

"The boy stays here," said Missy O'Brien, sniffing her disapproval. "With two servants. Those blacks there, I don't know their names."

"Lorena and Harper," said Henry.

"But why won't Jemima take Nicholas?" Nathan asked.

"Business," said Missy, her small mouth pursing. "That's the claim. Though if I was a betting woman, which I am not, I would wager my good right arm that they won't come back at all." Missy said this as though the idea met with her approval. She was always one to anticipate other people's misfortune.

Pete's wife, Georgia, was working herself into a temper as well. "They'll just leave the boy here with Callie. That's what Jemima does; she dumps her burdens off here and goes on about amusing herself."

Henry said, "You had best not be talking about our aunt like that." Henry had a temper, though it didn't often come to the surface.

"She wasn't talking about Callie," Pete said, pulling his wife away. "And don't you tell anybody otherwise. We got enough trouble without getting on the wrong side of your granddaddy."

Georgia looked like she wanted to argue the point, but just then

Jemima and Mr. Focht came out of the inn. Jemima didn't look at any-body at all; she just went to the carriage and went up the stairs, holding up her skirts with one hand and taking a servant's arm in the other.

"Off for a ride, Mima?" called Jed MacGarrity in his warbling old man's voice. He had arrested Jemima once, according to the stories, and so maybe it wasn't a surprise that she ignored him.

When Jemima had settled in the carriage with her husband beside her Birdie said, "I wonder if Martha knows."

"Oh, she knows," said Missy O'Brien from the back of the crowd. "Jemima and her number three there—Focht, is that his name? A strange name if you ask me—they come down from the mountain not a half hour ago. I don't think they were picking wildflowers. Look, they're about to go."

One of the servants climbed up into the carriage while two others mounted postillion.

Just then Nicholas appeared with a woman on the threshold of the Red Dog. Harper was just behind him, and neither boy seemed espe-cially worried or concerned. Birdie decided that she needed to get to know Harper. She had seen him out walking almost every day since he arrived, all over the village and the mountain too. That last memory gave her a twinge; she hadn't said anything to her da, and she was supposed to. They all kept an eye on anybody who wandered around Hidden Wolf.

But then again it was just a boy who liked to wander, and who had too much free time. There probably wasn't much work for one servant, let alone for the four that Jemima had brought with her.

"Maybe that was his wet nurse," said somebody nearby. "Maybe he won't care about Jemima being gone as long as he's got her."

Henry said, "That's Lorena. She's his favorite."

To Birdie the woman looked kind. She had a small but easy smile, and when she used it her teeth flashed very white. Her skin was not so black as some of the other servants; to Birdie it seemed more the color of cin-namon, rich brown tinged with red. Her face was built different from blacks Birdie knew. She had a full mouth but her nose was narrow, and her eyes weren't exactly black or even brown.

Nicholas seemed his usual cheerful self, smiling broadly, one arm ex-tended up and over his head so he could wave his whole body. The last Birdie saw of Jemima was her handkerchief waving in reply from the window.

"It don't seem right," said Henry.

"Should we take him with us?" Nathan asked. "Bring him home for dinner?"

"Maybe not today," Birdie said.

"I just don't understand it," said Henry again. "Why would they go off without him?"

It was a question that occupied them all that Sunday at dinner and for the entire school week. Of all of them, Adam was having the hardest time understanding why Nicholas had been left behind.

Birdie had heard him asking Jennet and Luke about it after dinner that very day, and by the end of the week he had asked every grown-up in the family, as well as Curiosity and all Curiosity's extended family.

Adam was worried, but Nicholas didn't seem to mind that his mother and stepfather had gone away. If anything Birdie thought he was happier, mostly because he didn't have to go straight back to the Red Dog after school, and he had more freedom to explore.

"Those boys move," Curiosity said, watching them from her kitchen window. "Put me in mind of Daniel and Blue-Jay when they was that size."

It was clear that Adam had appointed himself Nicholas's guardian, and the two of them showed up everywhere, very often with Harper in tow. At first Birdie wondered if the other boys might take offense, but it was summer and there was no lack of things to do. They formed themselves into loose tribes that shifted day by day, rotating from Curiosity's kitchen to their fort on the mountain to Lake in the Clouds to the apple orchard.

Once Birdie had followed them to the orchard after school, out of pure curiosity. Levi put her straight to work, as she knew he would. It was time to thin the apples on the branch, a tedious job. Only one in four or five apples could be left to grow, and the extras had to be carefully snapped off. The only thing that made it bearable was that everybody sang, following Levi's lead.

Birdie had never seen Nicholas shirk any task, no matter how hard or dirty, but he had never seemed particularly interested either. Now she couldn't tell if he liked working in the orchards, or if it was Callie who drew him back. She spent a lot of time showing him how to do things, explaining the why and how of it all. Some of it seemed to stick with him, but mostly he just gave her the same smile he gave everybody. She didn't seem to notice that he wasn't grasping things, or maybe she didn't care. It was odd, and Birdie didn't know how to explain it to herself.

"That Nicholas, he ain't nothing like his ma," Missy O'Brien had taken to announcing whenever she caught sight of him.

Ruth Mayfair was Quaker through and through and she never argued, but she made an exception and came as close as she ever would to calling Missy O'Brien rude.

"He is indeed a bright light in the world," she said with a solemn look that Missy O'Brien didn't care to notice.

"Must be Lorena's influence," Missy said. "She's got a good head on her shoulders, does Lorena."

There was another odd thing: Even people who were determined to dislike anything and everything having to do with Jemima took a liking to Lorena.

"The boy a little slow," Curiosity said of him. "But pure of heart. Most of all, they ain't the littlest bit of self-pity in him. He just take things as they come. That he did learn from Lorena."

The only person who seemed to have any doubts was Levi. Levi could be standoffish, because, as Ma had told Birdie once, he had lost everybody he loved—his little brother to a terrible accident at the mill, his ma drowning, and Ezekiel gone too, and within two days of falling sick with the measles. He could be standoffish, but he loved the orchard and could be won over by anybody who showed any real interest. If Nicholas was going to make a friend out of Levi it would be by means of his help in the orchard.

If you took the time to visit with him, Levi opened up. He knew hundreds of songs and stories and he was generous with all of them. Once in a while he would play the fiddle at a party, and then he looked like a different person altogether, happy with himself and the world.

And Levi listened. He listened close, even when other grown-ups didn't seem to take things seriously.

Birdie asked her ma about Levi and Nicholas, and from the look on her face she knew she had hit on something that troubled her.

"You know the stories about his mother's death."

"Cookie?"

"Yes. She died in a violent way, and some people believe Jemima was responsible."

"I know that, Ma," Birdie said. "Everybody knows that. When Cookie and Levi and his brothers were still slaves Jemima treated them awful. And then they got their papers—"

"Manumission papers," Ma reminded her gently.

It meant something when Ma interrupted. A new question occurred to Birdie.

"Where did Cookie get the money to buy herself and her boys free?"

"It's a complicated story," Ma said. "I think all you need to know right now is that the enmity between Jemima and the Fiddlers runs very deep."

Birdie took note of the word *enmity*, considered asking about it, and decided not to. Ma was looking for reasons to change the subject as it was.

"But why would Levi blame Nicholas? He wasn't even born yet."

"The deepest feelings are not always very rational," Ma said. "That is especially true for the kind of wound Levi has been nursing all these years. He may believe that Nicholas is part of some scheme of Jemima's."

"Nicholas?" The idea was so odd that Birdie had to smile. "There's not a false bone in his whole body."

"I don't know exactly what he suspects," Ma said. "It may have to do with Nicholas or perhaps with Harper. But it certainly has something to do with the orchard. Jemima tried before to take the orchard away from Callie's father. To Levi I think that was just as terrible a crime as what happened to his mother and little brother."

Birdie thought of asking again about Levi's brother who had died in an accident at the mill, but she decided that it wasn't the right time.

"He loves the orchard," Birdie had to agree.

"He has put everything into it," Ma said. "After his older brother died it was the orchard, the work in the orchard that kept him from losing his mind."

"But why would Jemima even want it anymore?" Birdie asked. "Half the trees got swept away in the flood. All they've got now are the Spitzenbergs and a lot of 'maybe' trees."

"I don't know that Jemima *does* want the orchard," her ma said. "But history has shown us that it's dangerous to underestimate her."

"So you think Levi's right to distrust Nicholas?" She had been wanting to ask this question, but it came up and out of her mouth before she could think of better wording.

"No," her ma said. "I don't think there's any reason to dislike Nicholas or to be suspicious of him. Callie has tried to convince Levi that the boy is no threat, but his distrust hasn't given way yet."

"It's sad," Birdie said, and got one of her mother's gentle smiles.

"It is very sad," Elizabeth agreed. "And for the moment at least there's nothing you or I can do to help. Levi must work this out for himself."

That night Elizabeth told Nathaniel about this conversation after the lights had been put out, while they floated in the calm time before sleep. There was a light rain falling and the air was crisp and sweet, but it was also very dark.

She raised a hand and couldn't see it, even when she touched her nose to her palm. In all her years in the endless forests she had never been comfortable on nights like these. But that was the difference between a grand house with two dozen servants—including one who did nothing but care for candles and oil lamps, as had been the case in her girlhood at Oakmere—and this place. Her place.

"You're very quiet," she said after a while.

"I'm thinking it through, Boots. You want me to talk to Levi?"

"No," Elizabeth said firmly. "Things are complicated enough as it is."

"Not that you need to go looking for things to worry about," Nathaniel said. "But I heard Callie and Martha arguing about the boy. Martha was coming out of the trading post and Callie was going in, and they were having one of those arguments where women whisper at each other and you can hear every word ten yards off."

There was a longer silence, and Elizabeth poked him.

"Boots," he said, catching her hand. "Hold on, I'm just trying to organize my thoughts. Callie wants to take the boy in, and Martha don't like the idea. And before you ask, I can't say what Martha was worried about, because she never came out with it. They caught sight of me and that was the end of the conversation."

"You just left it like that?"

She could almost hear him smiling. "You wanted me to run after Martha and demand more information?"

"You know that's not what I mean."

"Yes it is."

"All right, maybe I do mean something like that. It would have been—"

"Nosy?"

She pinched this time, and hard enough to make him hiss. "Ow. Boots, play fair."

"Fair play," Elizabeth echoed, "is very hard when you don't even know what game it is you're caught up in."

The bed creaked as he rolled to look up toward the ceiling. He said, "I wish you could just put down that worry basket you carry around with you, for a while at least. You got Daniel married off—"

"I didn't have anything to do with that!"

"—and he's going to let Hannah stick him full of pins to see if that might help him some. Ethan is settled too and it looks like things are coming along right well for him and Callie. Hannah and Curiosity both say Lily is healthy and there's no sign of trouble—"

"Of course, but—"

"Even Birdie is calmed down for right now, at least. Can't you do the same? Just put it all aside and enjoy what we've got. All the children nearby, everybody healthy, a couple new grandchildren on the way, crops in the ground, and a willing husband in your bed."

Elizabeth let her breath go in a long sigh. "What was that last part again? I didn't quite catch it."

"Come on over here, Boots," he said, "and I'll spell it out for you."

49

Martha had many things to be thankful for, and one of them was that Daniel didn't expect her to rise when he did. He left their bed at dawn or even earlier, and went about his business while she slept on. At first it had seemed a kindness, but then she realized she didn't like waking alone.

This Saturday morning she woke slowly, stretching in the puddle of sunlight that poured over the bed. Her first thought was of Daniel, and where he might be.

There was a way to keep him in bed, but it didn't have anything to do with sleeping, and moreover, Martha could not imagine herself suggesting such a thing. The closest she ever came was to touch his face, a small gesture that captured his attention completely, to her continual surprise and satisfaction both. Maybe she would have worked up the courage to be more direct with him if her courses hadn't interrupted the natural progression of things and kept them apart for—she counted—five days now.

She forced herself to tell him plainly, and then was a little put out when he took the news without the slightest hint of discomfort. He had nodded and kissed her briefly, changed the subject to something else entirely, and then simply stopped approaching her. Everything stopped; he didn't catch her up against the wall to kiss her or pull her to him when she walked by. In bed he kissed her good night as if she were a sister.

With her rational mind Martha understood that this was another bit of kindness and generosity, or at least, that he meant it to be taken that way. In fact, it hurt her feelings. There was no logic to it, nor could it be reasoned away.

Now her courses were finally over, but Martha found it was far harder to share that bit of news. Every way she could think to say what should be said made her nervous to the point of jumping. She was being childish and silly, and she had no idea how to stop.

Martha lectured herself at length. Sooner or later Daniel would turn to her, and in the meantime there was a lot of work to do. There was teaching, and the issue of young Nicholas Wilde which seemed to get more complicated every day; most afternoons when they came up the mountain they found that two or three of the Bonner men had come to work on the house. Even with help from Betty Ratz it was hard to keep up with the sawdust and dirt.

Betty took care of the washing and cleaning, and Martha the meals. She had once been a serviceable cook, and now it came back to her. She put egg pies and fried trout, thick soups and cornbread on the table for whoever was around that day. Whatever she produced Daniel ate with enthusiasm, and Betty made sure to praise her efforts.

Betty was a sweet girl of fifteen, nothing like her older and very difficult brothers who had gone to school with Martha. To Betty's way of seeing things she had the best work in Paradise, looking after the little house in the strawberry fields. She was delighted with everything, and always eager to go home when her work was done so she could report the news to her family: Lily's Simon had finished another chair for the table he made; there was a new cabinet for dishes, and a dozen new shelves, empty still, for the many books in the house all stacked in piles she dare not even touch for fear of putting things out of order.

When Gabriel had finished turning the new garden plot Betty began to collect seeds from neighbors and friends, and together Betty and Martha planted beets, carrots, peas, parsnip, cucumber, and three kinds of lettuce. Betty turned her hand to whatever work there was without complaint, but she was happiest in the house cleaning and arranging. The cushions Curiosity had sent up for the new settles put her in raptures, each of them embroidered with flowers in colored thread and smelling of lavender.

There were new bedsheets and pillows and pillow slips, and even a new bed, bigger than any bed Betty had ever seen before and so high that she needed a footstool to smooth the covers.

Martha had taken pleasure in all the improvements and gifts, but it was the new bed that gave her real pause. One day when she came up from the village after school let out it was already in place with a coverlet spread over it, one she had never seen before that was almost certainly a gift from Elizabeth.

The shock of the bed kept her right there, red-faced, until Daniel came to find her. She was perched on the edge, her feet dangling a good foot above the floorboards.

"What?" he said when he saw her expression. "Don't you like it?"

"Tell me," she said in a low whisper. "Please tell me you didn't tell your father or brothers that we needed a bed this high for any particular purpose."

She made him laugh, even when she didn't mean to. There was nothing cruel about it, and still sometimes it itched.

"Of course I didn't," Daniel had said. He was smiling at her in a way that meant he was thinking of crossing the room to sit down beside her—and maybe more. But then he remembered her courses—she could almost see the idea come into his mind—and instead he had gone back to work with Simon, who was making changes to the hearth.

Now Martha rolled over and pressed her face into Daniel's pillow to draw in his smells.

Outside the puppy was yipping in the high, excited half howl he used to greet someone well known. Daniel spoke a few calm words and Hopper settled. Another creature totally in his power, and really, Martha asked herself, wasn't it time to pull herself out of this mood?

But she stayed just where she was and listened as the cart came closer and Daniel called out. His father, hauling hardware or wood or more furniture. She should get up and put the kettle on, but instead Martha almost fell asleep listening to the easy back and forth of their voices. Maybe she did fall asleep, because she started when Daniel opened the chamber door.

"Martha."

She yawned and sat up. "I'm coming."

"Da brought up the last of your trunks, with your books."

She was suddenly very much awake.

"I'll make tea," she said. "Has he eaten?"

"Gone already," Daniel said. "But I could eat."

She climbed out of bed thinking of books.

The new shelves were of cherry wood, carefully sanded and rubbed, and Martha was pleased every time she looked at them. They weren't as intricately carved as Ethan's, but all she really wanted was a way to make the common room a little more her own, and her books would do that.

When Daniel came in he took a minute to admire the filled shelves, and then he sat down to his late breakfast of tea and boiled eggs sprinkled with salt and pepper.

Martha sat down opposite him. "Thank you," she said. "I missed my books. But there's still a lot of space. Shall I put your books on the shelves too?"

Nothing unusual about her tone or the request, but she watched him anyway. If he grinned at her now, then he knew what she was about.

Instead he said, "Good idea. It might take you a while to track them all down, though."

Daniel was very good at sniffing out mischief, no doubt a skill acquired in near ten years of teaching clever and often devious Yorker children, but it seemed he didn't have any sense of what she was up to. Because she did have an ulterior motive and a plan. It had been in the making ever since they came home from Johnstown, when she had waited in vain for Daniel to produce the promised book by A French Lady of Leisure.

Her choices were few: She could ask him about it directly, or she could go exploring and seek it out on her own. Neither option appealed to her overmuch. Married or not, Daniel had a right to his privacy, and she wouldn't go through his things until and unless he gave her specific permission. And now he had. She had his leave to look through his books.

He had a lot of them, many from his mother who passed them along when he took over the school. Some Martha recognized because

Elizabeth had read them to her class. *Gulliver's Travels* she remembered especially well, because Miss Elizabeth—as Martha had called her then—had been so delighted by the story herself.

Martha began with the table that served as Daniel's desk, piled high with stacks of books. *Geography Made Easy: A Short but Comprehensive System. More Speedy Attainment of the Latin Tongue. A Rhetorical Grammar of the English Tongue. Practical New Grammar. The Schoolmaster's Assistant, a Compendium of Arithmetic Both Practical and Theoretical. The Natural Sciences. The Art of Writing. Sketches of the Principles of Government.*

The books not related to teaching were more scattered and had been much more thoroughly read. Kant's *Anthropologie, The Autobiography of Benjamin Franklin, M'Fingal, Moll Flanders, Tom Jones.* She was surprised to see that together they had enough novels to fill an entire shelf.

There were dictionaries and grammars for Latin, German, and French. In general there were a lot of books in French; she found a dozen of them on the worktable, of all places, under a pile of shirts that needed mending. She sat down to look through them, her pulse picking up a notch.

Descartes, Toussaint, Voltaire, Balzac, Rousseau, Diderot, and a French grammar and dictionary. Dry as dust, all of them. No sign of the Lady of Leisure.

While she dusted and arranged all the books she had found, Martha considered. There were three possibilities, as she saw it. She could confront Daniel directly and insist that he either produce the book or confess he had made the entire story up out of whole cloth; she could continue to search; she could simply put it out of her mind.

She tied up her skirts so they wouldn't be in her way when she climbed the ladder into the attic to look through the boxes she had seen up there.

Ethan had plans to open up the attic into a sleeping loft, but that was further down his long list of improvements. For now it was nothing more than a raw floor with slanting walls that needed diligent dusting and sweeping. Moreover, it was tremendously hot even in May despite the open vents at either end.

The trunks were lined up in a row. Martha lifted the lid on the first box and dropped it as soon as she realized what she was seeing were packets of letters, all tied with serviceable string. She was curious, but the idea of reading someone else's mail—even her husband's—that she would never even consider. The letters were Daniel's, and Daniel's alone.

The second box was full of clothing carefully folded. She made a note to herself to ask him about these things, and then she went to the third and last box.

She hesitated, because a question had come to her, one she should have considered first. What was she going to do with the Lady of Leisure once she found her?

Daniel, look what I found in the attic.

Daniel, is this the book you were telling me about?

Daniel, your French Lady of Leisure's memoirs were very instructive. Would you care to join me in our room on our very broad, very high, very chaste bed so we can discuss them?

The sensible thing to do would be to walk away.

With one quick movement Martha lifted the lid.

It was almost a relief to see that the box was empty; she could put this nonsensical crusade aside. Except that there was a single piece of paper at the bottom. She picked it up.

In Daniel's hand, a single sentence written in ink as black as his heart: *I know what you're looking for.*

Outrage and laughter and embarrassment vied for the upper hand while Martha sat there looking at the message Daniel had left for her. Then she heard a familiar voice calling.

"Martha!" Birdie yelled. "Where are you?" And then Hannah's voice: "No need to shout, little sister."

"Maybe she forgot we were coming," Birdie said.

And she had. Martha had forgot completely about Hannah dropping by with her Chinese needles. She asked herself if she was mean enough to enjoy the discomfort the treatment would cause Daniel, and decided that she was not.

But he didn't need to know that.

Daniel came in, sweat-drenched and bare-chested, to find two of his sisters sitting with Martha.

She looked to be in a fine mood, which might mean she hadn't been up to the attic yet, or another possibility: She wasn't looking at him because she was mad and didn't want to show it.

It had been a calculated risk. The truth was, he liked Martha in a temper, because arguments led to lively discussions where she let her guard down. The note was supposed to make her just that mad and no madder.

That whole line of reasoning had required exactly as much time as Birdie needed to propel herself across the room like a spinning top.

"I knew you'd keep your word!"

"Your faith in me is much appreciated," Daniel said dryly. He took a towel from the washstand and began to wipe himself down while Birdie held center stage.

"Can I explain it to you? Hannah, can I explain to him?"

"Go right ahead," Hannah said, looking up from a thick stack of closely written papers.

Birdie held herself very straight and still, as though she were reciting in front of a class.

"The idea is, bad things get caught up in you and can't find a way out. And these needles, they make holes—tiny little holes—for the bad to come out of. So you'll feel better."

"Like a lightning rod," Daniel suggested, and she scowled at him.

"Not like a lightning rod. A lightning rod is there for the lightning to grab on to. A lightning rod fools the lightning into staying away from trees and people and houses. This has got nothing to do with grabbing on; it has to do with letting go. Helping the nerves let go. Isn't that right, Hannah?"

"In the essentials." Hannah had opened her bag on the table and was taking out bits and pieces and lining them up. To Birdie she said, "I will need water."

Birdie shot outside and soon the sound of the pump working came to them. Daniel found himself standing there, unobserved, while Martha talked to Hannah about what she might need, whether the bed or the table or perhaps even the floor would be the best place for Daniel to stretch out.

Daniel took the opportunity to open the carved wooden box Hannah had brought with her. Some twenty needles on a bed of silky green velvet overlaid with white silk. Thin needles as long as a finger, with small ivory grips at one end. Tucked into the velvet that lined the inside top of the box was a folded piece of paper that turned out to be a diagram of the human body. The writing was in Arabic and English printed very small in a neat hand.

"Daniel?" Hannah called again, and he turned to her.

"As soon as Birdie gets here with the water—" she pulled a jar of soft soap from her bag, "we can all wash and begin."

There was no arguing with Hannah when it came to washing before she treated someone. She and everyone else in the room would wash three times. Hands were then examined and if there was dirt beneath the fingernails or if the fingernails extended at all beyond the nailbed, that person would have to clip their nails and start again. She was unrelenting on this point, which she had learned from Hakim Ibrahim when she was very young.

Daniel had once asked her to explain the reasoning to him in more detail, which had resulted in a visit to the small building that had once been Richard Todd's lab. Hannah had brought her microscope out into the daylight and then had him examine all sorts of things from pond water to spit until he conceded that yes, there were beings smaller than the human eye could perceive and yes, it made sense to be as free as possible from such things when she was trying to fix something.

People who came to her for help gave in to her demands soon enough and few even remarked about it anymore. Except for Jennet, who made a needlepoint banner to frame and hang in Hannah's workroom: *Evil resides beneath the fingernails.*

In some things Hannah had no sense of humor, but she had smiled and allowed Jennet to hang the needlework.

The plain truth was, the citizens of Paradise had good reason to trust Hannah. If you listened to her and did as she told you to do, there was a pretty high chance that you'd eventually get up out of bed and go on about your business. But the respect she had in Paradise didn't extend beyond its borders.

"Are you thinking of Nut Island?" Hannah asked, bringing him up out of his thoughts with a jerk.

"That was the last time you operated on me," Daniel agreed.

"This isn't an operation," Hannah said. "But I hope it will do you some good anyway." She turned to Martha.

"You are very quiet. Does the idea of this particular treatment bother you?"

Martha pursed her lips and Daniel had to resist the urge to laugh out loud. She was mad, all right.

Before Martha could answer Daniel said, "Just don't let her get hold of those needles."

"Oh?" Hannah raised an eyebrow, glancing back and forth between them. "I gather you've given your new wife reason to be angry."

"Why do you jump to that conclusion?" Daniel said, vaguely affronted.

"Because she knows you," Martha said.

Hannah said, "Martha, if you'd rather not stay—"

Martha gave a short laugh. "I wouldn't miss it for the world."

---

50

*W*hen Birdie came along with Hannah on a call, she spent the whole walk home peppering her with questions. Why one kind of fever tea over another, how quickly a bone would knit, when a baby might be born, what Hannah heard when she put her ear to someone's back, and what those sounds meant.

But today Birdie was lost in her thoughts. She was working herself up to ask a big question, and Hannah thought she knew what it was going to be. And then Birdie surprised her.

"Can we go home the long way?"

There was a question within the question that Hannah heard quite clearly.

"You want to see how the beaver are coming along?"

There was a line of beaver dams at the far end of Half Moon Lake, an arc that stretched more than three hundred feet and was as tall as a man in some places. All of that had been destroyed in the flood, and Birdie had been worried about the beaver as much as she worried about her neighbors. Despite the assurances of her father and brothers and uncles and cousins that the beaver would rebuild.

"Not the ones trapped in the dens," she had said darkly.

Birdie was at the mercy of her imagination, as Hannah had been as a girl.

So they changed direction and started down the path that would end far from the village, where forest gave way to marsh and marsh to lake.

Hannah had work at home and this detour would cost them an hour or more, but she was glad to be in the forest where the heat—because it was unusually warm for May—gave way to cool shadows. The smells that rose with each footstep took her back to her childhood, when she had spent much of her time in these woods.

Birdie was still very quiet and her expression was grave.

"What is it?" Hannah asked. "Are you worried about Daniel?"

Birdie seemed surprised by the question. "No, not overmuch at any rate. Do you think the needles will do him any good?"

"I don't know," Hannah said. "The treatment has to be repeated many times before we'll be able to tell."

"It was kind of disappointing overall," Birdie said.

"Oh, really?" Hannah tugged on the younger girl's plait. "Bored, were you?"

"Not bored. But you hardly put those needles into him at all. Just the very tip. Not even a drop of blood."

"You look distinctly put out," Hannah said. "But it would have been a strange way to try to relieve him of pain, sticking a dozen two-inch-long needles into him."

"But it would have distracted him for a while at least."

Hannah laughed. "He wouldn't sit still for that."

"He would," Birdie said. "If Martha asked him." After a long moment Birdie said, "I'm glad they got married."

"So am I."

"They were fighting before we got there."

Hannah stopped and Birdie turned to face her.

"What makes you think that? What did you think you heard when you were at the water pump?"

Birdie could produce a look of dry disbelief that exactly mirrored their father's. "Nothing," she said. "It wasn't anything anybody said. It was the look on Martha's face. Or maybe, that she wouldn't look at him. You didn't see that?"

Hannah thought for a moment. "I did. But it doesn't mean that they're fighting. Married people disagree."

"You can say that again. Don't laugh, you know it's true," Birdie said. "You and Ben get into arguments all the time."

"And we get out of them again."

"Yes," Birdie said, her mouth twisting. "I know how you do that too."

In her surprise Hannah gave a full laugh, but Birdie wasn't at all put out.

She said, "Daniel likes getting Martha a little mad. He was thinking about it all the time you were putting those needles in."

"Are you in the habit of reading Daniel's mind?"

"Sometimes," Birdie said quite seriously.

Hannah said, "Are you worried about Lily? You know she is doing very well. If we can keep her in bed, I think she will come through this pregnancy with a healthy baby."

"Lots of women don't," Birdie said.

That was true, of course, and Hannah didn't try to deny it. They had lost a mother and baby just months ago.

The path grew very steep and narrow, and so for the next part of the walk they were too busy staying on their feet to talk.

The woods gave way gradually until they were surrounded by speckled alder, silver maples, and elm. The ground got wetter and wetter under-foot and then they stood in the clear, on the edge of the swamp.

It should have been very familiar, but it was not. The storm had come down hard and the shoreline and water were littered with debris from the flood. Shattered trees piled together like a game of pickup sticks, boulders, and uprooted bushes.

"Look." Birdie pointed to the remnants of a canoe hanging from a maple limb. "Gabriel's."

In spite of the damage, there was some comfort to be taken here in the certainty of another growing season. Human beings were the only ones who seemed to hold on to disaster. Birdie wondered why she hadn't thought to come to the lake to watch the birds. It was her favorite thing about this time of year, to keep an eye out for mallards, white-winged scoters and all-black ones, teals and buffleheads and loons.

A black-winged duck was moving across the water with a dozen ducklings fanned out behind her. There would be nests tucked out of sight, but many of the birds they saw today would be gone very soon, continuing on their way north.

Hannah and Birdie went on, moving carefully over or around dead-fall toward the sound of the beaver at work, great flat tails thumping the water. The debris and marsh stopped them just short of the point where the large stream that came off Hidden Wolf joined the lake.

The beaver were hard at work putting their world back together, though some of the younger ones seemed more interested in the large supply of food that had been deposited all around them. Hannah saw more than one lounging on its back in the water, nibbling the soft inner bark from a branch.

Birdie said, "Is Jennet well?"

The question startled Hannah so that she couldn't find her voice for a moment.

"Yes," she said finally. "I think she is. Why do you ask?"

The girl lifted both shoulders and let them drop.

"Something is worrying you. Tell me."

Birdie looked at Hannah over her shoulder. "She just seems tired all the time. More tired than you were when you were going to have Simon."

After a long minute in which Hannah thought very seriously about Jennet, Birdie said, "What's that?"

"What?"

"That. I thought at first it was just a log, there on the end of the dam. But there's something blue caught on it." And then, her tone calm and even: "Sister, I think that's a body."

Elizabeth was in the trading post to see if there had been mail when the door flew open and her youngest came bounding in, red-faced and out of breath. Hannah was just behind her, looking serious.

"Ma!" Birdie flung her arms around Elizabeth's waist.

"Is there something wrong with Daniel?" Her voice creaked and broke.

Birdie's expression was almost comical. "Daniel? There's nothing wrong with Daniel. But something awful—"

Almost of their own volition Elizabeth's hands touched the girl's head and back, searching for some hidden wound but finding only the rapid beat of her heart.

"A body," Birdie said. "At the beaver dams."

There were a lot of people close by, as was always the case when the post rider was expected. Even those who rarely got a letter wanted to know who had, and what news there might be. And now there was something much more interesting to tell at the dinner table.

The questions came from all over the room. Had Hannah seen the body too? Did she recognize it? Was it a local? How long had it been in the lake? Why hadn't she brought it back with her?

Hannah looked at Elizabeth, who inclined her head toward the counter where Magistrate Bookman and Uz Brodie were standing. Brodie served as a kind of sheriff and a substitute for Bookman when he was away on business. "We couldn't get very close," Hannah told them. "You'll need a canoe."

Baldy O'Brien snorted. "And where would they get a canoe?"

Before the flood there were close to a dozen canoes on the lake; the only one to survive had been up at the Ames place waiting to have a hole in its side fixed.

"What about Runs-from-Bears?" asked Brodie. "He started on a new canoe the day after the flood."

"Not finished yet," Hannah said.

John Mayfair said, "There's the raft. We took it out of the water once the bridge was done, but we never broke it up. It's right out back."

"Well, then," said Bookman. "The raft will have to do."

"I want to go back with them," Birdie said. "There's room on the raft. Please, Ma, can I go back with them?"

"Of course not," Elizabeth said, her tone more severe than she had meant it to be.

Tobias Mayfair raised his voice to be heard above the noise. "Friends, has anybody gone missing over the last few days?"

The sudden silence lasted only as long as it took for people to take inventory of their family and neighbors.

"We'll have to go around and ask," Brodie said.

The crowd shifted and in that moment Elizabeth saw her grandson

Adam and young Nicholas Wilde standing near the door. Nicholas looked intrigued but confused, while Adam seemed to be worried.

Birdie made straight for them, with Elizabeth and Hannah close behind.

Hannah crouched down a little so she could look the boys in the eye. "Is someone missing?"

"You had best speak up," Birdie said to the boys, and Elizabeth put a hand on her shoulder and pressed. Birdie gave her an insulted look, but she held her tongue.

"You aren't in any trouble," Hannah was saying. "But we need to know if someone has gone missing."

"Harper," Adam said softly.

Nicholas looked at Adam with surprise. "Harper wouldn't go away," he said. "He just goes exploring sometimes. He'll be back."

"Harper?" Elizabeth asked.

"Harper Washington," Birdie explained. "One of the servants the Fochts left behind."

Hannah said, "When did you see him last?"

"I see him all the time," Nicholas said. He was growing agitated.

"Early this morning," Adam said.

"Nicholas," Elizabeth said. "Does Harper like to swim?"

This time the boy's face lit up. "He's going to teach me," Nicholas said. "He promised to teach me. But Ma says swimming is for fish, and I had best stay far away from the water."

Lily was reading to Curiosity when Adam came to stand in the door. The older children had gone into the woods with Simon and Luke to haul timber, but Adam had stayed behind with Nicholas, who had been forbidden such outings by Lorena.

Lily held up her finger to ask him to wait, and finished the paragraph.

Curiosity turned then and saw him there. "Good God, Adam. What is wrong?"

"Where's my ma?" Adam said.

"Taking a nap with the littlest three. Come on over here and talk to us."

He hesitated for just a moment before he came into the room to stand between Curiosity's chair and Lily's divan. In Lily's experience

Adam was an even-tempered child, slow to anger and always willing to listen to reason. She had never seen him upset like this.

Curiosity was saying, "Come on, now, and tell us what's wrong. Where's Nicholas?"

The story came tumbling out at the mention of Nicholas's name. Hannah and Birdie had come into the trading post to say there was a drowned body in the lake and it turned out that Harper Washington was missing, gone from the Red Dog since early morning, didn't even come home for his dinner.

"And he's always hungry," Adam finished. "Lorena—she looked like she was going to faint when Hannah told her there was a drowned man in the lake. And now the magician and Mr. Brody have gone off on the raft to bring it back."

"Magistrate," Lily corrected him, fighting back the urge to laugh. "It might not be Harper," she heard herself saying. "A trapper might have got caught in the flood and washed up there."

Adam's head bobbed, as if he wanted to believe her but didn't dare.

"Where's Nicholas?" Curiosity wanted to know. "And where have your grandma and auntie got to?"

"I'm supposed to tell you," Adam said. "Auntie Hannah is waiting for the body to come back so she can look at it and Grandma is with Lorena and Nicholas at the Red Dog. Why do they want Auntie Hannah to look at a dead body?"

Lily gestured and he came close enough that she could put an arm around his shoulder. "Doctors look at dead bodies because sometimes by looking they can tell how a person died."

Adam looked even more distressed. "But dead is dead," he said. "What difference does it make, how it happens?"

Curiosity made a clicking sound, the one that said she saw trouble coming. To Adam she said, "You know there are bad people in the world."

Understanding came over Adam's face. "Do you think the dead man in the lake was killed on purpose?"

"We don't know that," Lily said, pulling him closer. "Most likely he just got caught up in the flood."

"Why would anybody want to kill Harper?" Adam said. He was shaking.

Curiosity said, "Come set here on my lap a bit, little boy."

He went willingly enough and climbed up to that safe place. Some of Lily's most vivid and comforting childhood memories had to do with sitting on Curiosity's lap, and she saw now that Adam was glad to be there.

"You just set," Curiosity said to him, one hand resting on his back. "You set here with me and when you feel a little better, we'll have a talk, you and me."

Lily said, "Hannah won't need your help?"

"Your sister and mama can handle things just fine without me," Curiosity said. Her gaze was fixed on Adam. "We got other work right here."

"I want Mama," Adam said.

"I know you do," Curiosity said gently. "But your ma has got to get some rest. When she wake up, we'll fetch her right down here to sit with us."

"I feel bad for him," Adam said. "I don't understand why his ma would go off and leave him in a strange place. My ma wouldn't ever leave us like that."

Lily didn't think it would be a good idea to get into a discussion of Jemima's motivations with a nine-year-old boy, but neither could she ignore the real concern he was showing.

"Does Nicholas talk about his ma very much?"

Adam's mouth worked for a moment, and then he shook his head. "He never does. Not once. It don't seem right."

"Sometimes when people are very angry they tuck it all away and never let on," Lily said. "In my experience, that only makes things worse."

"I don't think Nicholas is mad," Adam said thoughtfully. "He likes it here better than anywhere else he ever lived, he told me that. And he likes Lorena and Harper—" He broke off to clear his throat.

"Let's not borrow trouble," Curiosity said.

Adam pressed his mouth together and nodded. He blinked once and then twice, like a much younger child in need of a nap.

Curiosity shook her head gently at Lily.

Such a beautiful, perfectly made child and with such fragile sensibilities. It was hard for someone so young to see things so clearly. To understand and not understand all at once.

Lily closed her eyes and tried to see her own child at nine years old.

A boy or a girl, long-legged, skin browned by the sun. A child who was free to run and explore, as she had been, as Adam and all the others were.

She had the sense that this would be her only baby, a thought that would have filled her with sorrow a few months ago. But here in Paradise it wasn't as hard to think about. There was no lack of family or playmates here.

And just that simply Lily realized that she had come home to Paradise for good. There was nowhere else in the world she would ever be able to raise a child as she meant to raise this one.

51

———

*H*annah's strict instructions were that Daniel was to rest for a full hour after the treatment.

"Alone." Hannah's tone was pointed, but she was smiling too.

On the porch Martha said, "What is the most we could hope for?"

The question clearly surprised Hannah. After a moment she said, "He will never have full use of his arm, but if we are lucky the pain will be more manageable."

"Isn't it better now than it used to be?"

Birdie had gone off to play with Hopper, but Hannah still looked around herself to be sure they couldn't be overheard.

"Yes," she said. "It is better. Every year it is a little better, though it can flare up now and then, if he's not careful. You'll know when it does because he will go to ground. Daniel doesn't want anyone nearby when that happens, even those who could do him some good."

"Including me," Martha said. "Is that what you're trying to say?"

"Yes." Hannah looked away over the strawberry fields. She said, "His spirits seem high."

Martha coughed a laugh. "I should say so. He's a terrible tease."

Hannah smiled openly. "I'm glad to hear it. For his sake and yours too. You are blushing, but what I mean to say is that you are good for him. Better than any treatment any doctor might suggest."

"I'm not so sure I deserve such praise. I have been—unreasonable at times."

At that Hannah laughed. "I never said you were a saint. That's not what Daniel needs, anyway."

Martha might have asked the logical question: What does Daniel need? But it was not for Hannah to answer. She was still thinking about this when her good-sisters had gone.

After waving them off she went to walk through the fields with no intention but to think.

The little stream that separated the strawberry fields from the woods meandered its way downhill, and Martha walked along it until she was out of sight of the house.

She had a favorite spot where the stream was broad and just a few feet deep, surrounded by high grasses and wildflowers and a great tumble of rocks. Martha spent a few minutes picking flowers until she had a handful of bluebells, pussytoes, foamflowers, phlox, and long grasses. Then she sat down on the broadest, flattest rock and began to weave a fairy crown.

She was concentrating so hard that it took a moment to realize that she was being watched. A red fox stood at the edge of the woods, its bright eyes fixed on her. She blinked, and it was gone.

As girls she and Callie had sometimes argued about Martha's love of fairy crowns. Callie thought them a waste of time and always balked, but in the end she would give in. They would unplait their hair and settle the ring of flowers on their heads to play enchanted princess or bride.

Now they were both married, and Martha had lost the talent for cheering Callie up. Callie, who once had been sharp-tongued and witty and great fun. The events of the last weeks had taken that out of her, and Martha felt it as a real loss.

It was very hot in the sun, and so after a short debate with herself, Martha stripped down to bathe in the stream. The water, ice cold, made her draw in a sharp breath. In a moment she let it go again and settled in to wash. She had no soap with her, but she was glad of the cold water and the warm sun.

I am very fortunate in my husband. She whispered those words to herself every day. Today, somehow, she had forgot that basic truth.

Martha made a promise to herself. When she next saw Daniel, she would tell him the things she had wanted him to see for himself.

Now she climbed out of the stream and onto the flat surface of the rock, to lie in the sun and fall into an immediate sleep.

When Martha had been gone far longer than he liked, Daniel went out to look for her. It wasn't difficult to trace her trail across the fields, but he was in no hurry. The last thing he wanted to do was to startle her. In fact, he was going to find her in order to make peace between them. It had occurred to him, lying on the table while his sister placed her needles in spots along his spine, that he had been neglecting Martha. It hadn't been his intention, and in fact he might not have realized it but for Hannah, who waited until Martha was out of the room to point out the obvious.

"You hurt her feelings."

His first impulse was to deny this charge, but he held back for a moment and tried to make sense of it.

"And how do I fix that, when I don't even know what I did?"

Hannah was smiling; he could feel it. She said, "It doesn't matter what you did, not really. She's new to this business, Daniel."

"It's not like I've ever been married before," he said.

"You know that's not what I mean."

And he did know. Martha had come to him a virgin, unsure but willing. Insecure about the things they did and how they made her feel. He had responded with playfulness, and it seemed now that maybe that had not been enough.

"So how do I fix things?"

"My guess is that all she needs is a little wooing."

For the hour he had been ordered to rest, Daniel had contemplated his sister's advice, and then he set out to see if he could meet the challenge.

He knew where she was, because he liked the spot on the stream as much as she did. Daniel scanned the shadowed woods, the rocks, the water itself, and then he saw a flutter of color rise and fall in the wind.

Martha's hair. She had loosed her hair, and threaded flowers through it.

The images came hard and fast: Martha's pale shoulders breaking through the river of color, the feel of it sliding across his skin.

Now she slept in the sun, half turned on one side with one long leg crossed behind the other. She wore only her chemise, of fabic so fine that he could see the very color of her skin.

He called her name and she woke with a start. Daniel took in her breasts under the damp cotton, paper white and perfectly round, the shadow between her legs, and then more movement in the shadows, just behind her.

One part of his mind recognized that movement for what it was before he could put a name to it. Martha hadn't seen it, but from the expression on her face he knew she had heard the rattle. She froze, her eyes huge and round and fixed on him.

It all happened at once: Daniel's hand found the knife's hilt of its own accord, and his arm came up and over in an arc, even as the rattler's sleek head rose; the flash of sunlight on the blade as it flew, rotating once, twice, three times before it met the sinuous neck and severed head from body.

Then he was running those last few steps. He grabbed her up and held her away from the carcass, felt the flow of her rasping breath on his face.

"It's dead," she said. Not a question, but an assurance. "It's dead."

Gently Daniel set her aside clear of the rock, and went forward to look more closely. It was a good-sized timber rattler, but its bite would probably not have killed her, though it could have cost her a foot or hand. Daniel flung the head into the brush, picked up the body and did the same.

He retrieved his knife and wiped it on the grass. Martha said, "I could have made a stew out of that."

Daniel took in her loosened hair, the crown of flowers, and the brimming tears that she was holding back with such effort. She was trembling.

He pulled her up against him and put his mouth on her brow.

"You will joke at the strangest times." His voice came hoarse, and he realized he was shaking himself.

She raised her face to his to say something and he kissed her.

Martha in his bed had been a revelation. It was a delight and a surprise to watch her take in the unexpected, to see how she argued with herself about letting go and how hard she fell when she did. Little by little she had been growing more confident and courageous, and then had come the interruption that meant he had not yet got a child on her.

He said, "I missed you." She nodded and pulled his face to hers, answering a question he didn't know how to ask. She wanted this; she had missed him too, and he wouldn't have to start wooing her from the very beginning. Now she clung to him with such fierce purpose, her desire so unmistakeable that he might have laughed for satisfaction and joy.

He went down on his knees in the grass and she went with him. For the first time, she put one hand on the front of his breeks. The brush of her fingers was almost more than he could bear; he caught her hand and slipped it inside the flap.

Her fingers moved gently and then circled, taking his measure. He might have said something, but talk required breathing and there was very little air in the world at that moment.

She said, "The infamous cucumber," and he found he could laugh, after all.

He pulled her chemise off over her head and tossed it aside. Face-to-face in the bright sunshine her whole body seemed to glow. Her nipples, as pale and firm as berries just starting to ripen; the sheen of sweat at the base of her throat; the cascade of hair that fell from the circlet of grass and flowers to the ground. He touched her as she had touched him and she put her head back and gasped. Then she righted herself and put her hands on his face.

She said, "Why are you still dressed?"

It was as if her hands had been tied, and were now, suddenly, free. She touched him everywhere as he peeled off his breeks. He began to undo his shirt but she struck his hand away and pushed him, both hands on his chest, until he was sitting in front of her in the high grass, heels on the ground and knees raised. She paused, uncertain.

He didn't have the patience to talk her through what she clearly wanted to try, so Daniel pulled her onto his lap, levered her up, and then, with exquisite slowness, down. Flesh parted and gave way so that she caught him up, inch by inch, in wet heat that might have robbed him of his senses. That would have robbed him of his senses, if not for his need to watch her face as he opened her and filled her.

When he was fully seated, when they could be joined no further, he kissed her softly and pulled her tighter to him, his hand spread on the small of her back.

"I wondered," she said, breathless, her hips moving in response to the pressure of his hand. "I wondered if this would work."

"Of course it will, darlin'," he said, his mouth at her ear. "And the next time you get to wondering, I hope you'll just come on out and say so."

52

That evening Martha and Daniel ate a simple meal and went about the usual chores, talking easily about the week to come, the end of the school year, about Nicholas Wilde and Callie and what would come next. Callie was still determined to take the boy in.

"I don't see how I can stop her," Martha said.

Daniel was thoughtful, his gaze fixed in the distance. Then he turned to her, his expression grim.

"What are you worried about, exactly? What's the worst that could happen?"

It was an excellent question, one she had asked herself repeatedly. She said, "If it turns out that the boy is some kind of imposter, I don't know how Callie will react."

"That's the worst?"

Martha shook her head. "The worst is that Jemima is scheming to try to get the farm and orchard away from her, and using the boy to do it. But why? Why would Jemima with her fancy coach and rich husband want what's left of the orchard?"

Daniel put back his head and drew in a deep breath. "You know the answer to that as well as I do. Jemima wants. That's her nature. Doesn't have to be any reason or logic to it."

When the dishes were wiped and put away and the chores done, Daniel pulled out the tin bath while Martha put water to heat.

She needed this bath. Her whole body felt tender, like a piece of paper that had been folded and refolded so many times that it had gone soft with handling. Maybe a bath would help her sort things through, because there was a war going on. Her mind told her that she should be satisfied and sated and in need of nothing more than a good night's sleep, but there was a tingling itch between her legs that would not be ignored.

When the water was heated she climbed in and leaned back, her whole body relaxing with pleasure. Nerves jumped in the places she was most tender—she saw now she had a rash on her breasts and shoulders, all from Daniel's beard stubble. She slipped farther into the water and sighed with contentment.

Daniel pulled up a stool so he could sit next to her. For a long moment he just watched as she began to wash.

"Your mind is very far away," she said, a little put out that he was so uninterested in the sight of her in the bath.

He said, "Is it? I wanted to say something. Now that the books are all organized—" He cleared his throat. "I thought maybe we could read aloud now and then in the evening."

Martha closed her eyes and did her best to keep her tone even, but there was a breathless quality to it. "What a good idea."

"Well, then," Daniel said. "I'll just open this book up and see where we land."

There was a riffling of pages and a long pause that drew out and out and brought Martha to the edge of reason.

"This is one of my favorite passages," Daniel said, and he began.

"'The highest tax was upon men who are the greatest favourites of the other sex, and the assessments according to the number and natures of the favours they have received; for which they are allowed to be their own vouchers. Wit, valour, and politeness were likewise proposed to be largely taxed, and collected in the same manner, by every person's giving his own word for the quantum of what he possessed. But as to honour, justice, wisdom and learning, they should not be taxed at all, because they are qualifications of so singular a kind, that no man will either allow them in his neighbour, or value them in himself.'"

Martha opened her eyes. *"Gulliver's Travels?"*

Daniel could produce a very innocent smile when it served his needs. "Would you prefer something else? I've got my mother's copy of *Vindication*—"

"Gulliver will do just fine," Martha said. "Please, go on."

"'The women,'" Daniel read on, "'were proposed to be taxed according to their beauty and skill in dressing, wherein they had the same privilege with the men, to be determined by their own judgment. But constancy, chastity, good sense, and good nature, were not rated, because they would not bear the charge of collecting.'"

It was a good story, Martha reminded herself, and it had been a long time since she had last read any of it. Daniel's voice was deep and clear, and he had his mother's talent for accents and voices. After some time Daniel paused to ladle more hot water and then to put a folded towel beneath her neck.

"That better?"

She smiled at him sleepily and began to drift in and out, aware of the rise and fall of his voice and the crackle of the fire and little else.

"'For my own part,'" Daniel continued reading, "'I was far from pleased with his excessive regard for feminine modesty and fragility. He believed me to be innocent and so I took it upon myself to demonstrate a truth he, for all his sophistication and worldly experience, had failed to comprehend. And that is, if one wishes to attain full enjoyment of love, restraint must be overcome and modesty banished. My woman's body was made to give and receive pleasure, and we need fear nothing but artifice. There was no sin in our enjoyment of each other, and nothing to regret as long as the fucking brought pleasure for both.'"

Martha bolted upright so that water sloshed onto the hearth and the fire hissed in complaint.

"Daniel Bonner!"

He cocked his head at her, his expression calm, though a twitch at the corner of his mouth gave him away.

"What? Gulliver was putting you to sleep so I thought this might interest you more—"

She made a grab for the book, and he scooted backward out of reach.

"You—you—" She heard herself spluttering. Then she realized she was kneeling upright in the tub, naked, her skin rose pink from the heat. Martha sat down again and more water sloshed.

"I'll put it away," Daniel said, "if you don't want to hear any more." He was smiling broadly. "In fact, I'll toss it in the fire." He turned toward the hearth.

"Daniel!"

One eyebrow arched. "You object?"

"Yes. No. Yes!" Martha reached for the towel on the empty stool beside her, but Daniel was there first.

"Oh, look, it's wet," he said with great solemnity. "Let me hang it up to dry. Now what was it you wanted me to do with the French Lady of Leisure?"

Her choices were extreme. She could climb naked out of the tub and stalk, just as she was, into the bedroom to dress; she could sit back down, close her eyes, and listen to Daniel reading.

Martha made an effort to examine the book. Plain dark green binding, gold-edged pages, and a lot of them. A long book.

"Did you want me to keep reading?"

"You are merciless."

"Let me go on a little more, and maybe then you can decide. Where were we? Oh, yes. 'I am well spoken, it has often been said, for a woman, and in this instance I could see the power of my words working on his—'"

Martha cleared her throat and Daniel paused, one brow raised.

She said, "I thought this young lady was French? She sounds very English to me."

"She travels a great deal between England and France in pursuit of adventures."

"I suppose she'd have to."

Daniel turned back to the page.

"Where was I? . . . 'As I shared these thoughts with him he attained a fierce erection with a head as large as a plum—'"

"Plum?" Martha said. "Plum?"

"The French Lady of Leisure is prone to exaggeration."

"But a plum is—"

"Large?"

"Purple."

He inclined his head thoughtfully, and began to read again.

"'Now I almost regretted my speech, for he wasted no time in placing me in a position to receive his invasion and at once I felt him there at the threshold—'"

"Invasion," Martha muttered.

"The French Lady of Leisure has a wide and imaginative vocabulary. Isn't that water getting cold?"

Martha nodded tightly.

"Well, then," said Daniel. "Let's get you out of there and go to bed, what do you think?"

"I am very tired."

"I can see that."

In one movement he snagged the towel he had put out of reach and offered it to her.

Martha said, "Will you read to me some more?"

"Darlin'," Daniel said. "I'll read until you beg me to stop."

53

Official Inquiry into the death of
Harper Washington, free man of color, conducted by
James Montgomery Bookman, District Magistrate

I. Statement Submitted into Evidence
Signed by Hannah Savard, Physician
Witnessed by John Mayfair, Attorney-at-Law
and Ethan Middleton, Esq.

On the second Sunday in May in this year 1824 I examined the remains of a young man of African origin, about seventeen years of age. In life he stood about five foot eleven inches tall. The remains indicate that this was a healthy, active young man.

There were no wounds on the body visible to the eye or closer examination. The bones of the head, limbs, and torso were all intact. The examination of the internal organs confirmed the subject's health.

Upon opening his chest both his lungs were found to contain water, which indicates that he was alive when he went into the lake and drowned. There is no evidence of foul play.

Hannah Savard née Bonner, also known as Walks-Ahead by the Kahnyen'kehàka of the Wolf Longhouse at Good Pasture

II. Statement of Lorena Webb,
free woman of color and servant
to the Focht household.

I, Lorena Webb, hereby swear that the earthly remains showed to me this day were those of Harper Washington, free man of color. Harper was employed by the same family as me, Mr. and Mrs. Focht. He was no blood relation of mine. I have known him about six months. I am told that his ma died a few years back of a lung fever.

I can't hardly imagine that he's really gone.

Pardon? Oh, yes, I'm sorry to let my mind wander. I last saw Harper early this day, about an hour after sunrise when he brought my breakfast to me from the kitchen. Harper and me, we wasn't to eat in the dining room. His appetite was good and he was talking at a gallop, the way he always talked.

He did like to swim, that's true. Liked the lake too. Said it was all kind of cool on a hot afternoon. I guess maybe he got him a cramp.

No, sir, I can't imagine any reason Harper might do hisself harm. He was such a lively boy, always interested in everything around him. Uncommon smart too. Mr. Focht saw to it that Harper learned his letters and numbers. Sometimes he would lend Harper the newspaper and then they would talk about what was going on in the world. Mr. Focht put a lot of trust into that boy, and is going to be mighty disappointed to find him passed on.

I suppose I'll just set tight right here, looking after young Nicholas though truth be tolt I'd just as soon go back home. What choice do I have?

III. Statement of Joshua Hench,
free man of color, village blacksmith

I did know the boy, he come around here pretty much every day to visit. A friendly boy and curious about the world. Never heard anybody ask so many questions. The boy had a loose jaw.

He wanted to know about everything. How we make nails and where we got our charcoal from. Wanted to know everything about everybody. Who was courting and who was increasing, who was getting along and who wan't. But there didn't seem to be no harm in him.

No, I never did talk to him this morning, but I saw him setting off. I don't know where he was going, but it wan't the lake, at least not to start with. No, sir, Harper set off that way, downriver. How he ended up all the way on the far end of Half Moon, I fear we'll never know the answer to that question. May God have mercy on his everlasting soul.

IV. Statement of Alice LeBlanc
at the Red Dog

Yes, Harper come in to get his breakfast as usual and took it up to Lorena. The boy Nicholas who claims to be a Wilde, he had already had his fill and gone out to run with the Bonner children, and good riddance say I.

No, I don't like him. I don't like the way he looks at me. There's something wrong with him. Like he was blind on one side and can see more than the rest of us on the other.

I'll tell you once more. I don't know a thing about what Harper got up to when he left here. If you say he went swimming, well, then most likely he did. Ain't no concern of mine one way or the other, though I am sorry to hear he's dead at such a young age.

Did you ask Levi Fiddler? I saw them talking more than once. Maybe he can tell you more.

V. Statement of Levi Fiddler,
free man of color, farmhand at the orchards

My name is Levi Fiddler, and I work for Miss Callie. Yes, sir, I mean Mrs. Middleton. Been working in the Wilde's orchard ever since I got my manumission papers. I do all the heavy work at the orchard, and the pressing, come fall.

Yes, sir, I knew Harper to talk to. He come by to call almost every day, and he took up whatever work there was to hand. I got the feeling he was lonely ever since the other servants went off with the Fochts.

That's all I know to tell you. Can I get back to work now?

VI. Statement of Callie Middleton

I knew young Harper Washington through my half brother Nicholas. Harper was supposed to be looking after my brother.

I can't deny he was a helpful and friendly young man, but he was far too green and flighty to be looking after a young boy like Nicholas. Now I ask you, Jim Bookman, what if my brother had gone down to the lake with Harper? I hate to think of it. And that Lorena was just as bad. I have been saying it all along that Nicholas should be with us, and he will be by the end of the day, that I promise you.

54

The day after Harper Washington was fished out of the lake was Sunday, and on Sundays everybody came home to Uphill House for dinner at midday. There were so many of them that they couldn't fit around the dining room table, so the men set up trestle tables and benches in the open space between the house and the gardens, and the women spent all morning cooking. It was Birdie's job to see to it that the little people all kept busy and out of the way, which was a lot better than scraping potatoes or cutting up onions.

Ever since she got out of bed Birdie had been wondering how she could get to Daniel and Martha before anybody else. She wanted to be the one to tell them about Harper Washington, because she was the only one who would tell them the whole story and not leave anything out. But the little people were everywhere and impossible to shake off, and so she had just about given up the idea when the Hidden Wolf folks showed up early to help.

Susanna and Annie had baked pies and Birdie's ma came out to admire

them. There was a lot of talk about dried currants and strawberry preserves, and then Birdie couldn't hold back her question any longer.

"What about Daniel and Martha?" she asked. "Why didn't they come
down the mountain with you?"

Gabriel said, "You'll understand when you're newly wed yourself."

The kind of answer that made Birdie hopping mad. She said, "You
and Annie are newlyweds. And so are Callie and Ethan, but all of you are
here."

"Don't begrudge them a few hours sleep," Ma said. "They've had a
very strenuous week."

"That's right," Gabriel said, grinning. "They need their sleep."

Then Annie had stepped on his foot, hard enough to make Gabriel
squawk.

Blue-Jay said, "Let me at that other foot," and with that the wrestling
started.

It was the best chance she'd have. Birdie slipped away and headed
down to the village at a trot.

It was a beautiful day, warm but not warm enough to raise a sweat
unless you were working in the sun. She found a spot out of sight in the
shadows next to the schoolhouse, because it wouldn't do if some neighbor saw her. There would be questions about what she was doing sitting
there on a Sunday, and didn't she need to get home for dinner? She was
better off where she was if she could just stay awake. That would be hard
in such fine weather, because she hadn't got enough sleep in the night.

Because of the dead boy in the lake, the little people had whispered
among themselves. *Because she saw that dead boy.*

They were right, and they were wrong too. Birdie had seen more
than a few dead people. Her aunt Many-Doves, for one. People as old as
her grandfather Hawkeye, and as young as the little boy Friend Verena
Henry had brought dead into the world. There was nothing to fear from
dead people, but there was something about Harper that didn't sit right.

She had begun to drift off despite her best intentions when she heard
Daniel's voice. He was laughing. He laughed a lot these last few weeks,
and because he was laughing and happy, it seemed other people were
happier. Birdie realized she herself was smiling to hear him.

She startled Martha, coming out of the shadows the way she did.

"Is there something wrong?" Daniel could always read her face, even
when she least wanted him to.

And so she told them the whole story while they stood there, dumb-founded.

Martha said, "That's terrible. Poor Nicholas, he must be very distraught."

"He's at Uphill House with Ethan and Callie," Birdie said. "So you'll be able to see for yourself."

Daniel's brow pulled down low. "So Callie fetched him from the Red Dog, then."

"Last night," Birdie said. "Now Lorena's there all alone."

"Then let's knock on her door and invite her to Sunday dinner," Daniel said. Martha's face lit up at the idea, and Birdie had to wish she had thought of it first.

"Wait," Birdie said. "There's something else that's bothering me."

They waited, watching her face. For a moment Birdie was thankful that her people were the way they were. Mostly grown-ups couldn't be bothered with children who didn't know their place.

Birdie said, "When they pulled Harper out of the lake he was dressed. Shirt and breeches."

"Shoes?" Martha asked.

"I don't think he owned a pair," Birdie told them. "I never saw him wearing shoes. But I did see him swimming once—" She broke off, her determination to tell this story suddenly deserting her.

Martha smiled at her. "Go on, Birdie. No one is going to scold you."

"Maybe you won't," Birdie said, a little grumpily. "But other people will."

"Don't be a coward," said Daniel.

Birdie knew he was baiting her, but she couldn't help herself; she rose to it.

"I did see Harper swimming in the lake and more than once. But I never once saw him swimming in shirt and breeks. He shucked his clothes every time."

Daniel bent over to look her in the eye. "Have you been swimming this early in the season?"

"No," Birdie said on a sigh of relief.

"All right, then." Daniel tugged at her earlobe. "I'm glad to hear that your common sense hasn't deserted you."

"You swim in cold water all year," Birdie said.

"And so could you, if you cared to come up to Lake in the Clouds. Now, let me think a while about Harper. I need to talk to Hannah."

"But not with the boy nearby," Martha said.

Daniel nodded, but Birdie had the sense her brother was too far away in his thoughts, and hadn't heard Martha at all.

When the first round of roughhousing was done, the men carried Lily and her chaise longue outside and set her down in the shade of Elizabeth's fruit trees. Curiosity was waiting for her there, where they were surrounded on three sides by tables, two long and one short.

"Like Caesar looking over his troops," Lily said of her situation. No hint of boredom or irritation in her voice. In fact, she was in a teasing mood. Elizabeth knew there was reason for her good cheer and even a cautious optimism, but worry still had a strong hold on her own heart.

Curiosity squinted up from the rocker Nathaniel had brought out for her. She reached out and took Elizabeth's wrist. Her touch was very cool and dry.

She said, "You set too. All those young women in the kitchen, no need for you to be running around. You will just trip over each other's feet."

"She's right, Ma," Lily said. "Sit with us. Dinner's almost ready anyway. I wonder where Daniel and Martha have got to."

Just then Simon came out of the house with another rocker.

"I see I have been outmaneuvered again." Elizabeth sighed and sat down. "It's just as well. My feet are sore."

"They must be fallen off your legs for you to admit something like that," Curiosity said. "Girls! We need a basin of hot water and some Epsom salts for your grandmama."

"No, we don't," Elizabeth raised her voice. And to Curiosity: "That can wait until after dinner."

Curiosity grumbled, but she let it go.

"It is so good to be out of doors," Lily said. She stretched a little and yawned too. Then she seemed to remember herself and covered her mouth with one hand.

"Pardon me," she said. "Too long out of proper company."

"There's company, and there's family," Curiosity said. "Yawn if you've got a mind to."

Elizabeth watched the little people running back and forth with dishes and bowls, every one of them looking determined. Luke had probably offered some kind of prize for the chld who could cause the least disturbance and provide the most help.

She said, "Where is Birdie?"

Lily scanned the scene. "Not here, Ma."

"She'll be close by." Elizabeth said this out loud for her own benefit.

Curiosity made a harrumphing noise.

"Do you have reason to believe otherwise?" Elizabeth asked.

"No, but I know the girl," Curiosity said. "And I gave up trying to keep track of her long ago. As you will too, someday."

"Never," Elizabeth said easily, and they laughed at that, all three of them.

"Oh," Lily said. "Ma, the boys have got the bagattaway sticks out already."

Before Elizabeth could get to her feet to set things right Ethan was there in the middle of a crowd of children whose expressions ranged from guilty to insulted. In the end they went stomping off to put the long sticks away.

It was a familiar scene and a very rewarding one, watching the children she had raised taking up the care of the children they had brought into the world. Elizabeth felt the familiar but unwelcome prick of tears behind her eyes.

"Look at the family you made for yourself," Curiosity said. "I can still close my eyes and see the day you got here. You were the brightest light, Elizabeth. You lit up the room and you still do. Lily, you just about the age your ma was when she come to Paradise."

Elizabeth managed a smile.

"See how it is? Folks almost never change. Thirty years on and your mama still cain't take a compliment. Look at her blush."

Lily said, "I see. But that's because she's happy, Curiosity. She's so happy she's going to start weeping any second." This last bit came with a cheeky grin, and that was what Elizabeth needed. She sat up straighter.

Curiosity said, "While I got you two alone, let me ask you what is happening with young Nicholas Wilde."

Elizabeth scanned the crowd and saw that the boy was coming around the far side of the house with his arms full of firewood. The other boys followed suit, with the littlest carrying one piece of tinder in each hand.

"Callie and Ethan took him home," Lily answered Curiosity when it was clear her mother would not.

"That don't sit right with you, Elizabeth?"

She hesitated. "If they want to take the boy in, who am I to stop them?"

This question was still hanging in the air when Daniel and Martha came into the clearing, the young dog they had brought home with them racing ahead. Just behind them came Birdie and Lorena.

"They brought Lorena," Elizabeth said. "We should have thought to invite her."

At the sound of voices raised in greeting the children looked up from the wood they were stacking. Nicholas shot across the clearing, strong legs pumping, to throw himself into Lorena's arms with such joy that it made Elizabeth's throat clench.

Lorena bent her head down to listen as the boy talked, pointing to the tables, the other children, the firewood, the sky overhead. She listened as any mother would listen, with pride and joy.

"She raised him," Lily said. "She's like his—" she broke off, because Callie had come into their circle.

"She might have raised him," Callie said calmly. "But she's not his mother. She's not any blood kin to him at all."

All the frantic activity came to a stop when they sat down to eat. Even Lily was allowed to sit up at the table, but Curiosity kept an eye on her.

There was a leg of lamb stuffed with herbs, another of veal, and a ham, along with flour and cornbread, and the last of the squash, potatoes, and carrots from the root cellar. The Bonners liked their food, but the talk carried on, multiple conversations at once that ebbed and flowed together and then parted.

With her plate untouched before her, Elizabeth took it all in. Most of it she had heard hundreds of times before, old jokes and gentle teasing, comments about the veal, questions about the chutney, when the first new greens might be ready for picking, and was Luke planning on hoarding the whole plate of Annie's special cornbread or might he pass it down?

It was no small feat to feed so many, but it was worth it. These Sunday dinners stayed with her through the short winter days.

Nathaniel raised his head and looked at her. Reading her thoughts, again. Under the table he squeezed her hand.

"We've done all right for ourselves, Boots."

Then he leaned over and neat as a kingfisher Nathaniel hooked a piece of lamb from Lily's plate. She slapped his wrist, laughing and then held up her fork and waved it. "Do not," she said with a halfhearted scowl, "do not make me use this."

From the children's table came cries of encouragement, but Nathaniel held up his hands in surrender.

Callie got up to help clear the tables, and sat down again when Curiosity gave her a pointed look. "Little girl, walk with me, will you? My Dolly and her Joshua coming by this afternoon and I got to get back home."

For a moment Elizabeth watched Callie walking alongside Curiosity, head bent down to hear what the old woman had to say.

Lorena cleared her throat. She said, "Thank you kindly for dinner, but I should get back now."

Elizabeth turned to her in surprise. "I thought you might stay the afternoon. I hoped you would."

She looked around herself and saw that for the moment they were alone. Lily had been spirited away in Simon's arms, Nathaniel was off with the little people, and Jennet and Hannah and the others were clearing the table to set out sweets.

Lorena had a calm smile with nothing of artifice in it. "I don't think Miss Callie would like that idea," she said.

It was true, and Elizabeth hardly knew what to say. To explain Callie's behavior would require a long conversation and the breaking of more than one confidence. She could not take those things upon herself, no matter how sound the cause seemed.

Instead she said, "He is a fine boy, Lorena. You have done an admirable job with him."

Lorena studied her folded hands, because, Elizabeth realized, she was in a similar situation. There were things she might explain, but not without breaking confidences.

Finally she said, "The most important thing to me is that Nicholas is happy and busy and folks don't take advantage."

"There we agree," Elizabeth said. "And I can promise you I will do everything in my power to see to his welfare. You may not know that I had a brother, and that Ethan is his only child. I know that Ethan will never let the boy come to harm of any kind."

"Sometimes," Lorena said, "sometimes the best intentions do the most harm. Don't you think?" She stood. "Please, will you tell your husband I said good-bye, and thank you?"

"Of course," Elizabeth said. And then, quickly: "There's really no need for you to sit alone on a Sunday afternoon. I wish you would stay."

Lorena smiled. "But I won't be alone," she said. "I'm going to go walking with Levi, and then we're both invited to take tea with Daisy and her family."

"Oh," Elizabeth said, trying not to show her surprise. "That sounds lovely. I'll wish you a good afternoon, then. Will you come again?"

Lorena inclined her head. "Thank you. I'd like that."

Callie came back from taking Curiosity home and found a spot alone under the big oak on the opposite side of the clearing. It was a good spot if she wanted to watch the game that was rushing back and forth, and it was even better if she needed to be left alone with her thoughts.

She had feared the worst when Curiosity dragged her off, but then the talk had been easy enough. Mostly about Nicholas, what kind of boy he was, how he dealt with disappointment and sadness and the loss of his friend. It was clear that Curiosity liked the boy, and that pleased Callie, though she couldn't have said why.

What pleased her less was the way everybody was watching her. As if she couldn't be trusted to look after a nine-year-old boy. As if she were a child playing house, and unaware of the challenges ahead.

But they would see, soon enough, that she could take care of a household, a husband, and a child. She intended to make sure every one of them realized how wrong they had been about her.

Although Elizabeth had a strong urge to walk over and sit with Callie, she understood it would be a mistake. Callie did not like to be seen as weak and she would not thank Elizabeth for her interference, no matter how well meant. Instead Elizabeth went into the house, where the women were gathered in the kitchen. Voices and laughter came to her in the hall and she hesitated a moment before going in.

Hannah was nursing her Simon with her feet propped up on a stool. She sat beside an open window that provided a view of the children and the bagattaway game. The sun fell over her hair and made her skin glow gold and copper. It stroked her breast and the child's cheek, so that his lashes threw shadows as he suckled contentedly. It was a moment so clear that Elizabeth thought it would stay with her forever.

"Come sit," Hannah said.

"I've done enough sitting," Elizabeth said.

"Well, there's no room for another pair of hands over here," Jennet said from the business end of the kitchen. "So you might as well keep Hannah company."

Elizabeth could have argued that Jennet was the one who should be off her feet, but she didn't want to disturb the atmosphere in the kitchen any more than she had already. She sat.

Susanna brought her a cup of tea. "Peppermint," she said. "With a little honey."

"I wish you would come visit with us more often," Elizabeth said. She caught Annie's eye. "All of you."

"We've been in the cornfield every day," Annie said. There was something of pride in her tone; she knew what she owed to her family, and the work came easy to hand. It occurred to Elizabeth, and not for the first time, that young women were as competitive as men, but in ways men were not likely to see or comprehend.

For a few minutes they talked about the gardens and cornfields, who might have seed to share, and whether the early spring meant a longer or a shorter summer.

"But I do mean to come visit more often," Susanna said. "It's just that the days go by so quickly."

"And the nights too, I'm sure." Joan LeBlanc said under her breath. Elizabeth jerked around, but Joan had turned her back and was scrubbing the table.

If Susanna had heard Joan's comment, she was giving no sign of it.

Elizabeth asked about Lily.

"Upstairs," said Jennet. She arched her back and stretched. "Taking a nap with the weeest of the wee people."

"You need a nap as much as Lily," Elizabeth told her.

Jennet waved this suggestion off as if she were shooing away flies.

"When is the baby due?" Martha asked.

"That's a matter of some debate," Jennet said. "By my reckoning, early August. Curiosity insists July, and Hannah here is keeping her opinion to herself. I think it's odd they won't take my word on it. I was there when it happened, after all. Och, Martha, I've embarrassed you. I apologize."

Martha smiled to herself, and Elizabeth imagined she was enjoying the company of these women who she could now claim as sisters. They were, and would always be, a powerful force in her life. They would help her bring her children into the world, and stand by her when illness and misfortune struck, as she would stand by them.

She wondered, as she sometimes did since her last birthday, how many years were left to her, how long she would be able to watch Martha grow into her new life and family. Then she thought of Curiosity and took some comfort in that good example.

She said, "Martha, do you feel yourself come home?"

Everyone looked at her, as if she had said something out loud they never knew the words for. Martha's smile softened.

"Yes, I suppose that's what I'm feeling. I'm—" And she broke off.

"Pregnant!" said Joan LeBlanc. "I knew it!"

Martha turned very quickly, color rising on her cheeks. "I am not," she said, with great dignity. "And if I were, it would be none of your concern. I would like an apology."

Joan looked as though she had been slapped. Which she had, in a way. She mumbled something that might have been an apology and then something else about the parlor and slipped away, out of the kitchen.

Anje was worrying her lip with her teeth, her eyes wide.

"The lass is aye angry," Jennet said.

"At me?" Martha said, clearly upset. "Why should she be angry at me?"

Elizabeth said, "She's angry at everybody."

Anje said, "Don't send her off, please. It would only make things worse."

"What things?" Annie said, her brow drawn down.

Anje looked at the door as if she wished she could see through it, and then she lowered her voice.

"She had hopes of one of the Sampson brothers. I think it's hard for her to see all of you so—"

"Settled. Happy," Susanna suggested. "I'm sorry for her loss."

Elizabeth hadn't thought very much about the Sampsons, and she felt a pang of guilt about that. But the three brothers had lived alone, and there had been no grieving family to look after.

Hannah said, "Which one?"

Anje looked confused.

"Which brother?" Hannah said.

"Oh," Anje said. "I don't know."

"She didn't confide in you?"

Anje lifted a shoulder. "She didn't know herself. She would have taken any of them. She's worried she'll die an old maid."

They were all quiet for a moment, because there was little to say. Ethan and Daniel and Gabriel had all married very quickly; the Sampson brothers were lost in the flood, and most of the other single men were Quakers, who married among themselves or went to Baltimore or Philadelphia to find wives.

There were no men for the younger women like Joan and her sisters to marry, which meant they must resign themselves to spinsterhood, or leave home to take up work in some bigger town. And that, in turn, meant that should one of them find a husband, she could never come back to Paradise, unless there was money to buy land.

"Ethan planned so carefully," Hannah said.

"A few things did slip his notice," Annie said. "And then of course one of the eligible men went and married a squaw."

Elizabeth heard herself draw in a sharp breath. "Annie."

The girl raised her brows. "I'm not making it up, Auntie. People say such things to me."

"Who?" Jennet asked. "Who would dare to talk you to like that?"

Anje's color drained away and she turned back to her work.

"It's not important and I don't want to say. If word got back to Gabriel—"

"Och aye," Jennet said. "Better to avoid that."

Simon was sound asleep, and Elizabeth took him from Hannah so she could put herself to rights.

Just at that moment the kitchen door swung open and Callie came in, a pulse fluttering in her neck and her eyes very large in her face. She said, "I can't find Nicholas. I've looked everywhere."

It took a good five minutes to settle her down and get the story, which was very simple, in the end. Callie had dozed off in the shade of the trees watching the games, and when she woke there was no sign of Nicholas anywhere.

"I checked the barn and stable and all the outbuildings," she said. "I went over to your place, Hannah, and I checked there too."

"But think, Callie," Jennet said. "The boy makes friends so easily, there's no cause for panic. Our lads go off for days at a time playing in the fort at Lake in the Clouds or exploring—"

"You're thinking of Harper," Martha said. "That's what has you so worried."

Just that simply Callie dissolved into tears. "If something happens to him, I couldn't bear it."

In her calmest voice, Jennet asked Callie an obvious question. "Did you see the other bairns? What did they have to say about Nicholas?"

Callie's mouth crimped with irritation. "I wasn't looking for them," she said. "I was looking for Nicholas."

There was a small silence in the room, and then Martha came forward and sat next to Callie.

"Callie," she said. "The boy will be with the other children."

With a studied slowness Callie raised her head and looked at Martha so coldly that Elizabeth's throat closed for a moment.

"His name is Nicholas," she said. "Why can't you say his name? He's your half brother, whether you like it or not."

Martha closed her eyes and opened them again, and then she stood. "I'm going out to look for the children. When I find Nicholas, I'll send him to you here."

"There they are," Hannah said from her spot by the window. "Don't you hear them laughing? And Nicholas is there too. Callie? Nicholas is there."

Callie got up and went to the door, where she hesitated for a moment. Then she turned and looked at each of them. She said, "I know what you're thinking. You think I'm too attached to him. But he's the only blood kin I have in the world. In my place you'd feel the same."

Jennet said, "Callie, lass. What will you do when his mither comes to claim him?"

She heard the question, Elizabeth was sure of it, but Callie simply walked away, out of the kitchen and through the hall and front door, letting it close behind her with a sound as sharp as an axe meeting wood.

———

Despite the disconcerting episode in the kitchen, the rest of the after-noon went smoothly. Elizabeth returned to her spot under her apple tree and was glad when Martha and Susanna joined her. For a long time they spoke very little, half dozing in the shade while they listened to Jennet telling stories to the older children while Hannah and Annie finished in the kitchen. Over the next half hour they all drifted back together, sit-ting quietly in the shade to watch the game that ranged up and down from one goal to the other.

With a flick of his bagattaway stick Blue-Jay sent the ball flying and Gabriel leaped into the air to intercept it, as graceful as a deer. Elizabeth watched Nathaniel running, his long hair flying around him.

Martha said, "This will go on all day, won't it? Unless somebody gets hurt."

"Even then," Susanna said. "When they are in the grips of the game, they hear nothing else."

"Runs-from-Bears is as fast as any of the younger men," Jennet said. "And Nathaniel is faster still."

"They are a joy to watch," Elizabeth said. "I have never tired of it, even after so many years."

"I doubt that I will either," Susanna said.

Martha turned toward her. "How did you and Blue-Jay meet? I don't think I've ever heard the story. If that isn't too personal a question."

Susanna said, "There wasn't very much to it. One day when we had been here a few months, Ben came to our Seventh-Day Meeting. Ben's sister-in-law is a Friend, and he sometimes went to Meeting with her when he lived in New Orleans. He was homesick, I think. Blue-Jay asked to come along with him to see what it was like."

She put her head back to study the boughs overhead.

"My father met them at the door and directed them to the back bench, though there were spaces enough at the front." Susanna closed her eyes and then she sat up straight and looked directly at Martha. "Thou must understand. If Daniel or Lily or someone like thee came to a Meeting, my father would be gracious and welcoming, and room would be made at the front."

"Oh," Martha said, clearly unhappy to have raised the question.

"Yes, oh," Susanna said with a grim smile. "I was shamed by my fa-ther's lack of charity and fellowship. And so I went to sit with Ben and

Blue-Jay on the back bench. And that was the first time we spoke, though I had seen him before in the village. Thy expression, Martha. Have I surprised thee?"

"Yes," Martha said, "a little. So that's why you don't come into the village? Because of the way your family treated the Mohawk?"

"Every day I pray for an opening," Susanna said. "For a way to forgive my father and my mother too, for taking his part in what happened at Meeting. In the meantime, I have made my home with Blue-Jay at Lake in the Clouds, and I want no other."

Martha turned her attention back to the game, which had not slowed down at all in spite of the afternoon sun. Backs and shoulders, knotty with muscle, glistening with sweat. Martha's eyes tracked Daniel and Elizabeth was struck with the memory of the first days of her own marriage. The powerful hunger, the strangeness of it all.

To see Daniel playing was to see him truly happy. So much had been taken away from him, but here was one thing left from childhood that he could still do, even one-armed. He leapt into the air brandishing the bagattaway stick Hawkeye had made for him when he was a boy, and scooped the ball out of the sky into the net at its end. With a flick of his wrist he sent it flying again.

When Elizabeth looked at him she saw her firstborn son, who had come back to them when she had begun to give up hope.

Martha said, "I worry about being so happy."

None of the others had anything to say to that, because they knew too well what she meant. Rather than give her false assurances, Elizabeth covered Martha's hand with her own.

"Thank you," she said. "For my son, I thank you."

𝒻or Martha the last week of spring and the first of summer seemed to spin by like a top.

She learned to rise at first light, to have that quiet hour with Daniel. As soon as Betty came up from the village with fresh bread and new milk, the day would begin.

To Martha's great relief school came to an end without any terrible missteps on her part, but the newly free hours were filled straight away. She helped Curiosity make soap and Lily organize hundreds of drawings and paintings accumulated over the years. The little people came to visit and she fed them all pancakes while they told her their newest stories. When Hannah went into the woods to find the herbs and roots and barks she needed for her medicinals, Martha came along and paid attention until things she had once known began to come back to her.

She helped Annie and Susanna in the cornfields at Lake in the Clouds, so that her hands blistered, the blisters broke and then came again until finally she had calluses enough to protect her, and the hoe felt solid in her hands. Though she wore a broad-brimmed straw hat, her freckles multipled by the hundreds, much to Daniel's interest and amusement. His own skin tone deepened until the green of his eyes stood out and took on a silver cast, so striking that she sometimes found herself unable to look away from him.

After Martha had watched her new husband shave himself a few times, an awkward process he had trained himself to do with one hand, she offered, hesitantly, shyly, to be taught. At first she thought she had offended him, but the next day he showed her how to sharpen the razor on the strop and to beat soap into a lather and then, step by step, how to scrape the stubble from his cheeks and chin, from his upper lip and finally from his jaw and throat. She loved his neck for reasons she couldn't explain to herself, and running the razor down its length unsettled her in a way she would have found odd and disturbing, if she had not seen the same reaction on Daniel's face.

Betty looked after the laundry and the cleaning, while Martha found other ways to look after Daniel. Sometimes she washed his hair out in the open, Daniel on a chair tilted back and propped against the pump while she rubbed soap into his scalp and then rinsed it. Water ran in rivulets over his arched neck and down his chest, and it often took all her concentration to stay focused on the job at hand. As if she had set him a challenge, Daniel took over the brushing of her hair in the evening. It was her turn to sit in the chair, and she found herself looking forward to it at odd moments during the day.

They talked about everything. He told her family stories, sad and funny and outrageous, about his grandfather Hawkeye, his own adventures on the mountain as a boy, the time in the militia before he was shot and captured. The time in the garrison at Nut Island. He talked about his injury, and gave her extracts to read from books on anatomy and medicine, so that she would have a better understanding of the damage to his shoulder, and what it meant.

He told her the story he had heard from Lily about Gabriel Oak and his grandmother. It was hard to believe that Elizabeth's parentage was as unorthodox as Martha's, but it made her feel closer to her mother-in-law.

"She should have been Elizabeth Oak," Martha said, and Daniel looked directly surprised at that suggestion.

She told him more about the years she had lived alone with Jemima in the old mill house. Things she hadn't allowed herself to think about swam up out of the dark and Daniel listened while they sat together on the porch, his fingers laced through her own.

Elizabeth went to Albany and took Birdie with her, and for that week Martha went more often to Uphill House to help Jennet and visit with Lily. She sat with Nathaniel and Simon and Luke while they ate supper and listened to tall tales that made her laugh until her sides hurt and she wept tears.

Every third day Hannah came with her box of needles. Sometimes Birdie came along and sometimes Hannah brought her youngest, and Martha sat outside with him until Hannah had finished. Simon was a sturdy, cheerful child who was very serious about learning to crawl. Martha's courses came again and for all her affection for the little people, she was relieved. She wanted to remember this summer exactly as it was; she wanted to keep Daniel to herself for a while at least.

In the normal course of things she would have spent a year or more learning about him before they ever entertained a serious thought about marriage. He would have come to call on her, and they would have gone for walks and buggy rides, and little by little they would have given in to the attraction between them. She said this to him and he laughed at the idea outright.

"You think either of us could have waited a year?"

"Well, yes," Martha said. "Or at least, I could have."

He raised one eyebrow, which was his way of calling her less than truthful.

"You have a high opinion of your powers of seduction," she said.

"Oh, I would have had my work cut out for me," he said as he pulled the brush down the length of her hair. "But I imagine we would have had a good time, both of us."

It made no sense to argue with Daniel about these things—mostly, Martha admitted to herself, because he was more comfortable with the subject matter, and worse, he was usually right. And still, he did ask her thoughts and listen when she gave them. He valued her opinion, and he trusted her.

Martha understood the full measure of his trust the day he emptied his satchel out in front of her. Nothing there was much of a surprise: whetstone, handkerchief, string, compass, the stub of a pencil, a folding of paper covered with notes, and neatly trimmed newspaper clippings held together by a pin. The only item that gave her pause was a tightly wound ball of yarn that smelled of lanolin. Before she could think to ask him about it, he had taken it up and begun to squeeze it rhythmically with his injured hand.

After a few minutes sweat appeared on his brow and ran in rivulets down his face, but his expression was resolute and he continued on, looking neither left nor right, looking at nothing at all except whatever goal it was he set for himself.

She wondered if anyone knew he did this, and what Hannah would say. In the end she only brought him a cup of water and a damp rag to wipe his face. It was an hour before Daniel came back to himself, and then he spoke to her about the window sashes they expected any day, and how good it would be to have the renovations to the house done.

The next day Hannah came alone, and Martha stayed close by to watch. Daniel stretched out on the table, bare to the waist, so his sister could work on his back and shoulders and on the arm that had never healed. She worked in companionable silence, only stopping now and then to talk to Martha about what she had before her, as if Daniel were the subject of an anatomy lesson.

For the most part Martha kept her questions to herself. She wanted to know if Daniel thought the treatments might be helping, if the pain came less often, if he was feeling hopeful. But now was not the time to ask such things; maybe there would never be a good time unless Daniel raised the subject himself.

Hannah left, and they went to the spot on the stream where Daniel had killed the timber rattler. They spent the rest of the afternoon in the sun, napping or talking. Sometimes Daniel read aloud to her while she made flower crowns for both of them and for Hopper, who was growing fast out of puppyhood but still insisted on chasing every insect and inspecting every rustle in the grass.

Every few days Martha went into the village to the trading post. It seemed now certain that no one would ever call it the emporium or anything but the trading post, regardless of how big a sign the Mayfairs nailed in place. She stopped to talk to almost everyone she met, and realized one day that she had lost her reserve. She was too busy to be shy, too happy to be self-conscious. Even the sight of Baldy O'Brien's scowl couldn't stay with her for long.

The only worry was Callie, who seemed ever more distant and

preoccupied. She and Ethan had begun building a new house in the orchards—far too big and fancy for Paradise, according to the O'Briens—
with room for both the Misses Thicke and for Nicholas too.

Nicholas was so much a part of the village already that Martha
wondered if he ever thought of his other life. The urge to ask him about
that life she had been able to keep to herself. So many questions that had
to go without answer.

When Nicholas was not off exploring with Adam and the rest of the
little people, he followed Ethan around asking questions. Ethan had always been good with children and he had endless patience; he answered
Nicholas calmly no matter how often the question had been asked and
answered.

To Martha it seemed that Ethan was better with the boy than Callie,
who was always on guard. The circles beneath her eyes darkened and the
wit that had made her conversation so lively rarely showed itself. She had
no interest in talking about the new house or the orchards or anything,
really. Unlike Nicholas, who was eager to tell every detail.

To Daniel Martha said, "Nicholas can show you where the windows
in his room will be. He wants a dog, and snowshoes, and a hammer of his
own. And Callie promises him everything he asks for."

In the first fragrant quiet after sunset they were sitting on the porch
with a smokepot downwind to keep the blackfly at a distance. It would
be Martha's favorite time of all, if not for the blackfly. Even the pennyroyal ointment she had from Hannah only worked in part. When she
grumbled Daniel threatened to tie her down and smear her from head
to toe with bear grease, his own way of coping when he went into the
bush.

Daniel said, "I was hoping Callie would calm down after a bit."

"Is Ethan concerned?"

He looked at her, surprised. "I haven't asked him, and neither should
you. They'll work things out between them."

"Or they won't."

He didn't protest. For a long minute his thoughts seemed very far
away, and then he surprised her. "Have you heard Nicholas singing with
Levi when he's helping in the orchard?"

Martha sat up in her surprise. "Nicholas can sing?"

He pulled her back to rest against him. "Ma mentioned it to me. She said he has a pure tenor voice, clear as ice. According to Levi the boy can sing harmony to any tune, even ones he never heard before. It's a natural talent, seems like. To make up for other things."

It explained why Levi seemed less distant around the boy and less suspicious in general. When Callie's father had been alive, there had always been singing in the orchard. It made Martha glad, and it made her deeply uneasy.

Daniel said, "Are you going to tell me what has got you so worried? Does it bother you that the boy can sing?"

"Yes," Martha said. "My mother can sing, and so could Callie's father. It was the only thing they had in common."

"Were you doubting Jemima's claims about the boy's parentage?"

"I suppose I was," Martha said. "The tighter Callie holds on to the boy, the more I want to draw away. What is she going to do when Jemima comes to claim him?"

"Maybe she won't come back for him," Daniel said. "Maybe she really did mean to dump him here for you and Callie to take care of."

But Martha remembered the look on Jemima's face when she spoke about the boy. The obvious pride, and something that was as much like love as Jemima could produce.

"She's coming back," Martha said. "Like a bad penny. I can feel it in my bones."

Callie Wilde Middleton had just brought the workmen their dinner when she saw Lorena walking toward the cider house with a basket over her arm. Her pace was slow and she held herself like a queen, as if she owned everything she saw around herself. As if, Callie had heard said in the village, butter wouldn't melt in her mouth.

Lorena visited every day, and sometimes more than once. Callie had been ready to raise the subject to Levi when Ethan made a remark at supper that changed her mind.

"Did you notice Levi is smiling again?"

Callie had noticed. It was so unexpected that at first she had wondered if his bowels gripped him.

"I think he's pleased about the way the orchard is coming back from the flood."

Ethan had a look he used sometimes, not exactly sharp but certainly clear. As if he could see into a person's head to the worst things hidden in the deepest corners.

"It might have to do with that," Ethan said in his usual even way. "But I'm wondering if it has to do with Lorena. You don't like that idea?"

Callie often found herself guessing at the answer Ethan wanted to hear from her, because he seldom gave her any obvious clues. His tone left Callie with only two choices: to say nothing at all, or to tell the truth, which must disappoint even Ethan.

The truth was that Callie didn't want any outsiders talking to Levi. Not so long ago he had gone for weeks at a time talking to nobody but Callie herself. Now he spoke every day with Ethan, because, she had to remind herself, the marriage meant that Ethan was the legal owner of this land and everything on it, and as such, he was Levi's employer. To Callie's surprise and satisfaction, Ethan had paid Levi's back wages—two years' worth, since the last half-decent harvest—and had begun paying him every week on Friday, seeking him out wherever he was to put the money in his hand and spend a few minutes talking.

Levi was smiling these days, but it didn't necessarily have to do with Lorena or with wages or even with the fact that for the first time they had the tools and supplies they needed. Callie believed that Levi was smiling about the Bleeding Heart tree, hidden away in the nursery. Callie found herself smiling too, when she thought of it.

Just yesterday she had gone at sunrise to see for herself, and found that she was afraid to even touch the green fruit no bigger than walnuts.

Levi said, "All we can do now is pray."

It wasn't like Levi to depend on anybody but himself. She couldn't ever remember him talking about God, or anything to do with religion. Callie wondered if it was Lorena's influence, but she bit her tongue.

Levi scratched his jaw with a thumbnail and looked over her head to the orchard.

"I have got to ask you a question that maybe ain't none of my business."

"Go ahead."

"Your husband don't know yet about the Bleeding Heart?"

She had known this subject would come up sooner or later, but still she was at a loss. "I keep meaning to tell him," Callie said. "But I can never get started. I know I am being superstitious."

"You got reason to be touchy on the subject," Levi said. "Maybe it's best to wait until he can taste the fruit for hisself."

"Have you—" She almost stopped herself, but then pushed on. "Have you told anybody?"

His level gaze gave away nothing, not surprise or hurt or anger. "No, I have not," he said. "But then, I ain't got a wife. I wouldn't hold it against you if you told Ethan about it."

Now Nicholas appeared out of the cider house door and came hopping and jumping down the hillside toward her, his face alight with pleasure. Callie found herself smiling at that, the simple sight of her brother running through the orchard in summer.

He never slowed down, launching himself into her arms so that she dropped the empty basket and laughed out loud.

"Nicholas," she said. "Slow down."

"Where are you going? Can I come along? Do you want me to carry the basket? What did you bring the workers for their dinner? It smells like beef-and-kidney pie. I like pie, but I like fritters better. Lorena made fritters for Levi's dinner. And she let me have one too. Lorena makes the best fritters, Levi said so too, and so would you."

"I don't know that I can remember all those questions," Callie said. "But let me try. I'm going to see Lily with a message from Simon; yes, you certainly can come along if you like; it was indeed steak-and-kidney pie; and if you fill yourself up with fritters, you won't want a proper dinner," Callie said.

That made Nicholas laugh out loud. "I could eat fritters until my stomach stuck out to here." He touched fingers in front of himself as far as his rounded arms would reach. "And I'd still eat dinner. Wait and see. Oh, there's Friend Abigail, do you see her? She's got the longest plaits of all the girls at school and she smells of soap."

Conversations with Nicholas were like this; he rattled on telling stories at a nonstop pace. Callie wondered if he had always been like this, so full of joy and open to the world, or if that was something new.

She said, "Nicholas, do you miss Boston?"

His brow wrinkled as if he wasn't quite sure how he should answer. "I like it here," he said.

"Good, I'm glad. But you must have friends there who you miss."

"Are you going to send me back? Ma said you might not want to keep me. She said you might send me back. Are you going to send me back?"

"No," Callie said firmly. "I'm not sending you anywhere. I was just worried you might be lonely for old friends. You make friends so easily, I'm sure you must have had a lot of them in Boston."

His brow cleared. "Oh," he said. "Now I understand. My old friends aren't in Boston."

Callie hesitated, and he stopped to look at her. "My old friends are in Banfield. I never lived in Boston."

Her voice came out in a creak. "Banfield? You never told me about any place called Banfield."

"I didn't?" He seemed to be searching his memory. "I didn't tell you about the church or Reverend TenHouten or the farm?"

"No. I thought you lived in Boston before you came here."

"Huh," said Nicholas. "I never lived in Boston. You are making a face. Are you mad at me?"

"No!" Callie said. "No, I'm not mad at you. I'm just confused. Can you tell me about Banfield? I'd like to hear."

Lily and Jennet had got into the habit of napping after dinner in the shade of Elizabeth's few fruit trees, and Elizabeth had got into the habit of sitting with them until the conversation gave way to sleep. They were still talking when Callie and Nicholas came into the clearing.

"Company," Lily said, putting her hands on the swell of her stomach. Elizabeth understood that gesture; it meant that Lily was uneasy about something. It might be nothing other than the heat, or it might be the way Nicholas was running toward them. She got up to intercept him, holding his shoulders at arm's length while Callie came up at a slower pace.

Jennet said, "We were hoping for some company this afternoon."

"Oh, yes," said Lily. "Come sit, both of you, and entertain us."

Over the last month or so, it had seemed to Elizabeth that Callie was regaining some of her old spirit and quick wit. Whether that had to do with her marriage or with Nicholas or both, she could not be sure. Right now, though, Callie let Nicholas take the upper hand in the conversation and only answered when spoken to.

Elizabeth said, "Nicholas, if you haven't had your dinner you may go ask Anje to make you up a plate. We pulled the first of the radishes today, and I think there are some left."

"I'm still full of fritters." He plopped down next to Jennet and said, "Where is Adam?"

"Doing his chores with the rest of the wee monsters. He'll be by here soon enough."

Without warning Nicholas put his ear to Jennet's very round belly, and she squeaked in surprise.

"Nicholas!" Callie's tone was more surprised than sharp.

"Och, never mind, Callie. He means no harm." She put her hand on the boy's head. "Too bad, you've missed today's concert."

Nicholas's head came up so quickly that Jennet jumped.

"Careful," she said, laughing. "It may no be so much to brag on, but it's the only nose I've got."

"What's a concert?" Nicholas said.

Jennet raised a brow in Elizabeth's direction, but it was Lily who answered. "Do you know what a theater is, or a play?"

He nodded vigorously. "Punch and Judy."

"Of course. Well, a concert is something like that, except there's music instead of acting. People playing instruments—"

"Like the fiddle? Levi plays the fiddle."

"Like the fiddle and piano and other things. And sometimes people sing at a concert. I think Jennet was telling you that her baby sings to her sometimes. Is that it, Jennet?"

"Just so," Jennet said. "When this little one is feeling frisky, he sings to me. Sometime you might just catch a bit of a song, if you're aye lucky. As he seems to have gone to sleep, you can have a story from me, if you'll go off and have some proper dinner after, straight away."

"You needn't," Callie said to her.

"But I want to," Jennet answered. "Sitting under this apple tree on a summer's day has put me in mind of Thomas the Rhymer."

———

"Now Thomas," Jennet began, "was laird of the castle at Ercildoune in the Borders, and though he lived hundreds of years ago, people still talk of him."

"You're talking about him right now," Nicholas observed, and Lily called him over to sit with her, where she could keep him quiet.

"One day when Thomas was a young man he was out hunting near Melrose Abbey when he lost his way. The gloaming was coming on and it looked as though Thomas would have to sleep rough in the heather, when an old woman came out of the woods on a horse and offered to show him the way.

"Now note, my hens, she never said the way to *what,* and Thomas was too hungry and tired to ask.

"They rode along for so long that Thomas lost all sense of direction and time. His mind told him it must be late at night, but there was light all around, a glowing among the trees."

"A fire?" Nicholas asked nervously.

"No. Nothing like that. Listen now.

"And finally they came to the very heart of that endless forest and at that spot the path split in two. On the right the path led back to the world as Thomas knew it, and the other—that was a mystery. Between the two paths, in the fork of the road, stood the most beautiful apple tree Thomas had ever seen. No taller than he was himself, but full of fruit though it was long past harvest. At the sight of those bloodred apples his stomach gave such a growl that the birds stopped singing in the trees, and his hunger raged up and it was all he could do to mind his manners. Because as hungry as he was, Thomas could see that this was no ordinary tree. It was then he kennt that the old woman had led him into an enchanted place where man born of woman was rarely allowed.

"The old woman saw how it was with him, and so she got down from her horse and plucked an apple, and she offered it to Thomas.

"'Thomas Learmont of Ercildoune, will ye eat of this apple? It will grace ye wi the gift o truth.'

"Thomas was very hungry, but he hesitated nonetheless. For who cares to be burdened with the truth every moment of every day? What of stories and dreams? To always see the truth must be like going through the world without eyelids, so it seemed to Thomas.

"But in the end his hunger was larger than his misgivings and Thomas took the apple and bit into it. And the taste of it filled his mouth and belly both, it was so good. With that, the old woman shriveled up, just where she stood, and in her place a spark of light grew and grew until who stood there but a beautiful young woman, none other than the Queen of Elfland. Thomas was so overcome by her beauty that he kissed her, and together they went down the left-hand path to the Land of the Elves where they feasted for three days and Thomas ate his fill of fruits he had never seen before.

"At the end of the feast days, the Queen of Elfland told Thomas that he must return to his own world, where seven years had passed. Thomas did not want to leave his Queen, and so she made him a promise. If he stayed seven years in his own lands, he might come back to the land of the elves to stay. Because the Queen of Elfland liked Thomas just so much as he liked her, you see, but she understood that such choices must be made carefully, and with a freedom of spirit and clear understanding.

"And so Thomas was sent on his way with the gifts of truth and poetry and music, which delighted the folk of Ercildoune and surprised them as well, for the Thomas who had gone away for seven years had not one but two tin ears, and could no more carry a tune than he could a cow.

"For seven years he ruled his lands wisely, and in the evenings he would sing and play on the harp for anyone who cared to listen. The truth was with him too, all through those seven years, so that he saw things to come. These he put into his songs, and so he became known as Thomas the Seer or Thomas the Rhymer. And that is Thomas's story."

Jennet paused, and Nicholas closed his jaw with a snap. "Did he go back to the Queen of Elfland and the elves?"

"I canna say. The story as I know it stopped there. Can you imagine, so much fortune, good and bad, from an apple?"

Callie was smiling, as if she could answer that question if someone would only ask her.

"What kind of apple was it?" Nicholas wanted to know. "Maybe my sister has a tree like that in her orchard. Do you have a tree like the elf apple tree, sister? Do you know its name?"

"If the apple tree had a name, that was never told to me," Jennet said. "But I suppose you could give it one. Stories are passed from hand to hand, and some things fall away and others things stick as they go. Now will you go and get your dinner? Your belly is growling as loud as Thomas's."

"An apple needs a name," Nicholas muttered as he turned toward the house.

Lily's shoulders were shaking with laughter and Elizabeth herself was having a difficult time holding her smile in check.

"Such an earnest child," Jennet said. "He doesna ken the difference between stories and reality."

"Many never learn that," Callie said dryly.

"That's true," Lily said. "But it's also sad. His world is a much more colorful one than ours."

Just then Nicholas turned back toward them from across the clearing. "I know!" he shouted. "I know a name for the elves' apple tree! Let's call it the Bleeding Heart!"

"I was looking at her directly, as close as we are now," Elizabeth told Nathaniel later that day. "The color drained out of her, as though some-one had pulled a plug. I thought at first she would faint, but after a mo-ment she pulled herself up and just—walked away. She didn't even give Lily the message Simon had sent about coming late for supper, though we didn't find that out until much later."

"So what do you think this is all about?" her husband asked. "What gave Callie such a shock?"

"I have no idea," Elizabeth said. "I sent a message down to ask after her, but Nathan came back without a reply."

Nathaniel was quiet for a long minute. When he was like this, Eliza-beth let him be so that he could gather his thoughts.

"It's a nice evening," he said. "Why don't you and me take a stroll down to call on Ethan and Callie. See if we can be of any help."

"I was hoping you would say that." Elizabeth squeezed his arm and put her brow against his shoulder. "Something feels wrong, and I won't sleep for worry."

"You think this is about Jemima?" He cupped the back of her head with one hand.

"I don't see how, but I'm afraid it is."

"I think I could go the rest of my life without another one of Jemima's surprises," Nathaniel said. "I imagine Callie and Martha feel like they'll never get out from under."

Birdie said, "It's unfair."

"Maybe so," said Nathaniel. "But you'll stay right where you are or I'll have to take a switch to your backside, little girl. Your ma and me, we're going down to the village alone. Do you understand me?"

Birdie's face was ablaze with frustration and anger. She had folded her lips in so that her mouth was no more than a slit in her face, but she didn't dare ignore her father. She nodded.

Elizabeth waited until they were out of earshot before she let out the sigh she was holding.

"She is so very hardheaded," Elizabeth said.

"Comes by it honest. Ow! Boots, take care or I'll start pinching you back. What? You look like you forgot something."

"Curiosity," Elizabeth said. "Maybe we should take Curiosity along with us."

Nathaniel lowered his head to look at her down the slope of his nose. "You know that's not a good idea. You don't want to startle Callie. She needs careful coaxing."

For the rest of the walk Elizabeth considered what it would look like to Callie if her house were suddenly filled with people.

"She likes Curiosity," Elizabeth said finally. Nathaniel made a sound deep in his throat that was an admonition. It meant: You're missing the point, and you know it. She might have pursued this line of discussion, but they came out of the woods to the garden behind Ethan's small house, and the sound of Callie's voice raised in anger.

"Then who?" she was shouting. "If not you, then who?"

Nathaniel rapped on the kitchen door and then went in directly without waiting for an invitation, and Elizabeth followed closely.

Ethan and Callie stood in the parlor facing a visibly angry Levi Fiddler. Ethan stood poised as if he expected to have to put himself between his wife and the orchard manager.

"Seems like we missed the beginning of this party," Nathaniel said. "Callie, Levi. The glass is shaking in the windowpanes, you're making such a fuss."

"This doesn't concern you," Callie snapped. She was trembling.

"Callie," Ethan said. His tone was as close to sharp as it ever came, and Callie's gaze skittered toward him. "These are my family too, and I'd be glad of some help trying to sort out this mess. Do you object to them being here, Levi?"

The muscles clenched and rolled along Levi's jaw. "They welcome to stay. I got nothing to hide."

"Well, that's good," Nathaniel said. "So let's set."

"I'll make tea," Elizabeth said. It was a way to be alone for a few minutes in order to gather her thoughts and calm the beating of her heart, and beyond that, she thought, the tea might do them all good. While she stoked the stove and set the kettle to heat she was listening, but the house might have been empty, it was so quiet in the parlor.

Nathaniel called, "No bloodshed in here, Boots. We're just waiting for you to get started."

"So who wants to start?"

They had moved to the dining room where they could sit around the table. Levi's back was as straight and stiff as the chair itself. Callie was curled over, her arms crossed on her midsection.

Ethan cleared his throat. "Whatever it is, I can promise you—both of you—we are not here to find blame or make accusations."

"In other words," Nathaniel said, "one of the two of you had best start talking."

Callie was staring down at the floor. When she raised her head Elizabeth started to see the anger and misery there.

She said, "It's complicated."

"Most things are," Elizabeth said. "But we are here to listen and to offer what help we can."

"I'll start," Levi said. "As I'm the one stands accused."

"Of what?" Nathaniel said.

Levi glanced at Callie, but she had lowered her head again and she wouldn't raise it.

"Miss Callie here thinks I been conspiring with Jemima behind her back. I guess she forgot it was Jemima who killed my ma. I'd as soon snap her neck as lift a hand to help that woman. I'll do it too, if I ever get the chance."

Elizabeth caught Ethan's eye. She thought probably her expression looked like what she saw on his face: numb surprise.

Nathaniel said, "You know more about what went on back then than the rest of us?"

"Maybe I do," Levi said. "But that got nothing to do with this business we got to settle right now."

"So tell us," Nathaniel said. "You have got our full attention." Under the table he put a hand on Elizabeth's knee, and she covered it with her own.

"It has to do with an apple tree," Levi said. "We call it the Bleeding Heart."

Levi talked for a half an hour. For that entire time none of them spoke or even moved, but Elizabeth's mind raced back over the last weeks, back to the flood and further still. Callie's grim determination when her crop failed once and then again, her unwillingness to talk with any seriousness or in any real detail about the orchard. What it must have been like to harbor such hopes and to lose everything on the cusp of success. How she had kept it all to herself; how in the confusion and chaos of the flood nobody had seen her distress. She and Levi had supported each other in their common cause, and now something had turned them against each other.

That it had to do with Jemima did not surprise her. She should feel anger, but instead there was only a deep weariness.

Ethan was asking questions about the surviving apple tree, the reaction of the orchardists Levi had called on, the potential for earnings.

"Once we got enough trees bearing fruit, I reckon cider and jack will bring in two thousand a year." Levi hesitated. "If Callie wants to sell saplings, those will bring in quite a lot as well. I hope she doesn't. Sell saplings, I mean."

There was a small silence around the table, mostly, it seemed to Elizabeth, out of pure surprise. A small family could survive comfortably on twenty dollars a week; farmers, who traded for most things and grew a lot of their own food, could make do with less. An apple orchard that earned two thousand a year for its cider was a valuable holding.

Ethan and Nathaniel had a lot of questions, and between Callie and Levi they all got answered.

Then Elizabeth spoke to Callie directly. "Tell me about what happened today, with Nicholas."

"I'd sure like to hear that myself," Levi said.

Callie's mouth tightened. "You heard it yourself, Elizabeth. When Nicholas was carrying on about Jennet's story. You heard him say the words *Bleeding Heart*."

Elizabeth nodded. "Yes, I did hear that."

"About an apple, he said *Bleeding Heart*," Callie repeated. "And where did that come from?"

She wasn't looking at Levi, but her whole posture said clearly what she was thinking.

Levi said, "Before today I ain't never spoke those two words aloud to anybody in this world except you."

"You must have," Callie said. "It can't be a coincidence."

"Wait," Ethan said. "Levi, when you went to call on the orchards with the cider samples, you didn't say the name even then?"

"No, I did not," Levi said, much calmer now but with an anger very near the surface. "I handed over the letter Callie wrote and I answered questions, and that's all."

"You never told Lorena about the tree." Callie's tone was flat.

"Nobody," Levi said. "You want to send for her? You can ask her your own self."

"Callie, think. You wrote that name in your letters," Ethan said. He turned to Levi. "Did you go as far as Boston on your journey?"

"No," Levi said. "I went along the Mohawk trail as far as Greenfield, and then I was out of samples and so I turned around for home."

"Where is Greenfield?" Elizabeth asked, and Nathaniel glanced at her.

"Short of Boston by a couple days' walk," Nathaniel said. "Hard to imagine how the Fochts would have got word of an apple tree in the city."

Callie straightened in her chair. She caught Ethan's eye and took a deep breath.

She said, "Nicholas never lived in Boston. He told me today. He says he grew up in a place called Banfield but he doesn't know where it is, exactly."

Levi closed his eyes and opened them again. "Banfield is a small town on the Deerfield River. Farms, mostly. I don't know what Jemima and her husband would have been doing there."

Ethan said, "Callie is going to faint, Elizabeth."

Elizabeth steadied her, and then Ethan was there to take her. He didn't often seemed rattled, but Elizabeth saw his confusion and worry and she took over.

"On the divan, I think. Nathaniel, please fetch some water. Is there a facecloth?"

Levi stepped in closer, his fists clenched tightly at his side. "Should I fetch Hannah?"

"She'll come around in a moment," Elizabeth said. "And then she'll have questions. Perhaps you should fetch Lorena after all."

To Ethan Nathaniel said, "Where is Nicholas? He shouldn't come back here until things are settled down."

Ethan's wheat-colored hair was plastered to his temples by sweat, and his color was high. Then he made a visible effort to concentrate.

"He's at Curiosity's," Ethan said. "Unless they all went over to your place after supper."

"That's where he should stay for the time being," Nathaniel said. "Boots, if you can manage I'm going to head up and have a quick word with Curiosity. I'll be back as soon as I can."

---

56

*B*irdie loved the summer for the long days, when twilight stretched itself out like a cat before a fire and children were allowed out to play until it was full dark. They only had to stay in shouting distance of either the Uphill or Downhill House, but that gave them a half mile, from Birdie's own front porch to Curiosity's.

Even the blackfly couldn't take away her love of the summer evenings; she simply covered herself with Hannah's pennyroyal ointment after supper as she did after breakfast and dinner. It was also her job to make sure the little people did the same. Luke's twins turned up their noses at the smell, but would have tolerated much worse than stinky ointment to run free in the evenings with their cousins.

They played hide-and-seek, and its opposite, seek-and-hide, or Sardines, as Birdie's da called it. They put on theaters where they re-enacted scenes from their favorite stories, except this year the boys always wanted the same thing: the tournament of Ashby-de-la-Zouch from Mr. Scott's *Ivanhoe*. Birdie liked the story too, but, she wanted to know, how many times could you refight the same battles? Which made her da laugh in the way that meant she had come up with a good point that most grown-ups never thought about. The real problem was there was always a lot of argument about who would get to be Prince John or Cedric or Rowena, or Robin of Locksley. Usually Ma or Hannah had to step in and assign roles, which never turned out very well, in Birdie's opinion.

More often they played jumping games and guessing games and tag, but the best game of all was capture the flag, because the grown-ups could be wheedled into playing.

It's your favorite because it suits your nature, her da pointed out, and it was true. Birdie loved the mad dashing that paused only long enough for quick discussions of strategy. She liked trying to outwit her elders, and she had good mates in her nephews, especially. The little people loved nothing more than watching their own parents being marched off to gaol.

Once when she jumped down from a branch to tag Gabriel he had thrown up his hands in surrender and laughed all the way to the porch. He said, *Too bad you're a girl, little sister. You'd make a good exploring officer.*

Except he didn't say such things in Ma's hearing, because while even Ma had to admit that Birdie couldn't enlist in the army, she would still tell stories about warrior queens from long ago. There was a whole page of them in her notebook: Boadicea, Queen of the Iceni who drove the Romans off, Jehanne la Pucelle, and Tomyris, Queen of the Massagetae, who defeated Cyrus the Great. And Birdie's favorite, Caterina Sforza of Milan in Italy, who had been a tomboy and good at sports, and an excellent soldier and leader of armies who had saved St. Angelo. Birdie had a hard time imagining what St. Angelo could be and what it might look like, until Lily came home from Italy and explained it to her.

So Birdie couldn't join the army, but neither would she forget that things had once been different, and might be different again.

This evening, though, she didn't care to play. Instead she sat on the porch with Lily, who was sharing the role of gaoler, as she couldn't move from the spot where Simon had settled her.

"It's just as well," she told Birdie. "I wouldn't want to deny you the pleasure of gaoling your brothers."

And it was very satisfying when someone got tagged and Birdie was called over to take the prisoner to the porch. This evening they had had three prisoners so far, Daniel, Adam, and Isabel, but all three of them escaped when Birdie went to get a shawl for Lily.

"They took advantage of your condition." Birdie glared at the escapees, but they were too busy running off to notice.

Ma said they could play capture the flag only once or twice a week, for fear it would become routine. Birdie could hardly imagine such a thing; it was only during these games that she had seen Luke laugh so hard he got the hiccups and tears ran down his face. Jennet was everywhere at once, holding her pregnant belly as she ran and ignoring Hannah's scolding until Simon and Ben each took an elbow and carried her, feet flailing, protesting in a broad Scots, to the sidelines until Hannah declared she might play again.

Even Ma played, whooping with delight when she evaded capture, her cheeks flushed a deep red. When Ma got tagged the little people capered with delight to see her dragged off because she didn't go quietly, but argued all the way and reminded them that she had broken out of—and into—more than one gaol in her time. That made Da laugh like a boy.

But Ma and Da weren't playing tonight. They were gone down to see Ethan and Callie. And what was that about? No one seemed to have even the slightest idea, even Curiosity, though Birdie had asked more than one way.

A lot of outraged laughter erupted from behind the house, and Nicholas Wilde came trotting around the corner with the other side's flag—a piece of an old red flannel hunting shirt—raised high overhead. At the same time Anje poked her head out of the door and said Curiosity was asking for Birdie's help in the kitchen.

Curiosity didn't really need her help; that was clear to Birdie before she went through the swinging door into the clean and ordered kitchen. The fact that her father sat across from Curiosity at the table did take her by surprise.

"Da," she said. "I thought you were down in the village at Ethan's place."

"Came up the back way. I've got to go back right now, but I need to ask you to do something first."

Her da's voice and expression were calm and steady, but a shiver went up Birdie's spine anyway.

"What's wrong?"

Curiosity shook her head. "Why you got to jump to that conclusion, little girl?"

"Because there's something wrong, I can almost smell it."

Curiosity's expression softened a little. "Yes, I suppose you can."

"Da?"

He got up from the table. "We're trying to figure that out, daughter. I need you to keep Nicholas here until somebody comes to fetch him home to Ethan's."

Curiosity said, "And that might could be a while."

"Has he done something bad?"

"No," Birdie's da said. "But he'd be in the way just now. So will you do that for me?"

Birdie nodded. "If he starts to talk about going home I'll think of something."

He put his hand on her head and smiled. "I know you will." And then: "You got any good words lately for your notebook?"

It took her a moment to clear her thoughts. "One," she said. "Inscrutable. Do you know what it means?"

"Sounds like some kind of skin rash." But he winked when he said it.

"It's the word you use when you can't make out what somebody's really thinking from their face. Mostly you're inscrutable and Ma's scrutable, but just now I can see you've got something on your mind."

She hated it when grown-ups laughed at things she said when she was serious, but Curiosity and Da only looked at each other. Then he said, "Have you ever heard Nicholas talking about a place called Banfield?"

"He's talkative," Birdie said. "But I never heard him mention any Banfield. Do you want me to ask him?"

"No, don't ask him. We'll try to sort this out without that for the time being."

He went to the door and picked up his rifle from where he had leaned it against the wall.

"Nathaniel Bonner," Curiosity said. "Don't you walk out that door before you tell us what a place called Banfield got to do with anything at all."

He smiled, which put some of Birdie's worry to rest. Da wasn't one to put a false face on things.

"Banfield is a village on the Deerfield River. It's where Nicholas grew up, as far as we can tell."

"But I thought he came from Boston," Birdie said.

"So did we. That's what we've got to sort out before Callie goes and jumps to all kinds of conclusions."

Curiosity closed her eyes. "If you are saying what I think you're saying, I will see to it that Jemima pays. I swear it."

"You won't have to take that on alone," Birdie's da said, and he slipped out the door. Birdie watched him disappear into the woods, and then she asked Curiosity the question she couldn't hold back.

"Does this mean that Nicholas isn't really Callie's brother?"

Curiosity took a deep breath and let it out slowly. She said, "Pray the good Lord it don't."

They had started another game while Birdie was in the kitchen, and she was glad of the chance to sit down and think for a few minutes. Lily was knitting, glancing up now and then to follow the game, and smiling to herself. She was smiling a lot lately, which made Birdie glad and worried her too. More than once Hannah and Curiosity had stopped talking when she came into the room, and she couldn't help thinking it had to do with Lily and her baby.

There was something odd going on in the game. She looked more closely and looked again.

"Look," she said to Lily. "See that bush to the right of the low path? The one that wasn't there a quarter hour ago?"

Lily raised an eyebrow. "Brother Daniel has been teaching the little people some of his old tricks. And there's Nicholas walking right into the—"

The bush leaped in that moment, and two strong brown arms reached through the branches to grab Nicholas by the wrist. Nicholas jumped a good foot straight into the air and then fell.

"Henry Savard!" Hannah shouted. "Careful or you'll put an eye out!"

Henry was trying to rid himself of his cloak of ivy and pine branches, shouting at the top of his lungs all the time.

"I got him! I got Nicholas! Gaoler! Gaoler!"

Lily said, "You have work to do," and so Birdie went to get her prisoner, who was still laughing so hard he could hardly walk.

She said, "You weren't scared?"

Nicholas drew a quick breath, tried to answer, and gave up. Finally settled on the porch, he said, "Henry said he'd sneak up on me and he did."

"You sound happy about it," Lily said.

"I like Henry," Nicholas said.

It was an odd answer, but the right one nonetheless.

"He likes you too. We all like you."

"Does that mean I can get out of gaol?" Nicholas asked, looking back and forth between them.

"No," Lily and Birdie said together, and that set all three of them to laughing.

"You are the sunniest, most cheerful boy," Lily said. "I don't think I've ever seen you unhappy. We'll miss you when you go home to Boston."

Birdie froze, but Nicholas was still smiling. He said, "Oh, look. Martha almost got Jennet." And: "I'm not going to Boston."

"You aren't?" Lily said. She put down her knitting.

"Nope," said Nicholas.

Birdie heard herself ask the next question. "What about Banfield?"

Lily had a quizzical look on her face, but Birdie kept her attention on Nicholas, who seemed to be thinking about the question.

He said, "I miss the farm sometimes."

"What is Banfield?" Lily asked, and Nicholas turned to look at her.

"Banfield is where I live," he said. "And Lorena too. Can I go back to the game now?"

Lily nodded, and he catapulted himself off the porch and raced away.

"What is going on?" Lily asked Birdie.

"I'm not sure," she said. "Da said we should sit tight and he'll come talk to us soon."

---

57

*E*lizabeth had just made the third pot of tea when Nathaniel came back, followed closely by Levi and Lorena.

While she arranged cups and saucers on a tray she listened to the sound of talking. Ethan's tenor, Nathaniel's particular rhythms in baritone, Levi's voice, even lower, as he gave short answers. There was no sound from Callie or Lorena. She realized just then how little she knew Lorena, but the simple truth was that Elizabeth would gladly have foregone the coming discussion.

She scolded herself for being cowardly, and went out with the tea tray.

"No, thank you." Lorena wanted no tea, nor anything else. She sat straight-backed at the table, her hands in her lap. Beneath the brim of her straw hat it was difficult to make out her expression, but her voice was even. If she was expecting trouble, she was hiding it well. Levi might well have prepared her for what was to come. Seeing them sitting side by side made Elizabeth realize that they were not strangers to each other, and might be more than mere friends. Under other circumstances she would have been pleased for Levi, but now it seemed only like another complication in an already confusing and even dangerous situation.

Two small coins of deep red sat on Callie's cheekbones, and in the light of the candles Ethan had just lit, her eyes sparked silver agitation.

Nathaniel said, "Why don't you sit down, Boots. Folks can help themselves to tea."

What he was saying to her, she heard it very clearly, was that she was making everyone nervous. She sat.

Callie seemed to be trying to formulate a question, but Lorena spoke up first.

She said, "Levi tells me you want to know about Banfield."

Callie's voice cracked. "Is Nicholas my brother?"

Elizabeth's pulse jumped, but Lorena never blinked. She looked Callie directly in the eye and said, "I don't know."

There was a flicker of something, pity or compassion, that touched her expression so briefly Elizabeth wondered if she imagined it.

Callie let out a long sigh. "Martha was right," she said, dully. "Martha is always right."

Ethan put a hand on her forearm. "She didn't say *no*. She said she doesn't know. It would be a good idea to hear what she does know before we make up our minds about anything."

Beside Elizabeth Nathaniel was perfectly quiet, but there was a tension in the set of his jaw. He said, "Lorena, it might be a good place to start if you tell us a little about yourself, before you came to work for Jemima."

Lorena raised a brow and glanced at Levi, who closed his eyes and inclined his head. That gesture said more about their relationship than any verbal declaration.

Levi cleared his throat. "I want to say something first. Whatever Lorena got to say is new to me too. I ain't asked her about her past. Not because I don't want to know, but because I didn't want to have to keep anything from Callie."

He was looking at Callie as if he expected her to ask questions, but she only acknowledged him with a short bob of her head.

Lorena said, "I was born and raised up in Boston. My father was a preacher. At sixteen I went into service as a maid. I married at twenty-five."

These facts she laid out in a line on the table, one by one, with no inflection. As if she were reciting verses from a primer.

Ethan interrupted her gently. "Just tell the story your own way. Tell it to Levi, if that helps you gather your thoughts."

"I am breaking every rule Mrs. Focht laid down," she said. "Excuse me if I hesitate."

Then she turned to Levi, and concentrated on his face alone.

Lorena keeps house for her husband of one year, takes in sewing and mending so they can put a little aside, and waits for the birth of her first child. It is a simple life. They are both satisfied with their lot and each other.

On the day she loses everything, Lorena feels the first birth pangs early in the morning. She keeps this to herself. First babies are slow in coming, and there will be time enough for Jonah to worry when he comes home from work. She is thinking about what he will say to find the midwife with her when she hears the sound of something very large crashing to the ground.

She finds Jonah sprawled in front of the door, a hand clutched to his chest as if to grab hold of his heart and make it behave. That night she gives birth to a daughter who breathes fitfully for a quarter hour, and then stops.

The little bit of money they have put aside goes to the coffin maker and the grave digger. Then she walks home to find a note from Mr. George pinned to her door. Now that Jonah is gone, he needs the little house for another worker, a man with a wife and children. He can give her two more days. He is not a cruel man, Lorena knows this. She also knows that he will do nothing to help her.

She has no place to go. A hard birth has left her too weak to take on work in a scullery or washhouse; her clothes are so worn that she can't present herself as a house servant. Her people are in Philadelphia. She has exactly enough coin in her pocket to buy a simple meal.

Lorena dreams of the baby. Her breasts ache, and there is a hole inside her that seems to grow by the hour.

A woman who turns her away when she asks for work takes the time to give her advice. The almshouse is the place for your kind, she says. Except of course they don't take colored.

On her first day without a roof, Lorena finds a copy of the Boston Advertiser *on a bench in the park. At the very bottom of the last column on the last page she reads an advertisement:*

Wanted. Wet nurse. Clean, healthy, no thieves or degenerates.
Apply to 73 Barleycorn Street.

It takes her more than an hour to walk there. A house in a neighborhood of fine houses, the kind of place where successful businessmen raise their families with the help of nurses and cooks and maids-of-all-work. There will be meat on the table every night, fresh wheaten rolls for breakfast, ponies and pianoforte lessons for the girls, and when they are old enough, the sons will become members of the clubs their father favors.

The servant who answers the kitchen door is a true African, her English so turned around that Lorena has to ask more than once if she has found the right house.

The servant leaves her there with nothing more to do than study her surroundings. The kitchen is tidy and well scrubbed. On a long table are the makings of a cake: sacks of flour and sugar, a clutch of brown speckled eggs, a lump of butter. On a piece of paper are small hills of ground spices: nutmeg and cinnamon, cloves and cardamom. Lorena commands her belly to be quiet before someone comes into the kitchen.

Another servant who might have been a sister to the first takes Lorena through to the parlor where she will be interviewed by the lady of the house.

The parlor drapes are pulled so that the sun won't fade the expensive fabrics. With one part of her mind Lorena takes note of the figurines on the mantelpiece, the thick carpet underfoot, the fragile teapot on a tray inlaid with ivory. With the foremost part of her mind, the part that understands what is at stake, she calculates what this woman—Mrs. Wilde, she names herself—needs to hear that will convince her to hire Lorena.

Mrs. Wilde wears a gown the color of muddy water, with jewels at her throat and in her ears and on her fingers. A plain woman, who puts Lorena in mind of the old-time Puritans, those who made it their business never to smile. There is no sign of a cradle, or of a husband. She wonders whose child needs suckling, if it could be Mrs. Wilde's. There is nothing about her bearing that marks her for a mother.

She says, "Where were you born, Lorena?"

By rights she should be addressed as Mrs. Webb, but this white woman, like most of her kind, won't be bothered with last names for blacks.

The questions come rapid-fire. Lorena names her place of birth, her parents, their occupations; yes, her father taught her to read, she owns a Bible, and she writes a clear hand. Mrs. Wilde reels off a list of numbers and Lorena adds them together in her head. Divides them by three, multiplies by eleven. She tells the story of how she met Jonah and how he died. Yes, she has her marriage lines.

"Tell me about your child."

"A girl," Lorena said, her voice catching. "Died almost right away. Just three days ago."

"Ill-formed?"

Lorena shakes her head because she doesn't trust her voice.

The questions turn to her health. Has she had smallpox, measles, whooping cough, lung fever? Is she clean in mind and spirit and deed?

She says it like that, though Lorena would not have taken offense at a more direct question. She has never prostituted herself. The only man she has known was her husband.

"I suppose you sound white because your father was a minister," says Mrs. Wilde.

Lorena drops her gaze because there is nothing to say to this that won't shore up the world of wrong ideas Mrs. Wilde has built for herself.

"Well, I was hoping for a white woman but every one of them who answered that advertisement had gin on the breath. You don't take strong drink?"

"I never have."

"Tobacco? Laudanum?"

Finally Mrs. Wilde leans back in her chair, her lips pursed while she thinks. With her right hand she strokes the silk embroidery on the arm of her chair.

"Well," she says with a grimace. "Sugar water only goes so far. You'll have to do. Go wait in the kitchen until Marjory comes to fetch you."

There is no talk of salary or sleeping quarters, but those things can wait. She dare not make a sound that might change Mrs. Wilde's mind.

The servant called Marjory brings the infant to her in the kitchen. It looks like all new infants, its crumpled napkin of a face blotched bright red. It mewls like a kitten and then breaks into a thin cry. With trembling hands Lorena begins to undo her dress, but Marjory stops her with a sharp word.

"No time for that. The coach waiting."

She tells Lorena to bring her satchel, and leads her out into the rear courtyard where a coach is indeed waiting. The baby starts to cry in earnest. Lorena knows she should be asking questions, but she is so hungry and Marjory has put two baskets in the coach. From one comes the smells of roasted meat and new bread.

As the coach makes its way through the lanes Lorena looks to the child, who latches on to her breast with a furious purpose. Her bodice soaked with milk, she can no longer ignore her own hunger. With her free hand she reaches into the food basket. The bread is rough and dry, the mutton burned on the outside and blood-red at the bone, but she fills her stomach, pausing only long enough to burp the child and put him to her other breast. There is a bottle of elderberry water in the basket too, and Lorena finishes it off in three long swallows.

The child is asleep at her breast, its cheeks still working. There is the distinct smell of soiled clouts, and at that moment Lorena realizes she doesn't know if this is a boy or a girl, or what name she should call it. In the half hour of talk in Mrs. Wilde's parlor, she had said not one word about this baby.

There are fresh clouts in the basket, and she sets about undressing the baby. A boy.

Lorena's breath catches in her throat, in sorrow, in relief. When she puts this baby to the breast she might, one day, be able to put aside the memory of her own child.

When they stop to change horses Lorena learns that the driver knows no more than she does. He was hired only a few hours earlier, and his instructions are brief: He is to take the wet nurse and her burden to a house in Banfield, next to the Congregational Church, where Reverend TenHouten is expecting them. The rest Lorena can reckon for herself. She has been sent away from the city to take up the work of raising this unnamed, unwanted burden of a child who was most likely born on the same day, maybe in the same hour, as her own daughter.

He yawns, the silky white cheeks rounding like pillows, and Lorena wonders who she is weeping for.

Callie's color had risen while Lorena talked. She had folded her hands on the table, but still they trembled. "Do you mean to say Jemima had nothing to do with raising him? It was all you?"

"Reverend TenHouten was kind. Nicholas thinks of him as an uncle."

"But what of the baby's name? He went almost ten years without a name?"

"Reverend TenHouten wrote to Boston and got a letter back saying we were to call the boy Nicholas."

For once Ethan's calm seemed on the verge of deserting him. "Jemima?"

Lorena's brow lowered. "After the interview in Boston I never saw her again until the first of this year. First thing, she introduces Mr. Focht, says she's remarried."

There were so many questions to ask, Elizabeth could hardly order them in her mind. The others were not so hampered, and Lorena answered them one by one with a dignified calm.

"So you kept house for this minister—"

"TenHouten," Lorena supplied. "A widower. I cooked and washed and kept his garden for him because he couldn't anymore."

"Wasn't Nicholas frightened when Jemima showed up at your door? Had you told him about her?" Elizabeth asked.

"Of course I had," Lorena said. "I told him everything I knew about his mother."

"But you didn't know if she was his mother," Callie said. "You still don't know. He could have been hers or some child she got out of the almshouse nursery."

Lorena inclined her head, to acknowledge that Callie was right; there was no direct proof that the boy was in fact Jemima's son by Callie's father.

"What happened next?" Elizabeth asked.

Lorena was studying the table linen, her eyes tracing the pattern woven into the damask.

"They wanted to take Nicholas with them, to travel, they said. And they asked me along because Nicholas wouldn't have it any other way."

Ethan said, "Lorena, what do you know of Jemima's plans? Why she brought him here just now, and what she hopes to gain."

"They never talked about anything in my hearing," Lorena said. "But they did talk in front of the other servants. The Africans, and Harper."

That name hung in the air for a long moment.

"What did Harper know?"

"I don't know. I never heard him talking about the orchard or apples or any bleeding heart."

Levi put a hand on her shoulder in a gesture as simple and intimate as a kiss. He caught Elizabeth's eye, his expression resolute. He was claiming Lorena as his own, which must be a good thing for them both, but was likely to confuse things even further before the current problem could be sorted through.

Ethan cleared his throat, and all faces turned toward him.

"It's pretty clear to me that Jemima has been planning something for a good long while. The first step was making sure Martha didn't marry in Manhattan. A husband's claim nullifies a mother's, and she would have been cut off right then."

"Seems like Daniel and Martha handled that on their own. She is married now, after all," Nathaniel said.

"And so am I," Callie said. "But I think I understand now what is supposed to happen. If my father has a legitimate male heir in Nicholas, then the orchard and everything in it belongs to Nicholas and not to me. In that case it doesn't matter if I'm married or not. But there is a solution. I'll sell the orchard to Levi."

Levi himself drew in a sharp breath, but Callie went right on. "We can draw up a sales contract right now. Everything goes to Levi for— how much would he have to pay for the courts to uphold the sale?"

"I don't know that they would uphold it," Ethan said. "Most likely they wouldn't. But I am sure that any legal challenge they mount would take many years to come to trial."

Nathaniel said, "Levi, could you pay a hundred dollars?"

Levi shook his head. "I got thirty, saved up over the last years. But Lorena has got some put aside too. Don't you?"

In the silence that followed Callie said, "Does this mean you're getting married?"

"We were hoping to," Levi said.

"Well, then," Callie said. A pulse was beating in her throat. "If you get married tomorrow and we settle the sales contract right after—" She broke off.

"What?" Ethan said. "Finish your thought."

"Then I'd be free of it all, the cider press and the new house and the Bleeding Heart. And Jemima, once and for all."

Lorena said, "What about Nicholas?"

Callie pushed away from the table so suddenly that her chair almost toppled. She looked at each of them in turn.

"Nicholas isn't going anywhere," she said. "I'll see to it."

Martha said, "I have never had so much fun playing a game. My ribs are aching from laughing so much."

She yawned widely and put her head back against the wall of the new stable, watching Daniel as he went about the evening chores. Hopper was tugging at her skirts, and she tugged back companionably.

Daniel ran a hand over Little Jo's back and the mare nudged him affectionately. Beside her Abel rocked his head and knickered.

"Two days and the horses are already under your spell," Martha said. "Maybe horses talk to each other about men, the way men talk about horses. Maybe they heard from Florida that you speak horse and are generous with oats."

Daniel grinned at her. "And what do they say about you, do you think?"

"That's easy. They know I'm just another woman who sits a saddle well enough but is too dense to understand them when they talk to me."

Daniel was still laughing to himself when they left the stable, walking toward the house. Tonight the stars were bright enough to throw a shadow, so that they didn't even need a lantern. Hopper leaped ahead of them, and Martha yawned again.

Daniel opened the door for her and she went into the darkened house. Then he spoke a firm word and the pup slunk over to his blanket and settled down with a put-upon sigh.

Daniel said, "Does all this yawning mean that you're so tired you want to go directly to sleep?"

She bit back a smile. "What else did you have in mind?"

"Chapter twelve of the French Lady," Daniel said, his hand sliding down her back to cup the curve of her hip. "If you can stop yawning long enough to listen."

A half hour later Martha interrupted Daniel and said, "I hate that she calls it that, the little death."

Daniel slipped a marker between the pages and put the book aside. Then he took her wrist and pulled her up closer for a brief kiss.

"Wait," Martha said. "It doesn't bother you to compare that—that event—to death?"

He smoothed the hair away from her face. "You have heard how dramatic the French can be on this subject, but yes, I suppose it is a strange way to describe it. Do you have a better suggestion?"

Martha fell back against the pillows. "I have no idea. I don't think it's possible to name something like that. Could you describe what it feels like to sneeze?"

"What an odd conversation," Daniel said.

"Don't you see? Everyone knows what it's like to sneeze, so there's no need to worry about explaining it."

"You don't like *climax*? The word, I mean?"

She made a face at him. "It's a very cold word."

Martha started to roll away from him, but Daniel pinned her down. "Are we done talking?"

"Not yet," she said, and he kissed her through a broad grin. "I think I know what the problem is," Daniel said. "It's impossible to think clearly wearing clothes. Let's take care of that first."

Martha said, "I believe you could make a fortune wagering at cards. You are ruthless when you want something." She took a deep breath and then another while her nerves kicked and her heart settled into a normal rhythm.

Daniel had collapsed beside her. He said, "Is that a complaint?"

"Lord, no," Martha said, smiling in the dark.

"You haven't come up with a substitute for 'the little death,' I take it."

"Right now my own name is a bit of a challenge. And if you don't stop that, I'll have to pinch you."

"I don't remember you being so quick to retaliate as a girl," Daniel said. "Except maybe for that time the Ratz boys put a snowball in your boots."

"You remember that?" Her voice came muffled because she had turned onto her stomach. "I did love those Saturday afternoons playing in the snow."

She sat up suddenly.

"What?"

"It's like sledding," she said.

"What's like sledding?"

Martha wished she could keep from blushing and decided she should simply ignore what she could not control. She had something to say, and she could say it to Daniel. She could.

"You know, the—climax."

"Ah," Daniel said, one eyebrow riding up his brow. "Go on."

"Well, it's like sledding. You work your way up the hill dragging the sled. All you can think about is getting to the top so you can let go and feel the wind rushing over you on the way down. Sometimes you don't get to the top and you go slipping back down and you have to start all over again."

Daniel laughed. "Go on."

"You know the way your stomach drops when the sled tips over the top and starts down? That clenching excitement? That's what it's like. It takes your breath away and your whole body curls into itself to hold on to that feeling. And the longer the climb to the top, the greater the excitement. When you finally get to the bottom, you're covered with sweat no matter how cold it is, and you're breathless."

"Sledding," Daniel said.

She rubbed her face against him. "Isn't it like that for you?"

"No," Daniel said. "I can say with complete certainty that there's nothing even remotely snowy about it for me."

"Too bad," said Martha.

"Too bad?" Daniel let out something that could only be called a giggle. "There's nothing bad about it at all."

"I mean, I wish I could understand what it feels like, for you."

Daniel shifted her so they were lying face-to-face. "I'm right fond of sledding," he said. "And I'll chase you up that hill any time the mood strikes you. On the way down maybe I can tell you what it's like for me. Your heart just picked up a beat, Mrs. Bonner. You like talking about this?"

"Um," Martha said, a flush crawling up her breast. "I think what I like best is when you talk, and I listen."

When Callie thought back on her school days in Elizabeth Bonner's classroom, the lessons that came to mind first, the ones she took most to heart, had to do with logic. Or, as Miss Elizabeth had called it, rational thinking.

Many times over the last years she had felt herself on the verge of despair and even desperation, and in every case she was able to talk herself into a better frame of mind. Hard work was no guarantee of success; she understood that, because she had lived it. On the other hand, hard work was all anyone needed for a good night's sleep. She herself always fell to sleep straight away and she slept deeply. She woke at five every morning without a clock and without fail, and by six she was hard at work. Even in the deep of winter when blizzards held her captive she was busy. There were tools to repair or sharpen; the hearth must be fed, and if she did not cook, she could not eat. She made clothes for herself and Levi both; she traded her own cider for Molly Nobel's raw wool, which she spun into yarn, which she knitted into socks and mittens; she made soap and dipped candles. Once a year she bought a pig from one of the farmers and helped with the butchering in order to bring the price down, after which came salting or smoking.

It had never occurred to her to complain, because there was nobody to complain to. She did what must be done to get from day to day. Once in a while she met friends at the Red Dog and played cards and listened to stories or told her own. She had spent some nice evenings with Daniel Bonner and Ethan and a few others, but it all seemed a very long time ago.

Those days of constant work were over, at least for the moment. Now she had the Thicke sisters, who did everything. She never had to think about putting food on the table or hauling wood for the hearth; her clothes were always clean and neatly pressed, and she had never replaced her knitting needles and sewing basket after the flood. There was no need to spin or knit or weave, as Ethan went to Johnstown every few weeks and could buy fine cloth by the ell without hesitating over the cost.

So it was that Callie spent most of her time in the orchard or the garden Levi had dug for her near the foundation of the old house.

Somewhere in the course of all these changes, she had lost the knack of falling asleep. On the other side of the room Ethan was having no such troubles. In the less-than-dark she could see the rise and fall of his chest.

If she waked him he would not complain. He would want to know what was bothering her and wait until she was ready to talk about it. And maybe she did need to think harder about what she had set in motion.

In the dark she made herself whisper the words to herself.

I am selling the orchard. Tomorrow the orchard will no longer belong to me. It will be safe from Jemima.

It will never belong to Nicholas.

Her maybe half brother, who was asleep in the next room.

When Lorena had finished her story and answered every question, she and Levi had gone in one direction and Elizabeth and Nathaniel in another, leaving Ethan and Callie sitting in the parlor. It was easy to sit quietly with Ethan; it was one of the things she appreciated most about him.

When the clock struck eight he said, "Nicholas will be home soon."

She hadn't realized it was so late. Any moment Nicholas would come in full of stories and in need of a bath before he could be sent off to bed. A boy so full of life that his very presence had roused her from some kind of waking dream; there was no way to resist him,

Ethan said, "Does it matter?"

He knew where her mind was, and she couldn't pretend he didn't. Ethan was going to put it into words, and she was almost glad.

"Would you send him away if you knew for sure he wasn't your blood?"

"That's the kind of thing Jemima would do." Her voice was hoarse and she forced herself to swallow. "I couldn't do that to him." She met Ethan's eye. "He'd be better off with us. Can you see us doing that? Raising him?"

"Right now that's the only thing I can see," Ethan said. "No matter who he was born to, he feels like ours, now."

She wanted to tell Ethan that she admired him for his open mind and heart, that she would always be thankful to him, that she loved him, but her throat was tight with tears.

It was then that Nicholas came dashing in, chasing all the quiet out of the house. After that there had been heating the water for his bath, and warming soup, and laying out clothes for the next day.

Now, full awake, she wondered what Nicholas would say if he knew she was about to sell the orchard. Most likely it wouldn't mean anything to him, as long as he was still welcome there. He might miss the idea of the new house, but Callie thought he wouldn't worry about it for long. It didn't seem to be in his nature to covet. But then, she reminded herself, he had never done without, as he would have done if he had grown up with Jemima in Paradise. As she and Martha had done.

Once Martha came to mind Callie admitted to herself that sleep was out of reach. As quietly as she could manage, she got out of bed and dressed in the dark.

The night air was cool and warm all at once, with a breeze that touched her face and combed through her loosened hair with gentle fingers. She had forgot to cover her head, and how odd it felt to be so open to the world.

It was, strictly speaking, not terribly sensible to be on the mountain in the middle of the night without any weapon at all. It wasn't until she had reached the old schoolhouse that Callie really became aware of where she was, and how foolish she was being. She had no weapons beyond a quick mind and quicker feet, but nobody could outrun a puma or a charging boar. She picked up her skirts and ran, and by the time the path came out of the woods into the strawberry fields her breathing was hoarse and the taste of salt and metal was strong in her mouth and throat.

It took a few minutes for her heartbeat to return to normal, and in that time Callie took stock of Daniel's place. Of Martha's place. Her eyes were adjusted to the dark so that she could make out the lines of walls and roof. Since the last time she had come this way the house had expanded on two sides, like a tree putting out new branches. Ethan had told her about all this, but it was still a surprise to see how different things were. Once there had been a small house here such as any bachelor might build for himself, and now there was a homestead. The place where Martha and Daniel would raise children and grow old.

She sat on the porch for a few moments and considered turning back and going straight home. Tomorrow was soon enough to tell Martha about Nicholas and Lorena's story and to tell Martha another truth: She had been right to doubt. Martha knew her mother best, in the end. Callie felt the vaguest flicker of anger, but it was a poor thing with nothing to feed on. None of this was Martha's fault.

Just then the dog began to bark. She could hear him scratching at the door, eager to get out here and chase off whatever creature was trespassing. When he paused she heard voices that drifted from the window that looked out toward the valley.

"Probably a fox sniffing around. I'll go and settle him down." And: "Don't even think about getting out of that bed."

Before things could get any worse, Callie knocked at the door, two hard raps that could not be mistaken. The barking racheted up a notch, and Martha's face appeared at the window, craned around to see who was on the porch.

"Callie! What's wrong?"

Behind the door Daniel spoke a sharp word and the dog fell silent.

"Are you hurt?"

Under the long cascade of her hair the skin of her shoulder and throat and face shone, as smooth as cream.

Callie cleared her throat. "Nothing wrong with me. Except there's things you need to know about, and I won't get any sleep until I tell you."

Daniel stood in the open door. His smile was easy, as if it were nothing unusual to be disturbed in the middle of the night. As if she were family, and belonged here.

He said, "You had best come in, Callie. We'll put water on for tea."

Daniel lit the lamp and then announced his intention to go back to bed so they could talk, but not before he asked Callie if there was anything he could do.

"I just need to talk to Martha for a little while."

If he was curious, he kept it to himself. Callie was thankful to him for that, because she needed a moment to gather her thoughts while Martha moved around the room.

Then she came to sit beside Callie and held out a teacup. The lamp cast a soft light over the table, touched the pale hair on her forearm, and sparked the deeper colors of her hair. She wore a night rail of light cotton that moved against the curve of hip and shoulder and breast as she turned to pick up the milk pitcher and then the sugar.

She smelled of the warm bed and of Daniel, smells that were unfamiliar to Callie but ones she recognized all the same as belonging to the marriage bed. Where Martha had been with Daniel, where Martha spent every night with Daniel. It took all Callie's concentration to ban those images from her mind.

"Callie," Martha said. "You are covered with blackfly bites."

She touched her face. "I didn't even notice."

"I'll get you some lotion." Martha started to get up but Callie stopped her by taking her wrist.

"Not yet," she said. "Let me tell you what I came to say first."

Martha's steady gaze held hers for three heartbeats, and then she nodded.

When Callie had finished relating Lorena's story, Martha folded her arms tight against herself and then leaned forward to rest her brow on the table.

After a moment she felt Callie's hand on her shoulder, her touch as light as silk.

She said, "I'm sorry. I'm sorry I didn't tell you about the Bleeding Heart. I don't know what I was afraid of."

Martha raised her head. "My mother," she said. "And clearly with good reason. But Callie, there's no need to apologize to me. She's my mother, and it should fall to me to set things right. If I only knew how to do that."

"We've done that. It's safe now, from her."

"No," Martha said, almost too sharply. "I don't want you to sell the orchard. She can't take that away from you again; it's not right. How did she find out about the Bleeding Heart?"

"I don't know," Callie said. "But I intend to find out."

"Wait. What if Daniel bought the orchard?"

Callie said, "It's right that Levi should have it. I know you won't understand, but I want him to have it. He's lost more than any of us."

Martha studied Callie's face for a long moment. She saw weariness and resignation and something of relief, and anger, held tight in a closed fist.

"There's more," she said. "I can see it, Callie. How can I help you if I don't know what you're up against?"

Callie turned her face toward the window. The sky was lightening, the world moving toward dawn.

"All right," she said finally. "But don't interrupt me or I'll lose my nerve. It's about Harper."

"Harper? The boy who drowned?"

Callie drew in a sharp breath and nodded. "Right after Jemima went off and left Nicholas behind, Harper started hanging around the orchard, asking questions. Lots of questions about the trees and the harvest and pressing. How much money could a person make if crops were good and the jack was strong? What was the best apple we grew? Did we have to take our jack out to the cities to sell it, or did people come in to buy, and a dozen more.

"It made me more and more nervous, so I finally asked him right out,

why was he so interested in apples? Was there something he was supposed to find out for the Fochts? He closed up tight as a drum and swore
up and down it was all his own idea, Mr. Focht had no interest in farms
or orchards and especially not in apples. The more excuses he made, the
clearer it was to me that something was wrong.

"So I went to talk to Levi. I told him the whole story, and that turned
out to be a mistake."

"Callie—"

"Don't interrupt me. Levi gets real quiet when he's mad, you probably remember that. And he never said a word to me when I told him
about Harper's questions. He just nodded and walked away. The next day
Hannah and Birdie came across Harper's body."

She dropped her head. Martha was still clasping one of her hands, and
Callie pulled it free, gently.

Martha's thoughts began to spin; she imagined a trial, and reminded
herself there were no witnesses to whatever had happened on the lake.
As far as anyone knew Harper had fallen and hit his head on rocks or
a submerged tree trunk, just as everyone had come to the conclusion
that Cookie Fiddler's death was an unfortunate accident and nothing
more.

Except Levi and his brother Ezekiel. They had always believed
Jemima had had something to do with their mother's death, and they
had been right.

Martha said, "I don't think you should tell anyone else about Harper."

Callie's shoulders folded forward and began to tremble. The first tears
dropped on the table, and then Callie let herself be drawn up against
Martha.

She wept as Martha had not seen her weep since her mother's burial.
It hurt her to think what Callie had been enduring, the secrets sitting
like rocks in her belly. Levi was the person she had worked with every
day of her life, someone she trusted, someone who looked out for her
when no one else had taken the time. Even now, well married and secure, she could not bear the idea of losing him.

A healthy, friendly boy of seventeen years was dead because he had
shown an interest in the orchard and a particular apple.

"It is possible," she said aloud. "It is very possible he did just slip and
fall, and that no one had anything to do with his death."

It was as if Callie didn't even hear her, and the reason for that was clear: She was sure in her heart that Levi was responsible.

Very gently she said, "I've been thinking this through now for a while. You saw the carriage and horses and servants she brought with her. The house Lorena described, the one in Boston, all of that indicates that she has had quite a lot of money at her disposal. If all goes well with the orchard a good amount of money will come in, but not until you've got enough bearing trees, and Jemima has never been patient."

"Unless none of it is true," Callie said dully. "Unless she was play-acting and has no place to go but here, and no money to support herself. Then she'd want whatever she could get her hands on."

That idea stuck immediately, like a hooked burr that would draw blood.

"Yes," Martha said softly. "I suppose that is a possibility."

Callie was still weeping silently, her tears striking the table. Martha put an arm around her shoulders and Callie began to sob in earnest. Out of fear for Levi and herself, out of anger. Martha took it all in, like a beating she had earned and must accept without complaint, as she must admit to herself that Jemima was her mother, and her burden.

When the worst had passed and it seemed that Callie's breathing came in great shudders, she spoke very softly. Martha said, "There's something you should know too. It might be a help to you, it's about Billy Kirby."

Callie's eyes were still swimming with tears. "Your uncle."

"Yes. You remember the stories about Billy, how he beat my father, and the other things he did." She swallowed. "Do you remember how he died?"

"Not exactly," Callie said. "Was it something about a hunting accident, on Hidden Wolf?"

Martha said, "That's the story that most people tell, but the truth is, Nathaniel killed him. This was after Billy almost got Hannah killed. Nathaniel tracked Billy onto Hidden Wolf and ran him down. He could have taken Billy to Johnstown to be tried, but he—he didn't. He killed him. He killed him because he knew that sooner or later Billy Kirby would kill Liam or one of Nathaniel's own."

Certain parts of the story Daniel had told Martha remembered word for word. *The law has got no teeth when it comes to a man like that, who might go off like a powder keg at any minute.* It occurred to her now in a sudden flash of understanding that Daniel had been talking not just about Billy Kirby, but about Jemima.

To Callie she said, "The reason I know this is that Nathaniel told Daniel about it, and Daniel told me. He thought I should know, that it might change my mind about marrying into the family."

"But it didn't."

Martha was close to tears herself, and it took a moment to make her voice work. "Who am I to judge? My mother let your mother walk into a blizzard to her death. My father blackbirded for years. It was because of him that Selah Voyager died. It doesn't matter that he repented and tried to make restitution, because her little boy still grew up without his ma. Billy Kirby would have gone on hurting people. How could I hold anything against Nathaniel Bonner? No more could I judge Levi, if he is responsible."

"It was wrong," Callie said.

"Yes," Martha said quietly.

"Before Nicholas came, I think I was on the brink of real madness. I don't think Ethan could have helped me then, but Nicholas brought me back to myself." She drew in a long breath. "Martha, I'd die before I let Jemima get hold of that boy. Blood or not, I can't bear the thought of what she'd try to make out of him."

"Of course you're right," Martha said. "Of course he must stay here with us."

"She'll want to take him away. Could we hide him?"

"For a while, but not forever. Callie, we don't have to figure this out on our own. We have Ethan and Daniel and the whole clan, and you know that they will help."

"I hope so," Callie said. "I hope you're right."

Just before sunrise Daniel saddled the horses and took Callie down to the village, because she wouldn't stay even when he offered to take word to Ethan.

"The fresh air will clear my head."

"You'll need five, six hours of solid sleep to clear your head," Daniel said. Callie would usually have had a smart comeback, but she was half asleep in the saddle and wrung out. There hadn't been time for Martha to tell him what was wrong, but he could see for himself that Callie was in a bad way.

The day was overcast and the wind already fitful. His aunt Many-Doves would have seen an omen in the color of the sky. Daniel wondered, but he didn't have her gifts. Certainly he was at a loss when it came to saying the right things to a woman in Callie's state. His mother would know; even his father would know. For the moment the best he could do was not talk at all; not offer any false comfort or hope. Let her be in the world without distraction.

Once they crossed the bridge into the village she said, "Thank you. I can go on from here alone. I'll make sure the horse gets back to you later today."

Her tone left no room for argument, and Daniel watched her move away. He could turn around and go straight back to Martha, but she would sleep for a few hours at least, after last night. He headed for his mother's kitchen where he found nobody but the LeBlanc girls, who were baking. According to Anje, his mother and all the rest of the family had gone over to Curiosity's not a half hour before, to spend the day. If he had come up by the regular way he would have seen them parading along behind Simon and Ben carrying Lily between them on her divan.

For so much of their childhoods Lily had done her best to gain the upper hand over her brother and cousins, and now she was making the most of it.

"Your da is in the stable," Joan said in a surly tone. "And you're in the way." Martha hadn't been exaggerating about Joan, he could see that now. He wondered if he should say something to her, if that would make matters better or worse. There was no way to ask her about any of this without sounding cruel, but he would have liked to know exactly what wrong Joan thought Martha had done her.

Daniel went out to the barn and found his father sitting on a keg of nails in the open doorway, his face raised to the sky.

"That storm means business," Nathaniel said by way of greeting. "Things battened down at home?"

"Martha can manage," Daniel said. "I just wanted to talk for a few minutes before I head back. Can you tell me what's going on with Callie? She came up in the middle of the night, and they talked until light, her and Martha. From the look of her she's shed a bucket or two of tears."

"You don't want to wait to hear it from Martha?"

Daniel crouched down to rest on his heels. "If you tell me now that gives me the ride home to sort it through."

"Fair enough," said his father. And he told him.

Later Daniel said, "That *bitch*."

"That's one word for her."

He walked in a circle through the stable to think it through. "Da, is there any way to know who the boy really is?"

"Probably not," his father said. "Maybe she gave birth in Boston and couldn't stand the sight of him. Maybe her own child was born dead and she got another one from the orphanage to take his place. Lorena wasn't in the house long enough to get any sense of things."

"Jemima did the boy one favor," Daniel said. "She handed him over to Lorena instead of raising him herself."

Rain had begun to fall in heavy drops that raised dust in the door-yard.

"You know what Ethan's thinking? How he wants to handle Jemima when she comes back? I doubt she'll just give over when she hears Callie sold the orchard out from under her."

Nathaniel said, "I think most of us have an idea of how to handle Jemima, but your ma would object. You got any suggestions?"

"Maybe," Daniel said. "Let me think about it for a bit."

The wind picked up and began to drive the rain against the roof and walls. A warm rain, the kind that was made for children to play in. Daniel realized he was sorry to have missed the little people. Even more than that, he saw how things had changed. Just a few months ago he would have been glad to be left to his own devices.

"I got this idea," said his father. "Your ma wouldn't like me asking you such a thing straight out, but I'm going to anyway. You count yourself happy these days?"

It was a word Daniel seldom considered. He wasn't even sure what it meant, and he said so.

"You are your ma's son," said his father with a half smile. "If you cain't even take a word like *happy* at face value."

"Da, this is the best way I know how to say it. If one of Jennet's fairies offered me the chance to change one thing in my life, I don't know what I'd say. I like teaching, and I'm getting better at it all the time. I like where I live, halfway between Lake in the Clouds and here. I like coming here on Sundays especially. And—" He paused, because he wasn't sure he wanted to put the way he felt about Martha into words. His father waited, content with the quiet.

"And when it comes to Martha, I can't believe my own good luck. Even arguing is something to look forward to, and I don't think I've ever laughed so much in one day. There's nothing to not love about her."

And there it was, the word that loomed so large in his mind, bigger by the day. The word he had never spoken out loud, even to Martha. The word neither of them had said aloud.

His father watched the rain for a long minute. Then he said, "That's the way it's supposed to be, and I'm pleased for you. But what about your bad arm? Caught you off guard, did I? You weren't even thinking about it."

"I guess not," Daniel said. He looked at the hand that lay in the fold of the sling, and then, quite deliberately, he flexed his wrist and then, before he could lose his nerve, lifted his elbow. The pain was there, but was there less of it?

Maybe Hannah's needles were making some difference. He had never allowed himself to consider that possibility. He had accepted the pain and the loss of his arm, or he thought he had. The idea that there might be some improvement made him feel jumpy.

"So." His father got up and stretched to get the kinks out of his legs. "Rain or no, there's work to be done. You planning on staying around or heading back to that girl of yours?"

Daniel said, "I'm already gone."

58

Curiosity said, "You got a scowl on you would sour milk. You finally ready to tell me what's been eating at you the last couple weeks?"

Birdie came all the way into the kitchen and sat down on the stool next to Curiosity's rocking chair. It was a little easier here on the talking stool, as she thought of it. It was a good place to settle her mind when things were going badly.

"June," Birdie said, "has been a terrible month."

Curiosity pursed her lips. "Go on."

"First Levi and Lorena get married and don't even have a party after."

"I don't suppose you can forget that any time soon," Curiosity said dryly.

"And it's rained almost every day since."

"It has been some wet this year, that's true."

"The little people get awful fractious when they're stuck indoors for any length of time."

Curiosity looked at her down the slope of her nose, and Birdie heaved a great sigh.

"I get fractious too."

"Yes, you do."

"Auntie Jennet is so big she waddles."

"And just why does that bother you? It's a natural thing."

"It bothers me because that baby is sure to come on the Fourth of July and then *that* party will be ruined."

"She's pretty close," Curiosity agreed. "Might could be on the Fourth."

"It's not that I don't want her to have the baby. I'll be just as happy about the baby as everybody else, but first you and Ma and Hannah will close yourself up with her and you won't come out for a whole night or maybe even longer, and that will be that, no more Fourth of July."

"You always borrowing trouble. Why is that?"

"I'm just being prag-matic," Birdie said. She pronounced the word carefully, as she had only written it down in her notebook yesterday. "And there is real trouble. Daniel got a letter from Manhattan. The new teacher isn't coming."

That got Curiosity's attention. She put down the magnifying glass and the book she was trying to read, and looked at Birdie more closely.

"Do tell."

"His ma is sickly and he can't leave Manhattan."

"Now that is a disappointment. What does Daniel say?"

Birdie fluttered her fingers in the air as if to shoo the idea of her brother away.

"He's going to put a new advertisement in the newspapers, but you remember how long it took last time? I just know when school starts we'll all be crammed back into the one classroom. He won't even talk to Martha about taking the class. I asked him and he got all stony-faced."

"Not in front of you, he won't talk to Martha. That business is between him and her, and you had best stay out of it."

"So you think he might ask her?"

"Mayhap," Curiosity said.

It gave Birdie some hope. Some very little hope.

"You think she'd rather stay home all day looking after the house? That doesn't sound like Martha to me."

Curiosity pursed her mouth while she thought. Then she said, "Other things might keep her at home."

"Not another baby."

"I don't know about that one way or the other," Curiosity said. "But it's just a matter of time. That's all I'm saying."

Birdie said, "I wish people would stop having babies."

"You won't feel that way in another ten years or so."

"I will too," Birdie said. "I'm never going to have any."

Curiosity raised her brows, two strong white wings against her dark skin. "You say so?"

Birdie nodded. "I'm going to go places and do things, and babies just get in the way."

"Well, then," Curiosity said. "Duly noted."

Birdie looked at her closely and saw nothing of amusement in that familiar face. Curiosity wouldn't make fun when it was something really important, and it was a comfort to her.

"Tell me," Curiosity said to Birdie. "Was there any other mail?"

"Nothing for you. Ma got a letter from somebody famous about something she wrote in a newspaper; it came all the way from Germany. Luke got letters from his office on Whitehall Street."

Curiosity said, "Would you just go ahead and spit out whatever it is you come in here to talk about?"

Birdie said, "All right. Every grown-up has been whispering in corners for weeks, it seems like. Nobody will tell me what about, but it's something important. I asked Da straight out and he told me that it was serious business and none of my concern. Can you imagine that? None of my concern, as if I was one of the little people. If everybody is worried, then I have got the right to be worried too."

"Sound to me like you already worried," Curiosity said.

"You know what I mean. If there's something wrong I could help."

Curiosity's expression softened. "Your folks just trying to keep you safe."

"Safe from what?"

"Maybe nothing," Curiosity said.

"Jemima," Birdie said. "I know it's Jemima everybody is whispering about. Can't you just tell me that much?"

"Of course it's Jemima," Curiosity said. "She's that bad penny you always hear folks talking about. I can tell you this much—"

Birdie sat up straighter.

"It ain't none of my business, and none of yours either."

When Curiosity got a certain look in her eye, it was best to leave things be. Birdie got up and went to find her mother.

Nathaniel Bonner pushed back from the breakfast table late on the morning of the Fourth of July and ran a handkerchief over his damp brow. Elizabeth glanced at him from the newspaper she was reading, revealing ink marks on either side of the bridge of her nose.

She said, "You're grinning. I take it I have ink on my face?" And she held out her hand for his handkerchief.

"I'm guessing you got a headache if you're pinching the bridge of your nose."

"A little one. I'll ask Hannah for one of her powders."

He leaned over and kissed her on the brow. "Boots, it's time you admitted you need spectacles for reading."

Over the years she had seen at least a dozen people fitted for spectacles—at her own expense too—but now she avoided doing the same for herself.

"An occupational hazard." Whether she meant the ink or the need for spectacles wasn't clear, and she clearly had no intention of pursuing the subject. Instead she reached back to a basket of clean laundry and hooked a fresh handkerchief out for him.

He said, "I'm on my way down to the village to see how they're getting along with the fire pits. I'm hoping there won't be any fistfights tonight."

"Now that's a fib," Elizabeth said. "You look forward to the ruckus all year."

It was true that he looked forward to the Fourth of July celebration. The food was good and plentiful, there were contests and games and dancing. In the evening, Joshua Hench would set up his twice-a-year fireworks display.

"You saying you don't like the Fourth?"

"I love the Fourth," Elizabeth said. "And you know it. I just wish it weren't so very hot. I keep thinking of the July I was eight months gone with Robbie, when I thought I would suffocate in that heat."

She sometimes talked of the children they had lost so early, and in such warm tones that anyone who didn't know her would think she had got past the pain. The fact that the lost ones were on her mind meant that she was more worried about Jennet and Lily than she could even admit to herself. To Nathaniel it seemed that all the women were on edge these last few days, and he wondered, fleetingly, if there was something amiss they had decided to keep among themselves. If he asked her straight out she would tell him, but then again he wasn't sure he wanted to know.

Instead he said, "Why don't you come down with me? I'm guessing the little people will have all kinds of mischief going, and I know folks will be asking after you. Curiosity will have some harsh words for me if I leave you here."

"It just seems unfair that Hannah should have to stay behind."

"Hannah," he reminded her, "is a doctor, and if she thinks she needs to stay with Jennet and Lily, that's up to her."

He watched her turn the idea over in her mind. She said, "I could send one of the children up to check on them now and then."

"Exactly," Nathaniel said. "Fetch your sunbonnet, Boots, and let's get going."

In the deep shade of the parlor Hannah stood at the window and watched her father and stepmother start out for the party in the village.

"He did it," she said. "I didn't think he would, this year. But she's going."

"Well, good," Lily said. "Good for Da."

Hannah sat down in the rocker Simon had fitted with a system of ropes and pulleys. She put one foot on a small board that pivoted as she rocked, and in response a thin rectangle of perforated wood hung overhead began to swing back and forth, sending a current of cool air through the room.

"Och," Jennet said, putting her face up to catch the breeze. "Don't stop."

"I think Simon could sell these contraptions from Florida to Quebec," Hannah said.

Lily stretched and yawned. "He is clever, my good husband. Is it possible that I need another nap?"

"Take it while you can get it," Hannah said.

It was a luxury to have husbands and parents and children elsewhere, so that they could rest in each other's company. Even the LeBlanc girls had the day off, so that there was no one to overhear them and carry tales to the village. To Hannah it was worth a hundred firework displays.

For a long time they talked on and off, each of them slipping away into sleep for a few minutes, half rousing, falling back into slumber. When the baby roused from his nap Hannah fetched him to the parlor and nursed him in the pleasant breeze from the fan, and then they passed him around and entertained him until the heat made him sleepy again. Hannah took him back to the infant cot that had a permanent place in her stepmother's kitchen and saw him settled.

Then she put together a tray and they sat around it in the parlor— Lily still on her divan, Hannah and Jennet on chairs—eating boiled eggs with salt and butter and new bread. There was a jug of water she had retrieved from the springhouse, and cold mint tea.

"In the village they're eating pork cut off the spit," said Jennet. "But the very thought makes my stomach turn." She ran a hand over the great swell of her belly.

"That's the heat," Hannah said. "And a child ready to come into the world."

"It could hardly be more impatient than I am," said Jennet. She closed her eyes and without opening them she said, "What does it mean, do you think, that I'm so much more tired this time than the last, with the girls?"

"No doubt it's a boy," said Hannah. "Already set on mischief."

"And for Lily?" Jennet asked. "Another boy?"

"Oh, a girl," said Lily. "Ma won't have it any other way, though she wouldn't admit it. I hope she's right, though if it's to be my one and only—well, it seems that Simon should have a son to carry on the family name."

"Listen to her," Jennet said. "Have ye been keeping count of the Ballentynes at Carryck? Simon's brithers have been putting out sons one after the other. Like rabbits. And beyond that, why should you not have a daughter to carry on your mither's line? Is that no just as important?"

"She's right," Hannah said. "And beyond that, I don't see why this should be your one and only. You may have one a year for the next ten years, now that you've got the hang of it."

They laughed for a while, but then Lily's expression sobered. She said, "I am starting to wonder if the doctor I saw in Rome might have been right about my problem."

"The wee mannie who said you had to choose between art and childbearing?" Jennet snorted.

"No, that's not what he said, not exactly." Lily sat up a little straighter. "He said that if I insisted on painting I wouldn't be able to carry a child to term. Since Italy I've only used charcoal and pencil and ink, no paints of any kind because I didn't want the smell in Ma's parlor. It's probably just a coincidence." But the look she sent Hannah's way said she didn't believe this herself.

"There are herbals and medicines enough that interfere with a healthy pregnancy," Hannah said. "Dittany. Black cohosh. Vervain and rue. There might be something in paint."

Lily's expression was pained. "Do you really think—"

"It could be," Hannah said.

Lily's high color faded a little. "I may have to write and tell him he was right," she said. "If all goes well in the end."

"No need," said Jennet. "The idea that he might have been wrong would never occur to him."

"Well then," Lily said slowly. "If I seem so healthy to you, and there's no sign of trouble—do you think I might be able to . . . walk around, at least a bit? A few minutes every day?"

"We'll put the question to Curiosity and your ma this evening," Hannah said. "You'll have to win them over."

Lily collapsed back and blew out a breath so that the curls at her temples jumped. "I was afraid you'd say that."

Jennet sat up straighter to look out the window. "Who is that coming? One of the LeBlanc girls, but which one?"

Hannah stood up to see. "Alice."

"Alice LeBlanc?" Lily's tone was half amusement, half doubt.

"It is odd," Hannah said.

"Och," Jennet said. "Is she the one who's so angry that Martha got Daniel?"

"She is," Hannah said. "Good thing Martha isn't here. I'll go see what Sour Apples wants."

Alice was the prettiest of the LeBlanc girls, but she had earned her unflattering nickname. When Hannah's daughters asked her why Alice was called Sour Apples, Hannah had reminded them of one of Elizabeth's sayings: *Pretty is as pretty does.* There were many such expressions Elizabeth had brought over with her from England; this was one that made sense to Hannah.

It was one of the mysteries of life, how children born and raised in the same family could turn out so different from each other and from both parents too. Becca was one of the kindest and most generous women Hannah knew, but she was also very gruff. Alice had only got the gruff. The six LeBlanc girls were a mix that always took her by surprise, like coming across a white cat with a litter of kittens every color of the rainbow, from black to ginger to calico. It made sense to Hannah that Alice had it hard, the first girl after six boys, but why she held on to that resentment though it did her only harm, that was unclear.

Now Alice was coming on at a good clip, her frown focused on the ground at her feet. Then she caught sight of Hannah on the porch and her expression shifted from preoccupation to worry.

She called out, "I've been looking for you all over."

Hannah owed Alice LeBlanc no explanations, and so she cut right to the heart of the matter.

"Somebody hurt?"

Alice took a moment to catch her breath. "No," she said. "Sick. A lady in one of our rooms, she's been vomiting since last night."

"Is she in pain?"

"Belly cramps," Alice said.

Something was off about this, but Hannah couldn't put a finger on it. She said, "Good of you to come up here with word."

Alice's mouth turned down at the corner and she looked more herself. "Everybody else is at the games, and Ma's busy in the kitchen. It was me or nobody. If you don't care to come—"

"I'll be there," Hannah said coolly. "Start straight down and I'll follow you in ten minutes."

The truth was, she didn't mind being called out. Things had been very quiet in Paradise since the flood. Sore ears, a few broken bones easily set, two deliveries, fever teas. She considered the ailments that might account for the symptoms that Alice described, which was most likely nothing more than indigestion that camomile tea could put right.

Jennet dismissed her reservations about leaving them with a wave of the hand. "I can get to the kitchen when Simon wakes, and I imagine Elizabeth will be back soon, anyway. We're fine, aren't we, Lily?"

"More than," Lily said, yawning. "There's no reason to worry about us."

Hannah had her bag with her—she always did, these days—and so it was just a matter of tying a kerchief over her hair and washing her hands. Then she dashed down the hillside on a deer path that would take her to the Red Dog by the back way. It was a sensible precaution, because if any of the little people caught sight of her it would be next to impossible to resist their pleas that she come watch the foot races or bob for apples or buy them sweets. Just now she didn't have the time, but if this visit didn't take too long she could spend an hour with them.

She had just come around the corner to the back of the Red Dog when somebody caught her by the elbow and swung her around and up against a wall.

"What—"

Ben pinned her by the wrist held over her head, and he kissed her. He was good at it too, and always had been. Even when she was disinclined or distracted, Ben could bring her back into the here and now like this. He kissed her so expertly that she felt the tug of it in her womb.

When he pulled away she said, "How good to see you too," and he laughed and kissed her once more, this time running his hand up her leg to cradle her buttock.

"Ben!"

"Hmmm?"

"Anybody could come around that corner."

"I don't mind an audience."

She put her free palm on his chin and made him look her in the eye.

"You wouldn't mind Baldy O'Brien grading your performance?"

He went very still, and then he pulled away. "There's the schoolhouse," he said, wiggling one eyebrow.

Hannah closed her eyes briefly. "I know I've been neglecting you—"

"Hush. I'm as much at fault as you are."

It was true that they went to bed exhausted and fell asleep before they could even think about the things they were missing, but that was the price of bringing children into the world. The irony was, the thing they both wanted to do here, in broad daylight, would give them release, but the possible result nine months down the road would only compound the problem.

Hannah counted the days in her head as Ben did his best to win her over to his way of seeing things, and when she had calculated as best she could, she pulled away again.

"Here's what we can do," she said. "Tomorrow morning we can leave the house at first light. I'll make noises about going to see the patient upstairs—" She gestured with her chin to the upper floor of the Red Dog. "And we'll meet at the pond."

Oh, when he smiled like that. She'd be thinking about it all day.

Alice said, "That was more than ten minutes."

"Was it?" Hannah would not let Alice get the best of her, and so she only smiled. "If you'll take me to the patient—"

Huffing like a newborn with colic, Alice led Hannah through the empty public room and up the stairs. In Paradise folks took the Fourth of July seriously and nobody wanted to miss any part of it, not even the men who spent every free hour cradling a tankard of Becca's ale. And still Hannah had the strong sense that something was not as it seemed.

She touched the sheath that held her knife, and the gesture both calmed her and made her laugh at herself. Alice LeBlanc might be meanspirited, but she wasn't homicidal; and more than that, Hannah would only have to shout out the window to get someone's attention.

In the hall Alice opened the door and stood aside for Hannah to enter, a simple act that stopped her cold. The Alice LeBlanc she knew would never let Hannah precede her through a door; she had too high an opinion of her own worth.

Alice frowned at her. "What?"

"If you do not tell me exactly who is in that room, I will turn around and leave," Hannah said.

"It's all right," a voice called. "Alice, it's all right. Hannah, come in, and shut the door behind yourself."

Jemima.

Alice was smiling now, a superior and self-satisfied smile that said she was enjoying having got the best of Hannah Savard. Hannah waited until Alice had taken her smirk down the stairs, and then she went in and closed the door.

A sickroom has a smell all its own, and Hannah had entered enough of them to get a sense of what was waiting for her on that basis alone. Here there was bile and vomit and strongest of all, the oily stench of unhealthy stool. There was something wrong here, something far worse than indigestion.

Jemima was sitting in a large upholstered chair by the window. The curtains were drawn and the air in the room was close and hot and heavy. Hannah went to the windows and pushed back the curtains to let in light. Then she opened both sashes as far as they would go.

"I don't like the breeze," Jemima said.

"And yet you need fresh air." She drew in a deep breath and turned to face Jemima. "When did you get here?"

There were new lines in Jemima's face, brackets around her mouth that spoke of pain, along with streaks of iron gray in her hair. And there was a struggle going on too; Hannah could see it happening in her eyes. Jemima didn't like this situation, but she was forcing herself forward.

"Last night just before dark."

"Alone?"

"Alone," Jemima said.

"You came masked, in a costume?"

Jemima's mouth jerked at the corner. "I was wearing a veiled hat, if you must know the details."

"I find it hard to believe you traveled, as sick as you are, and by yourself."

"It wasn't so bad yesterday," Jemima said. "Came on a little after I got here."

"Your husband—"

"My husband is none of your concern. I have money, and I can pay you for your services. What I need, first of all, is laudanum. And then a diagnosis."

The anger that Hannah had been holding at bay kicked up, but she pushed it back down. "I am not interested in your money and I think you'd be better served by another doctor."

Jemima said, "I've seen eight doctors in the last six weeks, and none of them would or could tell me what's wrong with me."

That made Hannah laugh aloud. "And so you came to me? To me? You never had any opinion of me or my skills as a doctor. You accused me of killing children out of incompetence."

"I don't think much of you," Jemima agreed. "But others do. And desperate times call for desperate measures."

Hannah studied the woman sitting by the window for a full minute.

In that time Jemima never moved, though her breathing came quick and shallow. She was in pain, and trying not to show it.

"I'll examine you and charge what I always charge, and I'll tell you what I find. And that's as much as I'll promise."

"And laudanum."

"Yes. I see you are in great pain."

"And how that must thrill you."

Hannah looked at her calmly, and waited.

Finally Jemima said, "All right, I take it back."

Hannah put down her bag and sat down on the chair opposite Jemima. "Tell me," she said. "Every symptom and when it started. And leave nothing out."

Later Jemima said, "I came to you because I knew you wouldn't mind giving me bad news."

Hannah considered, weighing words and phrases, trying to recall extracts she had read and autopsies conducted long ago when she had been studying under Dr. Valentine and Dr. Savard—who would one day be her brother-in-law—at the almshouse in Manhattan. It was the thought of Dr. Savard that gave her a way to talk to Jemima. She imagined what he would say, and she said it.

"It will go like this. The pain will get steadily worse, far worse than it is now. Far worse. In a week or two, if you're lucky you'll fall into a coma and stay there until you die. You have questions?"

"Do you have enough laudanum to see me through?"

"No," Hannah said. "But I can send for it."

"You are saying I have cancer."

"Most likely, yes. In the digestive organs and the liver, at the very least."

"If I stop eating and drinking can I end this quicker?"

"Then it will be two or three days at most."

"I don't suppose you'd be willing to give me something to end it now. Think of the satisfaction you'd get. In fact, you could auction off the privilege of killing me." Her laugh was hoarse and phlemy.

Hannah stared at her.

Jemima sighed. "How much do I owe you?"

Hannah said, "You owe me nothing but answers."

———

Despite the pain, Jemima could laugh in a way that evoked memories Hannah would have preferred to leave buried.

"Go on," she said. "Ask your questions. I might even answer some of them. When you're done I want that laudanum."

There were dozens of things Hannah wanted to know, but she had never thought she might one day get answers. The idea was so strange that for a moment she couldn't think where to start. Old mysteries or newer ones? Once they had been schoolchildren in the same classroom. What Hannah remembered best about Jemima was the fact that she never smiled unless it was at someone else's expense.

Except that wasn't entirely true. The only time anyone got a sense of the person that might have been was when Jemima sang. Elizabeth had encouraged her singing for that reason, and maybe it had even helped a little, for a while. Then her father had been killed and her mother and brothers died of typhus, and Jemima had let anger and bile drag her down. Others had lost just as much; others had lost far more, and survived. They took comfort in the Christian Bible and its promises of another world, or lost themselves in work, or in founding another family. Some drank themselves to death. Jemima vented her fury at those closest to her.

Hannah said, "Do you still sing?"

Jemima closed her eyes, as if that could make the question go away. When Hannah thought she would never get an answer, Jemima opened her eyes again.

"Until last fall I sang almost every night."

That was more information than Hannah had expected, and it raised more questions than it answered. She considered.

"What made you stop?"

A flush of annoyance moved across Jemima's face. "What kind of questions are these?"

"You chose to pay my fee in answers."

"Ask something else."

"Did your coming back here have anything to do with that, the singing?"

Jemima scowled at her. "Ask something else."

"All right," Hannah said. "What was it that Harper was supposed to be finding out for you?"

"Harper is my husband's creature," Jemima said. "I don't know exactly what arrangement they had."

Hannah said, "Harper is dead. He drowned."

Jemima went very still. Then she said, "That boy could swim all day. He was half fish."

"Anybody can drown," Hannah said. "There was no evidence that it was anything but an accident."

"Of course you'd say that. It was probably one of yours who did it."

Hannah counted to ten. Then, very calmly she said, "For someone who wants favors of me, you are very free with unfounded accusations. And may I point out to you that there have been other accidental deaths over the years."

Jemima drew in a sharp breath. "Go on with your questions, but you are trying my patience."

"You want the orchard, and leaving Harper behind had something to do with that."

"Christ, no," Jemima said. "I wouldn't care if I never saw an apple or an apple tree ever again."

"Your husband is the one who wants the orchard, then."

"You must realize," Jemima said, slowly, "that by rights, the orchard should go to Nicholas."

She got up stiffly to walk over to the bed. Hannah waited until she had settled herself and she said, "So you know about the Bleeding Heart."

A flicker of a smile. "Now I do."

"You knew before. You heard about it by chance, from a farmer near Boston."

"If you know the answers, why are you bothering to ask?"

"So the long and short of it is, you came back here to claim the orchard for Nicholas. You are worried about what will become of him when you're dead. Did it ever occur to you to just ask Martha or Callie to take him in? Why do you assume they are as small-minded and selfish as you?"

"You always thought you were smarter than anyone else," Jemima said.

"Is your husband coming?"

"No," Jemima said. "He is not."

"Was he your husband to start with?"

"Another thing you'll never know for sure."

"You're here because you have no place else to go, and you need to make arrangements for the boy."

Jemima said, "I believe I've answered enough questions. It's my turn to talk. I want you to arrange for me to be carried up to Martha's house in the strawberry fields, by tomorrow morning at the latest. I don't intend to die under Becca LeBlanc's roof."

The idea so surprised Hannah that she had trouble collecting her thoughts. "What makes you think Martha and Daniel would agree to such a thing?"

"They'll agree," Jemima said. "Or pay the consequences."

"What could you possibly do to them at this stage?"

The pain was coming on stronger now, Hannah could see it in Jemima's face. And still she would have the last word, no matter what it cost her.

Her voice was unsteady. "I know things. I know things Martha and Callie and even your Saint Ethan wouldn't want made public."

"I see your game now," Hannah said. "You're trying to goad someone into killing you."

Jemima smiled. She said, "Is it working?"

Hannah took a deep breath. Then she picked up her bag and left, closing the door behind herself.

Alice and Joan were waiting for her at the bottom of the stair, both of them on edge. As well they should be, thought Hannah.

"I hope you two are proud of yourself," she said. "Does your mother know about this?"

Alice drew up, affronted, and launched into a lecture that Hannah cut off with a sharp look. She fished a small bottle out of her bag and thrust it into Joan's hands.

"Laudanum. Dilute a tablespoon in a half glass of warm water and have her drink it slowly, or she'll bring it right up. She can have that much every two hours."

"It's just her bowels gripping her," Alice announced, as if this would make it true.

"Among other things," Hannah said, and she walked out of the Red Dog into the bright July afternoon.

———

Martha put the flat of her hand to her brow to cut out the sun, and then she said, "Look, there's Hannah. She came down after all."

Daniel turned and saw his sister weaving her way through the crowd. She was trailing little people in a long tail, all of them plying her with questions and stories and requests for pennies.

There was something wrong. He looked around himself for Simon and Luke, but there was no sign of them here. Most likely they were down at the lake where some of the trappers were wagering on log rolling. If Lily or Jennet had gone into labor they would need to know.

Henry was saying, "Ma, can we stay until dusk? Can we stay and watch the dancing and the fireworks? Can we?"

Hannah came to a stop and looked down at him. "If you promise to keep an eye on your brothers and sisters and cousins."

"We'll all do that," Nathan said, and heads bobbed in agreement.

"Then off with you," she said, and they turned toward the trading post where some of the women were cooking doughnuts that were snatched up as soon as they were pulled from the sputtering fat.

Martha put her hand on Hannah's arm. "What is it? Should we fetch Simon?"

"It's not Lily or Jennet," Hannah said. "But I need to talk to you and Curiosity and Callie."

The last time Daniel had seen Hannah this distracted and curt she had been on her way to see about a little girl who had fallen into the hearth in the middle of winter. A little girl who had just begun to walk, and Hannah had been pregnant with Henry at the time.

He said, "What do you need me to do?"

"Send them both up to my shed," she said. "Your ma too. The quicker the better."

Martha left with Hannah, and Daniel set out at a trot to track down the others.

It was Birdie who caught him up before he had got very far. "Where are Martha and Hannah going?"

"To Hannah's shed," he said. "You could probably catch them up, if you don't care about the footraces."

He knew Birdie as well as anyone on this earth knew her, including their parents. If he had forbidden her to follow, she would have found a way unless he tied her to a hitching post, and probably even then.

He said, "You seen Luke around, or Ben?"

She wrinkled her nose at him. "When Martha's gone you get this look on your face like a dog that's being scolded. I guess you must be thankful to me for matchmaking you two together in the spring."

"I guess I must," Daniel said. He leaned down to touch his forehead to her brow. "Luke?"

"With Simon and Da at the lake. Oh, look, the races are starting." And she was gone without a backward glance.

He hadn't gone more than a couple feet before he ran into Daisy and her daughter Solange, who had a fussing toddler on her hip.

"Hannah is looking for Callie and your ma," he said to Daisy. "You know where I'd find either one?"

Daisy took more after Galileo than she did Curiosity, but once in a while he caught sight of her mother in the set of her eyes. She was looking at him like that now, concerned.

"Joshua took my mother home about a half hour ago," she said. "Is there something wrong?"

"I'm just looking for Callie," Daniel said. "Seems like the women are wanting to have one of their tea parties where men aren't welcome. You should go along too." It was a pure lie; he knew without being told that there was something bad going on and that Curiosity would not want her daughter and granddaughter drawn into it. But Hannah had given him no details, and most likely she had done that because she didn't want him telling anybody anything. He managed what he hoped was a reassuring smile, but Daisy saw right through it.

She said, "You'd break into a sweat if I took you up on that, that's plain. You come fetch me if need be. You know you don't have to ask."

Solange was looking around herself, and then called out. "You there, Markus! Come on over here, baby."

Solange's oldest boy had been running in the footrace and his clothes were soaked with sweat, but he was smiling too.

Daisy said, "You go find Miss Callie, and tell her Daniel is looking for her. Where you want to meet her, Daniel?"

"Send her up to your mother's," Daniel said. "That's where I'm headed right now."

"You planning on joining that tea party by force?"

He produced a grim smile. "If needs be," he said. "You know I will."

It was Richard Todd who had built himself the small laboratory at the edge of his cleared property, about a minute's walk from the kitchen door. It was as well equipped as any laboratory in Manhattan or Paris or London, with a reverberating oven that had been hauled upriver by keelboat and then over land at huge expense.

Hannah had inherited her uncle Todd's practice and his laboratory too, but while she made use of it for her medical papers and books and medicines, she balked at calling it anything but her shack.

Daniel knew his uncle Richard would find it amusing that Hannah shunned the scientific research that was his only real interest. He had found everything funny in the last years of his life, even those things that caused sincere trouble to others. He was a difficult man but a good doctor, and he had trained Hannah well.

As he came around the corner of the house Curiosity shared with Hannah and her family, he saw that the door stood ajar. Hannah leaned against the doorframe, a large open book in her hands that she was studying intently.

Curiosity appeared beside her and waved her cane at Daniel in a way that said very clearly that he had other places to be and if he hadn't figured that out for himself, she would show him good and proper. It would take a stronger man than he was himself to challenge Curiosity brandishing her cane, but Martha was there and Martha might need him. He'd stay as close by as Curiosity allowed. Now he went a little closer, if only because he knew it would make her laugh, and Curiosity's laugh was a kind of medicine all on its own.

"Just in time," she called to him as he came closer. "Go on and fetch me the biggest jug from the springhouse, would you be so kind?" There was a glint in her eye that he dare not ignore, but Daniel came still closer and looked over Curiosity's head to see Martha, who lifted her shoulders at him; whatever was causing such turmoil, she hadn't been told yet either.

"Nothing wrong with her," Curiosity said, thumping the ground with all the menace of an angry billygoat. "Nothing wrong with any one of your folks. Now fetch me that jug, will you?"

It was one of Curiosity's oldest tricks, and still there was no avoiding it. Daniel fetched the jug and then was sent on a half dozen other errands. Curiosity didn't want him to join them, but she did want to know where he was, and she was inventive when it came to errands.

First she wanted her fan, which might could be in her parlor or may-hap in the kitchen and praise God, won't it too hot to sit without one? Then, in possession of her fan, she realized that everybody could use one and she sent him back to look in the bureau below the looking glass in the front hall, in the cabinets under the stair, and a half dozen other places.

Daniel started with the last place she mentioned, but she had antici-pated him; it took ten minutes to find the fans. It was like being caught up in a conjurer's spell. By the time he had fetched fans, handkerchiefs, and a particular book, and filled the water jug three times, Callie and his mother had arrived.

Curiosity met him at the door again. "You can see for your own self, nobody in trouble here. So go on now, wait over at the house."

Once again Daniel considered challenging such a dismissal, but a life-time of experience told him it would be no use. Then he looked up and saw the rest of the men coming toward him.

Now and then Daniel had the strange idea that his father could smell trouble. It was less than rational, but then again his father had a way of showing up where he was needed, even if folks didn't know they needed him yet. This time he had come with backup. In the three quarters of an hour since Daniel came up from the village, his father had rounded up Luke, Ben, Simon, and not far behind them Gabriel, Blue-Jay, and Runs-from-Bears.

All together they made an army that few men would challenge.

Simon called out first. "What's gone wrong?"

Daniel recognized Simon's expression for what it was: worry for his wife.

"No trouble with Lily or Jennet."

They stopped at the edge of Curiosity's garden, where the smell of herbs in the sun filled the air, and waited for Daniel to reach them.

"Hannah wouldn't tell me anything," he said before they could ask. "All I can say is that she was agitated, and we aren't welcome in there while they're talking."

"That's not like Hannah," Gabriel said. And: "I'm low on powder; can I get some of yours, Ben?"

It was their way, to get ready for the worst, but this time Runs-from-Bears raised a brow. "I don't recall being so quick to prime my rifle at that age, do you, Nathaniel?"

"Huh," Luke said, winking at Gabriel. "I seem to remember a story about a battle at William-Henry when you two were hardly older than Gabriel. You volunteered, as I recall."

"And at Saratoga," said Ben.

"Then there was Crown Point," said Simon. "Not to mention—"

Runs-from-Bears held up a hand in surrender. "True enough. But unless I'm losing my eyesight I don't think I've seen a redcoat or a scalp lock around here for more than thirty years."

"Hold on," said Ben. "What kind of trouble are we talking about—talking trouble or shooting trouble?"

"I have no idea," Daniel said. "Except that Hannah went looking for Martha and Callie first."

The men looked at each other. "Sounds like Jemima," said Blue-Jay. "I think I'll check my powder after all."

They laughed on the way back to the house, but it was an uneasy laughter. Daniel checked his knives, and tried to imagine what could have put his sister Hannah into such a state.

When Birdie saw her father and Ethan set off on the hillside path she went and looked for the rest of the men, and at that point she realized that she had been tricked. Every one of them was gone, and she was pretty sure she knew where they were.

It was her own fault; she should have known better than to trust Daniel, who was inscrutable as inscrutable could be. Now all the grown-ups were headed home, and that meant somebody was in some kind of trouble.

She took five minutes to locate all the little people and another five to remind them what was expected of them as Bonners. The three oldest boys got mad at her, as they always did when she was looking out for their best interests. She didn't particularly care just at this moment. She was too busy thinking about what could be so wrong that everybody headed uphill at the same time.

It could be Lily, but as soon as the idea came to her she dismissed it. It was way too early for Lily's baby, and the grown-ups weren't quite moving fast enough for that kind of emergency.

Birdie slipped quietly through the crowd and into the woods behind the trading post. She waited a while to make sure the boys weren't following her, and then she started uphill.

If her father didn't know she was following, he couldn't send her back. In fact, he hadn't said anything about her staying put. He hadn't said anything to her at all about what she might and might not do this Fourth of July afternoon. Birdie filed that fact away in case she needed to defend herself.

She was a good runner, sure-footed and fast, but she had already run three races and she knew she wouldn't be able to catch anybody up. At the fork in the road she had to come out of hiding to see which way they had gone, home or to Curiosity's.

The most recent tracks were on the path that led up to Curiosity's, which put her mind to rest about Lily. And still when she got to the edge of the clearing, she was out of breath and hot enough to keel over. She knew better than to rush right in; she'd sit where she was until she had come up with a plan.

A good plan was crucial. Without a plan she'd get caught before she could figure out what was going on, as had happened in the cloakroom at the schoolhouse. A well-laid plan was built on good information; that was something she had learned from her father and mother both, and they were experts. In their long-ago youth they had both got themselves into bad trouble and then planned their way out again, and more than once.

Birdie approached the house from the blind side, and then walked around it pausing to listen at every window. She had started to wonder if maybe the grown-ups had gone on to Uphill House when she heard the sound of her father's voice in the kitchen.

The kitchen was hard. There were two windows on one wall, and there was the door that went out to the kitchen garden and pasture and outbuildings. Anybody standing at the windows could see her, and anybody in the garden or pasture or outbuildings could see her at the kitchen door. Birdie changed direction and stood for a minute with her back against the wall, considering.

Were the women in the kitchen too? If all the Bonner men were there, it seemed unlikely that anybody else would have room.

Birdie considered. She could go in the front door, but it was next to impossible to do that without making a floorboard creak, and Da would hear her. Ma claimed he had roused out of a deep sleep more than once at the sound of a step in some other part of the house. His hearing was as good as his eyesight, and he was known for his eyesight for a hundred miles around, and more.

There was a trellis on the far wall, where Curiosity had trained morning glories to climb. People mostly didn't come around that side of the house because it wasn't convenient—another word from her notebook—which made it perfect for Birdie's purposes. She would climb the trellis to the window that opened into the girls' room, and then she could sit in the upstairs hall and hear everything. As long as the kitchen door was propped open, which it always was in the summer to let the breeze through.

As long as the little people didn't come home before time, she'd find out what there was to know with the least possible fuss and then she could decide what she needed to do.

"It's not like you to be so jumpy," Curiosity said to Hannah.

Elizabeth was thinking the same thing, but she resisted the urge to agree aloud with Curiosity. Whatever was happening, Hannah must be left to tell them in her own way. Curiosity knew that too, but just now she seemed to have forgot. They were all jumpy.

Martha and Callie exchanged confused glances, and then Callie spoke up. "Is this about Nicholas?"

"No," Hannah said. "It's about Jemima."

The name drew a spark. "What about her?" Callie snapped.

"She's here. At the Red Dog."

Curiosity drew a deep breath and closed her eyes. "Lord God be merciful."

Elizabeth put a hand on her shoulder, and Curiosity covered it with her own.

"Let me tell it from the beginning," Hannah said.

Callie began to pace up and down the room, and when she finally came to a stop it was to interrupt Hannah.

"She wanted you to examine her? It must be some kind of trick."

Callie's anger was plain to see, but Elizabeth was more worried about Martha, whose expression was studiously blank.

"It isn't a trick," Hannah said. "She is sick."

"With *what*?"

Hannah looked at Curiosity, and the older woman nodded her encouragement.

"I don't know if it has a name. She has had episodes on and off for the last year. Swelling and severe pain—" She touched her own abdomen where it met the breastbone. "When the pain comes she can't hold down food or water. Laudanum gives her little relief. The nausea is so severe that she dry-retches for minutes at a time. Coughing or sudden movement makes the pain worse."

"I thought she looked on the thin side. What about her stool?" Curiosity asked.

"Full of fat and the stench is—I've never come across anything as bad."

Curiosity nodded. "Rash?"

"Yes," Hannah said. "A very strange rash. It surrounds her navel in a circle. It reminded me—" She broke off.

"Like a bad spot on an apple," Curiosity finished for her.

Callie made a sound deep in her throat.

"What," Martha said, her voice coming so rough that she had to swallow, "what are you thinking?"

Hannah turned to the anatomy book that lay open on the worktable and picked it up to hold it in front of herself like a teacher in the classroom.

"You see these digestive organs tucked up against the liver? The gallbladder, the ducts that empty the bile, the pancreas, the stomach itself. The simplest explanation for what is wrong with Jemima would be gallstones that are blocking the bile ducts."

Callie's face crumpled. "You did not call us here to tell us Jemima has a bellyache."

"No," Curiosity said. "She called us here to tell us Jemima is dying."

The silence drew itself out, and Elizabeth watched Martha. Her posture, the set of her shoulders, the tension in her jaw, none of that changed appreciably.

Very quietly Hannah said, "I said the simplest explanation would be gallstones, but her condition is far worse."

"You said these episodes come and go," Callie said. "Why is this one different?"

"Malignant disease progresses until it can't be ignored any longer. It is interfering with basic bodily functions and soon her organs will begin to fail entirely."

Elizabeth said, "Curiosity, are you familiar with this?"

The older woman rocked forward, her arms crossed on her belly. "I never saw a case," she said. "But I heard about it. That's the way John Glove's mother Ebby died. I never met her, but they say she had a problem with drink. Do you get the sense Jemima's been drinking hard, Hannah?"

"I asked her," Hannah said. "She denies it."

Callie's face was twitching almost convulsively. Elizabeth thought she would burst out in laughter or tears, that she would have done so already, if not for Martha beside her.

Martha said, "Is there any treatment?"

"Death," Curiosity said. "Death will put an end to it."

Martha flinched ever so slightly.

"So now we know," Callie said. She began pacing the room again. "Jemima's dying. I don't expect any of us will mourn her for long."

"Except Nicholas," Curiosity said, and Callie turned on her heel in surprise.

"He hardly knows her. He never met her until six months ago."

"Don't matter," Curiosity said. "She's his ma, and he's a tender-hearted thing. Harper dying took him real low."

Callie's mouth pressed itself into a tight and disapproving line.

To Hannah Martha said, "What now?"

That was the question, the one that Hannah had been dreading. Elizabeth knew her stepdaughter's face, and she thought she knew what she was going to say.

"That's where things get complicated," Hannah said.

"Send her home," Callie said. "Could anything be simpler?"

"There's no place to send her. I'm not sure the man she had with her last time was even her husband, and she says she has nowhere to go."

Callie shook her head slowly. "She came here to die, is that it? She wants us to watch her die. Or, wait—" She looked at Hannah. "She wants Martha to nurse her."

Hannah gave a sharp nod of her head.

Everyone's gaze shifted to Martha, who had lost all her color.

"You are not to even consider that seriously," Elizabeth said in a firm voice. "If she has nowhere else to go, she must stay at the Red Dog. She can pay one of the LeBlanc girls to look out for her, and Hannah—"

"Not Hannah," Curiosity said. "If Jemima needs doctoring, she will get it from me. I'll sit right there and do what needs be done until she's gone, and then we'll bury her and we'll be shut of her, once and for all."

Martha said, "Why would you do that for Jemima?"

"I wouldn't," Curiosity said. "I'ma do it for you."

Martha was surprised to come out of the shack and into sunshine. It seemed that much more time must have passed; she had come here one person and now she was another, and how could such a thing come to be in a matter of minutes?

Callie touched her arm and started to ask a question, but Daniel was walking toward them. She shook Callie off and went to him, her pace picking up until they met there in the middle of the pasture. Martha put her face to his shoulder and began to shake. She didn't want this; she didn't want Callie or anyone to see her like this, but she could not control it. Daniel's hand cradled her head and he was whispering to her, soft nonsense things that began to work, somehow.

She was aware of other people passing but she stayed as she was. Daniel was shaking his head now and then, telling people to stay away for now.

Then he led her to the springhouse and they went inside.

She leaned against the wall, cool and damp, and made herself breathe. Once, twice, three times she drew in air until her lungs were close to bursting before letting it go.

Daniel was concerned, there was no hiding it. But he would wait. He would wait until she could find the words to tell him that her mother had come back, as Martha had always known she would, to stay. Jemima would be here until she died, and there was no way to escape that fact.

She took a step toward him and he held out his arm, drew her to him, and tucked her up against his good side, and then they settled on the bench. A small bench like any other you'd see in a dairy or woodshed, the plank worn smooth with use. Martha saw now that Daniel's initials were carved into the corner, and she thought of him as a boy, bent over his work. It gave her comfort for a reason she didn't understand.

"Can you talk?"

To her own surprise Martha found that she could. Once she started the words ran like a flood. She was shaking again, and in one part of her mind she wondered if she might simply break into pieces.

When she was finished, Daniel said, "Tell me the rest of it."

She paused and tried to gather her thoughts. There was more, and he knew that without being told.

"I've never told anybody," she said.

He waited, nothing of tension in his body.

"When I was younger," Martha said, "I had a dream almost every night. Always the same dream. I come into the kitchen at the old mill house, and my mother looks up at me. She's sitting at a table. And I walk up to her and I hit her in the head with a hammer. That dream was always so real to me, I felt the force of the blow travel up my arm and shoulder to my own skull. And then I woke up. It didn't stop until I had been in Manhattan for at least a year."

"Martha," Daniel said evenly. "I don't think you're the only person who has dreams about killing Jemima."

A laugh caught in her throat and turned to a sob. "But she's my mother."

"She gave birth to you, but I wouldn't call her your mother."

"That's what Curiosity said."

"Whatever is wrong with her now," Daniel went on, "whatever is coming, she brought that on herself. You have no obligation to nurse her or even to visit her."

"It doesn't feel that way," Martha said.

She might have said the things that were in her mind, but Daniel knew them already, and she disliked herself for them.

What will people think of me turning my back on her now?

He would tell her that it didn't matter, and he was right and wrong all at once.

Daniel said, "I want you to tell me the truth, Martha. Do you want to take her in? If you feel you must, then that's what we'll do. We'll see to it that she has good care, and otherwise we'll stay clear of her."

She shook her head. "You cannot mean that."

"Of course I mean it. If you feel strongly that you must do this thing she is asking of you, then we'll do it together."

"No," Martha said. "I don't want to do it. I don't want her anywhere near our home. I'm not even sure I could be in the same room with her. It doesn't matter how sick she is, I've still got that hammer in my fist, and I can't put it down."

A harsh sound left her throat. "But she's going to drag it out. She'll make us all watch, and wait. She'll hold on to every minute just to make us suffer with her. You don't believe me, but I know it. I know she can do it. That's why she's here."

Daniel's chest rose and fell with his breathing. She pulled away to look at him, his familiar face. His beloved face. What she saw there was understanding and sympathy and concern and nothing of censure or disgust. He pulled her closer and kissed her, a sweet kiss that lingered no longer than a heartbeat. Then he pressed his mouth to her temple and he took a deep breath.

He said, "Martha Bonner, I swear to you, I'll do everything in my power to protect you. Because I love you, and your happiness is the most important thing in the world to me. Now, can we go home, if you're feeling up to it?"

How long had she been hoping to hear him say these things? She had imagined it happening in a dozen different ways, but certainly not like this, hiding away from everyone so she could weep in privacy.

"It's odd," she said. "But there is one good turn my mother did me. She didn't realize it at the time, of course. She just wanted to get me away from Teddy so he couldn't get control of my money, and so I came home to Paradise—"

She broke off, thinking of what might have been. The full truth was that if she had married Teddy and settled into Manhattan society as the wife of one of the sons of the founding families, she might have been happy. Or better said, she might have believed herself happy. She might have gone through the years attending receptions and giving teas, knitting for the poor and volunteering at the hospital, making sure that the cook remembered that Teddy had wanted ham for his dinner, or interviewing nurses who would see more of her children than she would herself.

If she was fortunate she might never have realized what was missing and counted herself fortunate to live as well as she did with a husband who never raised his voice to her. In time she would have become to Teddy what his mother was: a figurehead to be obeyed. Not a wife, not really.

And it was because of her mother that she had escaped that fate.

Martha shook herself and stood. "Yes," she said. "Let's go home."

They had come down from the mountain on foot, and they would have to go back the same way.

"But can we go the long way around? I couldn't bear to talk to anybody about this, and word will be out already."

"We can," Daniel said. "I was going to suggest that anyway, because I need to take you to Eagle Rock."

His expression was sober, his color high. As if he had been weeping too.

"Eagle Rock?"

He touched her lower lip with two fingers. "I have dreams about your mother too, and I think it's time I told you about them."

59

It was well past six, but Ethan's parlor was flooded with light so intense Hannah's eyes watered.

Ethan was saying, "How do you think this could possibly work? Nicholas is sure to hear that she's in the village. There's no way to avoid that unless you want to lock him up until she dies. And then he'll find out anyway, and he'll be hurt and angry. Hannah?"

This was one of the reasons that Hannah had walked home with Callie and Ethan, to be of help to them as they tried to sort out this very complex situation.

Callie's color was high and uneven, and she looked as though she might vomit any moment. "Hannah will agree with you," she said. "You may even be right, both of you, but it doesn't feel right to me."

"You want to protect your brother," Hannah said. "That is understandable. But what you are suggesting will do more harm than good, in the long run."

"I don't want to see her," Callie said. "I refuse to see her. And I don't want him to go alone. Ethan, it is cowardly of me to ask it of you, but would you take—"

"No," Hannah said. "I would rather do it, if you have no objection."

Callie's brow rose in surprise, but Ethan's expression was harder to read. Callie said, "But you needn't. Curiosity—"

"I have to go see Jemima again, at least once," Hannah interrupted her gently. "I promised her more laudanum. After that Curiosity can take over, and I'll be glad of it." Hannah was not good at lying, but she did her very best, and Callie seemed to take her at her word.

"When are you going? Could we get it over with today?"

Ethan frowned, but he held back whatever objection he had.

"I think that's a good idea," Hannah said. "I'll go find Nicholas now and explain to him what's happening, and then afterward I'll bring him home to you."

She felt Ethan's gaze on her, but she knew better than to look at him directly. Not now. Not yet.

"Yes," Callie said. "All right. Ethan, will you go with her to find Nicholas? He might be alarmed otherwise."

Hannah's understanding of Nicholas was so far different from Callie's that they might have been talking about different boys. In her experience he was not easily upset or frightened, and if he knew and liked someone, that person could ask the moon of him and he'd climb a tree to see if he could reach it. But this was not the time to discuss the boy or Callie, and certainly not Callie's grasp of the facts.

Ethan got ready to go, and Martha sat in silence for a moment. Hannah rose from her chair and hesitated.

"Do you have any other questions, before I go?"

Callie shook her head. "Just promise me you'll take care of Nicholas."

"Of course," Hannah said. "Of course I will look out for his best interests."

Though it was early evening the brilliant summer day showed no signs of giving way to twilight as Hannah and Ethan left the house. The seed of a pain that had been sitting between Hannah's brows twisted and turned and blossomed into a headache. Elizabeth had always warned her about the dangers of going about bareheaded in the sun, and now it turned out she was right. It had just taken much longer than anyone would have guessed.

Willow bark tea and a quarter hour in the shade would be enough to set her right. With that thought Hannah realized that she had left her bag . . . where exactly? At home? She tried to remember when she had last had it, and in response the headache dug in its claws.

Ethan would go look for her, if she asked him. She could sit in the shade of the beech trees up ahead, and maybe she would sleep for ten minutes or twenty while he retrieved it. She needed some time to sort things through before she told Ethan the things she thought he needed to know. She knew Ethan as well as she knew anyone in her family, but she was unsure how he would react to Jemima's threats.

What she really wanted was an hour with Ben, to sit down with him someplace quiet. He would listen and then they would talk, passing ideas back and forth, and in the end she would have a better understanding of the choices before her. But right now there was no time. Right now there was Ethan, who walked beside her, his hands crossed at the small of his back.

He had been a quiet, loving boy and he had grown into a good man. Thoughtful, observant, generous to a fault, but always at pains not to draw attention to himself. He had married Callie for reasons that were still unclear to Hannah, but those reasons were also none of her business. They made a good couple, Ethan's even temper complementing Callie's easily roused anger. If there was no obvious passion between them, then that was nothing unusual. She knew married couples who never even looked at each other in public, and who had five and six children—evidence enough that in the privacy of their homes they could give and accept affection.

Without any discussion Ethan turned onto a path that wound its way through the farmsteads to the far side of the village, and Hannah followed. The wind brought them the occasional faint sound of laughter, music, the shrieks of children at play. And the first rifle shots. The sharpshooting had begun. Ben was going to compete again this year, and she had wanted to be there to watch him.

Ethan said, "There's nothing you can say that will surprise me," and Hannah came up out of her thoughts with a jerk. He was looking at her with an expression that said he would have answers to his questions.

"What is she threatening?"

There was no help for it; she could not contain Jemima's seething anger, or protect her family from any of what was to come.

Hannah said, "It's about Martha and Callie."

"Go on."

"That's all I know. That's all she said. It was just—the look on her face. As if she were cherishing the idea of doing Callie—and you— harm. But she said nothing of the why or how. Why should she hate you so much? At first I thought she was bluffing to get her way, but afterward I couldn't stop thinking about that smug look. . . . You'll think I'm imagining things."

"Oh, no," Ethan said. "I'm sure you're right."

"Then what is there to do?"

"One thing I am certain of," Ethan said, "and that is that she stays where she is. Hannah, you can leave this to me now. I'll speak to her. I'll take Nicholas to see her too, so you need never step foot in that room."

Hannah said, "I promised Callie I'd take the boy, and I want to keep my promise."

"Fine," Ethan said, and after a long moment: "Thank you for bringing this to me first."

"Do you—do you have any idea what it is she's talking about?"

"Maybe," Ethan said, his expression both closed off and distant. "Can you leave this to me now?"

"I can try," Hannah said. "I'd like to find Nicholas and get this over with."

Ethan nodded. "The sooner the better."

60

Daniel told Martha the story as best he remembered it.

A hot summer afternoon, the sky clear overhead and he was a pathfinder, leading a family of settlers deep into the frontier. His face painted with clay and chalk as his uncle Runs-from-Bears had taught him. He had gone off trail because there was a war party of Huron nearby, and it was his responsibility to see that the settlers' scalps stayed on their heads where they belonged. He had a tomahawk, the one carved by his grandfather Hawkeye with a handle painted red. He used it to cut through the underbrush, and then stopped when he heard a step behind him. Maybe Aunt Todd had let Ethan come out to play after all. That would be good; it was hard work to ambush a war party by yourself.

But then his sister stepped out onto the deer trail. His twin, determined as ever to have her part in his games, though she was a girl. It did no good to argue with Lily but if he worked at it he might lose her, and so Daniel let out a war whoop meant to startle her and ran off, pushing hard up the mountain, wondering if she would dare follow him if he went as far as Eagle Rock. When he glanced behind him she was there, breathing hard, a scratch across her cheek, her mouth set in a line that meant she would get the best of him if she could.

She kept up and never once asked him to slow down or stop. By the time they hit the first crest his lungs were burning and he knew hers must be on fire. He was already a head taller and hard-muscled, but she was smart and stubborn, and her size didn't seem to slow her down. No matter what tricks he tried, she'd follow. Another time he could be proud of her, but just now he wished he could fly away and leave her behind, a little bit of a girl carrying a fistful of drawings. Drawings, in the bush.

She was three minutes behind at least when he came out of the bush just under Eagle Rock, a boulder as big as a cabin jutting out of the mountain. Standing on top you could see the whole world: the village and Aunt Todd's house on the hill where Ethan had been kept indoors to help her write letters, and a hundred, a thousand mountains. They came here sometimes with Da or Grandda or Runs-from-Bears, but never from below, as he had come this time with Lily following. From below it was crazy dangerous. A steep shifting incline, covered in many inches of loose scree.

He would have set off in another direction but for the voices that told him there was somebody on the rock. Somebody who shouldn't be there. His da would want to know about this and Daniel should run straight home to tell him, but first he needed to find out who was trespassing.

He crept up until he could see over the edge, and then he stayed longer than he meant to, trying to make sense of what he was seeing: two people rolling around on the ground, one of them a woman, her skirts rucked up so that her legs were bare to the sun. The other a man, on top of her, his breeches down around his knees.

Daniel dropped back down, eased himself down all the way until he was crouched under the ledge. He could still hear them, hear the noises they made. They were fucking, a word he had learned not so long ago from the boys in the village. Fucking on Eagle Rock in broad daylight, and who would take such a chance?

But he knew the answer. He had heard enough to recognize their voices.

Then Lily was there. He had almost forgot about her. She stood heaving for breath, and before she could make a single noise he pulled her down next to him and put a hand over her mouth. If she hadn't been struggling to breathe she would have bit him, he was sure of that.

The voices were louder now, an argument so bitter that the taste of bile was in the air. Daniel tightened his grip on his sister, feeling the jump in her pulse and his own.

Will you be quiet?

When she nodded he took his hand away.

It's all right, *he whispered.* They'll go soon.

Who?

Even whispered the names made her jump. Jemima was shouting now: I'll swear a rape.

The sound of a hard slap, and her laughter in response. It gave Daniel a sick feeling to hear that laugh, and still worse was what came next. They were struggling and the whole business started again, Jemima Southern and Liam Kirby fucking on Eagle Rock like snarling dogs.

Lily didn't know yet about fucking, and he wasn't going to tell her. He pressed her arm hard to keep her quiet.

It seemed to go on forever and then the sound of Jemima's laugh came again, sharper and shriller, like the hunting cry of a falcon. Then silence. It seemed that one of them must have gone away, but there was no way to be sure. Daniel wondered how long they should wait, when it would be safe, and with that thought came the rattle of scree.

Jemima stood in the sunlight looking at them where they crouched under the ledge. Her lower lip was bloody and her breasts free. Daniel looked away and Lily took that as permission to fling herself at Jemima.

And from there things went from bad to worse.

Daniel's story took no more than ten minutes. When he had finished he took Martha by the hand and they went into the woods. She allowed herself to be led to a fallen tree, and she sat there beside him.

After a while she said, "I was conceived that day."

"I think so, yes."

"She threatened you."

Daniel nodded. "But none of that came to anything. There was no real harm done."

She turned to look at him. "Why did you tell me this?"

"I haven't told you all of it, yet," Daniel said. "There was one more thing. Something I haven't told anyone, not Lily or my parents. Not anyone."

"Do I want to hear this?"

"Most likely not, but I have to tell it."

She closed her eyes and nodded.

"Lily's ankle looked to be broke, and so I set off to get help and I ran as hard as I could. You know the beaver pond where the stream drops real sudden about six feet? The little waterfall, we used to call it, about halfway between here and Lake in the Clouds. When I got that far I caught my foot on a root and I fell so hard I knocked the breath out of me. Took me a couple minutes to get moving again, but before I could go I heard her. Jemima. She had climbed down to sit on the edge of the pond, and she was weeping. The sound of it surprised me so that I couldn't help myself; I went around to the side where I could see her better, and she was sitting there, bent over for weeping. It was like her heart was being torn out of her, she was shaking and crying so hard."

"What did you do?"

"I am ashamed to say that the first thought that went through my head was to chunk a rock at her, I was that mad. But I was too worried about Lily, so I ran on home and got Runs-from-Bears. And still I couldn't get it out of my mind, Jemima weeping like that. It got all mixed up in my head with the things she said about Hannah."

They sat there in an awkward silence for a while, and then she let out a sigh. "I always had the idea that maybe there was something once between Jemima and Liam Kirby that wasn't ugly. Just for a day or even an hour. I don't know how I held on to that idea all these years." And then, a little sharper: "What were you thinking, that I'd forgive her everything because she shed tears?"

"No," Daniel said. "I'm just hoping you won't hold it against me that I was there that day."

By the time they got home the first fireflies had begun to float over the meadow. The smell of ripening strawberries was in the air, and Martha thought of the bears that would soon come to eat their fill. She would have to keep Hopper on a line for fear he would try to chase them away.

Daniel said, "What are you thinking about?"

"Hopper." And: "We left him with the little people. Should we—"

"They'll bring him by tomorrow," Daniel said.

She didn't like that idea. Hopper belonged here with them, tonight especially. Tonight she wanted to close the shutters and bar the doors to the rest of the world. It was a childish thought, but she could not shake herself free of it.

From the village came the faraway sputtering of the first fireworks.

A thought came to Martha and she spoke it before she could stop herself. "What if it's all a lie? What if she's not really sick at all?"

Daniel might have tried to calm her fears by reminding her that Hannah would not be so easily fooled. Instead he said, "What would that gain her?"

Martha lifted a shoulder. "She might want us off guard. She might have come for Nicholas and known we wouldn't give him up. Maybe it's got something to do with the Bleeding Heart and the orchard. Maybe she plans on kidnapping Nicholas and holding him until she gets what she wants from Callie."

Daniel said, "Would you feel better if I went to make sure Nicholas is safe? I'll take Abel and I can be back in an hour or less. Maybe Callie and Ethan will let me bring him back here, if that will keep him out of harm's way."

For a long moment Martha tried to convince herself that to send Daniel back to the village after such an exhausting day would be self-indulgent and selfish, but the truth was, she was uneasy. And something else she hadn't said, and could not say, was that she would be glad of the hour alone. An hour of quiet to try to make sense of the image he had put in her head, of her mother weeping in the deep of the woods on the day she was conceived.

So many of her memories of Jemima had to do with her mother's determination to get what she needed and wanted at any cost. Curiosity had asked if maybe that wasn't the worst thing you could accuse a woman of, fighting to survive. But Curiosity didn't know about what had happened on the bridge that winter.

"Martha?"

"It would be very good of you, if you aren't too tired."

Daniel kissed her on the brow, his hand resting lightly on the nape of her neck. "I'll be as quick as I can."

She was sitting on the porch when he came around from the stable a few minutes later, leading Abel. Daniel's smile was like a balm, and for a moment she thought of changing her mind and telling him that she was being silly; he needn't go back to the village again. They could sit together and listen to the fireworks, and then later there was their bed and sleep. She would sleep for a day, and when she woke up her head would be clear. Answers would present themselves.

Instead she said, "Could you bring Hopper home with you too?"

"Whatever you need, darlin'."

"I need you," she said, and she managed a smile. "Don't dawdle."

He winked at her, her beautiful husband who knew the worst, and who loved her nonetheless. When he was gone, she went inside to wait for him.

Lily's suspicions about Jennet were proved true just past dark when the fireworks began in the village and Luke came through the door.

He took one look at her and said, "When did the pains start?"

Jennet put out her hands and he pulled her out of her chair. "Och, dinnae fret. I've done this before, after all." She turned her head to wink at Lily over her shoulder.

"I thought you might have started," Lily said.

"And you kept your questions to yourself, for which I thank you. I'll be as happy as the next woman when I've got this child on the outside of me, but there will be no peace for months to come. This afternoon meant a great deal to me."

Luke was in the hall calling for Curiosity.

Jennet said, "You could come along, if you like." And then, in response to the look on Lily's face, "Aye, and why would you?"

"If you would like me there, I will come and gladly," Lily said.

Simon came galloping, bursting into the hall like a boy with an excess of energy. He had taken the time to wash at the pump, so that his hair was damp, his face was new scrubbed, and his expression alarmed.

"Lily," he said, trying not to scowl and failing, "where is it you think you're going?"

"She'll stay right where she is, Ballentyne," Jennet said, one hand supporting her belly. "I'm away to split myself in two. And here's Curiosity, to help me along."

"You are very calm," Lily said to her.

"For the moment, aye. I'll do my fair share of shouting by morning."

"You're going to walk to Downhill House?" Simon looked aghast. "Why not stay here in your own chamber?"

"Don't look at me," Luke said. "I've got no say in any of this."

Curiosity said, "That's right. This is women's business. Come, Jennet, a walk will move things along nicely and my guess is, the shouting will be over long before morning." Then she turned and gave Simon a pointed look. "You go on ahead and tell the story that has got to be told."

Then Lily was alone with Simon, who collapsed next to her on the chaise longue.

"So, my blueberry. Can you tell me why Jennet's been taken off to Downhill House?"

"Because that's where Hannah has all her supplies and medications," Lily said. "That's where she'll want me to be when my time comes."

"And the bairns?"

"They'll send them all over here for the night," Lily said. "So they can distract one another from worry about Jennet."

"And distract us too, forbye." He put a hand on her belly.

Recently Simon had taken to patting her and waiting for a response, which often came in the form of a solid thump or two. The first time this happened his surprise and delight told Lily that he had been afraid to hope. With that soft thump, he finally realized that this child was coming. Tears had filled his eyes, and that alone made all the worry and discomfort worthwhile.

"Blueberry is sleeping," she said. "And let's leave things be. My liver has been mauled enough for one day. Simon, what story was Curiosity talking about?"

He drew in a deep sigh and held it for a moment. His expression alarmed her, and she said so.

"It's just Jemima," he said. "She's back."

And in response to her sharp look, he told her the rest.

"If I were able," Lily said when he had finished, "I would march down to the Red Dog and have a word with Jemima, sick or no."

"Aye," Simon said. "I ken ye so far, Lily. But we must leave this to the others."

"It's our own fault," Lily said. "We were so surprised to see her again, we all backed down. She shows up and makes demands and carries on and we let her."

"And if that's so," Simon said, "it won't be the case for long."

"But she'll make everyone miserable between now and then. If we let her."

"Do ye no think," Simon began slowly, "that it's Martha's place to decide how best to act in this case?"

"No," Lily said. "Martha doesn't see any of this clearly."

"And who does?" said Simon. "In the whole Bonner clan, tell me, which of ye sees clearly how best to handle Jemima?"

---

61

*B*irdie had no memory of falling asleep. One minute she was stretched out on the floor straining to hear the men talking about things that might be interesting some other time, but which right now only got in the way. She never meant to fall asleep, but the sound of their voices was better than a lullabye and sleep came between her and her good intentions.

When she woke the house was quiet and she was aware of two things: She had slept for a long time and must be missing the dancing, and the men were gone without her ever finding out what exactly was going on. As soon as she sat up a few other facts presented themselves: her legs and arms were covered with scratches from climbing the trellis, and she had a cramp in her neck.

Birdie was halfway down the stairs when she heard people coming back into the kitchen. She sat right down where she was and hoped whoever it was was in a talkative mood, and that they'd stay out of the front hall where any grown-up was bound to ask her a dozen questions.

She heard Curiosity say, "Set there while I get some things together. By and by we'll get you settled upstairs. How close are the pains?"

Jennet's voice said, "A quarter hour or so. No great hurry."

There was a moment's silence and then Curiosity said, "I hope Hannah is staying away from the Red Dog, but I doubt she will."

"Jemima will cause as much trouble as she can manage," Jennet said. "And Hannah is drawn to trouble. We all are, who are of Carryck. It's in the blood. All ye need to do is look at the little people, and there it is, plain to see."

Birdie slipped out the front door after a short debate with herself on whether she should stay and help Curiosity until Luke found Hannah and brought her home, or whether she could go down to the Red Dog and find out for herself what it meant that Jemima was back. The fact was, she still did not know what had happened to make all the grown-ups gather in the middle of the day to talk about it. One thing seemed pretty clear: Something was wrong, and it had to do with Jemima. If that was indeed the case then she, Curiosity-called-Birdie, would just have to step in. It would be the quickest way to the answers that seemed determined to hide themselves.

And she was good at talking to difficult grown-ups. She had developed her methods in Daniel's classroom, and perfected them at the dinner table.

It would have been useful to know where everybody had gone, because if she ran into Ma or Da or anybody else who considered themselves in a position to order her around, she'd never get to the Red Dog.

She heard the music before she ever got as far as the main road, which meant the dancing was still going on, and that would make things much easier. Every non-Quaker in Paradise would be there. And then it turned out that her ma and da were in the common room at the Red Dog, which brought her up short for all of ten heartbeats. They were here either to talk to Jemima or because they had already talked to her, but there wasn't any time to waste and so Birdie took herself in hand and found her way around and up by way of the rear stairs.

Pressing her ear to the door gave her no information at all, and so she scratched, very softly. And then more loudly. In response the door thumped as if someone had thrown a book against it.

"Go away," came a woman's voice, rough and raw. "Leave me be."

Birdie took a deep breath and opened the door.

The room was dim and it smelled bad, and the woman on the bed—fully dressed, down to her shoes—was the color of new cheese, a sickly yellow-white. She smiled in a way that reminded Birdie of a hunting cat.

"You are the image of your mother," she said. "But take heart, she got a husband in the end, didn't she. So maybe there's hope for you."

"Oh," Birdie said. "You mean to say my ma's ugly. But that's not true, so it can't upset me." And: "You don't have to prove to me how mean you are. I know that already."

Jemima struggled to sit up higher on her pillows, glaring at Birdie as though she'd like nothing better than to take a bite out of her.

"You're sick," Birdie said. "I didn't know."

With a huff Jemima said, "As if everybody weren't talking about me already. You can keep your lies to yourself, missy."

Birdie sat down on a stool next to a table where a tray with a bowl of broth and a piece of bread had been left untouched.

"Usually people lie because they don't think they can get what they want by telling the truth," Birdie said. She was glad she had someplace to sit where she could watch Jemima that was more than an arm's reach away, because her face had gone pure red with irritation and she seemed the kind to strike out. "That's what Curiosity says. So why would I lie about knowing you were sick? And anyway, don't you hear the music? It's Fourth of July, so I doubt many people are talking about you, if any at all."

Very slowly Jemima said, "Go away now, and leave me be."

"I won't stay long," Birdie said. "I don't have many questions."

Jemima turned her face to the wall.

Birdie said, "What do you want with the Bleeding Heart?"

Jemima turned back. She looked like she was going to spit or laugh or both.

"What?"

"The Bleeding Heart, Callie's apple tree. What do you want with it? Do you want to take over the orchard?"

Jemima's mouth fell open in surprise. "Who told you I wanted the orchard?"

"Well, don't you?" Birdie wished she had written down all her questions because it was hard to keep track.

"I don't care if I never see another apple or apple tree or orchard," Jemima muttered.

"But maybe you wanted it anyway," Birdie said. "People sometimes want things they don't need. They fight to get them and then they don't want them after all, all they were after was the fight itself. Is that what you're after? Or maybe your husband wants it."

"If I could get out of this bed," Jemima said, "I would box your ears."

"Ma says, if people change the subject that's usually because they don't want to answer a question."

"You can spare me your mother's wisdom," Jemima said.

"But you still didn't answer my question," Birdie said. "Do you really want the orchard, or was it just the fight you want?"

"I want what's mine," Jemima said.

Birdie thought for a minute. "The orchard is a lot of work, you know, and it's not Callie's anymore anyway."

"So I hear," Jemima said, her voice hoarse.

"Well, if you're not here for the orchard, does that mean you came to take Nicholas away? Because I hope not. He likes it here and we like him. He's very good at games. He's not book-clever, but he's quick in other ways. He was the first one who figured out about chicken number two."

Jemima closed her eyes and shook her head, and Birdie took this as a sign she didn't understand. So she explained about the last day of school and Curiosity's chickens, and how it had worked exactly the way she had planned with the little people, everybody running around the schoolhouse after the chickens until they got the ones marked "one" and "three" and "four" and then running around again because they couldn't find "two."

Jemima's forehead creased. "You're saying Nicholas found a missing chicken?"

"No," Birdie said.

"Then what did he do?"

"The chicken wasn't lost. People just thought it was."

"So who found it?"

"Nobody," Birdie said patiently. "Because there wasn't a second chicken. There was just 'one' and 'three' and 'four' and Nicholas was looking for 'two' like everybody else, and then he jumped up on the teacher's desk and waved his arms over his head and shouted, *What if there never was a second chicken?*

"And then Daniel and Martha began to laugh—did you know Martha was teaching too?—and everybody laughed. The whole village laughed when the story got out. Except Curiosity, who was mad that we borrowed her chickens. She's fond of her chickens."

Jemima had turned to the wall, and her shoulders were shaking. After a while she got quiet. Still looking at the wall she said, "Who sent you to talk to me?"

"Nobody," said Birdie. "Nobody knows I'm here. I tried to hear what Hannah was telling but I fell asleep, and so I thought I better come down here and find out for myself. And I'll get in some trouble when they find out."

Jemima looked affronted at that idea, so Birdie tried to explain. "Ma wouldn't want me to be here, because she's afraid of what you might do. But I'm not, at least not now. Because I can run faster than you, and I could even if you weren't sick," Birdie said. "You are very sick, aren't you. I can see it in your face."

What Birdie saw in Jemima's face was the mask that came when somebody was sick unto death. She had seen it before, and more than once. She had seen it when Many-Doves was sick, though she was too young then to explain to Hannah. Many-Doves had understood without being told, and she talked to Birdie about what it meant to see such things, how it was a gift from the Maker of Life and with time she would learn how to use it to help people pass into the shadow lands. Because sometimes that was all a doctor or a healer could do, take the sick person's hand and get them ready to go. Especially white people, who were afraid of the dark.

"You haven't answered any of my questions, you know. Not about the Bleeding Heart and not about Nicholas either."

"I haven't," Jemima said. "And I won't."

"It looks to me like you're not well enough to travel," Birdie told her. "So Nicholas won't have to go." She didn't say, *because you're dying*. Instead she said:

"You don't have to worry about people being mean to Nicholas because of you," she said. "You don't have to worry about him going without, because Callie wouldn't let that happen and neither would Martha. And neither would my folks, because Martha and Callie belong to us now and so Nicholas is one of us. You may hate that idea, but the truth is, as long as he stays here he'll be happy. The same is true of Martha, because she's not going anywhere and you can't make her do anything. It's too late for that."

Jemima was staring at her again, but the heat was gone from her face. There was no anger there and not even any irritation, which was usually what happened when Birdie got to talking with grown-ups this way. She just looked tired and sick.

She said, "What about Callie? Is she happy?"

"I don't think she knows how to be happy," Birdie said. "Maybe she never got the hang of it, even when she was little. Because her ma was sick and because everybody went off without her and left her alone. All she cared about for a long time was the orchard, but that didn't make her happy either because the crop kept failing. Which is why I don't think you really want the orchard, even if the Bleeding Heart does turn out as good as Callie hopes."

"What difference would that make?" Jemima said. "She sold the orchard, to Levi Fiddler, of all people. Levi and *Lorena*—" She made a disgusted voice deep in her throat.

Birdie took a deep breath. "You don't understand, then. You don't understand how Callie thinks about the orchard. It don't much matter to her if she owns it, but it does matter that something comes of it. Her father loved the orchard and she loved it for his sake. Haven't you ever done anything for the love of it?"

For a long time Birdie thought Jemima had gone to sleep and she wouldn't answer, but then she did. She said, "People here think they know me, but they don't. They don't know the first thing about me."

"I don't think you want people to know," Birdie said. "I don't think you know yourself."

Jemima's face twisted. She said, "What do you want of me?"

"I don't need anything from you," Birdie said.

"Then get out of here," said Jemima. "And leave me alone."

62

$\mathcal{I}$t seemed to Elizabeth that in extreme duress a particular mood fell over the village, a living thing with tendrils that reached everywhere and bound everyone together. It had happened during the flood, it had happened when fire burned down the Maynards' barn, and when disease stole whole generations of children from one family or another. That same mood could turn abruptly and bring out the worst of man. The slaughter of a thousand birds for no reason but bloodlust, the push toward war. Her first year in Paradise she had seen the worst come to pass, when a few men had roused the village—much smaller then—to move against the Mohawk on Hidden Wolf.

Her father-in-law had been one of the few people who could put a stop to trouble with nothing more than a few well-placed words. Even the drunkest, most bellicose trapper had backed down when Hawkeye stood up and looked him in the eye.

Why those things should come to mind Elizabeth was not at all sure. The feeling of foreboding that followed her from home all the way down to the village had no grounding, as far as she could tell, in any observable fact. It was impossible to imagine that the village might rise up in outrage *for* Jemima, who had no friends here. Once word was out that Martha was refusing to take Jemima in, Missy O'Brien might try to work up outrage about a child unwilling to look after a sick mother. Then again, Missy's own husband had a complicated and unhappy history with Jemima—one that Missy would prefer to forget—and so it seemed unlikely that trouble could come from that corner. Nor could Elizabeth imagine a crowd storming the Red Dog to serve justice to a dying woman. That kind of mob needed a leader who was skilled at directing violence in a particular direction.

The situation, when she could make herself look at it dispassionately, was not very complicated. A woman they had thought gone for good, someone many people had cause to dislike or even hate, that woman had come back to Paradise to die. Why exactly she had done such a thing was a mystery that might never be solved beyond one basic and undeniable fact: She would suit herself, regardless of the trouble and pain she visited on her daughter and stepdaughter and their families.

Nothing Hannah had told them of Jemima's demands had surprised Elizabeth, but she had learned to trust her own instincts, and she knew somehow that there was more to this story. Turning onto the Johnstown Road she realized what it was.

Not the story Hannah had told, but Hannah's own manner when she delivered it. She had lost many patients over the years to disease and injury, old people and young. Even the most tragic cases, the ones that must break even the most stalwart of hearts, even then Hannah maintained her calm.

And now, less than an hour ago she had stood in a circle of women of her own family, and she had struggled but failed to completely hide her disquiet.

Elizabeth was irritated with herself that she had not registered this at the time, but the shock of the news about Jemima had made Elizabeth turn all her focus to Martha and Callie. She had missed the signs, but she was sure Nathaniel had not.

Once they had agreed on a course of action, everyone had scattered. Martha and Daniel left for home while Ethan and Callie and Hannah herself had gone in the other direction. Simon took Curiosity to see

Jennet and Lily, who had been alone far too long and who would need to hear the news about Jemima. Luke and Ben had gone back to the village to round up the little people, and she, determined to bring Jemima to heel, had set off to see her, alone.

As the Red Dog came into view Elizabeth realized that the news of Jemima's arrival would have already spread through the village. This was clear to her because there was a small crowd outside the Red Dog, people who normally would not have left the lakeside until very late, when the fireworks had come and gone. Jemima was come, and there would be more rumors about where she had been and why she was back like this, without her husband. They would be trading opinions and theories fueled by ale and high spirits. Elizabeth could almost read it in their faces.

Except they weren't looking at her, but beyond her, so that when Nathaniel's hand settled on her shoulder she stopped and leaned back against him in relief.

"Married all these years," he said. "And you're still making me run after you."

Becca came outside just then and started right for them, her arms crossed tight at her waist, as if she were in physical pain.

"Elizabeth," she said in a low voice. "Nathaniel. I want you to know I had no idea about Jemima coming back. She never wrote to me. I didn't even know she was here until an hour ago. It was Alice and Joan who arranged it all with her, and I hope you know they are sorry just now that they were ever brought into this world. Almost as sorry as I am for the trouble they have caused."

Elizabeth managed a small but reassuring smile. "Becca, you have nothing to apologize for."

"I have Alice," Becca said, bitterly. "And I have Joan. I have took the liberty of telling Joan she won't be coming back to work for you anymore. I'll see to it you get somebody better deserving of your trust. I just don't understand, after all the stories I told of Jemima as a girl, and the misery she was to me when we went into service together. How terrible she was after she tricked Isaiah into marrying her, to me and Cookie both. I said to them, I said, whatever she promised you, you can forget about. Jemima Southern never kept a promise in her life. She's using you like she uses everybody."

Becca drew in a breath to steady herself.

Nathaniel said, "Becca, there's no call for you to work yourself up this way. Put Jemima out of your head."

Becca took a darting look around herself, leaned forward, and dropped her voice even lower.

"Is it true she's real sick?"

Elizabeth nodded.

"And that tomorrow she's moving up to the strawberry fields so Martha can look after her?"

"No," Nathaniel said firmly. "Unless you kick her out she'll be staying right where she is. Curiosity and Hannah will manage nursing her between them."

"It's cowardly of me, but I don't want to be the one to tell her she's not going to Martha's," Becca said.

"On the contrary," Elizabeth said. "It is proof of your native good sense."

That got a smile from Becca.

"If you were hoping to speak to her just now, I don't know what to tell you," she said. "After she heard the news about Lenora getting married she threw a fit, and now she's locked her door and says she won't see anybody before Hannah comes back to talk to her." She bit her lower lip hard enough to break the skin. "I knew she'd be trouble. I knew I should have turned her out that first time she showed up. You could just kick down the door, Nathaniel. I wouldn't mind one bit."

"I think not," Elizabeth said. "We'll just wait for Hannah. She will be here very shortly."

"Maybe we could get some of your cider while we're waiting," Nathaniel said. "This heat gives a man a thirst."

63

$\mathcal{H}$annah cut across the Mayfairs' pasture, the most direct path to the middle of the village where she was most likely to find the little people. She wished she knew where her stepmother was. Elizabeth would be the right person to take along on this errand; she was one of the few people Jemima seemed to respect, in a limited way.

Sometime between this moment and finding Nicholas she'd have to think about how to tell the boy the things he needed to know, and prepare him for his mother's condition. She was still thinking about this when she was caught up in the crowd impatient to start dancing. They filled the open space that stretched from the trading post to the school-house, full of energy and excitement and, many of them, an excess of ale. In their middle Levi stood on a small wooden stage, his fiddle already tucked up under his chin. Next to him was Maurice Petit, a French trapper who had made a name for himself calling out dance steps in his own particular way. Over ten years he had developed a patter that added a lot of laughter to what had once been a fairly serious business of trying to remember complex steps. Some claimed that they couldn't dance anymore unless Maurice was there telling them which way to go, bouncing up and down on his toes like a puppet on a string.

People were calling out suggestions, and Levi was nodding and smiling. It always went this way; Levi held a cupped hand to his ear and made a serious face while people shouted up at him. Then he played what he wanted to play. While Hannah watched, Levi and Maurice launched into "Sweet Peas," and the crowd hollered its appreciation. Even over that noise Maurice could be heard, and in fact the children called him Moose Maurice for the way he bellowed.

In his heavy French accent he shouted out the moves—three-hand swing, cage the bird, ladies' ring—pausing now and then to bellow at somebody who was a beat behind or, more often, a young woman who knew how to move. He would break into rhymes he seemed to come up with spontaneously, because Hannah had never heard him repeat one.

> It's right by left by wrong you go,
> Step right lively, *à la fois,*
> Madame around, Monsieur bow low,
> Run the gauntlet and duck that blow
> Wheel left and greet your beau.

Another time she would have been here dancing with Ben, and enjoying herself mightily. Now Hannah made a circle around the dance, but there was no sign of the little people. She had turned toward the road down to the lake when she saw them coming toward her at a trot, each and every face grim and worried. Evidence enough that news of Jemima's arrival had already reached them. The boys walked in almost military formation, with Nicholas in their middle.

They stopped in front of her. As Nathan was the oldest when Birdie was absent—and where was Birdie, Hannah wondered—he took one step forward and cleared his throat to recite a speech.

"Auntie Hannah," he began. "We heard that Jemima is back."

"That much is true," Hannah said.

"And we heard she's here to fetch Nicholas and take him away, and there's nothing anybody can do about it. He has to go whether he wants to or not. And Lorena can't go with him because she married Levi, and Nicholas doesn't want to go. He wants to stay here with Lorena. And us."

Hannah said, "Who told you all this?"

"Lots of people," said Mariah.

"Maggie and Kate LeBlanc," said Adam.

"Jonah Ratz," added Nathan.

"Cam Cunningham."

"Georgia Blackhouse."

Hannah held up a hand to stop them. "So, everybody is saying these things."

Heads nodded. At least the news about Jemima's health had not begun to circulate.

She said, "What have I told you about rumors?"

Isabel leapt in the air, waving madly. "Rumor grows as it goes!"

John had come up beside her and now he leaned into her leg and rubbed his face against her hip. Hannah cradled his head and wished that she could still pick him up, but at five he was more than half her height. All the boys were big-boned and tall for their ages, and she mourned those days when she could carry them easily. It was to her the essence of motherhood, and it was why when she thought of Nicholas, she thought of Lorena. She had held him and rocked him and sung to him; she was, in Hannah's mind, his mother.

Nicholas spoke for the first time. "Do you mean my ma ain't here?"

"She's here," Hannah said. "But there's no talk of taking you anywhere."

He made a thoughtful face. "Does Lorena know?"

"I'm not sure. Will you come with me now so you can see your ma?"

The boy blinked at her as if he were on the edge of sleep. He let out a great sigh, came forward, and took her by the hand.

"What about us?" Amelie said. "Can we come too?"

"No," said Henry gently. "Let Ma take him on her own."

"You can all stay right here and watch the dancing," Hannah said. "I believe we should be back in time for the fireworks. Henry?"

"I've got hold of her, Ma," said her oldest. He took his littlest sister by the hand and then turned toward the dancing.

On the way to the Red Dog Hannah told Nicholas that his mother was ill, and then answered his questions, which would have been amusing, if not for the seriousness of the situation. As plainly as she could, she explained, and still she wasn't sure he understood; the words didn't make a picture for him. Jemima herself would have to do that.

She said, "If your ma seems crabby, it's because she's feeling so poorly," Hannah said.

"Ma is never mean to me," Nicholas said with great seriousness. "No matter how mad she is at other people. Once she threw a vase at Mr. Focht she was so mad at him, but when she saw me she smiled. Ma gets mad easy, but not at me. Maybe when I'm older."

Before Hannah could think how to respond to this speech, he was off again.

"Ma says if she doesn't fight for what's hers and mine, nobody will. She seems mad when she talks like that, but mostly I think she's scared. Did you know my ma used to sing in a theater? There was music and costumes and she sang. She told me some of the stories. Someday maybe I can go to the theater and watch."

Then they were at the Red Dog and Luke was coming toward them with a focused look that told her what he had to say before he ever opened his mouth. Elizabeth was right behind him, and Da. The sight of those three faces worked like a balm.

Nicholas dropped her hand and went straight to Luke who put a hand on the boy's head and smiled down at him briefly.

Hannah said, "Jennet?"

He nodded. "Curiosity's at Downhill House with her. Alone."

"I'm on my way already," Elizabeth said. "You needn't rush if you have something to do—" She smiled at Nicholas, and he smiled back at her, though it was for him a quiet smile.

"I have this call to make," Hannah said, meeting her father's eye. "And then I said I'd stop by the fireworks so I can fetch the little people home."

Nicholas looked up at her hopefully.

"Now see," Hannah's father said. "There's an idea that's got his attention. Do you want to come up the hill after the fireworks?"

Nicholas hesitated. "Will my sisters be there?"

The breath caught in Hannah's throat. "I don't think so. Why do you ask?"

"Because of Ma," said the boy. "Because Ma will want to see them."

"One thing at a time," Luke said.

It was the kind of thing adults said to children. She said such things to her own, when she wanted to reassure them without making promises. And Nicholas accepted it just as her children did, with a blind faith that was touching, and frightening too.

At the foot of the stair Hannah stopped and turned Nicholas toward her. In the light of a brace of tallow candles his expression seem to jump and shift, all nerves.

She said, "You understand how to act in a sickroom? No loud talking or jumping. Try not to excite her."

The boy's eyes widened. "You mean I can't tell her about Harper?"

"She's already heard about Harper," Hannah said. "Do you understand me, Nicholas? Your ma is very ill."

Nicholas glanced up and then jolted so violently that Hannah herself jumped, even before she saw that Birdie was standing at the top of the stairs. She closed her eyes briefly and when she opened them again Birdie was standing right in front of them.

"Little girl," Hannah said, struggling to contain her tone. "What have you been up to now?"

Birdie straightened her shoulders as if she were going into battle, but before she could answer Nicholas jumped in.

"Will you come with me now to see my ma? Please?"

It was the first clear sign that he was worried and agitated, and the only thing that could convince Hannah that Birdie should join them. She pointed up the stair with a movement of her head.

Birdie started to say something and Hannah shot her a look that made her fall silent.

"My ma's sick," Nicholas said to Birdie just as Hannah knocked at the door.

"Leave me alone!"

"It's me," Hannah said. "And I've brought Nicholas to see you."

They moved into the room, all three of them in a row. Birdie came last, and she came reluctantly. If Nicholas hadn't had her by the hand, she would have bolted.

Jemima said, "Oh, look, you've grown since I've been gone."

"Ma," Nicholas said, walking right up to her bedside and leaning in to look her in the eye. "Ma, is it true you wanted to take the orchard away from my sister Callie? They said you did but I said that couldn't be true. I said you wouldn't be so mean, and they said—" His voice trailed away.

The look Jemima sent Hannah was pure poison. "Have the Bonners been telling you these lies?"

He looked confused for a moment, and then shook his head. "I heard them right here," he said. "Downstairs in the common room. Callie doesn't even own the orchard anymore, she sold it to Levi, did you know that? Are you going to try to take it away from Levi? I don't understand why you'd want an orchard, that's why I told them it wasn't true."

Jemima took a deep breath and let it out slowly. She said, "Once I thought the orchard was rightfully yours, and that you should have it. Property passes from father to son; do you remember us talking about that?"

"Oh," Nicholas said, bright color coming into his cheeks. "But I don't want the orchard, Ma. I like helping there, but I wouldn't know how to take care of it. I'm just a boy."

Jemima was trying to control her urges, Hannah could see that. "Birdie and I could leave," she said to mother and son. "We could wait in the hall."

"Yes," Jemima said.

"No," Nicholas said. "Please let them stay, Ma, so if I forget what you said exactly they can remind me. Are you angry with me if I don't want the orchard?"

Jemima forced a smile. "I'm not angry with you."

His color climbed another notch, in pleasure or relief or both.

"You look awful sick, Ma."

"I am sick, but I feel better just now. Will you come to see me every day? I'm going to be at your sister Martha's house—"

"No," Hannah said. "No, I wasn't able to arrange that. Nicholas, you'll be able to visit your ma right here. She's only a few minutes away."

Jemima went still, all expression wiped from her face. "Son," she said. "Take Birdie and wait in the hall while I talk with Hannah, would you?"

In the hall, Birdie's legs were so shaky that she sat right down on the floor. She had thought maybe no one would ever know that she had come to talk to Jemima, and then to run into Hannah three steps out the door—that was bad luck. If she had had some good news to bring home, she wouldn't have minded, but she didn't. All she had done was to convince herself once and for all that Jemima wasn't interested in making things better.

And now Nicholas sat beside her, very quiet and still. She wondered if Hannah had said how sick his ma was, and decided she had not. It was not the kind of thing she'd tell in passing. It might be that Nicholas had reasoned some things out for himself, as he did now and then. Birdie tried to imagine how she would feel if her ma were as sick as Nicholas's, and a hot fear gripped her.

They could hear voices seesawing back and forth, but the words weren't clear.

Nicholas said, "What do we do if Ma starts to throw things at Hannah?"

"Hannah has been to war," Birdie told him. "Hannah has been in the middle of battles, taking care of wounded men. It's hard to get the best of Hannah." She wished she felt as sure as she sounded. She wished Hannah would come out so they could go home. She wanted to be somewhere else, and not in this hall with its bright white curtains at the window and the polished rail. She didn't want to be here when Hannah sat down with Nicholas and told him about how sick his ma really was.

And still it seemed like a very long time before Hannah came. To Birdie it seemed too as if Hannah had simply forgot they were waiting, because when she saw them she started.

"I'll bring you back tomorrow to see your ma," she told Nicholas. "Right now she is very tired and needs to sleep."

Nicholas looked uncertainly between the door and Hannah, and then he nodded. "Can I go home with you and Birdie?"

Hannah closed her eyes briefly. Birdie had never seen her so tired, and she still had to go help Jennet have her baby.

She said, "I think Callie would be very worried if you didn't come home first. Shall we go ask her? We can talk along the way."

Birdie felt the sudden sting of tears in her eyes. To her sister she said, "I think the fireworks are done, so I'll go fetch the little people and start home with them."

Hannah touched her cheek. "Thank you," she said softly. As if Birdie would want to be there when she told Nicholas that his ma was dying, and she was sacrificing something by leaving them.

Just at this moment Birdie couldn't remember why it had seemed so important to talk to Jemima. She wished she never had.

64

$\mathcal{D}$aniel meant to go straight home to Martha; that had been his firm intention. And yet he found himself in the dark schoolhouse while outside the dancing and drinking and hollering rolled along like a rock down a hillside.

Blue-Jay and Ethan were crouched opposite him. It was the natural way for the three of them to talk. As boys they had handled every challenge and cooked up every scheme just like this. How to remove a pan of maple sugar from under Many-Doves's watchful eye, where they might get nails for an addition to their fort, how they would fit chores around the smelt run, how to remind the Ratz boys that they had best keep clear of sisters, how many pups Blue was going to have and who had a claim to one.

They had been clever, almost as clever as they believed themselves to be. A few times they managed to get away with something small, though now, looking back, Daniel understood they had not got away with much at all. Parents had chosen their battles carefully, as was necessary with three boys as they had been. Full of ideas and energy, a combination that sometimes ended in high spirits, and sometimes in days of extra chores.

Now they were men. All three of them married, a thing Daniel had doubted would ever happen. He had doubted it for himself, and for Ethan. Both of them so cautious about the idea that it might have been avoided indefinitely. If not for Jemima Southern and the threat she posed, he wondered how long it would have taken for him to get down to business with Martha. Put aside his doubts and worries and ask her straight out if she wanted to be married to a one-armed school-teacher.

He had thought Blue-Jay lucky, back when they were young and before the war. It was the Mohawk way for women to handle such things. A girl's mother talked to a boy's mother, and if the boy liked the idea, the girl had the final decision. It had worked that way with Terese; Blue-Jay had married her because he liked what he knew of her and she had wanted him. The trouble that followed was a lesson to all three of them, though Blue-Jay bore the brunt and then learned from that. The day after he first talked to Susanna Mayfair at Meeting, he had crouched down like this with Daniel and Ethan and made a plan, how he was going to pursue her and what he wanted out of that.

Now that Daniel had gone through it himself he understood better what he had only sensed before. It could go wrong no matter how you approached it, and if you wanted it to go right, it took a lot of work.

For Daniel and Ethan things had moved too fast, and they had never had the chance to talk like this. In fact, they hadn't talked for a long time, since before the flood. Daniel realized how much he had missed these discussions.

Ethan was saying, "We have to do something."

"She'll be dead in a week," Blue-Jay said.

"The damage she could do in a week is substantial," Ethan said.

Daniel wondered exactly what kind of damage Ethan was worried about, but he kept that question to himself.

Blue-Jay studied the floor. "Are you saying we should put a bullet in her?"

Ethan was as angry as Daniel had ever seen him. It might have to do solely with Callie and Nicholas, but then Ethan had his own history with Jemima.

He gave a quick shake of the head: not that. Not yet.

"We could take her up to Lake in the Clouds," Blue-Jay said. "She'd be out of troublemaking range, and Susanna would nurse her."

Daniel said, "That would stretch even Susanna's goodwill to the breaking point."

"For you and me, sure. But Jemima has no power over Susanna."

"Jemima will fight the idea," Ethan said, but his tone was hopeful.

"We'll tell her we're taking her to Daniel's," Blue-Jay said. "And then we'll just keep on going. She can holler her head off. It won't matter."

Within a quarter hour they had sorted out the details: Blue-Jay would head home now so that Susanna had time to make a chamber ready, and Daniel would go home to Martha to put her mind to rest about Nicholas. When the village was quiet, Ethan would bring Jemima up the mountain to Lake in the Clouds.

"You think you can handle her on your own?" Daniel asked Ethan.

"I'll ask your da to help me," he said. "And Bears and maybe Gabriel. To keep me from putting that bullet in her head."

"Well, sure," Daniel said. "Just the men to take along if you want somebody to preach non-violence."

Any other time it would have made Ethan smile, but he seemed not to hear at all. That silence caught Blue-Jay's attention, and he lifted a brow in Daniel's direction.

"Ethan," Daniel said. "Is there something more going on here that we don't know about? That we should know about?"

"No," Ethan said. "Not a thing you should know about."

Daniel had the sense that he had asked the wrong question. It followed him all the way home, while Hopper snored in his saddlebag.

65

*C*harlie LeBlanc came to bed late, as he usually did, but he also came to bed sober, which was unusual. Especially on a holiday like this one, where ale ran so free. The oddness of it woke Becca, and she sat up.

"What is it? What's wrong?"

"Nathaniel and Ethan came by, and they had Callie with them."

"Was there news about Jennet?"

"She's still at it," Charlie yawned. "They were here to take Jemima away."

"What?"

He turned to look at her over his shoulder, the candlelight casting the planes of his face into stark relief.

"They told me she was likely to make a fuss, and I should stand by so she couldn't say they handled her rough. Ethan settled her bill."

"*Did* she make a fuss?"

Charlie shook his head. "It was right odd, Becca. Nathaniel was helping her down the stairs and when she passed me she smiled and she said sweet as pie, 'If you find my body at the bottom of a cliff, this time you'll know who's responsible.'"

Becca drew in a sharp breath.

Charlie said, "I told her not to talk like that."

"I'm sure she took it to heart," Becca said dryly. "How did Callie react when she said that?"

"You know Callie's temper. She lashed right out and said, 'Old woman, if I wanted to kill you I wouldn't go to the trouble of dragging you up Hidden Wolf first.'"

"I knew Jemima wanted to go to Martha's," Becca said. "But I didn't think they'd let her. You'd think she'd be happy to get her way."

Charlie lifted a shoulder and let it drop. "I don't think anybody will ever understand that woman. Or how she came to have such a sweet boy."

"I understand her," Becca said, lying down again. "She's as mean as a snake and twice as twisty, and thank the dear Lord that Nicholas takes after his da."

"It's not like you to be so uncharitable," Charlie said. "The woman is dying."

"Let her get on with it, then," Becca said. "It cain't come soon enough. Can you remember a time when she wasn't causing trouble?"

"If you put it that way," Charlie said, and blew out the candle.

Daniel came out on the porch and Martha said, "Did you really think I'd be able to sleep?"

He shook his head and put an arm around her shoulder. The night was warm and there was a breeze that stirred the grass and Martha's loosened hair. She smelled of soap and salt, and if there had been any real light Daniel knew what he'd see: her face swollen with weeping.

"I didn't think you'd want to wait and watch," he said.

"I'm not sure I do, but I don't seem to be able to stay away. Daniel?"

"Hmmm?"

"Have you thought much about having children?"

He knew she felt the jolt that ran through him, because she held up a hand. "I'm not."

"Not yet," he said.

She would be blushing, but her voice was calm. "Not yet. But I've been thinking about it. I don't know if I can. That is, I'm fairly sure I'm capable—" Her voice trailed away.

Daniel drew in a deep breath and let it go. "You are physically capable—"

"I assume so."

"—but in your mind you feel unprepared."

"In my heart and mind, yes."

"Who is ever prepared for a first child?"

"No," she said. "It's worse than that. For Lily it's different than it is for me. Don't you know what I mean?" A tinge of exasperation and unhappiness in her tone and she shifted uneasily on the bench.

"Yes, I think I do. You're afraid that you'll be a mother like your mother was."

"I'm afraid that I will turn into that kind of mother."

She seemed to be waiting for permission to go on. He said, "Martha, I'm listening."

"I know. I know you are. When I was young, I had this odd idea that every mother was like mine, but some were just better at hiding it. Becca, for example. She's gruff, but there's no doubting how she feels about her children. Even when she yelled at them, you could feel it. But I was sure that it was all for show."

"Maybe it was easier for you to live with that idea," Daniel said.

"Maybe."

"When did you figure out that some women do make good mothers?"

She was quiet for a moment. "I'm not sure I ever did. Sometimes when I see a woman who is loving and open with her children, I still feel some doubt. Even with Amanda, and she is the gentlest, kindest soul I know. Even there I wondered now and then what stories Peter might tell if I asked him the right way."

"So. Are you saying you don't want to have children at all?"

She turned to rub her cheek on his shoulder. "That's the problem, Daniel. I do want to have them. Whenever we're together some part of me hopes I'll catch, but then afterward—the thought frightens me."

After a long moment Daniel said, "Did you ever wonder what kind of mother Jemima would have been if Liam Kirby had loved her and married her? If he had been there to help raise you?"

She lifted her face to look at him. "I have to say that never occurred to me. I wonder why not, why I can't imagine her happy, and that's—I don't know what it is. Sad, or tragic. She sometimes told me that if I hadn't been born, things would have gone differently for her."

"And I thought I couldn't get any madder at her than I am already. She blamed you for her mistakes." His voice had taken on an edge, but he couldn't stop himself. "She's a sorry excuse for a human being. You know that you weren't responsible for her unhappiness, I hope."

"In theory, yes." She said it very quietly.

"I can tell you one thing for sure," Daniel said. "There's no simple explanation for why a person turns out the way they do. Good parents or bad, rich or poor. Your grandmother Southern was a good woman, but Jemima still turned out the way she did. And then there's Becca; you said yourself that she's a good mother, but her own mother was a drunk, and mean too. Maybe you haven't heard those stories, but it's true."

"I've heard them. Curiosity told me some of that, and she said something I forgot about until just now. She said, the reason Becca works so hard and never allows herself a moment's peace is because she's running away from the idea of her mother. Trying to prove to herself that she's not the same person."

"Yes, that makes sense," Daniel said. "I wonder she hasn't dropped dead of exhaustion long ago."

Martha laughed, a short tight sound.

He said, "All I know to do is to be here, Martha. You don't have anything to prove to me. You may doubt that it's in you to be a good mother, but I don't, not for a second. Maybe if we hadn't been rushed into marrying I could have had time to make you understand how I see you, and how fine you are to me. I should tell you more often, but words don't always come easy."

He felt her relaxing against him and it made him want to hold her tighter, to turn her to him and show her what he meant to say.

She said, "Listen."

In the clear night air there was no mistaking the sound of horse and cart coming up the trail. Hopper roused himself and growled, the fur standing up on the back of his neck until Daniel spoke a word.

Martha was up and moving slowly toward the sound. It drew her forward as steadily and unrelenting as a rope. He could call her back, but he doubted she'd even hear him. Following her at the right distance, that was the trick, but then she stood there in the dark, all the color leached away so that it seemed to him, for that moment, that he could see through her, see her bones and the flow of blood and the shapes of her muscles.

He took her hand. Her pulse was hammering high and fast, while his own heart seemed to be settling into a preternaturally slow rhythm. Daniel was aware of the knife at his hip, of the sweat trickling down his back, of the nightbirds in the woods and the stars overhead.

He wanted to take her back into the house, but she wouldn't thank him for his interference. She had decided upon a course of action, and he would not try to stop her.

Martha drew in a short sharp breath when Nathaniel came out of the woods. He was carrying a lantern that swung in rhythm with his step, with Florida following.

It was true, then. It was happening. They would take Jemima to Lake in the Clouds, where Susanna would nurse her until she died.

The cart Florida pulled was just big enough for a couple lambs or barrels, but it would handle the mountain trail all the way up. They had lined it with something, quilts or blankets, and turned it into a makeshift chair. A throne, of sorts, where Martha's mother sat wrapped in blankets despite the heat. The swinging lantern revealed a shoulder, a cheek, the jawline in turn.

Ethan followed with another lantern, and behind Ethan came Callie. Martha's breath caught in her throat.

Beside her Daniel said, "Callie'll do what she must, and so will you."

"I can't leave her to handle it on her own," Martha said.

"You can," Daniel said.

Nathaniel and Ethan raised hands in greeting but their pace didn't slacken. Callie's gaze was fixed on the cart. Martha had the idea that Callie wasn't even aware of where she was.

"I'll regret it for the rest of my life if I leave her to do this alone."

Daniel started to say something and then fell silent, because the figure in the cart shifted and a harsh voice was rising in question. It was Nathaniel who turned to answer, and in response Jemima's voice rose another octave. Callie's voice and then Jemima's, both sharp as sticks.

"Martha!" Jemima yelled. "I can see you there. Martha! Will you send me off to die among strangers?" She was struggling to free herself of the covers, shouting at Nathaniel to stop, to stop right here, to stop right here or by God she would put out his eyes.

The cart stopped, and Martha began to move forward with Daniel by her side.

Callie called out, "Go back. Go back. There's no talking to her. She's as mean and stubborn as she ever was."

"Martha Kuick!" Jemima shouted, her voice cracking. "You get over here right now or I will box your ears, I promise you that, missy."

Those words came out of the past and struck Martha with such force that she stopped, unsure of herself and the world around her. Everything folded in upon itself and narrowed to a small island of wavering lantern light on the border between open field and the dark of the woods, between herself and the woman who had borne her and raised her, the woman who demanded recognition, who would wring it from her like water from a rag, if Martha let her. Out of pity, out of guilt and a regret she could hardly explain to herself.

For that moment Martha met her mother's gaze and a great stillness came over her, an understanding. Jemima was dying, and she was afraid. Fear and desperation had brought her back to Paradise, and to this spot on the mountain. In her rage she would strike out, as vicious as an animal caught in a trap, and she would strike first at those who were bound by blood to care for her. The mother Martha had wanted, the mother she had wanted to believe lived deep within the mother she knew, she would not show herself in these last days. There would be no gentle words or kindness, because that woman had never existed.

The woman in the cart, and the people who stood nearby talking to her and to one another, their voices small and distant . . . Martha was aware only of herself and Daniel, standing so close that she felt the heat of his body. Close enough to touch, but not touching. Waiting.

She drew in a hitching breath and held it for three heartbeats. Then Martha turned and started back for the house.

Behind them the cart began to move again, Florida tossing her head so that her harness jingled. Jemima was still shouting, her voice so strained that the words came out first garbled and then not at all. She hissed and squawked like an angry goose, but the cart moved on and she went with it.

Martha was aware of Daniel looking over his shoulder to watch. Then he stopped so suddenly that she would have fallen if he hadn't steadied her.

"What?" she said. "What?"

Daniel said, "It's Levi. Stay here." And he ran off at a lope toward the group that had stopped again, just short of the spot where the trail turned into the wood.

Martha watched Daniel moving away from her, and then she jolted out of her waking dream.

She raised her skirts in her hands and ran after him.

Daniel was aware of his father's steady voice, talking in a tone most people recognized as something to take seriously.

"Levi," he was saying. "You won't mind me pointing out that laying in wait with a loaded musket ain't exactly neighborly."

"My business is with her," Levi said, jerking his head toward Jemima.

"I was wondering if you'd ever get around to it," Jemima said. She sounded almost pleased. "All these years you been thinking about this, haven't you. Getting me alone and making me pay."

Ethan said, "We could gag her."

"You should take your own advice," Jemima said. "Unless you want me to start talking about *you*."

Levi held the musket easily, like any tool a man might pick up to fix what was broken. Daniel felt the weight of the knife under his hand. It would be easy enough to disarm the man, if things got that far. If he could make himself do it.

"She wants to talk about my mother," Levi said. "Let her talk." He looked at no one but Jemima, even when he was speaking to someone else.

"He wants a confession," Jemima said to no one at all.

"Now see," Nathaniel said to Levi. "I know you're too smart to let her draw you into one of her traps. She'll poke at you until you boil over and point that gun at her. That's what she wants, Levi."

Jemima let out a barking laugh, but Levi's face was stony. He said, "I'd be glad to oblige you, if you want to die right here and now. As soon as you confess."

"You first," said Jemima. "You tell everybody how it was you schemed your way into buying the orchard out from under Callie."

"I got all night," Levi said. "I'll stand here until you feel like talking. I want to know how my ma died. Maybe it's too late to see you tried and hanged, but I'll have a confession."

"Levi," Callie said. "She's never going to tell the truth you want to hear."

"What truth is that?" Jemima said. "The one that makes you feel better?"

Nathaniel stepped right up so that he was towering over Jemima. He said, "'Mima, I've had just about enough of your nonsense. Another word and I gag you. You think I won't do it?"

The lantern light lit only half her face, which looked to Daniel like a mummer's mask, human and animal all at once.

"Now I think I got a solution that will satisfy Levi and won't run too contrary to the law. You listening, Levi?"

"I've got nothing to say about this?" Jemima tried to sit up straighter.

"Not a thing," said Nathaniel.

"Go on," Levi said.

"I say tomorrow we fetch Bookman up here, and we have a hearing. An inquiry, I think you call it, into Cookie's death. Will that serve?"

Levi uncocked his musket. He nodded. "Tomorrow morning."

"Tomorrow afternoon. I got a new grandchild trying to make its way into the world and I'd like to be close by for a while. And I don't doubt there will be some who want to speak to this on the record. Ethan, you think we can take care of this tomorrow afternoon?"

"Yes. As long as Bookman hasn't ridden off somewhere."

Jemima had been watching this exchange stony-faced, but now she turned her attention to Ethan. "You want a hearing, you had better be ready because I got stories to tell too."

Ethan seemed to have not heard her at all. To Levi he said, "If you need a hearing, then that's what you'll get. Right now I think we all need to get moving."

"I'm going up to Lake in the Clouds with you," Levi said. "I'm not letting her out of my sight."

66

Luke was a patient man and never balked at stepping out of the way when he wasn't needed, but for once his calm had been shaken. When Elizabeth came to find him he was red-eyed and his hair stood up in peaks. He was frantic with worry, and she was here to tell him that there was indeed reason for concern. Ben sat with him, and for once there was nothing in his expression of good humor.

"She never screamed like that before," Luke said. "With the girls, she didn't scream like that."

He hadn't been with Jennet when Nathan was born, something he had always regretted; Elizabeth had heard him say it.

"It is not the easiest of births," she said. She sat down across from him and wished for Nathaniel. Maybe Ben saw that in her expression, because he cleared his throat and leaned forward a little.

He said, "If you've got news it would be best if you'd come out with it."

"Yes," Elizabeth said. "The child is very big, and Jennet's not making progress the way we would hope. But it's not time to despair yet. She wants to see you, Luke."

He followed her up the stairs and along the hall, passing the empty rooms where his children would normally be sleeping. They had all been sent to Uphill House with Birdie, to sleep two and three to a bed with their cousins.

There was no reluctance in him, but dread and confusion and a contained fury.

Jennet's moaning could be heard clearly, though the door was shut, and as they approached it spiraled up into a hoarse scream, the kind of scream a man has rarely heard unless he has been in battle. Elizabeth hesitated, and Luke reached past her and opened the door.

The room was well lit, at Hannah's direction, so that shadows danced on the walls. Both windows were open, but covered with cotton gauze pulled tight and pinned in place to keep the insects out. Whatever breeze this would have provided was countered by the fire in the hearth, where water was kept at a simmer and Hannah burned herbs.

Hannah and Curiosity did not even look in their direction. Curiosity was bent over Jennet's straining form, her head turned to one side as she felt her way by touch alone, measuring what progress there might be.

Jennet's scream fell away and Curiosity straightened to look at her while she took a damp cloth from Hannah and wiped her hands.

"You working hard, I know it. The child has got itself stuck, and I'ma have to turn it."

"Then turn it," Jennet whispered, her voice cracking. "But let me talk to Luke for a moment."

Hannah said, "Just a moment, Jennet. Time is of the essence."

She stood with one hand resting lightly on the mound of Jennet's stomach, waiting for the first sign of the next contraction.

Elizabeth went to the far side of the bed to refold the pile of linen that needed no refolding, because while Jennet and Luke deserved privacy, it was a luxury Jennet could not afford. Curiosity turned to tend the fire, and Hannah began to organize the tray of medications and herbs. All of them trying not to listen, but of course they heard, every word.

Jennet said, "I've made a muddle of this."

"So you have." Luke's voice firm and tender at the same time. "But you'll figure a way out, you always do."

"If things gae wrong—Luke, dinnae shake your heid, ye mun hark. Should things gae bad, then the bairns should be raised here. Lily and Simon wad take them, I've already talked to her about it—"

"You what?"

"As women wi a speck o sense talk of sic things before the travail starts," she said with a hint of her old spirit. "Mind me, man. Will ye do as I ask?"

"No," Luke said. "Because you'll come through this. You will come through this."

"Ordering me aboot," Jennet said. "As ever. I will do my best, but ye mun promise."

"I promise," he said.

"Then leave me tae my work. But kiss me first, before ye go."

It was a full minute after Luke had closed the door behind himself before Elizabeth could trust her voice enough to speak.

"What do you need me to do?" she asked Hannah.

"Talk to me," Jennet said, answering for her sister-in-law. "Tell me the story of the first time ye saw Luke."

Hannah turned suddenly. She said, "Oh, I can do better than that. Look Jennet. I found this letter you wrote me more than twenty years ago when Luke first came to stay with you at Carryck." She pulled it from her apron pocket. "I think it would make you laugh to hear your first opinion of the man who got you on your back—"

"Hannah!" Ma sounded truly shocked and so was Birdie. Curiosity laughed out loud.

"Oh, I hope you do want to hear it," Curiosity said. "Because I surely do."

When the next contraction had passed, Jennet blew a damp hair out of her face and agreed that, yes, it would divert her to hear that letter read aloud. Elizabeth opened it and adjusted a candle.

She read:

"Now that your half brother and his mither have settled in at Carryckcastle, I suppose it's time I keep my promise and write and tell what there is to say. Truth be tolt, tis no an easy task. Ye'll want to hear guid tidings, and there's little comfort in the tale I've got to tell.

"He's a slink mannie, is Luke. Tall and braw and bonnie, and slee as a fox. Cook calls him luvey and bakes him tarts wi the last o the pippins. The Earl bought him a mare the likes o which ye'll no see in all Scotland, as black as the devil and that smart too. The lasses come up the brae—"

Jennet drew in a long gasping breath in response to something Curiosity was doing. Then she said, "Go on, please."

"The lasses come up the brae for no guid reason but to sneiter and bat their eyelashes at him, and then run awa when Giselle catches sight o them. Even my mother smiles at Luke for all she looks daggers at me and makes me wear shoes. . . ."

The scream started low and spiraled up. Elizabeth dropped the letter and positioned herself behind Jennet to support her shoulders, and it took all her strength to steady her.

Hannah was talking to everyone at once. *Just a moment more* and *Yes, see here* and *Curiosity, do you* and *Take a deep breath.*

It was not meant for her, but Elizabeth took a deep breath even as Jennet went limp in her arms.

"It's all right," Hannah said. "She's just fainted. Curiosity?"

"Just another inch, and—there. Jennet!"

Jennet stirred, and Elizabeth took a rag from the bowl beside her and ran the cool water over the younger woman's mouth.

"Wake up now," Curiosity said. "It's time to have this baby. The next contraction you got to push for all you worth."

Jennet nodded wearily, leaned forward with Elizabeth's help, and took the rope made of braided linen and tied to the bedpost.

"It's starting," Hannah said. "Now."

Jennet heaved a deep breath and pushed, and with that brought a son into the world.

Much later, when spirits were high and Luke had come in to sit with his wife and youngest child, Elizabeth remembered the letter. She found it under the bed and held it out to him.

He looked up from his examination of the infant's crumpled red face. "What is that?"

"Read this aloud to her," Elizabeth said. "I think you'll both appreciate it."

Luke began to read, almost reluctantly at first, and then with growing interest. When he had reached the point where Elizabeth stopped, Hannah and Curiosity turned toward him to listen.

"I must be fair and report that Luke is a hard worker and there's naught mean-spirited in him, but he's an awfu tease and worse luck he's guid at it, in Scots and English both. I'll admit that he's no so donnert as he first seems, for all his quiet ways. It would suit me much better were he witless, for my father has decided that since my guid cousin kens French and Latin (taught to him by his grandmother in Canada, he says, and what grandmother teaches Latin, I want to know?) I must learn them too, never mind that I speak Scots and English and some of the old language too, having learned it from Mairead the dairy maid. But the Earl would no listen and so I sit every afternoon wi Luke, no matter how fine the weather. And just this morn I heard some talk o' mathematics and philosophy, to make my misery complete.

"He's aye hard to please, is Luke, but when he's satisfied wi my progress, he'll talk o Lake in the Clouds, and then it seems to me that he misses the place, despite the fact that he spent so little time wi ye there. And he tells outrageous stories o trees as far as a man can see and hidden gold and wolves that guard the mountain and young Daniel catching a rabbit wi his bare hands, and then I ken that he's a true Scott o Carryck, for wha else could tell such tales and keep a straight face all the while? But my revenge is this: I wear a bear's tooth on a string around my neck, and he has nothing but the scapular my father gave him when first he came and took the name Scott.

"I'm sorry to say that I canna like your brother near as much as I like you. But tell me this, as you're as much my cousin as is Luke, do ye no think it's time for me to visit ye in Paradise? Perhaps the Earl would let me come, if your grandfather were to ask him."

Luke put the letter down and laughed out loud. Then he leaned over and kissed Jennet soundly.

"I had no idea you started your campaign to leave Scotland so early," he said. "Or that you were scheming even then to get away from me. That's one trick you'll never master."

"I didn't mean it, even then," Jennet said. "But then you knew that."

"Of course I did," Luke said. "Of course."

67

$\mathcal{J}$im Bookman was a good neighbor and a respected magistrate, well liked except by those who would not or could not stay out of trouble. Bookman wasn't afraid to use his fists or his weapons; and he was all too willing to drag troublemakers off to the small gaol he kept, nothing more than a lean-to built up against his cabin. In the Red Dog the regulars liked to tell stories about Bookman's militia days, and they often debated what he would do were he to come face-to-face with a crime that called for hanging. Some thought he would string up the offender without a qualm or hesitation, while others claimed he would restrain himself and drag the culprit off to Johnstown. He was a law-and-order type, for all his years on the frontier and in the bush.

Daniel and Blue-Jay had served under him in the militia and they had seen him fight, but they kept those stories to themselves, out of simple respect and because the conversations at the Red Dog amused them.

Uz Brodie, who served as Bookman's unofficial sheriff and stand-in, had fought in the same war, but on the other side of the border. A fact that nobody seemed to remember at all, which was all you needed to know about him, Daniel's father had said more than once. There wasn't a British bone in the man's body, and he was quick to help a neighbor.

The idea that these two would have the running of the hearing was the only thing that could keep Daniel's worry within bounds. And still he was preoccupied enough that Martha had to call his name more than once.

They were picking strawberries, so fragrant and full of juice that their hands were stained a deep red.

"The idea is to have something to take to Jennet," Martha reminded him. "Which means you should stop eating every berry you pick." She was short with him, and had been since she woke. When Betty came to start the day's chores Martha had found it hard to speak even a whole sentence, though Betty brought the news that Jennet was safely delivered of a son.

"They've named him after his father," Betty said. "Luke Alasdair Scott Bonner. And why a boy needs so many names, that I'll never understand."

At that Martha just walked away.

Betty was a Ratz and so she knew more about short tempers than most; in fact, Daniel realized, she probably didn't recognize Martha's temper for what it was. In any case she went about her business as cheerfully as ever.

Part of the problem was that Martha didn't want to go to the hearing at Lake in the Clouds; she had made that clear enough. She had also made it very clear that she would go, no matter how many logical reasons Daniel offered to stay away.

He picked up his pace, and resisted the urge to remind her that they needn't visit Jennet and her newborn today either. Tomorrow would be soon enough, or the day after.

The trick, his father had told him, was to know when to let a woman be mad because she had a right to it. This was one of those times.

They saddled the horses and by ten they were crossing the bridge into the village. It was a perfect summer's day, not yet hot enough to be uncomfortable, and it seemed that everyone was out of doors. A good number of those were cleaning up after the Fourth of July party, laughing and talking among themselves as they worked. When Martha passed they paused and then dropped their gazes.

So word had spread, then, as they had known it must. He wondered how many of them would come to Lake in the Clouds this afternoon. Baldy and Missy O'Brien would be the first through the door, no doubt. Set on getting their names on the record and making as big a fuss as possible.

Sometimes you have to settle in and wait. That was another piece of advice from his father. What he hadn't said was, sometimes a man didn't have a choice.

What Martha wanted, what she needed most of all, was an hour alone with Curiosity. By the time they got as far as Downhill House, she had worked up the courage to say as much to Daniel, only to discover that she had worried about his feelings for nothing. He was neither hurt nor rejected; on the contrary, he was distinctly relieved. Why she should be irritated with him because she had failed to offend him, that was too confusing a question for the moment.

Instead she turned her attention to Jennet and her new son, and said all the things that were required of her. She stopped just short of pronouncing him a beautiful child, and Jennet caught her hesitation.

"He looks like a crabbit auld man," Jennet volunteered. "With his bald pate and empty gums and that scowl. You'd think he was the one who did all the work." She had a whole slew of unflattering things to say, but every word was spoken in so soft and caressing a tone that the baby only blinked at her, entranced already.

After the little people had been congratulated, Daniel went off to find Luke, and Martha was finally free to seek out Curiosity.

She found her in her garden, sitting on a low stool and pulling up the first of the carrots. Curiosity smiled her slow smile, the one that said she had been expecting you and she knew why you had come even if you didn't know yourself.

In the bright sunlight Curiosity looked her age, and more. Her face was as lined as a map folded a hundred times too many, and there were deep hollows in her cheeks. She looked as tired as Martha had ever seen her, a thought that made the knot in her belly pull tighter. Jemima might be dying, but Curiosity could not.

Martha said, "Are you unwell?"

"Help me up," Curiosity said, holding out one arm. "Let's you and me talk a while."

It took all her self-control to contain herself until Curiosity was settled in the kitchen, and then Martha asked the question again. It earned her only an amused shake of the head.

"I'm as well as any old woman who spent most of the night at a difficult birthing. Were you wanting to talk about my health? I thought me not."

"You heard, then. About last night."

"Oh, ayuh, I heard. Nathaniel told me early this morning when he came by to see his newest grandbaby."

"He told you about the—" Martha hesitated, and Curiosity sent her a sharp look.

"About the hearing. Yes, he did. Come on out with it, girl. Say what's on your mind."

"I don't want there to be a hearing," Martha said. And in a rush of words she could not have stopped, she said all the things she had been holding back.

"What good will it do? What earthly good? She won't admit to anything, and she'll do her best to draw blood. She'll be gone within a week, Hannah says. Can't Levi be satisfied with that?"

She drew in a long hiccupping breath and realized that her face was wet with tears. Curiosity held out a handkerchief, and Martha took it. Then she bent forward and put her forehead on her knees, and she let the tears come.

Some minutes later the kitchen door began to swing open and Curiosity made it close again with a single well-aimed *shoo!* Then she put a hand on Martha's shoulder and she lowered her voice.

"You been keeping this all pent up inside you because you afraid what people will think if you let it out. That they'll think you want to protect your mama, and she don't deserve to be protected. But that ain't what got you tied up in knots, is it? You ain't worried about Jemima's well-being. You thinking about the last hearing, when you was just a girl. Where they made you sit up there in front of God and man and tell what you knew with your ma looking at you. Ain't that so?"

Martha nodded.

"That was a terrible thing to do to such a young girl, and everybody knew it. They did it anyhow, and all for nothing. Jemima walked away. That must sit like a rock in your belly still today. So it ain't no wonder that you cain't abide the idea of another hearing."

"What am I going to do?" Martha said. "I can't stay away and I'll die if I have to sit there and listen. When they were talking about it last night nobody stopped to ask me. Nobody thought to ask me, and I couldn't make myself say anything. Levi has a right to know what really happened to his mother, but she won't leave it at that. You know she won't."

Curiosity made a comforting sound deep in her chest.

"All last night I was awake wishing she would die right then. Put a stop to everything. Make it all stop. Curiosity."

"Hmmm?"

"I shouldn't be here. I shouldn't have come back here. I should have gone someplace she'd never find me."

"I expect it feel like that to you," Curiosity said. "But you all twisted up in your mind just now. And no wonder."

Martha let out a raw laugh. "You're going to say that you can't tell me what to do."

"Why, no," Curiosity said. "I'ma tell you exactly what you have got to do. You are going to that hearing. You have to go and hear whatever it is people need to say, your ma included. Because no matter how bad it might be, not being there would be worse. Not knowing is the worst thing of all, because until you know you cain't put a thing done and let it go. That's why Levi wants this hearing, and that's why you have to go too. So you can start to put it all away from you. So you can be free."

"I thought I was free," Martha said.

"I know you did," Curiosity said. "You married into a good family, and you got a good man. A strong man. And you was thinking it would be enough to turn your back on what used to be."

"You told me this day would come," Martha said. "But I didn't really understand what you were saying."

"I hoped this day would come," Curiosity said. "It's a gift your ma is giving you, and she don't even know it. She is handing you a key, but you got to be brave enough to take it."

Martha felt light-headed and weighed down all at once. "I just want it to be over."

"And it will be," Curiosity said. "Soon enough it will be behind you and you can get on with your life."

———

Because she would have it no other way, Nathaniel took Elizabeth to talk to Magistrate Bookman about the hearing.

"I don't know what you want from the man, Boots. He's honest, you know that, and he won't promise you anything." ·

She had on her most resolute look, the one that said she would brook no contradiction. It was not something he saw often. It was not something he wanted to see today.

"I won't ask him for promises," she said. "What I want to do is to make sure he has the official record of what happened at the first inquest. You know what kind of fabrications and exaggerations he will have heard over the years."

It was a reasonable enough idea, but Nathaniel had the sense that she had other plans she wasn't ready to talk about.

They found Bookman at the Red Dog, surrounded by people who weren't afraid to ask the most outlandish questions and keep asking them, though they knew they'd never get an answer. When Bookman looked up and caught sight of Elizabeth and Nathaniel Bonner he stopped the talk with a wave of his hand and got up.

"Let's go outside," he said. "A man can't hear himself think with all this yammering."

Missy O'Brien's face began to twitch in anger, but that didn't seem to bother Bookman. Instead it seemed to Nathaniel that the magistrate got some satisfaction at having riled her.

Once outside Bookman turned down a lane that ran between two open pastures, so that they could be seen by anybody who happened to come out of the Red Dog, but not heard.

For once Elizabeth dispensed with all niceties and came right to the point. She took a thick pile of papers tied with a string out of her basket. The handwriting on the topmost sheet was easily recognizable as Ethan Middleton's.

"What's this?"

"The full record of the original inquest into Cookie Fiddler's death."

For once Bookman looked taken aback. "O'Brien told me all records had been lost in the flood."

"Which is true, no doubt. But I had a second set made at the time. My husband thought I was being overly fastidious—Nathaniel, you must admit you didn't see the need—but I doubted Mr. O'Brien's ability to keep such records safe. You must correct me if I'm wrong, but I suspect he offered you his memory of the proceedings as fact."

Bookman cocked a brow. "You doubt his memory too?"

"Wouldn't you?"

He inclined his head. "I should have time to read this before the hearing. If that's all?"

"There is one more thing we need to talk to you about," Nathaniel said. "Boots, don't look so surprised. I see the roadblocks just as clear as you do."

"What roadblocks are you talking about?" Bookman said. He was rifling through the papers with considerable interest.

"Jemima has a long history in Paradise," Nathaniel said. "You've heard the stories. What we're worried about is people who'll show up because they've got some score to settle and want to be heard."

"You object to that?"

"At the hearing this afternoon, yes. As far as I'm concerned you can have a hearing every day, one for every man jack in Paradise who has a bone to pick with Jemima. But today we'd appreciate it if you could keep things focused on Levi's complaint."

"I can't turn people away from a public hearing," Bookman said. "In fact I was just on my way to ask John Mayfair if he'd come to serve as her counsel."

"That's a fine idea," Nathaniel said. "Nobody will accuse John of favoritism. Beyond that, we're not asking you to close the hearing."

"Then what did you have in mind?"

"I'm not sure," Nathaniel said. "But my wife has an idea. Don't you, Boots?"

She gave him a sour look. Later he'd get an earful about his methods, but the truth was they depended on each other in situations like this.

Elizabeth said, "Of course the hearing must be open," she said. "Have you made it public yet? Provided any details?"

"I have. Four o'clock at Lake in the Clouds, is what I gave people to understand."

"Very good," Elizabeth said. "Then here is my suggestion: May the principal parties plan to see you there at three?"

Bookman's expression was half surprise and half admiration.

"I think that could be arranged," he said.

"Then we'll leave you to your reading," Nathaniel said, taking Elizabeth by the arm. "And be on our way."

When Martha and Daniel started home just before noon storm clouds were beginning to muscle their way into the Sacandaga valley. Below the lowering thunderheads the light took on the odd cast of copper touched with green, the kind of light some people called gloaming. It made every tree stand out from its neighbor, and every leaf on those trees began to twist and flutter in the wind, as fitful as anxious children. It seemed as though the clouds were leaching the heat from the sky, so that flesh slick with sweat just minutes before suddenly rose in gooseflesh.

The only thing Martha had wanted just a half hour earlier was her own bed and sleep; now she was fully awake and aware. The horses tossed their heads anxiously and nickered to each other.

Daniel picked up the pace as the first fat raindrops began to fall, and then again when the wind shifted and brought a scattering of hail that stung face and hands. Just when Martha began to worry that the horses might really bolt, they came into the center of the village. Daniel rode straight for the livery behind the blacksmithy, hardly slowing as he passed through the double doors.

He was on the ground in a single leap, reaching out to grab Abel's harness with calming words. Martha took that opportunity to dismount and then nearly staggered, her knees were shaking so.

The hail drumming on the tin roof made so much noise that they would have to raise their voices to be heard, so instead they went to stand side by side in the open doors and watch. Hail the size of a child's fist bounced off the ground, pummeled wash hung out to dry, and knocked flat the few chickens that had not been quick enough to find shelter. It stopped as suddenly as it had started, and the first wave of rain came in on a buffeting wind.

Martha took a few steps back, shivering so that her teeth clacked. The sound seemed to rouse Daniel out of a trance. He looked around himself.

"There," Martha said. "Blankets."

"I think we can do better than horse blankets. Hold on a minute."

When he had taken care of the horses, Daniel put his hand on the small of her back and steered her out of the stable and into the smithy itself, empty now as Joshua Hench closed for business during the dinner hour. In the hearth that fed the forge a low fire still burned. Martha put her back against the warm chimney and the warmth of it made her sigh.

She watched Daniel tending the fire. He concentrated so completely on what he was doing, she knew that she would have to call his name twice to get his attention. There was a great deal of comfort in this moment, watching him tend to the simplest, most basic chores. He had his father's quiet competence that never drew attention to itself.

The fire roared into life and lit his face with its strong jaw and deepset eyes. He might have felt the weight of her regard, because he raised his head and grinned at her.

"Warm?"

She nodded. "Getting there."

The rain was coming down so hard that the glass in the two windowpanes rattled, and yet the first flash of lightning took Martha by surprise, so that she jumped in place. Daniel brushed his hands off and came to stand with her.

They leaned against the rough brick, shoulder to shoulder as the storm shook the world around them. It was then that Martha realized that the anxiety she had been fighting all day had gone. Somehow in the dash for shelter and warmth she had lost the tightness in her chest and throat. For the moment, at least, she could think about the hearing without breaking into a sweat.

"It would be nice," she said aloud.

"To stay here like this?" Daniel inclined his head. "Until we got hungry." And, after a moment: "We could sleep for a few minutes, if you like. Until the worst of the storm passes."

It sounded like a wonderful idea, a half hour's sleep in the soft warmth smelling of sweet hay and charcoal. And then it seemed that sleep was not possible, because a question forced its way into the clean stall where they made a nest for themselves.

"What if Jemima has done something even worse than we imagine?"

He heard her. She felt the question being taken in and then turned over in his mind but he wouldn't answer until he had thought it through, which was another thing to appreciate about him, though it did make her pulse pick up a beat.

"I don't care what she's done," he said finally. "It can't change the way I feel about you."

It wasn't the question she had asked, but it was a good answer anyway.

Daniel turned a little so he could see her face in the half light. "I don't think you understand it yet, Martha, so let me say it once more, as clear as I can. You bore the burden of your mother as a girl, and you bore it alone. But you're a woman, and you're not alone. Just the same way we'll stand together at the hearing this afternoon and face whatever comes. You and me and my whole family at our backs. No matter what she has to say, no matter how bad, none of that matters. I know you're afraid and you've got reason to be afraid, but sometime or another you're going to have to trust me."

"But I do. I do trust you."

"No you don't," he said. "Not down deep. Not where you've got all that history with your mother bundled up and tied with a knot. You can't let it go for fear of the damage it'll do, so you keep it to yourself."

"How do you know?" Martha said. "How do you *know*?"

"Because I know you," he said. "Because I know you in your bones. Because I know without a doubt that you are not your mother and you could never be her."

"I wish I were as confident of that as you are."

Daniel said, "So do I."

The storm passed and the sun came out to set the world on fire. Every raindrop on every leaf sparkled, and the air smelled new-washed, as it must have smelled on the day the earth was created.

Elizabeth had walked this way so often she would never have believed that it could take her by surprise, but it seemed that she was wrong.

The very first time she came to Lake in the Clouds, on a snowy winter day, it was Hannah who had showed her the way. How young they had both been. How unaware of the things ahead. The natural beauty of the place had overwhelmed her, and beyond that she was aware of her life shifting and changing with every step in ways she had never expected to find, certainly not here on the frontier with a man she had only known for weeks. A backwoodsman.

The jutting shoulder of the mountain curved abruptly inward like a mother protecting a child. The result was the glen the Mohawk called Lake in the Clouds. It measured almost a mile from the precipice to the falls at its innermost corner. Many things had changed here over the years, but the falls were constant.

"Boots," Nathaniel said. "You look like you're dream-walking."

"It feels that way too," she said. "I'm glad we came on foot."

They caught sight of Gabriel. He was draped over a rock on the edge of the cornfield, bare-chested to the sun, and anyone else might have thought he was sleeping. Elizabeth knew he was not.

He sat up when they were within talking distance and raised a hand in greeting. Then he picked up his rifle, got to his feet, and trotted over. His expression was purposefully blank, and that seemed almost proper given what was about to happen.

Nathaniel said, "I look at him and I see my father."

Gabriel had been almost grown when Hawkeye came home to Paradise. The resemblance had always been obvious, but when they finally stood side by side it seemed as if the past had come forward to merge with the present. Elizabeth was glad of it for Nathaniel's sake, and for Gabriel's. He would never have a moment's doubt about where he belonged.

He leaned down to kiss his mother. "Everybody else is inside, waiting for you."

"Who all would that be?"

"Bookman, Daniel and Martha, Ethan and Callie, Hannah and Levi. John Mayfair; he came up with Bookman. And Susanna. She's there to see to Jemima if need be."

"I'm sorry this burden fell on you," Elizabeth told him, and he looked directly surprised.

"Not on me," he said. "Susanna took one look and made Jemima her concern. You know how she is when she lets her Quaker side get hold of a problem."

"What problem does she mean to solve?" Nathaniel asked.

"A peaceful death, is what she said to me. How she plans to get Jemima there, that I don't know beyond the fact that the two of them sat out in the sun near the falls for most of the morning. Now Jemima has stopped talking to anybody but Susanna."

Nathaniel said, "As much as I like and admire Susanna, I don't think anybody could reach Jemima anymore. If anything has tamed her, it's the cancer."

"Maybe," Gabriel said. "I suppose you're about to find out."

———

Hawkeye built the original cabin nearest the falls when he brought Cora there as a bride. That cabin was gone, burned to the ground in the year '06. In its place Nathaniel had built a proper house, far more comfortable and conveniently laid out, but Elizabeth couldn't approach this spot without missing the simpler cabin where she had borne all but her youngest.

"My mind keeps wandering away to the past," she told Nathaniel. "Looking for an escape route of some kind, I suppose."

"We'll get through this, Boots, and so will Martha and Callie and the boy."

Elizabeth was trying to decide if that was true when they came into the main room. Someone had rearranged the furniture to suit the purpose at hand—benches in a half circle around the chair where Jemima sat, a table for Bookman and one for Ethan, who would record the proceedings. Someone else might have taken on that task today, but Elizabeth kept that thought to herself. There was no one she'd trust more.

Jemima sat apart, bundled like an infant. Her color was off and there were unfamiliar hollows in her cheeks, but the surprise was her expression. Dampened, was the word that came to mind.

The most striking thing about Jemima when she was in health was the intensity of her gaze, always alert for injustice against herself. Now Jemima sat quietly with her hands folded in her lap, her mouth slightly open. She blinked slowly, and Elizabeth realized that Hannah had given her something—had given her quite a lot of something—for the pain.

Magistrate Bookman was at his table looking over the papers he had received from Elizabeth a few hours before. The others sat as though they had been sworn to silence, unwilling to talk in front of Jemima for reasons that might be called superstitious. Callie sat alone on a bench with Levi standing behind her, rocking back and forth on his feet, his chin cradled on his chest.

Jim Bookman looked up from the papers and cleared his throat.

"We're here at the request of Levi Fiddler to hear evidence against Mrs. Jemima—Focht, is it?"

"For the moment," Jemima said.

"John Mayfair is here as your counsel."

"If he likes," Jemima said. She sent a glance to Susanna, who sat in a corner, straight of back, her head canted to one side as she listened.

"I call this hearing to order. In the matter of the death of Cookie Fiddler, a manumitted slave, on or about the eighteenth day of November in the year 1812. At the time there was no clear decision on the nature of Mrs. Fiddler's death—Mr. Middleton, will you read the findings?"

Ethan had been waiting. He began without hesitation.

Statement Submitted into Evidence
Signed by Hannah Bonner, Physician
Witnessed by Mrs. Elizabeth Bonner
and Ethan Middleton, Esq.

On the 26th day of December I examined the remains of Mrs. Cookie Fiddler in the presence of Mrs. Bonner and Mrs. Freeman of this village, as Dr. Todd is recently deceased and there is no other with the training to perform this last service.

The subject was a mulatto Negro woman of about sixty years, very small and slight of stature but well nourished and without obvious external signs of illness. Both ears pierced. The body bore numerous scars, primarily of whippings to the back and legs. The right fibula was once broken and set crookedly.

First observations indicated that the subject died by drowning when the water was at or very near freezing, for her remains were well preserved. On autopsy it was determined that her lungs were in fact filled with water, which indicates that she was alive when she fell into the lake. All other internal organs appeared unremarkable for a healthy woman of her years.

The only wound on her person was on the back of her head, an indentation about a half inch deep, three fingers wide, and a half foot long, regular in shape, as might have been made by a blow with a wood stave or by falling and striking the head on a wood structure such as the handrail or edge of a bridge. The blow was severe enough to slice the scalp to the skull, cleave the skull itself, and render the subject insensible. There were no other signs of struggle, that is, no broken fingernails or wounds as might have been received in a struggle for her life. In addition, there were a few grains of sand clutched in her hand and found in the folds of her clothing.

Thus is it my opinion that Cookie Fiddler's death may have been an accident or a murder, but it is not in my power to declare which on the basis of the evidence I had before me. I surmise that she received a blow to the head and fell unconscious into the lake, where she drowned.

This statement dictated to and taken down by Ethan Middleton and signed by my own hand and sworn to be true to the best of my knowledge and ability:

Hannah Bonner, also known as Walks-Ahead by the
Kahnyen'kehàka of the Wolf Longhouse at Good Pasture
and by Walking-Woman by her husband's people, the Seneca,
this first day of January 1813.

"This is an unusual situation," said Bookman. "Maybe the oddest I've ever come across since I've been a magistrate, up in Plattsville or here. Mr. Fiddler, is there some new evidence come to light these eleven years later that makes you believe a trial is warranted?"

"Should have been one back then," Levi said.

"Be that as it may," said Bookman. "Is there new evidence you wish to present?"

"Just what never got said last time."

"Well, then," said Bookman. "The accused is very ill, as I understand it. Is that so, Mrs. Savard?"

Hannah agreed that it was.

"A mortal illness."

"She has very little time."

"Mr. Mayfair, do you consider Mrs. Focht to be well enough to take part in these proceedings?"

"She is in her right mind. As far as her physical well-being is concerned, that question is best answered by Friend Hannah."

Hannah stood again. "She has had a large dose of laudanum which will keep the pain within bounds for a while. There are side effects, but she is able to speak on her own behalf."

"Of course I am," Jemima said. "With laudanum all things are possible."

The peculiar smile on her face was far more unsettling than any diatribe she might have delivered.

"Mr. Fiddler," said Jim Bookman. "Your statement."

It seemed for a moment that Levi wouldn't speak at all. Then he raised his head and straightened to his full height.

"My mother and my brothers and me were born in slavery, into the Kuick family that used to live here in Paradise. The same family Mrs. Focht married into."

He must have rehearsed this speech hundreds of times over the years, because it flowed easily, from one point to the next without hesitation or reaching. Levi told about the Kuick household and his mother's responsibilities in the kitchen, about Jemima's first arrival at the house as a maid, and the changes once she married Isaiah Kuick. In quick strokes he drew a picture of Jemima as a woman who disliked his mother on sight and did what was in her power to make Cookie's life miserable.

"Because Ma wasn't afraid of her," Levi said. "That's what made her so mad. We were still slaves or we would have left right then. Once we got our manumission papers and we went to work for Mr. Wilde at the orchard things got better. All three of us, Mama and my brother Zeke and me. Mama in the house, me and Zeke in the orchards. That was the best time, until the day Mrs. Wilde and my mama both went missing and never were seen alive again."

His voice was a little more strained as he told the rest of the story; how Jemima had stepped in to comfort Mr. Wilde in his loss, how quickly they had wed, and what life had been like for Levi, still mourning his mother, once Jemima came into the household.

When he seemed to have finished, Bookman looked at him over the top of his reading spectacles. "Mr. Fiddler, what you have got here is a sad story about a mean and vindictive woman, but the law requires more before a person can be charged with murder. Motive, method, and opportunity are the cornerstones of such an accusation. Are you saying the motive in this case was simple hatred?"

"No, sir," Levi said. "I'm saying she was a widow woman and wanted a husband and Mr. Wilde was her object. She did what she had to do to make that possible, and that meant getting rid of my mother so she could get shut of the first Mrs. Wilde."

Bookman made a grumbling noise that rattled in his throat. "This still leaves the matter of method and opportunity, but let's put that aside for the moment. Mrs. Focht, what do you say to these accusations?"

Jemima looked surprised to be asked. "I've heard them all before. What is it you want me to say? That I needed a husband? A woman with a child to raise and no money must have a husband. Of course."

The magistrate worked his jaw as if he were chewing something tough.

"Mr. Fiddler, you are by my observations a careful man and fastidious. Surely you must see that if I send Mrs. Focht to Johnstown for trial, there's little chance she'd live long enough to stand before a judge, and it's almost a certainty that if she did, the judge would throw out the case. Can you be satisfied with the knowledge that she'll be standing before her Maker soon enough, and that he'll be better able to mete out punishment than we are?"

"I want to hear her admit it," Levi said. "Then I'll be satisfied to let the devil deal out her due."

"Anything to say, Mrs. Focht?"

"Let Callie talk next." She said this with no emotion, as though she were asking him to open a window or pass the salt.

"Mrs. Middleton," said Jim Bookman. "Did you want to make a statement?"

"Yes," Callie said. "I have some evidence to give. I should have given it long ago, and I'll ask Levi to forgive me for holding back. Jemima did kill Cookie Fiddler, and I know because I saw her do it."

The sharp silence that followed was broken by Levi. He said, "You weren't even in Paradise that night."

"I was. I'll tell the whole story now if you want to hear it."

Bookman said, "You saw Mrs. Fiddler die, and you never told anyone? Mrs. Middleton, why would you keep such information to yourself?"

Callie looked directly at the magistrate. "I was a little girl. I was afraid. And nobody ever asked me. Martha they called down to the meetinghouse to give testimony, but not me. It never occurred to them to ask me. And later . . . I don't have an excuse. There is no excuse. I can only ask for pardon."

"There's a difference between an excuse and an explanation," said the magistrate.

Ethan cleared his throat and the magistrate shot him a strict look.

"Mr. Middleton, your wife is capable of answering this question."

"Yes," Callie said. "I suppose I am. The closest I can come to an explanation is just that I was angry. I was so angry, it filled me up and pushed everything else out, every reasonable thought. I was angry at Jemima and at the whole world."

The magistrate pushed out a sigh. "What of the claim that you were not in Paradise at that time?"

"That's what I wanted people to think," Callie said. "But let me tell you the whole story from the beginning."

68

"*I* never thought I'd ever tell this," Callie began. "I tried to put it out of my head, but it just wouldn't go. So I'm only going to look at you, Mr. Bookman, and nobody else and maybe I'll get through it. I'm also going to ask Ethan and Martha and anybody else who gets the urge not to speak up. To leave me the telling of this.

"This is what happened. I was supposed to go to Johnstown with my father, that much is true. But Ma was poorly and Levi was away, so at the last minute Da said I should stay to help Cookie.

"Late that afternoon Ma was getting worse, as bad as I ever saw her. The day got darker and colder and she started talking to herself, talking loud. About all kinds of things, but mostly just rambling. She was running a fever too, and Cookie decided she had to go fetch help. She said I was to stay behind because Ma was quietest when I sat with her.

"All I can say in my own defense is that I was young and disappointed about Da leaving me behind. When Cookie said I couldn't even go into the village I got mad and I decided I'd go anyway.

"It was full dark when she left. I waited a few minutes and made sure

Ma was quiet—she was resting just then, half asleep—and then I set out to follow Cookie. I knew she would send me home so I hung back a ways, but not very far. I didn't want to lose sight of her lantern. I remember thinking I would catch her up by the bridge because she'd have to stop and scatter sand—you remember how icy the floorboards on the old bridge got in midwinter? But when I got that far I saw Jemima was coming across from the other side, and I stopped right where I was. They both had lanterns and I could see just that much of them, faces and hands that caught the light.

"I have thought it through for years now, and I'm pretty sure it was just a coincidence that they met up on the bridge. But then once they saw each other neither one of them was going to back down. I wasn't close enough to make any of it out but they were both fighting mad. I could see it in the way they were standing.

"Just when I was going to run for help, Cookie tried to push past Jemima and she slipped and fell. She fell real hard.

"I was so scared, I could hardly breathe. I was scared Cookie was bad hurt and I was afraid that if I showed myself the same thing would happen to me. I wanted to run away but I couldn't move my feet. I wanted to yell for help, but I was sure if I did Jemima would come after me.

"It wasn't even a couple heartbeats before I heard a rider coming. Jemima heard it too, by the way her head came up sharp. And then— That's when she leaned down and just pushed Cookie over the edge. One shove and she was gone. Sometimes I still dream about it, and in the dream I can hear the splash.

"I stayed in the shadows for a long time and then when I was sure Jemima was gone, I went down by the lake. It was too dark to see anything and it was cold, but I had to look. I think I was hoping that Cookie might have swum away, but there was no sign of her. So I went back home.

"Now I have got to confess something that has bothered me every day of my life since then. I loved Cookie and I was worried out of my head, but I was just as much worried for me as I was for her. I was thinking, *Please don't be dead. Please don't leave me alone with Ma, please don't. I can't take care of her myself.*

"Once I got home I climbed into bed with Ma because I was so cold and scared. I wanted to tell somebody what I saw, but I was so tired and Ma wouldn't have understood anyway. And when I woke up the next morning, Ma was gone and the blizzard had just started up. I was so scared I was shaking, but I got on my clothes and I went out after her.

"I don't know if anybody will recall that when my ma wandered off she often went to call on Daisy Hench. She always liked Daisy and somehow or another Daisy was good at calming her down. So I set off to see if I could catch her up. I got about three quarters of the way when I realized I wasn't dressed warm enough. I thought for a minute I might die myself, and that I wouldn't mind so much if Ma and Cookie were both gone. I might as well go too.

"Just then I came to the Steinmeissen place. I suppose something in me wasn't ready to die yet because I knocked, thinking they'd let me set by their fire until the weather let up a little.

"But they weren't home. I was so beside myself I forgot that Margery died the winter before, and Anton had gone off into the bush to drink himself into a stupor.

"So there I was in the Steinmeissen cabin. It was so dark with the blizzard coming on, and not a single candle anywhere, nor a bit of oil for the lamp. But there was wood stacked right outside the door and a tinderbox on the mantel, and I managed finally to get a fire going. I just wrapped up in every cover and blanket I could find and I lay down in front of the hearth and I fell asleep.

"Martha, if you keep weeping like that I won't be able to finish, and I need to tell all of this. Let me tell it.

"Even after the blizzard let up, I couldn't make myself go out. I found a crock of bacon grease and a few crackers, and I melted snow to drink. So I stayed another night and then the next day when I was going to give up and go on home I heard my da's sleigh bells. I ran right out in the middle of the road, and I scared him bad so that at first all he could do was yell at me and ask what was I thinking, being so careless and what was I doing all the way on this side of the village.

"To this day I don't know how much I told him, or what he understood. Didn't matter anyhow, because not five minutes later we were in the middle of the village and people were running from all directions shouting at us to stop, stop, something terrible had happened. And that's when we heard Ma had died on Hidden Wolf and that Cookie was missing. That's what people said, and that's what they believed, that Cookie was missing and nothing more.

"Da and me, we never talked about it, after that. Why I was at the

Steinmeissen place all alone, or what happened to Cookie, or how Ma had wandered off to die on the mountain. I don't think he even thought about it, he was so broke up about Ma and Cookie. Levi came back and he was so upset, I was afraid to talk to him for fear he'd run off and kill Jemima and then they'd hang him.

"If I had known Da was going to end up marrying Jemima, I would have made myself tell him. But I didn't. Sometimes I wonder what the world would be if I had obeyed Cookie and stayed behind that evening. I wouldn't have slept so deep, and Ma couldn't have wandered off, and Jemima couldn't have got my da to marry her, and all the trouble later about the orchard would never have happened. They might still be alive today, both my folks. I am sorry to say that no matter how hard I looked at it, I couldn't find a way to save Cookie. There wasn't anything I could have done. When she and Jemima got within striking distance of each other, it was like fire and gunpowder. Something was going to happen.

"That morning after Cookie died, when I woke up and found Ma gone, I knew right then. I knew that if Ma was dead, it would be my fault. And so she was, and so it is."

Martha held Daniel's hand tight, and her gaze cast downward. If she concentrated, she might be able to clear her mind and find some way to think clearly. Some way to rid herself of the images Callie had put there, of blowing snow and dark water and of Jemima, standing on the old bridge looking down at the water closing over Cookie.

For all those years Martha had a different image, one she had never told Callie about, though she had testified to it in front of the village. Mrs. Wilde, underdressed for the weather, her hair flowing loose down her back, walking up the mountain on the morning of that same blizzard. Standing at the kitchen window Martha had seen it all very clearly. The woman in a dress the color of dried blood, bent forward a little as she walked into the wind and first gusts of snow. Her skin already translucent, as if she were melting away into the weather.

She tried. She asked again and again. *Ma, Mrs. Wilde's got out somehow; let me take her home. Ma, there's something wrong with Mrs. Wilde. Ma, let me go get Cookie.*

Her mother's answer she remembered clearly, and the tone: firm, cool, inflexible.

That's her concern and none of ours.

Knowing that Cookie was dead, Jemima had said that.

Now Martha looked at the woman who had borne and raised her, sitting wrapped in blankets on the hottest of July afternoons. Her face composed, even blank. The idea came to Martha that the spark that animated her mother for all her life was already gone, and the woman who sat there was somebody else entirely.

Callie was sitting down again. Levi put his hand on her shoulder, leaned over and asked her something. She shook her head. Then Ethan came to her and crouched in front of her and took her hands. He talked for at least a minute, in a hushed voice. The kind of voice you might hear someone use in a church or a sickroom. Again Callie shook her head.

Martha wondered if it was her own turn now to go and comfort Callie. To tell her that she wasn't responsible, that she wasn't to blame. To say, *I don't mind that you kept all that to yourself all these years, that you didn't speak up back then. I'm happy that you made that decision for yourself without asking me what I wanted.* But those were things she couldn't say. She might have said something closer to the truth of what she was feeling: *Look at all the pain and trouble we might have been spared if you had told somebody what you saw.*

Jim Bookman was saying, "Mrs. Focht, do you wish to respond?"

Jemima raised her head as if the sound of his voice had called her up out of a daydream. "What?"

"Do you wish to respond? Tell your own story?"

"My story." The idea seemed to amuse her. "Of course, I'll tell you my story."

69

"First before I start, John Mayfair has drawn up a last will and testament and I've signed it. The little bit I have in the world—and it is just a very little bit—I am leaving to my boy. To Nicholas. I have asked my daughter Martha and her husband to act as guardians until the boy reaches his majority, but I have named Susanna as the person who should take over his upbringing. She has agreed that she will take him in and raise him here at Lake in the Clouds.

"You can tell yourself I am doing this because I want to keep Nicholas away from Callie just to make her mad, but the fact is I don't want the boy raised by somebody who hates me. If that causes Callie pain, why, that's an added bonus and nothing more.

"See how Susanna is looking at me, so's I remember that I promised her to be civil. I will try harder, I promise.

"As a girl the thing I wanted most was to be here. Right here, at Lake in the Clouds. When Hannah started home after school everyday, I wanted to follow her. I never let on, of course, but this place was like some kind of palace in my mind, back then. Maybe because I knew I didn't belong and never could belong. Don't things out of reach just glow in your mind? And then sometimes when you do get what you've been hoping and planning and fighting for, the glow is gone. Rubbed off in the getting of it.

"Most things I fought for turned out that way. I'd think, that's what I need to be safe and happy, and I'd fight and fight, and then when I got it in my hands, it wasn't gold but brass needing to be polished and polished if it was to give any service at all. That's the way it was marrying Isaiah. I knew he didn't want anything to do with me and that was fine. I thought the money would be enough. I thought I could withstand anything if I had nice clothes and enough food and firewood and a house to call my own and servants. I told myself it didn't matter how he hated me or if I disgusted him, as long as he kept up appearances. But I found out soon enough, pity is much harder to swallow than hate. You all think I'm made of stone, but I never was.

"The thing is, everybody I ever wanted, every single person, wanted somebody else and only made do with me. My father was mad I wasn't born a boy and the minute my brothers came along, he couldn't see me anymore. Liam Kirby was bound heart and soul to Hannah, who didn't even want him back. I took what he wouldn't give me of his own free will, and to this day I'm glad I did it. If you're honest you'll admit you're glad of it too, all of you, or Martha wouldn't be sitting there, precious as she is to you.

"Nicholas wanted Lily, he wanted her so bad he was sick with it, but she didn't want him. Not really, or she wouldn't have fallen so hard in love with that Scot. So I took things into my own hands. Yes, I did. Levi wants to hear me say it, and so here it is: I did what needed to be done. When Cookie fell and knocked her head I did the rest. I lied to Nicholas about Lily, and I let Callie's ma walk away into a blizzard. I did all that because I knew I could be a good wife to Nicholas and that he would take care of us. By that time I had given up the idea of an easy life. I just wanted to know there'd be food and firewood.

"A man goes out and fights and kills sometimes for his family, and that's honorable. Nathaniel knows what I'm talking about, don't you? That's what it means to be a man. A woman is supposed to take what fate hands her and be satisfied with that. She's supposed to be *thankful* for that. If I had any strength left that idea would still make my blood boil.

"When things went bad and Nicholas was close to losing his mind for grief and anger and hurt male pride—because that's what it was, even if you refuse to see the truth of it—I knew I had to go before he killed me or I killed him. Of course I left the girl behind. I couldn't look after her. If I had taken her, you would have raged about that. Sometimes I wonder who got the brunt of your anger once I was gone.

"It didn't matter that I left without Martha. She wouldn't have wanted to come with me anyway. Can't say as I blame her, to tell the truth.

"So I went. I went and I found my way and I had my boy.

"You'll be surprised to hear me admit this, but there's something sour in me. Something spoiled. It has been there since I was a girl, since Ma and my brothers choked to death with the quinsy. I nursed them as best I could. I went to Curiosity and got tea and medicine, and none of it did any good. I begged them, but they died anyway. Something settled on me then, and I never did get rid of it. Like a tattoo on my face, I could scrub at it but it wasn't going nowhere. And after a while, I liked myself like that. I looked in the mirror and I liked what I saw. I'm crabbit and mean and vindictive, always have been.

"But I did mean for the boy to grow up healthy. So I sent him away with Lorena to look after him, and every month I sent money. I couldn't have kept him in any case, because by that time I had regular work singing in the theater. You didn't know that, did you? I sang every night under the name Monique Moreau. And I'd still be singing but for this cancer in my belly.

"I hate that the cancer has got the best of me. I hate that after all I did to keep my head above water, my own body has betrayed me. They told me a year ago I didn't have long, but I was determined to see that the boy was took care of. So I spent the last of my money hiring Dan Focht to play my husband, hired the carriage and horses and the extra servants. Dan wanted his boy Harper along and I didn't object. If I hadn't been sick maybe I would have realized the boy was quick-fingered and always looking for easy money. He's dead and no doubt he deserved it, whoever did it. I can't hold a grudge on his account.

"I went and claimed my son and we lived all together for that short time so I could know him better. And what I found was a child so sweet and good, I could hardly believe he was mine. But he is mine. He's the only thing I can claim as my own.

"All I wanted was for the boy to have what is rightfully his. Martha has money enough to raise him proper, but I wanted him to have something of his own, something of his father's. You all thought I wanted the orchard because of that apple, the Bleeding Heart, but the truth is I didn't know anything about it. I'd swear it on my son's life. What I did know was that my boy had some property owing him, and I wanted to make sure he got title to it before I died.

"Then Focht wanted more money to keep up the charade and I didn't have it, so he left and I went too. I had a few ideas, how to raise a little more money, take the boy's claim to the courts. But time caught up with me and the money ran out, and there I stood, sick unto death with the almshouse staring me in the face.

"I stole a horse and buggy to get here, but I don't think they'll track me down in time to hang me. You all may decide to hang me anyway, or maybe Levi will put a bullet in my head to avenge his ma. It would be a blessing, truth to tell. I'm ready to go, now that I know the boy will be looked after. I like to think of him growing up here on the mountain. Not because I'll die here, but because it's a good place and Susanna is a good woman for all she married a Mohawk.

"So now you can sort things out among yourselves. I'll sign anything you care to put in front of me, as long as John Mayfair says I should. Susanna, could you help me? I feel the need to lay my head."

70

PUBLIC DECLARATION

*F*ollowing from a hearing held this 6th day of July in the year 1824, I find sufficient evidence to charge Mrs. Jemima Wilde (known also as Jemima Focht, or Jemima Southern, or Jemima Kuick and also as Monique Moreau) with Manslaughter in the death of Mrs. Cookie Fiddler on or about the 18th November 1812. She is charged also with Depraved Indifference in the death of Mrs. Dolly Wilde on or about that same date.

Because the accused has signed a statement confessing to both these crimes, and further because she is close to death, no trial will be ordered. A report will be submitted to the district court in Johnstown.

May God have Mercy on her Soul.

James Bookman

Magistrate

Paradise on the Sacandaga

---

*O*n a bright September morning Curiosity-Bonner-called-Birdie flew down the hill into the village and then straight to the schoolhouse where her brother and sister-in-law were getting ready to start classes for the day.

Then she was too winded to tell them what they needed to know, and so they stood there asking her questions while she heaved breath and her voice came back to her. It came out in a rush.

"Lily's having her baby and Curiosity says you should come, Martha. Lily wants you there."

Martha's eyes went very large and round and she pressed her fingers to her mouth as if she was afraid of what she might say.

"Won't you come?" Birdie looked between them. "Daniel, won't she come?"

Martha found her voice. "Of course I'll come. Daniel can manage without me for the day. Unless you wanted to come too?"

The look on Daniel's face might have made Birdie laugh out loud if she wasn't in such a hurry. The idea surprised and even alarmed him, but there was something else there too, some curiosity or simple concern. Lily was his twin, after all.

In the end they left a note on the door saying school was canceled and all three of them walked back up the hill together. Walked fast, with Hopper galloping along behind them. They passed Downhill House, where nobody seemed to be home at all, and then they passed the new clearing where Simon had begun to build a house for Lily, and finally they got to Uphill House where all the men were sitting on the porch as if it were a Sunday and nobody had any work to do. It made Birdie cross, that they should sit there all day at their ease while Lily worked so hard.

"You could go build something," she said as she passed by, but they were too busy talking to Daniel to take note of what she had to say.

"Never mind," Martha said. "They're only men after all."

She looked as nervous as Birdie felt, and that was a comfort.

It still surprised her to come into the kitchen and see only half the little people. Luke and Jennet had taken theirs home just a few days before, and Birdie was glad to have some peace and quiet back. She could even admit she missed having Jennet and her children in the house now and then, but that was mostly when Ma had a long list of errands and nobody to pin it to but Birdie herself.

There was water warming on the stove and a basket of clean cloths that Martha picked up as they passed, as if she knew what was needed in the birthing room, though she had never attended one. Neither had Birdie, but this time they were allowing her to stay. It was very exciting and it made her stomach hurt too.

Lily was in Ma's chamber, the biggest one in the house but it seemed to be filled up anyway. She had argued with Hannah until she got her way: Lily would bring this child into the world under her parents' roof.

There was the bed with Lily in it, Lily with her belly like a ripe melon that rippled when the pains came, like a bald man wrinkling his forehead.

They gave Martha the job of getting the cot and the swaddling clothes ready, and she seemed relieved. Birdie was relieved too. Martha might be squeamish about such things, but Birdie wanted to see it all and she didn't want to have to worry about Martha.

Ma was saying, "Lily, you're very close now."

"Not close enough," Lily said through clenched teeth.

"You can't breathe with your jaw all clamped shut like that," Curiosity said. "What did I tell you about breathing? Birdie, come over here and sit by your sister's head and remind her about her breathing."

But Hannah winked at her, as if to say *This is all good, there is nothing to worry about.*

"Can I push now?" Lily said, her voice cracking. "I feel like I have to push."

"Not yet," Hannah said. "But almost."

"Ma," Lily said, "How did you do this so many—"

And then the pain took her away. Birdie leaned over and whispered in her ear about breathing and after a while it seemed to her that maybe Lily was hearing her and maybe that was helping. Her hair and face and the sheets were soaked with sweat and little red veins had come out on her cheeks, but she was breathing the way Curiosity had showed her.

"All right," Hannah said with some satisfaction. "Now you can push."

"Steady," said Ma. "Steady. Your baby is almost here, Lily. She's almost here."

"It might be a boy," Martha said. She had left the folded swaddling cloths to come stand with them around Lily. They made a circle with Lily at the center, like a flower.

"Oh, no," said Lily. "I promised Ma a girl."

"Don't be silly," said Ma. "You did no such thing."

"Of course I did," Lily said, panting now as she wrapped her hands around the pull rope. "Wait and see."

When the clock in the hall struck ten, Lily pushed one last time and gave birth to a daughter. Small but perfectly formed, with a head of dark curls, all rounded elbows and knees and belly and open mouth. Her eyes were open too.

"Oh, look," Lily said, when Hannah put the baby in her arms. "Look, Ma, she's smiling at us. Maddie, say hello to your grandma."

"Now look at that," Curiosity said. "Look at that beautiful child. Lily Bonner Ballentyne, look what you made."

For once Birdie had been completely forgotten, and she found she didn't mind at all.

EPILOGUE

_____

PARADISE SUN
Light for All

The Week of Monday, March 3, 1828

ADVERTISEMENTS

Friend John Mayfair has opened a law office in the new building next to the schoolhouse. Please stop by to consult with him any weekday morning between eight and twelve of the clock.

Curiosity Freeman would like all to know that she has chicks ready for sale. Potential buyers should remember that these are the descendents of Chicken Number Three, who was an excellent layer and of an unflappable temperament.

Daniel Bonner invites all schoolchildren and their families to stop by the schoolhouse to meet Mr. Lawrence March, who will be taking over the junior classroom now that Martha has withdrawn from teaching to care for her sons.

NOTICE

As you may be aware, the printing press that made publication of the *Paradise Sun* possible arrived in Paradise six months ago. In recognition of that fact, the editor invites suggestions from any interested party on how the newspaper might better serve the needs of its ever-increasing readership. This includes anyone who would like to offer an editorial on matters of public interest, with no restrictions as to political affiliations or world views. Please stop by the newspaper office on the town square to share your thoughts.

Elizabeth Middleton Bonner, Editor

PARADISE SUN
Light for All

The Week of Monday, June 8, 1829

ABOUT TOWN

Ethan Middleton would like it known that he has taken on Nicholas Wilde of Lake in the Clouds as an apprentice builder. Given the rapid expansion of the town, Ethan is likely to be hiring again within the month. Those interested should inquire at Ivy House.

Levi Fiddler tells us that this past winter's success of the Bleeding Heart cider has enabled him to add another two acres of trees to the orchard.

Mr. Bookman has announced his intention to petition the county for funds to cobble the main road into the village. Friend John Mayfair will assist him with this task.

PARADISE SUN
Light for All

Special Edition
Monday, July 19, 1830

PUBLIC SERVICE ANNOUNCEMENT
OF GREAT IMPORT

Doctor Hannah Savard reminds the residents of Paradise that all drinking water and water used in preparing food *must be boiled*. Further, it is of crucial importance that the new guidelines on the digging of privies be observed. These measures are our best hope to bring the quickest possible end to the typhoid epidemic that has struck at the very heart of our families.

In the past week three children and five adults are dead of typhoid or complications of typhoid. They are
    Mrs. Lorena Fiddler and her daughter Margaret, age four
    Mr. Baldwin O'Brien
    Friend Margery Blackstone
    Friend Magnus Allen
    Mrs. Jennet Scott Bonner and a stillborn daughter, in childbed
    Friend Alois Farmer
    Mairead Ballentyne, age three

PARADISE SUN
Light for All

The Week of Monday, November 7, 1831

OBITUARY

On last Wednesday, November 2, Runs-from-Bears of Lake in the Clouds was struck down by a sudden apoplexy and died within the hour. He was seventy-three years old.

Runs-from-Bears was a member of the Turtle clan of the Kah-nyen'kehàka at Good Pasture. He came to Paradise in 1792 when he was joined in marriage with Many-Doves of the Wolf clan, also originally of Good Pasture.

Runs-from-Bears fought in the French and Indian War and the Rev-olutionary War and was renowned for his bravery and daring. The trip he made to New Orleans during the War of 1812 together with his life-long friend Nathaniel Bonner is still spoken of both in that city and here. In peacetime he was considered the best tracker in a hundred miles or more, and his furs were sought after for their quality.

Runs-from-Bears is survived by his son Blue-Jay and good-daughter Susanna, their children Callum, Grace, and Sarah; by his daughter Annie and her husband Gabriel Bonner and their children Tobias, Jay, and Liza; and by many dear friends. He is preceeded in death by his wife Many-Doves, and by his adult children Kateri and Sawatis. On a personal note, this loss is an especially painful one for the editor and her family. Runs-from-Bears was the best of men, and we mourn his passing.

Elizabeth Middleton Bonner, Editor

PARADISE SUN
Light for All

June 6, 1832

ABOUT TOWN

Nathaniel and Elizabeth Bonner would like their friends and neighbors to know that they are in receipt of a letter from their daughter Birdie, who has arrived safely in New Orleans to take up the study of medicine with Dr. Paul de Guise Savard and Dr. Phillipe Savard at that city's Free Clinic. The doctors Savard are the brothers of Ben Savard of Downhill House.

Further good news from the Bonner clan: This past week Lily Ballen-tyne née Bonner was delivered safely of a healthy girl, her fourth daugh-ter. On the same day Martha Bonner née Kirby added twin boys to her brood for a total of five sons. It seems that age and wisdom have not tempered the spirit of friendly competition between the original Bonner twins, Lily and Daniel, and their respective spouses.

Ethan Middleton has announced plans for yet another addition to the schoolhouse.

PARADISE SUN
Light for All

Tuesday, September 17, 1833

ABOUT TOWN

Yesterday three of our young men departed Paradise for Manhattan, where they will take up studies at Columbia College. They are Henry Savard of Downhill House, and Nathan and Adam Scott-Bonner of Ivy House. All three will take up residence with Nathan and Adam's father Luke, a face well known to us here in Paradise.

We wish them great success.

With this issue of the *Paradise Sun,* the editorship is passed on to Mr. Lawrence March, one of our teachers. Mr. March would like to thank Mrs. Bonner for her hard work in establishing the newspaper, and hopes she will continue to contribute editorials on the topics of the day.

Lawrence J. March, Editor

PARADISE SUN
Light for All

Friday, January 3, 1834

OBITUARY

With great sadness we report that Mrs. Curiosity Freeman, the oldest surviving citizen of the original settlers of Paradise, died quietly in the first hours of this new year, 1834. Her daughter, Mrs. Daisy Hench, and her dear friends Mrs. Elizabeth Bonner and Mrs. Hannah Savard were by her side. She was 99 years old.

Mrs. Freeman was born into slavery on a farm in Pennsylvania in the spring of the year 1734. In 1762, when a Quaker Abolition Society purchased manumission papers for herself and her husband Galileo, the young couple came to Paradise to take up employment with Judge Alfred Middleton and family. After Judge Middleton's passing, she kept house for Dr. Richard Todd for many years.

Burial services were conducted on Thursday, January 2, in the course of an unusually mild and pleasant winter afternoon. There were more than two hundred people in attendance on very short notice. Many of those who attended had been helped into the world by Mrs. Freeman, who was an exceptional midwife.

The wisest and most generous of souls, Mrs. Freeman was a loving mother, the most caring of friends, a gifted healer, and a constant source of stories. War, disaster, illness, in all of life's challenges she remained the steadiest of lights. It is not too much to say that Mrs. Freeman was the rock on which Paradise was built. She will be sorely missed.

She is survived by her daughter Daisy Hench and her son Almanzo Freeman, as well as six grandchildren and five great-grandchildren. Her beloved husband Galileo preceded her in death by more than thirty years.

The Savard, Bonner, and Ballentyne families, with whom she was especially close, and who considered her one of their own, are also in mourning.

PARADISE SUN
Light for All

Monday, April 11, 1836

ADVERTISEMENTS

Gabriel Bonner of Lake in the Clouds has a large number of especially fine marten and beaver pelts taken this winter. Before he arranges to have them taken to market in Manhattan, he would like to offer them for sale to any resident who might be interested.

This past Saturday Mrs. Daisy Hench, a widow since her husband Joshua passed on five years ago, married Levi Fiddler, a six-year widower. A small party was held at Orchard House. We wish the couple every happiness.

Mr. Daniel Bonner and his wife Martha announce the birth of their sixth child, a daughter to be called Jennet. We wish this newest Bonner good humor and fortitude growing up with the five Bonner boys, well known in Paradise for their abundant energy and inventive natures.

PARADISE SUN
Light for All

The Week of Monday, May 28, 1838

We have received word of a steamboat accident on the Hudson River which has taken the lives of two of our citizens. Ethan and Callie Middleton were returning home from Manhattan when the Steamboat *Reliance* was rocked by an explosion and sank almost immediately. There were no survivors.

Nicholas Wilde, Callie's half brother and Ethan's partner, traveled to Albany to bring the bodies home to Paradise for burial. He was accompanied by Levi Fiddler.

The Middletons were much admired by their friends and neighbors, and dearly loved by the families they leave behind. Ethan was responsible for the revitalization of Paradise by means of careful planning, innovative design, and meticulous building practices. While they had no children of their own, the Middletons took in the five children left behind when Ethan's cousin Jennet Scott Bonner died in the typhoid epidemic of 1830.

They leave behind Nathan, Adam, and Alasdair Scott-Bonner, Mariah Mayfair, and Isabel March, their spouses and children, as well as grieving aunts, uncles, and cousins.

PARADISE SUN
Light for All

Tuesday, May 5, 1840

Gabriel Bonner was in town today and stopped by the newspaper office to announce that his wife, Annie, has given birth to their fourth child and second daughter, who will be called Carrie. With such unanticipated incentive, Gabriel plans to move ahead quickly with the plans to rebuild the old homestead at Lake in the Clouds.

We are delighted to announce that Curiosity Bonner, better known to us here in Paradise as Birdie, is newly married to Henry Savard of New Orleans, and further that the young couple, both certified physicians, will be coming to Paradise to take up residence. They will join Hannah Savard's practice, which has long been stretched to its limits.

Henry Savard is the nephew of our own Ben and Hannah Savard of Downhill House.

Please join us in welcoming Birdie and Henry home.

It is our understanding that Becca LeBlanc, widow and innkeeper, intends to sell the Red Dog to her daughter Anje and Anje's husband Jeremy Reed. We wish Mrs. LeBlanc well in her hard-earned retirement, and Anje and Jeremy on their new business venture.

PARADISE SUN
Light for All

Friday, October 22, 1841

Mrs. Lily Ballentyne is returned from Boston where a selection of her drawings and watercolors were on display at the establishment of Messers Johnstone, Purveyors of Fine Art. The event was mentioned in both Boston and Manhattan newspapers, as Mrs. Ballentyne's work is in great demand.

Mrs. Ballentyne, who was widowed last year, was accompanied by her mother and father, Nathaniel and Elizabeth Bonner. The Ballentynes' four daughters joined the family party in Boston. During this trip Mrs. Elizabeth Bonner's second collection of essays was first offered for sale at Boston bookstores. Copies are available for sale in the *Paradise Sun* office.

PARADISE SUN
Light for All

Wednesday, September 27, 1843

OBITUARY

At sunset on Thursday, June 15 of this year, after a particularly beautiful autumn day, the town of Paradise lost one of its leading, most respected and admired citizens.

Nathaniel Bonner died at Downhill House, the home he shared with his wife Elizabeth and his daughter Dr. Hannah Savard, son-in-law Ben Savard, and their family. All the Bonner children and many of the grand-children (all of whom he still referred to as Little People) were with him. His mind remained clear until the very end. He was eighty-five years old.

The son and only surviving child of Daniel (Hawkeye) Bonner and Cora Munro Bonner, two of the town's founders, he was born and raised at the family home at Lake in the Clouds. Later in life he moved in to the home known as Uphill House, originally owned by his father-in-law, Judge Alfred Middleton. For the past ten years he and Elizabeth have been living with their daughter Hannah and her family at Downhill House.

Nathaniel fought in two wars and returned home to take up trapping and hunting, skills he learned from his father and grandfather. Like his father before him, Nathaniel was a marksman of astounding skill.

His first wife, Sarah, bore him three children, of whom only Hannah survived. Some eight years after Sarah's death he married Elizabeth Middleton, with whom he lived in harmony for the rest of his life.

Nathaniel is survived by Elizabeth, by his children Luke, Hannah, Lily, Daniel, Gabriel, and Birdie, and their spouses, by twelve grandsons and eleven granddaughters, and eight great-grandchildren, and by many friends. He was preceded in death by his parents, his infant sister Alice, his first wife Sarah, his infant children James, Robert, Michael, and Emmanuel, his daughter-in-law Jennet Scott Bonner, son-in-law Simon Ballentyne, and his granddaughters Mairead Ballentyne and Fiona Scott Bonner.

On the last day of his life, Nathaniel rose at dawn and spent a full day helping his grandsons make repairs to the meetinghouse. In the evening he ate alone with his wife, a simple meal of soup, cornbread, and cobbler made with the first apples of the season.

PARADISE SUN
Light for All

January 1, 1844

As all of Paradise's citizens are aware by now, Mrs. Elizabeth Middleton Bonner passed away yesterday after a short illness. She was eighty-one.

Mrs. Bonner left explicit instructions that she wanted no obituary, and requested instead that we print this statement written by her own hand on the day before her death. As a lifelong author of hundreds of editorials, articles, and essays on politics, education, abolition, and the rights of women that appeared in newspapers all over England and the United States, we at the *Paradise Sun*—the only newspaper she founded—are honored to comply.

30th December in the Year 1843

To my dear family and friends,
The facts of my life are well known to those who have reason to be interested in such things and need not be recorded again here.

My life, as extraordinarily full and happy as it has been, did not truly begin until December of 1792, when I arrived in Paradise and met Nathaniel. Neither of us will ever leave you as long as you remember our stories and pass them on. I relegate this right and responsibility to our children and grandchildren, who brought both of us great joy and fulfillment.

I trust you will miss me, but I hope you will not mourn me

for long. Each day is unique and precious, a coin to be spent thoughtfully. Waste nothing and your regrets will be few.

The young cannot imagine death and for that reason they fear it. I am not afraid of death. I greet it as anyone who has a long and satisfying day's work behind them greets sleep.

I have loved the stars too well to fear the night.

Elizabeth Middleton Bonner

Author's Note

When I was writing *Fire Along the Sky*, the fourth novel in this series, I asked Diana Gabaldon if she had found the fourth in her Outlander series hardest.

No, she shot back immediately. The fifth is.

She was, of course, writing her fifth at the time. This is more evidence of a phenomenon well known to those who make a living telling stories: Fiction writing is one of the few things you can do with your life that doesn't get easier as you go along. To provide balance to that unfortunate truth, the writing of fiction is enormously satisfying after the fact.

At the end of this series I am as confident as I can be that I have told Elizabeth's story, but I also find myself confronted with an unavoidable truth: I cannot possibly name all the people who have helped me in one way or another along the line. In the sure knowledge that I am leaving out many who deserve to be mentioned here, I would like to thank:

- my editors at Bantam, first Wendy McCurdy and then Shauna Summers, and Nita Taublib, who stuck with the story when it wasn't clear it would ever take off;
- my agent, Jill Grinberg, my own personal buoy in the rough seas of publishing;
- Jill's kids, for giving me a reason to spend time thinking about monkeys;
- the librarians and researchers and experts who took time to answer often ridiculous questions, or to point me in the right direction to find those answers for myself;
- Pokey Bolton, the very first reader to ever introduce herself to me, for her enthusiasm and early support;
- Lynn Viehl, who read this manuscript again and again and never threw it at me—her help was invaluable;
- Kaera Hallahan, wherever she disappeared to, for encouragement at a crucial juncture;
- Penny and Suzanne, the best accidental sisters ever;
- the other participants at the now defunct CompuServe Writers Forum, who were by turns blindly supportive and constructively critical;
- Rachel Gorham, for her help with matters technical and not-so;
- Judith Henrickson, for her tireless work on the Wilderness Wiki;
- the editors at Baronage Press, most especially William, for the back-story research that made *Dawn on a Distant Shore* more historical than fantastical;
- Kathy Jones, genealogy queen, who made sense of the Wilderness universe in ways that were endlessly helpful and sometimes surprising;
- Katey Burchette, who runs a book-discussion website with unparalleled panache and exactitude;
- dozens of other regular visitors and commenters at my author weblog, including but not limited to Pam Shaw, Rachel Auclair, Carol Baughman, Bruce McCorrister, Kenzie, Robyn-the-MySpace-guru, Meredith Rigter;
- the original Women of the Wilderness from the first discussion board.

Thank you, one and all.

ABOUT THE AUTHOR

SARA DONATI is the pen name of Rosina Lippi, under which she won the PEN/Hemingway Award for her novel *Homestead*. The first five novels in the Wilderness series—including *Into the Wilderness, Dawn on a Distant Shore, Lake in the Clouds, Fire Along the Sky,* and *Queen of Swords*—have more than one million copies in print.